W9-BFA-550

Homeward Bound
Love is a Gentle Stranger

Homeward Bound
Love is a Gentle Stranger

THREE BESTSELLING NOVELS COMPLETE IN ONE VOLUME

Love Leads Home
Love Follows the Heart
Love's Enduring Hope

JUNE MASTERS BACHER

INSPIRATIONAL PRESS

NEW YORK

Previously published in three separate volumes:

LOVE LEADS HOME
Copyright © 1984 by June Masters Bacher
LOVE FOLLOWS THE HEART
Copyright © 1990 by June Masters Bacher
LOVE'S ENDURING HOPE
Copyright © 1990 by June Masters Bacher

All rights reserved. No part of this work may be reproduced or
transmitted in any form or by any means, electronic or mechanical,
including photocopying, recording, or any information storage and
retrieval system, without permission in writing from Harvest House
Publishers, 1075 Arrowsmith Street, Eugene, Oregon 97402.

First Inspirational Press edition published in 1998.

Inspirational Press
A division of BBS Publishing Corporation
386 Park Avenue South
New York, NY 10016

Inspirational Press is a registered trademark of BBS Publishing Corporation.
Published by arrangement with Harvest House Publishers.

Library of Congress Catalog Card Number: 97-77412
ISBN: 0-88486-193-7
Text designed by Hannah Lerner.

Printed in the United States of America.

Contents

PART I

Love
Leads Home

Dedicated to
The Rev. Richard Huls,
my minister and my mentor.

Contents

Cast of Characters

"True" North (Trumary North, daughter of Mary Evangeline Stein North and Wilson North's stepdaughter)

Angel Mother (Mary Evangeline Stein North, Wilson North's first wife and True's mother)

Daddy Wil (Wilson North, settlement doctor and True's stepfather)

Young Wil (Wilson North's nephew and adopted son)

Aunt Chrissy (Christen Elizabeth Kelly Craig North, second wife of Wilson North and True's aunt)

Joseph Craig (Uncle Joe, first husband of Aunt Chrissy and settlement minister)

Marty (adopted son of Aunt Chrissy and Uncle Joe)

Grandma Mollie Malone (Mrs. Malone, wife of the Irish O'Higgin)

O'Higgin (second husband of "Miss Mollie")

Michael St. John (shareholder in transcontinental railroad and most eligible bachelor in Atlanta)

Cousin Emily Kincaid (Michael St. John's cousin and powerful ruler in the Kincaid-St. John household)

Preface

Love Leads Home is the fourth book in a six-novel series depicting romance and courage in the wild and beautiful Oregon frontier. Artists find it difficult to paint the region. It is so green and fertile that it lacks the contrasts of most regions. One depends on words as tools—words from such old-timers as the Irish O'Higgin (in *Love Is a Gentle Stranger, Love's Silent Song, Diary of a Loving Heart, Love Follows the Heart,* and *Love's Enduring Hope*), to catch the spirit of the country.

In one of the rich valleys protected by ancient and sometimes mysterious mountains is a special settlement where *Love Leads Home* continues this Western saga. The valley is held to its distinctly different sister-valleys by the mighty arms of the Columbia River, one of the four great streams of North America. Heading into the Canadian Rockies, the river has the strange power of becoming like the countryside through which it flows. Aimlessly it meanders through Washington, but then, as if by unseen Power, it becomes an awakened giant in Oregon—gouging through mountains with gathering force to rush to Celilo Rapids, the Grand Dalles, and into the Cascade Gorge.

Or that's the way it used to be—before its power was harnessed by the building of a dam. But the "Old River" will not be forgotten as long as folklore continues among the "Oregon children" who gather to hear repeated stories of the red men paddling up and down these white-capped rapids . . . coming of the palefaces with their wagon trains (meeting here the greatest hardships of the trip across the continent) . . . and it will not be forgotten that underneath the now-still waters of the dammed-up lake lie the fallen rocks of the natural bridge which once spanned the river, "Bridge of the Gods."

Yes, Oregon is home to its inhabitants. But in the heart of young True North, "home" could be elsewhere as well. In searching for her real identity, True feels she must go back to her mother's homeland in Atlanta . . . and then to Boston, where her father, whom she never

met, was killed. But there she finds more conflicts, more displace-
ment of her heart, and more questions. Maybe she should go home
to Oregon to sort things out . . . especially three men in her life. . . .

A gentle love story, *Love Leads Home* will leave you with a more
clear and inspiring definition of love . . . a loving heart which finds
and cherishes all earthly love . . . and a more faith-filled heart which
recognizes the origin of our being.

For God Himself is love!

June Masters Bacher

1
Going Home—Or Leaving It

❧

God bless you one and all, my wonderful family. Know that I will remain with you always. I will blossom with the dogwood in the springtime and hum with my bees in the summer sun. I will sparkle with the snowflakes and in the ribbons of each rainbow. I will laugh when you laugh. Cry when you cry. So long as you are together! For I leave with you my legacy of love.

Your Vangie

The final entry in the diary of Mary Evangeline North, True's "Angel Mother."

The conductor paused to look down at the Dresden-china beauty of the sleeping girl. Must date back to royalty, this one. Only rarely did such appealing mixture of fragility and strength show up among the few women passengers, at least on his run between Portland and San Francisco. The big violet eyes, so childlike, gave vulnerability to the girl's face. But the little way she had of thrusting out the rounded jaw spoke of courage.

Well, of course, this young lady had courage! Otherwise, would she be crossing the country by train alone? Why, the rails linking East and West were hardly laid before this one was traipsing to—where did her ticket say? Atlanta? That was it—Atlanta, Georgia!

The slender figure of the girl stirred as the train's whistle cut through the stillness of the afternoon, echoing and re-echoing against

9

the autumn-painted canyon walls. As the train snaked around a sharp bend, the man heard the girl murmur something almost inaudible.

"Home," he thought she said. "I'm going home—or am I leaving it?"

A finger of sunlight found its way through the smoke-darkened windowpane, turning the pale gold braids to molten copper. The conductor sucked in his breath in admiration. About the age of his Midgie, she was. And then a frown crossed his weathered face. Sometimes he worried about his daughter. Alone there in Portland since they'd lost her mother . . .

Suddenly aware of another presence, True North opened her eyes. Aunt Chrissy had cautioned her about strange men who sometimes tried to become too friendly. She relaxed when her eyes met those of the conductor, her self-appointed guardian. She would miss him when his run ended in San Francisco. He would go back home and she would have to change trains after a long layover and resume her journey alone to the land of her mother's childhood. True shivered with a mixture of anticipation and downright fear. Fear? Yes, she admitted it for the first time: fear . . . fear of traveling alone, and fear of what she would find when she reached the big city where she knew nobody.

Oh, it's not that she would have let Daddy and Aunt Chrissy know. Or, for that matter, Marty (had she known his whereabouts), or the twins. And certainly not Young Wil! He had opposed her leaving like this more than all the family.

"True, you are out of your mind!" he had said, his brown eyes showing more emotion than usual. "At your age—"

"Leave my age out of it!" True had snapped. "I'm 19!"

He raised a submissive hand. "All right then, a girl—"

"That, too!"

I wouldn't have been so snappy, True thought now, *if I hadn't been about to cry . . .*

True came back to the present with a start. Conductor Callison was speaking.

"Anybody meetin' you when you change trains?"

"No, but I'll be all right." She had said the same words over and over to her family so much that they were automatic.

The conductor took off his cap. His large head with the silver mane of hair wagged back and forth. "I don't know about young folks these days. Worries me havin' you girls out on your own. You and Midgie need men looking after you, what with danger lurkin' around every corner."

True turned back to the window. She'd heard all about his daughter. She did not want to hear it again. Already she would recognize Midge Callison if she met her aboard this train . . . gray-green eyes, slanting upward at the corners "like her mother's, rest her soul," lots of heavy, dark hair "done up fancy-like," but not easy to understand—his Midgie . . . but there was a young man now . . . and he was hoping . . .

True kept nodding politely, concentrating all the while on wiping away enough film on the window to make a peephole through which she could catch one last glimpse of the beautiful Columbia River below. She succeeded just as the train's whistle gave a last shrill warning and turned sharply to begin its long, tortuous crawl up the mountainside. Her beloved river lay like a silvered mirror below. Bordered on both sides by mountains, the trees seemed to float on the surface as the late-afternoon sun turned their needled boughs from green to gold. A lump rose to her throat. She couldn't be homesick already. To get herself under control, True turned her attention back to the fatherly man beside her.

"I'm going to miss you," she said. It was true. No matter what pretense she made at being independent, inside she was scared out of her wits.

"It's been a pleasure, miss—a real pleasure," he said with a pleased smile. "I still think young ladies as pretty as you hadn't ought to be runnin' around alone, but—" Mr. Callison paused, scratched his head as if in despair, and put his conductor's cap back on.

Then, seeming to brighten, he said, "There's somebody aboard I'm hopin' to introduce if ever his business is finished—shareholder on the railroad and—er, well, most attractive."

"Most attractive" would mean *male, unattached. Well, no, thanks!* The last person True wanted to meet was a man, attractive or otherwise. And she had her reasons. She had given up trying to make Mr. Callison understand that she had had enough experience with young men. True found herself confused sometimes trying to figure out the relationships. Marty, adopted at birth by Aunt Chrissy and Uncle Joe, must be a "cousin." Yes, that was right, *cousin;* because, even after Uncle Joe's fatal accident Aunt Chrissy had married Daddy Wil following Angel Mother's death, that would still be right—wouldn't it? And, as for Young Wil—oh, dear! He was Daddy Wil's nephew, so what *did* that make him to her? *Cousin? Stepbrother?* She only knew that they were *family*, and that she loved them very much—except when Marty was a brat and Wil was so bossy . . .

"I—I—" True began. But the conductor was gone. Just as well. It was all so confusing. She turned back to the view below, watching every detail—half-wishing the train were going the other direction. Closing her eyes, she saw the family . . .

Lost in thought, True was unaware that the conductor had returned until he spoke. "Like I said," he began, "you ought not be alone in all them big cities. Should have a man at your side as a—well, means of protection—"

"I don't need protecting." If she kept her eyes closed, maybe he would go away.

Mr. Callison cleared his throat and tried again. "There's someone you oughta be meetin'—"

"I don't *want* to meet 'a someone'!"

"How can you know when you haven't even met him—I ask you, now, *how?"*

The man had been a gem. Getting started on the long journey had been the hardest part, and he had taken her under his wing. But now he was doing what Mrs. Malone back in the settlement would have called "overeggin' the pudding," and it was adding to her misgivings, just as Aunt Chrissy, Daddy Wil, Marty, and Young Wil had done. It was best that she set things straight once and for all. She was intelligent, self-sufficient, and *determined.*

"Really, Mr. Callison, I am capable of being very rude. If you come dragging some man up here, I am apt to prove it!"

"You just did."

Startled by the strange, male voice—low, throaty, and deeply amused—True bolted upright, her violet eyes wide with surprise and embarrassment. To add to her confusion, she felt hot color stain her cheeks. Before her stood a tall, sandy-haired stranger, hat in hand, and hazel eyes twinkling with amusement.

Bowing low, the young man said, "I am that someone!"

2
No Longer Strangers

❧

THE CONDUCTOR INTRODUCED Michael St. John as a shareholder in the railroad line between Portland and San Francisco, and then hurried away on his duties. True wondered if Aunt Chrissy would consider it a proper introduction. Perhaps she should dismiss this man with a glance or a word—no, she had been rude. Good breeding demanded an apology first. So thinking, she turned to the man who seemed to be waiting for her to make the first move.

She met his eyes, then blushing, glanced down. His gaze was bold and complimentary—out of keeping with the boyish-looking face.

True inhaled deeply in preparation for trying again—and quickly, lest this man get the impression that she was engaging in the age-old game of letting eyes meet as if by chance, with each glance exchanged becoming a little longer. She had never engaged in flirting. But she had watched other girls, and she knew the pitfalls.

When she lifted her eyes again, there was no mistaking the pleasure in the beginning of a smile below his closely cropped mustache. There was an uncomfortable knotting of her stomach muscles—the kind that came whenever she met a new man.

One would think the year in Portland would have given her more poise. Fumbling for her bag, True pretended to look for a lost item. When Michael St. John laughed softly, she realized that he had taken her behavior for affected mischievous disdain—a mistake that must be corrected, and quickly!

"I owe you an apology, Mr. St. John," she said with gathering courage. "I'm afraid I sounded abrupt. You must think me a terrible prude."

13

"Not at all," he said, "but may I sit down for a moment?"

True hesitated.

"I assure you that I don't eat young ladies. Poor digestion, you know."

Surely there could be no harm in that.

"Of course," she said, trying to sound hospitable but distant.

"Now," he said, easing into the seat beside her and crossing one gray-checked leg over the other, "I have a theory about the little wrongs we commit. It's not enough to apologize. We need to go back to Point A and proceed cautiously until we find where we went wrong, then correct it."

"I don't understand."

"Well, I should have asked the conductor to get your permission before disturbing you. You, on the other hand, feel that you were rude—so I suggest that we start all over. I want us to be friends. How do you do, Miss North?"

True laughed. It undoubtedly was happening too fast, but he *was* entertaining—

Without awaiting a reply, Michael St. John continued, "I am Michael to my friends—and may I call you True? Someday I would be interested in knowing how you came by that name."

Again, True felt color creep into her face. Her name was something she would never discuss with anybody, excepting Young Wil.

They had read the story over and over in her mother's diary . . . talked about their pasts together . . . and gathered the rest from Daddy Wil and Aunt Chrissy. But it concerned nobody else! Without realizing it, her chin went up in defense.

The look was not lost on the young man beside her. "I've a feeling the lady guards a secret," he said as if the idea pleased him. "But, alas! She will never confide in me until we are no longer strangers. Should I tell her now that I am 25, the most eligible bachelor in Atlanta—"

"Atlanta! Atlanta, *Georgia*?" True's heart picked up a speed that was frightening.

The man who wished to be called "Michael" smiled. "Is there another? Not to us natives."

Unaware that her blue eyes were like twin violets in her excitement, True whispered breathlessly, "Natives—you're a native? Because that's where I'm going!" True blurted out, regretting the impulsive words immediately. How forward the man would think her. "I—I mean, it's a coincidence," she finished lamely.

"My good fortune," he assured her. And, to her relief, he had failed to notice anything amiss in her words, it seemed. "I seldom get out this direction—second trip, in fact. But my father's health is failing and he has shifted most of the railroad business to my shoulders. Most of my traveling takes me to one of the branch offices since the consolidation. So I divide my time between home and Boston."

"*Boston*?" The word was a whisper.

"You've been there too, I gather. I had no idea you were so widely traveled—but, again, my good fortune."

"I've never been to either city," True said slowly, wondering how much to tell him. "My ancestral roots are there."

"Then I take it you'll be staying with relatives?"

Relatives? True was not sure she had any. In her bag she had all sorts of names, maps, and family history, but she still was not sure where she would be staying in Atlanta. Perhaps in a suitable boarding house . . .

True realized then that Michael St. John was looking at her quizzically. Then his expression turned to one of friendly concern.

"Never mind, I foresee no real problem. Atlanta has built back considerably since the war between the states. Many of the old mansions are still intact, and the owners take in boarders. By the way, would you care to join me in a late supper? I have a partial coach, such as it is, near the back and—"

"Oh, no—no, thank you," True said quickly. "I have enough food with me to furnish a diner."

"Which we'll have once we change trains in San Francisco. The rails out West are newer, you know, and as yet lack the modern conveniences. I shall insist on your company once we are aboard for Atlanta."

"That would be nice," True said, feeling a thrill of excitement. It was hard to believe her good fortune—meeting someone who could help her change trains and find a place to stay in Atlanta.

Could he also help her trace her ancestry in both cities? Of course, she would have to work carefully, revealing only so much.

There were things one did not discuss outside her family.

"I shall say good night, then—and I'm glad I met you, True North. The gods were smiling on me this day!"

"*God*," True corrected softly before offering him her hand. "I'm glad too," she added—"glad we're no longer strangers."

3
To "Point B"—And Beyond

❧

THE MIRROR IN the section marked "Women's Powder Room" was cracked, and some of the silvering on the back had sluffed off.

Even so, True's reflection was reassuring. Aunt Chrissy would have discouraged her from changing clothes so quickly. The long leg of the journey lay ahead, and she would need several changes. Well, she wasn't responsible to her mother's sister or anybody else now. It was essential that she make decisions on her own if she were to accomplish her mission this first time away from home.

Well, not the first, exactly. There had been Portland while she prepared herself to follow in her aunt's footsteps and become a teacher.

But alone? Never! Not with Young Wil to lean on, confide in, and lend a broad shoulder when she cried herself dry of tears when she was homesick. She was going to miss Daddy Wil's nephew—*so* much.

True squared her shoulders determinedly. *Stop it*, she told herself. *Stop it right now! He saw you as a little girl!* She had thought he saw her as a young woman until he realized she was really serious about making this trip into her past.

That hurt. It hurt maybe more than saying good-bye to the rest of the family. His opinion had always been her mirror . . .

She must take one last look at her reflection and get back to the coach. Michael St. John had spoken of bringing coffee from his compartment, and it seemed only proper that a lady should look her best.

16

Yes, the front view was fine—dark skirt unwrinkled and flaring out at the bottom as it should. Blouse—well, becoming. She was right in changing from the navy polka dot to the white, tucked-in-front one with the deep yoke and elbow-length sleeves. It was "the acme of elegant simplicity," according to the mail order book from which she had ordered.

Somehow she thought Michael would like simple things. Oh, it wasn't that she was dressing for *him*, True assured herself, as she took a small compact from her bag and, turning her back to the mirror on the wall, examined the back of her hair.

It was good that the women in her family had no need to resort to the puffs, wigs, and switches shown in Portland. But she did wish her hair would stay in place and stop curling like a schoolgirl's around the nape of her neck and tumbling down over her forehead in front. It made her look younger than she was. No wonder Young Wil felt so superior—as if eleven years older made him so.

Then, contradictorily, she thought, *Oh, Wil, I miss you so much!* She owed him so much—always knowing her thoughts, her wishes . . . only *he* would have known how much it meant when he located the family brooch and bargained with the Portland jeweler for it. He had cautioned her to have the valuable pearl-and-sapphire piece of jewelry locked in the train's safety box for her own protection in case of train robbery.

Train robbery indeed! she had scoffed, feeling that such talk was only another scare tactic to keep her from making the trip.

Gone was the need for bravado. In its place was a longing to hold onto something tangible—something that tied her with her family back in the Oregon Country.

Pulling the brooch from her bag, True looked at it with the usual fascination. Always she had loved it, even before knowing its full history. The blue lights of the sapphire seemed to light the dismal room. And then, on impulse, she pinned the heirloom on the bosom of her white blouse before stepping from the powder room to wait for the young man who had been so kind to her.

Back in her seat, True took the small Bible she always carried from her bag. As usual, she read the fading message from Aunt Chrissy to Uncle Joe, given to her then-new husband when he accepted his first ministerial position.

And, as usual, her eyes misted over. Brought up in a loving environment of family and friends, True had always been "best friends" (as she, Young Wil, and Marty called themselves) with God. But it was dear Uncle Joe who had baptized her in the shallows of the valley's river. He held a special place in her heart, as did each member of the unusual family to which she belonged.

How did one hang a label on love, anyway? There were so many kinds, and she loved each of the wonderful ones in the Craig-North family differently.

Almost, but not quite, she could identify the special feeling she had for Young Wil. But it was best not to try.

Pushing the idea into a corner of her mind, True opened the Bible. Almost automatically it opened at the Old Testament page from which Uncle Joe had read at the close of her baptismal: "The Lord bless thee, and keep thee: The Lord make his face to shine upon thee, and be gracious unto thee: The Lord lift up his countenance upon thee, and give thee peace" (Numbers 6:24–26).

True remembered wishing Marty had accepted the Lord along with her. He had refused, and she had felt very lonely in spite of the crowd on the riverbanks—lonely, that is, until Uncle Joe took her hand in his big one reassuringly and read the Holy Words. Almost symbolically, a mourning dove had flown over the water that orchard-scented spring day. And she was no longer alone.

"Good morning, True North!" The voice was rich with feeling, but low, as if the young man she had met yesterday had no wish to startle her again. "May I offer you a cup of morning coffee?"

True smiled a good morning and accepted the tin cup gratefully.

"You have been most kind," she murmured, dropping her eyes when she saw the look of admiration in his face. His own eyes traveled from the pointed toes of her button shoes to her upswept hair. Then slowly they came back to rest on the bosom of her blouse. She felt herself color under the scrutiny.

"My pleasure—and you will forgive me for staring, but that is the most beautiful brooch I have yet to see. The sapphires must have been chosen to match your eyes."

True hesitated, taking a small sip of hot coffee before answering.

"I'm afraid the jewelry was purchased long before my time," she said. "My mother's—a gift from my father—"

"I'm sorry if I've embarrassed you. Those blue eyes illuminate a certain sensitivity I want to explore after we progress to Point B!"

We have—and on beyond, True thought, uncertain whether to be happy or frightened.

He reached across and closed her Bible.

4

Growing Fear

❧

IT WAS HARD to determine how much time passed. There seemed to be a lot to talk about, considering that Michael St. John was a stranger.

Of course, people who traveled together had an opportunity to become better acquainted than those who met casually on occasion. At least, True told herself that was why she confided more in him than she had intended to.

The man was easy to know. Or was he? Something gave True the feeling that, although his eyes crinkled often with a smile and his manner suggested goodnatured candor, he held something back, especially when he talked business, which he tended to do after polite encouragement.

But invariably the conversation came back to True. It was flattering but embarrassing—and more than a little disconcerting. There was a lot which True planned to keep to herself—and for good reason.

Did her father or her mother live in Atlanta—or was it Boston? Both places, True explained guardedly. Was either still there? No— her father was dead . . . and there she stopped.

Even after all these years, it was hard for her to say that her mother was dead. So she had kept the childhood image created during her years of formative theology.

"You mentioned an uncle and an aunt in Oregon. I gather you have been staying with them while attending school in Portland? Tell me, did you like teaching?"

"I only taught a part of one year—Aunt Chrissy's unexpired contract," True answered quickly, hoping that he would not push further into why she was in Oregon, or why she chose to go to Atlanta and Boston.

Let him think she was "visiting" Oregon—or whatever he might be thinking. Better that than saying she was going back to trace her way, if possible, to her mother's and aunt's home (where they both had been hurt so cruelly) and to search for her natural father's grave—the man who was responsible for their broken hearts.

"Tell me about your work!" True said, putting more enthusiasm into her voice than she felt in hope of steering the conversation away from herself. She met Michael's eyes.

Tall and broad-shouldered, with well-groomed hair framing his face, he had looked stern in repose. Now the handsome face lighted up as if in response to the flare of excitement in his hazel eyes.

Obviously, here was a man who loved his work. And obviously he had done well in the railroad business. His clothes had a tailor-made look and he wore them with the confident air of a man accustomed to wealth.

True tried to concentrate on what he was saying.

"As you know, good times did not climb the Rockies and smile on Oregon. When the gold boom failed, settlers—so my father tells me—began blaming their troubles on the railroads. There was plenty of beef, lumber, fish, apples, and even mined goods going to waste without the railroads, which were bringing prosperity to other regions. Well," Michael said as he combed his blonde hair with his fingers, "am I boring you?"

"Oh, no, not at all!" True said truthfully.

Laying a light hand on hers momentarily, as if in gratitude, he allowed it to remain only a proper time and then resumed talking.

"When cross-continent rails were first planned, things looked rosy. We're traveling on a spur of the first efforts—but quarrels broke out and there were those like Ben Holladay who controlled the stages between Missouri and the Oregon frontier—ever hear of him?"

Hear of Ben Holladay? True smiled, remembering the wonderful winter evenings when Daddy Wil and his Vangie (before she became "Angel Mother"), Uncle Joe, and Chrissy used to gather around the fire and dream of the prosperous days ahead as she, Young Wil, and Marty monitored the conversations. The railroads would come through. Produce would be hauled away. The mill the men co-owned would flourish. The Pony Express would come on to Turn-Around Inn to delight the O'Higgin Malone clan . . . steamboats . . . the land flowing with milk and honey, they'd said. There would be a growing need for Daddy Wil's medical services as a doctor, and certainly there was always a need for God-called ministers like Uncle Joe . . . on and on went their cotton-candy dreams, their low-pitched but excited young voices echoing softly against the time-mellowed beams of the great living room of the North home, where True was born. The children's eyes would droop sleepily . . . but her mother had captured the dreams in her diary.

True came out of her reverie with a start. Michael St. John had stopped talking. Guiltily she looked at him. What had he asked? Oh, yes, Ben Holladay.

"Forgive me," she said, "but the name brought back memories. Please go on. It won't happen again."

Was the look in his eyes annoyance? Amusement? No, it was something else. More curiosity.

But why? Then, to her relief, Michael was speaking again.

"Well, if you're sure?" When she nodded, Michael went on: "Holladay bought up a line of steamships running between Portland and San Francisco, then decided to build railroads. Big spender that he was, he built a mansion, brought in Eastern people, and filled the lobbies at the State house—only to go bankrupt.

"Along came Villard, sharing the grand vision with Holladay that the Pacific Northwest would become a great empire. All it needed was railroads. They had the mistaken idea that if the country would fill up with people, the rails would pay off."

Michael laughed, as if the idea were amusing.

"But wasn't that part true in a sense?"

It seemed important somehow that she know if the laugh had been directed at the immigrants. Did he think that money determined *worth*?

He shrugged.

"People with money, yes. But some of the people were pretty low-lifed—"

Anger rose inside True—a defensive kind of anger that refused to be denied a voice. Her words, when she spoke, however, were low and calm.

"I fail to see the connection."

Michael, apparently unaware of her strong feelings, simply shrugged again and went on with his railroad history. Northern Pacific crews building across Montana at the rate of three miles a day . . . killing off buffalo . . . and at last driving the "Golden Spike" which linked East to West . . . then his family had bought shares from them all and "come in for the kill" . . . but there were still hard feelings . . .

"Oh, I doubt it," True said. "The Oregon people are too grateful to hold grudges about squandering of some of the pools to which they contributed—and, besides, they aren't like that. They are friendly and warmhearted—"

"Not when it comes to having the railroads run through their lands, they aren't!" Michael's eyes lit up strangely.

True sucked in her breath. "If you mean the few train robberies—" She paused and held his gaze.

"I do!" he said. And something in his tone frightened her.

5
Change of Plans

⁓

"SAN FRAN-*CIS*-CO!"

When Conductor Callison sang out the words the next morning, True eagerly raised the faded blind to see the waking city.

Her first glimpse was one of disappointment. Smoke emitted from the slowing train mingled with the early-morning fog to enshroud the city.

Then, as the train came to a hissing stop, the smoke cleared and she was able to see enough to make her gasp with wonder.

Almost surrounded by water, enthroned on hills, San Francisco seemed to go on forever. She had read so much of the city's landlocked harbor, one of the largest in the world, according to her geography teaching manual.

Oh, it would be so wonderful if she could see it even from a distance! Her students would want to hear all about it. *If* she went back, True reminded herself. At any rate, she would want to tell Young Wil about it in that long, long letter she had promised him.

Strain as she would, however, True was unable to see the water of the bay or the ships it hosted. The dense fog persisted, seeming to billow in like clouds and settle around the tall buildings, climb the steep streets, and become a part of the sullen skies.

Depressed by the scene, she was about to turn away in hope of seeing Michael St. John when the conductor came into the coach again. He paused at her side.

"Unable to see Alcatraz on a morning such as this, I s'pose? Easy to confuse 'The Rock' with a battleship—lonely island, isn't she just?"

24

Shivering, True nodded. Recently printed history books had a lot to say about the disciplinary measures taken in the barracks.

"Military prison, isn't it?"

"Yep—oh, there she is, a little to the north!"

With mixed feelings, True turned her face to the direction Conductor Callison pointed. In the distance she could make out the faint outline of what indeed did appear to be a ship. Then the fog closed in. Something about the scene tore at her heart. It looked so cold. So lonely. And, unaccountably, she felt the same way.

It was the weather. It had to be the weather. "Grandma Mollie" Malone would be complaining of her rheumatism and Daddy Wil would be assuring her she would feel better once the sun broke through.

But they weren't here. And she was alone—unless Michael showed up, as he had promised. True longed to ask his whereabouts. The conductor would know. But that might seem forward—

And then she saw him!

At first True thought it was only her imagination. This fog was tricky, winding itself like evil fingers around anything it seemed to touch. But then, as if enjoying the game, the fog moved on, only to thicken again.

It had parted long enough, however, for her to see distinctly that it was Michael St. John.

Michael and three or four other men, all well-dressed, wearing hats and carrying canes and briefcases, standing together as if in an important conference just outside the coach behind her. And then the others had moved away like the fog, leaving Michael standing alone.

Mr. Callison had seen, too.

"Makin' arrangements for changin' trains and the like, no doubt," the man said, seeming to feel a need to explain. "I just learned from the switchin' yard that there'll be no layover for you. Real blessing— probably time enough for coffee. Me, I'm glad I was able to find a fine-appearin' young gentleman to look after you on that long, lonely trip. If 'twas my Midgie—oh, here's Mr. St. John!"

True made a futile effort to sweep the tendrils of curling hair from her forehead, a motion not wasted on Michael.

"Leave it alone—please do," he said with a warm smile. "It's very becoming, you know. And I'm happy to see you're wearing that splendid brooch again."

I'm wearing all the clothes I wore yesterday, True thought with embarrassment. There was so little time. And certainly the ladies' room afforded little space or privacy for a lady's toilette.

True thanked him and then asked anxiously about the change of trains.

There was no cause for concern, he assured her. He would see to it personally that she was safely aboard and comfortable. Oh, very comfortable! His eyes narrowed slightly as if he were about to reveal a secret.

He had strange eyes, she found herself thinking. Sometimes they were amused. Often they were pensive. And today as he talked with the strangers there in the fog she had observed a certain shrewdness she had not seen before. She knew very little about this man really. . .

Which was the same way he felt about her, True realized with a start. For his next words caught her completely off guard.

"Just who are you anyway, my Mystery Lady? You know, it occurs to me that you have told me very little—about yourself, I mean."

True studied her hands. The nails needed buffing. "There's nothing to tell," she said, buffing a thumbnail across the folds of her long, dark skirt. The skirt had picked up lint, she noticed. She must look a fright . . .

True paused. Then, realizing that he was waiting for more, she made a hasty decision. It would be better to handle the problem lightly. He was not one to be put off.

But she couldn't help wondering what his reaction would be if she told him the real story of her life. Not that she intended to. Now or ever!

"Really, Mr. St. John," True said coyly—glancing up to be sure Michael knew it was a game—"my name, as you know, is True North, age 19, of good family and excellent health. None of my family has been hanged—"

His laugh sounded forced. "There's more to your life story—"

True interrupted with a light chuckle.

"Yes, oh, yes! Lean closer and I will share with you that I am a—*shh-h-h*—teacher! I am earthbound and I am a free spirit. That's about it."

Michael was no longer smiling.

"Banter is fine, up to a point. What I had in mind was this. Are you betrothed?"

A strange warmth crept through True's body. She might have known where the conversation was leading. Here she was avoiding one issue and another cropped up.

When she did not answer, Michael leaned forward to look into her face.

"Is there someone *else*, True?"

Use of the word "else" startled True. That meant *he* was interested. Why, they had just met. There could be no doubt that the relationship was moving too fast. It was dangerous in more ways than one, particularly since they would be running into one another either by arrangement or design.

A shrill warning whistle sounded, jolting True back to the present. If she should miss this train—

Involuntarily, she reached for her bags and would have risen to her feet except that Michael St. John sprang up ahead of her, blocking her passage. The suddenness of his movement and a certain glint in his eye was startling and a little frightening.

"Really—I must go," True said quickly. "Please let me pass."

Michael did not budge.

"I shall in due time. But not until I have my answer."

"You have no right to ask—"

Another blast of the whistle rose above the sound of foghorns.

"That's not quite true," he said. "You see, I am about to offer you the use of my headquarters from San Francisco. And certainly I have no desire to be getting myself into one of those triangles where somebody gets shot!"

"I have no idea what you're talking about. But I do know we must go—*please*! But, no, there's nobody else—at least, nobody to whom I am engaged to be married—not now anyway—"

Michael's hazel eyes were suddenly dark.

"There *is* a rival, but I take it not a serious one at the moment. Very well, then. Now to explain. I've been detained and you will use my coach."

6
Beginning of a Fairy Tale

❧

LEANING BACK AGAINST the fringed cushions of the velveteen couch, True tried to put into proper perspective everything that had happened since her tearful good-bye to her family until this moment.

It was impossible, of course. How could she put events in order when she was unable to recall events themselves?

Michael St. John's handsome, slightly mocking face floated around the luxurious compartment of the private coach—smiled at her from the gold-framed mirrors, glowered from the silver-gray of the shirred, sateen drapes, and studied her every move from the soft glow of the shaded gas lamps.

What on earth was she, True North, fresh from a homespun community in the Oregon Country, doing here?

A mellow toot of the southbound train assured her that she was not dreaming. Perhaps it would have been better that she had been. There had to be a price to pay later. Things like this just did not happen in real life. And then in panic she tried to recall where her host had said they would meet.

"Get hold of yourself, True North!" she said aloud sternly. "You wanted to be on your own. Well, you are. You very much are!"

With that, she felt inside her handbag to make sure Michael's note bearing his aunt's address was there. She relaxed when her hand closed around it. Of course, it would be in the small compartment right beside her Bible.

Feeling better, she took out the Bible and decided to read until supper was served, as the porter had told her it would be. But she did not open the Bible right away. Something else troubled her about Michael St. John.

Why had he deliberately closed her Bible on one occasion? The incident had gone unnoticed at the time, but she remembered it now. True found herself wondering if he were a Christian. Somehow she doubted it.

Well, that was sad. Just as it was sad when *anyone* had missed the joy of knowing the Lord. Michael belonged on her prayer list. But she was going to explain to God just why he was on that list—and it wouldn't be because of any personal interest in the man!

Still . . . she was grateful to him. But for Michael St. John she would be in one of those straight-up, green chairs in an overcrowded day coach (probably half a dozen cars away from the ladies' room and maybe leading through the men's smoker!).

So she must thank the Lord for bringing this stranger to her. At peace with the thought, True began to read.

A light rap on the door interrupted her reading. The knock was followed immediately by the tinkle of a chime.

"Last call to dinnah, Miss No'th, ma'am," a soft-voweled voice said outside the door of the compartment. "Mistah St. John s'posed you'd be wantin' dinnah in his qua'tahs? 'Stead of the dinah?"

True closed her Bible and hurried to the door. There she was greeted by the white-coated porter who had introduced himself as "Mose" during the rush of her getting settled in the elaborate coach and Michael's hasty departure from the train.

Unaccustomed to such service, now True could only stare at the beautifully laid-out tea cart with the starched lace topcloth not quite covering the pewter bud vase holding a single red rose.

When she nodded mutely, Mose's ebony face wreathed with smiles which showed rows of startling white teeth. Immediately he rolled the tea cart in, uncovered it, and began to lift lids from the silver tureens.

"Here, I'll do that!" True said quickly.

Mose shook his head doubtfully.

"Mistah St. John he won' be likin' that. The mastah dun said—"

True smiled.

"I appreciate your loyalty to your employer, Mose. But he is not your master! Only the Lord is entitled to be called by that name."

The black man smiled shyly. True wondered as she took the silver serving spoon he was holding if he had never received a compliment before.

"Yessum," he said and smiled again.

Before leaving, Mose opened a lavishly curtained corner which converted into a little booth—a private dining room—surrounded by brass rails which held the curtains.

True was glad she was to be alone. She was sure the food would be unfamiliar—sure, too, that she should have dressed for dinner. The closest thing she had which qualified as a dinner gown was the tea-rose taffeta that Aunt Chrissy and Grandma Mollie had hand-stitched for her. Aunt Chrissy had mentioned several ladies' shops in Atlanta which used to offer a seamstress for a reasonable fee but cautioned that the fire during the war had most likely taken them.

Well, her clothes would have to do. Nobody was going to know her identity anyway.

Correction! Michael St. John knew too much already . . . oh, how had she gotten herself into this web?

Aware suddenly that Mose was waiting to be dismissed, True murmured a thank you. When the door closed behind him, True turned to the table.

No matter how it had happened, she was here. And it *was* a glorious adventure—maybe just what she needed as prelude to the search for her real identity—the identity she knew intellectually, but the one she must know in her heart before she could decide where she belonged.

She wished again that Young Wil had been more in favor of this trip. But he, having no desire to locate his wayward mother who had deserted him when he was a baby, was unable to understand her quest. Her letters would win him over . . . beginning with the fairy-tale existence on the train.

But as to how it came about? What would he think of her accepting favors from a strange man? Well, *fiddle-dee-dee!* He saw her as a sister. He saw her as a child. He saw her as a sometimes-pest. So why not shock him into seeing her as a grown-up young woman capable of managing her life?

Aware that she stood foolishly in the center of the little booth with the spoon in her hand, True seated herself, hesitated a moment, then lowered her head in silent prayer before lighting the candle beside the rose.

Then she took in the sight that danced before her in the candle's glow. Salad of shredded carrots, slivered almonds, baby corn, and miniature shrimp . . . chicken soup laced with some kind of creole seasoning . . . and whatever could this main dish be? Certainly it was a display of color . . . bright yellow cheese sauce over still-warm muffins, surrounded by turkey rolls with broccoli filling. Alongside this medley was an enormous lettuce leaf accented by what appeared to be fresh pineapple and strawberries! Another tureen held crepes stuffed with mushrooms and seafood in some kind of sauce.

True caught her breath in a mixture of admiration and despair. How could half the world as she knew it live like this while the others lived in need? Which were the lucky ones?

It's a shame, she thought, *that my fairy tale has to be spoiled!* True wished she were less sensitive to the inconsistencies of the two worlds. Food, but not for the hungry. Except her!

As if in a dream, she picked up her fork.

7
Unexpected Delay

❧

IN A VERY real sense, True wished the dream could go on forever—
that the glass bubble in which she was encased could float high, high
above the world and all its inevitable problems. For the luxurious
quarters afforded her were indeed a bright bubble.

But bubbles burst suddenly, or else they fade and die. They never,
she was sure, reach a point beyond the pull of the earth where they
are free to orbit forever in happy weightlessness.

Like a bright bubble, True gravitated between gravity and levity.
One moment she was light-headed and giddy. But the next, like a
bouncing bubble, she was brought back to stark reality. Her surroundings were temporary at best. And before her lay all the problems she
had brought along plus newly-created ones.

For one thing, there was the matter of meeting Miss Emily Kincaid.
At Michael's urging, she had taken the elderly woman's name and
address. Now there were misgivings.

What would this aunt think of a total stranger's descending upon
her without warning? Maybe Michael would send a telegram, she
thought hopefully. That would prepare Miss Emily.

But True herself would be unprepared. Back in the settlement one
took gifts when calling. Aunt Chrissy had failed to tell her what the
customs were in Atlanta. Of course, they would have changed considerably since Aunt Chrissy and Angel Mother were there as young
girls. They would have left when they were about her own age.

What would life have been like, she wondered, had they remained in their Southern home, one of them marrying Jonathan Blake? She wondered which one it would have been of the two young women—Christen Elizabeth Kelly, whose engineer-father had perished in an explosion, or her own mother, Mary Evangeline Stein, the second-marriage daughter?

Even now True's heart would not accept her mother's father as a grandfather. A grandfather gathered his offspring close and loved them. He did not reject his daughter just because she was misused by a man she trusted and, in her innocence, loved.

How could Jonathan have done such a thing? Been engaged to Aunt Chrissy, only to betray both her and Angel Mother . . . and how did she, proclaimed the brightest member of her class in both Centerville School and Portland Normal School, entertain ridiculous ideas that maybe the man still lived . . . even that one day he—rich, famous, and remarkably handsome—would come riding up in a stylish carriage to bear her away, the heir of her rightful fortune? Especially when she didn't want to leave!

Anyway, men didn't claim illegitimate daughters. Still . . .

In her younger years, True recalled as she watched the green hills give way to a flattened, sun-baked valley, Young Wil had been patient. He had called her "highly imaginative" and had told her she should write a book, as he was doing in botany. Then, after the quarrels began when she emerged into young womanhood, he had cautioned her to rid herself of the foolish "adolescent fantasies." She had become infuriated and, at one point, bitten him in the hand.

Marty had thought her wild imaginings were exciting. And he had loved the way she tore at Young Wil with words and teeth! But it wasn't Marty's approval she wanted . . . it was Young Wil's . . .

Aware suddenly that the train had slowed, True forced her mind to slow with it. Undoubtedly, they were about to start upgrade again. Or the locomotive could be taking on water at one of the watering tanks. They were far apart.

So thinking, she leaned back and took out her writing tablet. All resentments toward Young Wil were gone. She wanted to begin her letter—one that would give the facts and more. No matter what decisions she was to reach, she needed his help—and something more, which she was unable to identify.

My dearest Wil:

True looked at the greeting. She had never called her stepfather's nephew anything but "Young Wil." But that would sound rather foolish in a letter, wouldn't it?

Maybe it was time he used some of his own medicine—outgrew her childish name for him. So let the shortened version stand.

> You would never believe all that has happened! You thought I would be alone and in danger, and that is not the case. First, the conductor took me under his wing and then I met a young man . . .

True reread the last line, frowned, and crossed out *young*. She was in the midst of telling him in detail what had happened and describing the elegant coach she was privileged to occupy, when there was a loud knock at the door followed by the sound of men's voices.

None of them belonged to Mose. Who could be wanting her?

Quickly she closed the tablet and laying down her pen staff, True was about to cork the ink bottle when the knock was repeated— louder, more insistent. And something in its sound caused her heart to beat a little faster.

Prepared to steady herself against the motion of the moving train, she was aware suddenly that the train had stopped. Something *was* wrong!

"Yes?" she managed to answer without opening the door.

A deep-throated voice on the other side said, "Open up, lady!"

For a moment she hesitated. Just what did a lady who was traveling alone do under such circumstances? Well, Aunt Chrissy and later Angel Mother had made it alone by stagecoach. She could make it by train!

Lifting her chin bravely, "Who is it?" True asked.

This time another voice spoke. The accent was softer and the tone more gentle.

"No need for alarm, miss. We are officers of the law."

True opened the door a crack. The uniforms, all different, were reassuring. But she had not expected to see so many men in the group. Not certain what was expected of her, True nodded a greeting and waited.

"Do you want we should inspect your quarters, ma'am—er, miss— er—" one of the younger men stammered.

"Whatever for?"

"Just a routine inspection at this point," another of the officers said. "Miss—"

"North," she supplied. "Is this customary?"

"In these parts, yes—but unless you have seen something which aroused your suspicions—"

"Suspicious characters, he means. *Train robbers.*" The younger man spoke again. His voice was overly dramatic.

True relaxed a bit. The whole idea was ridiculous—so silly she wanted to laugh. Train robbers indeed! Just how was she expected to recognize one?

But the desire to laugh dissipated with one of the older men's next words. Spoken quietly, they carried a heart-chilling warning.

"This is Jesse James country."

Jesse James! But she thought the Missouri-born outlaw belonged farther in the Midwestern states.

"Are you all right, lady? Look mighty pale. We didn't have a notion of scarin' you, just cautioning you—and, by the way, 'twould be best if you put that piece of jewelry you're wearin' in safe keepin'."

Automatically, True's hand went to the brooch pinned to the lapel of her dark jacket.

"I'm all right—I guess," she said, aware that the trembling of her hands gave her away. "It's only that I thought Jesse James and his brother were captured—and certainly I never expected them here—"

"Them outlaws ain't gonna be took alive," the gruff-voiced man with a heavy growth of beard said. "And they can be anywhere. Governor Critterden's got a reward fer 10,000 dollars dead or alive. They've joined up with the Younger Brothers now and could be anywhere. Yep, anywhere, so be careful, lady! Travelin' alone ain't recommended. Ain't safe anywhere."

It was sometime after the men left before True was able to bring herself under control. She brushed her hair and took a sponge bath. That should have relaxed her, but she was unable to eat much of the carefully prepared food Mose brought later.

And her dreams that night were troubled.

8
Trouble Ahead!

~

BUSY WITH HER letter to Young Wil and fascinated by the intricate patchwork of changing scenery, True lost track of time. As the conductor kept telling passengers that they had entered another Standard Railroad time zone, she would set her watch forward—thinking all the while that she had entered a time zone all her own. The past no longer seemed to count. Neither did the future or what it held.

She all but forgot her mission, except in her subconscious mind, because of the new world of elegance that surrounded her. Repeatedly she felt an overwhelming desire to pinch herself awake, only to wonder if she really wanted to wake up after all.

I'm no snob, she kept telling herself, *but is it wrong to enjoy this?*

For a while there were feelings of guilt. Then the feelings gave way to pleasure—temporary, she knew—but maybe that's the way all pleasure was.

So, living in her personal "time zone" of the here-and-now, True was surprised when the conductor announced that they would be arriving in Atlanta the next day. The terrain had changed to deep woods, most of the trees garbed in the sad-sweet red-golds of autumn.

But where were the swamps that Aunt Chrissy had spoken of? The bayous, switch cane, and mosses? Some trees had been cut away for the railroads, others destroyed during the war. Maybe the rest wasn't like her aunt remembered it either . . .

True wondered sadly if Oregon would change for her in the same manner. Oh, it mustn't! It was the most wonderfully beautiful country in the world, populated by the world's most wonderful people!

A wave of homesickness swept over her, and she was about to give way to tears when there was a sudden jolt of the compartment in which she rode—a jolt so sudden and severe that it set the overhead gas lights in frightening motion and all but threw True to her knees. A prickle of fear ran down her spine.

Grasping the side of the chair where she had been gazing pensively out the window, True tried to pull herself up. But there was another jolt—a shuddering which she could hear running through the entire train. And then stillness which said the train had stopped.

Steam poured from beneath the train, making it impossible to see what was going on. True could only guess the worst.

Jesse James and his gang! They were about to be robbed.

Her first reaction was to tear the brooch from the lapel of her jacket—pricking her finger painfully. Oh, why hadn't she listened and had the piece of jewelry put into the safe?

Quickly she stuffed it into her handbag. Then, realizing that her finger was bleeding, she stuck it in her mouth just as there was an insistent knock on the door.

True's first reaction was to ignore it. If she didn't answer, maybe the robbers would go away. It wouldn't work, she knew immediately.

So, paralyzed with fear, she forgot to remove her finger from her mouth, and asked incoherently, "Who's there?"

"Conductor, miss! Sorry about the delay. Just wanted to let you know there's trouble with the tracks. Crews ought to be here soon. Suggest you stretch your legs a bit. Could take a bit of waiting when there's trouble ahead."

Weak with relief, she leaned back against the cushions until her heart resumed its normal pace. Even then, her legs were still wobbly when she tried to stand.

Maybe Young Wil was right. It was best for a man to be along when a woman was traveling.

What nonsense! she was telling herself the next moment. There had been no danger at all. Just silly fear—fear he had helped bring on by all those silly warnings!

Determinedly, she smoothed her hair in place and brushed the wrinkles from her skirt as best she could. A walk through the other coaches would do her good. Maybe she could find another woman and make small talk while they waited.

It struck her then that she had no idea how many coaches the locomotive engine pulled or what the accommodations were like.

There were countless cars, True was soon to realize, but very few passenger coaches. And crossing between the coaches was frightening. She felt that she was walking without support when forced to cross alone. But crossing when others were present was even more frightening.

Bewhiskered men seemed to enjoy inhabiting the small enclosures—all of them staring openly, a few grinning suggestively. Panicky, True hurried past them each time, dreading the time when she must retrace her steps to the safety provided by Michael St. John.

She was growing to appreciate him more and more.

The two coaches she passed through on her way toward the back of the train were a disappointment. How few women there were! And none of them gave signs of wishing to be bothered with company. They were surrounded by large families of children whom they were attempting to pacify with unpalatable-looking, stale food. Most of the men looked up with interest, but she avoided their eyes and moved on quickly.

Head down, True almost bumped into the conductor, who approached from the rear of the train. She murmured an apology and was about to move on when his hand, placed lightly on her shoulder momentarily, detained her.

"I wouldn't be going any further, miss," the man advised, pointing a warning finger at the lettering above the entranceway.

True's blue eyes followed his finger and then widened, turning violet in their surprise. The sign read: BLACKS.

"Does that mean—" she began.

The portly, ruddy-faced conductor nodded.

"Niggers. Sorry. Tried our best forbiddin' 'em, but it was sure to come even before the government mandate. Rest assured they won't be botherin' you in the dining room or powder room."

There had been actual apology in the man's voice—an apology which was misdirected. Trying to hide the annoyance she felt, True spoke in low tones.

"But how do you expect them to manage—I mean—" she stopped, embarrassed.

The conductor snickered.

"They're herded together in th' rear car. How they *manage*, as you so delicately put it, is their problem!"

Hot words rose to her lips. But it was not the conductor's fault, she supposed. His job was to carry out orders.

But if the colored people were still in social bondage, then the Civil War made even less sense than she and Young Wil had thought when they read of the killings and burnings.

Marty, on the other hand, had found all the war stories more fascinating than Aunt Chrissy's Bible stories and fairy tales. But Marty was always a strange one. While Young Wil pored over the Latin terms in Daddy Wil's medical books or labeled a new leaf in his botany collection, Marty drew pictures of cannons and interrupted her studying with his explosive, "Boom! Boom! Boom! Surrender or you'll all be blasted to bits!" She wondered where he was and what he was doing.

"Something botherin' you about the niggers bein' on the train with you, you so fine a lady 'n all?" It was the conductor's voice.

Something was bothering her all right. Her mind had wandered. But all the while a part of her had refused to allow her to turn and start back to Michael St. John's private compartment.

"Would you mind if I went in there?"

The eyes of the conductor narrowed and the furrow in his brow deepened.

"Yes'm, I would mind. I would mind very much. I promised Mr. St. John I'd be lookin' after your needs—"

That came as a surprise. Doggedly she continued, however, as if directed by some force greater than herself.

"I appreciate that, but I see no reason why I wouldn't be safe among them. I hardly think they would be that hostile."

The light hand on her shoulder tightened, slowly but surely turning her around.

"Not *them* I'm speakin' of. But the others. White folks in these parts don't like their kind associatin' with niggers—"

"Please don't use that name!"

The words were out before True knew she was going to speak.

The conductor looked surprised.

"You'll be pardonin' me, ma'am—er, miss. I never realized you felt different. 'Course, you're not from these parts."

True felt herself being firmly propelled back down the aisle as he continued.

"Main reason, though, is that 'llowing you to go in back there would cost me my job. Too near pension time for the risk."

True stopped and turned to face him.

"You mean—"

"I mean Mr. St. John would have me fired for not lookin' after you proper. Come on, now. Let me escort you back."

True did not know why she reacted as she did. Perhaps it was the nagging thought that she had let herself become too indebted to Michael St. John already.

"That man has no right to take over people's lives the way he does!" she said hotly. "Yours. Mine. Everybody's, the way I see it! For your sake, I will obey your wishes. But let me assure you that Michael St. John will hear from me loud and clear when we meet again!"

Then, when she saw the look of pleading in the man's eyes she added an additional statement.

"Not about you, sir. I will only let him know he has no hold on me!"

Anger gave way to exhaustion. The walk back seemed an eternity. Once back inside the private quarters, True felt unutterably weary and depressed.

9
Robbery!

~~

THE DAY DRAGGED on. True read her Bible, choosing passages suggested by her aunt's first husband, "Brother Joseph," whom the settlers had loved so much. Uncle Joe had penciled notes in the front of his Bible, and she had copied the references before leaving home.

When in sorrow, read John 14 . . . *Men fail you,* Psalm 27 . . .

Quickly, letting her finger slide down the list, she located the ones she wanted.

When you want courage for your task, read Joshua 1 . . . *When the world seems bigger than God,* read Psalm 90 (and finally) *When leaving home for labor or travel,* Psalm 23 and 121.

True read the passages. Then, closing the Book, she prayed for each member of her family, admitting to God that no remnants of her mother's family in Atlanta or her father's in Boston could ever replace the people who had loved her, nourished her body and soul, and taught her of His unconditional love and forgiveness. She prayed for courage in what she herself was undertaking. She thanked Him for bringing Michael St. John into her life and asked God to touch Michael's heart if they were yet strangers.

Somehow there seemed more she should say about that, but she was unable to put the thoughts together. About to close her prayer, True remembered her rude awakening earlier to what she saw as injustice and possible suffering among the black people in this part of the world.

41

"Forgive them, Father, for they know not what they do," she said of the white people responsible. "If there is something I can do, just whisper it in my ear, Lord."

Feeling better after her *Amen*, True continued her letter to Young Wil. As she wrote, the hunger grew so strong to see her childhood idol that she wandered far from the facts of her journey and dipped into her storehouse of feelings—the way the two of them had always done.

As she wrote, True was aware of the *pick-pick-picking* outside her window. She had been too engrossed in her meditations and the letter to Young Wil to notice more.

But, pausing now, she was aware of singing. Beautiful singing! The kind she remembered hearing in the settlement when the black families came through.

"Goin' over Jordan and what did I see? Comin' for t'carry me home . . ."

Rising from the couch, she walked to the window. In the gathering twilight she saw a large crew of smoke-streaked faces, beads of perspiration rolling from their foreheads. All black.

Why? True wondered. *Why?* Something was going on here—something she did not like.

Why, the situation now seemed more unhealthy than what Aunt Chrissy had described during the time of slavery! She and Angel Mother had grown up with a mammy whom they dearly loved and respected.

She would find out more from Michael . . . he had shown *her* great compassion . . . but what about others?

It was growing dark. Was that why everything was suddenly so quiet? Mose had not come in to light her lamps. And, for that matter, supper was late. She was more than ready for the train to get underway.

But why was she feeling so apprehensive? Maybe another turn through the coaches—no, wait!

Did she or did she not hear a woman scream? Probably her imagination. But the thought decided her against another stroll.

And then without warning the door burst open. Unable to grasp the reality of three masked men standing before her, their faces caked with dirt mingled with sweat above the red bandannas and hair matted to their foreheads from days in the saddle, True could only think dully that she had forgotten to lock her door.

Her next thought was that someone was playing a joke, trying to keep passengers amused until the journey could resume.

But when she saw the three guns aimed directly at her, she realized that this was the robbery of which the officers had warned!

"Keep your head, lady, and you won't git hurt," the tallest of the group said, his beady eyes boring into hers.

"This is a holdup," he added unnecessarily.

"Don't stand there gapin', lady!" The older man with shifty eyes stepped from behind the first speaker and raised the barrel of his gun. "Want that purty face blasted off?"

The taller man stepped forward again, pushing the other man's gun barrel down.

"Easy, pardner. Our pals'll take care of the rest of the crew like they done that nigger boy in th' prissy white suit—"

"Mose! You've hurt Mose?" White-faced, True faced him.

"Seems he was kinder sweet on you—and no wonder, boys. Take a gander at this one! Never mind about the black boy, girlie—git your cash out, lady. *Now!*"

Paralyzed with fear, more for Mose than for herself, True was unable to move. But she must! Her life depended on it.

For a wild moment, her mind sought an avenue of escape. Train windows too small. Crew injured—maybe some dead. She was alone. And she must find a will to move. To cooperate.

"I don't have money, just a small amount—"

The two men laughed coarsely as they started toward her. The third man slunk in the shadows.

"Ain't no mistake and if you value that purty neck, you'd best be forkin' over the dough before one of these guns goes off! Think we don't know it's the rich shareholders that ride in this grand style? I'd sooner shoot you than a sidewinder, and don't be forgettin' it—you've took our land, busted our fences, ruined the range—"

"There's been a mistake. I can explain—"

The taller man sprang forward, his movement so quick that True was thrown against the couch as he grabbed her hair and yanked her head back furiously. Pain shot through her neck and for a moment the room whirled in black confusion.

"Git your bag if I decide to let go—hear?"

Biting her lip until she felt the salty taste of blood, True tried to nod her head.

"Please," she tried to whisper, "just let me go—and I'll do what I can—"

"'Course you will. You see, boys? Git a move on, kid!"

At the command, True was aware that the man who had stood in the shadows moved forward uncertainly.

The man holding her hair commanded, "Empty that bag of hers there on the table."

He bent his face frighteningly near to True's, pressing his unshaven cheek against hers and pulling her body close.

"You know, it might be wise if we just took you along fer security—and fer other reasons—understand?"

She understood only too well. And understanding caused her blood to curdle.

"Please," she whispered again. "Please, you're hurting me—"

Maybe the yell of triumph from the younger man who had stayed behind until ordered to dump the contents of her bag saved her life. True was never able to remember clearly what happened next.

The shifty-eyed man moved over beside the younger man, grabbed her pearl-and-sapphire brooch, and yelled, "Whoopee! Will you take a look at what she was hidin'!"

"Aha!" The younger man's eyes lit up with new interest. "This is no ordinary woman we have here." His tone was mocking. "'Tis a lady, she is! Either a shareholder in this railroad or," his eyes roved about the compartment, "his mistress! What say we take 'er along—good way of teachin' 'im a lesson and collectin' us a ransom at the same time!"

There was a round of laughter while True stood rooted to the spot. Fear of what the men might do to her and heartbreak over loss of the precious piece of jewelry and all it stood for had taken its toll.

But something else had moved in to dull her senses to fear and loss—the fact that the eyes, seen only in the shadows, of the youngest of the gang were familiar. The man was someone she knew.

It was terribly important that she get a good look—*terribly* important, some flash of insight told her. She must make every effort . . .

But at that moment there was a shrill two-fingered whistle from the mouth of a rider outside the window. So there were more, True thought dully—not that they mattered. She had to get a better look at the young man.

Maybe she would have except that her captor let go of her hair so unexpectedly that she felt her neck snap. An overwhelming dizziness resulted, and before she could regain her equilibrium the three men were gone as suddenly as they had arrived.

Reaching out to steady herself against the table where her empty handbag lay, True stooped to look out the window.

There, to her surprise, was a large party of men—all masked—riding sweat-soaked horses. The horses were stamping impatiently, causing dust to swirl and eddy up around their bellies, and the men's masks made them look much alike.

Except for the man standing in the center! Even at a distance, True could see that he looked out of place in their midst, dressed immaculately and wearing a rakish beaver dress hat.

If only she could see better! Straining her eyes, True tried to see his face. And then one of the horses bolted. Someone fired three shots, probably a signal, and the gang was gone.

In the whirlwind of dust they left behind, the well-dressed man was lost. When the dust settled a bit the man was gone.

Who was he? What part did he play in this?

But, more importantly, whose eyes had she seen above the bandanna when the three men broke into her quarters?

Then she dismissed her fears and brought her pounding heart under control. She had escaped with her life. What more could she ask? And with that thought True realized that others might not have fared as well. Mose, for one, was hurt!

She must get into the coaches and help. But there was a need for strength—lots of it.

"You'll have to help me, Lord," she whispered. Then, with as much courage and dignity as she could muster, True North left her compartment and walked calmly down the aisle.

"My mother was a nurse. My stepfather is a doctor. Let me pass," she said, using a gentle but authoritative voice.

The soft command had an immediate effect. White-faced mothers who had been moaning in shock and terror seemed to borrow of True's strength and busied themselves comforting their crying children.

Nobody was injured in the first coach, and, after asking the occupants to sit down quietly unless they were willing to help, she moved to the next one.

There a group of men was busy untying the hands and feet and removing the gags from the mouths of the engineer, conductor, and brakemen. Once freed, they too moved forward to check on the other passengers.

"Here's the first-aid kit, miss," the conductor said, handing True a box. "Ain't a doctor on board, but I got a doctor's kit of sorts—some ease medicine and ointments in the caboose. Can you manage 'til I go for 'em?"

True nodded, then looked around her. The woman on her left had a bad bruise on her forehead. Cold pack. Was the child's arm broken? Better splint it as best she could. She worked rapidly, all the while wondering about Mose.

And then she saw him! Lying between two rows of seats, he was so limp and still that at first she feared he was dead. Quickly, praying all the while, she felt for his pulse. Finding it, she bent to check his injuries. There was a jagged cut on his face, but the wound seemed to be superficial. Blood was seeping through his jacket, however.

With her handkerchief, she stopped the flow of blood, then ran to meet the conductor for help.

10
Strange Appraisal

❧

ALTHOUGH EXHAUSTED, TRUE was unable to do more than doze after the terrible nightmare had ended and a degree of normality had been established throughout the southbound train.

She had been awake since the first gray blades of morning knifed through the window blinds. Listening to the noisy *clackety-clack* of steel against steel, she reviewed the incidents of the night before.

None of them made sense. There had been warnings and danger signals, but none of them prepared her for the awfulness of the desperadoes who had robbed and wounded so many of the passengers. The victims, her tired mind realized, were those who appeared to be the most affluent.

But it could have been worse. So much worse! The outlaws could have taken her with them . . . could have killed their victims so there would be no witnesses. Who was the well-dressed man? *And whose eyes had she seen?*

Pulling herself up on her elbows, True lifted the blind and looked around her at the smoky beauty of the mountains the train had entered during the night. The first rosy fingers of sunrise touched the peaks to mingle with the blue haze.

This must be the Blue Ridge portion of the Appalachian chain she had heard Aunt Chrissy talk about so much! But, even as she watched, the chain terminated abruptly to appear again and again in short purple ranges and detached peaks.

"Does one have to pray with her eyes closed, Lord?" she whispered. "This scene is too beautiful for me to miss. How great You are, Lord—how great! Great enough, I know, to put some of this beauty into the lives of those who view Your handiwork!"

The train had picked up speed in the sharp descent of the Blue Ridge. True saw that it was now crossing what appeared to be a swamp. Moss-covered cypress trees and gnarled tupelo gums huddled together, seeming to shudder with fright at the giant Iron Horse which invaded their land.

And then a crude sign loomed up, the misshapen lettering reading: SUWANEE RIVER.

Oh, yes, the river that Angel Mother and her natural father had crossed to seek privacy . . .

But this was no time to work at trying to put together the puzzle that was her life. There was the more recent past to deal with. And then the strange meeting that lay ahead with Michael's aunt.

Hurriedly, she pulled a robe around her shoulders and began the 100-stroke brushing of her hair.

"Miss North!" True, recognizing the conductor's voice, laid down the hairbrush and answered his knock.

"I come to invite you to the diner, miss. Hopin' you don't mind under the circumstances."

True knotted the cord of her robe and, sweeping her hair back, opened the door a crack.

"Of course, I don't mind!" she said quickly. "But the others—how are they?"

"A miracle," the man said, shaking his head with wonder. "In all my born days I never had a prayer answered so quick! I prayed for an angel and there you was—a fine lady like you, makin' the rounds like—"

"Oh, come now, please don't go putting a halo on my head. I did what any caring person would have done—and your words, well, they embarrass me, sir."

Then, lest he feel scolded, True asked quickly how Mose was progressing.

"Oh, good as new, that boy! Them folks got a tough skin, you know—"

Not wishing to hear any more about "them folks," True said politely that she would join him shortly. Then, padding barefoot back to the dressing table, she picked up her hairbrush . . . 88, 89 . . .

True jabbed the hatpin into her flat-topped felt, smoothed her rumpled skirt, and picked up her suitcases. Foolishly, she had hoped that Michael would find a way somehow to be here before her arrival.

The morning haze had risen from the river to create a strange fog that mingled with the smoke of hissing trains. Hundreds of them, it seemed! She was surrounded by the black monsters.

It was a strange contrast to the little depot where Daddy Wil had flagged the midnight train and, surrounded by a loving family, she had boarded—how long ago?

It seemed like a million years . . .

"Can I hep you-all, ma'am? You-all want I should call a carriage?" a rich voice asked at True's elbow. Gratefully, she handed her bags to the capable hands of the elderly, dusky-skinned man.

Feeling increasingly alone, True watched for some familiar landmark from her mother's diary or Aunt Chrissy's descriptions of Atlanta. There were none.

In place of the mansions they mentioned there were charred ruins in the midst of weed-grown lots, rotting fences with sagging gates, and neglected magnolia trees which looked as if they had forgotten how to bloom.

"This part's a heap bettah," the driver said suddenly. With that promise he pulled the reins to guide the horses into an area which either had escaped the worst of the Atlanta fire or had been built back Gardens were groomed to perfection. Fall flowers crowded one another for space. And giant oaks appeared to link their arms in leafy bowers above the widely separated mansions which centered the immense estates.

The carriage stopped with a jerk.

"Miss Emily lives heah," the driver half-whispered, as if afraid he would awaken the occupant.

True stiffened with surprise and half-fear.

Here! Why, this was a mansion . . . a great, white-pillared mansion . . . and she was here to meet a woman whose name she had never heard just days ago.

The hand she gave the driver was shaking and cold, and her legs wobbled as the two of them walked toward the massive white door after he helped her from the carriage. Her sense of adventure gave way to uneasiness.

Michael had made it sound so simple. True had found herself a little excited as she tried to imagine his maiden cousin. At least she would have one friend.

But now she was no longer sure it was a good idea. There was something forbidding about the place, unwelcoming in spite of its Old-South grace.

The intrigue was gone and she was on the verge of telling the driver she would return with him.

But the door opened before she could decide about ringing the chimes. It was as if eyes were watching from behind the heavy gold drapes.

A black butler in full dress opened the door but was pushed aside immediately by a circle of other people.

"I'll take over, Hosea," a softly musical voice said with a note of dismissal.

The owner approached, and even as True appraised the other woman, a part of her was aware of piercing, measuring eyes surrounding her.

She must be standing in the center of Michael's family. A group of "instant friends"? An anchor to cling to in case her plans crumbled?

Somehow she doubted it. If only she could escape . . . well, she would, at the earliest possible moment. Right now she must introduce herself and explain if she could.

But before there was an opportunity, Miss Kincaid was speaking.

"I am Michael's Cousin Emily," she explained. "And I bid you welcome to this house—"

"But—but—" True began uncertainly. "You don't know who I am—"

Cousin Emily's laughter was mellow, reminding True of evening chimes.

"Oh, but I feel I do! Michael's night letter was glowing with excitement. But, come, come, let us not be standing here at the door. You must meet the others here."

Then, turning, Miss Kincaid directed her words to the driver, her tone becoming clipped and abrupt.

"What are you waiting for?"

The driver! True had forgotten him completely under the seemingly hostile observation of her hosts. Remembering that she had neglected to pay the man, she suddenly realized she had no money. The robbers had taken all except that pinned to her corset.

"I-I'm sorry," she whispered, feeling a hot flush creeping from her neck to her cheeks. "You see, there was a problem—and my money was taken—at least," her flush deepened, "any that I can get to now—"

"So the lady needs a loan?" One of the men stepped forward, obviously a relative of Michael's because they resembled each other greatly. He bowed to her almost mockingly and his tone said more than he asked.

Is that ALL you want of us?

He paid the driver. True thanked him. And Emily Kincaid motioned the group to the parlor. As they gathered in the vast room, True was aware only of the modernization which had gone into its renovation.

It was a blend of the old and the new, with the kind of workmanship which required more than skilled workmen. Only an architect could do it—and architects charged handsomely.

But that was no deterrent to this family, apparently. And "this family" meant Michael's family, she thought dazedly. *Michael!* What had he told them, anyway?

Later, during the course of the odd conversation, True was to think a bit more coherently, taking in every detail of her surroundings— the intricate carved mouldings above the great marble fireplaces (*three* of them in one room) and the Tiffany windows alongside; the high-arch ceiling; the soft plum-and-apricot hangings; the fine paintings in heavy gold frames . . .

But for now it took all her strength to concentrate on the people around her and try to make some sense of her strange position.

"You come as a complete surprise to us, you know, my dear," Emily Kincaid repeated.

"I'm sure," True murmured, not sure what was expected. Words were poor tools in such a situation. All she was able to manage was to stare at Michael's cousin.

The slender woman stood as tall as True. Her skin was like finely webbed parchment but was kept magnolia-white, undoubtedly by expensive creams and use of parasols to ward off the sun. The regal head was crowned with heavy hair, not braided and wound about her head like Aunt Chrissy's, but pouffed on the sides and piled on top in curls.

Cousin Emily's dress was lavender silk with a creamy white bertha laced with black velvet ribbon. Beside her, True felt dowdy. Out of date. And untidy in her travel-wrinkled suit. Her hair needed a rainwater shampoo. Her nails needed buffing. And she felt that her usually pink-and-white skin must be streaked with soot. Else why would they all be looking at her so intently?

"Now, tell us about your trip, my dear . . . oh, forgive me, I must introduce the rest of the family. Sit here beside me."

Emily sounded cordial and at the same time commanding

Numbly, True sat down at the opposite end of the velvet couch. Cousin Emily made an arc around the room with a slender, jeweled hand. True would never remember the names—cousins, she supposed. No closer, since the woman made a point of Michael's being an "only heir." Later she would meet his father, who was confined to his chambers . . . but for now, she must need a cup of tea, poor child . . .

Cousin Emily rang for the butler and ordered tea and crumpets. Hosea was back almost instantly, setting out the sparkling silver tea service. Once tea was poured, Cousin Emily leaned back against the pillows and repeated her request.

"Your trip. We want to hear all about it—and you."

True fumbled nervously with her teacup. She disliked tea without sugar, but her hands were trembling too badly to risk spooning sugar into her cup.

"There's little to tell," she began. Little that would be of interest to this group, she felt. But a look around the room told her that they were interested spectators. Vaguely, she wondered why.

The silence became embarrassing. Obviously, they expected her to continue. So, choosing her words carefully, she told of the interesting scenery. Maybe small talk would suffice.

But no. The man—hadn't Cousin Emily called him Oscar?—who had paid the driver leaned forward.

"You spoke of misfortune. Did someone take your wallet?"

There seemed to be nothing left to do but tell of the robbery. It was not an interesting account, True felt. She was troubled by the focus of so many appraising eyes. She avoided telling her reaction to Mose's injury, her assistance to the injured, the well-dressed man she had seen with the outlaws—and certainly her feeling that she had seen a pair of familiar eyes.

Later, True realized that she had also avoided mention of when she and Michael had met. She had no idea what he may have told the family.

But she had a fair idea of the wrong conclusions they would draw if they knew that she had been so brazen as to occupy his quarters on such short acquaintance.

There were questions, mostly for conversation, except for the excited ones posed by two small children who had entered.

Then, without warning, an auburn-haired woman about her own age said, "North? The name is unfamiliar. Was your father from Atlanta?"

"No, my mother," True said quickly, then added, "and my father was from Boston. That is one reason why I am here—to sort of trace my ancestry. The Kelly and Stein family—"

"*Kelly—Stein—*" Cousin Emily's voice was little more than a whisper, and her face had grown pale. But she recovered quickly.

"We must ask no more questions. You must be exhausted. I shall have the maid draw your bath, because, of course, you are to stay here! You're one of us now."

One of them? Something was wrong . . . something she must correct. But for now she was exhausted. Wrong?

Of course! They were looking at her as would a groom's family. And there wasn't a groom!

11
Mistaken Identity

⟿

TISHA, ONE OF the several maids, brought a breakfast tray the next morning. True was scarcely aware of what she ate. She was too overwhelmed by the cherrywood furniture against the silk-covered apricot of the walls, the beige carpet with apricot-and-plum roses, and the vases of silk flowers.

Soft pink-gold sunlight filtered through the curtains drawn against the sun, giving a soft lampglow to the guest room in which she had slept.

But she did not belong in this mansion. Today she must leave . . .

Her thoughts were interrupted by a knock. Michael? Could it be Michael? It occurred to her that the man was a stranger. With a thudding heart, True reached for her robe.

But it was Emily Kincaid's voice.

"May I come in, True?"

The tone of voice presupposed an affirmative answer. The older woman entered before True could respond.

"And did you sleep well, my dear?"

Emily, elegant in a morning dress of muted blue, moved about the bedroom, opening drapes of the windows which looked out onto a wide veranda lined with swinging baskets of blossoming vines that formed a green screen to create an underwater look.

The antique furniture was arranged formally, and behind it True could catch a glimpse of well-manicured hedges, all ignoring fall and

54

in brilliant bloom. A huge fountain centered the scene. It was all so lovely that True could only gasp with sheer pleasure.

"It's lovely," she murmured.

Emily Kincaid only nodded. Then she seated herself on the slipper chair near the bed.

"And now," she said, "I should like to hear about your family."

For a moment True felt a little flare of anger. What did her family have to do with this? Why was she under inspection here?

But immediately she put the thoughts from her mind. After all, she was a guest in the house. She had accepted their hospitality. And, yes, she remembered suddenly, she had mentioned tracing her past— even mentioning the name of Kelly, Aunt Chrissy's father, and Stein, Angel Mother's father.

Now she regretted that. She could never bring the cruel man who was her grandfather into her heart. Never in a million years! Why, he had hated Aunt Chrissy, his stepdaughter, and had thrown her own mother out when he found her "with child" out of wedlock . . .

What would this woman say if she knew I was that child . . . what was it people here used to call illegitimate children—"briar-patch children"? Except that I'm not illegitimate. Angel Mother married Daddy Wil so I would be a True North! True's chin went up defensively.

True was suddenly aware that the other woman was studying her closely through narrowed lids. She colored under the level gaze that seemed to penetrate the invisible wall she had built around herself.

"Your family?" Emily Kincaid prompted.

"Yes—my mind was wandering, I'm afraid. I'm sorry—"

Why was she apologizing and what for?

"There is little I can tell you. What I mean is that I am here to sort of—well, retrace their past." She hesitated, and when her hostess did not speak, True added without necessity, "Which would be *my* past."

"I can help you," Emily said without expression. "You see, I knew your—er—Mr. Kelly, whatever relationship he was to you. He and I kept company once upon a time—which is of no consequence. But it is not my past we are tracing."

She paused, and True wondered in the moment's silence if *investigating* would not have been more appropriate. But there was no time to concentrate on the interest these people showed, for Emily was speaking again.

"It would help if you had brought along some photographs?"

Maybe the woman would help, after all. It was worth a try and, besides, there seemed no graceful way to refuse.

"I have one or two," she said, fumbling in her handbag. Seeing her wallet, she paused. "I have money now, and I want to repay the man who came to my rescue yesterday—"

Emily waved a slender hand—her way of dismissing an idea.

"Your Cousin Oscar would not dream of accepting it."

Your Cousin Oscar! What on earth . . . with all her heart True wished she knew more of the practices here. Maybe everybody was "Cousin"—after proper examination.

Then, locating the pictures, she turned her attention to what had brought her here in the first place.

On the surface, the Kincaids and (as far as she could ascertain) the St. Johns—all under one roof—were making an effort to be hospitable.

But, in the luxury of their home and amid their appraising glances, True was uncomfortable among these wealthy people. She was an alien, a foreigner—not ready or willing to be a cousin. She belonged in the picture she was about to hand Michael's Cousin Emily. But, first her grandfather . . .

"Is this the man you knew?" True asked, handing the photograph to Emily.

Emily's eyes lighted up, making words unnecessary as she studied the dark, good looks of the then-youthful man. At length she spoke.

"Jimmy," she said. And then the woman added something almost inaudible. Surely True's ears deceived her. *Could* Emily Kincaid have said, "*My* Jimmy"?

"I never heard him called by that name," True said. "You're sure—"

Emily stiffened.

"I'm very sure. How could I have forgotten? Had your grandmother not come to spend that fateful summer . . . or even if we had played a different game! I will never believe she did not know Jimmy was behind the door when girls guessed the identity," Emily colored, "and discreet young ladies guessed wrong purposely—lest they be—oh, this is indelicate!—*kissed*, and in this very house."

In spite of herself, True giggled. Her hostess did not join her, and True sighed inwardly. That stolen kiss, planned or otherwise, very well may have been the only one exchanged in this place.

Well, this woman's love affairs, or lack of them, had nothing to do with her. It was good, however, that she knew something of the Kelly family—

Emily broke into her thoughts.

"Fine family, the Kellys. Fine, indeed, regular bluebloods like the Kincaids and St. Johns. And background is *so* important—essential when choosing one's mate, since it ties together two families forever."

True did not meet Emily's eyes. She had a strong feeling that there was more behind her words than the long-ago romance which never blossomed. It was a relief when the other woman asked to see the other photograph True held.

"Maybe you will remember the daughters—"

"Jimmy, my personal name for him, only had one."

In the short silence, True could hear the pounding of her heart. This was thin ice.

"Yes," she said, choosing her words carefully, "but my—I mean, when the man you call Jimmy Kelly was killed, his wife remarried."

"My dear young woman," Emily Kincaid said crisply, "I do not need you to jog my memory."

Rebuffed, True was on the verge of snatching the picture, thanking her hostess for her questionable hospitality, and ordering a carriage. But then Emily was speaking normally again, as if nothing had happened.

"Jimmy's widow let no grass grow on his grave after the explosion before finding herself another mate! And, as for that Stein man . . . but, wait, am I speaking of your grandfather? There was another daughter. Ah, yes, here she is—Mary Evangeline, wasn't it? Exactly like her mother, face of an angel—but who knows what evil lurks in the heart?"

There was a wild desire to run at this woman. Tear at the delicate skin. Break down this regal shell.

But it would defeat the cause. And nothing would touch her anyhow. *Caution. I must use caution.* Over and over she told herself that.

True realized that Emily was speaking. Hoping she had missed none of the words, she listened carefully.

"—She left here, of course, and in disgrace, I might add. Rumor had it that she got into trouble with some Eastern man. Could have been anybody, of course. You never can tell about women like that. Once they go bad, there's no changing them—"

"Oh, I don't agree! I don't agree at all—"

"You know nothing of such women. They may delude themselves into thinking they'll make their hearts right, but the road to hell's paved with good intentions. Made by evil people . . . but why are we speaking of someone you never knew? Although, I must say, you inherited your aunt's dangerous physical features. Sad, indeed, that you didn't take after your mother. Odd, isn't it, that your mother looks so like her father and that blonde gene continues to travel through the generations! Now Christen Elizabeth, your mother, was different in every way."

Speak up, True. Speak up now. Correct this deception. But the tongue that could have told the truth clove to the roof of her mouth.

Was she afraid of this woman or was she trying to gather information she could not have gleaned as the "bastard child of the wayward Mary Evangeline Stein"?

Part of both, she decided with the only corner of her brain that was able to think in the cloud of confusion. But of one thing she was certain. She, True North, was not ashamed of her heritage. She was proud of her family. Never mind blue blood!

Overcome with an overwhelming desire to get out of this house, True reached for the photograph.

But Emily drew back.

"The rest of these people—who are they, True?"

"It's hard to explain. No, easy to explain, but hard to understand. They really have nothing to do with—"

"If they are descendants of Jimmy's, they concern me!" Emily's voice carried an edge.

It was hard to imagine why. But, then, everything about this situation was unimaginable. So why not get it over with? And quickly!

"Part of us are his descendants," True said, choosing her words

carefully. "It will be easier if I use full names—if that is all right?"
Safer, too . . .

Emily nodded in agreement.

"I'll know the relationship."

True studied the photograph. How well she remembered the day the traveling photographer came to Turn-Around Inn, an unforgettable Easter Sunday.

Swallowing the lump in her throat, True began, "This is Christen Elizabeth Kelly, as you know—"

"Your mother."

No, my aunt! Should she say it? Quickly True went on.

"The man to her left is Joseph Craig, a wonderful minister. And between Christen Elizabeth and Mary Evangeline is Dr. Wilson North. The tall, dark boy holding me is Young Wil, Dr. North's nephew. The boy my age, holding Young Wil's hand, is Marty. Marty's parents died in a flood and the Craigs took him in—"

"In a sense, then, Marty is your brother?"

In a sense, yes, but not the way you think. You have identified the wrong young woman as my mother. True realized then that there was no way that she could tell of Angel Mother's death, followed by Uncle Joe's—and the subsequent marriage of Aunt Chrissy to Daddy Wil.

Well, that did make Marty her brother . . . better let it go at that.

She was about to replace the photograph in her bag when Emily Kincaid's shrewd eyes focused on her, compelling her to look up. Dark, young eyes locked with faded blue ones and the gazes held. Even before the question came, True—careful as she had been—knew that it would concern something she had touched upon quickly if at all.

"Am I to gather then that the wayward Mary Elizabeth came to that wild frontier to give birth to that—that—"

"Baby," True supplied. Emily Kincaid did not know her well enough to detect the dangerous quiet of the voice.

"Her baby was born dead, then?"

"Mary Evangeline lost one child, yes," True said, remembering the painful account of her mother's trying to bear a child to her beloved Wilson.

It was something that this unfeeling woman would be unable to understand—an unselfish act of love. Angel Mother had known the risks . . . even then had been in fragile health . . . but nothing mattered except her love, which could never die, no matter what happened to her flesh.

So let the woman think the lost child was True herself.

"It has nothing to do with us, Miss—"

"Cousin Emily," the woman corrected. "Michael should be home tomorrow, as I am sure you are aware, and we must have another long talk—this time about our own relationship."

No, she did *not* know when Michael was returning. And there *was* no relationship. Whatever was going on here had to be corrected. And at once! She was glad, for that reason, that Michael St. John was coming home so soon.

True glanced at the grandfather clock at the far end of the great bedroom.

"My!" she said, "I had no idea it was so late. If you will excuse me, I must get dressed."

Emily rose to stand her full height. Did she never make an ungraceful gesture?

"Yes, you will wish to see the ruins of your home. I will accompany you—"

True swung a foot onto the carpeted floor.

"No, please—this is something I must do alone. Also, I must mail an important letter and locate a telegraph office to let my family know I am all right."

"I will order the carriage," Emily said as she turned to leave. "It is good that we got to know each other better."

Only we don't! True's heart protested. *It's a case of mistaken identity . . . one I may NEVER be able to correct . . .*

12
Magnolia Manor

❧

ONCE SHE HAD sent Aunt Chrissy and Daddy Wil word that she
was safe, True felt a sense of relief. The night letter would arrive the
following day, the telegrapher said.

She only wished her bulky letter to Young Wil would go through
as fast. Miss Emily had said it was perfectly all right to receive mail
at the Kincaid-St. John mansion, so True had given the address without explanation.

It would be wonderful to hear from Young Wil again. Actually, she
understood very little of what he told her concerning his studies in
pathology. But she clung to his every word, honored that he would
choose her as the one in whom he confided. At those times they were
very close. Young Wil didn't tease about the two freckles on her nose.
And he did not treat her like a child!

Remembering their countless tramps through the Oregon forests,
forever in search of new forms of plant life for Young Wil's botany
courses or animal fossils for zoology, True wished that he were with
her now. Young Wil knew how to turn everything into an adventure—
and how to make her feel safe and cared for at the same time.

Maybe, she thought slowly for the first time, it was better to be
thought of as young and inexperienced than pushed into the foreign
role of maturity. Especially when one had to cope alone . . .

A brisk breeze had risen. Autumn leaves pattered down noiselessly
at her feet. True realized then that she had been so engrossed in her

thoughts that she surely must have passed the home where her mother and aunt grew up.

The section of the city that she had entered was in shambles. Here and there a few stone fireplaces, once a part of the great houses they had warmed, stood as if waiting for their owners to return. Rotting foundations, barely visible through the tangle of brambles, marked where other mansions had stood.

Some of the places, she saw, were posted with NO TRESPASSING signs. Nobody seemed to have bothered with the others. Nothing here resembled the Kelly home.

She was about to turn when she spotted the lonely-looking figure of an elderly black man. Sitting on the edge of what had once been a wishing well, the man appeared to be dozing. In his hand was a pair of shears.

True cleared her throat. Startled, the man sprang to his feet. She saw then that he was even older than she had supposed.

"'Scuse me, missy—I don't mean no harm bein' here abouts. Lemme git from yore way—"

And like a frightened rabbit, the old fellow stepped aside for True to pass through the gate. He had removed the ragged straw hat to reveal a head of frizzled, cotton-white hair which he now held in his hands.

"I jest come heah t'wish—"

"It's quite all right," True said quickly. "And you needn't be afraid. I don't belong here either. I'm looking for a house and I thought perhaps you could direct me." She handed him a slip of paper carrying the address.

The man shook his head sorrowfully without looking up.

"I cain't read th' words," he murmured.

Compassion filled True's heart. Feeling as embarrassed as the man looked, she was about to thank him and move on when the ebony face brightened.

"Did she have uh name—th' house? Mostly, they did, I recollects."

Of course! She should have thought of that.

"Magnolia Manor," True replied.

Dropping the shears, the man forgot his shyness and raised a pair of dark and shining eyes.

"I knowed it," he whispered in a near-croon. "I tole my Mandy afore she went to be wid th' Lawd that someday one o'you-all wuz shure t'come home."

It was True's turn to be taken aback.

"You mean—you mean, *this* is it? This is all that's left of Magnolia Manor?"

"The' buildin's all went blazin—and th' lootin' follawed no mattah how hard us colored folks tried t'save th' only home we evah had. But th' trees is heah—'member them mossy oaks wheah you-all and yo big sistah used to swing? Allus wantin' I should swing you highah than yo mammy thunk was safe." His laugh was mellow with recollection of another generation.

"How wonderful that I've found you," True said warmly. "And forgive me for not introducing myself. I am True North. What is your name?"

"Name's Joshua—and I allus added Kelly on, secretlike." The man scratched his head in confusion. "But the name ain't right fer you-all. I got no book larnin', but I got myself a memory—Miss Vangie, we all said, Miss Vangie, our Li'l White Chile!"

True moved over to take the gnarled, black hand in hers.

"You're close, Joshua—very close. I'm her daughter."

A look of sheer joy crossed the weathered face, and he favored her with a toothless grin.

"Don't mattah none. You-all'll wan' the' yawd puttin' shape 'fore the buildin' starts. Best I be workin', Miss—"

"Just True, please, Joshua." True inhaled deeply, wondering what to say next. But he mustn't be allowed to count on something which would never materialize.

"Let's hold off on any more work—at least, for now. Agreed?"

For a moment the old man looked disappointed. Then his countenance brightened.

"Ain't no rush. Nobody's to bothah us none, 'ceptin' maybe th' feller from the courthouse."

"What fellow, Joshua? Someone you know?"

Joshua shook his grizzled head.

"Lawman mebbe—sumpin' 'bout railroad bizness fer Miss Vangie."

13
Homecoming
❧

THERE WAS SO much that True would have asked of the old gardener if there had been time. Later she was to regret hurrying away, for the two of them were never to meet again.

But Emily Kincaid had said that dinner would be early this evening, and her request that all gather in the library by six o'clock was a command.

One simply did not cross the woman, True thought a little resentfully, as she hurried away from the ruins of her mother's childhood home and the only living person, as far as she knew, who might have helped her put together the missing pieces that her mother's diary had omitted.

Buried in her thoughts, True was at first unaware that somebody or something stood before her. And then she realized that Michael St. John had appeared from nowhere like an apparition.

"I know I should have waited at the house," he said apologetically, taking another step toward her, "but I could not wait to see if I was right—without an audience!"

He looked at True with hazel eyes which in the slanted rays of the setting sun looked bright and innocent. A little smile of appreciation played about the corners of his mouth above the carefully trimmed beard.

Feeling a mixture of emotions she was unable to identify, True could only murmur, "Right? Right about what?"

Even as she waited for Michael's answer, she felt herself smiling in return. Here was a friend in what she could only assume was enemy territory, although the "why" of either was yet a mystery—one he could help resolve.

"Right about your beauty, my dear. And you may rest assured that is not intended as idle flattery. Through those dull meetings I kept seeing that special golden look of yours. 'But, Michael,' I said, 'no young lady's hair can outshine the moon. No pair of eyes can change from sky blue to royal purple—and no face can be shaped like a delicate cameo—' "

At the word *cameo*, he stopped short. And True felt her own quick intake of breath. Automatically her hand flew to her throat, pausing at the spot where she ordinarily wore the pearl-and-sapphire brooch.

As important a part as the precious heirloom had played in the lives of her mother, her aunt, and herself, how *could* she, even in this strange new world, have forgotten until this moment that she had been forced to surrender it in the holdup or be taken hostage?

The sunset glow turned to a peculiar white haze. The cobblestone street was rising up to meet her. And the moss-bearded oak trees were dancing about her in a dizzying quadrille . . .

Through it all she was only dimly aware that Michael reached out to steady her and then gathered her into his arms. She clung to him as one clings to a lifeline. Caught in a riptide of emotions, Michael was solid ground.

Not thinking of his arms as an embrace, True relaxed against the smoothness of his vest and let her eyes droop closed.

Michael was speaking, but she paid no attention to the words—just their tone, which was smooth velvet. Soothing her. Making her long to sleep.

Was it possible to go to sleep standing up? *Surely she must be dreaming*, True thought. Dreaming the words she heard. And surely sleep accounted for her feeling of helplessness. Weightlessness. Her total levity. What was the handsome, sandy-haired man in her dreams saying?

"Rest, my darling—that's it, rest. They've worn you out. I should have known it would be too much. Rest, my Sleeping Beauty, and when you awaken, there is much—so much—we must talk about. A lifetime of planning—but for now, *rest*."

And when she would have opened her eyes, he kissed them closed. *Darling*, he'd called her . . . the wrong man . . .

Later True wondered how long the two of them stood there beneath the oaks. She began to regain consciousness when the gathering evening breeze swept the Evangeline moss against her face; and then—not satisfied—wrapped itself about them as if to bind them together.

When she opened her eyes, the sun was down and there was a strange, yellow glow where the sun had been. How could she have let this happen?

"Oh, Michael—we must go," she murmured hastily. "Miss Kincaid, your Cousin Emily, doesn't like to be kept waiting!"

Reluctantly, he released her. Then, with a little laugh, he reached for her hand and tucked it beneath his arm.

"I see she got to you, all right. Was the meeting very awful?"

Matching her steps to his, True tried to appraise the situation.

"Not awful, I guess," she said slowly—"more frightening. I'm sure none of them like me—but, then, why should they? Oh, I'm not making sense at all!"

They were nearing the mansion. It looked even more ominous in the shadows than by daylight.

True had had a feeling of foreboding earlier. Now the feeling was worse—as if the night moths which were beginning to fill the air around them were loosed inside her as well.

The mansion was so tall. So dark, except for the windows—all angrily ablaze at their tardiness—which seemed to watch their every move as True and Michael moved up the narrow path left by the heavy growth of hedge.

The veranda, she saw now, wrapped both sides of the great house. Bay windows jutted out at every corner and, in spite of the vine-draped pillars, something about the recent architecture changed the plantation-period house from a colonial mansion to a Victorian castle.

Maybe it was the round tower on the back roof, shaped like a witch's hat. Involuntarily she shuddered, realizing what was wrong with the house. It lacked love.

Michael lowered his voice.

"You make all the sense in the world, my dear. Meeting them, especially Cousin Emily, can be a fiasco. She's our self-appointed guardian of the family fortune." He chuckled. "And the family's good name, I might add."

True drew back.

"And she thought I had designs on you? Is that why she was so remote and—well, cautious? Oh, Michael, I never should have accepted your hospitality. I had no right . . . but, tell me, how could she have suspected such?"

Pulling her behind a giant magnolia, as if to hide from the staring windows, Michael gripped both her hands.

"I accept full responsibility for that impression, True. I wanted you to be cared for—looked after—until I could get here to do it. And it was necessary that I imply that we—well, had an arrangement."

True tried to pull away.

"I feel used somehow," she whispered. "Used and rebuffed—and, yet, guilty, because I let it happen."

She felt on the verge of tears.

Michael's voice was low and pleading, something which surprised her about the caustic man with all his polished social graces.

"Wrong on all three counts, my dear—*wrong!* You must believe that. Oh, we should have talked before the gathering of the clan. My intentions are strictly honorable—and you have not led me on. I want to make you mine—"

"*Michael!* Is that you in the garden?" Emily Kincaid's voice, though pleasant, carried an edge which sliced through the balmy night air.

Anticipating her inward rage, True shuddered again. Her hostess would be wearing an elegant gown, her neck encased in pearls, while she herself was rumpled and untidy.

There would scarcely be time to wash up before joining the clan of (she hoped the Lord would forgive the word) *vultures* in the library.

Ducking in (a bit ungracefully, she feared), True made a flying trip to her room. Pouring water into the china basin, she recalled that she had told Michael nothing of the robbery. Neither had she thanked him for use of his quarters.

He was right. They *must* talk. . . .

14
On Trial

ぐ

"DINNAH IS SURVED, Miz Emily."

With Hosea's softly spoken announcement, Emily Kincaid rose in signal for the others to rise also. Oscar escorted the hostess through the dining room arch. Michael politely waited for all the others (whose names and relationships True was still unable to identify) to follow.

Then, with a slight twinkle in his eyes, he offered her his arm. Gratefully she took it. Whatever else Michael St. John might or might not be, he was gallant, "a gentleman of fine breeding," she supposed they would phrase it here.

How could he have failed to see how she stood out—in a wrong way—in her tailored navy suit, simple, high-necked blouse adorned only with a single-strand pearl necklace, while the other women were bustled and ruffled as if for a gala party?

He himself was dressed so impeccably—everything about him giving off an aura of fastidiousness—that he had to be comparing her unfavorably. If so, he gave no sign of it. That gave True confidence to get through the grueling evening which was to follow.

She wished he had warned her what to expect, but he probably knew no other world himself.

Tisha brought turtle soup. Did True like turtle soup? Emily inquired. True didn't know. Then Tisha was pleased to have the finger bowls ready for Miss North in case she did not care for the flavor.

The maid stood ready with the fragile, cut-glass bowl on which rose petals floated. Small talk went on around her. But True had the

68

feeling that all eyes were focused on her as she lifted the soup spoon and, careful to dip away from her, touched the creamed, green liquid to her lips.

Why were they all staring? The soup was flat and tasteless, since she was in no condition for her taste buds to work.

But if it had been made of green persimmons, she would have gone on with the silly game they were playing. So she forced a smile.

"Isn't True all I told you she was?" Michael's voice, laced with pride, broke into True's consciousness.

Emily Kincaid laid down her spoon and rang the silver bell beside her.

"I'm sure she is, Michael—and much more."

The small addendum was not lost on True.

Please, Michael, she willed. *Please say no more—* "Has she told you that some of her ancestry goes back to Boston?"

"You may bring the salad, Hosea," Emily instructed. Then she turned to True. "How interesting, my dear! An old established family?"

"Boston-Irish," True remembered Aunt Chrissy's calling the Blake family.

Then, in an effort to lighten the moment, "But I doubt if they were able to crowd into the *Mayflower.* Surely it must have been overloaded!"

There was no laughter. Michael saved the moment by reaching out to place a steadying hand on hers.

"I kept True a secret, Cousin Emily, in the hope that I could be here for the trial! Does she pass the test?" Light words, but meaningful.

True colored under Emily's scrutiny. The older woman was comparing her, of course, to the other women in the room . . . the other women in Michael's life . . . and some Southern belle she had chosen for her cousin as a suitable wife.

Well, it was best to get the whole thing out in the open. Let them know that she was here for the exact reasons she had mentioned. Her stay in the city would be brief. And it would not be here in this house!

Where should she begin? With her mother's secret—or the fact that she had never eaten turtle soup before?

Before she could think of appropriate words, Emily spoke again.

"I regret that you were late this evening—"

"We've apologized." True was unable to hold her tongue.

As if she had not spoken, Emily continued, "We were to make some plans regarding your introduction to our circle of friends. As soon as your trunks arrive."

And have something suitable to wear. They were ashamed of her. Tears sprang to her eyes. She did not belong in their shallow, glittering world. She felt on the very top of a high cliff about to topple into a canyon below.

How silly of her to feel that way! All she had to do was walk out! Why, then, did she feel trapped?

True gripped Michael's hand, hoping it would signal her desire to escape. The tightened fingers brought a look of pleased surprise; but, before she could convey a further message, Emily spoke over his head.

"Tell me, my dear, did you find what you were looking for this afternoon—yes, you may remove the plates and bring the main course, Tisha. Did you not like the salad, True?"

True looked at her untouched plate, aware of the salad's presence for the first time.

"I—I'm sorry—I seem to have little appetite—"

"All the excitement has been trying. I should have gone with you uninvited this afternoon. Tell me, was that eccentric colored man there again? He rambles on so foolishly—"

True answered briefly. She was reluctant to talk about the afternoon, or, for that matter, herself. But, yes, a nice man who called himself Joshua was there, she said.

Emily leaned forward, her face strained. And around her True felt the raised eyebrows of over a dozen members of this family up and down the table.

"Did he make mention—"

So that's it! They want to know about the "feller from the courthouse." But why?

And then Michael exploded a cannon.

"Let's not exhaust True. Bear in mind that she has not said, 'Yes' to me yet."

15

I Want to Go Home, Lord!

∽

AFTER THE TENSE dinner hour, True pleaded a headache and escaped to her room.

"Please don't linger, Michael," she begged. "There is so much we must discuss—I'm so confused—so bewildered—but not tonight. I have to be alone!"

Later she wondered if she had been rude. Certainly she had all but shut the door in Michael's face. And he had done nothing to deserve that . . . or had he?

Who was responsible for this mess, anyway? And how had she veered so far off her course? Or maybe she hadn't. Everything was so shrouded in mystery . . .

Too exhausted to think clearly, True turned up the wick on the gas lamp beside her bed and read Uncle Joe's Bible. But the words ran together and she did not find the usual comfort in the Scriptures.

Michael's face kept drifting between her and the pages, his hazel eyes sometimes admiring, sometimes quizzical, and sometimes frighteningly shrewd.

When the shrewd expression came, True squeezed her own eyes closed to shut out the part of him that bothered her.

And then the face wasn't Michael's. It was Young Wil's—so real that she felt she could reach out and touch him, push the boyhood cowlick away from his broad forehead so she could look into the dark, thoughtful eyes that could turn roguish and back to pensive without notice.

A carbon copy of Daddy Wil, his frame was a little taller, a little more powerful than his uncle's—which accounted for his looking equally at home in lumberjack garb of the Northwest or his Sunday best.

Oh, how she missed him! Given the opportunity, she would put up with his teasing—even welcome it! How long did it take a letter to reach Portland, anyway?

Better yet, maybe she would be finished here before his answer came . . . or the Lord's . . .

With that thought, True sat straight up in bed. What was it she had said? That Atlanta might be home, after all? Or maybe even Boston?

It occurred to her suddenly that she had not had a heart-to-heart talk with the Lord for too long.

Quickly sliding from between the linen sheets, she knelt beside the bed. Then, tucking her long nightgown about her chilled feet, True poured her heart out to God.

"Why is it, Lord, that I forget You even when I know You never forget me? Forgive my neglect. Forgive my disloyalty to You—and maybe to my wonderful family—although You know I never intended that . . ."

And then the tears came as she prayed for each of her loved ones by name: "Daddy Wil, Aunt Chrissy, Young Wil, the twins, and Marty— wherever he is—"

True stopped at that point, aware that something she was unable to pinpoint bothered her. When no insight came, she continued.

The great clock by the window seat interrupted her rudely.

"Funny thing about clocks," Young Wil had said once, "they fold their hands but can't learn to keep quiet even during our family prayers!"

Family prayers . . . that was something else amiss in this house. Nobody prayed. At least not aloud.

Seemingly satisfied with its 12 strokes, the clock was silent and True finished her prayer.

"I need Your guidance, Lord. I really don't know who I am or where I belong. I had hoped this visit would teach me—but I am only more confused. Lead me home—wherever home is. Right now I want to go where I *think* I belong. But something is holding me back . . ."

The time that followed was a confusion of people, each—it seemed to True—with a hidden motive, each different.

She had resolved to have a private talk with Michael. It was imperative, to save further embarrassment and possible heartbreak, that they come to an understanding. He had given the impression that theirs was a friendship of long standing—*more* than a friendship, actually, something this clan seemed to have sunk their collective teeth into. Surely that was why Emily Kincaid had put her through the third degree.

Well, she thought with a glow of pride, *nobody could say she was not of gentle breeding!* Aunt Chrissy had seen to that. And, although Daddy Wil's income as a country doctor was small and she herself had left just as she was to the age of helping out, True had felt that her mode of dress was well above the average afforded other girls her age in the Oregon settlement.

Willowy-thin, her regal bearing compensated when she had to make do with a new scarf or flower in place of a new gown. Until now!

Now everything about her was wrong . . . but was it only the clothes? There was the matter of background. Well, there again, she had nothing of which to be ashamed!

Aware then that she was on the defensive, True pushed the unworthy ideas aside. After all, she reminded herself again, she was a guest here—until she could get around to her second resolution, which was to find a place to stay until she had checked out a few other details concerning her past . . . and something else.

What was causing the vague uneasiness? In a sense these people had been hospitable—maybe in the only way that "monied people" knew how to be.

Were they always suspicious of newcomers? Or was she a special kind of interloper? The uneasiness went deeper. It had to do with Magnolia Manor.

Sometime she must get around to seeing how to check on her losses in the robbery, some facts of which still puzzled her . . .

Had any girl ever been confronted with more? Yes, of course! Her mother and aunt had been in much worse circumstances . . . *only they had escaped by running away.*

Well, she wasn't going to run! Whatever was wrong here, she would stay and fight it to the finish. Her rounded chin jutted out as she decided that the first priority was to have the talk with Michael St. John.

But it was slow in coming. True desperately needed to get her simple wardrobe in order. She asked Tisha about an ironing board and almost regretted it, so great was the young girl's reaction to the question.

"I's so sorry, Miz True. I shudda dun yo things."

"We'll work together, Tisha," True offered, which seemed to frighten the girl all the more. In the end, Tisha allowed her to take the garments away one by one to be aired and pressed as she removed them from the suitcases.

The clothes were still wrong. But True felt a little more at ease once they looked smoothed free of wrinkles. And fortunately there was a lot she could do with her hair. Flowers seemed to be in eternal bloom here, and a camellia pinned to the crown of her long hair was most becoming.

Or so were her thoughts as she went down to the evening meal on Saturday.

Michael had been out riding "over the plantation," according to Tisha. And so she saw him for the first time as they met with the usual ritualistic formality in the library.

"Charming, my dear." His voice had a ring of sincerity.

There was an exchange of small talk, the grand march into the dining room, and then Emily's announcement: "We will all be attending church tomorrow morning. Tell me, True, are there organized churches on the frontier?"

Angry words rose to True's lips, but she put them aside. Churning inwardly, but outwardly calm, she answered simply, "Many of them."

She was about to add that her uncle had been a dedicated minister, but thought better of it. Certainly she had no desire to get into family relationships again.

"And do you attend?"

Emily Kincaid's question caused True to choke on the bite of fillet-of-sole mousse she was supposed to be enjoying. Reaching for her water goblet, she all but tipped it over.

The other woman did not seem to notice.

"I mean, with all those savages around—well, I would think any public gathering would be unsafe. Does one dare wear her jewelry?"

Praying for strength, True took a sip of water from her glass. What did this family want of her, anyway?

"I hardly know how to answer your questions." True realized that her voice was cold, but suddenly it did not matter.

"Yes, I attend church. And we do not refer to the Indians as 'savages.' As a matter of fact," she felt her voice rising, "we do not consider Oregon a 'frontier' anymore. We are quite civilized! As to the jewels, I have very few, as I am sure you have observed."

True paused, not so much for breath as to let the full implication of her words soak in and let Emily Kincaid see that she, "the homespun frontier woman," was not blind.

When she resumed, her words opened a new topic—one she felt needed further discussion.

"As a matter of fact, it was in these environs—not in the Oregon Country—that I was robbed of a very precious piece of jewelry."

Emily Kincaid was not enjoying the turn of the conversation, as evidenced by the high spots of color in her cheeks. But nobody was going to break through her facade of affected poise.

"And we must be looking into recovering the brooch for True, Michael. I will get in touch with Inspector Devore Monday. He will wish to speak with True . . . and now about church tomorrow, have you suitable clothes, True?"

"Really, Cousin Emily, I feel that could be offensive." Michael's voice was low, almost a growl.

"Why, I meant nothing at all—except to offer a light wrap in case there is an autumn chill. Her trunks have not arrived—"

True laid down her fork.

"Would you mind terribly if Michael and I skipped dessert?" Could that deadly calm voice be hers? "I have lost my appetite and there is some talking Michael and I need to do—in case," she added with a growing acidity, "the outside air is no chillier than this—"

Rising, she stood her full height. Let her chair tilt backward. Let her water glass upset and splash water the full length of the formal lace tablecloth. Let Michael remain seated. Whatever! *She* was going to escape. And now.

None of it happened, of course. Michael was behind her chair in one swift, fluid motion. And together they left the startled diners.

Home? *This?* It never could be . . .

The outdoor air was sweet with night-blooming cerus. Somewhere in the gathering darkness a cicada, reluctant to let go of summer, chirped for a mate. In the light of a half-moon, Michael's eyes turned from hazel to coffee, True noted dully. Coffee with cream, the moonlight adding mellifluous tones.

He was a part of the setting—unreal. Reality lay back home in Oregon, and she must escape this strange land, else she would become a part of the unreality.

It was unreal, too, that Michael's arms were reaching out and she was walking into them for comfort.

"I have to get away, Michael." Her voice was dead of emotion.

"True, listen to me, dear one." Michael withdrew one of his arms to cup her chin in his hand and bring her eyes to meet his. "They are not as bad as they seem. There's a lot of stiff-necked pride—and money—"

"I never would have guessed," she murmured, but she could feel blood flowing through her being again.

"And, of course, Cousin Emily pulls the strings. The others are puppet heirs."

"I wouldn't have guessed that either!"

Michael laughed.

"Ouch! Do I fall into that category, too, True? Your answer is important. *Very* important."

True inhaled deeply.

"I don't know Michael. I honestly don't know what I feel about you. There has been so little time. And everything has moved so fast that it seems like a dream. One doesn't think in a dream."

"Love requires no thinking. It's a matter of the heart."

True's heart skipped a beat.

"We weren't talking about love, Michael—"

"But we *have* to talk about it! Isn't that one of the main topics we need to discuss?"

When Michael would have tightened the circle of his arms about her, True ducked playfully from reach and laughed. A few minutes earlier her spirits had plummeted. She was a frump. A nothing at all.

Now, unexplainably, she felt better. And the laugh she managed was light.

Michael responded to her mood. Twirling his sandy mustache in mock-villainy, he said, "Ah, me proud beauty, so it pleases you to play hard to get! But it is I who will pay the rent."

The words, so playfully spoken, brought True back to the problems at hand.

"Oh, Michael, what am I going to do?"

"Why, you're going to marry me, of course! There has been no doubt in my mind since I first laid eyes on you. And get it out of your pretty head that my feelings have anything to do with background or money. I hoped you would like the family and I know they will accept you—"

True felt the beginnings of another headache.

"They don't have to *accept* me, Michael! I'm not staying on. Why should I?"

"As my wife!"

The headache materialized.

"Nothing's decided," she whispered. "Nothing at all. I have to go on to Boston . . . and there's Magnolia Manor . . . I need to see who owns it—"

"You do." Michael's answer was immediate.

"I'm not sure—"

"About an answer to my proposal or who owns that piece of property? I know the answer to both! And, incidentally, there's land that goes with the house—quite a large parcel. Rundown, of course, but land all the same and maybe valuable sometime."

Land? No, she hadn't known. She wasn't sure it even mattered. *And, she thought foggily, who would be entitled to the property? Originally it was the Kelly home and would have been Aunt Chrissy's. But when Grandmother married my grandfather . . .*

"Why the frown? A moment ago you seemed almost happy." Michael's voice carried a note of concern.

"I was thinking, for one thing, that we've been discussing family and seeming to get nowhere. And in all this time I have not met your father."

Michael's face became sober.

"Don't think I've forgotten that! But I have been waiting for the right time. Father has his good days and his bad. He has suffered almost total paralysis and has lost some of the power of speech. He occupies the upstairs east wing of the house—owns the house, incidentally, and 50 percent of the railroad shares—that is, among the owners we know about. One is missing."

He frowned and looked away.

16
A Week of Revelations

~∂~

THE WEEK THAT followed was the strangest of True North's life. Later she was to look back on it as a week of revelations . . .

SUNDAY.

The day dawned bright and clear. "Shirt-sleeve weather," O'Higgin would have said. No need for a wrap.

True dressed in her dark blue suit and added a faceveil to her flat-top hat. The other women of the house wore fur-trimmed suits.

Maybe she should have brought along a shawl just for appearance—an idea she shrugged off. She was unaccustomed to people who did things for appearance sake and she wasn't sure she liked them very well.

Emily Kincaid kept her distance as the group waited for the carriage to be brought to the front of the mansion. The woman had been coolly polite, nothing more, since True had spoken her piece—which suited True fine.

One more mention of the "overdue trunks" and True was going to tell her there were going to *be* no trunks. And just maybe, she thought spiritedly, she might add a few more tidbits about herself that would prove as shocking for this overpowering woman.

But when Emily spoke, her words were addressed to Michael.

"It was good of you to come along, seeing that you attend only Easter and Christmas services—or some other special occasion."

"This is a special occasion," Michael replied. If he planned to explain, there was no opportunity. The carriage had arrived.

Carriage? No, a Cinderella's coach! True stared in disbelief at the cut-under body style of the fringe-topped surrey, constructed of hardwood and steel, carpeted in red velvet. And the seats—weren't they upholstered in genuine leather? And in white! How long could white hold up?

"May I help you, True?" Michael's voice broke into her reverie.

True, suddenly aware that she had been gaping, clamped her mouth shut and lifted her skirts slightly in preparation to stepping up to the wide step and into the "pumpkin coach."

Seated between Michael and Oscar, True continued to look around her in admiration.

"How beautiful!" she exclaimed, seeing the oil-burning lanterns on either side of the carriage. "Daddy Wil has to hang a lantern in front of his old buggy when he makes an emergency night call. Maybe Young Wil can—"

Aware that she was thinking aloud, True stopped in mid-thought. A flush of embarrassment stained her cheeks.

Oscar was talking over his shoulder to the red-haired cousin—Audrey Anne, wasn't that her name? The others were listening to him so that only Michael heard True's words.

"That makes a good dozen times you've spoken of him," he said softly. "What is he to you?"

What was he to her? True gulped and tried to smile. Then she swallowed and tried again. But it was no use. Her chest was tight. Her throat hurt. And there were tears burning behind her eyeballs at the mention of his name.

Strive as she would, True was sure that her imitation of a human voice was not creditable.

"Why, he's—Young Wil's my—uh, cousin—well, stepbrother—no, none of those—not really. I mean he's my friend, the one who helped bring me up."

The glance she turned to Michael would have to plead for understanding. Certainly she had no words to cover the relationship.

"Does that clear things up?"

"Oh, perfectly!" Michael's laugh was as low as his words. He reached out to touch her hand. "It tells me nothing, except what I really wanted to know—that this fellow's the rival I've been asking you about!"

The carriage stopped. A liveried driver helped the group from the carriage. And, with Emily Kincaid sweeping grandly ahead, the procession filed down the aisle to a pew marked "Kincaid-St. John."

Once she was seated in the straight-backed pew, True had a sudden sensation of something indefinable, a sense of *deja vu* that was frightening. She had never seen this place before, and yet every corner was familiar.

The high ceiling would be arched . . . the pulpit draped in gold cloth . . . and there would be a multitude of stained-glass windows darkened by pre-Renaissance art in which the flesh tones were deathly pale, the eyes of the subjects filled with sorrow, and the background shrouded in gray-on-gray to give the illusion of smoke.

Shuddering, True forced herself to look slowly about the shadowy room. When her gaze came to rest on a dismal painting of Moses descending Mount Sinai, his outstretched hands holding the tablet of stone on which the commandments were engraved, she closed her eyes. The picture was too horrible for her mind to accept. For Moses wore a pair of grotesque horns!

It was comforting when Michael reached and covered her white-knuckled hands with his own. But she was unable to thank him with a look because her eyes, when she opened them, were pulled as if by magnet to the scene of horror on the window.

And somehow she knew even before looking that the name below it would be "Stein."

Maybe I never quite believed what they told me, she thought wildly. *Like Doubting Thomas, I have to feel a nail-scarred hand! But, dear Lord, don't let my faith be like that . . .*

In that moment, she knew what her mother and aunt had endured.

Then, with closed eyes, she listened to the "hellfire and damnation" sermon delivered by an austere man in a long, dark robe. There was no choir and no group singing. And there was no fellowship afterward. True walked out of the church in a state of depression.

"True, I beg your indulgence at this question. But do you really believe like the Reverend Father Holtz?" Michael asked as True was about to go freshen up for Sunday dinner.

"No, Michael," she said simply, "I don't."

"Then why, for heaven's sake, do you put yourself through it?"

Again, she said, "I don't. You see, I grew up knowing a God of love. Does the man never touch on that subject?"

Michael gave a small laugh.

"Like Cousin Emily said, I don't darken the door very often."

"I can't say I blame you!" Her words surprised him, True thought. And then she added, "But why not give some thought to God's love?"

Michael shrugged and saluted slightly. Which could mean anything . . . giving her more to think about . . . as if she needed more!

MONDAY.

It was one of the senior Mr. St. John's "good days."

"I want you to meet my father, True," Michael said at breakfast. "And, if you don't mind," he said to the rest of the family, "I prefer that the two of us go alone."

A frown creased Emily's face. She erased it quickly.

"Of course," she said abruptly, then to True, "but don't be surprised if his mind wanders—particularly without my presence."

Imagine 36 rooms in this house! True had written to Young Wil in her second letter. This morning she felt that she and Michael passed all 36 rooms before they reached the east-wing suite his father occupied.

Michael opened the door softly, without knocking, and motioned for her to follow him into the quarters. The rooms were full of shadows and a fire flickered sulkily in the grate behind a great four-post bed.

There had been bright sunshine downstairs, she remembered. And then she saw that heavily fringed velvet drapes were drawn against the light of the outside world.

When her eyes adjusted to the semidarkness, True was able to see the features of the man who occupied the oak bed.

His face was so wax-white and he lay so still that for a moment she wondered if he was alive. She was about to express concern to Michael when, to her complete surprise, William St. John lifted a feeble white finger and curled it in their direction.

"Come closer." The voice was faint.

Cold with perspiration, True accepted the hand Michael offered and allowed herself to be led to the older man's bedside.

"This is True North, Father. I told you about her—"

"I remember!" The voice held more strength. "Come closer, my dear, so I can see you—my eyes are failing of late."

"Good morning, sir," True said cautiously, hardly knowing what was expected of her. Then, without thinking, she added, "Wouldn't you like the drapes opened a little? It's such a lovely morning!"

At her words, his eyes flew open with a suddenness that startled her. Even in the shadowy room she could see how alike they were—father and son—the same hazel eyes that pierced shrewdly, but not unkindly.

"That voice—it's familiar—come near!"

He was fighting laboriously for breath. Should he be talking? True looked questioningly at Michael. When he nodded, she moved to the bedside and took the feeble, outstretched hand.

"Say something more," Mr. St. John begged, his fingers clinging to hers.

There was something compelling about this man, something True liked instinctively.

"What would you have me say?" she asked lightly, relaxing somewhat.

"The voice—and, yes, even in the darkness, I see the face is the same! Open the drapes a crack, Michael!"

"But Cousin Emily—"

"Drat Cousin Emily! Do as I ask, please."

When a shaft of light appeared in the room, the wan face of the ill man was filled with wonder.

"Mary Evangeline Stein," he said almost reverently.

"You knew her?" True's heart raced with joy. She was about to add, "I am her daughter," when Michael spoke up quickly.

"This is her niece, Father. I understand that the resemblance is quite remarkable. We must not tire you, but I wanted you to know that I have asked this beautiful creature to be my wife—and although as yet I have no answer—"

Had Michael really proposed? Formally? The way a girl expected? Young Wil had always said that love needed a long growing season . . . but she must listen . . . something else was going on in this strange house.

"No answer—never gave me one either—" The voice had grown more feeble already. "Oh, you're beautiful, my dear, so beautiful— and if I had my time to go over—"

Michael signaled to True that it was time to leave, but when she tried to disentangle her fingers from his father's hands, the grip tightened.

"No," he whispered, "don't go . . . I need your promise to use what is yours wisely—your beauty . . . the land . . . and the share of . . ."

The faint voice drifted away and True was able to make out only the word, "Father . . . fath-er . . ."

"I promise," she said to calm him, having no idea what she was agreeing to. But the faint smile of happiness was enough.

William St. John closed his eyes again and slept. Michael and True tiptoed from the room.

"What was he talking about, Michael? Was he calling for a priest? Or was he speaking of his own father?"

"I don't know," he said. "I'm as puzzled as you—and more than a little surprised that you fitted into the picture. It's all very strange . . . let's not discuss it with Cousin Emily."

"All right," she answered, carefully keeping her eyes on each polished step of the stairs lest he see the immense relief she felt.

Emily Kincaid was the last person on earth with whom she would wish to share *anything!*

TUESDAY.

There was little opportunity to speak with Michael alone; Emily always seemed to be on hand. True had a growing sense of preplanning on the other woman's part.

But in one of her moments with Michael he had made mention of taking her to see the rest of Magnolia Manor on Wednesday. They would take a picnic lunch and have that long-overdue talk.

Looking forward to the midweek plan, True caught up on the long letter to Daddy Wil, Aunt Chrissy, and the twins, then started a third letter to Young Wil. She would ask both of them concerning Marty's whereabouts, if they had heard, so she could get in touch with him.

Marty's wandering around and shifting from one job to another was a source of sadness for them all. How long had it been since she had seen him, anyway? Poor Marty! As much as she loved him, True pitied him even more. Not as quick to learn as she and Young Wil, he was at a disadvantage, but she wished he had been less resentful . . . more willing to develop his own potential without feeling threatened by his adopted siblings.

Of course, he was easy to ignore, as he said so often . . . easy to forget, too . . .

Right now she could scarcely remember his face . . .

Having let her mind wander across the miles that separated True from her family, she was surprised when she was joined by three men, only one of them familiar. One moment she was sitting in the porch swing beneath the wisteria-draped gazebo alone. And the next moment they were there unannounced.

"Sorry, we didn't intend to startle you, Miss North," the man with the familiar face said. "There was no response at the front door—oh, I beg your pardon for not introducing myself. I am Charles Devore, insurance adjuster—"

True accepted his proffered hand.

"I believe we've met," she said slowly.

"No," the man's dark eyes smiled engagingly, "I'd have remembered, I assure you!"

True was unconvinced, so she only half-listened when he introduced the two other men.

Where was it? In spite of his gallant words, she had sensed an uneasiness about him, as if he did not wish to be recognized.

But why? And even after the other two men began asking her questions regarding the train robbery, a part of True's mind kept returning to the identity of the familiar face.

The memory was there. But, like the fragments of a dream, one moment the face was clear and the next moment it was gone. Realizing that she was staring at him in a manner that might be considered rude or even flirtatious, she forced herself to concentrate on the investigation.

How many men came to Mr. St. John's quarters? *Three.*

Description? *One about six feet tall—dark-haired, in need of a haircut. Another, medium height. The third, short.*

Distinguishing marks? *Well, it was dark. And they wore masks. Tall one had a little scar right here,* pointing to her temple. *And there was something about the shortest one's eyes . . .* but there she stopped vaguely.

Something kept her from saying that the eyes, like the face of Investigator Devore, were familiar. Involuntarily she glanced in his direction again, only to find him surveying her, his eyes probing deeply through narrowed lids.

Well, no matter who this man was, he was not one of the bandits. Eyes too dark. Too tall of stature . . .

Her losses? True described the brooch and, in a choked voice, explained its sentimental value.

A little money, yes, but (she blushed) *not all of it. Some of it was—well, tucked away . . .*

One of the men whose faces were unfamiliar nudged the other knowingly, at which time Charles Devore stepped back into the picture.

"We will do our best to recover your losses, Miss North—"

"How did you know my name if we've not met?" The question surprised True herself.

"The conductor, of course."

Well, of course. So, synchronized and efficient, the men took turns asking questions and writing down answers. Finally they were finished.

But True was not.

"You should know that the men threatened to take me hostage and that they dealt cruelly with some of the passengers. The conductor and I worked at caring for the injured as best we could—once I was safe—but it was more than a robbery."

Did she imagine it, or was there an exchange of looks between members of the investigating trio?

"Anybody hurt but the coloreds?"

"What possible difference could the color of one's skin have to do with what I'm telling you?" True asked heatedly.

Angered by the attitudes she had seen, she realized too late she took her wrath out on these three. "You know, I get the impression that you're still fighting the Civil War down here—and the South's winning!"

"Anything wrong with that, Miss North?" Devore asked.

"There's plenty wrong with it!" Then, spreading her hands in despair, she said sadly, "Oh, what's the use? Let's get on with this investigation."

The men turned to the door without replying. With his hand on the knob, Charles Devore turned to nod a wordless farewell.

Only it wasn't a farewell. And they both knew it. He was angry with her and she sensed a vindictiveness within him. As for herself, there would be no rest until she knew . . . but suddenly she did know!

When the door closed, she ran in search of Michael. He was shaking hands with the men at the front gate. When they were gone, she ran to him, white-faced and out of breath.

"True, what is it? What's wrong?" He reached for her limp hand.

"That man," she panted, "the one who calls himself Charles Devore—I know his face, Michael! He's the one I saw through the window the day of the robbery—with the outlaws—a part of them. He *has* to be!"

"Are you sure?" Michael's voice was filled with shock. "He's been in our employ for years—investigates everything concerning our losses. And they were great in the recent robbery."

"Oh, Michael," she whispered. "I'm sure—and being sure makes me afraid!"

WEDNESDAY.

To her disappointment, True heard a tattoo of raindrops on her window before daybreak. And this was the day for the picnic.

She had hoped that having time alone with Michael would help put recent events into some kind of shape. Each day brought a new set of questions without clearing up the ones of longer standing. What she did not know, as she dressed in the half-light of a gloomy dawn, was that today was to be no exception.

Quickly securing her hair into a coil on top of her head, True picked up a sweater in preparation for going quietly downstairs for coffee. Then she could have her morning's devotionals, continue with her letter-writing, and—time allowing—go back and review her mother's diary.

Time was slipping past rapidly and as yet there had been no opportunity to plan for the trip to Boston. The diary would help prepare her, providing she could settle a few things here . . . find a place to stay, for one thing . . . somewhere reasonable, as money was dwindling . . .

A soft knock at the door interrupted her thinking.

"Missy True, ma'am—you awake?" It was Tisha! At this hour?

"What is it?" she asked as she fumbled with the lock.

The voice on the other side was low and somewhat anxious.

"Mr. William, he dun wants to be seein' you-all 'fore the others come. Can you come soon-like? Me, I'm takin' coffee—"

But before the girl finished speaking, True had joined her in the hall and locked the door behind her. Together they ascended the stairs soundlessly, with Tisha looking back frequently.

"Thank you, my dear, for coming!"

Mr. St. John's voice sounded much more clear today. "How lovely you are—and would you do a dying man a favor? Would you pour the way *she* used to?"

"Of course," True smiled. Dismissing Tisha with a nod, she picked up the heavy silver pot. They drank the strong coffee silently while True waited for him to speak.

"There's a box in the highboy there by the closet. Sort of tricky to open."

He explained the combination and asked her to bring it to him. The key was in another compartment. Would she bring it, too? True did as he asked.

Wondering what all this had to do with her, she watched as the thin fingers of Michael's father struggled with the lock of the box. Something in his manner begged for independence and so she did not offer to help.

The papers inside were yellow and emitted the telltale odor of age.

"You will want to examine these," Mr. St. John said, his voice still strong.

Obediently she accepted the sheath of paper. Old slave ownership papers . . . Confederate money . . . a bundle of letters bound with faded ribbon. Time had dimmed the spidery writing on the documents, and she was unable to make out names or places. Only the block printing remained on legal documents.

"The ownership papers carry a rider on back, freeing slaves who were so vital a part of the plantation."

Why was he telling her this?

"Some here—some at Magnolia Manor."

"But the war—didn't it free them automatically?"

His small laugh was bitter.

"You'd be surprised how many continue to violate—and there's really no enforcement except man's conscience. Hosea, Tisha, and the rest of the staff's ancestors chose to stay. The younger ones are paid—"

When the voice gave way to a cough, True felt a rush of concern. She probably should not be here at all, and certainly she should not allow him to talk.

"You are a kind man, Mr. St. John, but I feel that I am taking your time—intruding, actually—that I should go."

"Stay!" The weak voice carried a command. "These matters concern only you and me."

His mind wandered, Emily had said.

"Really—" True began.

William St. John ignored her interruption.

"The letters are from *her*, your grandmother. You're Chris Beth's daughter? But we both know better, don't we, True?"

Too surprised at the suddenness of the question to think clearly, True was unable to respond.

"Your grandmother, wasn't she? There can be no doubt in my mind that you are that all right. But you are Vangie's child."

There was no question in his voice.

The room was suddenly stifling her. Air. She must have air. Else her lungs would burst.

"Please," she whispered, "please—I must go—what difference could it make? It is past—"

His answer was to extend a large brown envelope taken from the bottom of the box. True accepted it with trembling hands and found herself opening it at his command.

Her eyes refused to focus—as is the way with dreams. And that's what this was—a dream. One from which she could not awake.

"What is it?" Her question came through stiff lips.

"The shares. Railroad shares. There's a third owner, you know. We've looked for years . . . trying to find some trace. Your grandmother came of wealthy stock . . . married Kelly instead of me . . ."

The voice was failing, but True was powerless now to stop the conversation. She lacked both strength and will.

More. She must hear more.

"A family arrangement . . . fragile, like a flower, powerless against them." The piercing eyes turned toward her. "You're like her . . . but different . . . more like a piece of Dresden china that won't let itself be dropped."

The eyes fluttered and closed. Maybe she should terminate the visit. But he had left so much unsaid.

Then to her surprise the determined voice went on, "You are intelligent . . . not going to let Emily, wily as she is, put anything over . . . and I admire your independence . . . Michael will need it." He reached to touch her hand. "You *are* going to marry him?"

"I—I don't know. We—we've reached no agreement. I came here to think—and, well, I think my being here has created a wrong impression. I just can't answer Michael—or you."

"Don't let me press you—it's just that we must draw up the papers while I have the breath . . . so you will be protected . . ."

"I still don't understand, Mr. St. John."

"Don't be so formal—that pains me deeply when you should have been my daughter . . . or granddaughter—"

"The age difference—what—how?" The words were out before True knew she was going to speak them.

The man's sigh was barely audible above the sounds of the first autumn storm. The rain had stopped, but a blustery wind was tossing leaves against the windows.

"I vowed not to marry after your grandmother broke my heart . . . waiting for her, maybe . . . then, just before she was widowed, I married into the Kincaid family . . . then she married your Grandfather Stein."

The white face twisted in remembered pain. Even now he could not bring himself to speak of the two men who had married her grandmother by their Christian names.

How he must have loved her—loved her the way a woman needs to be loved. Did Michael love her like that? Did he love her at all? Slowly her mind cleared, and she saw something she had failed to see before. Yet how could she have missed it?

"Michael's finding me—it was no accident, was it?" Her whisper seemed to echo in the room.

"No . . . been searching . . . knew you by the picture . . . and by some things you said." The voice broke and was silent like the dying fire in the grate. "Only you are entitled . . ."

The room had grown chill—a chill which seeped into her bones and squeezed at her heart.

"Does he know about the circumstances of my birth?" True hardly heard her own words.

The papers lying between them appeared to rise and fall. The beams on the ceiling slanted crazily, and before her very eyes the antique sterling chest seemed to change places with the lowboy from which she had taken the documents tying her into this family. Her mind would no longer function.

"It would make no difference—" William St. John's hoarse whisper was interrupted by a spasm of coughing. "No difference in the railroad stock . . . belonged to *her* . . . no difference in the inheritance either . . . an attorney this afternoon . . ."

"Inheritance?"

"What I choose to leave you . . . go, dear child, before they find you . . ."

Not sure that her legs would support her, True rose. She should say something. But what? That he had made her feel she belonged here? But that was not true.

With a sinking heart she knew she could never fit into a family who had money to buy anything they wanted—even the respect of other . . . the ones they wanted to cultivate, anyway . . .

And then it occurred to her that she, True North, was about to fit into the same class. Dully, she wondered whether to feel happy or sad. Like a sleepwalker, she moved to the door.

Then, spinning on her heel, True went back to the bed. No matter *how* the others behaved, *he* had welcomed her. And for the right reason: love. If not for her, at least for someone in her family. Not for money or background—just love.

Leaning down, she brushed the pale brow with her lips.

"That's for Grandmother," she said softly. And then when she saw the tears flood unashamedly down his cheeks, she repeated the kiss. "And this is for me—Grandfather."

The white face was suddenly a bright sun which lighted the entire room.

"I could die happily now—only I'm not going to! That would please the parasites too much . . . must rest to be ready to see the lawyer . . ." The voice drifted away and then resumed faintly, ". . . must stay . . . don't go away . . . *promise* . . ."

"I promise," True said quickly, seeing that he was no longer able to talk. Only later was she to realize what the commitment would cost her.

THURSDAY.

Although True's dreams the night before were a crazy kaleidoscope of seemingly unrelated events, she awakened with an unaccountable sense of excitement. Oh, yes, the picnic!

She needed to get back to Magnolia Manor to find out if it truly belonged to her (and, yes, if she belonged to *it!*).

There was more ground, Michael had said. They would look at it. And, eventually, she would have to make some decisions about it— and a million other things.

But, oh, she thought (stretching luxuriously one leisurely moment before getting dressed), it would be good to get away from problems. To have some time with Michael!

That, of course, accounted for her excitement. With that thought she was unable to stay in bed to finish the stretch.

Two hours later, with a wicker basket packed with what looked like enough food to last them a week, she and Michael slipped furtively down the stairs.

"Have you ridden a bicycle?" Michael whispered.

True shook her head at the bottom of the stairs.

"I supposed we'd walk."

"With *this*?" He pointed to the basket.

True stifled a giggle.

"Well," she said tentatively, "maybe I can—if it's anything like riding a horse."

"I can't say." His reply was muffled by the sound of the door opening and then closing behind them. "I've never been astride a horse!"

"Such a lot we don't know about each other—" True murmured more to herself than to Michael, who was busy depositing the picnic hamper into a carrier. His next words told her he had heard, however.

"Which is one of the purposes for our day together. Now, let me help you—you'll have no problem, so relax against me. It's a bicycle built for two. Two lovers!"

True laughed self-consciously as she tried to settle herself with some grace onto the unaccustomed seat.

"Lovers," he had said. *Are we lovers?* A thrill prickled her spine and then stopped. *Would Michael love me if he knew?* And then came an even more startling thought: *Would I want him to?*

Her thoughts were interrupted when Michael climbed astride with easy grace and, as he started to pedal slowly, gave True instructions when and when not to pedal. At first she felt 100 feet off the ground with nothing below.

But once she got the feel of the team effort, it was fun to feel the wind in her face and watch it billow her skirts past the fast-flying wheels.

"Hang on tight!" Michael called above the whistle of the wind.

When she hesitated, he called again, "Arms around my waist! The new pneumatic tires are guaranteed against blowout. Still, it's safer—"

Frightened, she grasped his waist with both hands and relaxed against him. His shoulders were broad in their tweed coat.

Safe. It was such a nice word. There should be safety in marriage . . . but Michael's kind or hers?

His family saw security in power—the kind that money and background afforded. But something vital was missing. Why, they were not a real family at all. More of a pack. That was it, a pack of animals—snarling, biting, fighting primitively underneath their polished finish—never ready to accept a new member until it was established who was leader!

Her own family found power only in love. And, feeling as they and the other settlers did, they reached out with open arms to embrace the whole world. God was their Leader . . .

"A penny for your thoughts!"

True jumped at Michael's words. She had been so absorbed in her thinking that she was unaware they had stopped.

"Where are we?" she murmured as Michael helped her dismount.

"Magnolia Manor, but we approached it from the other road. It's smoother."

True looked around her in dismay. Once this neglected ground had been a vast plantation—something she had not known. But now weeds and brambles had taken over. The ancient oaks, like bearded prophets, looked saddened by the change.

"Were the shacks ever occupied?"

"Still are—one of the many decisions you'll need to come to. Slaves' quarters and sharecroppers. Some of both still around. Guess they think they have squatters' rights now."

"I only saw where the big house stood—which reminds me, there's someone I want to ask about: Joshua, the gardener."

"They won't tell you here. Mostly, they act like scared rabbits—"

True silenced him with a finger to her lips. Her ears had picked up a faint moaning sound, followed by a mellow hum of voices which seemed to rise and fall in a melody that was a combination of poetry and music. The croon seemed a part of the setting.

Michael directed her gaze to the tumbledown shack, larger than the others, only a short distance away.

"Their church. These people spend more time on their knees than at the plow!"

"Maybe they know something we've not talked about," she said slowly. "Grandma Mollie, a wonderful friend of my family, used to say, 'Neither belly nor purse takes the place of God.'"

Michael sucked in his breath.

"And you believe that?"

"Of course I believe it!" True was unable to say more, as an unexpected need swept over her. "Michael, I want to go inside. Will you come with me?"

"In *there*?" Michael made no effort to hide his dismay. "Down here we don't mingle—by mutual agreement."

"I'm not sure it's mutual," True said. "And, after all, this is supposedly my property, so I don't have to have a welcoming committee. Back in Oregon we join together in caring for and nurturing one another . . . are you coming or not?"

Inside, the black worshipers, with heads bowed, continued the sadsweet croon. The voices blended together in the sweetest music True had ever heard—music of the soul, born of suffering, yet triumphantly proclaiming that there was nothing—*nothing*—that God could not heal.

Entranced, True listened—how long she did not know. Maybe she would have stayed all day. But there was Michael to consider.

Reaching out to touch his hand, she signaled that they should go. Nobody had noticed their arrival. Nobody noticed their departure. Their spirits were in the "other world" of hope and faith.

"May I breathe now?" Michael grinned once they were outside. Then, more seriously, there in the shadow of the old building, he grasped her shoulders and gently turned her to face him.

"True, tell me something—just how important to you is all this?"

"These people—or my faith?"

"I have a strange feeling that you equate the two."

True nodded.

"The Bible gives us no choice . . . have you given any thought to it, Michael—love, in the context I mentioned?"

"Mostly I've wondered if it's a qualification for your husband."

True bit her lip in concentration. Then she spoke truthfully: "I don't know, Michael—I honestly don't know. Let's take it a step at a time about the husband . . . but as a father? I would have to say, yes, it's essential . . . that's the best I can come up with right now. You see, I too am searching for answers—"

"And we won't find them here!" Michael's voice was lighter. "Can you walk in those shoes? Oh, yes, I see you can. Thank goodness you wore something sensible."

"I'm a pioneer woman, remember?" Her tone matched his. "Let's go!" And, picking up her skirts gingerly, she followed him as they hiked for what seemed miles over land which lay idle for lack, she suspected, of tools with which these deprived people could work.

Adults were either at the church or chose to remain out of sight in the buildings which leaned against giant oak trees for support. Several times True stopped to speak with the near-naked children, but they seemed so frightened that she gave up trying to visit with them.

When Michael asked if she had seen enough, True nodded. "But I would like to find out what happened to Joshua."

Michael shrugged.

"Drifted back to Shanty Town, most likely. Most of them are pretty shiftless."

True bit her lip.

"Don't spoil my day, Michael."

"Oh, darling, I didn't intend to. Forgive me. Please—let's make this our day. We are entitled to that."

Yes, they were. And with that, she took the hand he offered. Together they walked back to the spreading oak where Michael had left the bicycle. Gathering up the lunch basket, he smiled broadly.

"I really am a romantic soul. Look!"

True's eyes followed the direction that Michael's finger pointed. And there, chained to a gnarled cypress tree, was a canoe, complete with two paddles.

"I—I don't know," she began uncertainly. "I've never ridden in a boat. Our rivers are so swift—"

Michael laughed and, grabbing her arm, forced her forward.

"Fear not, Fair One! This is a shallow bayou."

The water, she found, was stale, stagnant, and murky. All the same, she stepped carefully into the canoe with a growing sense of adventure. With her offer to help, Michael tapped her nose lightly with an index finger.

"That's one of the things I like about you—your willingness to learn. But not until we're safely past this trap of water hyacinths. Just relax and let me tell you now the things I *love* about you."

"Not now, Michael. Please not now." True leaned back, allowing the sun to slope soothingly across her face only to disappear in the long drapes of Evangeline moss at frequent intervals.

Enjoy the sun and shade. Enjoy your companion. Time enough for talking, thinking, resolving later . . .

Michael rowed on in silence. There seemed to be no room for words—even those which must be spoken. Now and then he pointed out a rare bird haloed in shafts of sunlight against the patches of blue. There was no sound but for the unbroken song of the birds and the slap-slap of the oars against the water.

"Hungry?" Michael's question reminded True to note that the sun had passed high noon. "There's a clump of trees to the right with a little island in their midst." Without waiting for an answer, Michael turned the canoe toward it.

A few minutes later, True, leaning lazily against a rough-barked cypress, was engaging in Michael's game of trying to catch wild grapes he tossed at her mouth.

"Come now, is *this* all we carried in that hamper?" she laughed, missing a grape.

"I thought the belly wasn't important—" Michael began. Immediately, interrupting himself, he raised a conciliatory hand. "Strike that one and have a sugarcured ham sandwich. Lucky for us Tisha saw to our needs. Cousin Emily would have suggested watercress— ouch! I beg your pardon again . . . she represents the 'purse,' doesn't she?"

In spite of herself, True laughed as she bit into a ham sandwich so reminiscent of Grandma Mollie Malone's that tears unexpectedly filled her eyes.

"I'm sorry," she whispered at the look of concern on Michael's face. "It's a day of sun and shadows—on the bayou and in my heart—and I can't ask you to understand. I don't even understand myself! I don't know who I am—"

In an instant Michael was by her side, having upset the lemonade in the middle of the tablecloth. Neither of them paid the slightest attention to the liquid's spread beneath the pile of sandwiches and toward the mint-jelly layer cake.

She was in his arms and they were clinging to one another. She should be pouring out her troubles. Telling him all about herself.

There must be no secrets in love. But instead she had needed a shoulder to cry on. And Michael's was there.

The lunch went unfinished. Michael's lips brushed her cheeks again and again. They should be getting back. But a heavy languor held her still.

True let her half-closed eyes drink in the beauty of the afternoon sky, barely breathing, engulfed in warmth. And for a fleeting moment she was back in the glass bubble in which she was encased when she occupied Michael's luxurious suite en route from the Oregon Country to Atlanta, weightless, high above the earth.

Then she was brought back to earth.

"We must talk." This time it was Michael who said the words. "I have asked you to marry me. We can't keep putting the issue off."

"I know." True's voice was still dreamy, like that of a child who is not yet quite awake. "I know." Idly she tickled his ear with a blade of grass. "And I'm grateful."

"Grateful! Is that all you have to say to a proposal, True?" Michael's voice carried a faint edge of impatience.

"You deserve better, but there's so much we must clear up first . . . and there's something more," she added. Wide awake, True realized that she had to begin somewhere. Where better than with love itself?

"I have to consider what we talked about this morning—faith and all it involves. And, too, it seems to me that love has to grow slowly, steadily, based on—well, so many things."

Until, she thought, *two hearts beat as one . . .*

Rising, Michael began to gather up the remains of the picnic. The dappled sunlight had turned gold with the promise of sunset. It was a beautiful time of day, but something had gone wrong—something she alone could correct.

Sadly, True stooped to fold the ends of the sodden linen tablecloth, wishing for her sake and his that she were ready to commit herself.

By the time they reached home the sun had set, leaving behind a rich burgundy glow to color the horizon behind the great house. As always, it looked silhouetted in mystery—some of which she must help clear. Screened away from the windows by heavy shrubs, True paused to look at Michael, trying to think of some word which would break the tension.

But caught in the transition between dusk and dark, Michael's face was closed—like that of a stranger—which, she realized, in many ways he was. With a sigh, she turned and walked toward the door, aware that the beautiful day had offered everything but what she had intended. She and Michael had not talked. And she had hurt him deeply.

FRIDAY.
True was breakfasting with the family when the package arrived. When the butler announced that there was a parcel for "Missy No'th," she was aware of all eyes turned her direction.

Emily's were like burning coals and True was careful to avoid direct contact with them as she carefully folded her napkin, excused herself, and—with the small package in hand—hurried to the privacy of her room.

Wil, her heart sang out, *Wil, Wil, Wil!* She was expecting nothing from him, but whatever it was made no difference. It would put them in touch again.

Wil . . . Wil . . . it was like the heartbeat she had wanted to describe to Michael.

Clinging to the moment, True held the package to her pounding heart.

Savor the moment. Make it last . . .

But when she saw the address her heart sank. Her name, crudely printed, appeared to have been done by somebody who intentionally wished to disguise the handwriting. Unfamiliar, of course . . . and yet there was something about it . . . never mind!

She was weary from trying to solve unsolvable problems. Sick with disappointment, she tore the wrapping from a small box. Then, lifting the lid, she could only sink weakly into a chair, her mind unable to believe that the beautiful sapphire-and-pearl brooch lay there winking back at her.

What . . . who . . . well, she must find out. Quickly she picked up the wrappings and reexamined them in hope of finding a postmark. There was none.

"Now, Lord," she whispered, "you'll have to help me decide which ones to tell—"

At that moment there was a sharp rap on her door.

"True, there are two men downstairs wishing to speak with you!"

Emily! But why hadn't she sent one of the servants? Curiosity, of course, True realized angrily. Quickly, tucking the brooch away inside her bag and picking up all signs of the hastily opened package, she joined the older woman at the door without inviting her to come inside.

True followed Emily's straight-backed lead into the sunroom, where tuberous begonias, odorless in their confinement, separated great pots of Boston fern. One of the two men rose from an opulent chair. Stern-faced, he offered his hand.

"I am Edward Keith," he said, sweeping back thin, white hair with long fingers, "a private investigator whose services Mr. William St. John has engaged."

He turned to Emily, dismissing her with a look before introducing his companion. True was acutely aware of the rustle of angry skirts as Emily retreated.

Then she obediently sat down in one of the needlepoint-covered chairs, large enough for the three of them, to which the investigator pointed an inviting finger. Emily would be furious at being denied the privilege of being hostess.

"And this is Albert Berkshire, attorney-at-law." Wondering what the two men were doing here together, True found herself looking into a pair of merry eyes in a round, good-natured face, topped with a thatch of bright red hair. It was easy to answer his smile.

Edward Keith cleared his throat.

"Since Mr. St. John also wishes to have Attorney Berkshire draw up some legal documents, his business may take more time. If you will simply respond to my questions regarding the robbery first, then I shall be on my way. I am a very busy man."

"I'll be glad to cooperate, but it puzzles me why you are here— that is, were you aware that the adjusters have spoken with me?"

"My dear Miss North, that is precisely why I am here. There seems to be some irregularity—a matter," he paused significantly, "that you brought to the family's attention."

Michael had told his father, then. True wondered about Emily. And then she listened carefully to Edward Keith.

The investigation was brief. What else could she tell him about the man she had recognized? True described the man who had stood in the midst of the train robbers.

Seeming to agree, Edward Keith nodded, then asked her to get in touch with him immediately should Charles Devore make contact with her.

"Contact?" True frowned. "What would he want of me?"

"Never mind. I would not wish to frighten you—just do as I ask. If he suspects you recognized him, he might try to cover his tracks. Even pretend to recover the brooch . . ."

The brooch! As if from a great distance True heard one of the two men ask if she was all right. Yes, but it was so warm.

A glass of water? Yes, that would be nice. Then she was shaking hands with the investigator, and Albert Berkshire was asking if she felt up to continuing.

Yes, she was fine now.

The lawyer shuffled through his briefcase, bringing out a fistful of papers.

"Now, nobody suspects you of being an impostor, Miss North. This is all routine. Strictly routine."

"I don't understand." Why had she said she was all right?

"My error. I took it for granted that you knew yourself to be an heir to Magnolia Manor. I will handle the details on the property for you. But it is not entirely because of the old plantation that I've come. It seems that Mr. St. John has evidence leading him to believe that you are entitled to railroad shares belonging jointly to the Kincaid-St. John-Kelly—er, Stein joint ownership but—" He paused, a frown creasing between his bewildered blue eyes.

"Is there a problem?" True found it hard to breathe.

"Well, yes, there does seem to be some kind of error made here." Then his merry face brightened. "Nothing you should worry your pretty head about, just confusion with names. I am sure you brought along identification."

"Identification?" The word was a whisper.

"Any statement by an attending physician would have sufficed." Albert Berkshire tapped on his teeth with his pen. "Oh," he said brightly, "a family Bible!"

"I never thought—I—the family Bible is in Oregon—"

He inhaled in concentration.

"Ordinarily, we could send for it. But in view of Mr. St. John's condition—tell me, can you give me the names of your four grandparents, including your grandmothers' maiden names? That would be a start. And your own father's full name—family lineage, you know?" He smiled.

Stunned, True could only stare at him.

"I have nothing at all," she said woodenly. "I only brought along maps, a little Bible, and my mother's diary to direct me—"

"Diary!" The ruddy face fairly glowed. "That is admissible!"

Admissible. And revealing. Tearing away every shred of privacy. Wordlessly, True handed him the diary.

SATURDAY.

There was a brief encounter with Michael early in the morning. Brief, and yet it took up, as if by plan, where the two of them had left off on the bayou. Michael was on his way upstairs to see his father. True was on her way downstairs to check on the morning mail. They met halfway and stood looking wordlessly at each other for a moment on the shadowy landing.

Then Michael spoke.

"I understand Father sent the investigator and attorney to see you. How did it go?" His question was made warm and personal by the reach of his hands to grasp and hold onto hers.

"Very well," she said without withdrawing her hands. "I guess I wondered why they came together—"

"Expediency. Time is a factor. It's running out."

"For us all," True murmured without meeting Michael's gaze. "I want you to know that I'm thinking—"

Help me say it, Michael. But he was silent. Her question, when it came, was too abrupt.

But somewhere below there was the sound of a door opening and closing, so hurriedly she whispered, "Would you have been attracted to me if you had not recognized me from the photograph? Your father told me—"

"He has told me everything—"

"About the circumstances of my birth?" she gasped. "That too?"

"That too. Did you think it would make a difference?"

"Yes. No. I don't know. I hadn't planned to discuss it—certainly not with the others—"

Footsteps below. Michael spoke quickly.

"I think we're talking about different things." His hands tightened and he drew her to him in a quick embrace. "Nothing could alter my feelings—nothing." His voice was husky with emotion. "And to answer your question, which somehow got lost in the conversation, yes, I would have been attracted to you—and come to love you just as my father loved your grandmother and your Aunt Mary Evangeline who looked so like her!"

Her *aunt*. Michael didn't know. *Explain! But how!*

Now there were footsteps on the stair. The two of them drew apart, each going his separate direction. Even as Emily greeted True on the stairway (with unaccustomed warmth), her mind was on the secrets contained in her mother's diary.

They had been sacred to Angel Mother, then later to Aunt Chrissy, then to herself. Evidently, Albert Berkshire and William St. John intended to preserve its secrets, even from Michael.

Downstairs, True thumbed through the large stack of mail for the household. She had looked for mail from home for so long that she had all but given up hope of receiving any.

Home, and all those wonderful people who had been bigger than life so recently, now seemed to be receding into the past—diminishing in size as they faded into the beautiful background of her childhood. Maybe this was the real world . . . her past, the dream . . .

But there were letters! Two from Aunt Chrissy and a bulky letter from Young Wil! She ran back up the stairs three at a time to be alone.

Lying across the great bed, forgetting to turn back the silk coverlet which just cleared the dust ruffles, True held his letter to her heart. It had begun the relentless tattoo again.

Young Wil . . . Young Wil . . . then wildly, *Wil, Wil, Wil!*

But dessert comes last, Grandma Malone had taught her. Daddy had said it another way—that one did the toughest tasks first, then the others seemed easier. And from these teachings Young Wil had devised a game for her and Marty called "Anticipation." They *anticipated* how good a chocolate cake would be before testing a crumb. *Anticipated* the joys of opening gifts . . . and childhood habits are hard to break. Even if she wanted to!

So, happily anticipating the contents of her childhood idol's fat letter—all resentment dissolved like the morning fog along the bayou—

True happily opened her aunt's letter bearing the earlier of the two postmarks.

Quickly she scanned it to make sure the whole family was well and safe. Later she would read it again and again. But for now, the heavy pounding of her heart forbade any deep thinking. Except anticipation!

Everyone was fine, Aunt Chrissy said. Fine and missing True . . . oh, how they missed her! Her being in Portland was different . . . within reach . . . "But Atlanta—oh, darling, it's so distant in every way. Has it been kind to you?"

True raised her eyes to the high arch of the beamed ceiling, realizing for the first time what it must have cost Aunt Chrissy to leave home and family and make the long trek by stage alone.

Oregon was younger then, and more primitive. More dangerous, too. Prior to the Civil War, Atlanta must have possessed a beautiful culture, one which its colonial inhabitants fully planned would go on forever. What courage it must have taken to leave when Aunt Chrissy found herself jilted . . . jilted by the man she was to marry! And the reason still pained her . . . jilted because of True herself!

Which of the two half-sisters must have suffered the greater agony? she wondered. The one Jonathan Blake jilted or the younger one whom he promised to marry for the sake of "decency."

Decency? True shuddered, wondering if thinking had changed here much today. The thought bothered her. She turned her full attention to her aunt's letter.

"You know how spectacular Oregon is now, wild apples ripening along the fencerows trying to outdo the orchards and the leaves on fire with color. The twins have staked claims on Halloween pumpkins, feeling sure Young Wil will be here to carve them the way he did for you and Marty. No, we don't hear . . ."

Daddy Wil was keeping neighbors in good health . . . Miss Mollie was making green tomato pickles . . . the church had been able to find a new minister, recently retired and a fine man that Young Wil had worked with in Portland . . . in need of another teacher . . . the board was hoping True would return . . .

The second letter was from the twins. The kittens were growing. They had a new dog, a shaggy one named "Beowolf." He was afraid of cats, though. Would she be home for Halloween? Thanksgiving was too far away . . . and "On Christmas everybody has to be here.

Young Wil will hang up six-foot stockings like always and Daddy will get a ten-times-bigger tree than ever!" That was Kearby.

"About Christmas," Jerome wrote, beginning where his sister left off, "we have to start early, so you'd better hurry home. We want the house real fancy—and there's a program at church. I'm a Wise Man who knows a lot. Kearby just sings in the angel chorus, but she'll do good. Daddy says she's got lusty lungs! Oh, True, come home . . ."

And at the bottom, Daddy Wil had penned, "They're right, you know; Christmas began with a Child. It remains a time when each of us can be a child again—when we can celebrate our most precious possession, our family. A time for love!"

True had smiled through the children's letters. But at reading Daddy Wil's postscript, she wept.

Oh, darlings, her heart cried out, *don't you know how much I love you?* To which they would have asked, "Then what are you doing so far away?" And she would be unable to answer. But soon. Yes, soon now.

Anticipate. Anticipate! But, try as she would, waiting was impossible. True tore into Young Wil's letter, not caring that the tattered envelope fluttered all about the room.

My dear little True:
No broken bones since you left. Come to think on it, no bitten hands either! I still bear that scar. But no grudges. I have forgiven your transgressions since you went away. I simply never knew it was possible to miss anyone so much . . .

True hugged the letter to her.

Oh, don't spoil it now, she whispered across the miles. *Don't tell me I am a "burden," "brat," "nuisance." I am a grown-up now. Remember how at Daddy Wil and Aunt Chrissy's wedding you said "Yes" to my proposal and promised we'd have an even bigger cake with three feet of white frosting?*

You really were a raw nerve "back when," but somehow you and I always understood each other. And I guess you were right. Even raw nerves heal in time! Meaning that your letter indeed sounded like my little-girl monster is growing up! Well, I've been waiting for that . . .

Say it, say it! True's heart begged. *That I would make a suitable wife for a country doctor. A little of me's a teacher. A little bit's a nurse after my experience on the train. And ALL of me's head over heels in love with Young Wil North!*

Hungrily she read on. But the letter went on to other matters. They had always shared everything, so it made sense that he would continue the pattern.

His studies in pathology were drawing to a close. Following in the footsteps of Uncle Wil, his research of the common cold was up for review for possible publication. He was doing an internship in "bedside manners," and, of course, he continued the botany collections. Church work took up a lot of time, so it was good that he had found a young lady at the rooming house who could help him "the way you did with my notes."

True's heart sank. Someone had replaced her? Why, Young Wil had said nobody, absolutely nobody, else could read his writing—and his mind.

Halfheartedly she read on. But the rest of the letter was mostly in response to her account of the long trip ... expressing the proper amount of concern over her having been a victim of the robbery and showing thankfulness for her safety—but also having the good sense not to imply an "I told you so!"

Of course he wouldn't do that. He was never accusing, just protective. Overly so, she used to fume. Now she longed for his care ... but why was it necessary to find another girl? Weren't there boys who could assist?

Yes, there was Marty, if he would stick around long enough.

She reread the sentence, anger rising a little. After all, did he have to say *young*? She had avoided the adjective when describing Michael. Well, not anymore! She would begin a letter right away, and her words, she hoped, would be as biting as her teeth once had been! How could he understand her and be so blind?

True was to read his letter until it was frayed about the edges and the writing smudged with tears, reading into it something new each time, like the game they had played as children, chanting "He loves me," "He loves me not" as they plucked petals from the daisy fields in the summer sun.

Always her daisy promised "He loves me." But, admittedly, she had cheated a little sometimes. Maybe she was doing the same with the letter, making the first part read "He loves me" and allowing mention of this girl who had usurped her place to deny Young Wil's love.

But for now she must not sit "mooning around" (Grandma Mollie's expression). There was a quick letter to Young Wil to write, another to Aunt Chrissy.

And then she must find Emily Kincaid and explain that she would be going to Boston, and then perhaps back to Oregon, as soon as business here was finished.

Something else bothered her, a little feeling of something she had left unsaid. Oh, yes, she should explain that her reason for staying on at this house for the brief time remaining was because of William St. John's request. Emily would be displeased.

But she wasn't. To True's dismay, the woman was cordial.

"Well, I should hope you would be staying! Haven't we appeared hospitable?"

"Well, yes—" True, off guard, realized she sounded tentative. But Emily, like everything about this place, confused her.

"As a matter of fact, I have planned a party for you next Saturday evening. It will take the servants that long to prepare properly. And I suppose you will wish to do some shopping?"

Buy yourself a new gown. Don't embarrass us.

True inhaled deeply. A party in her honor. Without a "by-your-leave." How was she being presented? As a *shareholder*? Surely not "family." Not until she and Michael talked again.

What would this arrogant woman say if she refused to attend? True was on the verge of speaking when Emily, having settled the matter in her own mind, glanced at the tiny jeweled watch pinned to her blouse and said, "Oh, I was to tell you that Cousin William wishes to see you in his quarters. I wouldn't stay long—"

Woodenly, True rose. Why wasn't she able to say no to these people? Obviously she didn't belong here. Emily had made it clear from the beginning—until now. There was a sudden . . . what was it? *Softening?* No, more like resignation.

"By the way, dear," Emily called to True's departing back, "I'm so glad Michael found you!" True stiffened and waited, knowing what would come next. "We needed to locate the missing shareholder and set matters straight. No longer a need to fence!"

And then be off with you! Who knew what this woman was thinking? True realized anew as she hurried up the stairs that she was unaccustomed to such complicated people.

Family and friends in the Oregon Country nurtured one another. "Fencing" to them meant patching up the zigzagging rails—not holding one another at sword's point!

William St. John looked even more fragile than when True had seen him before. It was hard to tell if he was breathing except for the small rise and fall of the brocade coverlet.

In the shadows she moved toward him, like one of the shadows herself. But he saw her, motioned her closer, and motioned a white-uniformed nurse to bring something from one of the large wardrobes which lined the east wall of the bedroom.

True gasped with delight when the woman wordlessly held up a dress for her inspection. Of exquisite silver net, the gown was trimmed below the sweetheart neckline with all-over silk-lace medallions. Minute white satin bows rippled in row after row around the blouse, stopping at a wide, crushed-velvet belt of palest blue at the waist. There insertion of valencinnes lace raced in vertical symmetry up and down the floor-length sweep of the wide skirt. And underneath there seemed to be a dozen daintily ruffled silk petticoats—pale blue to match the belt.

"How beautiful!" True whispered when she could breathe. "A wedding gown?" She moved to touch the garment. The fabric seemed to take on life when her fingers touched the sleeping folds.

"Hers . . . for our almost-wedding . . ." The voice was faint.

Hers! That would mean Grandmother's dress! True touched it again, almost reverently.

"Yours now . . . wear to the party . . . just for me . . ."

True gave a little cry and ran to kneel beside the man who might have been her grandfather.

"Oh, I would be so honored!"

William St. John stirred slightly and turned his head so he could meet her eyes.

"I saved her trunk . . . from fire . . . no other wedding dress . . . two husbands . . . but loved me!"

The last three words came out triumphantly in spite of the beads of perspiration spelling exhaustion on the pale forehead. The nurse motioned her to go—when there was so much to say.

Gently, True kissed the old man's cheek and left the room.

17
Unfinished Business

THERE WAS MORE unfinished business here than True had
thought when she spoke to Emily about leaving. Before going to Boston, she wished to visit the cemetery where her grandparents lay and,
if possible, to locate the grave of her mother's first husband.

Aunt Chrissy had wanted her to do that and had drawn a map
so complete that she would need no help. That was good, for True
wished to make the journey alone. Only in that way could her ancestors "come alive" completely, though already she was seeing them
in a new light—the too-fragile spirit of her grandmother and the clay
of her grandfather.

Their common blood flowed through her own blood. And yet, True
realized, they were as foreign to her as the occupants of the strange
mansion.

There was a Sunday-feel to the air the morning True set out alone
to visit her grandparents' graves. Church bells tolled an invitation
all over the city, but after the depressing experience at the old church
in which her mother and aunt had been forced to "worship" in a kind
of piety they could never understand, she felt no desire to respond.

She would have preferred going to the falling-down building on the
premises of Magnolia Manor.

"I could identify with them—I know I could," True had insisted
to Michael.

But he had said (perhaps wisely), "Yes, but could they identify with
you?" Probably not—not now, anyway.

So today I will worship God in my own way, she decided as she dressed the minute the family carriage was out of sight. Taking her Bible, she hurried along the cobblestone streets toward the ruins of her mother and aunt's childhood home.

Getting away alone had been difficult: first pleading a slight headache to appease Emily, then convincing Michael, who refused to attend services without her, that she needed a walk to clear her head. No company. *Alone.*

Pausing at a sun-dappled corner to get her bearings, True fanned herself with the folded map before opening it to see if she were nearing the site.

No breeze swayed the moss, and the hot sun drew up unpleasant odors from the stagnant bayou. Mosquitoes buzzed about her head, and somewhere among the bullrushes a bullfrog complained hoarsely. Otherwise it was quiet. Too quiet. So still that True could hear her own breathing on the heavy air.

Feeling alone and uneasy, she checked the map quickly.

"Here it is!" She said the words aloud, for to her surprise the cemetery joined the far corner of Magnolia Manor—just a stone's toss from the building where the ex-slaves and sharecroppers worshiped together. Somehow the discovery pleased her.

The cemetery was all but hidden by a dense forest of bearded oaks. Once inside the grove, which seemed to hover jealously over the churchyard, True stood and looked around in dismay.

From the outside it had appeared overgrown with blackberry vines. But inside all the brambles were cleared away from the gravesites. True wondered who was responsible. She had to pick her way slowly through the mounds as there were soft bogs and oozing pools, some of which looked treacherous if she should stumble and fall.

It was hard to see in the deep shade of the hanging moss. Here and there tombstones showed dim white in the darkness. Crudely constructed wooden crosses marked some of the graves. The other mounds, appearing more recent, were unmarked.

Nervously she made her way from one headstone to another, reading names and dates in the yellow twilight of the moss's shade. The old church stood some distance away, but there was no sign of life.

Remembering the warning from Investigator Edward Keith that

her life might be in danger until Charles Devore was apprehended, a shudder passed through her body. The idea was no longer as ridiculous as before.

With a pounding heart she moved on unsuccessfully until suddenly a tall, white monument—largest and most elaborate of them all—loomed ahead. Even before she could reach the site, slipping and sliding from time to time, she knew it would be the place of her grandparents' interment.

Lifting her skirts above the oozing earth, she leaned down and found their names, rechecked Aunt Chrissy's notes, and found that the dates matched.

There were no children belonging to the Stein family except her mother, who was buried back in Oregon beside Uncle Joe.

Why then should there be three graves here with a common gravestone? Curiously, she moved slightly in order to read the lettering, only to feel her head reel with surprise. KELLY!

Why, that would be Aunt Chrissy's father . . . why wouldn't her aunt have known? And what were the remains doing here when the map showed the grave in a secluded southeast corner? It had been a long time, but her aunt was one to remember details.

This was something she would want to share, but for the moment True felt a need to search out her own feelings . . . to meditate . . . and somehow identify with a past she could never share in order to understand herself and her strange feelings of being torn between the two worlds in which her mother had lived.

Quietly she knelt at the foot of the center grave. This was her grandmother, with a husband lying on either side. And yet True was disappointed that she felt nothing but curiosity concerning the woman like whom her own mother and she herself looked.

Something, however, compelled her to remain, to open her Bible, and read some of her favorite passages: "The Lord is my Shepherd: I shall not want . . ."; "In my Father's house are many mansions . . ."; "Lo, I am with you always. . . ." Then, closing her eyes, she prayed for a long, long time.

When a twig snapped behind her, True jumped. Fully expecting to see Charles Devore, it came as a great surprise to see the face of Michael instead. But his words were an even greater surprise.

"Which of the two men was your grandfather, True?"

His voice was low and expressionless. True answered in the same tone. "Does it make a difference?"

"In the will, yes. Even though the money and property came from the Kelly family, it went to the Stein chap—due to, I would say, a lack of business acumen on your grandmother's part."

"But to you—would it make a difference to you?" Michael's answer was to reach down, pull her to her feet, and brush the caking mud from her skirt.

"Look at you. You're a mess!" Lightly. As if the previous conversation had never been.

That was one of the things that infuriated her about this man. One second he was cold, aloof, probing shrewdly. The next he was warm, charming, and often teasing. He was a puzzle, like everything and everybody else here. Well, what had she expected of him anyway?

Being a Stein entitled her to money, a source of power. But it admitted illegitimacy . . . how had Emily phrased it? "Bastardy child!" Well, there was no power in a "bastardy wife"! His hesitation had answered adequately.

True jutted out her chin and was about to say she had an answer for him when something in the shadows stopped her. Just a slight movement. It could have been the wind, except that there was no breeze. Wordlessly, she pointed a shaking finger toward what appeared to be the figure of a man squatting behind one of the gravestones. Michael's eyes followed her finger.

"A man," she whispered. "He's gone now—but there was one—"

"Let's get out here!" Michael grasped her arm and hurried her from the churchyard.

18
Fast-Moving Events

❧

"WE MUST GIVE all our attention to the party this week," Emily said as she and True shared an early breakfast.

True had risen before the sun, hoping for time to write to Aunt Chrissy, give her a report, and make sure everything was all right. Something about her aunt's last letter had bothered her. It was nothing she could put her finger on—just one of Miss Mollie's "feelin's" that something was amiss.

Was it Marty's long absences—or could she be right in suspecting that Young Wil was involved with the girl he had spoken of and her aunt did not want her to be hurt?

One minute she was telling herself that it made no difference. But in the next one, she knew better. Any woman who tried to take her place . . .

"True!" Emily, who had interrupted her plans, now interrupted her thoughts.

"We'll open the entire downstairs into a ballroom . . . chamber music . . . banks of flowers there . . ."

True only half-heard. Ballroom? Emily was giving a *ball*? And in her honor? It made no sense. She had thought of only a few selected friends. But this was too much!

"You have given thought to the proper gown? I can help you choose what is correct."

"I have the proper gown," True said softly, taking pleasure in the look of perplexity that crossed Emily's face. "I—"

111

But whatever else she felt must be said had to wait. Hosea appeared at the door to announce that there was a gentleman to see Miss North. Would Missy True join him in the library?

Edward Keith rose from one of the ladder-back chairs when True entered the room.

"I wanted you to know, Miss North," the investigator said without preliminaries, "that two of the men you helped identify as bandits are in custody. One, however, remains at large—as does Charles Devore. May I remind you how important it is that you stay in touch with us? If either should make contact in any way or you see anything suspicious—?" Inspector Keith ran a hand through his white hair, pale eyes questioning like his tone of voice.

True was tempted to tell of the mysterious return of the brooch. But something made her ask instead, "Which of the men did the authorities take into custody?"

The man looked at her, his eyes boring into hers.

"You would recognize names?" When she shook her head, feeling foolish that she had asked, he went on, "I can only say then that it was the tall one with the scar and the other one you described as medium height. The third—have you remembered what you saw that seemed familiar?"

That his eyes were familiar, True wanted to say. But the words would not come. It was her duty to cooperate. To tell of the brooch and help identify the man if she could . . . but the moment was gone. The inspector, hat in hand, was giving her another warning to be cautious.

"Your life could depend on it!"

"Wait!" As if suddenly awakened from slumber, True's words tumbled over one another. "There was something strange—a man in the cemetery. I know I saw him dodge behind a marker."

Inspector Keith scribbled a note on his pad.

"Alone?"

"He was. I wasn't. Michael was with me. But he didn't see the man and rushed me away. He seemed alarmed, but he has nothing to fear from this man—and I doubt if I do either."

"Let me be the judge of that!" His words were sharp. "As to the younger Mr. St. John—no, nothing to fear from Devore. His hasty departure was most likely to avoid trouble with the—uh, people who live on the property."

"The colored people?"

"And poor white trash."

True felt her back stiffen, and the pulse at the base of her throat begin to throb.

"I will never understand you people—never in a million years," she said in a voice that was carefully low and controlled. "You speak of the poorly educated and culturally deprived people as if they were less than your horses! How can they be other than they are when they're so ill-used—kept living in a world of unrelieved grimness?"

Unaware that her eyes were purple with rage, True turned her burning gaze on Edward Keith and was pleased to see that he was unable to return her gaze.

"I would be careful down here, Miss North," he said as if determined to make a point. "Even when they've done you a favor—"

"Go on!"

"Well, like moving the remains of your grandmother's first husband—pretty poor taste, if you ask me."

"I didn't ask!" True's words came out sharper than she intended because of the emotions stirring inside her. So the pitiful poor who inhabited the land she was about to own were responsible for seeing that their loved ones were together. The idea had such a strong appeal that she spoke her thought aloud.

"Jesus would have loved these people."

True hardly heard the man leave. Two plans had taken shape in her mind. One she would discuss with the good-natured lawyer, who reminded her so much of Grandma Malone's Irish husband, O'Higgin, back home. The other she would manage herself. On the night of the great ball!

"You're quite sure, miss, that this is what you want to do, now are you?" Albert Berkshire's red eyebrows that matched his flaming hair rose in astonished arcs above his blue eyes. "Really, you're a remarkable young lady!"

True smiled at the attorney.

"Thank you for the compliment, Mr. Berkshire. And, yes, I'm quite sure what I want to do with the land if you're sure I own it."

"Mr. St. John, Sr., and I have gone over every word!"

"Does Michael know?"

Albert Berkshire stroked his forehead with a pudgy finger.

"No, nobody knows besides Mr. St. John, you, and me. And I'm not sure anybody else should be informed—not yet."

True answered quickly.

"Oh, I agree! But you *do* think we can count on the government to help—I mean, offer a means of protection against protests?"

"Oh, they'll cooperate all right—even if it means sending in a militia! The government gave a land grant some time ago as a possible site for the school adjacent to Magnolia Manor. Major Radfield was pleased when I located the legal owner of the property and is drafting a letter of appreciation to you. As to the new church, how much of the planning will you leave to the—"

"New owners?"

The attorney smiled broadly.

"Sure enough!" He smiled. "They won't be 'squatters' anymore!" He turned to look at her thoughtfully. "Are you sure you wish to break the news this way? I mean, if you change your mind—"

"I won't change my mind! This has been one of the reasons Emily didn't like me, hasn't it, Mr. Berkshire? She wanted the colored people and the poor whites out—am I right?"

Mr. Berkshire scratched his head.

"That she did, but to say she didn't *like* you—well, now, let's not be jumping to conclusions. Young Michael has some say—there now, I'm out of line, having made you blush. Back to business—you want what funds as are left after settlement costs to go into the building fund which I'm to hold in trust?"

"Right," True said, feeling a thrill of sheer joy race up and down her spine. "Let the new owners do their own planning . . . advising only as you need to. It may take some time for them to grow accustomed to making choices . . ."

Mr. Berkshire blew his nose, reminding True again of O'Higgin.

"You know, Miss North, you've a great big heart."

True smiled mistily.

"Big hearts run in my family," she smiled. "And speaking of families, you have drawn up the proper papers regarding the railroad stock?"

"Sure enough! Half in your name, hereinafter known as the 'party of the first part'—meaning Stein—and the remainder in your aunt's name, Christen Elizabeth Kelly Craig Wilson." He smiled, then continued, "'party of the second part—meaning Kelly,' splitting dividends . . . reimbursing Oregon investors!"

"Affirmative!" True smiled. And then they burst into shared laughter. First at the legal jargon, then for the sheer joy of having conspired to do something daring which would bring more happiness to the impoverished people of Magnolia Manor and back home than they ever knew existed.

With all the problems that faced her, True had never felt as happy and fulfilled in her entire life. She knew now that she had been right in coming here. She also knew where she belonged.

"I can't thank you enough, Mr. Berkshire. Now, when I finish in Boston . . . tell me, do you think it is safe for me to go?"

"Alone? Negative! I shall accompany you, of course."

19

The Daughter You Never Knew!

֍

DISPLEASURE COLORED MICHAEL'S face and his disposition when True announced that she would be going to Boston the following day. Why hadn't she told him? Well, they had had little time together, True tried to explain. But inside she was thinking that even those short times were tense. There were silences . . . spaces . . . unvoiced questions . . . and something akin to suspicion. There was everything to say. Or was there nothing?

"I thought you understood you were not to go alone," Michael said darkly, his voice in tune with a low rumble of thunder.

"Mr. Berkshire will accompany me. I need his advice." *Not yours.* True had not intended the implication. But it was there.

"I see." It was hard to tell if the tone said he was angry, annoyed, or hurt. Whatever they had shared had never been solid, and now words left unspoken were undermining any hope of permanence. True found herself thinking that although in every way he was the more sophisticated, it was she who saw farther. She could stare from the window of her heart and see something his eyes were unable to discern. Another world. Another way of life. Compassion. Love. *Family*—real family, born of trials, tears, and togetherness. And the even-larger family of God . . .

As if reading her thoughts, Michael said almost angrily, "It's your religion, isn't it?"

Nate Goldsmith, chairman of the board of trustees back in the settlement, used to advise, "Ain't fittin' t'answer in anger, best run

116

through th' books of the Old Testament." Only there wasn't time, so True inhaled deeply instead.

"I prefer the word *faith*, Michael. But, by either name, what could my beliefs have to do with the trip to Boston?"

"And you can deny that something has come between us?" The words were scornful.

"We have settled nothing," she said slowly. "Or have we?"

"That, my dear, was to have been *my* question . . . well, you run along to Boston on your secret mission—"

"There's nothing secret about it! I told you all along—"

"You've told me nothing really!"

We're quarreling. Actually quarreling. And I'm not sure what it's all about. Maybe they had better get everything out in the open. But when True turned to face him, the sound of Mr. Berkshire's voice reminded her that he was waiting.

"Michael—" she began. But he spun on his heel and was gone.

There was rain all the way to Boston. The train trip could have been lonely and frightening without the company of the red-haired attorney. Away from the environment of the Atlanta mansion, he became almost boisterous—laughing, reminiscing about his Canadian boyhood, and even singing some of his native songs. He was easy to talk to, and True found herself sharing a great deal that she had felt would be of little interest to the Kincaids and St. Johns. They talked of the forests, the streams, the mountains, and their mutual love for the kinds of people who had given their all to conquer the frontier and be conquered by it.

"Can you be happy away from the wild beauty of the Oregon Country, really happy?" Mr. Berkshire asked suddenly. His question did not seem out of order.

"I don't know," True said honestly. "I've wondered."

"You haven't said yes to the young man, then?"

True smiled. "Neither have I said no." Then, before she knew the words would be coming, she mused aloud, "I'm not sure—not as sure as I think a girl should be . . . and I have a strange feeling that Michael isn't either."

Mr. Berkshire's merry eyes suddenly sobered. "Now what would make you think that? He proposed. He told me so!"

"But that was before—before he knew that I was conceived out of wedlock . . . and that I have chosen to give most of my inheritance away . . ."

Albert Berkshire sighed. "I am only an attorney who deals in facts—not at all skilled in matters of the heart. But, you know," he cocked his round head to one side, "I would say that if those things make a difference, you are indeed wise in postponing a decision!"

True was silent, weighing his words.

"Will you teach if you remain here? There is a need for governesses—"

"Nothing like that!" she assured him. "What I would enjoy is impossible. If I could help out in the school that's coming one day to Magnolia Manor . . . or even go in as a nurse there . . ."

She told him then about Aunt Chrissy's teaching, her mother's nursing, and her love for both. "I'm prepared in both fields—but mostly I guess I'm more prepared to be a wife and mother."

"And I beg you to wait for just the right man!"

"I know who the right man is—it's only—"

The train lurched at that point. And shortly afterward the conductor was singing out, "Boston, capital and largest city of the Commonwealth of Massachusetts, latitude 42 degrees and 21 minutes north . . ."

His long, well-rehearsed orientation for passengers was still in progress when Albert Berkshire and True North stepped out and walked on. Visit the old cemeteries, monuments, and memorial tablets . . . like the King's Chapel Bury Ground and the Granary, where Boston's earliest celebrities lay resting.

But there was no time for this, of course. True looked around her at the busy, bustling city and wished with all her heart that she could tour it all. There was so much history here, so much she would want to share with the family, particularly Young Wil, who shared her interest in the Puritan values and their influence on the New World. It would soon be Thanksgiving, a good time . . .

But the map that Aunt Chrissy drew (all guesswork, she admitted) did not fix the churchyard as being near the points of interest. "It looks closer to the sea," she said, pointing to the "X" her aunt had made. Mr. Berkshire agreed.

The cemetery was easier to find than True expected. So was the grave of Jonathan Blake. A caretaker pointed out a grassy knoll surrounded by a wrought iron fence as the Blake family's burial ground. "Fine old family. All gone now. You're the first visitor I recollect," the white-haired man volunteered. "Relative?"

True squared her shoulders. "His daughter," she said.

Albert Berkshire tactfully remained outside the enclosure. True stood silently at the foot of her father's grave, trying to picture the once-boyish, carefree manner . . . his devil-may-care attitude toward life . . . his ability to ruin the lives of the two women she loved. But the vision would not come. She felt only sadness that sometimes that's the way life was.

And in that moment she forgave her father.

"A new headstone you'll have—which says *IN MEMORY—from the daughter you never knew.*"

20
Brief Encounters

$\sim$

WITH THE ELABORATE reception so near at hand, True tried to feel happy. Let anticipation take over. After all, wasn't this what every girl dreamed of? Something right out of a novel? But such reasoning brought no happiness. Instead, she felt vaguely uneasy and depressed. A certain air of expectancy hung over the great mansion. But it seemed born of frenzy. People hurrying, checking lists, speaking curtly. Undoubtedly, everything was perfectly executed. Exactly on schedule. Time for everything—except each other.

True had her share of rushing to do, too. Tisha, who thrived on secrets she had found, located a dressmaker who could nip the waist of her grandmother's gown a wee bit. And the seamstress, a nonstop talker, knew just the right hairdresser.

"Why, I've never had my hair done!" True had tried to object.

And the dressmaker replied, "But you've never been to a ball, you tell me—and certainly any young lady who's the honoree—"

So why not concede? Make it a dream come true. But True wished with all her heart that she could generate enthusiasm, feel the way she felt the night Young Wil took her to her first square dance, following the roofraising of the new school. She had missed every call . . . been late getting back to every corner . . . hearing and seeing nothing but her partner's face as he sashayed back and forth, meeting her eyes, making her feel alive, grown-up, and head-over-heels in love. How odd that a memory could start her blood circulating faster, while present anticipation only slowed its flow . . .

The memory refused to go away, but True forced herself to work around it. She paid a quick call to Mr. St. John, giving him a briefing on what had been accomplished and what remained to be done. It hurt her to see that he was failing, but the hurt was eased by his tight grip on her hands even with his eyelids closed to all but words. It was as if he clung to her for life—life she felt would end soon after his present mission was done.

"I will come to you for final inspection before the ball," True promised, to which he said, "God bless you, Granddaughter!"

Granddaughter! That might have been. But, had circumstances gone another direction, perhaps she could have been the granddaughter of Emily Kincaid. The thought wiped away her smile. Like Grandma Mollie Malone said, "Best leave them things to the Lord. He knows a heap more'n the storks He created!"

Emily seemed to be everywhere at once. "Only the *grand monde* will be appearing. Make sure you reserve time for your personal appearance—if you're through poking around in graveyards . . . " When her voice trailed off, True assured her that she had found what she needed, keeping her voice as civil as possible.

Emily allowed a list she was checking to flutter to the floor. "You found that they—those *terrible* people have exhumed my Jimmy's body—moved it by *her*—" True held back any words she might have spoken. For in that one revealing moment Emily had shown her vulnerability. What a lonely, barren life of hatred and distrust she had built for herself! What a prison for her tortured soul, on which everyone she met must help pay the taxes! "Yes, I saw," True said, her voice appropriately sad. But the sadness was for Emily . . .

The days sped by. A letter came from Aunt Chrissy saying Young Wil had heard from Marty. Nothing more. True took a small margin of one afternoon to respond, giving a summary of her findings here. Then she mailed another novella-length letter to Young Wil, mentioning Michael liberally, but closing with "Love." The day before the party there was another bulky letter from him. Reluctantly True tucked it away for reading later, as Mr. Berkshire had some papers needing her signature and a report to make.

On the way to the conservatory where he waited, she had a brief encounter with Michael. His eyes looked restless and hungry—as if to say he had missed her. But they did not touch. His hand made a small movement toward her, then fell to his side, as if he felt there should be some more on her part.

Don't ask me now . . . I'm not ready! Her heart cried out, even as she wondered why he waited. His voice, when he spoke, was strained. "You seem different somehow," he said. He seemed less certain of himself.

"We all change," she murmured. "But I still don't know who I am . . . and I can't plan a future until I know *which* past I am!"

21
Love Leads Home

꒜

TRUE FOUND YOUNG Wil's letter infuriating, frightening, and heartbreakingly beautiful. *What a hybrid you are, Wil North!* She laughed and cried at the same time. And then she lay silent and pensive, eyes violet in concentration as she gazed at the ceiling of her bedroom on Saturday morning. There were a million details needing her attention—none as important as the wonderful man who could do battle with words or tame the wild creatures of the forest. Nobody, *nobody*, she lay thinking, could string words together—like his thoughts—in a strange necklace of subordinate clauses and make them come out making sense. Nobody but Young Wil North, the one who claimed logically that he had loved her before she was born!

Why, then, did he choose to break her heart? And always in grandstand-play style!

It was infuriating and downright humiliating to have him speak so boldly of "this young lady." His too-casual references (too frequent, too!) were an open taunt. He might as well have quoted their Grandma Malone who dished out such phrases. Their surrogate grandmother loved saying, "When the cat's away, the mice're bound t'play!" just to make Irish O'Higgin's face turn redder.

"Me Mollie girl's causin' me heart t'miss!" he would say, plunging a fork into another of his wife's sourdough biscuits. "Well, yer hand shure ain't!" And, with that, she would swat the big, capable hand for its transgression against good manners. *Goodness! How I would like to see them . . .*

123

True dried her eyes and forced her mind back to Young Wil's insults. Miss Mollie and O'Higgin were funny. Young Wil was not!

The letter repeated a list of "this young lady's" fine qualities—even made mention that Marty found her most appealing. Marty! Aunt Chrissy had said Young Wil was in touch. Why, then, didn't he tell her more? And why on this green earth was he introducing "this young lady" to their adopted brother? It would be like him to take her to meet the rest of the family! Which is exactly what he told her in the next paragraph he might do.

Oh, the nerve of him! If he were here to see her, she would tear this letter to shreds and say, "There! So much for your skirt-chasing, Portland ways!" But, without him as an audience, what was the use? And, besides, something else caught her eye.

"Glad about the railroad shares! Doesn't that make you a grand duchess or something? At any rate, the ownership will ease some tension on our brother's part, wouldn't you say? He never did, as our self-appointed 'Grandam' says, 'cotton' to the right-of-ways they claimed through the farm grounds . . ."

True read on, hoping he would say more about Marty. Instead, he expressed concern over what he called "Chrissy's anxiety." The two of them had always been close, True recalled. Aunt Chrissy had favored Young Wil when, orphaned, he came to live with the man she was later to marry—favored him and loved him above all the other children in her class. Partly, True suspected, because the little boy understood rejection, just as Aunt Chrissy did. She frowned.

If Young Wil had noticed, it wasn't only her own imagination that something was wrong at home. That was the thought that frightened her about the letter. Maybe Aunt Chrissy needed her . . . certainly not "this girl"!

But, infuriated and frightened as she was, True could only clasp the letter to her heart in sheer joy when in it Young Wil became the man she had toddled after in her babyhood, worshiped in her adolescence, fought with in her stormy teens—and now loved in the way that comes only once in a lifetime. A soulmate, helpmate—a man she could never do without! How could she ever have thought she could get along without him?

It's unfortunate that I can't paint words—use tinted ones or set them in slow motion . . . or write them in music, so you can see them rustling between the lines and spaces, ready for synchronizing into dream-flutes and dream-drums (including some remembered half-notes of your frowning, fuming, and raging!) . . . or perhaps add the fragrances they deserve. Yes, unfortunate, that words, as Paul wrote, are "become as sounding brass or a tinkling cymbal," depreciating their value when I would so like to describe my feeling about the sights, sounds, and *feelings* we have shared. The beauty was there Halloween, but I didn't see it. The beauty will be there Thanksgiving, but I will not taste it. But Christmas? There is so much we must say, so I take heart from Uncle Joe's last sermon. Remember? "Love leads home," he said . . .

22
Cinderella's Ball

❧

EVERY CRYSTAL PRISM on the age-old chandeliers was dusted to shine like new moons. Every potted rubber plant, glistening from a coat of oil, reflected the rainbow colors. Chair rails glowed with rubbed-down wax. All doors leading to the verandas were swung open to admit a balmy breeze and give a view of the gardens beyond. Marble floors, stripped free of furniture except for chairs lined against the walls of three-rooms-made-into-one for the evening, waited for the whirl of dancing feet. The voices of those occupying the chairs were pitched low with expectancy. The chamber music was soft and sweet . . .

And now there is a hush, a pause in the music, and the golden princess at the top of the stairs begins to descend. The stairs are long and winding—wide enough for an escort, but she is alone as she seems to float down. She is beautiful, so beautiful—her lemon-colored hair piled high, held in place by a little bouquet of violets placed there by her grandfather. The guests twitter, wondering if the owner of this mansion did not indulge in some youthful indiscretion. At the landing, the beautiful princess pauses, allowing the reflected light from the stained-glass window to tangle in her hair—turning it from pale silver to purest gold. Then, looking quickly over her shoulder as if for some sweet prince, she gathers her voluminous blue-and-silver skirts and, with a faint smile on her cameo-face, moves down the vast expanse of steps.

Who is she? What is this all about?

126

True can feel their questions. The frowning, fuming of them. The raging, racketing, rioting—and, for some, weeping in the words unsaid. How right Young Wil was! Words could never "phosphoresce." Words would not tell that she, an outward Cinderella, was unchanged inwardly. Just weeks earlier this same girl was in what they would have termed "rags." Admittedly, when she and Young Wil ran wildly over the meadows looking for a first daisy, her hair had hung down to her shoulders. All this was before these "fairy godpeople" undertook to transform her . . . away from her world—not of sweeping ashes from the hearth necessarily, but living an uncomplicated life among all kinds of people who exchanged recipes, waited on the sick, and knew little of each other's background and less about railroad shares and mansions . . .

The Cinderella story had staked a claim on True's heart when Angel Mother and Daddy Wil told tales before the wood-gobbling fireplace in what the family called the "Big House." Later, in her little-girl grief over the loss of her mother, Young Wil repeated it over and over . . . and she cried . . . cried for her mother . . . cried for Cinderella, who, at the stroke of midnight, went back to her cinders . . . and cried for a whole world of sadness she was unable to understand. But now here it was again. The Cinderella story. As powerful as always. And beckoning, beckoning. Promising that she could inherit the world. If she would but sacrifice her soul . . .

True closed her eyes for a brief moment to clear her head. Then, lifting her chin as one would expect of royalty, she let her eyes travel about the room in search of Prince Charming. At first she did not see Michael. Instead, her eyes met those of Emily Kincaid. Emily's eyes held a strange mixture of pride and hostility—part fairy godmother, part wicked stepmother. No matter what her identity, the other woman looked stunning in a forest-green velvet gown, trimmed richly with ecru lace.

When their eyes met, Emily said something to the distinguished-looking man at her side and came forward. She greeted True with such a warm embrace that anyone would doubt there existed any tension. True felt a rush of gratitude. Emily was trying to make the evening perfect, letting True be the center of this strange stage—the embrace serving to remind the guests, of course, that it was Emily herself who placed her there.

"How lovely you look, my dear," Emily said, her voice inaudible to all ears but True's in the spattering of polite applause. "How elegant the sapphire-and-pearl brooch would have been—"

Strange that she would think of the brooch, a piece of jewelry she had never seen and certainly did not know had been returned. True had wanted to wear it, but something warned her to keep it in her bag. The warning of Investigator Keith? No, something more—the eyes of the one member of the trio she had been unable to identify. Because she knew now that whoever owned those eyes had recognized her, too. It was he who returned the brooch.

With her thoughts so far afield, True had missed her cue. Somehow she was being handed over to Michael. And together they stepped back into the pages of the Cinderella story. She, adorned and beautiful (her only dowry), exchanging offerings with a Prince Charming who could lay material things at the toes of her glass slippers. But he had no spiritual offerings.

Michael extended his hand. "We are to dance, first," he prompted. The faint smile that curved the handsome lips beneath the sandy moustache was not reflected in his eyes.

As if in a dream, True accepted his hand. And, with Michael holding her the proper arm's length from him, they gracefully circled the polished floor. Then as, remembering her part, True smiled shyly up at the tall, handsome man, she realized that all around them—but worlds away—a million other dancing couples whirled and swayed. The magic transformation was complete.

"You look ravishing—absolutely ravishing," Michael whispered. His voice, like the dancers, was worlds away. "That was a fitting introduction the mayor gave!"

The mayor? Oh, yes, the man Emily had stood beside had joined them—but what had he said? Something to do with her being rightfully named—"True North, the *true* owner of Magnolia Manor . . . shareholder . . . perhaps other holdings . . ."

"'Other holdings'?" Blankly, True repeated the words in search of an explanation.

Did Michael's arms tighten or had his body gone rigid? "Why, my claim on your heart."

True did not look up, and his voice, muffled by the whisper of feet against the marble floor, lost its tonal quality. "You have no claim on my heart, Michael."

Michael skillfully dodged a dipping couple. "You're saying I mean nothing to you?"

True missed a step, murmured an apology, then said slowly, "I didn't say that—but isn't this a strange place to be talking about—well, matters of the heart?"

"Yes!" And with the one word, he swung her inconspicuously past a group of nodding chaperones dozing against the wall, and onto the oleander-screened veranda.

Once alone, Michael allowed his arms to drop to his sides. "Have you reached a decision?"

"Have *you*?"

Michael groaned in the darkness. But True knew that the question had struck home. She had been right in thinking that he was weighing the pluses and minuses of a "nameless" wife.

"All right, *all right!* If we're going to be so brutally honest, I did want to make sure I could beat my wife with a clear conscience—not because of her lowly birth—" He paused, seeming to sense that his attempt to light-touch the words was out of keeping with the emotional strain between them. When True was silent, he said, "Well, you can understand that, can't you?"

"No—no, Michael, I can't. If you'd loved me, you would not have had to consider. But then," her voice dropped, for it was now that True realized something she, in her newfound glory, had failed to see clearly: "You never laid much claim on love, did you? You sought me out because of my holdings—I was a necessary piece to complete the railroad puzzle."

"My father wanted to find you!" His tone was defensive.

True, hardly hearing, went on more to herself than to him. "Then there was Magnolia Manor—and its undesirable people—'two birds with one stone'—finding me would solve everything—"

"That was Emily's concern, yes, but True—"

We should have talked like this long ago, some part of True was saying. The other was saying, "Never mind who was responsible for what. I am at fault, too. The 'Cinderella complex'—I almost succumbed, Michael."

"*Almost? You* mean you're turning us down? Any girl in her right mind would jump at this! Oh, True, listen to me—"

Turn us down, he had said. "Apparently your family is aware that you planned to marry me. Do they all know why? Will my decision

disrupt their lives? Oh, I understand your father's tie with the past
. . . but Emily's? How much stock does she hold?"

There was a silence. Then Michael said in a low voice. "She and I
own the same number. Yours will be the swing vote."

"I see. Let's go back, Michael." Her voice, like her heart, was dead.

23

The Uninvited

❧

IT WOULD BE best if I tried to think of tonight as being like any other, so I can act natural, play out this role, and prepare for the stroke of 12. So thinking, True went through the motions of acknowledging introductions and managing to make small talk with the people around her. How would Emily and Michael dispose of them? Bring the story to a satisfactory conclusion? And the rest of the family? True realized with a jolt that she did not even remember their names. A family of which she was to have become a part—and she only recalled the names Oscar, Audrey Anne . . . and wasn't the rotund little man who quoted liberally from Edgar Allan Poe named Edgar, too?

Sometime during the evening, which seemed to run on and on, she caught sight of Inspector Keith's watchful eyes. And once Attorney Berkshire signaled as if he wished a word with her. But her mind was too muzzy to question presences, interpret signals, or make sense of anything. She felt feather-light. She was a piece of thistledown released from its pod. Drifting. Floating aimlessly. She was no longer the drab, insecure person Emily had taken her for. Neither was she the beautiful princess William St. John saw in his euphoric dream. She was True North, wanting with all her heart to get back to the balanced center of things—and not knowing how. And all the while, drifting . . .

"Have you found Atlanta as you expected, Miss North?" "You will be staying, Miss North?" "How romantic, Miss North! Tell us how you ever came to meet our most eligible bachelor!"

Did she make sense as she moved from one group to another? The present was a dream. All the while, as she moved through it—her heart dead inside—her mind was trying to go back, to put events in order, so that the world would seem real.

Then, suddenly, the languor of unreality was shattered. There was the ear-splitting sound of a gun, followed by harsh voices outside. Somewhere a woman screamed. And the brilliant candles of the chandeliers paled in a cloud of smoke that billowed in from the open windows. Another shot . . . more hoarse voices of men outside . . . and then, in spite of the mayor's pleading for calm, there was a wild stampede in all directions.

Michael! Where was Michael? And Emily? With a pounding heart, True hurried about the room, which was emptying quickly. Unable to find either of them, she rushed up the stairs. Mr. St. John's nurse may have left. He must not be alone.

Before making the turn to William St. John's suite, something compelled True to glance in the opposite direction toward the guest room she occupied. There was indeed a twang of smoke in the halls, but she believed the source came from below. Michael's father would be in no immediate danger. But she or something she owned was! For in that one quick glance True saw that the door was open. Quickly, for fear her footsteps would be heard, she slipped off her shoes. Then she padded noiselessly in her stockinged feet, feeling her way in the darkness. At the door, she listened. No sound except for the hammering of her own heart.

When True was reasonably sure she was alone, she eased the door open a little wider and would have entered except that she stumbled over some seemingly large object. With a little cry, she fell helplessly to the floor, her leg twisted painfully beneath her. At first she was afraid the leg was broken, but when the pain subsided some, she pulled herself up by holding onto the chair over which she had stumbled, and felt her way to the table lamp. She hesitated and then lighted it, feeling sure that any intruder who meant to harm her would have made a move when she was at such a disadvantage.

The lamp flickered as if sharing her fear. Then, more certain of its safety, it bathed the room in light. What True saw caused her to raise a hand to her throat to choke back a scream of terror. The entire room was in disarray. Drawers of every desk, bureau, and dresser gaped open like fledglings waiting to be fed. The contents lay on the floor. Her precious letters, once neatly stacked, labeled, and tied with ribbon, were scattered about the room. Envelopes split, pages rumpled . . . and then her eyes came to rest on the French doors which opened onto a private balcony—wide open, the silk draperies fluttering inward. The avenue of escape the intruder used!

Taking no time to think, she hurried to the open doors. There, still dangling to the ground, was a knotted rope. This must mean that this person could be only moments ahead of her. Cupping her hands to her mouth, True called, *"Help!* HELP!"

The echo of her voice was only a ghostlike whisper against the hallway walls. And there it died away, unable to rise above the bedlam below, where many more people than appeared on the party's guest list were pushing, shoving, trampling one another in mass hysteria. What was it all about? Or did anybody know?

I ought to be helping, True thought. But, not understanding and in a state of shock and fear, she could only stand on the dark balcony in speechless horror.

When minutes—or was it hours?—later she would have turned, True found herself suddenly caught in a pair of strong arms, her own arms pinned to her sides. The face of her captor was indistinguishable. The thief? A murderer? An arsonist? It hardly mattered. No matter what the danger, she was unable to move.

"It's all right, True. It's all right."

Michael! She should feel relief. But she was incapable of any feeling whatsoever. With a shaking finger she pointed to the knotted rope.

"I know." Michael's voice sounded far off. "Just be thankful that your timing was a little off and you did not actually catch him in your room." He inhaled deeply and then continued, as if the words pained him. "And we can all be thankful that the rope's there—not shaped into a noose—"

Him, Michael had said. Who? And doing what in her room? But those questions were trivial in comparison . . . did her ears fail to hear or had Michael said the horrible word?

"Noose?" True could manage only the single word. She twisted to free herself, but Michael held onto her as if fearing she would make a wild attempt to climb down the rope herself and join the mob below. And maybe she would have, she realized later. For she was in such a state of lunacy that it was hard to bring meaning to Michael's obviously hurried explanation.

"Charles Devore . . . looking for something sent to you in the mail . . . tie him to the robbery, but that fool kid . . . do you hear, True?" She heard but she did not understand.

The brooch! Mutely True nodded, trying hard to concentrate. ". . . irresponsible thing to do, withholding information *if* something reached you . . . and why, of all times, did you spread word of your alms? I thought those were to be done in secret!" His voice had grown bitter. "But, no, on the night of the ball . . . forgive me . . . not myself . . . maybe your foolishness saved a lot of lives . . . "

The pain had returned to True's leg. The excitement, the pretense of it all, followed by the ugly fingers of fear that had squeezed her heart dry were too much. She swayed against Michael as her legs were about to give way beneath her. He enfolded her in his arms then, but True was unaware. So near was she to the netherworld of unconsciousness, she was able to discern only key words.

"Squatters came . . . crazy way of paying tribute . . . burning torches like savages . . . then threat of lynching . . . " *Lynching!* ". . . warned you that the squatters don't 'belong' . . . till now . . ." *Till now!* "Well" (reluctantly), "when Devore attempted to slip through the net set by officers, it was the squatters—*new owners by your decree*—they stopped them in their tracks! Suffice it to say that for a time there it appeared that the nooses and torches intended for them—well, would be used on the self-appointed posse! A lynching in reverse . . . are you hearing?"

Now she heard—even understood. But she could not *believe!* What a peculiar chain of circumstances—no, *mysterious* was the word— brought this strange miracle about. The inspector-turned-traitor was in custody. Various agencies of the government would take over now, Michael explained, because the case involved a government payroll, money had been transported over state lines, and some other reasons True did not hear.

Her mind was on the brooch. Michael was sure to ask about it. What kind of answer could she give? Even though she expected it, when the question came True was still unprepared.

"Why did you deceive us, True? You could be helping to harbor a criminal, you know. The third robber, as far as we can ascertain, is still at large. Could you not have taken at least me into your confidence? Am I not to be trusted? Surely our relationship means *something!*"

True reeled uncertainly under the hammer-blows of his reasoning. With all her heart, she wished this man had no power over her—even when his reasoning fitted his own ends.

"Oh, Michael, try to understand—yes, of course, our relationship is important—but it has nothing to do with the brooch—and I still can't explain." *Brooch!* It was she who said it.

"Very well." Michael's voice was cold. He dropped his arms to his sides as if granting permission for her to leave.

"I wish things were different—" True's words were cut short by blinding lights. Lighted lanterns, held high above the heads below, formed pools of light in the balcony, illuminating her face.

"Miss True North! Miss True North!" Voices chanted in unison. "Come down . . . come down . . ."

With a thrill of joy in her heart, True turned a radiant face to the crowd of blacks, whites, sharecroppers, landlords . . . nobility and peasantry. The *grand monde* mingling with the uninvited. And it was the uninvited who, responding to some secret whisper of the Lord, found the courage to bring this miracle about.

The miracle enlarged. Even as True waved from the balcony and indicated with a downward-pointing of her finger that she would join the group, work-hardened hands linked with jeweled fingers to press into the great mansion. It was, True found herself smiling, as if the castle were under siege. By the Spirit of the Lord!

Again, lifting her blue-and-silver skirts, the Princess floated down the stairs—this time glancing over her shoulder only to make sure that Michael followed. At the landing, again she paused. Michael, as regal as any girl could expect a Prince Charming to be, placed a hand lightly on her shoulder.

Then, ever the crowd-pleaser, he bowed. Smiling, as if whispering words of love, he said, "This, my dear, is your shining hour!"

Obediently, True smiled back. "The Lord's!" she corrected softly. Together they descended the remaining stairs.

So the Cinderella story was closing. Only, just as Young Wil changed the ending with each telling, the outcome had been unpredictable. Except that she wore no shoes! Then all such thoughts dissolved as True heard the beginnings of the most beautiful words she knew: "Amazing grace," timidly, then boldly, "how sweet the sound . . ."

24
Missing Links

❧

"Now that you've traced the missing links of your genealogy, I suppose you'll be leaving us?"

Nothing in Emily Kincaid's voice told True whether this woman wished her to stay, to go, or was indifferent to the decision. The two of them sat sharing tea in the conservatory, one of the few breaks either had taken since the party.

True set her empty cup on the carved ivory table in front of them. "Yes," she said simply, hoping the conversation would end.

Emily reached for a scone. "Tell me, have you accomplished what you hoped to? And learned what you intended?"

"More—much more. About myself. The world—"

"And love!" Michael's voice came from the door. Emily's cup clattered to the table in surprise. "You'll excuse me, ladies, but I do have three announcements to make. For one thing, the young lady here has turned down my proposal of honorable matrimony—" His voice was falsely light.

"Michael, please—" True tried to interrupt.

Michael was undaunted. "Second, the young lady is to hear this! By special request, she is expected to remain here—my father's, yes— but add to it, the request of the United States Government. She will need to identify one Charles Devore *and*," he paused significantly, "declare any new evidence which may have reached her!" Dully, True realized that he should know the brooch was safe.

136

Emily's eyes sparkled with curiosity. When there was silence, she said, "You said three announcements, Michael."

"That I did," he answered, turning toward the door. "The third is to set all minds at rest. I shall not be gracing the premises for some time. There is much that needs attention concerning railroad business—particularly in light of our new findings. Rightful heirs. Divine rulers. And their kissing cousins."

The words, so stiffly spoken and formal, were intended to draw laughter or at least a smile, True supposed. Instead, they made her heart ache. Not for love of Michael, but for lack of it. And the fact that he was brokenhearted but stiff-necked in his pride. There was no way she knew to approach him. So thinking, his next words came as a great surprise.

"So will you pray for the state of my soul, Miss North?"

Oh, Michael, don't speak so lightly of so grave a matter. But aloud she said, "Of course, I will pray for all of you."

"Like you, I need to find some missing links—except that I'm not out searching!"

True turned away so that he would not see the tears in her eyes.

"It's my feeling that He's searching for you. Goodbye, Michael."

25
Solace on Thanksgiving

❧

AT FIRST TRUE was impatient with the delay. But she busied herself with the loose ends of her life here in Atlanta. Then, where once
it had seemed to drag, time sped forward.

She spent as much time as possible with William St. John because
she realized, even before the doctor told her, that there was little life
within his frail body. His talk was fragmented, sometimes making
little sense, and he often confused True with first her grandmother
and then her mother. Her presence, however—by any name—never
failed to fan the faint spark of his life. On one subject his mind was
remarkably clear, his instructions concise: his will and his wishes
concerning an unceremonial burial in the little churchyard adjacent
to Magnolia Manor instead of the St. John plot.

"But your family?" True ventured once.

"*She* is my family. And now you are all I have left of her."

With tears in her voice, True explained over and over that, yes,
the attorney had drawn up the papers properly for distribution of his
property. It only upset the dying man when she begged that her name
be stricken from his list of heirs, so in the end True saw that it was
best to submit to his wishes, with two conditions.

He was to instruct Mr. Berkshire to notify the relatives prior to a
reading of the will. To that he consented. Her second condition was
that the money he wished her to have might be set aside legally in
a special memorial fund. Her request came on one of Mr. St. John's
bad days.

"Ah, yes," he agreed in a voice so faint True was hardly able to discern the words, "a stained-glass window in St. Mark's Cathedral—"

"No! I mean—please, please don't do that." True's voice was even fainter than his. He mustn't. Oh, he *mustn't!* Memory of the terrifying stained-glass art had been like the plunging of a knife into her heart. "I want something living—something in which a part of you will go on . . ." She groped for words, ". . . like the children you and my grandmother would have had—"

The wan face lighted in a way she had not seen before. "Bring him— *now!*" Accustomed to his fragmented speech, True was sure she understood. Calling Tisha, she asked the girl to summon the attorney. Shortly after the papers were drawn up and signed, designating the money to go into a medical research fund naming Wilson North, Jr., as guardian, William St. John slipped into a coma. Three days later he died with nobody knowing the exact whereabouts of his son.

Albert Berkshire, his usually merry blue eyes now sober, went over all the papers with True, explaining the parts she was unable to understand. Yes, he would be glad to handle her proxy in case anything came up here needing a vote regarding the railroad shares. True thanked him warmly, explained that she would be returning to Oregon as soon as the robbery investigation was over, and said a tentative good-bye. There were tears in his eyes. The good man was, she suspected, the only person besides her who mourned William St. John's passing.

To True's relief, Emily remained discreetly out of sight. "After all," True overheard her say in a voice pitched properly low, "there is a black wreath at the door." Which made the situation all the more depressing, seeing that none of the family had loved him.

Longing now to be out of the house and on her way home, True went shopping on two occasions. "Nothing perks up a lady's spirits like a new bonnet," Grandma Mollie always said. Well, a new outfit or so would be uplifting. She would be seeing the family . . . and, of course, Young Wil would meet her in Portland! Her clothing must be—well, convincing that she was indeed a grown-up young lady. Ready for love!

Her spirits soared as the saleslady helped her into what True blushingly admitted "very well may be my 'Going Away' dress." Wedding dress? No, she had one already. "My grandmother's—and it's never been worn!" True was to laugh as she shared that with Young Wil later. But at the time she was too giddy with happiness to wonder why the saleslady looked at her so strangely.

"We will not observe Thanksgiving since we're in mourning."

Emily Kincaid's flat announcement left True shaken. Not that the woman could any longer surprise her. Just the fact that Thanksgiving was here—and so was she. She should be home, where the air was filled with anticipation and the winey scent of cider-ready apples. Every woman in the settlement would be baking, and Grandma Mollie's brood would be scouring the walls of Turn-Around Inn in preparation for the holiday feast. Well, there was something she could do about the distance between. Wouldn't a telegram, delivered by a runner about the time O'Higgin said "*Amen*—now, dig in, folks!" be wonderful? But, she frowned, whoever heard of not *observing* Thanksgiving—even in the heart?

The day came and went. True was alone but not lonely. The telegram was on its way. She had written long letters to Aunt Chrissy and Young Wil and, for the first time in her life, written out her prayer of thankfulness. Then, finding that she liked the words, she made a copy for Young Wil and tucked it into his letter.

One thing they *always* agreed on was the love of God—His tenderness, mercy, and love, which began, Young Wil explained, before He made the frame for the mountains or lighted the stars.

Dear Lord, I thank You for so much—most of all, Your patience while I shed bits and pieces of myself, trying to become some other person You never intended me to be. But thank You for Your *impatience*, too! I'm glad You woke me up before I cast off so much of what You molded that I no longer bore Your "likeness." My self-made punishment would have been the inability to go back where I belong, Lord. Today, though I long for those I love, I am grateful in my chosen exile. Otherwise, Lord, I might have gone on with my "Cinderella fixation," placing hope on earthly things instead of *You* when life seemed bleak. Here I have found that I do not want glass slippers, Lord . . . just give me a pair of work boots and send me home. . . .

26
The Greatest Promise

❧

TRUE HAD DREADED the identification visit for so long that when it came she was almost disappointed in its anticlimactic brevity. Two clean-shaven, young officers—obviously in training—accompanied Investigator Keith. They were clumsy, and the older man made it his business to prompt them frequently.

Did this drawing resemble the man who conducted the first investigation concerning a Mr.—er—(one of the men consulted his notes) Devore? *Yes.* Did Miss North give him any information she had withheld from Mr. Keith? *No.* Then, because the matter had bothered her constantly, True said that it was quite the contrary. At their look of puzzlement, she opened her bag and drew out the brooch, which she had kept tucked away in a section of the original brown-paper wrapping.

"Meaning that I did not show him this." Her hand trembled as she held out the ornament. One of the three whistled softly in admiration. Otherwise, the men seemed surprisingly disinterested. "It came after we talked—"

Edward Keith shrugged. "No point in taking it," he said, more to the other two men than to True. "The lady had described it already and it would have been returned to her."

The feelings of guilt were removed. True was first relieved and then puzzled. "But—but the sender—" she faltered, "you said—"

Running a hand through his thin, gray hair, the Chief Investigator seemed more preoccupied with a form he was completing than her words. At length he spoke. "They've all been apprehended, in-

141

cluding a young man from Oregon. Ready, fellows?" He snapped his leather briefcase shut. "Case closed."

"Young man from Oregon," he had said. The words, so casually spoken, caused True to sway on her feet. As if seeing the awkward printing on the wrapping for the first time, she examined the letters. Of course! Why hadn't she noticed before that the *N* in North was upside down? And the eyes—those little-boy eyes that always looked to her and Young Wil for approval—could belong only to Marty! Little Marty, who had never been whatever it was he wanted to be but jumped on every bandwagon that passed through! Little Marty, who wanted to take justice in his own hands, who identified with Robin Hood's robbing the rich to help the poor! Running . . . running . . . out of breath, but running anyway . . .

The men were moving toward the door. "Wait!" True's voice sounded unreal to her own ears. "The boy—who was he?"

"Can't say for sure, but nothing for you to concern yourself with. First-timer, they say—opposing policies of the railroads. Probably get off lighter than he deserves."

When the men were gone, she sat down weakly—not knowing whether to laugh or cry. Why hadn't she recognized him? And how had she missed the little clues in letters from Aunt Chrissy and Young Wil? Maybe she hadn't wanted to see! Maybe—just *maybe*—Young Wil was right in saying she wasn't through growing up.

Well, she was growing! What she had learned here had given her a certain maturity of heart. And what she had done here would help so many, in both "homes."

A long sigh began at the tips of her toes and traveled the full length of her body, freeing her of the long-restrained guilt and fear. In its place was a gnawing hunger to be with her family to share their sorrow if Marty had been convicted; their joy, if the courts had seen fit to give him another chance. Everything was all right. Everything was so wonderfully all right!

True was filled with a joy that was like the spring rains that greened the Oregon meadows . . . the autumn sun that mellowed the fruit . . . warming her heart the way the sun warmed the earth after the winter cold.

"Thank You, Lord, thank You for all You've shown me. That I must stretch and grow . . . that life is for giving and the two words combined, *forgiving!* That the great tragedy in life is not death but what we allow to die within us while we live . . . let me take that thought with me . . . while leaving it here . . ."

Two days later she was ready to leave. Her trunk was packed, her reservation made for the train ride back. And then came the surprise delivery. A special messenger brought her a package from Michael! The postmark was Boston.

It was, she realized, Michael's first gift to her. And his last. What had he chosen in farewell to a love that had never been? When the heavy outside wrappings fell away, True carefully removed the tissue from the small gold figurine and read the accompanying card.

"My gift to you—Statue of Aphrodite, Goddess of Love. Michael."

A little sadly, she rewrapped the statue and placed it carefully in the bag along with her gifts for Daddy Wil and Aunt Chrissy's twins. Then, removing one of the several copies of the New Testament she had purchased for the Sunday school class she undoubtedly would resume teaching, she wrote a note inside the cover.

"My gift to you—The Holy Bible, God of Love. True."

"The carriage is waiting!" Emily Kincaid's last command. Hosea picked up her bags.

True tried to thank Michael's cousin. "I'm grateful," she said, and tried to embrace her. There was no response, no bending toward love. Emily simply handed two letters to True and turned back to the dark corridors of the great house.

It was she—True realized—not herself, who must return to the "ashes." The ashes of a past she refused to leave. True sent up another silent prayer of thanksgiving to the Father who made it so clear that she could not—even to make a dying man happy—live out the life of her grandmother. Neither could she live out the life of her own mother here. And no fairy godmother was going to transform her into the girl Michael sought in the photograph.

She accepted Hosea's hand and stepped into the carriage. Only Jesus could save, heal, and make whole. He made no promise of "castle life" on earth.

Just love—the greatest promise of all!

27
Answer to a Prayer

ONCE THE TRAIN journey began, True opened the letters she had clutched in her hand—not even trusting her handbag to care for them. The one from Aunt Chrissy she scanned hurriedly, knowing she would read it over and over before reaching Portland, where Young Wil would meet her. She had written him the date, then sent a telegram to make doubly sure he knew.

Her aunt's letter bubbled with happiness . . . True's arrival would be one of Miss Mollie's "rainbows formed by Oregon's mixture of sunshine and showers." True smiled mistily, understanding now, but what she did not understand was the liberal sprinkling of "the young Portland lady."

Young Wil had brought her to Turn-Around Inn for Thanksgiving . . . such a lovely girl . . . so alone, in need of understanding of the family. "You can be a great help to her—to both of them, True. Her name's Midgie—"

Midgie? *Midgie Callison!* True threw the letter onto the seat beside her, feeling her heart drop to the toes of her new pointed, button-down shoes, which were beginning to pinch.

There was no need to read further. True knew exactly how this "lovely girl" looked. She ought to—considering the distance between Portland and San Francisco! Midgie's conductor-father had used up the miles describing the "gray-green eyes slanting upward at the corners and heavy, dark hair done up fancy-like." Why even *he* had given a hint that his daughter had a "young man." And his Midgie had to be "this young lady" in Young Wil's letters. And now Aunt Chrissy had referred to "both of them."

Well, we'll see about that, True thought furiously. *I can still bite, grown-up or not!*

Angrily, True ripped into the second letter. She had known it came from Young Wil and, foolish one that she was, had saved it (as always) in anticipation. Little had she known what the man she had loved all her life meant in his *heart* when he wrote of finding someone to take her place. Taking notes for him indeed! When it came to men, all women were just "ugly stepsisters" awaiting their chance to try on the glass slipper . . .

Recognizing that she was in no mood to read, True began repeating the books of the Old Testament to gain control. "Genesis, Exodus, Leviticus . . ." At "Joshua" she burst into laughter. Why, she was being pouty and jealous, *very* immature. And she was glad that Young Wil was not here to see such a mood.

She read the letter then, the laughter on her lips dying and tears filling her eyes, transforming them from blue to deep purple.

My darling: *(Darling! He'd said DARLING!)* I had a long talk with the Lord when your letter came, and this is in answer to your prayer. If, as you confessed, you've a "Cinderella fixation," it is I who put it there. I, your Prince. You see, not all Princes are rich and charming. But not all rich and charming Princes make tender, loving husbands. Riches cannot buy health, happiness, or heaven . . . but riches would make my dream of the research lab come true. For now, we must live on love with a cabin for a castle . . . happy forever after!

28
The True Magic of Love

❧

THE EARLY-DECEMBER sun dipped into the Western horizon. The days, having stretched their length, had shortened noticeably since True left. She had forgotten how quickly night fell in the mountains, blotting out everything but the glowing outlines of snow-capped peaks—and the glow within her heart.

Any moment now the train would come to a stop . . . and the moment had come! Love had led her home.

Quickly she smoothed imagined wrinkles from her dove-gray travel suit and touched the rosy softness of the feathered plume on her hat, hoping it was angled properly the way the milliner showed her. Almost unaware that her feet touched the ground, she made her way toward the station.

Wil . . . Wil . . . Wil! The wild pumping of her heart was suffocating her. *Walk like a lady . . . stand tall . . . show him how you've grown up!*

But when she saw Young Wil's handsome face, lighted with those unforgettably expressive brown eyes focused on her and her alone, True let out a squeal of delight. And then, guided only by her heart, she was in his arms.

His strong arms closed around her possessively.

"Pardon me, I'm looking for an awkward girl in pigtails who has been known to bite!"

"And I," True's voice was muffled against his rough, wool-plaid jacket, "am looking for the most handsome, the most wonderful, the most *bossy* man in the state of Oregon!"

Young Wil laughed against the top of her head just beneath his chin.

"I'd say you've found your man!"

"Oh, yes, Wil—yes, *yes*, YES!"

"Here," he said, drawing a large handkerchief from his breast pocket. "You'll be crying any minute now."

"Wil North—" True began, then promptly burst into tears.

"Blow!" When she obeyed, Young Wil pulled her close to him again. "Such an advantage, knowing each other forever. This lifelong courtship's going to save a lot of red tape. Right?"

She snuggled closer. "If you say so," she said meekly.

And then fear gripped her heart. There was so much they had to talk about. Most of it could wait. But not this.

"Midgie?" Her whisper was faint.

"Ummm—you smell nice. Midgie? It's supposed to be a secret— but she and Marty are to be married Sunday, providing your train made it on time. Grandma Mollie's hinting that Turn-Around Inn's used to double weddings—so—?"

For the first time, his voice faltered. It was her turn to laugh.

"If you say so!"

There was no need for further words. Wrapped in each other's arms, they had found the true magic of love—one that grew slowly, steadily, recognizing no barriers.

Until two hearts beat as one. . . .

PART II

Love Follows
the Heart

To
the Wilsons and the Bachers,
Family of My Husband, George Wilson Bacher,
Who Are Vital Links of
Oregon's Pioneer History
in the Fields of Railroading, Agriculture, and Medicine

The kingdom of God is not meat and drink, but righteousness and peace and joy. . . . Let us therefore follow after the things which make for peace, and things wherewith one may edify another.
—Romans 14:17,19

It is astonishing how little one feels poverty when one loves.
—Bulwer

Contents

1

Wedding with a Vow "To Keep"

&

ALONE, IN THE still of the night, True North pressed a warm cheek against the age-smoothed gallery post. It was cool and comforting. Motionless, face lifted to the stars, she breathed in the mystic fragrance of the June night. Something tugged at her senses. Some small demon of apprehension which had no right to be there clawed at her inner peace as if in effort to destroy her Joy.

"Go away!" she commanded. "You are unwelcome—uninvited—"

And then the slender, blonde girl laughed at herself. Why should there be a sense of fear or dread, or even the tiniest molecule of uneasiness? After all, it was not as if she were marching to the gallows tomorrow! She was marching down the stairs of Turn-Around Inn, where she and Young Wil had spent so many childhood hours—straight into his waiting arms. And with her would be . . .

Happiness flooded her being again, rendering her incapable of completing the thought which, in some strange way, might be the culprit disturbing her tranquility. Nothing, *nothing*, was going to spoil the perfection of her wedding day. Up, up, up through the golden glory of the heavens her spirit climbed to God.

"Please, Lord," she prayed, "let me be the right wife for this wonderful man You have chosen for me. Together let us work always for the highest and the best, because we have lived it with Your help—"

The prayer would have included Marty and Midgie, who were so fragile in their fledgling faith, had there been no interruption. But the soft twitterings of nightbirds broke the sacred silence of the dark, their tender flute-notes an undeniable "Amen."

Surprisingly, True slept late. The sun was peeking into her bedroom window inquiringly, reminding her to rush. Food was out of the question, although a tempting aroma of coffee trailed up the stairs. Any minute now Aunt Chrissy and the twins would be here, meaning well but actually being more hindrance than help. She smiled tenderly as she stepped out of the long nightgown. Always she would remember her aunt and Grandma Mollie's attention to detail during the prenuptial shopping. How Aunt Chrissy had shocked the saleslady with her disdain of the flower-splashed silk material which the woman had tried to lure her into purchasing, parading the length of Centerville's Ladies' Best Apparel Shop! Rolling her eyes ceilingward with practiced skill, the enterprising lady had clasped her hands, their nails highly buffed, as she paraded before them draped in an entire bolt of the cloth. This dress, she declared to her obviously "classy" customer, would rekindle her husband's interest and outshine the bridal gown—to which Aunt Chrissy had answered coolly, "My husband's interest needs no rekindling. It is the flame of love we hope to pass on to our daughter, whom I have no desire to outshine!"

A lift of her hand to smooth the widening gray streak that striped the midnight black of her right temple had settled the matter. The clerk sighed and brought back the navy crepe de chine. Christen Elizabeth North nodded and joined Miss Mollie in search for the proper fabric for the grandmother-of-the-bride gown.

Heart aching with love for the two women who had shaped her life, True had watched Grandma Mollie (Malone O'Higgin), hair now whiter than the winter snows atop Mount Hood, select patterns for the event which rounded out their dreams. God bless them! Their definition of love cut a pattern for her to follow which was far more important than the dresses which their clever fingers would design.

And their sentimentality was an added trim. "I would settle for a barn, horses as witnesses," Young Wil had laughed. "But I will go along with *anything* that makes them happy and enables me to claim one Miss Trumary North as my bride!"

From inside the circle of his arms, True agreed, knowing that he would have preferred the third-generation "Big House," where he had grown up as the namesake of his uncle, Dr. Wilson North. True herself might have preferred a church wedding. But they were little more than consulted. The wedding was to take place at Turn-Around Inn, once a home-away-from-home when stagecoaches instead of trains were the means of transportation in the Oregon Country.

Trains! True leaped to her feet, moving with the sense of urgency to finish dressing as if she were chasing the last coach of a rapidly disappearing freight train. Thank goodness, there was no question as to what *she* would wear, for Aunt Chrissy and Grandma Mollie had taken care of that matter too: her aunt's wedding gown, of course (and Miss Mollie's before her). Midgie, bride-to-be of True's adopted brother, Marty, would wear the pale-blue gown that Evangeline, True's natural mother, had worn when the sisters had a double wedding

Dressed now, she stood before the mirror, molten-gold curls caught up in a snood until the moment Aunt Chrissy would adjust her veil. Both girls would carry nosegays of sweet-scented wood violets. There would be few jewels (Midgie wearing Grandma Mollie's only jewelry of value, a single-strand pearl necklace), and True's only adornment would be the sapphire-and-diamond brooch around which so much of the family history would remain forever in orbit.

The girl in the looking glass twisted and smiled. Her lips made no movement. But from somewhere True heard the greeting loud and clear: *Hello, Mrs. Wil North.* The sweetest words this side of heaven . . . the words she had waited for all her 20-year life . . .

And that was the last clear memory she preserved of the preparations other than Aunt Chrissy's slipping a pair of white gloves over the ones that True was wearing to keep them as spotless as her vows. As unblemished and undefiled as the sweet virginity of body and soul, the most precious gift a bride could offer her husband. True understood the symbolic gesture. She had been conceived out of wedlock and marveled now at her aunt's ability to bring her sister's daughter up so genteelly while preserving the memory of "Angel Mother" so beautifully. Her delicate, childlike mother was blameless, Aunt Chrissy explained. That was how God worked—when one asked His forgiveness.

True and Midgie, daughter of Conductor Callison (True's self-appointed guardian in her West-to-East trek in search of her identity), now "given" by their fathers, stood side by side—two near-identical

Dresden-china beauties, trembling like aspen leaves in a gentle breeze. But there the resemblance ended. True's violet eyes, now cast downward behind her veil, gave vulnerability to her face. But even her maidenly blush did not deny the courage of the rounded jaw jutted out ever so slightly. By contrast, Midgie looked uncertain, almost afraid.

And that is how their eyes met those of their respective husbands. True, adoringly. Midgie, imploringly.

The timelessly beautiful vows were made: "to have . . . to *keep* . . ." There was a fractional pause when Marty claimed a brother's right to kiss the other bride, the words "to keep" lingering. It was as if somehow True had pledged herself to two men.

2
Departure and Return

THERE FOLLOWED A flurry of good wishes and congratulations.
Somebody was pumping away at the old organ, and guests had to
shout above it. The smiling clergyman, in futile effort to quiet the
jubilant guests in order to introduce the newlyweds with proper dignity, upset Miss Mollie's improvised altar, so carefully woven with
bright flowers and wood ferns, causing a new pattern of wrinkles
across her face. The Reverend Mr. Brewster raised an apologetic hand,
erasing the pucker from Miss Mollie's brow. After all, a beginning
minister could be forgiven a few transgressions.

Where had the man gone in this hour of crisis? *"O'Higgin!"*

The surrounding hills had no more than ceased to echo the summons in Miss Mollie's voice when there followed a stream of words.
"Oh, no, you don't! Get that tin can off'n the mare's tail! Want the
newlyweds to be spilt before the honeymoon gets goin'? That mare's
spirited 'nuf as is—always in th' lead. An' stop laughin'—it ain't
funny, O'Higgin. Be gittin' in here to hep!"

Laughter filled the vast rooms. The long diningroom table, presided
over by a subdued O'Higgin, creaked and groaned with its burden of
food. It was a miracle, everybody said, that the North twins managed
to bring in the enormous wedding cake without stumbling.

True heard herself addressed the first time as "Mrs. North." A surge
of pride, then something akin to laughter, resulted. Had anybody
counted the number of women who bore that title? Across the table
Midgie was responding to it now. "Such a pathetic little waif," Miss

Mollie had called the girl who was now Marty's wife. "You'll always be lookin' after her—but then you're used to that, lookin' after Marty th' way you did."

Grandma Mollie was right. Although the two of them were the same age, True had always been more mature. She remembered with a pang the bitter disillusionment which Marty's scrimmage with the law had brought to the family. Of course, Midgie Callison was only a description then—the "little girl lost" in Portland, according to her worried father, motherless and left alone while the conductor made his back-and-forth runs between Portland and San Francisco. Marty needed a mothering wife. Young Wil disagreed: A wife who depended on him for strength would give him a sense of worth. But what about Midgie? A wife had a right to become her own person. Thankful that she herself had a near-perfect husband, True's heart filled up with prayer for the other couple. Life had hurt Midgie enough already. Marty must bruise her no further. She was so trusting, as easily amused as a child, and so grateful for small kindnesses True doubted if Marty could do anything she would not forgive. If only he would be open and honest with her . . . he owed her that.

"You are a beautiful bride, my darling," Uncle Wil, a more mature version of his nephew (and still as handsome as ever), said softly.

Before she could reply, Young Wil came to claim his bride. "They want the four of us to cut the cake," he whispered. "Then we will make our getaway. I love you—brat!"

"Wil North!" True began, then stopped short. They had an audience. And the playful gleam of triumph in his dark eyes dared her to forget that he had the advantage. Just because he was ten years older and her idol did not mean that he was to continue his bossiness.

"Stop playing the heavy-handed husband," she warned between clenched teeth as they smiled and waved the crowd toward the diningroom.

His hand closed over hers as she and Midgie prepared to cut the first slice of cake, and her silly heart began to thud. Her fixed smile melted under his warm gaze and all else was forgotten. *Oh, Wil, Wil, wonderful Wil!*

"Come on, you two, stop dillydallying," Miss Mollie said; blowing her nose. "You got the rest of your life t'be starin' moon-eyed at each other 'crost th' breakfast table!"

A twitter of giggles brought the rosy-cheeked bride back to earth. It was good luck for the newlyweds to feed the multitudes, Grandma Mollie had coached. So the two couples moved about the room, greeting their guests and hand-feeding each with a tidbit of the fluffy, white, 14-egg wedding cake. Chris Beth stood in the shadows of the O'Higgins' new brocade drapes until all others were fed—smiling, though her dark eyes were misty.

When she stepped into the light True dropped the plate onto the nearest table with a clatter. "Oh, Aunt Chrissy—*Mother*! It was lovely!" Then they were in each other's arms, laughing and crying.

It was Chris Beth who let go. Holding her sister's daughter at arm's length, she looked deep into the steady blue, blue eyes (so like Vangie's), noting the carriage of the head, the character and tenderness of the lovely mouth, the determination of the finely chiseled chin (so uniquely her own). "I am so proud," she whispered.

The three-day honeymoon was all that a honeymoon is supposed to be—only shorter than planned. It began with laughter as the new husbands helped their lovely brides into the two-seated buggy while attempting to dodge a barrage of rice. More laughter followed as the horses galloped across the countryside, paint buckets and old shoes clattering behind them. It had always been like this, even when Young Wil had to be cross with little True after she and Marty tampered with his botany collections. Marty would cry, but True would make faces that caused Young Wil to burst into laughter. Even then she had been in love with him, knowing with women's intuition that they would be married. Now they could do anything, absolutely *anything*, together—with the help of the Lord. And, just as she had known that Wil was for her, she knew that the Lord had plans for them together. Who knew but what one day they could even teach Marty how to laugh?

The hotel suite was the best that Portland had to offer—not that True would have cared. What mattered was their being together, registered as Mr. and Mrs. Wilson North. In a dream, she slipped into the white velveteen robe that Aunt Chrissy had folded so carefully, and then brushed her golden hair until it was even more golden. One hundred strokes . . . 101 . . . 102 . . . 5 . . . 10 . . . until a rap at the door reminded that she was working overtime. "I'm seeking a bride!"

With a bubble of laughter True opened the door. "Wil! You—"

The expression on his handsome face stopped her. Wil was study-ing her face as if he had never seen it before, his eyes widening in admiration. "Any regrets?" he whispered huskily. "I'm just a poor—"

"Don't tease me—not tonight," True whispered, then rushed into his arms where she belonged as he turned out the lights . . .

The next morning the telegram came.

3

It Is Always Today

❧

THE AIR IN the quaint old hotel diningroom was bright with sunlight and gaiety before the telegram came. Every eye was on the center table awaiting arrival of the two sets of newlyweds. The balding manager, who talked as if his tongue were oiled, saw to it that the rumor spread. Everybody enjoyed watching young couples in love, and to be sure it was good for business! And 'twas mighty rare when a groom was as cooperative as this Mr. North—standing that sign up in the middle of the table: HAPPILY MARRIED. No hen-husband, that one. The other one—hum-mm, must be a brother, the name being North too—left doubt in the mind. Sort of unsure of himself, maybe even a little shifty-eyed. Could be a "shotgun weddin'" . . . oh, here the four of them came down the unstable stairs, stopping on the one that squeaked.

At the caretaker's signal, the other diners (just plain folks like himself) burst into vociferous song:

> "Here comes th' bride,
> Big, fat, 'n wide—
> See how she wobbles
> From side-to-side—"

"Enough a'ready!" the little man said, adjusting his nose-glasses uncertainly. Those log-rollers and fur trappers sang like their pipes were rusty. Might be embarrassing to his classier guests.

161

Wilson North waved good-naturedly. Marty tugged at Midgie's arm almost dragging her to the table. True, in keeping with Chris Beth's training, carried the situation off with becoming dignity, managing a small smile and nod in spite of what she considered a breach of good manners. But once at the table, seated with her back to the well-wishers, she turned flashing eyes toward her husband's face. "Wil North, you are impossible—you—you—"

"—wonderful man," he finished, eyes adoring her. "You loved it just as you love me. Shall we kiss and make up?"

"Don't you dare!"

She was saved further embarrassment by the arrival of a breakfast obviously intended for a dozen hay-balers, all of them starving: sourdough biscuits, almost as tasty as Grandma Mollie's fried potatoes, eggs (sunny-side up), and sage sausage swimming in cream gravy.

Wil reached out his hands to indicate linking them with his wife and the other members of the family. True took his hand without hesitation and waited until Marty and Midgie overcame their confusion and completed the circle. Young Wil's voice was low with reverence.

"Lord, we praise You for each other. Erase our yesterdays and take care of our tomorrows. But remind us that today belongs to You—for the miracle of our marriage is that it is *always* today."

A lump rose from True's heart to her throat, threatening tears. Then, like sunshine after a shower, it spread over her soul. *Oh, dear Lord, how I love this man!* She squeezed his hand so hard that it hurt her own. Young Wil answered with a lovelit glance and seemed about to say something when the keeper was back, wearing a look of importance mixed with curiosity, to deliver the yellow envelope, the color which could only spell out "Telegram!"

How strange—it was addressed to the four of them. Wil accepted the telegram and thanked his host with a "Thank you" in a dismissal tone. Then the four of them pushed aside the "Happily Married" sign and leaned forward in a huddle in effort to achieve a measure of privacy.

"Shall I do the honors?" Wil asked, already reaching for the flap.

Wordlessly, True, Marty, and Midgie nodded.

The message was brief: TAKE CARE OF BUSINESS AND COME HOME. The command was signed simply "O'Higgin."

All was silent at the table, causing a silence to fall over the other diners. Young Wil was first to speak. "O'Higgin would have been last on my list of guesses as to the sender." There was perplexity in his lowered voice. Marty and Midgie's eyes were question-mark blank.

True bit her lower lip, trying to ease the queasiness which the mountains of food caused in her middle. "Something must be wrong with Grandma Mollie—no, O'Higgin would have managed it. Oh," she said breathlessly as fear clutched her heart, "could it be Aunt Chrissy—Daddy Wil, the twins?"

"Let's not borrow trouble, darling," Young Wil said, touching her hand reassuringly. "Note that he said to take care of business, so that hardly means a matter of life and death"

Marty had not spoken. But Midgie, disappointment filling her childish voice, almost whimpered. Raising the gray-green eyes that slanted appealingly upward at the corners, she touched her near-perfect upswept hair. For the first time True noted in some far-off corner of her mind that Conductor Callison had used up the miles between Portland and San Francisco describing his Midgie—referring always to her "dark hair, done up fancy-like." Fancy it was, but dark it was not. The girl must have had it bleached—something only the more daring young ladies would do. And her next words confirmed it.

"I needed to have my hair done—and wanted to see a stage play—and shop. Daddy always wanted me to shop—"

"You will have time, Midgie," Marty began, then stopped. "Or will she? How long do we have, Wil?"

"How long will it take? is the question. We can return then and get the mysterious matter all settled." He attempted a smile which in True's mind did not quite come off. "I can close my office, such as it is—about the size of my clientele—"

"No criticizing my husband, you! He will be the finest doctor in the Northeast, and," caught up in her dream, True talked on as was her lifelong habit when she was alone, "we will build ourselves a nest and—"

"Careful—it's too soon to feather it," Young Wil laughed.

True blushed but went on unabashed. "You'll love the role of Father Bird—being so bossy by nature!"

"I should paddle you here and now like I used to when you were naughty."

The crisis-to-come forgotten in their banter, True turned to Midgie.

"The man was always a bully. He took every advantage of being ten years older than Marty and me—"

"Eleven," Young Wil interrupted, "just missing by two months."

True wrinkled her nose at him. "If you measure your medicine the way you estimate birthdays, you will lose the few patients you have."

"I do not dole out pills. You married a pathologist—remember?"

"But you will be both once you put in an internship with Daddy Wil—become the greatest doctor in the valley—make that the world!"

Her sudden mood swing brought Wil's rich, throaty laugh—beautiful, the kind that caused her heart to jog, at the same time arousing her ire. What an interesting life they were going to have! They would live in the little house across the creek where the sisters, her mother and aunt, used to live . . . close to her doctor-uncle and aunt . . . while Marty and Midgie—well, where *would* they live? For that matter, what would Marty do to support a family? He had never stuck with a job, and now it was harder to find one if a prospective employer knew his background—

"I don't have much to do—just see a few people—" Marty traced a pattern on the red-checked tablecloth, his eyes cast down.

"'Then you can help *me*," Young Wil briefed as if it were important that his brother's time be spent profitably.

In the end True and Midgie helped too. True was delighted, Midgie disappointed. But, she admitted, she was familiar with Young Wil's filing system, having helped him before. That was before meeting Marty.

As if reading her thoughts, Midgie stopped, putting a slender finger in the M folder as a placeholder. "This is Marty's file, started when he had an earache. Complete medical background, but nothing about family history—you know, diseases that run in the family—I hardly know who I am. I guess," she said slowly, "I never did."

True dusted her hands while searching for the right words. "I understand, Midgie, having lost my own mother—and never knowing my father. At least you had Mr. Callison—"

"But who am I *now*? What is my real name?"

"It is North, Midgie, just as my name is—"

"Before marriage and after," the other girl said impatiently. "What are you holding back? What are *all* of you keeping from me?"

True felt her spine tighten with surprise. "Nothing—actually, I supposed you knew, that Marty had explained our wonderful family." *And,* she wanted to add, *it hurts a bit that it should matter so much—providing you are in love with your husband.*

Instead, she suggested a break, sinking gratefully into one of the worn black-leather chairs. "Aunt Chrissy will tell you anything Marty has left out." It occurred to her then that included everything. She explained briefly: "We know very little except that his parents, a very young and struggling couple by the name of Martin, were drowned in a terrible flood and by miracle the baby, Marty, was saved—thanks to Daddy Wil's expertise.

"And adopted by my Uncle Joe, Wilson North's lifelong friend—closer than a brother. Known and loved by the entire valley as Brother Joe—he was a minister, you know—" she hurried on after a pause.

"A *minister? A friend?* But the name," Midgie groped.

"It *is* confusing," True said. "Uncle Joe's name was Joseph Craig and he married Aunt Chrissy, Christen Elizabeth Kelly—after Marty was born."

"Marty's name was Martin—then Craig—I would have thought Wilson North was the stepfather—why didn't the doctor take him?"

"Daddy Wil was raising Young Wil, his nephew—and," she inhaled, determined to leave nothing untold, "planned to marry my natural mother, Aunt Chrissy's half-sister. It was a double wedding like ours, but with a more complicated plot. You see, Midgie, my mother, Mary Evangeline Stein, was," she raised her head proudly, "pregnant with me."

Midgie's eyes widened. "You mean—oh, me and my big mouth—"

"Never mind, it's no secret. And you are family, Midgie."

"But North? How can all of you have the same name?"

"When my mother died of consumption—" she swallowed hard, a faint memory of the fragile beauty of Angel Mother's face floating before her, "dear Aunt Chrissy took me to her heart just as she had taken your Marty. Both of us leaned on Young Wil—he was so wise—and I guess we learned more how to love Jesus through him than through Uncle Joe's sermons. And then—and then—my heart broke again when dear Uncle Joe was killed in a senseless accident. Had it not been for Daddy Wil, the family would never have survived. We *wanted* his name—begged for it—"

"I'm so sorry," Midgie said uncomfortably, "I—I'm no good at trying to say things right, something consoling. Nobody taught me."

"There is no need for consolation, darling. God did that through Young Wil a long time ago. Oh, Midgie, I all but worship him!"

For the first time, her brother's wife grinned. "I wouldn't have guessed! Are you mad at me?"

True laughed. "Now, why would I be angry? You have a right to know—and to know that there is a strong tie between us in ways that are harder to count than the stars. Uncle Joe baptized us children, you know, when we accepted Christ with the same unquestioning love that all these loving people accepted us. We are so blest, so blest. Now," she said practically, "any more questions?" Then she remembered the twins.

Midgie hesitated. "Jerome and Kearby were born to Daddy Wil and Aunt Chrissy when, after years of loneliness, they were married," True said.

"And none of you are jealous of the younger ones, the twins?"

"We adore them! Being jealous of them would be like jealousy of ourselves. I would like a family *filled* with twins, just to put those two through what they have put us through—and what we put Young Wil through in our growing-up years. And now shall we make ourselves beautiful for our new husbands? They—I see a question in your eyes. So?"

"I still wonder about the Martins—and you never knew your father?"

"I never saw him alive—Michael St. John helped me find the tomb."

Immediately True regretted mention of his name. He, like her father, belonged to the past. Fearing another question, she said quickly, "I have built a strongbox and locked my heartaches and troubles there. I share them with nobody except the Lord. When I try to go back and look at the contents, He has taken them away. That's how He works!"

Midgie considered the words. "I hope He will take mine—about— well, everything in the future—maybe what we'll find wrong at the Inn—"

True tucked her own concerns away. "He will. He gave us *today*!"

4

Home—Forever Home!

HOMEWARD BOUND, THE carriage topped a familiar knoll, allowing a first glimpse of True's beloved valley. The sylvan setting belied the hustle and bustle of the city. Abounding in the thick, shadow-filled woods and sunny groves where furry creatures and sunbeams played together, and dotted with orchards of unforbidden fruit, it was the land flowing with the biblical "milk and honey," Young Wil so often remarked. To True it would forever remain her secret "Sugarplum Valley"—a place to dream and to make those dreams a reality, a land she could never, *never* leave behind for new horizons. True smiled now, remembering that her fertile imagination of childhood years led her to confide to him that she was a sylphid, a young diminutive creature of the air, created to keep watch over the unbelievable beauty of the valley and its people, to see that they never changed, but just remained tucked away from the woes of the world outside its realms, where life was simple and needs were few. She would tell God—

Young Wil stopped such thinking in short order. "Sylphids grow up to be slender and graceful sylphs, little lady, *but* if they existed— which they don't!—sylphs would be mortal, and have no soul!"

That time True had cried instead of arguing. And he had ended up comforting her, reassuring her that she possessed the sylvan beauty of body and the far greater beauty of a God-given soul. And now she knew that the entire valley was one giant soul, bound together forever.

167

Delighted shrieks, punctuated by welcoming barks, broke into True's reverie. In moments the carriage was surrounded by swarms of children and dogs.

"Dog Star had puppies!" Jerome yelled above the others. "Daddy helped her, and I helped *him*!" There was pride in the little-boy face.

"We have 'em named already—and saved the best of the litter for you!" Kearby, the twin sister, beamed as they ran alongside the buggy the remaining short distance to Turn-Around Inn.

Both panting, the children interrupted each other in their haste to tell the news. "'Tonsils' for True and Wil . . . got his name 'cause he can't bark yet . . . and Lucy Lungs' for Marty and Midgie . . . she barks *too* much . . . like Kearby sings too much and so loud she drowns out all the others in the church choir!"

The grown-ups came flying from the house, separating the children, hugging both couples until they were breathless, and everybody talking with speed that matched the children's.

"See what I told you?" True managed to whisper in Midgie's ear. And to her surprise she saw that the girl was crying—crying when she should be laughing at the crazy names the twins had hung on the helpless puppies. Tonsil and Lung indeed! That could mean only one thing: Midgie had spent more time in tears than laughter. And she was starved for love. She hoped that Marty knew.

And then all was bedlam. Valley folk swarmed from the great rambling house, beating pots and pans in wild sharps and flats of welcome. Then True too found herself crying, partly because of the genuine goodness and caring of these wonderful people with whom she fully expected to spend the rest of her earthly life, and partly from an overwhelming gratefulness to God for hearing her prayers. Nothing could be seriously wrong—not with this kind of earth-shattering welcome! Nothing mattered now . . .

5

Gifts with Condition

❦

THE QUIET IN the room so recently filled with a Tower-of-Babel happiness was now subtly portentous. Where was everybody? True wondered as she entered the enormous livingroom of Turn-Around Inn. Only Irish O'Higgin was waiting for his guests, his giant presence seeming to fill up the room. Omitting his usual blarney, the big Irishman motioned her with a finger to a nearby chair without lifting his red head from arms crossed and extended almost the full length of the mantel, where a few withering sweetbrier vines remained from the wedding.

"What are you doing—fire-worshiping in midsummer?" True tried to make her voice light, although she felt that she was speaking to a stranger.

"Where be the others?" O'Higgin asked, removing his arms from the mantel and thrusting hairy, hamlike hands deep into his pockets.

"I was about to ask you the same question."

"I asked me wife t'be makin' herself scarce—this bein' a soul-searchin' matter, a matter of me heart. Ever' man 'as 'is weak joint, 'n Miss Mollie be mine. That woman, a jewel she be, could change me thinkin', 'n me 'n the Lord's got it all figgered, we 'ave."

This was a different O'Higgin than True had known. What he had to say was a secret to all except himself, she supposed, since Aunt Chrissy and Daddy Wil were unaware of the telegram until they heard of it last night through Young Wil, herself, Marty, and Midgie.

Daddy Wil had brushed it away with a wave of his hand. "Probably just a whim," he smiled affectionately. "I have never known a

169

human being to love a family in the way he loves all of you—and that includes Miss Mollie's brood."

"They have a family?" Midgie had ventured. "Somehow I thought—"

"That we were their only family?" Aunt Chrissy had laughed. "That man has a heart so big it can house us all—with room to spare. And, of course, he *is* lonely since all the other children are gone."

"That's another complicated story, Midgie, so complicated that even I get bogged down in an explanation. You fill Midgie in, Marty," True suggested.

"You're doing fine," Marty said shortly.

Fine? She had not begun. What was the matter with him? She glanced at her sister-in-law, hoping that she had failed to note Marty's attitude. Her red face said otherwise.

True covered the awkward moment with a brief explanation of how Miss Mollie had married a Mr. Malone, a widower with seven—wasn't it?—children. How his death left the wonderful lady alone to support them. And how happy everybody had been when the widowed Mollie Malone said "Yes" to Irish O'Higgin's flamboyant "beholdin'." "So, you see, Midgie," she ended softly, "we pay little attention to blood-line here. Love takes its place."

True realized that her wandering thoughts had kept her from responding as to the whereabouts of Young Wil, Marty, and Midgie. And now they answered for themselves. The tuneful, vibrant whistle of her husband filled the hall, flooding her heart with joy, pride—and relief. The dirgelike atmosphere faded. Young Wil could handle any problem their beloved friend needed to share, and O'Higgin knew that. Yet it *was* puzzling just where Marty and Midgie fitted in.

All too soon she was to find out.

The question then would become: "But what has this to do with Wil and me?" She would find that out, too.

At sight of O'Higgin's troubled face, Young Wil stopped until the others seated themselves and the echo of his whistle trailed upstairs.

"Something is wrong." Wil's words were a statement, not a question.

O'Higgin's bushy brows drew closer together. The twinkle in his usually merry blue eyes was gone. And his voice was unsteady when at last he spoke.

" 'Tis no easy matter tellin' of me folly. And 'twould be breakin' me Mollie's bonnie heart should she come t'know. An movin' the likes o'her from Turn-Around—" O'Higgin stopped. Not a sound except the ticking of the clock as the silence lengthened into minutes.

The gravity in the ever-Jolly man's voice unnerved True. She sought Young Wil's eyes, but they were focused on the pattern of the rug— lids narrowed as they had a way of doing when he was thinking.

"But I thought—" she began, then faltered. What *had* she thought? That trouble could never touch them? That they would go on for- ever like the wide river hugging the valley? Just for her security?

"That we be well off, lassie? Time was when 'twas so. But it takes a heap o'money raisin' and educatin' a family—be it known there be no regrets now that they've all of 'em paired off and settled most proper. But the inn—oh, me achin' heart! 'Tis mortgaged to th' roof- top. Me'n me Mollie ain't ones t'be askin' charity, but—"

The big Scotch-Irishman turned to face the four he had summoned while his wife was away at a quilting bee. His haggard eyes would haunt her forever, True thought, unless there was some way to help.

Young Wil spoke for her. "So it's money you need?"

O'Higgin's high color receded to its natural ruddiness. But his voice was strained with humiliation. "Shure'n it is—then shure'n it ain't. Meanin' I got meself some cash—" O'Higgin paused to pat the breast pocket of his plaid cotton shirt. "But—with condition."

Young Wil chuckled, a welcome sound in the tensionfilled room. "So far, if you'll pardon my saying so, you've made no sense, kind sir. Care to explain just what we're talking about? *Condition?*"

"On condition Marty here'll cooperate—and 'tis a man-sized job."

"Me?" Marty's lips whitened. The startled question brought Marty North to his feet. "I have no money—no job—"

The older man's lips twisted into something that would pass for a smile. And all the while he was carefully scrutinizing the boy.

"Then 'tis likely the condition will be meetin' a need. Now, no ragin' 'fore ye be hearin' th' story. 'Tis a bit o'mystery—and was I 20 or 30 years younger, me lad, 'twould be me Mollie and meself who'd take this adventuresome trail 'stead o'ye an' yore lassie."

As if warned by a sudden flare of fire in O'Higgin's fading eyes, Marty dropped back into his chair, his deeper blue eyes smoldering as he listened to the incredible story.

True became so engrossed that she took no notice of Midgie, who strained forward, white-knuckled hands laced together around the floor-length sweep of her shepherd-checked voile skirt. True's first impression of the girl was that she feared the world and its inhabitants. Yet now her eyes, darting between Marty and O'Higgin, held a flare of hope. She looked excited and then uneasy, and a closer look would have revealed a tremble to the rounded chin. Only once did True glance her direction. That was when she unclenched her small fists and raised an uncertain hand like a child in need of "being excused" during a history lesson.

"Don't interrupt, Midgie!" Marty had said curtly. Half-frightened, half-defiant, the slight figure perched on the edge of the chair, her red lips clamped shut.

Still listening intently to O'Higgin, some far corner of True's mind longed to reach out to Midgie, to still her fears, to reassure her that nobody was going to hurt her. But from that same corner came a denial as if from Midgie's own lips. "I want to believe you—and I do *almost*. But not all people are kind like you. Sometimes they abandon you . . . ignore you . . . even put you in prison—like they did Marty . . . I had to learn in the orphanage what Marty learned in real life . . . a girl had to look out for herself . . . sometimes she can trust . . . sometimes not."

True shook off the illusion and gave full attention to O'Higgin, the trusted family friend, and his story, too incredible to be true, while too incredible not to be! Nobody could put together such fiction— and, most certainly, not O'Higgin, a devout man who firmly believed that God walked beside him every step of the way—sometimes taking his arm when his arthritic knee refused to support his weight—

"None o'ye knew I had a brother," his story had begun. True, very true. Nobody knew, or cared, about the good man's background. The gentle folk in this valley took newcomers at face value. No questions. No prying. They simply offered hands from every side to widen the "family circle." "Name was Artemis—smooth-haired, smooth-faced, smooth-talkin' one, Artie. Talked 'is way right into th' heart o'me Uncle Art afore 'im, sweet-talked 'is way, he did, right into steerin' Uncle Art's financial ship 'n sunk 'er—so I be thinkin' all these years. Never knowed much 'bout me good mother's brother—never liked 'im much, but th' ole coot musta been smarter'n I be thinkin', holdin' a wee somethin' back like he done fer me. Th' Lord works mysterious-like. Maybe all th' time He be teachin' ole Uncle Art t'be aware o'dogs like th' Good Book tells us mortals. Guess He 'ad a hand in lookin' out fer th' likes o'me—givin' me sweet Mollie—an' now this—yep, He did all right, all right—"

At that point, O'Higgin obviously began to enjoy himself, licking his lips from time to time as if he had finished a crisp-fried drumstick and was reaching for another.

Which, where words were concerned, he was. He had his audience in his hand and he knew it. "Know anything 'bout how t'ride, rope, round up cattle, Marty? How t'tell th' difference 'twixt wheat 'n chaff? Ever work 'til ye be fallin' stiff 'n sore on a bunk with yore boots still on? Know about work, boy—*real* work?" O'Higgin interrupted his own story to question. "Now, don' go talkin' when ye elders be speakin'—jest nod 'Yea' or 'Nay.' Ye hear?"

Marty, jaws tightened, eyes smoldering, nodded his head.

"Sooooo—why *you*? Well, a boy has t'become a man sometime. Gone 'n took yerself a wife—not a boy's job, ye best be knowin'. There be a *house* t'build an' little mouths t'feed. So here be yore chance. Here's yore chance t'hep yoresef 'n yore Gran'ma Mollie, well as please yore family 'n th' good Lord. Yep, by jiminy, ye best be listen', ye had!"

"What do you want of me?" Marty's voice was low and uncertain, and his still-boyish face wore the exact expression on his childish features as when Uncle Joe and Young Wil (a junior deacon) had led him and True into the river to be baptized, wanting to swim but fearful of water.

"Patience, lad, patience," O'Higgin admonished. His voice was rough, but True had the feeling that he was stalling—not for words but to assess the situation, study Marty's reaction, and calculate the outcome of the proposal yet to come. After all, wasn't Marty released to the older man's custody when he foolishly allowed himself to be led into an act of rebellion against the railroads, that of a minor part in the train robbery? Authorities had demanded someone outside the immediate family.

True felt her husband's gaze and lifted her eyes to meet his. Young Wil's dark eyes showed a rare touch of anxiety. But they were turbulent with affection. Boldly he winked. She blushed. Gentlemen did not wink at ladies. And then she laughed inwardly. When was she going to get used to the idea that she was his wife? The wink had

communicated love and intimacy—and more. They were sharing a
secret, she realized. No matter how serious O'Higgin's revelation of
the "condition," the prankish man was enjoying his role.

The idea dispelled a bit of her apprehension. And, right or wrong,
Young Wil's look of pride made her happy about something she would
never voice lest others think her vain: True was glad her husband
was proud of her. She paid little attention to the mirror, but for her
husband she was thankful that she was, although a wee bit too slight,
not of the Amazon variety, had eyes larger than a garden pea, and a
laugh that nobody had ever said would wake the dead. Of course,
nobody had said she was kittenish (like Midgie) either. She was too
independent; but for Wil she could be anything he wanted her to be
and everything the Lord found pleasing as a proper wife. Already she
found herself fidgeting, wanting this meeting to be over, eager to
establish a home here . . .

With an effort True brought her self back to the now of things.
Finally Irish O'Higgin was coming to the point. Forgotten were her
ambitions. Forgotten, too, her appearance, although the sun sent red-
gold waves shimmering through the natural gold of her hair and filled
with sunbeams the pools of her violet eyes where myriads of tiny stars
made daytime homes. The shock of O'Higgin's words were far too
great for ambition, vanity, or frivolity.

Somebody had asked if Uncle Art had died. O'Higgin's answer had
been to blow his nose, apologize, then say that his uncle had been a
cross, crotchety old man and that there was no need to mourn the
passing of a very old man. Still, he could have been kinder to his benefactor . . . and now that his carousing brother had sat in a drunken
stupor while a slow train ran over him (at which Midgie gasped with
horror and Marty, to True's surprise, placed an awkward arm around
her narrow shoulders)—well, things looked different. Lots of regrets,
but life must go on.

"So!" O'Higgin withdrew a crumpled paper from his pocket with
all the black-crepe severity of a lawyer preparing to read a will in a
tone that sent premonitory thrills down the spines of the hearers.
"'Lastly, th' property, real an' personal—includin' homestead grazin'
land 'n stock thereon—I bequeath t'me—my—nephew—on condition. One Irish O'Higgin's t'occupy—or have occupied by another of
'is choice and a suitable wife, one versed in th' Word an' abides by

it—populating the earth—which means bearin' of one heir within th' year o'their required occupancy an' provin' up on th' claim as well as provin' their worth, which is that Irish, or 'is chosen, will show before suitable witnesses, also designated and sent together with said heir, that he be—is—capable o'managin' rangeland an' further—re-peatin'—wife of same bear—' "

A white-faced Midgie gasped. "I won't—won't—" she choked.

O'Higgin's eyes lingered on the girl, weighing, testing. "Then ye be willin' t'rob th' man ye vowed t'stand by of 'is chance? An'," his voice dropped back to its original tone of defeat. " 'Low th' roof t'be taken from me'n me Mollie? Be ye so cruel?"

A fountain of sparks ignited in Marty's eyes. "Leave her alone—I refuse the conditions, too." Then, with every drop of color drained from his face, he met O'Higgin's eyes squarely. "I can't refuse, can I? You've got me cornered and you know it." His voice spilled over with bitterness, and the rebellion True had seen in the child now reappeared in the man. "You are right—that uncle of yours knew how to mess things up all right!"

"Or straighten 'em out. Give a wee bit o'thought t'that!"

Midgie's eyes brimmed with tears and a small blue vein throbbed on her forehead. "You married the wrong wife—I—I tried tellin' you. What am I? Not able to live up to your family's classy standards—and not able to face life in a wilderness—"

"You're an okay wife, Midgie. Nobody had any right to involve you in this mess. I can't ask you to make such a sacrifice—"

"No sacrifice, laddie—if th' lass loves you. What 'bout it, gal, be ye thinkin' love's important?" O'Higgin boomed.

"You don't have to answer that!" Marty's voice had grown stronger and more protective than True had heard it heretofore. Now, if only he would not drop his head sheepishly. But he did.

It was Midgie, surprisingly, who took up the matter again. "I will go with you, Marty. Remember I promised to forsake all others—wasn't that what we said? They've always forsaken me, so I'm thinkin' it's my turn." The laugh she attempted was unsuccessful. It came out pitifully.

Young Wil let out a breath that sounded as if he had held it a long time. "I commend you, Midgie. Let's find out where 'said property' is. Who knows but what this will turn out to be quite an adventure?"

O'Higgin looked alive again. "Oh, shure 'n I got me map—land lies over th' range—very private-like, no neighbors, 'ceptin' coyotes—how about it, Marty, be ye man 'nuf t'swing all th' terms?"

"Will I have a helping hand?"

"Best helpin' hand's th' one on th' end o'yore arm! But—" and he cast a scheming glance at Young Wil and then at True, "yes, terms included witnesses—an' I got me witnesses picked."

True had wondered where they fitted in. And now she knew! *Oh, no, Lord . . .*

6
Understanding—and Explaining

❧

"WHAT WILL YOUR Daddy Wil and Aunt Chrissy say?" Midgie ventured, her face whiter than her blouse.

"They are *your* family, too, Midgie—call them whatever you choose," True said gently as she touched the frightened girl's hand.

The two of them had suggested that they occupy the back seat of the buggy in order that their husbands might try to make some sense of the strange news. Too, True had hoped to bring solace to Midgie, who was finding marriage too much in such a short time—and yet had come through in Marty's time of need like a real trouper.

"As to what our family says," True continued, choosing her words carefully, "I think their reaction will depend largely on how we present the situation. We must sort out our feelings, darling— and may I say here and now that I was proud of you back there? Marty needed that. We must all take this a step at a time." She swallowed, then continued, "Please believe me when I say that I am shaken too. But—but—if we all stand together, we can build for ourselves a marriage like Daddy Wil and Aunt Chrissy's. It is more than fair-weather vows—"

"Oh, I will do my part. I don't want to be embarrassin' in high society—"

"Oh, my dear, we are not 'high society,'" True assured her. "We—"

But Midgie was not listening. Instead, with lifted chin, she averted her eyes and half-whispered, "Me—I'd walk over burnin' plowshares

177

in my bare feet before I'd hurt any of you—and—and if I could make Marty love me," she gulped.

True felt a tightness in her chest. "Oh, Midgie, you don't have to make a burning sacrifice, darling. We love you just as you are—and, as for Marty, surely you are sure of his love. What bothers you?"

"Young Wil was so nice to me—gave me a job in his office when other people thought I was dumb—and then he introduced me to Marty—" Midgie's childish voice shook and her breath came in little gasps. "I—I—think Wil may've thought I would be—uh—good for him. And, me, I up and fell in love. I'll make him love me, True—I promise I will!"

What was there to say? True made a weak protest, then paused. There might be a measure of truth in what Midgie was saying— not on Wil's part but on Marty's. Had he taken the vows seriously? "Please—*please*, Midgie, try to be happy. Smooth going does not necessarily result in happiness. In fact," she said, realizing that the idea was new to her, "it may very well be the other way around. And you will have us with you—"

"Honest to gosh—I mean, honest to goodness, True? You're sure enough *going*?"

True bit down on her lower lip, feeling a sharp pain shoot around her heart. What business had she to make such a commitment? Why, she didn't even want to go on this wild goose chase that some mischief-making old man may have dreamed up in wild delirium. And, most important of all, she would never, *never* make a decision without listening to her husband. Leaving here meant surrendering all their plans . . . his practicing medicine with his Uncle Wil, the only father he knew . . . serving the needs of the valley folk he loved so dearly . . . and it meant putting an end to her aunt's dream of her teaching as Chris Beth had done before her . . . and, small as the matter sounded, she and Young Wil had wanted to live in the little cabin that was just whistling distance across the creek . . .

"Some fathers would never consent to their daughters going to a wild, new country—Oooooo, those coyotes—but I guess my father wouldn't care where I went as long as I was out of his way. He put me in an orphanage, you know, and said he would come for me. I waited and I waited—" Midgie's chin quivered and her eyes glistened with unshed tears, as if she had waited all these years to weep her heart out.

"There must have been a good reason," True soothed. "It would be difficult for a man to care for a baby alone. Mr. Callison *did* come for you, and he looked so proud—"

"Proud because I'd made a good marriage—"

"You have been hurt, Midgie, but try to be fair to your father. He showered you with gifts—"

"Which never quite make up for love," she retorted, then added bitterly, "like I told Marty. But—I promised." Then quickly she went back to her previous comment. "What will *your* father say? Will he try to stop your going?"

"Daddy Wil would never stand in my way of happiness, no matter what. He loves me too much to hold on too hard, and yet he refuses to allow me to cling. And," she smiled in effort to lift the other girl's spirits, "our fathers have no right to make our decisions now, Midgie. Our husbands have that responsibility. Our place is with them—"

"I know—I said I'd go and I will, takin' whatever crumbs I'm offered. Whatever will we do for money?"

"We will work for it, Midgie. Yes, it will take hard work, and a whole lot of faith. Has it occurred to you that God may have had a hand in this—that there is a job out there He had in mind that even—"

"Old Nick didn't know about?"

"*Uncle Artie.*" Midgie laughed. Then True sobered as she said, "Midgie, trust yourself. Remember, darling, that sometimes detours offer more thrills and adventures than beaten trails." True wished she were sure of her words.

The Big House was ablaze with lights as the two couples reined in before the front gate. A lump that True found hard to dissolve rose to her throat. No matter what the hour, there would always shine a light in the window when one or more of its inhabitants had not reached the protection of its loving wooden arms. How could she leave them again—something she had vowed in her heart never to do when she returned from Atlanta? But life never revealed its pattern.

In minutes the twins, with a pack of dogs (including Tonsil and Lung), surrounded the four of them. There were embraces without questions—just an invitation for all to wash up for dinner, which, True knew, was over an hour later than they usually ate. Bless them!

Prayers said, Aunt Chrissy, refusing help, brought in a hearty stew and cornmeal muffins. She had been out calling on some new neighbors and Daddy Wil had delivered two new babies. Conversation seemed so normal. True wished she could erase the happenings of the day, just settle back, and live life as she knew it and loved it. But somehow she must find a way, once she found out what Young Wil had planned, to accept it—even try to make it sound appealing to Midgie and Marty. Her double role would not be easy. But she squared her shoulders and let a warm flood of joy flood her being: She had Young Wil!

True had a chance to talk briefly with Chris Beth once an exhausted Midgie was tucked in. The men remained in Dr. Wil's office in conference. True planned to wait for a report, but once alone with Aunt Chrissy in the upstairs bedroom that was always hers, she found herself spilling out the whole story. Her aunt listened without change of expression, nodding only on occasion.

Then with a faint smile she said dreamily, "History repeats itself."

"It *does* parallel your life story and my mother's in some ways," True said slowly, letting the revelation sink in. "What should we do?"

"Talk it out with your husband, pray together, and review your mother's diary. Whatever you two decide, we will stand by, my darling."

7

Charting a New Trail

⭗

A MILLION CONFLICTING questions crossed True's mind during the week following O'Higgin's outlandish proposal. *Outlandish* was the only word she could think of to describe its strangeness. The man was a born tease, known all over the valley for his shenanigans. But this? A man as devout as Irish O'Higgin would never stoop to so cruel a hoax. Why then did the uncanny feeling persist that there was more to the story than the red-whiskered giant had revealed?

Where was this mysterious land? How would they get there? And what would they take? These practical questions must be answered, and there could be no answers until the men could provide more information. True longed inwardly for time alone with Young Wil. In fact, she found herself resenting the invasion into what should have been her honeymoon. She felt robbed of sunlit days and star-dusted nights that should have been theirs. Honeymoon indeed! Why, she hardly saw her husband. He, Marty, Daddy Wil, and O'Higgin spent hours and hours poring over maps, talking with Thomas J. Riefe (the big-jowled president of Centerville's largest bank), and a stranger who wore half-moon glasses, had pink skin which looked as if the sun had never touched it, and carried a black umbrella even when there wasn't a cloud in the sky. Isaac Barney was his name, True learned in a brief introduction. He was the lawyer who had prepared Uncle Artie's last will and testament.

True wished she were a child and could pout. Not a single preparation could she make until somebody gave an order!

181

Well, she was no child; she was simply behaving like one. Certainly she could prepare—prepare for unemotional farewells, prepare her heart by reading the Bible, which she had been neglecting, and by leafing through Mother's diary again. The hardships recorded in its pages would make her own troubles seem trivial.

So, while Aunt Chrissy spent time getting to know Midgie—answering her questions about Marty, reexplaining the complicated family relationships, and reducing some anxieties about the girl's "fitting in"—True devoted herself to the demands of the twins. "Little pitchers have big ears" (Grandma Mollie's axiom) certainly applied to those two! Somehow they knew that their three idols were going away again, and they dogged her every footstep, accusing her with great, round eyes. How could she reassure them when she had no answers herself? Trumary North, the iconoclast. She hated herself in those moments. Then, feeling like a martyr who would never be catalogued as a saint, she turned her fury on her husband. How dare he show such neglect!

But she would reckon with him later. For now she must think of the children. So, as she had always done, True devised games (that nobody else in the world knew, she whispered in conspiratorial tones). Then, noisily and gleefully, they romped up and down the stairs with the dogs yelping at their heels. "Tonsil's learned to bark!" the twins shrieked.

Chris Beth shook her head in mock despair. "True is to Jerome and Kearby what Young Wil was to her and Marty," she explained to Midgie, supposing True to be out of earshot.

"I wish I could let go that way. I never got to play—or be *me*!"

"You will, darling, you will. Just wait until you spend a year around those two!"

Two. Even Aunt Chrissy failed to count Marty in—a fact which did not escape Midgie. "Marty never did count," she said to herself wistfully.

That night True spoke to God a long time about her brother. "I guess You are using this delay to help me develop patience, Lord, and to reach a decision in my own heart about this unexpected move. I guess You know what my answer has to be. Other people must come before my own selfish desires. So, if that means sacrificing a year for Marty, I will—providing You give me some sign that it is Your will and my husband's choice. Maybe he needs a sign too."

Mary Evangeline North's diary lay on the lowboy within reach of where True knelt beside the bed, her face pressed against the sweetness of the sun-dried doublewedding-ring quilt. She reached for it and read her mother's last entry:

God bless you one and all, my wonderful family. Know that I will remain with you always. I will blossom with the dogwood in the springtime and hum with my bees in the summer sun. I will sparkle with the snowflakes and in the ribbons of each rainbow. I will laugh when you laugh. Cry when you cry. So long as you are together! For I leave with you my legacy of love.

Your Vangie

So long as you are together. True turned the wick of the lamp on the nightstand low and extinguished the blaze with a ragged puff of breath. The words continued to burn in her heart. She squeezed her eyes shut, but they continued to glow in the dark. Then tears of acceptance came in a flood of relief. "Angel Mother" had said a sadsweet goodbye to a heartbroken little girl—leaving behind a legacy of love.

"All right, Lord, You've had Your say. You'll have to help me—"

And there, fast asleep, her husband found her.

"Hey, sleepyhead, the bridegroom is in your chambers. Is your wick trimmed?"

True blinked. There was so much to say! Instead, she flew into his outstretched arms . . .

8

By Rail and by Trail

❧

MIDGIE HAD SCARCELY spoken since boarding the heaving, obsolete, inland-bound train. White-knuckled, she gripped the rough boards of the wooden bench that she and True shared. True gave up trying to draw the frightened girl into conversation. *If only Young Wil were here*, her own heart kept whispering. But orders from a shirtless man with freckled shoulders and a chest like a bear were that Wil and Marty must ride the cattle cars: "An' iffen you two got a gun, she better be loaded, less'n you plan on losin' them prize cattle yer transportin', an'" (he grinned, revealing the absence of two front teeth, the remaining ones yellowed by tobacco) "them purdy women—they look like prize stuff, too."

Young Wil, face whitened with restrained anger, nodded. Marty, always impetuous, doubled a fist and stepped forward before Wil could place a restraining hand on his shoulder. "I'll not have you speaking of my sister and—uh—wife in that tone. They are not cows!"

The big man spat, leaving a brown tobacco-juice trail oozing down his chin and lodging on his massive chest. "More like heifers," he leered, "not yet full grown. Keep yer shirt on, Little Britches, else them two'll not be reachin' cowhood! Injuns in these parts ain't human—too lazy t'work—'n I'm here t'tell you greenhorns they'd steal you blind, bust yer bellies, 'n leave th' insides fer th' buzzards. Dunno who begun th' rumor back in yer Injun-lovin' settlements that th' savages are *people*. Dum' animals'd ruther have a white woman's

184

scalp than her body! Keep yer distance, Boy, from th' bloomin' redskins, from me—I ain't took myself no likin' t' th' likes uv you neither—'n from train robbers, white men—"

Marty's face blanched, all bravado gone. He slumped forward as if shot by an arrow. True understood. How far was it that the men figured they would travel by rail? O'Higgin had arranged through Isaac Barney for a so-called "foreman" (a squatter who gladly exchanged his services for "squatters' rights") to meet them. The sooner the better for Marty's sake, but how far was it that this rangeland was from the railroads? Maybe Midgie would remember. But Midgie's face was a white mask of horror, her young body stiffened against reality. And that was when she seemed to drown out reality. She appeared to be dozing now. True pulled a lightweight shawl around the girl's thin shoulders and glanced around her.

She had known all along that the two of them were the only women aboard the wheezing locomotive, so different from the modernized train she had taken in her cross-continent trip. Each time the train stopped, True had hoped that another woman would be among the rain-drenched passengers who entered. But always it was gawking men, soaked to the skin, their ragged jackets smelling like wet wool. The smell, added to the ever-thickening cloud of cigar smoke, was almost overwhelming.

Would any of these men be their neighbors? True's eyes traveled the distance of the now-crowded car as she moved an inch toward the sleeping Midgie in order to accommodate still another rider. Aunt Chrissy had told her about the long ride West by stage, where, interestingly, she had met Miss Mollie, O'Higgin, Wil North, and "Brother Joe." Certainly there were no such persons riding on either side of this narrow aisle. Across from them sat a man with a paunch in his middle, head down and lost in sleep. His left nostril twitched when he exhaled and his domino vest appeared ready to split until he sucked in another noisy breath. Beside him a man wearing bright yellow doeskin gloves kept fumbling in his pockets as if counting his change. And next to the narrow door marked "Use only when necessary" a rangy man sat soldierly-straight, a beaver hat covering his entire face except for the point of a skimpy goatee.

Gooseflesh prickled her arms. Why search here for a neighbor? She would rather die of loneliness. Only she would not be lonely! Lone-

liness was a state of mind. *Solitude*—that was the word. A lovely solitude that she and her husband would enjoy together. She would consider Aunt Chrissy's suggestion about taking the correspondence
courses in order to further prepare herself for teaching. The two of
them would study together, since Young Wil planned to pursue his
medical research. Their happiness would rub off on Marty and Midgie,
given time.

Forcing her eyes from the unsavory faces, True's gaze wandered
to the clerestory roof of the rattling confines, examining the three
brass kerosene lamps, so badly in need of polishing that they appeared
to droop as they swung ceaselessly to the jerking movement of the
clang and clatter of the segmented column of the centipedelike creature called a train. Up and up they crawled now without conversation, the quiet broken only by the rusty squeak of the "Necessary"
door's periodic in-and-out swing. It was fitting, she thought, that
nothing was visible beyond the smoke-stained window except a white
sheet of driving rain. Try as she would, it was hard to maintain the
lift of spirit sensed a moment before. Doubts and fears kept nipping
at her heart as she reviewed the peculiar twist that her marriage had
taken. All for Marty, she thought a little bitterly. Marty, who had
maintained a somewhat hostile aloofness as the rest of them prepared
for the journey.

At True's request, the family did not accompany the four of them
to the station. O'Higgin and Grandma Mollie took them instead. True
wondered how much the older woman knew, but she did not question the "why" of the journey. Instead, there was a constant homey
flow of conversation centered around domestic matters. Did they
bring along enough dried beans and canned fruit? Surely they remembered the blanket spread, enough quilts, and the black dinnerpot? Yes,
yes, yes, True kept saying mechanically. And, yes, of course she
would write often. Nothing of real significance except at the last
moment.

As Mollie Malone O'Higgin hugged her for the third time, she
whispered, "Now, you brung them stout boots. Jest make double-sure
you keep that sweet heart as stout, my child. It was right generouslike
of th' parents of this brood to make all of you feel comfortable with
cashmoney as a weddin' gift. Th' Good Lord's gonna be watchin' out
fer you, but, well, marriage takes work 'n understandin'—just you

be promisin' me one thing, that you're a-gonna remember that God gave you a husband at that altar 'stead of a brother!"

True promised fervently, although her smile felt faulty and uncertain.

They all would have to do a lot of adjusting, she knew. She had devoted a lot of time checking out the region of the Inland Empire, once she heard the name. Living there would be far different. There had been no gold rush, nothing to bring the wagon trains into the area in search of a fortune. So population would be sparse. Well, the ground was rich—or would be if there were more water. But clouds from the ocean dropped the needed moisture in the beautiful valley system first. Having dumped their burden, the thin clouds climbed the higher mountains, whose peaks squeezed them even drier. By the time they reached the eastern Oregon plateaus, the clouds were drained, weak, and tired. The land was all right for grazing; it welcomed stock, cattle, and sheep (if one could avoid range wars, dodge poachers, and chink up the cracks of his cabin against nasty winds and bitter cold). In fact, there were sections of land tilting up to the south that were receptive to wheat and gardens, especially when situated near a lake. Thank goodness, the vast acreage edged against a lake on one corner, according to the lawyer's crude sketch.

"Trees I can sacrifice for a time—maybe. But to give up fresh vegetables and bright flowers would be like giving up my life."

True spoke the words aloud without realizing she had spoken until curious eyes turned invitingly her direction. "Eh, Miss?" "Well, whadda ya know? Th' doll can talk." "Got ye'sslf a man, Woman?"

True gasped in relief when the conductor in greasy overalls ambled in to punch tickets, asking and answering questions amiably. His eyes lit up noticeably when they focused on True. "Better wake up your pretty companion, Missy," he said, punching True's ticket, "next stop bein' yours. Now, I do hope that you two ladies ain't plannin' on goin' it alone here."

The words renewed the interest of the uncouth passengers. There were suggestive remarks, a few whistles, and, in the eyes of some, unmistakable lust. True felt her blood curdle. *Oh, Wil, where are you?*

Praying for strength, she received it. "Our husbands are with us," she said in a dignified manner, her voice much louder than necessary.

For some unaccountable reason, True felt stronger. She had met one crisis. God would help her through those to come, maybe in ways she did not expect or understand. But help He would!

"Wake up, Midgie, darling," True said almost gaily. "We're there!"

"There" proved to be far removed from what was to become home, True realized as she looked at the vast grasslands with not a dwelling in sight. However, it seemed a good omen that the unusual gift of late rain had kissed the whole plateau with its special favor, then skipped away. Now the sun sifted gold dust on the stand of cottonwoods, which had appeared like an oasis in the open country. Meadows were ripe with sweet-breathed clover, bitter-scented white poppies, and wild daisies bobbing their heads as if to shake free of the rain. The train whistle startled a flock of quacking ducks, back from the warmer climes and now dining without conscience on a wide field of wheat. Alarmed by the din of human voices and complaining bellows of the cattle being unloaded, the fowl took to their wings, circled, and regrouped, finally wedging in departure. Were human sounds so foreign to them? Whatever True had expected, this was not it. This was surely another state, another country, another world.

Taking no note of the new surroundings, Midgie's anxious eyes searched the length of the train for sight of the men as the black monster puffed out a cinder-studded doughnut of smoke and prepared for departure. True followed Midgie's gaze and felt her heart leap with joy and relief when she spotted Wil. With customary efficiency he was instructing a dazed Marty in the art of coaxing cattle down the gangplank. One by one they hitched the cows together by means of securing their halters with ropes. And all the while Young Wil talked to the frightened animals in low, soothing tones. How wonderful he was at everything he did! Perhaps she judged her brother a bit too harshly, expected too much. It was unfair to compare him to her husband. Still—

"Look! The dogs!" Midgie's startled exclamation broke her long silence and passed it along to True, who stood speechless. How on earth had those twins managed to smuggle Tonsil and Lung into that car? And then she realized that it was comforting to have companionship, which obviously was a scarce commodity in this strange land. Too, the fat, wet-nosed puppies would be a constant reminder of home—and, yes, she was homesick already. She smiled to cover the sadness—a smile which was cut short by a scene, innocent though it might be, which caused her heart to lurch. Maybe she should try to distract Midgie.

"Midgie—wait!" True tried to stop her sister-in-law's flight. But Midgie either failed to hear or chose to ignore her. She ran as fast as her long skirt would allow. Stumbling over the wagging puppies, she failed to see the short interlude which gave True her first hint that trouble was brewing

The tall man with the beaver hat had approached Marty, said something which caused Marty to pale, and reentered the train. The stranger's face was still partially covered by the wide brim of the hat, so there was no recognition on True's part. All the more reason that a thrill of apprehension tightened her spine. The man had lifted a long-boned finger, resembling a talon, in salute to *her*!

There was no time to give the incident further thought. Young Wil spotted True, and in what appeared to be one long stride was at her side, his arms around her. Undaunted by the tedious ride, he grinned broadly. "Do I smell like a cow?"

"How would I know? My nostrils are too filled with smoke to do their duty. Who cares about smells anyway?" True snuggled closer. Over his shoulder she saw Midgie reaching her arms imploringly to Marty like a small child begging to be scooped up. Marty obliged with about as much emotion as if lifting a sack of grain. His face looked strained and morose, the expression which spelled out a touchy mood. Inwardly she shrugged. Marty North best read his Bible and heed the words of Paul: "Every man shall bear his own burden."

"Are you all right, sweetheart?" Young Wil's voice was filled with concern.

"Perfect!" And she was—*now*. They were a perfect team *anywhere*—

He was about to answer when a drawling voice drew them apart.

"Hi'ya, Mister North, I'm guessin'—th' bossman of Double N— gave 'er a name when we heered you wuz comin'. Welcome, Boss!"

They turned to see a withered little man with a face like a prune beneath a high-crown felt hat, some two sizes too large, with the brim turned up and secured with a nail. His legs were bowed out either by a quirk of nature or from riding horseback more than he walked. But the grin was genuine and heartwarming. True liked the little fellow at once, comical a picture as he presented.

"And you must be the foreman," Young Wil said cordially, seeming to ignore his appearance. "I am *one* of the Norths," he continued, "but neither of us is the owner of the ranch. Since his name is O'Higgin, I suppose rightfully we should call it the Double 0."

"No sir—it was him that ast fer th' N—'n me, I carry out orders."

"Good for you! But I failed to catch your name?" Young Will extended his hand.

The man took it awkwardly. "Goldish—Billy Joe Goldish. But th' fellers never could say it proper—pure devilishness, I'm guessin', when they dubbed me 'Goldfish'—so, jest call me 'Beetle,' what I'm knowed as."

"Beetle it is, Mr. Goldish—and may I present my bride?"

Beetle turned twinkling eyes on True. "Oh, my my! How purdy, jest like a picture—my wife'll be liken' th' sight of you—yep—"

True favored him with a bright smile. "So you have a wife. Oh, that makes me happy! I had hoped to meet another woman—well, several—"

The little man shook his head sadly. "Ain't many, ma'am. An' sad t'say, but—but my Mariah ain't able t'speak no English—jest Spanish—"

True felt absurdly near tears with disappointment. The disappointment then focused on Billy Joe, the Beetle. The little man was regarding her with unqualified approval—and hope. Hope, True supposed, that she would be able to teach Mariah to communicate other than in her native tongue, when the only words in Spanish she knew were *Señora* and *Sí*! But why dash his hopes at this point when the cross-currented lines of his mouth increased with a broad grin? Instead, True smiled back, wondering if Young Wil had also noticed that his foreman's hat flattened his ears so that they looked as if the Almighty had fashioned them as a hat tree. The answer came when his twinkling eye caught hers.

Billy Joe scratched his right temple in concentration beneath the ill-fitting hat. "I'm plum outta idees 'bout ho we're gonna get all that stuff 'crost th' trail," he said doubtfully with a nod toward the household belongings and trunks piled alongside the tracks. "So muddy sometimes th' gumbo gits right up t'th' hubs uv th' wagon wheels. Glad I brung th' burros—stubborn critters, but they come in handy."

"Thoughtful of you, Beetle—you know, I like Billy Joe better—any objections?" A look of pleasure crossed the man's face, and Young Wil continued: "Marty, how about a hand here?"

Soon the three men were loading the bundles and boxes onto the protesting wagon, leaving some of the heavier items for the slat-ribbed donkeys in order to provide seat room for the ladies.

"The rest of you are going to walk?" True said with concern. "How far is it?" Young Wil and Marty turned questioning eyes to Billy Joe.

With palms up he guessed it to be "'bout 25 miles down-slough," then up a little rise from Slippery Elm. "Got er name from a grove uv elmwood, but, by jiminy, sure wuz a fittin' name follerin' sech a rain."

So it was decided that they would spend the night in a sleazy little hotel in Slippery Elm. Midgie wondered about bedbugs. Marty complained about the situation in general. True ate cold mutton, white with tallow, and a muffin that failed to rise, and held onto Wil's hand—with a smile.

9
Mixed Feelings

❧

WASHING DOWN THE tasteless meal with water, True suggested stepping outside for a breath of air. Only Young Wil accepted her invitation. Midgie had chosen bedbugs over Indians and Marty—well, who knew what he was thinking?

Slippery Elm was no town—never would be—although it showed signs of lost ambition. There were no boardwalks and no plan laid out—just remnants of sod slabs, half-roofed with heavy thatch or canvas. The weatherbeaten hotel, which served as an inn, post office, and telegraph center, bore a proud sign: SLIPPERY ELM. Underneath it, more visible than hoops beneath a lady's skirt, was the peeling paint of the original sign: SQUATTER SOVEREIGN. The only other building was something passing for a general store. It would pass for Aunt Chrissy's description of what Centerville's first store looked and smelled like. It was more of a barn in appearance and was filled with barrels of sugar, flour, and coffee beans. The lid was off the vinegar barrel, allowing emission of such tartness that one was forced to clutch the throat to clear the windpipe. True had taken one glance, eyes misted over by the tartness of the vinegar, and expressed that they would not be doing their shopping here.

To her embarrassment the operator, a man with a mastiff face, bald head shining like a mirror, overheard her. Lifting hands that looked like 12-pound sledges to tear off six yards of calico for a waiting male customer, the proprietor stopped short. He set her at ease, however, by favoring her with a surprisingly gentle smile. And his voice, when he spoke, was apologetic and almost sad.

"Guess they's no choice—nothin' else in these parts. 'Silver 'n gold have I none, but I will give thee such as I have'—ain't that th' way th' Good Book says it, now? Meanin' I'll carry you folks from one crop to t'other. Right glad t'meetcha. North, ain't it, now?"

"News travels fast," Young Wil had smiled. "And your store's fine."

"Ain't much, but what we git, we share."

Telegram and all, True found herself thinking as she acknowledged the introduction and stepped over a hound stretched full-length between her and the door. "Curly" Caswell lifted the hinged board which would allow True to enter the dry goods section (where bolts of material were stacked along the walls) and bade her come in. She declined politely.

Once outside, True determined to make the most of what was beginning to look like a bad situation. She held onto the wooden banister of the sagging porch and concentrated on the sunset until Young Wil joined her. The total absence of fir-clad hills imbued True with a sense of loneliness. But the grasslands were green and the twilight was a beautiful blend of crimson and gold. The air was still fragrant with freshly scrubbed earth, and a meadowlark trilled across some distant meadow. In a final goodnight, the sun sent a last afterglow that rivaled a blazing forest. Just as it died away, leaving the old buildings squatting in shadowy shapes, Young Wil's hand closed over hers.

"Are you sure you'll be all right here, darling?" His voice held a curious choking sound. Her own emotions found vent in a little cry of delight as she turned to be swept into his arms. All right? She would be all right anywhere with him. *Nothing* could defeat her!

"I will be perfect, darling—once I wash off three layers of dirt and soot, and get a decent night's rest. Two nights jostling on that wooden bench have shattered my backbone. No way to wash up or brush my hair without being invaded by one of the men in need of the 'Necessary.' My teeth need brushing, and I must smell like a stogie—"

"Better that than cows and chips!"

Together they burst into laughter. Then True sobered. "Where did you sleep?"

"Sleep? What's that? I did well to find squatting room in the straw, most of it being taken up by bellowing, four-legged critters."

"Oh, darling!" Then, in retrospect, it all seemed funny again.

When the air grew chill, they went upstairs to a barren room dominated by an ancient iron bed with a straw mattress. Young Wil looked at it and claimed to feel right at home in the straw while True wearily poured water from the granite pitcher into a cracked pottery basin and splashed her face. As she was brushing her hair, the sound of Midgie and Marty's voices came through the thin walls. Midgie was sobbing while Marty's voice was low but angry. At least, whatever the problem, he had the good sense (and through Aunt Chrissy, good breeding) to keep it between them. But honeymoon? What could he be thinking?

True told Young Wil about the little scene between Marty and the stranger in the beaver hat then. It seemed important that he know.

Wil nodded thoughtfully. "I saw that—what do you make of it?"

"I don't know—I just never did know how to help Marty, I guess, although goodness knows I have tried hard enough—"

"*Too* hard, True. We will stand by him, and keep our prayers going up for him constantly. But promise me that you will let him grow up. This is his chance. It will either make or break him."

True agreed and climbed into the bed of thistles, too tired to flinch. Anyway, she was with Wil, so . . . what . . . did . . . anything matter . . . ?

She was fast asleep.

10
The Double N—Home?

❧

OVERNIGHT THE GROUND appeared to have soaked up the water thirstily. Not so with the trail, hardened and rutted as it was. The heavily loaded wagon began complaining while it was still on level ground. The wheels moaned and groaned as they hit pools of water, churning up fountains of mud over the two passengers. Midgie, eyes still red-rimmed from last night's weeping, gasped in horror as the murky water splashed onto her clothing, then struck her face. And then, as if almost relieved to have some way of explaining the tears, she began to cry again. Little sobs. Sounds of despair. It was best to let her cry.

True glanced away tactfully. "Oh, dear! Look at our poor husbands!"

The exclamation drew Midgie's thoughts away from herself. "Oh, how awful—they're like mudballs—" she hiccuped once, then went into a regular spasm, causing more tears. "How—how—can—we—h-hel-p?"

As True looked at Young Wil plastered in mud (and looking for all the world like an amateurish sculpture turned out with the aid of an eggbeater), she was tempted to join Midgie in tears. But for now, action was needed.

"I'm going to help."

"You stay put, young lady!" Young Wil ordered. "I don't want to have to worry about you!"

"Then don't!" True said saucily as she leaped from the wagon and put her shoulder to the front wheel right alongside Wil.

Together they hitched forward, paused to inhale, and—with eyes closed against the mud—hitched forward again. The mules strained in their harness, their mouths white with froth. True lost track of time and eventually her sense of reality. They were on board an ailing ship, helpless on a high, choppy sea—unable to move forward or backward, with water washing over their heads. And yet some determined captain was bellowing, "Heave—ho! Heave—ho!"

Crazily, True realized that she had heave-hoed all she was able to. And they were sinking, sinking—to the hole in the bottom of the sea. One more heave, no more.

The tactic, whatever it was, worked. The wagon lurched forward with such a lurch that True fell forward, biting her lower lip in the fall. But they mustn't stop now! They must push as never before. She was on her feet instantly, and, hooray! they *were* moving forward as if by pull of an unseen force! True kept pushing with Billy Joe's every command, spitting mud in the process, and squinting in an effort to see.

And what she saw caused her to falter and almost fall again. Midgie, helpless little Midgie, was pushing with all her strength on the opposite side of the wagon. Something about that touched her heart. She hoped it touched Marty's, too. The girl looked so beautiful in spite of the sad condition of her clothing. Her eyes shone and her lips curved in a smile of triumph. True knew the feeling. For a moment, Midgie and Marty had conquered the world all by themselves.

Feeling invigorated and oddly refreshed, in spite of still walking in a dream, True allowed her face to be wiped free of mud by her husband's clean white handkerchief. And for once she made no reply to his scolding, for she was seeing a vision: of their new home glowing like a precious stone, blessed with Mariah's colorful touch; of a blazing fire which would dry out her matted hair; of firelight dancing from bright saddle blankets, beaded garments, and vivid landscapes captured in oil and resting in hand-carved frames to the book-lined walls, where a giant white cat, now rosy with the changing color of the burning logs, stretched lazily on the mantelpiece. How cozy . . . warm . . . alive . . . welcoming!

The vision was to fade suddenly, for there was an abrupt stop at the foot of a little slope. "Thar she be!" Billy Joe announced.

This? *This* was where they would live—this cabin roofed with dirt and hay? True tried to tell herself that it was a mistake. But Wil's quick intake of breath said otherwise, allowing her dream (which had grown with beanstalk rapidity) to wilt just as quickly. Not a tree. Not a shrub. Just a single-story shack over which desertion had cast an evil spell. In the bright sun two dirty windows, panes cracked, stared sadly through their sagging frames. Stained and weather-warped, the boards of the crude building appeared ready to give up the effort of standing. A creaking door, standing ajar, told its story without words. Someone had inhabited the place recently and had hurriedly boarded it up, but another person (Billy Joe, undoubtedly) had made a vain attempt to rip away the boards and make the place respectable.

While the others stood pondering what to do, True moved forward as if drawn by an invisible magnet. With her heart winging its way into her throat, she pushed the door open cautiously, giving no thought to possible danger inside. Her concern was simple: What could she create from such chaos. But the interior held no answer.

Once over the threshold, she sensed a recent presence. Could it still be occupied? In the dimness, the sparse furnishings were shapeless. When her eyes adjusted to the shadowy interior, the cracked stove, orange with rust, came into focus. Then a table with remnants of food and abuzz with flies crawling along the faded oilcloth covering. True shuddered and forced her eyes to traverse the rest of the room. Benches made from packing crates. A three-legged desk leaning against the wall for support. A dilapidated bunk. And a door leading to another room, which lay in total darkness. It was easy to imagine a man or beast lying in waiting. She was going to be sick. She must escape—now. Spinning on her heel, True hurried out.

It was good to feel the warm rays of the sun and to see the *real* faces of her family. Real, yes, but concerned. And all eyes were focused on *her*. God had given her another assignment.

Valiantly, True North squared her shoulders. "Well," she said, forcing a smile, "welcome home—to the Double N!"

"Is—is it *hor*-rible?" Midgie's teeth were chattering.

"It is that! I need some volunteers who have no fear of dirtying their hands, a barrel of soapy water, and a good disinfectant!"

Young Wil's eyes flashed appreciation as he and Marty went inside to inspect. Midgie clung to True's hand. "What—can—can we do?"

"We can be brave—like you were on the trail—and wait for our men to make some decisions, darling. And I guarantee you an adventure!"

The men came outside. Marty looked ready for burial. Young Wil, bless him, looked ready to split with laughter—something only she could understand. But he pulled the corners of his mouth up stoically and nodded when Billy Joe offered assistance with unpacking. Maybe they could just bunk, he suggested. Then, come tomorrow, he and his Mariah would be back to help clean—oh, his Mariah *could* clean! Right shamed he was now, not being able to invite them to bed down with them. But, well, they had only a tent, and what with three "young 'uns"—they did understand? But at least they'd not be starving, not with Mariah's dinnerpot chuck-full of red beans (with lots of pepper) and lip-smackin' good.

The next morning Young Wil announced some emergency steps. He and Marty would go back to Slippery Elm and pick up a few emergency supplies. As he recalled, there were stacks of lumber in the shed of the combination inn-store-and-whatever-else-you-need building.

"If you girls are game?" His voice was sober with concern.

Marty answered before they had a chance. "Midgie's going home."

"Your decision or hers?" Wil's voice demanded an answer.

"This *is* home," Midgie said, her small chin lifted in pathetic appeal.

Marty could not meet her gaze. "I guess we have no choice, have we?" he said bitterly. "And you're enjoying my misery—"

"Get with it, Marty!" Young Wil said sharply. "Life always offers choices. God gave us free will and expects us to take charge *of* our lives. As I remember O'Higgin's terms, *you* are in charge—so, what's your pleasure?"

Put that way, True thought with a desire to laugh, Marty *didn't* have much choice! She felt a thrill of joy that Young Wil had placed the burden squarely on their brother's shoulders. They would go!

Once the men were out of waving distance, the two young women looked at each other, first in desperation, then in grim determination. And without words they understood each other.

Thank goodness Aunt Chrissy and Grandma Mollie had thought of everything—even rags for cleaning! Midgie drew a bucket of water by hand from the well (the pulley having rusted beyond repair), and the two of them shredded lye soap into a large granite pan. Then with rags, brooms, and brushes they went to work.

True's back was breaking, and her hands were bruised and bleeding, but in her heart was a song. "Work, for the night is coming!" she sang out, and, to her surprise, Midgie joined in. Why, the girl's voice was beautiful. Something told True that she had sung before under different circumstances.

11
Renovations

THE SOUND OF hoofbeats startled Midgie, bringing her to True's side. The child had a million fears—strangers, new situations, bugs, and mice. Now she was sure that she and True would be murdered. By whom made no difference. Child? True told herself for the thousandth time that she and Midgie were the same age, with Marty but three months their senior. She *must* stop treating them like children.

"See who it is, Midgie," she said briskly, wiping her hands and laying aside her mud-stained apron.

"Halo, halo—anybody home? I brung Mariah 'n th' brood—"

"Billy Joe!" Midgie whispered in relief. "Thank goodness—"

The two young women moved to the door to welcome their first guests. Billy Joe, "foreman" of the Double N, looked as relieved as Midgie. "Never can tell who might be lurkin' inside. But thangs are a-gonna be diff'rent with me 'n yer men in charge." He exhaled as far as his flat chest would allow.

True had hardly heard. She was preparing to welcome their neighbors—"squatters," wasn't that how O'Higgin referred to them? Billy Joe dismounted the aging mule so that Mariah, who rode behind him, came into view. Heavy, braided, dark hair swung forward and the near-black eyes, fixed on "El Señor's" family, were questioning. The high cheekbones showed signs of former beauty, weary and weathered though her face was. There was a plea in the woman's face, a begging to be accepted.

The three children, all boys (who, True guessed, ranged between five and seven), rolled dark eyes from their mother to the two strang-

ers standing in the doorway. Poor dears. They were all but hypnotized with curiosity but had obviously been instructed to "behave or
else!" In that split second, True lost herself in a dream of possibili-
ties ... Young Wil would make a wonderful father ... a quickly
spawned fantasy which ended abruptly with a startling memory: A
part of this strange bargain had been that Marty and Midgie bear a
child, preferably male ... how foolish could conditions of a will get?
An eccentric old man trying to dictate people's lives from his very
grave! Then came the realization that Midgie had reacted with a stout
refusal. "I won't!" She wished the memory had lain dormant.

Billy Joe's family continued to observe True and Midgie in fascination. "Forgive me, Billy Joe," True said quickly. "Bring them in by
all means!" She flashed them a warm smile and beckoned an invita-
tional finger. Her reward was a beautiful, pearly-toothed smile from
Mariah and then the wordless scramble of the three boys as they slid
from the back of the other mule obediently and came to her shyly.

"*Buenos dias, Señora*," they said in unison, then scuttled away.

"They know how to work, too!" Billy Joe said with pride, which
signaled the trio back to the mules (burdened, she saw then, with
crude tools). Billy Joe helped Mariah to the ground, keeping up a flow
of conversation. Wonderful woman, his Mariah—sole survivor, as far
as he knew, of an ambush. Indians? Billy Joe scratched his thatch of
hair that looked as if he'd borrowed it from the shack's roof and said
it was more like a bunch of "white trash" that attacked the lone
wagonload of Mexican immigrants bound on stock-raising. Stole the
livestock, of course, and some right good horseflesh excepting one
stallion that galloped to the hills faster than the winds could blow.
What with Archibald—yep, that was the stallion's name—and wild
horses abounding, there was a great opportunity.

Of course, horses needed good grain for wintering. And wheat
needed watering. For winter, that was. No problem in summer, with
grass belly-deep. No problem with milk-giving critters either, excepting for poachers. Great opportunities if men had a will, and it was
plain to see that at least one of the two North bosses had horse sense.
Billy Joe paused to laugh at his joke, glancing at Mariah, and then,
seeing that Midgie had established a friendly communication, lowered his voice confidentially.

"My Mariah warn't so lucky as th' stallion, tryin' t'run fer th' brush
like she dun—" Billy Joe's voice trembled with anger. "She was cap-

tured 'n th' whole shebang taken after her—'n—there wuz a life-'n-death struggle 'fore public fornication—"

"You mean—" True was too horrified to go on.

Billy Joe's mouth twitched pitifully as he nodded. But beneath the ill-fitting hat his eyes were live coals. "They ravished my Mariah—all th' stinkin' filthy cowards. Me, I went no fu'ther—runnin' ain't no answer. It settles nothin'—'n me, I'm a-gonna square thangs one day. Lucky I found her wanderin' 'round like th' stallion—jest her 'n her *git*-tar—them purdy eyes glazed like th' dead 'n sangin' words I didn't com'prend—but I'd seen enuf t'know—I know how t'shoot—them animals 'll pay—"

True could understand his feelings, wrong though they were. What she could not understand was Midgie's reaction. Having apparently overheard some of the conversation, she had stopped scrubbing and stood as if carved in granite. True shook her own head to clear away the image that floated before her eyes of an angel chiseled in a tombstone.

Without speaking, Midgie dropped back to her knees and resumed scrubbing. A throbbing pulse on her white neck like the delicate wings of a dove beating against a cage was the only sign of the inner turmoil that True knew was there. It was as if her sister-in-law faced some uncompromising danger from which there was no escape. Even if freed, inevitably she would be caught. What was the look? One of total change. As if being Mrs. Marty North—maybe even this faraway place—had offered refuge. And now the haven was but a thin illusion. Instead, something sinister and forbidding had taken its place. Maybe life had taught the peculiar man known as Uncle Artie more than any of them realized; how quickly values change to shift like shadows in crises!

All day they worked as if driven, each buried in a private vault of thought. Even the children—Carlos, Rafael, and Eduardo (who, Billy Joe explained, insisted on being addressed as Carl, Ralph, and Eddie)—were quiet as they brought fresh water into the shack and pulled weeds from around the doors and windows outside. There was no mention of lunch.

The afternoon sun dropped behind distant hills. Inside the air was sultry, but there was the smell of freshness and livability. A tinge of rose replaced the gold of the afternoon, the changing color now visible through the windows. Almost without warning the color faded, and twilight came like the flapping of gray wings to let in the dark. Somewhere a coyote howled. Resolutely True shook off the eerie feeling that they were being watched as Billy Joe struck a match on the sole of his shoe and lighted a lamp polished by his wife's capable hands. Immediately the room was flooded with a warm, mellow glow.

Mariah said something to the children, who shyly whispered to their father. Billy Joe nodded. "Time to wash up," he beamed, "fer my Mariah's corncakes, pepperpot, 'n coffee—puts grit in th' craw and greases th' innards, 'sides bein' lip-smackin' good!"

Mariah's cooking was all that her husband promised—and more. Several times True found herself grabbing for water to put out the fire in her mouth. But the food filled up the empty spaces in her middle that all the stooping, lifting, and scrubbing had created. She was grateful to the stouthearted woman who had endured so much so bravely, yet clung to her faith—a faith evidenced by the simple gesture of dampening a finger with her tongue and making the sign of the cross on her forehead before partaking of food. The children followed her pattern. True was uncertain what was expected of her, so said a quiet "Amen." Mariah smiled at her across the table, which, thanks to her husband, now had four legs. True was eager to have the men see the change.

The lean-to kitchen would accommodate no more than two, so True walked to the front door. The men should have been home long ago. She listened for the sound that might signal their return. Nothing. Nothing except the hair-raising howl of a hungry coyote. Billy Joe was at her side in an instant, shotgun raised.

"I—thank you, Billy Joe—I dislike those creatures—"

"No need fearin' 'em, ma'am. Cowards they are—iffen a sheep wus t'turn 'n look 'em in th' eye they'd hightail—jest like some men I know—'course now, a body's gotta be watchful, make ready."

"Life in such a place is challenging, isn't it?"

Billy Joe thought the statement over, then answered with judicial-like deliberation. "Ain't th' place fer them what don't cotton t' quiet. Me, I call it God's Country—ever'thang here a man could be wantin'."

True stepped out the door and stood breathlessly staring at the overhead canopy of shimmering stars—so close she could pluck them from the sky. The breeze was fragrant with nightbloom—and wasn't that—?

All thought of danger gone, she ran out toward the trail with a small cry, her feet flying in her haste to meet the loaded wagon that Billy Joe had lent them. "Wil, Wil—*Wil*!"

In his arms, she whispered, "Is it wise to be out—in—the—dark?"

"Wise? How can a man be wise and in love at the same time?"

12
One Step Forward—
Two Back

❧

IN THE DAYS that followed, the group was to see a lot of one another. The Goldish family spent every waking hour assisting with repair. Spreading canvas salvaged from covered wagons which had collapsed, been abandoned, or fallen prey to marauders, Billy Joe proceeded to remove sod from the roof. The little man, hopping about in the dirt, *did* bear a comical resemblence to a beetle, True thought with a smile as she handed him tools for prying away and replacing the sagging boards underneath. Later they would chink up the cracks between the logs, he said, and 'twasn't much, but—

"We'll make do, Billy Joe. Wil and I'll spend only the remainder of this year—"

The foreman stopped his work, turned his head aside to spit, and accepted a board he had asked for. "Yer meanin' that th' other 'un— th' one what don't look *at* a body, jest *through* it—*that* boy'll stay?"

"*Man*, Billy Joe, and his name is Martin, Martin North. He may stay—"

"Well, now," Billy Joe said as he scratched his chin, "Martin North's got hisself a heap t'learn—'bout ranchin', human bein's, 'n bein' a husband—"

True started to say that they would all have to help him, then paused. That was against the new rules she and Wil had agreed on.

Billy Joe took her silence as a rebuff. "Sorry iffen I offended you some, Miz True. But a man'd be stone-deaf 'n blinder'n a bat not t'take notice. Thick-skinned as a buffalo 'n sharp as a thistle with that tongue—sorta like he's a-tryin' t'duck out on life—"

Billy Joe may have talked on. True was thinking about Marty and Midgie. In fact, she thought about the four of them. A house—no matter about size and location—should be a refuge, a *home*. A home meant peace, love, and protection. How could this be so unless something was done? And indications were that her brother was unwilling to do anything to stem the emotional tide that was washing his direction. True had hoped it was only her instinctive desire to protect Marty that caused her concern. But an outsider's taking notice dashed that hope. This would become a house of strangers—alienated and fenced off in the private domains of their hearts unless they could talk the situation out. Up till now she and Young Wil had done all they could to make life normal and bring happiness to the other couple. But they were battling a formidable adversary. Marty's sulkiness spelled out a single-mindedness on some problem too great for him to handle. He was sick but unwilling to attempt recovery. His attitude now was one of bitter resignation. *Face it, True, an ingrate!*

Wil, on the other hand, had remained pleasant, even enthusiastic, and—unlike herself—determined not to allow their brother's problem to grind him down. But something had to give. The strain was more than Marty had a right to expect any of them to contend with, especially Midgie. She was trying so hard—*too* hard—to win the love of a downright spoiled brat! True suddenly wished that Midgie would simmer inside, warn Marty with signs of reaching a rolling boil by coloring with indignation at some of his insults, tighten her fist and voice, and then explode. Wouldn't that clear the air? Shake some sense into him?

And then it occurred to her that perhaps Midgie had no idea what this was all about. That in her naivete she felt she deserved no more— that "this is just the way the world is for people like me."

True determined then and there to have a talk with her.

For just a moment she feasted her eyes on Young Wil, so handsome in canvas-colored Levi's, sinewy arms—slightly sunburned and soaked with perspiration—hammering away at the window frames. Odd the effect he had on her. One look at him gave her a feeling of homecoming. Well, why not? They were of one flesh—one house which was God's temple—neither complete without the other. Feeling her gaze apparently, Wil paused, wiped the sweat from his bronzed forehead, and pushed at a rebellious lock of hair which crowned his smile. Oh, how God had blessed them! Even in this ridiculous situation they were happy.

On pretext of needing a cup of water from the barrel, Young Wil dropped his hammer and came to where she was picking up rusted nails. Then, pointing to a log, he led the way to it. There they sat down, his arm around her, a teasing forefinger tickling her ribs.

"Problems?" he queried, pushing a straw hat to the back of his head.

"Stop that tickling, Wil North. This is serious!"

"I know, darling—that's why I teased," he said gently.

True told him her concerns, leaving nothing out. "I'm sick with worry about poor Midgie—passive as a little lamb and just as docile, letting Marty walk over her. She tries to see life as sunshine and roses and what is her reward? He—Marty's going to destroy her, Wil."

Young Wil was silent for a time. At length he said, "Marty has been insulated from hard knocks, True. But no more. It's too bad that it has to come all at once, but that's the way he chose it—meaning that I am going to lay it on the line this time. I am tired of his childishness—one step forward then quick-stepping back two when nobody's looking!"

And she would talk with Midgie. But much was to happen before the plan materialized. There was so much to do. But, thank goodness, the cabin was hardly a shack anymore. It actually looked like a house now.

13

Strange Encounters

❧

JULY CAME IN hot and sticky. But the sky remained a constant blue, and True noted with glee that the sparrows which nested along the eaves of the cabin had hatched and were trying their soft-feathered wings. They touched her heart, striving as they were to cling to life as opposed to establishing a degree of permanency—somewhat like Slippery Elm, which was little more than a tent city and was apt to stay that way. Unless, of course, the vague plan materialized that she overheard mentioned in the lobby on the night she, Young Wil, Marty, and Midgie were guests.

The disheveled-looking town had come to mind because of plans to make a trip for wiring to patch up the corral fence at "roundup" time (Billy Joe insisted he could bring the stallion down and that the wild mares would follow), for some plants for a fall garden, and to search for a few temporary laborers to harvest the grain that Billy Joe had seeded by hand. The wandering harvesters would work for a dollar a day, he said, and it would cost a dollar thirty-five to feed them ordinarily. But his Mariah knew the shortcuts and could stretch a buck and still stretch a man's stomach. Not much profit in this year's harvest, to be sure, but a man had to look ahead, save good seed—improve 'em—

"Feed that horde, try to stay alive through a devilish winter—what kind of future is that?" It was Marty who spoke—bitterly as usual.

Midgie opened her mouth, obviously hoping to soothe his anger or cover for his rudeness, then closed it.

Billy Joe had eyed him with ill-disguised disgust. "What kinda future you got elsewheres? A man's gotta carve out his own by th' sweat o'th' brow, 'cording t'th' Good Book. Any venture's a gamble—iffeny' ladies 'll be pardonin' th' expression. They's a way t'survive. Hunt, man, hunt! We kin larn a heap from our red brothers 'bout harvestin' th' fowls, deer, 'n rabbits—like hare stew?"

Marty's lip curled slightly in disdain. This man he thought crazy had touched a nerve with his mention of gambling. Any onlooker could see that Marty was not a man committed to work out a friendship with the new land. He was condemned to it.

Billy Joe Goldish made a lot of sense. True agreed with Young Wil in discovering a lot more intelligence than they had first attributed to him. Marty had dropped out of the conversation when Billy Joe referred back to the talk overheard at the inn. "Shippin's always brung problems even if a man can turn a profit, but some o'them pipe dreams 'bout extendin' th' rails could be more'n cracker-barrel talk. Folks 'round here stick to th' idee with leechlike conviction!" Billy Joe said.

"Not that we have much need for transportation," Wil laughed. "Unless," he sobered, "we *can* develop a new strain like you say—"

His voice trailed off and True recognized the look. Always interested in botany, Young Wil's fine mind was out there somewhere climbing trees for a better view of the land, sorting seeds for developing a hardier hybrid strain, and finding a method to irrigate. She saw his dark eyes light up with inspiration as he said, "Maybe we can do the same with horses, not concentrating on how many we can breed, but creating a finer breed—improving—"

"Righto! That's 'xactly whut I'm meanin'!" Billy Joe's short legs bowed out dangerously as he literally jumped up and down. "Iffen th' weather cooperates 'n we kin find them hands tomorrow, hang onto th' harvest, it's possible t'git this place in th' black ink—providin' we gotta 'nuf cash money fer winterin'—"

"We have it."

"Then, by jiminy, we'll do it—it's our bounden duty t'prove it! Ain't that th' whole purpose?"

"Well, in a sense, yes—proving up on the claim there in the western corner." He made an effort to catch Marty's eye, but failed. "And certainly it will be a challenge," he finished, flashing a jaunty smile at True.

True smiled back. If her husband needed her support, he had it. He had Billy Joe's too; seeing the entire matter as a "duty," he was a willing serf, tied to the land, and he knew all there was to know about ranching. His family was a delightful bonus.

Her thoughts traveled on in a strange comparison of the three men. Duty for Billy Joe, yes. Challenge for Wil, yes again—but more. It was a moral charge, a sacred obligation. And Marty? While the dwarfed foreman would crawl on all fours to fulfill his self-imposed responsibilities, Marty's face revealed the awful truth about his own attitude: He was being punished, condemned, scourged to do penance for some heinous sin he did not commit.

True sighed. If his older brother had talked to him, it had accomplished nothing.

On the way to Slippery Elm, Billy Joe commanded the team to the right with a loud "Gee!" where the trail forked. "Been hankerin' t'show this," he said with pride. *This* proved to be a broad expanse of farmland where wheat shocks, scattered like a disorderly army, waited for orders. "Scythed it myself 'ceptin' my Mariah 'n th' boys— could'n git no help er no loan—so we jest had t'let a heap uv it be."

"Did the rain sour it?" Young Wil asked with concern.

"Nope, me now, I covered jest 'bout all with them wagon sheets. Ain't no noticeable damage done."

Billy Joe pointed to sections remaining for harvest—acres and acres. Farther north lay a narrow band of uncut grain still green with summer and stretching away to the horizon to lose itself beyond a rise in the terrain. In the clearing, nature had repaired the damages by sending squadrons of golden-yellow poppies and purple daisies to cover the stubble. The flowers stood at attention until a playful breeze set their heads to bobbing, their slender stems bending in exaggerated salute.

"Oh, True, look!" Midgie reached out her hand and pointed to where the road appeared to fork again. "That's where I'd like to build our cabin—no," she dreamed on, "make that a sprawling white farmhouse and matching picket fence . . . shakes for a roof . . . a fat chimney attached . . . and—what am I saying? It—ain't—isn't possible—"

"Of course it is!" responded True, caught up in the dream. "Anything's possible with the Lord. It will work out, darling—it has to!"

That would have been a perfect beginning for the talk that True so wanted for them. But this was neither the time nor the place. Even the wagon seemed to know. One wheel dropped into the deeply rutted trail and took its toll. The wagon, already flirting with collapse, shuddered. The two pine boards on which True and Midgie sat bounced, almost tossing them overboard. And then the wagon stopped with a telltale splintering sound. The wobbly wheel had made good its threats. A spoke was broken, Billy Joe announced without irritation. No problem—good place for a rest. Take no more than an hour to fix it.

Whistling, he set to work. With Wil's help and some grumblings from Marty, Billy Joe made good his promise.

Slippery Elm looked even sadder to True's eyes than before—just remains of a conglomeration of thrown-together buildings with dirt floors and rusting single-pipe contrivances through which smoke could escape. The few windows with glass looked like blind eyes wearing glasses, staring hopelessly as if waiting for those who had passed through to return. Silence hung over the treeless town like a plague, except for the tinny notes of an out-of-tune piano coming from somewhere in the inn. A few men sauntered past as Billy Joe tethered the mules at a hitching post—grizzled, ragged, and unwashed men, some gaping, others smirking at True and Midgie. They seemed to be the only women around.

"What's all the ruckus, boys?" the innkeeper barked from inside.

A tall man with a hacking cough and a withered arm yelled back: "Women!"

Marty took a long stride forward, coiled and ready to strike. "Ladies!" he ground out as if something about the town or its people rekindled a fire within him.

The man fumbled at his belt with his one good arm as if in search of something. A gun?

The swinging door creaked and Curly Caswell, the proprietor, stepped out. "Plannin' on usin' that weapon, eh, Gun Slinger? I wouldn't be advisin' it—be gittin' on home!" Wiping his massive hands on an apron that was none too clean, the big man turned toward the prospective customers, recognized them with a smile that sent half-moon wrinkles up from bushy brows onto his bald head, and bade them come inside.

"Tillie!" he called loudly, "come on downstairs 'n meet th' lovely ladies I tole you 'bout!" Again, the smile of pleasure.

Tillie Caswell, hair tousled from the cleanup work upstairs, appeared wearing a cheap gingham floor-length dress, ill-fitting and washed free of its original design. Her eyes were lovely, True noted, but as blank as unstamped coins. Life must have been cruel to her. Starved as she was for the sight of another woman, she was shy and fearful of strangers.

There were introductions, and True drew her into conversation. "I'm glad you're here, Mrs. Caswell. While the men stock up on supplies, I would like to have you show me some material for curtains. Too, I wondered if you had some colorful fabric for a special dress— what are they called, these full-skirted ones with lace that Spanish ladies wear for—"

When she paused, Tillie Caswell supplied the word, "*Fiestas*? Oh, then you are one of the two Mrs. Norths." Her voice was low and musical, her diction perfect. "You must be meaning Billy Joe's wife, Mariah? Oh, she's never had anything so nice!"

True smiled. "She has more than earned it." And this time she entered when the swinging board leading to the yardage was lifted.

Mrs. Caswell suggested a soft fabric of sunny yellow with small red flowers in circular design, plus black lace for trim, and wished for some patterns but assured True that Mariah was clever enough to make her own. True agreed and felt a surge of happiness when she saw light come into the woman's eyes, an awareness of her surroundings.

In fact, she appeared downright excited as she led True to a remnant counter. "I wish I had more selection, but very few peddlers come this way. Feel free to look these over just in case something here will fit your windows—or I can order from Meier and Frank's—"

"In Portland?" Midgie asked excitedly. It was the first time she had spoken after the brief "How do you do?" The rest of the time she had wandered around restlessly, casting her eyes up the stairs frequently as if in search of something she hoped not to find.

"The same," smiled Tillie. "Your home, too? I came from there—"

She paused as if talking too much and went on to tell the story obviously dear to her heart. Aaron Meier was himself the welcome peddler once upon a time—made door-to-door house calls on foot with his bags of calico, by-the yard elastic, paisley shawls of breathless beauty, and mysterious Eastern gadgets. Oh, how Aaron lightened the hearts of pioneer housewives—lightened their thankless burden of mending threadbare garments, too, with his gift of a darning needle.

"A darning needle?" Midgie looked puzzled. "One?"

"The same," Tillie Caswell said, biting off a thread that wrapped the soft pink-checked material that True thought would fill the bill. "And how precious it was! It was passed from one household to another, miles apart, by children—runners, they called themselves. The needle was stuck for protection in a raw potato and always threaded with red yarn. My, my! how that paid off," she smiled, remembering. "Once a boy stopped to gather some hazelnuts along the slough and was startled by a she-bear and her cub, so he dropped the spud— not that a soul blamed the child—"

"A *bear*?" The pupils of Midgie's eyes enlarged, but her curiosity overcame her fear. "And then what happened?"

"Will that be all, Mrs. North? No? Well, just make yourself at home and I'll answer the other Mrs. North's question. Oh, the whole family went hunting for the precious commodity—found it, too—do you know how?"

"The red string?" Midgie clapped her hands like an excited child. "I guess we don't have it so bad after all, True. But," she opened her oversize purse, "maybe we'd better take a supply of needles just in case."

The three were laughing together when the men returned. As they shopped among the tools and coils of wire, True prepared to pay her bill. That was when Midgie moved close to Tillie Caswell and, her face as pale as death, whispered: "This place—uh—it isn't a place—"

True was shocked. But Tillie Caswell's voice portrayed no emotion.

"A brothel? No, my husband's a God-fearing man. Just wish there could be a church here." Two questions answered, True had intended to inquire about the church, holding little hope that one existed.

But Midgie? Why on earth would she ask such a question? And why the look of relief? Surely she didn't suspect Marty—

Quickly she put the revolting thought from her mind. It had been a strange encounter, as if both Midgie and Tillie were leaving something unsaid. Or was she imagining things?

Certainly she did not imagine the next two incidents which happened almost simultaneously.

True was unaware that a train had arrived. Probably the continuous slashing away at the keyboard by a self-styled pianist who knew only one song had drowned out the noise. The arrival of a few newcomers and the sight of a cloud of cinder-studded smoke sweeping close to the ground beyond the single front window alerted her to the activity. Peering out the window for sight of the men, she noted that the sun, trailing ribbons of crimson through the smoke, had dipped below the horizon. Twenty-five miles of travel in the darkness held little appeal.

Looking anxiously for sight of Young Wil, who surely must be loading the wagon, her eyes caught a glimpse of Marty. What she saw stopped any attempt to get his attention. He was talking earnestly with the man she could only identify as "the stranger wearing the beaver hat." Both were gesturing and in turn glancing to see if they were detected. Thank goodness Midgie was looking on a counter marked "Milady's Toilette" and asking Mrs. Caswell if she could hope to find peroxide for her "roots."

True had grown more uneasy by the moment, and now this. If she could get the mail and find the men—yes, she preferred traveling in the darkness to—what?

"Mrs. Caswell," she called, "I failed to inquire about the mail. Have you anything for True North or—"

"True North! As I live and breathe, it's you. True North," the remembered voice repeated as if tasting the word, "so she did not marry, after all—"

Michael St. John!

15

"Let There Be No Misunderstandings!"

SEEING MICHAEL WAS no dream, True realized as her eyes roamed the darkness of the hotel room that Tillie Caswell had assigned to her and Young Wil. "I always try to accommodate newly-marrieds with a room having a door instead of a drape," the woman had said with a smile, "and the latch works. You see, it is safer that way—not that we expect trouble. But it's best being prepared."

Fleetingly, True hoped that the hospitable Tillie had made no such statement to Midgie. Looking around for spiders was enough for her to cope with for now. True herself had been relieved when Young Will suggested staying overnight. They could get an early start and . . .

Her thoughts drifted back to the events of the afternoon. Marty, Tillie, and Midgie, and then Michael. Why did she feel a connection?

After a plunge bath, scrubbing with a cake of coarse yellow soap that left her skin feeling stretched across her body, True had braved the mattress with Young Wil. She had planned to speak of the three incidents but he dropped off to sleep. Careful not to awaken him, True lay so still that a stiffness began at her neck and spread over her entire body . . . a long accumulation of fatigue, which she chose to ignore. It would be nice to get away from this place. On the other hand, she almost wished for some time to explore it further, enduring the gibes and leers of the stragglers, to learn what puzzled her: the background of the ranch that Uncle Artie had left to O'Higgin . . . the real status of the railway's present and future . . . and, most importantly, how

215

Marty and Michael would fit into those plans. Both were deeply involved, but in entirely different ways. She would keep her ears open and her mouth shut.

Sleep came fitfully. The stiffness had traveled down to her heels, and in turning carefully she thought there was the sound of footsteps outside their room. Was it locked? Barefoot, True padded to the door. No sound. But her motion had awakened her husband.

"Morning?" Young Wil sounded wide awake, rising on one elbow to look at the low-in-the-west moon shining palely through the loosely woven burlap serving as drapes. "Doesn't Slippery Elm bother to go to bed? I'm sure I smell coffee."

True dressed hurriedly, then lighted the stub of a candle on a stool table. By its sputtering light she took note of the pole bedstead with the tick mattress that had been about as comfortable as a sack of broken crockery. Their featherbed sounded like a luxury . . . as was their breakfast when they joined Marty and Midgie downstairs. Eggs 50 cents apiece! She was afraid to ask Young Wil what the coffee cost. It was strong enough to walk, so worth whatever it cost, but not bracing enough to stop Midgie's complaints about the eggs. She would get some chickens, that's what. Maybe *sell* eggs. Or exchange them for staple groceries.

"Just set a trap," Marty suggested, his mood seemingly improved. "I saw some wandering around the ranch, looking wild as quails."

"They belong there but have gone sort of native since—well, for a long time," Tillie Caswell said as she leaned across the scarred oak table to heat their mugs of coffee. "With a little grain, you'll have the birds eating right out of your hand."

"Good idea," was Midgie's reply. And the faraway look in her eyes said that she was speaking of more than chickens.

Tonsil and Lung came bounding out to meet the foursome returning to the Double N. The puppies were becoming dogs . . . a reminder of how time was slipping past. Seeming to read True's thoughts, Young Wil suggested that they get the fall cabbage and collards set out at once. Yes, the late-summer sun would do them in unless they were watered by artificial means. Marty was skeptical, saying there were no means out here in the "wilds." One needed pipes and know-how. Billy Joe, who was equipped, Young Wil said, with more than one set of ears, heard the dogs and appeared from nowhere.

"Smart young feller like'n yourself oughta know ir'gation's older'n history," he said, his voice rising a fraction with annoyance. "Read Genesis, my boy, secon' chapter: An' a river went outa Eden t'water th' garden.' 'N iffen that ain't convincin' 'nuf, flip over t'Kings—you do read th' Good Book, I'm a-takin' it?—sez there 'Ye shalln't see wind er rain—yet th' valley'll be full up with water that both ye 'n yer cattle 'n beast kin drink'—ain't that th' way it goes, Wil?"

"Close enough," Young Wil answered. "With three-fourths of the earth's surface covered with water, one day man will discover how to distribute it 'and the desert shall bloom.' For now, nature does a satisfactory job, what with the snow—at least, here. However, now and then nature needs a hand—"

"So we're to make a Persian wheel or Archimedes screw like I saw you reading about?" Marty's voice carried a jibe which Young Wil ignored. His attitude troubled True, however. Why must he behave like a wary foe, thrusting and retreating on the slightest pretext? Puzzling.

Young Wil and Billy Joe went on with the conversation. It would be a simple matter to plow ditches from the little lake. Walled up a bit, the lake would serve as a reservoir for capturing melted snow. Good that gravity flow was on their side. Would it work? Course 'twould, Billy Joe said smugly. "Look what them Mormons done in Utah, 'n that's desert, man, real desert."

Young Wil's dark eyes were alive with excitement. Of course, there would come a time when all the creeks and lakes would be fringed by more farms—then they would have to work out a more complicated system. But for now, "Well, let's get those cabbages planted!"

Marty scowled. "At least we have enough ground here so settlers can't inch in much, tap into our water lines. We'll see to that."

Billy Joe's small eyes became smaller. "Well, leastwise, yer thinkin'—allus a good sign. We're bound on makin' a good rancher uv you. An' one o'these days that mouth o'yorn's a-gonna open 'n let somethin' good come out!"

Marty actually grinned. And then the frown was back. "Could be we're facing a bigger problem than poachers, carpetbaggers, squatters, wild animals—and more. If those railroad thieves try cutting in—"

"Marty, please—" Midgie's voice was that of a pleading child.

"We'll worry about that when the time comes." Young Wil's answer declared the subject closed.

For the next month they all worked together, including Mariah and the three boys. Nobody complained, although True was sure that every bone felt twisted out of place, every back fractured. The men plowed a sizable square of virgin soil and pulverized it with a harrow before going on to break furrows for the water to follow. Midgie helped Mariah stake even rows by using string while True and the children crawled on hands and knees to drop tiny seeds, pausing only for drinking water or driving away the troublesome canines, who between chasing rabbits used the newly seeded garden for a speedway.

When the job was finished, the timing was right for presenting Mariah with the makings of her fiesta dress, True and Midgie agreed. Something had warned them that the woman was proud and very well might mistake any gesture of kindness as unearned charity.

But they were surprised when she refused the material even after her hard work. Vigorously, she shook her raven hair in refusal. But strangely, her dark eyes were shining as her tapering fingers made a desperate try to communicate in sign language.

What could she be trying to say? First, Mariah held the precious cloth to her own face and nodded. Then she shook her head sadly and pointed to Midgie, still clinging to the fabric possessively. When she pointed her direction, True felt a flicker of understanding.

"She loves the material—probably the loveliest thing she has ever owned—" True began.

Midgie caught the message and interrupted excitedly. "But she wants to make similar dresses for us. Oh, True, could we?"

"Of course we can! What a lovely thought, Mariah." True hoped that her smile and nod would fill in for the English words.

They did. Mariah jumped over a row marked "BEANS" and, with many a "*Gracias, Señoras,*" she smiled through a mist of tears.

"The men will be going for the laborers the last week in August," True recalled aloud. "We can see if Tillie has more selection—and both of us must have letters ready to mail the family."

"The dress will be the beginning of my new wardrobe ," Midgie said dreamily. "Nothing I have is right—and you are too nice to say so. It's wrong here—and there with your—our family—wrong in Portland. No wonder Marty got the wrong impression—we still have to talk—"

Her voice trailed off at the sound of Young Wil's whistling and Billy

Joe's singing (which was more of a croak). One day, True had prayed over and over, their attitudes (admittedly taken from Paul's—"I have learned in whatsoever state I am, therewith to be content") would rub off on Marty, allowing him to be happy.

"Yes, we must talk. We all need to be open and honest—"

Although the back door was opening, Midgie tugged at the folds of True's long dirndl skirt. "Can we be—and still love each other— I—I mean—*really* be truthful?" she whispered.

"It's the *only* way," True whispered back with a reassuring smile.

But Midgie needed proof. "Then tell me I am right—that my clothes *are* wrong—*look* at me, True!" Her voice was desperate.

True looked. Midgie was wearing a gimp two sizes too small, making her look 12, its colors screaming for attention. Inhaling deeply, True said kindly, "Yes, darling, the dress is wrong—but believe me, there is nothing wrong elsewhere. You are growing—truly you are—and your spirit has outgrown that dress!"

It was true. There was a change in Midgie's face. Her eyes were still searching, sometimes filled with fear and confusion. But she no longer looked lost, utterly defenseless. There was a look of discovery, as if she had looked deep inside herself and found a certain strength. And now she was ready to look *outside* herself.

"It's true, isn't it? I am stronger—I can face the truth—and share it! If I can just make Marty see—he just has to love me. Losing him would be second-worst to losing the Lord. Why, I'd be like an elephant without a trunk!"

True laughed. "You aren't going to lose either of them," she promised. "Just let there be no misunderstandings—"

"Let there be no misunderstanding about this, my beautiful brat— your man's hungry. This cow-punching whets the appetite, creates a desire for food, drink—and love!" The man with the appetite had his arms around her.

"Wil North—" she gasped and then stopped. His hug was so tight that she saw seven varieties of stars.

16
Developments at the Double N

⭗

THE FURROW-CANALS finished, the men experimented with allowing some of the little lake's water to trickle down to the gardens and field. The men watched with pride. Midgie watched not at all, her mind devising a way to capture the roaming chickens she had caught sight of. True, while sharing Young Wil's enthusiasm, found her mind taking an unexpected detour in fantasy. The earth-tone water, picking up loose soil in its downward course, turned to silver froth winding and coiling from a laughing waterfall. The scrawny stand of timber changed complexions from sunburned green to crimson-blushed forests climbing up the timberline to where forbidding rock peaks lost themselves in the ragged edge of gold-lined clouds. *Mount Sinai!* The mountain to which Moses had climbed to receive the Ten Commandments. Now his garments in her mind's eye blended with the filmy-white of the clouds obscuring his shining upturned face while below the whole of Israel stood in awe—seeing, hearing, believing . . .

True blinked away the vision, but another took its place: The foothills of home, junction for the five-fingered streams created by melting snows of towering mountains to water the broad valleys below, loomed before her eyes. The bountiful gardens. The endless expanse of cultivated fields. Aunt Chrissy's undisciplined flowers, which Daddy Wil vowed were soon to reach over the rooftop of the two-story house.

Face it, True North, you are homesick. Homesick for the protection and familiarity of the Big House and its beloved occupants.

Family and home. A lump rose to her throat, a lump which dissolved quickly with another startling realization: She was equally homesick for the loving fellowship of her church family. True, she and God had remained in close communion, but didn't He expect more? Something told her that, yes, she had a mission in addition to helping Marty and Midgie, but she wished the Lord would speak up, tell her . . .

The trend of her thoughts was interrupted by a commotion. Midgie was screaming, and with a different quality from when she spotted a mouse or expected to be scalped. She was laughing victoriously. And Marty was laughing with her—*Marty?*—while the dogs went crazy.

A loud squawk told the story even before Midgie yelled, "I got him—I got him—cock-of-the-walk—only rooster in the crowd . . . and the ladies'll follow. I—I—done—did it by myself—and now I can sell those golden eggs—"

True looked up and burst into laughter with the others. Midgie had tolled the feisty rooster to her by using up most of the precious cornseed. But the results were obviously worth the price. When the cock had paused to scratch coaxingly to his harem, Midgie had leaped from a furrow and grabbed him, managing somehow to avoid his deadly spurs. What she *hadn't* avoided was the rush of water released from the lake. She was an absolute mud ball, her hair an inverted mop.

It was a riot. And it was—*Oh, thank You, Lord!*—the very first time the four of them had laughed, genuinely laughed, together . . .

True inhaled deeply of the air, now gloriously a sparkle with bubbles of life. It was all going to work out. One day there would be a rambling structure with an inviting sign reading WELCOME TO THE ABODE OF MR. AND MRS. MARTIN NORTH! And, as if to guarantee that welcome, True, dreaming again, foresaw well-graded roads approaching the ranchhouse . . . corrals . . . barns . . . bunkhouses . . . towering silos. All spick-and-span with whitewash. To the east, looking down on fenced-off hayfields and meadows dotted with thoroughbred stock and cattle grazing in a varicolored mosaic, there would be—

Raising her eyes to the top of the tallest hill of which the terrain boasted, she finished the dream with a dread reality: There at the top was a natural gap through which pioneers had passed. There was now a man-made one, newly scarred, familiar to those who knew the method as a sort of divine-right move employed by the railroad to declare a right-of-way. Unfortunately, the law was on the side of the shareholders. And True's experiences in Atlanta had taught her that ruthless men encountering any resistance with landowners were not against use of force at gunpoint. Unfortunately, too, there were land-owners who believed in fighting fire with fire. That had been the youthful Martin North's downfall. Easily led, he had fallen in with bad company. While her adopted brother in his emerging selfhood saw an opportunity to protect the senior Wilson North's rights, lead-ers of the gang were mercenaries, and knew a scapegoat when they saw one. It was easy to convince him that their Robin Hood tactics were acts of heroism.

What had Marty learned, if anything? Which side was he on now? If only he were less aloof, more approachable! She was tired, tired, *tired*.

That night, after a sponge bath (most of the available water reserved for the disheveled but happy Midgie) and a hearty meal, True snuggled close to Young Wil in the confines of their bandanna-sized bedroom, their only place of privacy. She tried to tell him everything, whis-pering for privacy which the thin walls failed to provide. The gap . . . the feeling about Tillie Caswell and Midgie . . . Marty's meeting with the "beaver hat" stranger . . . and, finally, the surprise appearance of Michael St. John.

"Not sorry you came?" he whispered. But True was fast asleep.

17
Discoveries in Slippery Elm

❧

THE LATE-AUGUST TRIP to town was destined to be hot and sultry. But the sunrise was beautiful. Having left before the pink of dawn, True, Young Wil, Midgie, Marty, and Billy Joe (looking very much like "the Beetle" astride a skimpy-tailed mule) viewed the sunrise in awe from the sun's lavender warning flares until its sleepy golden rays spread over the luxuriant green of native meadows to the even greener glow of scattered grain fields, now taking on a harvest glow. The wagon wheels were surprisingly quiet, as if listening while staggering along the aged pack-trail—so quiet that a lone rabbit ventured out curiously, wriggled his nose in greeting, then scurried back to cover. True wanted to laugh, but Young Wil's hand squeezed her hand to warn silence as the team came to an abrupt halt.

Nobody spoke and, strangely, Midgie did not let out a single whimper. Instead, all eyes followed Wil's pointing finger. Billy Joe had dismounted and crept stealthily alongside the wagon, obviously struggling with a *"Yippee-yea!"*

And small wonder. There beneath the protection of a mushroom-shaped rock stood the most beautiful animal True had ever seen. An enormous shiny-backed bull, a perfect specimen looking carved in the rock, stood motionless, ruminative eyes upon the group. True did not recognize the breed, but she knew the look. The satin-coated beast reminded her of women that Michael St. John's aunt introduced her to at society functions in Atlanta: in doubt as to her social status; arrogant and superior; and all the while fearful and on guard of invaders.

223

"Great-blooded Shorthorn," Billy whispered in near reverence. "Prob'ly a runaway uv some Eastern immigrants—gone wild now—'n—"

Seeming to hear the sounds almost inaudible to human ear, the great animal snorted and pawed the earth, sending showers of debris between himself and his audience. When the dust settled, he was gone.

"I tole you—I tole you," Billy Joe, hoarse with excitement, said over and over. "I'm a-gonna ketch that sucker—I'll find me a way—an' we're boun' on havin' ourselves th' finest herd this side uv th' Ole Miss River. Now as t'how—"

"Ride him in," Young Wil teased, his eyes alive with excitement.

"Or let Midgie here capture him!" Marty grinned.

Oh, how good to hear him speak lightly! Better yet, to note his enthusiasm. There was no opportunity to point out the change to Young Wil. The men were too busy devising schemes to corner the magnificent animal before he was slaughtered for beefsteak or lassoed by some poacher who knew thoroughbred cattle. "Now that you seen queen's evidence, you willin' t'believe me—'n take my word that my plan's boun' on workin'?"

Billy Joe posed the question just as they entered the outskirts of a bruised and battered Slippery Elm, where a bar fight had obviously taken place the night before. True shuddered and slipped her hand into her husband's. The place gave her the creeps—or, as O'Higgin was fond of saying—made possums crawl over her grave! All thoughts of asking the excited foreman of the Double N about his plan were gone. She and Midgie would do their shopping quickly and hope that the men would do likewise. To get out of this so-called town *immediately* was not soon enough! How long did it take to find harvest hands?

Was last night's brawl too much for Tillie Caswell? She glanced at True and Midgie when they entered the store, her eyes vacant.

"Remember us? We're the Norths." It was Midgie who spoke first, reaching out with a small gesture of friendliness to touch the older woman's hand. Tillie's expression remained as blank as that of some store window's mannequin.

True wondered if Mrs. Caswell was reliving some chapter in her past. She wore an outdated cheap satin dress and her tassel-trimmed boots, once so stylish, were run over at the heels. But the pathetic part of her attempt at prettiness was the faded clump of velvet rosebuds tucked into her heavy hair.

Tillie's husband stepped in front of her unceremoniously. "May I be of assistance, ladies? My wife here's poorly today. We run a respectable place, but—" Curly Caswell paused to scratch his shining head where the hair used to grow, "well, I'm guessin' you fine folks have gathered some ain't so legitimate—oughta be burnt t'th' ground 'n them alley cats be scorched all th' way back t'St. Jo. Th' roughhousin' ain't good fer my Tillie—ain't good a'tall. She's been through a heap 'n it left her bundle o' nerves. Any excitement can trigger it—even when it's no relation uv what she's suffered—"

Midgie's face was white. "In Portland?"

"Thereabouts—in a flood, with lootin' 'n shootin' after, whilst she was all-time searching—"

The proprietor was unable to finish whatever he was about to say. Later True was to look back on his words and regret that. But for now she was relieved to see that Tillie was coming around, speaking in broken monosyllables, but present tense, with no reference to the past.

"I feel as weak as water," she said at last. "If I could have a cup of tea?" Quickly she unpinned the roses and dropped them to the floor. "I've a feeling you've come for more of that material. Did you run short? Too bad, but I am out completely. But," her tired eyes brightened almost feverishly, "guess what! We received a shipment of the loveliest dry goods ever—bee balms, scarlet, pink—reminds me of a late summer meadow. Makes you almost drop to your knees and gather in the flowers, praying a bit while you're down there."

Functioning now, she stepped behind the counter and began unrolling bolts. The fabric was every bit as lovely as she described. Excitedly, the two Mrs. Norths made their choices. As Mrs. Caswell's shears snipped away and she tore across the bolt in completion, she said dreamily, "I guess you ladies are making these for the roundup? It's the biggest thing we can boast of here. My husband told me that you planned on roping in some wild horses. Maybe the men can break them that day just before the barbecue?"

True thought of the beautiful bull and hoped he would not fall prey. But, after their near-total isolation, a gathering sounded exciting. It would be like the old days at the Big House or Turn-Around Inn. Tillie, her rational self now, made small talk while assisting with the selection of notions for completing the fiesta dresses.

"*Hola, Señor!*" Tillie said in greeting to a leathery-skinned customer who had entered noiselessly in his beaded moccasins.

Flailing his arms in excitement, the wiry little man began an endless reel of Spanish. Tillie, her voice low and musical, answered in equally rapid sentences. Then she turned to True and Midgie.

"Augie hears that there's work at the Double N. He's of fine character and as loyal as they come. Without him," she smiled, "my passing might go unmourned. Do you want me to tell your men?"

The man had an honest face and clear, dark eyes that could look another person squarely in the eye. His worn clothing spoke of need. "Yes," True and Midgie said simultaneously.

"It will take Mariah's help," True said thoughtfully. "None of us speak Spanish. Which reminds me, Mrs. Caswell, Billy Joe wants her to learn English so badly—"

"I will help her," Tillie said with a note of gladness in her voice. "And I will help Augie here—"

"And we'll *all* help at the ranch!" True was surprised to hear Midgie volunteer. For some reason it made her want to cry.

Young Wil entered. Tillie Caswell introduced Augie, explaining his background and desire to work, and made no effort to conceal her delight when her Mexican friend was signed on for the harvest. Augie was overcome with gratitude, murmuring, "*Gracias, Señor! Gracias, gracias—*"

True was only dimly aware that arrangements were made with the aid of Tillie's translations for Augie to sleep out-of-doors, there being no bunkhouse. Would a temporary shelter of canvas stretched over supporting poles be acceptable? And hay would be the best they had to offer by way of a bed. Young Wil's voice was apologetic, something Augie failed to hear. He was too busy adding to the sum total of his "*Gracias—gracias, gracias*" song of appreciation.

Resolutely, True tried to appear hospitable, but it was as if some irresistible magnet pulled her eyes to where Marty stood engrossed in conversation with a portly man dressed nattily from his proper black suit to his shining patent button-on shoes. His terraced chin showed lack of exercise, as did his pale skin in contrast to Marty's.

For the first time she noted how tanned and fit her brother had become from his hard work and exposure to the sun.

Suddenly a woman appeared from nowhere. "May I have a glass of water, please? This dreadful place is enough to drive one to madness. I shall be happy to bid it goodbye—if my brother and I are fortunate enough to escape with our scalps!" The voice had a metallic ring.

Before accepting the water, the woman touched her elaborately coiffured yellow hair. It glittered with some sort of glaze, totally unlike the satiny sheen of True's—where, Young Wil said, the stars were entangled.

Tillie Caswell obligingly took the almost-untasted water from the other woman's jewel-frosted fingers. "It is nice to see you once more, Mrs. St. John—Mrs. North, I believe you met Mrs. St. John's husband?"

Mrs. St. John! Michael's wife! Taken by surprise, True found herself tongue-tied, quite capable of committing some dreadful social blunder. Worse, she was staring, actually staring at this obviously wealthy person, no older than herself but already showing symptoms of middle-age curves, corseted into an expensive green frock, which was no greener than her cold eyes.

True was never sure whether either of them acknowledged the introduction. The woman—had Mrs. Caswell called her Felice?—turned away. "I do wish my husband would give up this silly notion of attempting to civilize this country—railroad or not—"

Tillie Caswell colored furiously. "Come now, Mrs. St. John—"

True heard no more. Midgie, missing the encounter by stepping outside, was walking toward Marty. Marty terminated the conversation immediately and motioned her back to where Young Wil was talking with a small knot of other men. Probably recruits gathered from their previous trip to Slippery Elm, True guessed.

The guess was correct. Marty, seemingly composed, nodded approval of "Pig Iron," a giant with an engaging grin but appearing to possess more brawn than brains. Pig Iron motioned for "Tex," a lad who looked as if he belonged in grammar school but was amazingly well versed in the ways of wheat. "Tough work, raisin' wheat—feller's gotta keep his eyes peeled on th' elements 'n bugs. My ole gran'pa use' ta say, 'Now, Junior, lis'sen t'th' Injuns. Wheat's gotta have a

lake with a mouth fer waterin' it—soil with ears that'll screech when
it's thirstin'—'n a windbreak uv trees that set there 'n watch, fer
protection from storms 'n fer reaching up t'th' Great White Spirit.
Golly-gee, it's work, but me, now I need work 'n there's somethin'
'twixt my brain 'n them yeller heads uv ripe wheat—you ready fer
threshin'?"

Young Wil looked amused. "The wheat has to be cut first."

"Yeah, 'n cured—then comes th' flailin'—beatin' 'til yore eyeballs
drop outa their sockets—"

Tex's voice had risen. He lowered it as if trying to avoid the adolescent crack he had learned to anticipate. But the crack came anyway, comically and uncontrollably. His unshaven face flushed, his
bravado gone, Tex looked as if he had been caught stealing sheep.
Clearing his throat, the boy tried to make amends for an imagined
transgression.

"Mr. North—Mr. Norths—I mean, uh, Mr's. North—I want you
t'be knowin' I ain't seen a lotta years, but they've been hard 'uns an'
learnt me a heap. I'll work hard 'n," he gulped, "I'm a nothin'-but-
th'-truth maniac—honest. 'N that ain't all, I brung a new strain uv
seed from th' east—hardier—"

"No need to keep talking, Tex," Marty said briskly. "You're on as
far as I'm concerned. Wil?"

Young Wil extended his hand. "Indeed. Welcome to the Double N!"

Excitedly, as if afraid that to stop talking would cancel the handshake agreement, Tex explained that his wheat could be planted right
after the first frost but before the first freeze. Red winter wheat.

"I'm glad you like your work," Wil said with a pokerfaced wink at
True. "Our foreman may need help with rounding up livestock—"

The boy was off like a cannon. "What a day!" Wil laughed. True
nodded, knowing that their meanings were different.

18
Secrets of the Harvest

❧

An EVENTFUL MONTH passed, 30 days of dawn-to-dusk labor for Wil, Marty, and the hired hands, including a "long drink of water" (as Billy Joe described him), friend of Tex's called "Slim" and, to True's dismay, the man with the withered arm that Mr. Caswell had called "Gun Slinger." Young Wil confided that he too distrusted the man but that he knew a lot about stock and cattle. Billy Joe had put him through the third-degree on longhorns, shorthorns, Holsteins, Jerseys, Ayreshires, and all the in-between mixed breeds of cattle. As for horses, Gun Slinger used to ride in a rodeo, to which the withered arm was a testimonial. A wild burro had rolled over on him—

True listened and prayed that everything would work out. In fact, she suspected that she kept God busy with her constant talk as she and Midgie worked their once-soft hands to the bone cooking and delivering meals to the fields at midday, since there was no pause for lunch. She and Midgie took turns at taking the food to the men— their only chance to keep alive the fact that they had husbands. They saw the North brothers only by lamplight at breakfast and supper.

Aunt Chrissy had done a commendable job at teaching True the art of cooking, but Midgie had had no training at all. True marveled at her, cooking as she did, awkwardly at first, but—under the supervision of True and Mariah—systematically, with no wasted effort and with every detail carried out to perfection. "I could feed a regiment," she beamed with pride. True believed her.

The only breaks in the strenuous routine were the fittings of the fiesta dresses which Mariah's nimble fingers somehow managed to

229

stitch together between the other demands on her days, plus Mrs. Caswell's weekly calls. If Mariah was to learn English, she must have regular lessons, Tillie declared, and besides, the trip got her away from the confines of Slippery Elm.

"Mariah's a fast learner," she declared. "Has a tuned-in ear. Do you know if she plays a musical instrument?"

True did not know. But she did wonder at the way Midgie's pale face went even paler at such a simple question. She welcomed Midgie's suggestion that the two of them take along a lunch for themselves when they delivered the noon meal to the men the following day. There was so much to talk about, and the few minutes' rest would do them good.

Beneath a little grove of elms, they spread the still-warm sourdough biscuits with blackberry marmalade from Grandma Mollie's pantry. The jerked beef tasted saltier than usual, as if Billy Joe had dunked it into the salt barrel for curing instead of smoking it slowly over a hickory woodfire. Midgie chewed on a piece, made a face, and spat it onto the ground. "This stuff needs soaking before cooking with dried beans," she said. Her face looked wretchedly white, as if she were going to be ill.

Small wonder. True herself felt as if during the past few weeks they had been traveling around the world—uphill all the way. She was tired, so tired, as if every step would be her last. Poor Midgie. She was less accustomed to the rural way of life, and certainly not this style. True had written cheerfully to Aunt Chrissy and Daddy Wil about their tribulations, making them sound like a game, but admitting that she would be happy for them all when the game was over. If they could see the overwhelming exhaustion on Midgie's face, they would find her accounts less amusing. For the first time, True noted that the other girl's legs were swollen above her heavy shoes, the ones she called "combat boots."

Before she could comment, Midgie lay back—head pillowed on hands laced together behind her—and moaned slightly. "It would take more than food and drink to restore me," she said in a small voice. "Physical strength just won't keep me going—"

True's heart filled with admiration and compassion. "I know, darling, and I am so proud of you. You have overtaxed your body. Only your will, heart, and purpose have sustained you."

"Keep watch, will you, True sweetie? I couldn't run if we were attacked by Indians or a pack of wolves. I feel as if life were tracking me down—watching me grow more helpless with every day—"

"You should have told me, Midgie—drink this water, close your eyes and rest."

Midgie gulped with an effort and returned the half-full glass to True. "I'll obey all except the *resting*. You watch and let me talk."

True began to gather up the crumbs. Any smell of food *could* invite a bear. Considering the possibility, she hurried—then stopped. Midgie's story was too incredible to allow for anything but listening.

"You know something's wrong between me and Marty—Marty and me. It all started before we married, and I thought if I tried hard enough I could prove myself—make him love me the way I thought he did be-be-before he found out the truth. But I guess I killed his love—killed it dead—only I didn't know—honest, True, I'm not a bad woman like he says—"

"Marty said *that*?" True dropped the canteen from feelingless fingers and mopped at the puddle of water with her cotton petticoat.

A tear slipped from beneath Midgie's closed lids. "Oh, I wish God could take us back—let us live some of our lives over. I wish that being 'born again' really meant another chance—"

"It does, darling—it does—you have to believe that! God does not require that we do that, just ask forgiveness and *He* wipes the slate clean—"

"Then why won't Marty do that, too?"

"I think," said True slowly, "that you will have to explain the situation instead of beating yourself unnecessarily—then we can talk. And, Midgie, remember that I love you no matter what the problem is. I also trust you—and find it impossible to believe that you have committed some heinous crime. Tell me only as much as you feel like—"

"I will tell you all of it—it's not that much, really—just a terrible, terrible misunderstanding—and me being so stupid—and lonely. Now, I ain't—I'm not excusing myself. But I've got me this weakness—about playing a guitar—folks say I have talent—"

Relieved, True laughed. "That's no weakness—"

"I guess," Midgie said slowly, opening her eyes to squint sightlessly into the sky, "you better let me finish—it gets worse."

It did. Listening, True was transported to Portland's back-street business section, where men with tobacco-stained teeth and no morals catcalled to any passing woman without hesitation. After all, no "lady" was going to venture down Rum Road without knowin' man did not live by bread alone. Ignoring them, the girl hurried into the door bearing the sign WANTED: YOUNG WOMAN PLAYING STRINGS. Summoning courage, she knocked and was admitted to a room with shades drawn. At first only the woman's thick, homely lips painted a violent red stood out, then the myriads of flashing sequins, lending an air of tawdry elegance to the sweeping folds of her black taffeta dress. A rush of footsteps said that they were not alone, but there was no one in sight as the woman led her into a large room with hob-nail-scarred floors. Scattered tables and tops supporting upturned chairs spoke of night trade, as did a battered piano, now idle, in the corner. Stale tobacco smoke and the sour-mash smell of a bar were enough to make one retch. But a girl couldn't be choosy if she wanted to break into the music business, could she? The opera house was hardly a starting place. She could gain some experience here and then—

"Whatcha lookin' fer, missy? Don't look dry behind th'ears."

"I—I—came about the sign. I play the guitar—"

The woman licked her lips, looked her over from head to toe, and nodded. "You'll do—had any experience?"

"No—but," eagerly, "I'm willing to learn!"

Denver Belle, her name was, rubbed fat palms together. "So much the better, missy—startin' tonight with th' strings—then, we'll see jest how well your act goes over 'fore—"

The girl heard no more above the tom-tom of her heart. Neither did her inexperienced eye recognize that the woman had a heart of pure flint, the temper of a rabid skunk, and the morals of a she-coyote.

"Now, I provide a necessary bizness, missy. Now, they's them psalm singers wearin' black hats 'n shirt collars on back'ards what'd have me horsewhipped jest fer givin' sweet young thangs like you a chance—fer gettin' on in this world. Better git them clothes stitched up tighter, uv course, 'n drop that Sunday-school drawstring neckline down over th' shoulders—git up there sang, knock 'em dead."

That was the first night. And sing she did. Even the men at the bar stopped their raucous talk and listened, yelling, "More, more!"

For a week everything went well. In her ecstatic state, Midgie paid no attention to the clientele and was oblivious to the other girls who must have "boarded there," since they seemed so much a part of the place, swishing up and down the stairs the way they did.

Midgie went on with her part-time job of helping Young Wil with his paperwork, and also continued seeing Marty. Young Wil, seeing that they were becoming serious about each other, encouraged them both. And the relationship grew, drifting into a sort of "understanding." Life was beautiful, and so was Midgie. She glowed in the warmth of being in love, something she was sure in her simple heart would be doubled when her beloved discovered that she had found success— real success—that she was a celebrity bound for the stage. She held the secret close to her heart for just the right moment. Then she would reveal her talents.

But the revelation came sooner than expected, the night of the Sod-Busters' Ball. Midgie could remember little of the preparations, she said, except Denver Belle's frenzied state of preparing for the big night when patrons would expect "quality goods." The rooms went wild with colored streamers and the scent of cheap cologne, which all but asphyxiated her as she practiced intricate strumming and fretting of the guitar, saving her voice for the performance. Denver Belle's attitude began to change. She screamed, cursed, and threatened, her face as white as the pottery washbasin, her eyes glinting with ambition that amounted to downright evil. Midgie had known all along that it was a less than ideal place for her to be; but a girl with no stage experience couldn't expect to go looking down her nose, could she? But this night she felt—well, threatened somehow. Her uneasiness grew each time her employer's eyes met hers—cold, calculating, and as hard as black diamonds in a way that drew the upper and lower lids together.

And then the crowd. The terrible crowd of leering men—full-bearded prospectors, filthy buckskin-clad trappers, and some decently dressed businessmen with uneasy glances darting back and forth to the door as if hoping not to be recognized.

"You're on!" Denver Belle hissed in Midgie's ear. "But first git some paint on that innocent face. This is your big night!"

There was no time to protest. No time either to put her blouse back onto her shoulders when the woman jerked it even lower than usual. Midgie made up her mind then and there that this would be her last night. But first she must fulfill her obligation. She must sing. Sing as

she had never sung before. Who knew who would be in that crowd?
Hadn't Denver Belle said this was her big night?

And then it happened. Midway of her performance, her eyes caught
sight of a table in the corner where five strangers sat. Quieter than
the others, they stared at her unbelievably, the one in the shadows
glowering. A regular powder keg, sitting there waiting for a fuse . . .

He found one. A drunken patron leaped to his feet and staggered
forward to mount the step to the stage, where he grabbed at her thin
blouse, tearing it to bare her flesh. "Ain't she purdy, boys?" And with
that Midgie screamed as his filthy face neared hers.

The shadow at the table was no shadow any longer. Taking substance, the man leaped forward, jamming a gun into her attacker's
ribs. "Move and I'll blow you apart! Let go of the woman I'm going
to marry!"

"Marty." True could only whisper the word.

"Marty—and with him some railroad men. Maybe some he'd been
in trouble with, maybe not. I—I was no longer aware of my surroundings—except that everybody went crazy. Marty's friends came to help.
Somebody shot out the lights. And me not helping just sitting there
wondering how I'd ever make Marty understand how nothing like
this had happened before—and—and that I wasn't one of the madam's
(yes, that's what she was) 'girls' who swarmed out of the rooms, half
dressed—"

Midgie burst into uncontrollable sobs, near hysteria at the memory
of the nightmare. True wished for the water spilled from the canteen
as she wiped the girl's feverish brow with the still-damp petticoat,
soothing her all the while. "Oh, my darling, you know Marty would
never think that. All you had to do was explain—"

"He—he wouldn't believe me—" Midgie whispered brokenly. "He
said he—could never trust me again—that I couldn't possibly have
been so blind—and that I deceived him—"

"Perhaps in a way you did. You should have told him, Midgie, but
we all make mistakes. Someday I will tell you about my trip to Atlanta—but for now—"

True paused, suddenly furious at Marty's behavior. "What right
had *he* to throw the first stone?" And then, "Did you tell Young Wil?"

Midgie was calming down, but there was defeat in her young face.
"Yes, and he called Marty a whippersnapper—said he would talk to

him—and I guess I'll never know if—if Marty married me out of duty—or because of what Young Wil said or did—or, oh, True, do I dare keep hoping that he does love me—and is suffering from what Young Wil called wounded pride?"

"The latter, probably," True answered, wanting to add that she wondered at this point why Midgie gave a fig for his pride. "You have been a wonderful wife. You've done everything possible—"

"Even had my hair bleached because he—Marty kept saying how pretty your blonde hair was. But—but about the child I—I'm supposed to—"

"Give yourselves time, Midgie. Babies wait to be wanted sometimes."

"Wanted?" Midgie's voice was hoarse. "*Wanted*? When he—he never touches me? Just once—on our wedding night. I—I feel so unclean—unwanted. If—if I ever conceived, he—Marty'd disclaim it—oh, True!"

19
Sorting the Wheat from the Chaff

꘎

THE WEATHER BEHAVED. The few dark clouds which bellowed
threateningly withheld their rain and there were no heavy dews to
sour the fallen grain. Sun-ripened into golden sheaves, the wheat was
ready for threshing now. Some of the choice crop would be saved for
seed and some ground into flour for home use, as staple groceries were
hard to come by. The hay was sweet enough for fodder, Tex declared,
fine for livestock, "providin' we save back 'nuf fer us stayers-oners
t'have fer beddin' down." The youngster planned to remain? True had
made an attempt to catch Young Wil's eye but failed because Tex
was going nonstop with next year's plans for his new strain of wheat.

"Back home we wuz always callin' wheat th' 'worry crop,' but
added onto th' veg'tables, eggs, milk, 'n stuff, uh body kin do right
well, sure 'nuf—'n that ain't countin' bringin' in them horses—"

True wished that her brother were half as enthusiastic about the
red winter wheat whose case Tex pleaded so hard. But Marty appeared
determinedly indifferent. It was almost as if he had set a no-win goal
designed to prove himself a failure—including his marriage.

The morning that threshing was to begin, True left her breakfast
unfinished in order to join her husband before Marty came outside.
She wanted to exchange hurried impressions of the situation. Would
the year help Marty get his life put together? Get his values straight?
Recognize sacrifice, opportunity, and responsibility when they stared
him in the face? Or would he continue to look the other way until
something bigger than all their efforts brought him to his senses?

But the moment was too precious to waste on words. Dawn was creeping slowly up in the east to transform the world into a fairyland of beauty. The air was sweet-breathed with hay and woodsmoke of the early-risers. Somewhere toward the lean-to barn Midgie's rooster announced that the last star had twinkled out. True reached out a hand to touch her husband's. The way he clutched it, lacing his work-worn fingers through hers, said that he too was reliving the fairyland of pantomimes of their childhood. Only the two of them knew that wood nymphs danced among the columbines at this sacred time of day, granting wishes and endowing children with magic passwords. But whatever magic lay in the lap of this God-given morn, True held no illusion about the raw reality behind the closed door.

"Have we made a mistake?" True whispered out of context.

"You may have—*I* didn't!" Young Wil declared, pretending to misunderstand. "I got myself the kind of wife every man needs—one who can stand the wear and tear of daily companionship and put up with my moods without being irritable and snappy—one with the saving grace of humor—"

"Wil North! One would have to have that to put up with you! Here we are allowed 30 seconds—"

Wil sighed. "And you want to talk about Marty," he said tiredly. "So let's face it, I am getting weary with our brother's seeing us as intruders. As a doctor, I see him as a patient with a weak heart and high blood pressure! Our coming here should have been therapeutic. Just seeing what a perfect pair we are under any circumstances ought to spur him on." He pulled her gently to him and talked over her head, his eyes watching the door for Marty. "After all, any dumbbell can get himself married. It's *staying* married that proves one's mettle."

True nodded against the roughness of his denim shirt while a vision of Midgie's white face floated before her . . . the steadiness of her gaze, behind which there was always the hint of tears. She would keep her marriage promises at any cost. How reverently she had repeated her wedding vows, although her heart must have been breaking.

"I talked with Midgie—or listened—" True began.

A creak of the door said they had only a moment alone remaining. Wil grabbed at it, speaking rapidly. "Midgie has done all she knows to do to save their marriage from the scrap heap—but I do wish she would learn the persuasive value of a laugh against his sulks—and stop knuck-

ling under to the ingrate! I am unable to get through his thick skull—
well," he shifted quickly as Marty's footsteps neared, "we outgrew the
wood nymphs, sweetheart, and Jesus took their place! Ask Him to walk
alongside us today—today will be no playhouse."

"You know I will! You, Marty, and all the others. Is—is—I can
hardly bring myself to say the name—how is Gun Slinger doing?"

Young Wil laughed as he brushed her brow with a kiss and swung
astride his horse. "Relax—no need for the name anymore. I said something of the same and he confided it was a name he'd dreamed up
himself—something to improve, in his mind, his self-image. Not that
I blame him much for a switch. Gervinus is hard to handle—so we
call the man Gerry. Slinger's his last name."

"Which doesn't weaken his aim, you'd better believe," Marty said
almost to himself as he bridled his horse. "He can shoot if need be."

Young Wil's head jerked erect. "You knew him, Marty?"

"Knew *of* him. That bother you?" Marty flung over his shoulder.

Young Wil made no reply. Instead, he was looking where True's
finger pointed to a lone rider silhouetted against the painted sky of
the gap.

After that, True made several sightings of the man. It unnerved her
to see him sitting there motionlessly, surveying the vast ranch. There
was nothing to arouse suspicion except his very presence. Once she
and Midgie had ridden to the gap to check out the newly gouged earth,
where stakes waving red flags were driven. True recalled her concern.
Then the morning sun shot up through a fleece of clouds to dye the
sloping hillside with radiance and transform their cabin into a habita-
tion of gold. Was the rider considering robbery or poaching? Could he
be connected with the railroad? Or was her imagination simply working overtime? Midgie had enough on her mind, so True made no mention of the stranger's reappearance time and time again.

September brought harvest to a close. Trees, which nobody realized were there, burned with color. Midgie's hens grew too fat and
lazy to forage for themselves, so content were they with her oversized
helpings of wheat. The fall garden flourished, necessitating the building of a tightly woven fence to keep out deer and rabbits, who ignored
Midgie's NO TRESPASSING sign. September also brought the fiesta
closer. Plans were underway when unexpected company came.

True and Midgie were canning tomatoes one sultry afternoon when a horse whinnied a warning from the hastily constructed corral. A light breeze sprang up, causing dust to swirl and eddy around the approaching buggy and muffle the labored breathing of Tillie Caswell's aging mare. In spite of the dust, the kindly woman's clothing suggested a soap advertisement. Her starched petticoats rustled as she hurried up the little path that True and Midgie had bordered with zinnias, now at their peak of brilliance. Making a megaphone of her hands, Mrs. Caswell called:

"Yoo-hoo, yoo-hoo! I've brought a guest—down, Tonsil! Down, Lung—let's not drive the Reverend away!"

The dogs looked at her in tawny-eyed reproach, sniffed the Reverend gentleman's pant cuffs and ministerial black frock coat, then went back to the holes they had dug in search of cool, damp earth.

"Mercy! Those two have grown. What do they plan to be when they grow up?" Mrs. Caswell laughed with more feeling than True could recall.

"Shepherds," True laughed back. "Do come in—it is nice to have callers."

Midgie hurried to set out the tea service, one of her wedding gifts, after accepting Mrs. Caswell's kiss and acknowledging an introduction to Reverend Randall. True hugged Tillie Caswell, thinking that her friend looked exceedingly fit, then turned her attention to her companion. Reverend Randall appeared to be middle-aged, although the white hair bushing from beneath the brim of his broad felt hat added to his years. He wore a broad black tie which, even after looping into a generous bow, flowed over his shoulder like a scarf. Reflection of the afternoon sun on his glasses gave him an owlish look, an effect which would have tickled the ribs of a stoic. But his handshake was warm and firm, his manners impeccable, and his speech carefully correct.

"Randy—" Tillie Caswell's face reddened at the slip of her tongue, a slip she corrected quickly, "Reverend Randall and I once knew one another in Portland. He still brings me news when he comes this way to conduct a revival. He's one of the last of the circuit riders."

True took his hat while he mentioned his denomination—a matter to which she paid little attention. A minister of any faith was a joy to have in her household. She told him so with heartfelt warmth.

"Oh, yes, I feel a need to make the rounds—conducting memorial services for those who have passed on, performing marriages, and making an effort to mend together the broken relationships. It tears at my heart, you know, seeing couples marry only to unmarry without regard to the tragic consequences to their children—and society—"

In the small kitchen a cup clattered to the floor and there followed the unmistakable sound of splintering glass. Above the swish of the broom, True was sure she heard a muffled sob. She longed to rush into the kitchen, put her arms around Midgie, tell her everything would be all right—that the cup could be replaced. But, even as she covered the moment by chatting with the guests, True wondered if the softhearted Midgie would accept a replacement for the original. She probably was as shattered as the cup, seeing the breakage as the beginning of the end, imagining herself to be one of the "unmarrieds" soon, her heart chafing at their caller's mention of the city where it all began . . .

"So," Mr. Randall was saying, "I envisioned the Double N as a possible dude ranch—"

"Oh, far from it," True managed to smile. "We hope to turn the fertile acreage into a real ranch one of these days—you know, good grain, thoroughbred cattle and stock—"

Mrs. Caswell took over from there. What fine folks the Norths were! How they had enriched her life and the lives of others they had chanced to meet already! Then followed a lengthy discussion of Mariah's progress with the English language. Blessings, all of them. Much to accomplish here if they all worked together. Randy did understand? The minister was nodding. Yes, Yes—time to sort the wheat from the chaff, so to speak. And, yes, yes, he'd love to attend the roundup . . .

Midgie was quiet over tea and thick slices of apple-prune cake. And her smile was far away when Reverend Randall broke the news that he was acquainted with the senior Norths in Centerville and had brought a package of books they ordered: all kinds—medical encyclopedias, educational textbooks, new Bibles—yes, yes, all kinds.

"Don't cry inside, Midgie," True wanted to whisper. And then she saw that Midgie's eyes were fastened on the gap. This time the horseman galloped down the hill a piece, stopped with a suddenness that threw the animal on its haunches, then turned and galloped away. Uncanny indeed!

20
The Roundup

❧

"NOW THAT THE grain's finished, I suppose you'll be letting the hands go?" Marty asked of Wil the day the wind-rowed hay was tossed into mows and covered against approaching winter. He looked as if the question were important to him—as if he too wanted to leave.

Young Wil, busily saddling the roan, turned to catch his brother-in-law's eye. "Isn't it time you made the decisions, Marty? The Double N was supposed to be your project—yours and Midgie's. I suggest that you look around, see what's to be done, and do it before letting the men go, regardless of the shortage of funds."

True, washing dishes, placed them noiselessly in the drainer in order to hear Marty's answer. She was sorry to hear Billy Joe's input. Welcome as his wisdom was, his suggestions were often ill-timed.

"Let 'em go, man? You gott a be loco—what with them horses we got corralled up yonder ready t'brang down fer th' breakin' 'n matin'—"

True's heart missed a beat. So some of the animals were penned, gradually getting to know the human race before being herded into civilization. This was news—with more to come, she supposed. Not that Young Wil intended leaving her out; time simply ran out.

"Not t'mention th' cows 'n that bawlin' bull. Th' critters is gettin' a little less spooked if them trespassers 'ud keep their distance. Marty, my lad, they's gonna be a iron horse passin' this way 'n th' likes o'you ain't a-gonna stop it. Now, now, none o'that sass!" Billy Joe wagged a warning finger in Marty's angry red face. "I dunno what y'got agin' th' rails—long as they don' go cuttin' our fences 'n lettin' them valu-

241

able herds stampede—you got somebody on th' lookout? Don' answer that—guess I'm a-knowin'—an' you got th' unmitigated gall t'ast iffen we let th' few men we got go? Shucks! You gotta be plum sick—"

"I'm not listening! You're like the rest of them—think I'm a nothing! You and your whole pack can go straight—" Marty's voice had risen angrily.

Billy Joe jerked erect. "Keep a civil tongue in yore mouth, I'm a-warnin' you, son. I'm only tryin' t'help. After all, yore th' bossman, 'cording t'Mr. Wil. So, straighten up 'n *be* one. Shore, shore, y'can fire me—fire th' whole crew, but y'better be knowin' it's a sick world out there. Iffen I wuz a young man with half yore opportunity 'n brawn—well," he sighed, "never mind, what cain't be changed, cain't. But afore y'let us go, best be considerin' th' vast majority figger it's uh whole heap easier t'rob, steal, murder—whatever it takes—than do sweatin' labor. One uv th' coyotes'll knife you 'n take that herd well as yore wife less'n you larn t'lower that voice 'n raise yore sight!"

Young Wil's comment was an understatement of what he must be feeling. "Think about it, Marty. He's right, you know. I understand the railroad's hiring on men, so the powers must be sure the contract is in the making—maybe signed. Better hold off letting our men go. Pig Iron's loyalty is without question, and he can do the work of ten. Tex is as well-versed in the ways of wheat as he claimed. Slim and Slinger—well, there's no reason to question their morals, and as far as handling horses goes, they've proven their skill—Augie's a marvel—"

"'N me, now, I vowed t'brang down that bellowin' bull, 'n by jiminy, I'm a-gonna—yep, yep, yep, so hurry them dogs along fer herdin'. Time they paid fer their board 'n keep. As fer th' heifers, they're boun' on follerin'—one o'them oddities uv nature, ain't it now, how purdy womenfolk knows us strong leaders? Th' Lord knowed what He wuz doin' when He created Adam powerful 'nuf t'go losin' uh rib without lettin' it cripple 'im up! Soooo, Mr. Marty, sir, what 'bout it—gonna keep me on?"

Marty made no direct response. Instead, he swung expertly astride the sleek chestnut mare and said, "Let's go."

"He *has* made a decision," True whispered, turning a thankful face heavenward. Then, wiping her hands—reddened from oversoaking in the lye-soap lather—she turned and all but bumped into Midgie. How much had she overheard? Enough, her white face said, so her words came as no surprise:

"Poor Marty. What a dreadful way to start such a beautiful morning! We—we had a fight—"

"Good!"

"Good?"

True nodded. "You've tried all else. Maybe standing up to him will do him good, Midgie."

Midgie's face said otherwise. "He said some ugly things—about me—that I—I had lost my pride—didn't care how I looked—but he was right—"

"Midgie, stop putting yourself down! Marty had no right—"

But the white-faced girl was not listening. "It's true that my hair's awful—half black, half-yellow from the peroxide—and it's true that I've gained some weight. I let all the tight dresses out—the ones he hated me in—but now they're tight again—"

True remembered the swollen legs. "Midgie," she suggested, "have Wil check you over. He is a doctor, you know."

Later True wondered how Midgie would have answered had Mariah not arrived, her face aglow with ill-concealed pride. And with good cause! Behind her, where the three boys used to ride before becoming "cowboys," were the three fiesta dresses, more spectacularly beautiful than True had imagined—and the first new garments that any of the women had owned in what seemed like forever.

October first—the day of the fiesta so looked forward to by so many, most of whom, True realized with a jolt, were strangers to the hosts. Undoubtedly that was the cause for the weak feeling in her middle, the sort of gnawing dread. It was understandable—the few inhabitants being so widely separated in this vast area which for the most part was unclaimed—that they would have met so few of them. What she failed to understand was the seeming lack of interest in neighborliness, their suspicious attitudes, and their lack of desire for improving the situation when there was a need for roads, schools, and churches. Her mind bolted ahead on an investigative journey as to why no church.

Thought of a church was like rubbing the magic ring. From around the bend of the narrow trail the Reverend Randall appeared like the Arabian Nights Tale genie. If possible, he looked even more likely to challenge the risibilities of other human beings: same black Stetson, same oversized frock. But, oh, it was too much—his wearing rubber hip boots (revealed by the lifted folds of the black material) in order to avoid the dust! "Dry land fishing," it must be called here, True thought, stifling a giggle. Then, remembering her manners, she ran out to offer assistance, for the good man was as heavily laden as a back-peddler. His Bible, a large basket, and—what was this? Fish! Real fish, beautiful rainbow trout, the first she had seen since leaving home. So he *had* been fishing!

"Come—let me help you!" True urged with starry-eyed excitement as she grabbed the string of trout which would pass inspection even back in Centerville, where they were so plentiful.

"More in the basket," Reverend Randall panted, "lots more. May be needing loaves and fishes, according to all reports—already on their way. 1 passed some resting in the groves—travel for miles, you know, this being the once-a-year custom, as I guess Tillie and Mariah explained." Guests, she supposed he meant, not fish!

"Where on earth did you find these—and how in these parts?" True asked in admiration. "I would hardly have expected a fish to know how to swim around here, even if there were water—"

The travel-weary man dropped to the ground, removed his hat, and wiped his sweating brow. "I always come—only this year it was lonely, camping out beneath the stars without my friend Artemis. We always spent a week just sitting on the bank of the stream that few know about—yonder about, oh, say, 30 miles or so—sometimes talking, sometimes speculating on the Next World, and," he chuckled, "sort of hoping the fish wouldn't interrupt us by biting. But," he dreamed on, "they always did—God's way of reminding us that we're not Up There yet. Ever wonder what it's going to be like?"

"I guess we all do sometimes," True admitted. "But I've decided it makes no great difference as long as I and my household are there together, sitting at the Lord's table."

"You are wise, very wise for your age. But," his eyes roamed the illimitable spaces overhead, "with Artemis gone on, I find myself wondering what he knows that I don't—sort of looking forward to following to see if flowers have the same fragrance and birds sing the same songs. They should have learned *something* on this earth. Sitting out there all alone this past week, I kept thinking of all the Creator has given us down here, all the beauties that too many fail to see, and I got to wondering if they would see them Up There either. Maybe the blind will stay blind, refusing to see the light in both places. But I think it's going to be twice as nice when this spirit's no longer hampered by a body—that is, when my work's all done. Which reminds me, it's my job to fry the fish."

True laughed delightedly. "I'm sure you will have no competition, although the men have the barbecue pits dug and the beef has been giving out mouth-watering smells throughout the night." She pointed to a mound where a thin spiral of smoke rose, source of the tantalizing aroma of hickory-smoked beef below the bed of coals.

The minister sat up with an effort, massaged his legs, helped himself to a shovelful of coals, and kindled his own fire. "Folks gather early. They like to watch the sunset, and," he wiped his watering eyes that smoke had filled when a frolicsome whirlwind whipped at his fire, "they like inhaling the special ozone that only the wideopen spaces have to offer. I always take care of the Lord's work while the food cooks; soaks in better than on a full stomach—"

"You mean," True found herself reaching for words, "there's to be a prayer meeting, a sermon—or?"

"All of those—maybe some baptizing up in the slough. It happens sometimes. Some want their babies dedicated. Some want to be married. And would you believe there are those who want their animals blessed? Right or wrong, I draw the line there."

True grew increasingly excited. What fun to entertain and have absolutely no idea of what to expect at her own house! Hers? It occurred to her then that Midgie had failed to make an appearance. She must check. But Mariah and her excited brood arrived on pack mules, the only draft animals strong enough to bear the burden of her pots and pans, tons of paper streamers, extra lanterns, and mysterious boxes.

"*Buenos dias, Señora,*" Mariah called out with brown eyes dancing. "*Mis*—my—*flores*—roses bloom brighter seence you come—yes?" She held out a lovely bouquet which, judging by her gestures, were intended for the ladies' hair—scarlet, yellow-gold, baby-pink, and pure white. "*Senora* will pardon pleese—I speek so leetle *ingles*—English—"

"The roses are beautiful, Mariah, and you manage English far better than I manage Spanish." Nevertheless, True was relieved to see Tillie Caswell's buggy rounding the bend.

Mrs. Caswell looked fresh out of a mail-order catalog, and her wealth of dark hair wound becomingly around her head, giving the lady-proprietor a regal look. The blank look once dominating her face was erased by a wholesome smile. What had happened to change her?

There was no time to think on it further, as the practical Tillie

had taken over, talking first in Spanish to Mariah, then remembering to address her in English. The pair worked with feverish enthusiasm which was highly contagious. True found herself looking forward more and more to the event while feeling, strangely, that it was
out of her hands. The gnawing sense of near-dread lodged around her
heart and refused to dissolve. How could one be excited and afraid at
the same time? she wondered as her feet took her back and forth to
the kitchen storing the Mexican chili beans (which must have been
prepared in a washpot, judging by the amount), greasing the potatoes
for baking whole in the coals, and scrubbing the tin plates left behind by previous occupants of the shack.

Once she knocked on the door leading to the bedroom that Midgie
and Marty occupied. There was no answer, but the sound of tearing
cloth was reassuring. Midgie was putting her hair up on rags, something she never dared do when Marty was around. The men, of course,
had been working at rounding up the horses and cows in preparation
for the big drive (carefully timed, Tillie told her, for an hour before
sunset). There was plenty of time, yet Tillie and Mariah seemed to
rush, as if they too felt a sense of urgency. True wanted to help Midgie
dress, and there was need for a dishpan of garden greens for salad.

Stepping out the back door, she inhaled the deeply wood-smoked
fragrance of the Indian-summer air. October had suddenly awakened
to soften the sun's rays and bring the bees humming back as if it were
spring. The sun was still warm enough to bake sweetness from the
stubble, the sky swept clean by a light breeze. Against its intermi-
nable blue, three black-enameled birds circled as if looking for a landing field. Crows? No, they were too large. Not hawks either. The color
was wrong and their wingspread too wide. Lower and lower they
circled, swooping down at a point just below the gap. There, caught
in bright sunlight, their heads revealed their identity. Buzzards! How
could the vultures hope to find anything nonliving on such a day?
Had some wild beast killed a domestic animal—or—?

Poachers! The word came from the nowhere of True's mind, causing a shudder that rivaled a physical pain to run the gamut of her
being. Hurriedly she finished picking the fresh vegetables from the
fall selection, then joined Tillie and Mariah. There she stopped,
awestricken. The transformation was amazing. The entire yard, and
on beyond in all directions, had taken on the air of a carnival. Lanterns, strung on wires overhead and winding through the fences, cre-

ated a million rainbows, and far to the right, toward the gap, men were nailing together rough boards which would serve as bleachers.

"My Curly closed up early," Tillie said with pride, "and took charge over there, bringing with him two neighbors and," she laughed, "all the guests at the inn—lots of railroad men, including the noted Mr. and Mrs. St. John—"

"Michael." The name came out flat and unbidden.

Tillie Caswell's eyes bored into hers. "So you two *had* met—I just had the feeling." A faint smile twisted her mouth. "Forgive me, True dear. It's a fault of mine—getting 'feelings,' one of them being," she lowered her voice, "one that concerns me gravely—a certain sense that your brother's suffering from an inner seething, a kind of protest. But against what? There I go—" Tillie spread her fingers out as if for counting. "But I suspect that you have the ability of looking inside the hearts of others too. You sensed that I had known Randy— the Reverend Randall—and you are right. Someday I will tell you about it, what a help he was to me before I met my Curly—back when the floods came and—" Tillie's face turned blank again momentarily, then sparkled alive, "I promised a *someday* talk, not today. Let's look forward to this glorious togetherness. What a grand night it's going to be! Do you realize the moon will be full?"

The crowd closed in. Later True supposed that there were far fewer than it seemed. To her, "thousands" would be a conservative estimate, so long had they been isolated. There was not a familiar face among them, and she probably would never recall their names, she thought with a spring of laughter bubbling up inside her. Maybe it made no difference. When, if ever, would she see them again?

And then she spotted Michael's wife. She stood, lips compressed tightly, straight as a ramrod. Her new fall outfit with a silver trim of fur looked out of place amid the ginghams and calicoes and out of season in the autumn-bright sunshine. True wickedly hoped the snobbish woman was uncomfortably warm, then felt a little ashamed.

"If you'll excuse me," she murmured, "I will help my sister-in-law dress," and hurried inside.

A few minutes later the two of them emerged—not unobtrusively as planned, but greeted by a round of applause. A hostess should remain in the background, according to Aunt Chrissy. It was her undisputed duty to see that guests were comfortable, their needs met. And here were two of the North wives dominating the scene. True's flush came from embarrassment at the sudden reversal of roles; but Midgie's, she felt, came from excitement. Well, proper or not, it was good to see a near-forgotten sparkle of happiness about her. And truly she looked lovely. The turquoise complemented her pale skin, camouflaging the pallor, and the white-lace trim circling the scooped-out neckline, the huge puffed sleeves, and the hemline of the skirt's four-yard sweep added to the China-doll resemblance. True had done Midgie's hair, carefully disguising the darkening roots by heaping curls on top and pinning the white roses above her ears where the "kiss curls" bounced playfully.

Mariah and Tillie had joined the two of them for a stolen moment—Mariah to hand each of them folding lace fans, and Tillie to tuck Spanish tortoise-shell backcombs in their hair. "All the rage in Paris, according to the peddlers," she confided, "although I must say that the two of you look more angelic than Spanish with those complexions."

Mariah slipped quickly into her own fiesta gown of crimson, the black lace mantilla floating over her hair, which she had impulsively unpinned and allowed to droop almost to her waist while Tillie wound a pinkdyed Spanish boa around her own neck playfully. It was a festive moment—one that True was to remember forever as a beginning and an end . . .

Now, more than a little flustered at the sea of admiring faces, True was relieved when Billy Joe's wife stepped forward to bow boldly in her new role, and then, leaning gracefully from side to side as if keeping time to imagined music, pirouetted in practiced ballet rhythm.

Spectators mounted the bleachers. For a moment the world seemed to hold its breath. Then, as Mariah picked up the tempo, swinging and swaying with a red rose clenched between her white teeth, the crowd went wild. Stamping. Clapping. Shouting, "Bravo! Bravo!"

True was seeing a new Mariah, a Mariah who was unknowingly urging the old Midgie to emerge further from her cocoon, she was to realize later. But for now she could see it only as a means of escape, a chance to do a quick fade away. Beautiful as it all was, the uneasiness within her was growing. Which was it, she tried to recall, that came first—appearance of the animals trailing down from the gap or Reverend Randall's sermon? The cattle drive, no doubt, as the air of expectation was growing. The man would have difficulty holding their attention. So where were the men? Why the delay?

Afternoon was waning. Traditionally they would watch the sunset—that was it. She scanned the sky for the buzzards, wondering why. *Stop letting your imagination run wild*, she scolded herself, only to wonder if the filthy creatures of the air had landed on a carcass. Shuddering a little, True would have hurried back to her guests except that the Mystery Man had appeared like a phantom at the gap. And what was this? This time he was joined by one, two—*four* others, all of whom disappeared so fast that she wondered if she could have imagined their appearance. In her haste to escape the thoughts invading the lovely afternoon, True all but fell into the arms of a man.

"Michael!" Did her voice sound as startled to his ears? There was nothing unnatural about his presence, considering that his wife was somewhere among the spectators. On the other hand, what was either of them doing here? She made an attempt to regain her poise. But it was difficult with his eyes sweeping over her with the kind of approval that claimed a certain propriety.

For the first time she was aware of her own appearance. Dull, she supposed. Surely she paled beside Midgie and Mariah's bright costumes. The pale yellow must give her an all-of-one-color look, blending as it did with her skin, now slightly ivory from the sun, and her blonde hair, where, without her knowing, Michael's eyes had focused to watch the sun rest in her upswept curls, turning them to gold.

"You look lovely," he smiled. "Yellow roses are my favorite—may I adjust this one? It is about to escape—"

His tone was inoffensive, but True reached to re-pin the blossom herself—a gesture that seemed to amuse him. "Forgive me," he said with only a hint of his old mocking tone. "I guess I was seeing us back in Atlanta—the elixir of the air having gone to my head. I always behave badly out here—"

"You have been here—before?" Why should that surprise her, detain her return to the party?

"Oh, of course. Old Artie and I were friends—always talking land values, the railroad, petitioning Congress for help in extending aid to both. This land was his life, as you probably know?" When she failed to answer, Michael continued: "He staked a claim—rather, his father did before him, I guess—back when guns spoke louder than fenceposts and barbed wire. Always had his heart set on raising thoroughbreds, so he'd appreciate what your men are doing up there.

Or," he grinned engagingly, "do you entertain the idea that the old devil's watching from some cloud up there?"

"We've had this conversation before," True said coldly. "I must get back—"

Even as she spoke she could not resist looking uneasily at the gap again. Michael saw. "One of the calves is missing."

The buzzards! But Michael's maddening patronage attributed her anxiety to another channel. "Surely you aren't reliving the days of armed bandits, masked men who robbed trains and stole cattle. That's over now, you know—"

"Which of us are you trying to convince—oh, there they come!"

Relief swept her being, followed by a thrill such as she had never experienced before. Nose-to-tail the chestnut horses, muscles rippling in the slanting rays of the sun, trailed down, nostrils flanged but otherwise making no effort to return to the wilds. It occurred to her then that Young Wil had saved this event as a surprise. The herdsmen had broken the steeds already. There would be no need for the frightening scene of roping and tying the animals, risking injury to both men and beasts. *Oh, thank You, Lord . . . thank You . . . thank You . . .*

"I was prepared to dislike the lucky man you said 'Yes' to, but I find it difficult when he appears to be such a decent sort of chap. Of course, I will envy him forever—because of us—"

"Michael," True said firmly, "there is no *us*. You are married—"

"A matter of convenience, family background, money—Big Brother's shares—"

"Don't make me lose respect for you completely. I refuse to engage in such conversations ever again. In fact, there is no reason for any contact between us—"

"Oh, but there is, my dear True!" True turned away angrily and ran forward to meet Wil, who was bringing up the rear, where the cows (fatter than she had pictured from feeding on the hillside pastures) were shaking their massive heads and making sportive attempts at escaping the halters of their keepers.

"Stan' back, Miz True honey, lest some o'these mavericks git too frisky," Billy Joe called out importantly. True obliged, eyes on Wil.

Wil dismounted. "Did you find the calf, darling?" True asked as he embraced her quickly, eyes still scanning the hill. "We did—dead—mutilated—in a way that told the story—the work of man, not beast—"

21
Unfinished Song

❧

THE SUN HAD dropped behind the western hillocks, taking with
it the dancing heat signals of the afternoon. But the air remained sultry except for an occasional refreshing breeze. A tinge of warm rose
replaced the day's gold. And far to the southwest True spotted an
innocent-looking cloudbank—innocent to those unskilled in sky-
watching, but she had learned to be wary. Was the hay covered?
Would the livestock panic in their new environment in case of a
storm? The party in progress seemed trivial by comparison. But why
borrow trouble?

The men were washing up after the long drive. They must hurry
or miss what remained of the sunset. Already the foothills were crimson in remembrance, and, although the purple twilight would be long,
nightbirds were foretelling end-of-day already. True, joining the
group, realized suddenly that all activity had stopped. The men sat
motionless, not one of them contaminating the air with smoke or
words. Where were their thoughts as they waited almost reverently
for the Reverend to take his place on an improvised stage? Some, she
suspected hungered to hear the Lord's Word. Others were curious.
Nobody seemed to take note of the distant grumble of thunder.

The sky flamed with secondary glory as Randy Randall, Young Wil,
and Marty stepped onto the rough-board platform. There was a
moment's discussion as the three obviously debated which should
greet the guests. The Reverend, undoubtedly a volunteer appointed
by default, won out.

Introductions were short and applause delayed because the serious-faced minister went into his message immediately. Eyes scanning the horizon frequently, he appeared to be on guard against the enemy. Intruders or the storm?

"Bless you all for welcoming these wonderful people that God has seen fit to send into our midst," he began. "Now, in view of existing circumstances, I promise to follow the rule of the effective sermon: 'Be sincere; be brief; be seated!'"

The light words conditioned his congregation for listening. The man was human, faces of the newcomers said. Maybe he *did* have word from On High instead of Down There, the way most of the wandering Bible-beaters harped on and on. His humanness would naturally outfit him with a taste for good food, and those barbecued smells were likely as not to make the "Holy Joe" into a man of his word.

Their assessment was correct. Reverend Randall went straight to the point. There had been trouble with a missing calf, he explained—trouble which delayed the roundup. Any rancher worth his salt would never abandon a little lost animal—no sirree, the good rancher, like the Good Shepherd, would search until the lost was found.

Obviously surprised by the news, the audience leaned forward to hear more, clinging raptly to each word. True, happy with the wisdom of making use of an analogy with which those present could identify, prayed that he would make use of the parable of the lost sheep. He did.

"I read to you from St. Luke, chapter 15, verses 3 through 7." Then, placing a finger between the pages to hold the reference, he further drew the congregation to him by returning to another situation with which they were familiar. "If ever any of you want to read my Book, it is yours for the asking—lots of wisdom here on how to handle animals, rotate crops, build houses—not to mention manage wives!"

Little snickers passed through the crowd as men nudged one another in the ribs and a few dared reach forward to shake the shoulders of women seated on the lower bleachers. "Most of you are familiar with the story well-known in these parts about Aaron Meier, the peddler, who furnished the one darning needle for sharing. Seems few know the rest of the story—how he came one day with a needle for every single household! Well, one day that's what I hope to do—

put a Bible in each home as your almanac, your guide for days when the going's tough—and your road map to heaven!"

Randy Randall reopened the Bible and read to the open-mouthed listeners:

And he (Jesus) spake this parable unto them, saying, "What man of you, having an hundred sheep, if he lose one of them, doth not leave the ninety and nine in the wilderness and go after that which is lost, until he find it? And when he hath found it, he layeth it on his shoulders, rejoicing. And when he cometh home, he calleth together his friends and neighbors, saying unto them, 'Rejoice with me, for I have found my sheep which was lost.' I say unto you that likewise joy shall be in heaven over one sinner that repenteth more than over ninety and nine just persons which need no repentance."

"Oh, friends, Jesus loves you! Right now He is searching here among you, longing to bring you home. If you want to be found, simply raise your hand and we will pray for you—if I sound like a tyrannous, radical old Turk to you—well, it's only because Jesus and I care—"

At that moment the last remnant of color faded and there was the curious calm that precedes a storm. The fast-spreading clouds slowly rolled down a curtain of premature darkness so that buildings began to lose their outlines in the deepening gloom. But hands were visible—one, two—they became countless—waved back and forth desperately. There could be no doubt about the sincerity of their gestures.

"Then let us be merry—the lost is found! Right now the weather seems up to some mischief, and I know most of you are hungry enough to digest a mountain lion, so rejoice in your new state and join us at the Lord's table!"

There was a flurry of activity—men pumping the minister's hand, some tears, and men whistling and laughing softly among themselves as if they had heard some good news, which indeed they had. Women bustled about with such urgency that True failed to make note of Midgie's disappearance again. Once the men had uncovered the browned-to-perfection barbecued meat and carved it, the ladies busied themselves with dishing up the remainder of the feast and set the enormous granite pot of steaming coffee back on the coals to keep warm. The men dived in hungrily, smacking their lips in appreciation, the older ones struggling to hold back beards from a bath in the bowls of rich, thick beans as—when eyes were turned safely in other directions—they lifted bowls to their mouths. An occasional dentured guffaw tattled when one of the male diners was unsuccessful. The air was charged with excitement—and electricity that none seemed to have noticed.

True cast an anxious glance at the threatening sky and slipped toward the corral unnoticed. The buildings were nothing more than a blotch of darkness, but the rustlings in the pens told her that Young Wil, Marty, and the hired hands were checking on the livestock. She caught sight of her husband as the shadows crisscrossed from the lanterns that someone had thoughtfully turned higher.

"True?" Wil was beside her in a moment. "Don't worry, sweetheart. Everything is perfect here—just keep the party going—"

Billy Joe, panting from exertion, rushed to join them. True was a lady—wife of the boss man—and therefore to be impressed. "Play 'possum, Miz True—you know, dead t'th' storm what's boun' t'pop. Thet wind's blowin' up a balloon—boun' on bustin' any minute— callin' fer help with these beauties. So see thet they're fed 'n calm— get my Mariah playin' t'soothe th' atmosphere—"

Billy Joe drifted over to where Marty was talking low and soothingly to a disturbed filly. Pleased, True took time to smile up into Wil's face. He nodded. "I had a chance to talk with him again," he whispered above the uneasy lowing of the cattle. "Things will be better if—"

Young Wil was unable to finish the sentence. There was a warning zigzag of lightning and he motioned True back to the group. There the thoughtful Mariah, accustomed to the sinister pranks of the elements, had begun strumming the strings of her guitar, gradually increasing the volume as the thunder grew closer. Mrs. Caswell had joined her. "Why not have everybody join in singing the words—or humming, whistling, even stomping their feet?"

For a time it worked. And then the unexpected happened. Her face glowing in the lantern light, Midgie slipped forward and seated herself beside Mariah. And strapped over her shoulder was her guitar!

True held her breath, remembering the terrible incident which so far had held Midgie and Marty apart. Surely Marty would appreciate his wife's overcoming her fear of crowds, her valiant efforts to help.

And yet she felt sawed apart, like the illusions created by a magician, her eyes seeing one thing and her heart convinced it was untrue.

But there was no time to stop the show. In response to Mariah's smile of welcome, Midgie drew a long, tremulous breath and joined her in a mellow Mexican sonata, softly at first, and then—gaining confidence—taking the lead. Her playing was beautiful, True realized. In it there was a rare brightness, an ethereal quality to the classical music which musicians usually took too gravely, causing the average listener to turn a deaf ear to intricate numbers. Her slender fingers slid from note to note in slow motion in a way which brought a lump to True's throat. Midgie was speaking to Marty with each strum of the strings, begging, pleading—for the slow movement of the sonata gave the sense of a glorified voice.

"An angel—sure as shootin'—a real live angel," one of the men marveled in a near-frightened voice. What had that preacher done to him? "Angels *do* play on harps, don't they?"

The man beside him shrugged. "Dunno much 'bout angels—but I knowed a girl once what sung like that in Portland—an' she sure 'nuf warn't no angel!"

True's spine stiffened and she prayed that Midgie had failed to hear as she and Mariah exchanged a few whispered words. Mariah was lowering her instrument. Then Midgie was going to solo? True felt choky inside as she surveyed the eager, wistful faces turned to her sister-in-law from the now-overflowing bleachers and benches that someone had brought from the picnic tables.

And suddenly Midgie, looking like a slowly unfolding blossom, began to sing in a voice so clear and sweet that one could be charmed easily into guessing that she had dropped from the Great White Way. The men were mesmerized, their weather-browned faces resting on the girl's white throat where the music originated—or was it sent from Above? The women wore different expressions—more dreamy, reliving another time, another place, before hard work robbed them of romance. And something more, a sparkle of hope that romance, like the wild horses, could be recaptured and brought home.

Midgie sang on and on—soft, sweet melodies, then ballads. And finally rollicky folk songs. Once she would have stopped, but Mariah leaned forward to whisper, "Pleese, Señora, a leetle more—*usted* fine ladee—sing on, so they be good, never bad—or have hunger eeven

wheen bellies have no *mucho* food. They fill bellies with fine music—yes?"

Midgie looked into the pleading face where the black eyes, appearing too large for her thin face, glowed with spirit—a spirit seemed to
overwhelm her and tranfuse lifeblood to those around her.

"I will close the musicale," Midgie said boldly, as if addressing an
audience in a fine concert hall, "with a composition of my own. Listen to the words, then join me."

> Day is done and night has come
> As stars turn on one by one,
> Lighting lanterns in the sky,
> Giving light to travel by,
> Till we join God in the sky . . .

The exquisite, languorous notes floated over the countryside as
she paused to repeat the words. Then, strumming a few chords,
Midgie nodded. The men moved forward toward the stage and took
up the song. The women followed and knelt as if seeing once more
the tender picture of mother, brothers, and sisters—now gone—and
perhaps a small village church where they had surrendered their lives
to God. They were watching their men do so now. For this angelic
little singer had taken over where the Reverend Brother left off.

Playfully, then—almost coquettishly, Midgie, sang out: "Good
night, ladies, good night, ladies—" drowning out the nearing thunder. As she reached the final line, "I'm going to leave you now!" there
was a jolt of thunder, so loud it was as if some resident giant of earth
suffered a passionate rage and prepared to jerk the rocky crowns from
the mountains, clashing them together to destroy the broad valley.

Which indeed was what happened—except that Martin North was
the giant and little Midgie was his victim. Glowering, he rushed at
her, ignoring her touchingly uncertain smile of welcome. For a split
second his half-crazed eyes rested on her hair, which the first wind-
driven raindrops had whipped into little-girl tendrils of silvered bronze.
Then, with shaking hands, he grabbed the guitar, jerked it none too
gently from her neck, and dashed it to the ground. It splintered.

22

Gone!

❧

As IF TIRED of being ignored, the storm struck with all its fury. The wind inhaled, seeming to suck up everything movable, including the benches and chairs, then exhaled with such gusto that it shook the windowframes and doors of the small house in much the same manner that an angered chaparral cock would shake a rattler. The lanterns flickered, steadied momentarily, then sputtered out. The world lay in total darkness, void and without form, except for otherworldly tongues of fire that bruised the sky.

There was bedlam as the crowd sought cover. They huddled beneath a straggling cluster of trees until Reverend Randy screamed against the snarling wind, "Don't tempt nature's forces by behaving like cattle! Get from beneath those trees—lie flat if need be—and pray while crawling on your bellies—"

Men fumbled in the darkness for a tarpaulin, waterproofed with tar for protecting the hay. If only they could erect it on the poles which held the now-unlighted lanterns—but the wind snatched it heartlessly away just as the rain came down in sheets, rattling and crashing against the distant hills. The frightened crowd pushed toward the cabin, some crawling beneath the wagons, as the wind gave one final gnash of its teeth—and stopped. In the final flash of lightning, True saw to her horror that the remains of Midgie's guitar had been picked up, twirled in midair, and carried away—broken and bruised like its owner's heart.

Where *was* Midgie? She should look after her chickens. The downpour could drown them unless they were cooped. True called her

257

name softly, then more loudly, knowing in her heart that it was use-less. Her voice would never carry above the roar of the storm and the frenzied sounds from the barnyard and corral. Knowing, too, that Midgie was crouched somewhere in the purgatorial darkness, shak-ing with fear of the storm, and weeping her eyes out with hurt and humiliation.

The men had managed to light a lantern in the barn, and through the cracks between the imperfectly matched boards True saw shift-ing shafts of light, enough for her to crawl on hands and knees to-ward the cabin as fast as her wildly thumping heart would allow—the kind of thump that a well-regulated organ gives when its owner is frightened for others but brave enough to act, knowing the risks. She must find Midgie, check on the safety of Young Wil and the others, try to bring Marty back to beg forgiveness—

The wind changed to a high-pitched nasal moan. Or was it the wind? The question had no more than occurred when the answer came. For in her path lay a human form—injured, judging from the sound of pain. A shift of the light from the barn allowed one quick peek at the face. "Mrs. Caswell—oh, Tillie—you're hurt!" The light shifted, but True could feel the hot stickiness that said blood. She felt for the wound and found it—a wide gash on Tillie's right arm. Without hesitation True ripped the bottom ruffle from her new dress and went to work. "There—that should stop the bleeding—now, to move you—"

However, the flesh wound was less serious than Tillie Caswell's emotional state. There was no budging her body, stiffened with fear as it was. The voice was thick and gutteral—beyond recognition.

"The flood—the flood," she gasped hysterically. "They'll all be drowned—and the baby is overdue. What did you say—they're dead? Dead—all dead—all three—Oh, I don't want to live—" she sobbed senselessly. "Let me die with them—they're all I have—bury me—"

And then, miraculously, the full moon peered from between the scudding clouds—its face innocent, seeking out and finding the dis-oriented victims below. Somewhere a shot pierced the sudden silence. But True's nerves were too taut for her to take notice of the rever-berating echo. Somebody would be on guard. And surely the crack of the rifle would be less disturbing than the thunder drums to the livestock.

That the firing of a gun signified trouble far greater than what they had all experienced did not occur to her at that time . . .

The storm was over. It was time to assess the damages, correct what could be corrected, and get on with living. There were conflicting reports from the hands. One of the choice heifers, probably the best for breeding the fine herd, was a spirited critter, Tex said, his schoolboy face lighted with challenge. He could cut her off at the pass and bring her home before Papa Bull knew that a member of his harem was missing. Fortunately, he knew every square foot of the wide valley, having fished the streams in order to exist between harvests before landing what he referred to as a "steady job." Billy Joe, obviously a little jealous, said the boy had miscounted—better be getting his bearings and checking on the horses, which were still somewhat crazed from the storm—flare of a match could undo them. Thanks to Pig Iron's locomotive strength, corral fences were under repair, and Slinger, unhampered by his withered arm, dragged poles to him as fast as the stronger man could nail them in place. Slim was running the fences. Hands cut and bleeding from the barbs, he snipped, cut, and nailed, aided by Augie's holding a lantern high above his head to aid the moon. Loyal group . . . but True must check on those closer to her.

Tillie Caswell had regained control of her emotions—uncannily, almost as if nothing had happened to trigger the memory of her bitter secret. While other guests prepared to depart—*no, no, they had no dread of the long journey, just needed to be home by daybreak*—Tillie and Mariah busied themselves collecting the soggy remains of drenched food and shelter. Tillie talked all the while.

"It was a wonderful thing you folks did here, True. Life here becomes intolerable compared to what women knew in Portland and Seattle. Some never had much human tolerance. Most of them see all this as ugly, a land of punishment, hobbling them and shrinking their hearts. Bad weather, no trifles that color their lives—and the men are no help—here's your fan, Mariah, want to try drying it out? Husbands are too exhausted to see that the girls they once loved enough to court and buy trinkets for are becoming prisoners. Or they blame the women—have to have somebody to take out their frustration on, I guess—"

"But they aren't all like that," True protested, while letting her glance travel to every lighted spot in search of Midgie. "Your men are caring and loving—and Reverend Randall is so understanding—"

Mariah, pushing heavy hair, around which she had wrapped a heavy towel, smiled broadly. "Si, Señora—'tis true—"

"But the exception," Tillie Caswell persisted as she shook the tarp, attempting to dodge the unexpected downspout of water and succeeding in showering them all. "Oh, mercy! A thousand pardons!" When True and Mariah laughed, she went on: "I guess our men are different partly because *we* are! We have our problems, but we've learned to trust the Lord. Everybody with one iota of sense can see the all-too-evident conditions around here. So why waste words? A low opinion of a place—or persons—grants no license to harp on it. But when one loses respect for self and faith in God and others—well, it takes somebody like you folks to bring a special sparkle back. And that's what you did tonight—storm and all—True, I'm worried about Midgie—"

"I must check on her," True replied. She thanked the two other women and went to the barn, almost throwing herself in the arms of her husband. "Oh, Wil—darling, I'm so sorry—is everything going to be all right?"

"Of course," he said, but there was less certainty in his voice than usual. "I hope we can save the hay, keep it from souring. Billy Joe is spreading the hay on the canvas to prevent sprouting. And," glancing around uneasily, "Marty's supposed to be with him—what took place just before the storm? Nobody seems to know for sure, except that Marty behaved like a madman. Is he with Midgie?"

"That's what I came to find out," True said. "He hurt her—hurt her terribly, darling." Then she gave him a quick account of the ugly scene. Young Wil made a snort of disgust. "Oh, there he is with Billy Joe, working off his fury, I guess. But what about Midgie?"

The chicken coop? No, she was not there, and the chickens were her life—Henny-Penny, Chicken Little, Half-Chick—all of them.

"Midgie!" she called in the kitchen as she lighted the closest candle to send sinister shadows scurrying about the small room. There was no answer. A quick search failed to reveal anything—but wait! What was this propped on the dresser of the room that True and Young Wil occupied? Yes, an envelope! Midgie's childish scrawl said: TRUE.

Dear, dear True:

Don't be too mad at me—please don't. And don't worry. I will be all right. It's just that I can't go on like this—and I know you understand. A woman needs love. I never was a right wife. So I have no right to claim love. Just let Marty know that he is free of me—that I'll no longer be an embarrassment. Don't let him look for me. He ain't (the word was smeared by an eraser and corrected) isn't obli—how do you spell it—obliged to be burdened. Maybe someday me and you'll meet again. I'll try to learn how to be a real lady by then. Thank you for never making me feel ashamed—and pray for me. Oh, and one thing more, look after my chickens. They *do* need me and will miss me when I'm gone . . .

I love you,

Midgie

23

Awakening?

⤫

THE NORTHS HAD had no sleep. Surely the men must be famished, True mused as she kindled a fire in the monstrous black kitchen stove and busied her hands with breakfast. Her mind was harder to control. Poor Midgie—where could she be? How and with whom had she escaped what to her must have been one of the prisons that Tillie Caswell described? It had been hard deciding how to break the news to Marty. She dreaded his scowling and sniping. Left alone, maybe he'd come to his senses. Why not let Midgie's note speak for itself? So thinking, she had propped it on his pillow, where to her surprise was another envelope, different only in that it bore no name.

Now the coffee boiled in the planished pot while bacon sizzled in the heavy iron skillet. The sourdough biscuits were rising, and she wished one of the hands would find a new hen nest in the hay. Midgie's little flock was faithful, but would the three dozen eggs she had hoarded for swapping to Tillie for "something nice" for Marty's birthday be enough to feed the overworked men? They could fill in the cavities with biscuits. The butter was still sweet and the honey had not sugared. Should she add fried potatoes? Probably—

That done, True glanced out the small kitchen window, hoping to catch sight of Young Wil. She did, and laughed at herself for the silly flip-flop of her heart. Just seeing her husband was like seeing the morning sun, which was now rising from a downy bed of tufted clouds to scatter gold coins into the placid pools left by last night's storm. For a moment it seemed to rest comfortably between the low hills, only to spread glory over the rain-washed sky. She felt so close to God . . .

"Umm-m-m, do I smell coffee? And is that my bride of long ago? Admittedly, these old eyes are fading—"

"Oh, Wil," True laughed, "sit yourself down and—*Wil*, the other men will see you—"

"Kiss my wife? Through *that* window? Not much of a view—"

When he released her, True poured coffee for them. "All's under control for now. But the storm served to show how much there is to mend." He paused. "Including a broken marriage. I've seen mulish people, but compared to Marty, they're as flexible as grass in a summer breeze."

True swallowed coffee which was so hot that it burned her throat. "He's a stiff-neck all right—and I don't know what more we can do—"

Young Wil extended his cup for a refill. His hand was shaking. From fatigue or emotion? Both, True suspected. "We're not going to do *anything*. It will be hard, sweetheart, but—well, this will either finish him off or bring him to his senses."

True poured his coffee. "But Midgie? What about Midgie?"

"'What God has joined together, let no man put asunder.' Helping could be interpreted as meddling, doing more harm than good. Maybe she was too patient, too clingy, too whatever. Apart, she may gain new insight, see things from a new perspective. Right or wrong if they can bring their thinking together—and it *must* be theirs— what I am trying to say is that O'Higgin (secretly I've always thought of him as the Fourth Wise Man!) had their marriage in view as well as their success here." Wil lowered his voice, "Here's Marty," he said.

Marty's face was whiter than a flour sack when, minutes later, he emerged from his bedroom. In the breast pocket of his soiled blue chambray workshirt was the envelope bearing no name. He tossed it on the table and poured himself a cup of coffee. Making no mention of it, what he said was "Smart move you made letting Billy Joe, the Beetle, remain as foreman, Wil. Straight as a barbedwire fence, and a good judge of character. If I doubted *your* judgment, I changed my mind last night—" Marty paused to take a swallow of the scalding coffee, winced, and helped himself to scrambled eggs.

Young Wil waited for him to go on. When he did not, Wil said slowly, "I thought we, you and I, agreed on it. Decisions around here are to be agreed upon until the time you take over completely—"

"Minor ones maybe, but domestic—or shall I say," a shade of sarcasm sliced through his voice, "affairs of the heart?"

"That too," Wil said shortly. "That is, if you refer to Midgie—"

"Ha! Who else?" Marty laid down his fork, having tumbled the eggs around without tasting them. "Take a look." He fumbled with the flap of the envelope. "If my beloved's note to you—none to me, mind you—didn't make that clear, this *will*!"

He withdrew a tiny circle of gold. Midgie's wedding ring! So she really meant that their marriage was finished? True's heart bled for her brother even though she could understand Midgie's pain.

"End of a perfect marriage," he said. "So what shall I do—go into Slippery Elm and get drunker than a hoot owl?"

"If you want to lose the respect of all the hands, yes, go ahead and drown yourself. But don't expect me to defend you when O'Higgin asks for an accounting."

"You make it sound like Judgment Day!" Marty pushed his chair from the table with a loud scrape.

"That'll do, Marty!" Young Wil's voice left no room for argument. "You know better than speaking in those terms, no matter how angry or hurt you are. There will be no more lecturing, no more coddling, no more protecting from me. And from you I hope I can expect a change of behavior. We are sick of the 'poor little me' attitude. If you wish to let the loss of your parents wreck your life, go ahead!"

True had never seen Young Wil so angry. It frightened her, but she kept still, breathing a silent prayer. God and her husband were smarter than she. Together they would figure this out.

"Easy for you to say—" Marty began, then stopped. "But I guess that's hitting below the belt, since we all lost out where parents are concerned."

"Then spend some time thanking the Lord for Aunt Chrissy and Uncle Wil—and while you're at it, say a prayer for Midgie. Praying is much better than some of these childish tantrums. You know what the Bible has to say about prayer."

"'The prayer of a righteous man availeth much.' But me, *righteous*?"

"That's another decision you have to make."

Marty sat down and, to True's amazement, took a mouthful of the cold eggs. By now they had to taste like cardboard. But it was his way of knuckling under—a first experience!

"How long do you suppose," he said meekly, "it will take to get last night's damages repaired?" Marty flinched at his own words. The question led right back to his marital problems.

Young Wil tactfully took it as Marty had meant it. In control now, he was brisk and businesslike. "That's about like asking how long we're going to live. It all depends on how we pull together—and then we'll have to get to the source of the slaughter of the heifer, as well as some of the other suspicious activities. Are you with me?"

Marty was. He made no further criticism of his wife. Had he awakened?

24
Planting, Planning, Plotting

❧

AN EARLY FROST allowed the men to get the planting done in mid-November. It also blackened the aboveground vegetables. Thank goodness the potatoes were bedded down in the haymow with dry onions and winter squash, True mused as she checked on the kraut. Lifting the heavy stone from a plate which weighted down the shredded cabbage (to keep it below the brine solution), she pronounced it perfect. The test, according to Grandma Mollie, was in the throat's reaction. If it constricted from the sour aroma, causing the tastebuds to lock the jaw, 'twas just right. True tried to smile, but the effort was less than successful. She was homesick for them all in a way that doubled the discomfort of the aching throat. Homesick—if one could use the word to describe her emotions—for Midgie, whose little hands had grated cabbage until her knuckles were red and raw, refusing to stop even as the handfuls of salt ground into the open wounds. Trying so hard to please . . .

Tex, coming into the woodshed for a shovel, interrupted her wandering thoughts. "Pardon, Miz True, but it ain't only th' implement I'm needin'; smellin' th' sauerkraut made my mouth set t'waterin' like a thirstin' horse. I'd swap jest 'bout anythang fer a handful right outta th' crock—"

True laughed. "You have earned it already. Do you think your red wheat will grow here?"

The boy reached into the crock, grabbed a giant-size handful, and crammed his mouth so full that it resembled a suitcase packed so

266

tightly for a trip that the lid could not be fastened. The sight made her throat tighten again, giving her an excuse for turning her head aside to hide a threatening burst of laughter.

Then she sobered. The boy was hungry—not only for kraut, but just plain hungry. How could she have been so blind?

"We're going to have to do some arranging here, Tex, if you're still considering staying on—although there is no proper housing—"

"Oh, I hafta stay," he choked, face red, and strings of the fermenting cabbage forming a green-white goatee down his chin. "Ain't no choice—I've invested all I got in this world, my wheat seed—an' I'm much obliged fer th' boss men a-lettin' me use th' ground." He swallowed so fast that True wondered if the mass wouldn't be brought back up in a cud to be chewed a second time like some ruminating animal. Then, covering his mouth to avoid the belch that threatened to erupt, Tex rushed on: "I—me 'n th' other boys ain't astin' much—"

"You mean—you mean they *all* want to stay?" True sat down.

"Oh, yessum! 'N we'll be no trouble—fact is, we kin hep avoid what's boun' on happenin'—th' rustlin' 'n th' like. Ain't safe out here without numbers—'specially fer th' ladies. We dun foun' a place—" he reached for more kraut, changed his mind, and continued, "saplin's are fine—'n I'm experienced. Why, onct I built me a shack in a week with my bare hands—got me a roof over my head in seven days, same time as it took th' Good Lord t'build th' earth. 'Course now I'm guessin' He didn' break His back like I did. But y'all know what? He up 'n helped me, knowin' it'd get my goat, but we made it, me 'n Him, 'n that's how I got them precious seeds. I plowed roun' boulders 'cause I had me no kegs uv black powder 'n couldn' budge 'em. That's 'fore I met Pig Iron—now, he's valuable, too—he could do it. We kin 'n will do anythang fer y'all—anythang a'tall."

His pleading humbled her. "Oh, Tex," she said, tears gathering in her eyes, "you needn't try to justify your being here. It's *your* welfare that concerns me."

In her mind she was seeing Atlanta again—seeing the "haves and have-nots" of the St. John-Kincaid family of which (had God not intervened—of that she was sure!) she might have foolishly become a part. Their wealth and "fine old family background" had made them into hopeless snobs, looking with disdain upon those whose skins were black. Even now, the remembrance of their superior attitude caused her back to stiffen and her eyes to turn purple with rage at the injustice of their narrow world which they called "Christendom."

"I will never understand you people—never in a million years," she had said in a voice that she hoped was low and controlled. "You speak of the poorly educated and culturally deprived people as if they were less than your horses! How can they be other than they are when they're so ill-used—kept living in a world of unrelieved grimness?"

Brave words. Yet here, like a ghost of the past rising up to meet her, was a case not too far different. The boy, Tex—could he be more than 17?—was willing to make any sacrifice in order to follow his dream in a world of injustice which cared more about its headache than his demise. "Poor white trash," Michael St. John's Cousin Emily had called salt-of-the-earth people like Tex and the other faithful hands on the emerging Double N Ranch.

"Jesus would have loved these people," True had said—a statement which had served only to raise aristocratic eyebrows. She had stuck with her conviction. How then had she allowed personal problems to blind her to the needs of others here? She was as selfish as Marty, petty and small.

"I'm proud of you, Tex," True said warmly now. "You have stood fast in your faith—"

The boy nodded shyly. "My grandma took care uv that. When I lost her, I lost ever'thang—'ceptin' my faith—"

"Faith opens the door to all good things. I will talk with my husband and our brother, and somehow we'll manage," True promised, wiping away a sudden tear.

"Now, don' y'all go cryin', Miz True. I—I'll feel so bad—'n Mr. Wil 'n Mr. Marty's got 'nuf t'settle. What we're facin's gonna take blood 'n sweat—then Mr. Marty's got hisself a pack uv other problems. He's battlin' with th' future 'n th' past—meanin' th' railroad which jest maybe ain't past after all. Then he's all tore up inside—losin' Miz Midgie 'n all. I tell y'all, Miz True, iffen th' Good Lord ever sees fit t'send me a woman so lovin', I'll be handlin' her like a prairie flower." Tex scratched a tuft of hair which stood at attention on top of his head. "Sad part bein' he's crazy in love, too—"

The boy mumbled some more, but True did not hear. *I should have stopped the conversation when it became personal*, she thought. But the boy meant well, bless his simple heart. And besides, his last sentence—in fact the entire conversation—had given a new brightness to the November sky . . .

True to his word, once he had the go-ahead from the North Brothers, Tex enlisted, without pressure, the services of the other ranch hands. The bunkhouse, such as it was, was ready for roofing by the end of the month. "Jest poles, Miz True Ma'm," Pig Iron said modestly, "but it'll keep th' wind an' wolves out. Even made ourse'ves some bunks, puttin' hay on 'em 'n kin cover ourse'ves with saddle blankets—right, men?"

"Right!" they all sang out in pride while Augie nodded his weathered brown face and kept smiling to reveal more teeth than True knew he possessed.

Marty was nodding too, although it was plain to see that his mind was elsewhere. It was he who had granted permission for the men to help themselves to the root crops. It was Marty, too, who suggested taking the leftover grain to town for milling.

"We'll share what we have—pool it, which will take honesty—"

True's heart sang to hear him take that much leadership. But there was little time to dwell on the change.

"That include th'—uh, beef, Mr. Marty?" Slim asked uneasily.

Beef? True's eyes questioned Young Wil.

"Slim found another heifer—calf, really—slaughtered," he said grimly. "Down in the hollow—still breathing but mortally wounded by gunshot, so—"

"It had to be destroyed?" True whispered, heart pounding against her ribs. She swallowed hard and steadied herself. "Was there a brand on it?"

"Ours," he replied. "Steady, sweetie—are you all right?"

"Perfectly," she said, stretching a point but feeling a curious touch of courage. "Then if you fellows will build a fire and put the beef to smoking—I—I'll watch while you search. I guess you'll have to?"

There was silence. Then all talked at once. They had searched high and low. No sign of human life except for hoof tracks. And, well, gunfire. No real casualties except for the one shot that whizzed past Augie's ear—and one thing more.

What? True had asked woodenly. But even before the answer she knew what it would be. Well, could be only a phantom, they said. Man's imagination had a way of tricking him—something call hal-halu—

Hallucinating, Young Wil supplied. No, it was no delusion. There was a man on horseback on top of the ridge—

"Who simply disappeared," True nodded without inflection.

"Up where the railroad has strung out red flags," Marty said, his voice as flat as her own. "Hadn't we better get the fire going?"

Leaving the other field hands to grub out stumps, mend harness, and—most important of all—keep an eye on the livestock, Young Wil and Billy Joe prepared the wheat for milling and the shelled corn for grinding. Enough, Billy Joe predicted, to last all winter.

"Mind if I go along?" True asked. "I need to do a bit of shopping."

Her husband answered question with question. "Think I'd go without you?"

How blest she was? She and Young Wil had each other, and even though circumstances had compelled them to plunge from wedding to marriage without the preparation period of a rightful honeymoon, life itself had prepared them. She often laughed at the memory of Young Wil's phrasing. "Such an advantage, knowing each other forever. This lifelong courtship's going to save a lot of red tape." *Bossy*, True had called him, while knowing he was right. This kind of love that grew slowly and steadily, recognizing no barriers, had every advantage. Their dearly familiar association had led them naturally and unhesitantly into two hearts beating as one. All this she wanted to tell him, but Marty had entered the door to say that he would be riding ahead for "some business."

Slipping into a tailored gray Sicilian skirt, side-pleated to allow for stepping high into the service wagon, she noted that the garment was showing its age, as was the box jacket that completed the suit. It was out-of-date, too, but warm. The day held promise of fair weather, but here one could put little trust in nature's promises, she had found.

For warmth, the three of them sat in the front seat. Young Wil tucked the lap robe over their legs, teasingly giving her knee a possessive squeeze just before taking the reins. The little gesture served to remind her again of her good fortune, and to wonder about Marty and Midgie. Marty had behaved much more calmly than she would have expected, but underneath the calm, conflicting thoughts and emotions regarding their problem undoubtedly boiled about. On the surface nothing resembling a solution had presented itself, but she had adhered strictly to the hands-off agreement that she and Young Wil made. They *cared*, but wordlessly.

So busy was True with the thoughts she had tucked away during the whirlwind days at the ranch that, if there were a warning above the drone of the men's voices discussing business, she failed to hear it. It was as if, on sudden impulse, the four corners of the earth simply folded together like a man's handkerchief, leaving the three in the wagon in the middle to soak up the drenching downpour. True would never look back on that wild ride without renewed thanksgiving that the prayer in her heart reached heaven—that God heard her plea and answered, giving Young Wil superhuman instinct as he bent over the buckboard and negotiated the twisting turns in what (fortunately) was a short distance, although harrowing. Overhead the sky sizzled with glistening tongues of fire to send thunder, like Thor avenging, rumbling through the passes. The swift transition from blinding light to black ink darkness blinded her. Yet somehow between flashes she managed to find the great canvas umbrella she had learned to tuck in for emergencies. She raised it, a move which seemed to aggravate the wind. It was an inexplicable miracle that the wagon did not capsize when it struck a deep rut. Oddly, she felt no fear—then. That was to come later. For now she could feel only relief that rounding the next corner would bring them to Slippery Elm—or would have had a monster far greater than the one with which they were wrestling not reared its head. Immediately in front of them it was as if a thousand furies had been released, bound on destroying the earth. And, through the blinding sheets of rain, one evil eye—

The train! True realized then that Young Wil, in his rush to get them to safety, had taken the shortcut which crossed the railroad!

"Wave, wave somethin'—anythang!" Billy Joe screeched.

True yanked at her sodden petticoat, gave it a yank, and began waving the wide-sweeping garment as a white flag. She could hear nothing, see nothing. Would the engineer see, stop? *Could* he? Strange how she could be so objective, go on waving frantically, while facing the deadly monster that was so close now that she could see it. Long. Black. Sinuous. Sinister. Writhing like some earth-swallowing black snake shining with rain, its one eye blind.

"We're stuck—jump, darling, jump—you amazing girl!" Wil shouted.

There was no time to jump. A frenzied warning from the train whistle. A groaning and grinding of brakes and wet wheels sliding to a shuddering stop. And then bedlam. People laughing, crying, praying. While True, exhausted and dazed, and bedraggled in appearance, could think only: *I hope I do not encounter Mrs. St. John. She would love my backwoodsy appearance.*

She did—but not before she met someone who shocked her even more!

"Th' saints be preservin' us! What have we here but pea-brains, th' whole trio—what be ye tryin' to do, me lad, me lass, and me crazy ole leprechaun who, be th' legends true that roll o'er th' Scottish highlands, live forever and ought t'be versed in takin' proper care—"

"O'Higgin!" Recognition of the Irish burr, softened by a velvet heart, identified the speaker to True, who—taking no time to ponder the circumstances of his presence—was in his brawny arms even as she spoke the name.

"For the luvva Mike—if it ain't me True—and Young Wil in th' flesh. I was to be meetin' with Marty—"

"I'm Billy Joe, the foreman—remember me?" Billy Joe ran between them.

"The Beetle!" O'Higgin boomed. There was backslapping and a rumble of talk as True allowed herself to be led inside the Inn by an anxious Tilly. "We have to get you dried off, child—"

True nodded numbly. The shock was wearing off and her vision, like the sky, was clearing—only to cloud over again by a second shock wave, and then a third.

Stepping gingerly off the train was none other than Felice St. John. Her haughty eyes surveyed True with amusement and something else—what was the look, *triumph*? Looking like she had stepped into the latest in fashion worn by a Meier and Frank window mannequin, the woman had taken advantage of True's sad plight. Soaked to the skin by drenching rain, hair freed from barrettes by the wind and clinging damply across her face (then dripping down her back), she must look like a blonde witch. True felt herself coloring to the roots of her hair when Michael stepped from the coach to be greeted by his wife's crooning voice: "Oh, darling, did you see your former friend, Mrs. North?"

"True!" Michael's voice held concern. "Are you all right? And, to set the record straight, Felice, we are not former friends—"

True mumbled something and stumbled away as she heard the hiss of scathing words from Felice St. John. Michael was answering angrily. Well, what they said to each other was no concern of hers. But what she saw simultaneously was. For to the right side of the front door, in the shadow of the overhang, stood Marty engaged in earnest conversation with the man wearing the beaver hat. Instinctively she knew something was wrong. She also knew that it was wise to get inside without being observed—a feat she was unable to accomplish. A strand of wet hair blew across her face, blinding her and causing her to stumble against a chair. The small motion escaped her brother's attention but attracted the other man's. His head jerked up warily and for the first time True saw his face. All eyes. Gray as concrete and just as hard. Immovable and focused on *her*. Tillie followed his glance and nodded in recognition. A million questions rose to her mind. What were they plotting?

Only then did her heart begin to pound.

25
Talk and More Talk

❧

DRESSED IN ONE of Mrs. Caswell's robes big enough to wrap around herself and Young Wil both, True allowed herself to be coddled as her hostess busied herself boiling water and setting out cups. True let her mind fly on wings of the wind—straight to Centerville, where last she had received such attention. How wonderful it would be to sit down with Aunt Chrissy and Grandma Mollie again just to talk and talk and talk . . .

The flight was shortened by Tillie's voice. "Would you believe you're the first woman I've entertained—you know, in a neighborly sort of way—in years!" she announced a little breathlessly. Hastily she cleared off an end of a table in her own small quarters, and, pushing a cup toward True, poured fragrant, amber tea with trembling hands. Her eyes, True noticed, glowed and her cheeks flushed.

"Are you lonely?" True asked, watching the thick cream spiral downward to color her tea. "There are so many people around, and you seem to know so many more than I realized."

"Lonely?" Tillie did not meet her eyes as she busied herself shrugging out of the Mother Hubbard apron and spooning sugar into her own cup. "Oh, not lonely as one ordinarily thinks of lonely. There are people in and out, but I get lonely for things as I once knew them. And I guess," she sampled her tea cautiously, "you and Midgie brought back Portland to me—except for the part I want to forget."

Forget, Tillie? The gold in the woman's eyes predominated, put there by some mysterious circumstance which was too painful to remember but too wonderful to forget. Except in part. And it was that part which puzzled. From somewhere deep down inside True had a growing conviction that at some point in the past the lines of their lives intersected. It took courage to follow a man into a wilderness like this, a land so vast and unpeopled that one could get lost just looking at the vast spaces about her. The thought startled her. She had never thought of herself as being courageous. Right now she was so filled with the home she had left—just as had Tillie Caswell.

True brought herself back to the present, realizing that her hostess was answering the second part of the question she had posed.

"Yes, there are people around—but in and out, not neighborly. And in my position I have come to know them all. Some, of course, I knew before coming. Randy and I are lifelong friends. In fact—well, what's past is past, but my life might have been different except for family responsibilities—then emptiness."

The gold had left her eyes, and so had all expression. True felt that she must do something—*anything*—to bring her back to reality.

"Tillie, did you know Irish O'Higgin—did he visit with his kin here?"

Mrs. Caswell seemed to concentrate. "I—think now—only after the property came to him—or maybe I saw him in Portland—"

No information there which was helpful to either of them. "And the man with the beaver hat—do you know who he is?"

For some reason the question amused Tillie. "That description could fit anyone, including women. According to *Godey's*, ladies will wear beaver hats this winter—winter is almost here, isn't it? Are you going home for the holiday?"

Would she! Wild horses could not keep her away if she had her druthers. But there were so many factors to consider that planning was impossible; it was inviting heartbreak. She must put the hope aside. And besides, she wanted to steer Tillie back onto the trail. The men would be in soon, and there was so much she wanted to discuss with O'Higgin. But first, back to her line of questioning.

"I have given no thought to Christmas—yet. But," True laid down her spoon and leaned forward, "do you know who the man is, the one," she smiled, "wearing the beaver hat?"

"Yes!" The answer came so quickly that it caught True unprepared. "But I am unable to reveal his identity. Please do not ask me to."

True's lips quivered betrayingly in spite of her effort to hide deep disappointment. Tillie saw. "I'm sorry, my dear." Her eyes lighted then, "But I can tell you a little about the mysterious man we saw in the gap the night Midgie left—forgive me—the night of the fiesta. At least, what I *don't* know, I should have said. Seemed he just dipped down out of the sky—let's see, about the time we were discussing the railroad shares and the rights of the government—"

We? Tillie must have seen the question in her eyes. "I own some," she said almost reluctantly, "as did Artie, as I'm sure you know now, since they came with the Double N, giving them to O'Higgin and then to you Norths—"

Railroad shares? True heard no more. Her mind was awhirl with conflicting thoughts and questions. Did Wil know? And what would this do to Marty, with his hatred for the railroad? And then: *So here we are again, Michael St. John and me—enmeshed in something between us. I should have known.* Would he stop at nothing in order to gain power?

Mrs. Caswell was still talking, apparently about the Mystery Man.

"He never asks for mail—never speaks, in fact, the few times he has ventured down. Whatever it is he does, he's dedicated to it. Strange thing about the man—he seems to drop out of the sky and go up in smoke with nary a word. Some say he's a being from another planet, and truly he plays a harmonica—the only human sound anybody has heard him make—like it was an angel's harp. If you can imagine grand opera notes made by inhaling and exhaling on a mouth organ! Asked to describe him, I couldn't. And yet I seem to know when he's around—sometimes feeling he is here even when I don't see him. Sometimes a Mystery Man, sometimes an Invisible One. Sort of spooky, but I'll wager he knows every train schedule."

An idea took shape in True's mind. "Then," she said slowly, "he may have been listening to the music that Midgie made? If so," she mused slowly, "that would eliminate him from suspects—I'm speaking about the slaughtering of the heifer. There was so much commotion—"

"And Midgie's going. Not meaning to pry, but I care about her more than you could understand, and," Tillie swallowed, "I'm wondering if you feel you could confide in me as to her whereabouts."

"I care too, Tillie. I care so much it hurts me to remember—but I can tell you nothing, including who took her away—"

Tillie jerked erect. "You don't suspect foul play!"

True's heart have a lurch and leveled off in painful beats. "I never thought of that—oh, Tillie, Tillie, keep her in your prayers."

O'Higgin's *haw-haw* laugh rang through the Inn. Mrs. Caswell picked up the tea things and True rushed upstairs to dress. Dinner was simple but sustaining—a rich potato soup with loaves of fresh-from-the oven black-crust bread. The latter Billy Joe dunked in his soup unself-consciously, sucking on one end as one sucks through a straw. The sound was less than pleasant, causing Mr. Caswell to cast him a shriveling scowl. Billy Joe took note and cast his host a superior glance. After all, the foreman of the Double N could take his food as he pleased.

"Where's your sense of humor, my good man?" Billy Joe jibed. "Remember, eatin' ain't quite th' same onct a body's teeth is falsified."

"Down, boys!" O'Higgin ordered as if addressing Tonsil and Lung. "Ye both be causin' me ears t'ring like bells." He rose and felt inside the pockets of his mackinaw tossed carelessly on the pier table alongside the high-domed clock beside the front door. What he found was cotton, which he promptly stuffed into his ears. "Protects me from th' bloomin' noise o'th' train," he bellowed, unable to hear his own volume. And then he grinned widely. "Glad His Majesty and Lady St. John ain't amongst us—too rich fer our blood they be—dinin' in th' special car o'th' Iron Horse. Big laugh, thinkin' he owns th' monster while us commoners hold th' purse strings."

True saw Marty's eyes widen. What he heard was news. So the man in the beaver hat had nothing to do with the railroads—or did he? Perhaps he felt as strongly against their coming through the rich farmlands as her brother. She tried to read Young Wil's face but found no expression there—just an admiring smile.

When at length he and she were alone with O'Higgin, they fired questions at him so rapidly that he threatened to stuff the cotton balls back into his ears. Yes, all was well at home. And, no, he was not here to check on the ranch—wasn't the agreement for a year? All seemed to be going well from her letters, he told True. Too bad the family couldn't have Thanksgiving together, but better that way—the weaning away, you know? They'd have one glorious celebration when the "trial period" was over (no mention of Christmas, no mention of Midgie). The twins? Oh, pimple-faced and giggling over "the facts of life."

O'Higgin checked his gold watch. "Oh, I'll be leavin' 'fore th' mists is off th' heather come morn—th' rest o'th' night is Martin's!"

26

Winter's Lock

❧

"**M**ARK MY WORDS, sumpin's brewin'." Billy Joe's voice had the ring of a bad-weather forecast. "What's th' world comin' to when Caswell, peaceful man as he is, goes totin' a pistol holstered t'his hip—sez murderin' renegades are gittin' thicker'n puddin'—strangers, too, added t'them unsavory-lookin', impoverished prospectors who know full well ain't no gold hereabouts but stay on. Cain't tell who's who—meanin' both sides uv th' coin looks th' same—like that satchel-carryin' St. John." His eyes scanned the rising terrain on either side of the return trail. "Then *him up* yonder in th' gap—I tell ye'both somebody's gonna git his skull separated from his body, er worse—"

"Worse?" True found it hard to keep a straight face even though his words made her shudder.

Young Wil seemed unaware of the conversation. His eyes, too, were on guard. "Did you pick up anything new concerning the railroads, Billy Joe?"

"Oh, they're boun' on railroadin' their way through, some kind uv merger's in th' wind—already recruitin' hands." Billy Joe's voice was nervous and hurried. "Even as't me 'bout our fiel' hands—'n since you wuz tied up in conferrin' with O'Higgin—good t'see that ole wheeze!—I up 'n took charge, sayin' we'd all look after ourse'ves. Oh, 'n sumpin' else peculiar-like. I ain't never knowed Tillie, who's so tight-lipped, askin' s'many questions—mostly 'bout Marty. Wonder why."

"I have no idea." Wil's dark eyes were resolutely on the road, but there was tension in his body wedged so closely to True, as if some inner

278

magnet were tugging at his eyeballs elsewhere. True wished, as she did so many times, that they were alone, that she could reach up and stroke the furrows from his forehead, reassuring him of she knew not what. Life simply seemed unfair sometimes. *Stop it!* She told herself; *it's only for a year.* Until then she must think of others beside herself. She was relieved when Marty's horse overtook and passed them.

"Did Mrs. Caswell—or anyone else—ask about Midgie?" She aimed the question at Billy Joe, but it was Wil who answered.

"I did not hear her name mentioned. I wonder how Marty handled that part in the long talk with O'Higgin. By the way, this is a small matter, but did you notice that O'Higgin addressed him as Martin? We've never used the name—"

"How'd he come by that handle—uh, name?" Billy Joe parried.

"Family name—I explained about his parents' drowning to Mariah—oh, there she is!" True replied. Mariah's feet took wing, the boys running a close second.

It was a joyous homecoming for them—and suddenly for them all: Tex, Pig Iron, Slinger, Slim, and Augie, who was trying to greet them in bilingual tongue (Tillie called it "Spanglish") above the shrill barks of the two dogs as they bounced, ran circles, and set the hens to cackling. Yes, this was a part of her family now. Yet she had shared physical food with them but neglected the Bread of Life. *This I will correct, Lord, her heart promised, beginning now!*

"We are all going to have Thanksgiving at our quarters. And that's an order!"

Great smiles carved their faces into jack-o'-lanterns of joy.

Their reaction gave her the needed courage: "We have so much to praise God for—"

"And I have more than anybody!" Young Wil whispered in her ear.

The next three days were spent in preparing for the feast. Using Grandma Malone's recipe, True set cracked-wheat loaves to rising. The bread promised success by filling every cranny of the house with a tantalizing smell of yeast. Aunt Chrissy's walnut-prune cake looked so good that True hid it behind the lard can from which she dipped in making pastry for the sweet potato custards. From the garden came carrots and collards. But meat? The men were tired of venison and bacon.

"I'm so hungered fer chicken 'n dressin' with thickenin' gravy," Tex said on one of his excessive visits to the kitchen, "I kin smell it—it's like my granny wuz back agin—say! I've got uh idee, we could use one uv them hens. They're lookin fat 'n ready fer th' pot—"

Marty had been busy nailing a storm window into its frame. Suddenly he slammed into the house like the storm he prepared for. "Get back on the job!" His voice was an angry order. "And no! You are not to lay a hand on Midgie's chickens—*not ever*—is that understood?"

Mumbling a "Yessir," the boy stumbled out hastily.

True gasped, but before she could make sense of the scene, Billy Joe rushed in like a spring squall. "S'matter with Junior?" he asked in his usual let's-get-to-the-bottom-of-this manner. "Come outta here with his tail between his legs, eyes as watery as uh fresh-opened can uv oysters. Been cryin'—huh?"

There was an awkward pause—a pause which True broke with the truth. "Tex was wishing for family, I guess—asking for a dish his grandmother used to prepare—"

Marty did not allow her to finish. "Wanted to kill one of Midgie's hens. Over my dead body!" he spat out.

Billy Joe's eyes narrowed to slits, which he fixed on Marty while fingering his grease-spotted hat. "When'er y'goin' after her—yer wife, I mean, not th' chicken?"

"She left of her own accord—" Marty began angrily, then stopped. His fury had bounced from Tex to Billy Joe, veered off to Midgie, and now returned to the foreman. "Did anybody ever tell you what a meddlesome busybody you are? If I had my way—"

"I'd be gone, I reckon, but iffen that'd solve yer problem, it's uh sac'erfice I'd make. 'N thet's th' gospel truth." Billy Joe shook his head sorrowfully, "Y'young' uns ain't never been tolt, I'm guessin', thet gittin' hitched is easy. It's *stayin'* thataway what counts—wisht I could come up with sumpin' surefire fer salvaging th' pieces fer'ye."

"Who said I wanted my marriage salvaged?"

"Hit dawg allus hollers—" Billy Joe commenced. He stopped as Young Wil entered the back door.

"May I have a moment with Marty—alone?"

Billy Joe, unabashed, strutted out the front door. True, her heart in turmoil, turned toward the bedroom door. Young Wil motioned her back. Marty was about to let go with a barrage of words—words he withheld when his older brother lifted a hand for silence. When Wil motioned to a chair, he took it, more from respect than meekness, judging from the hostility in his eyes. True slid into a chair beside him, knowing that the air must be cleared if there was to be a proper Thanksgiving.

"Marty," Young Wil's voice sounded weary, "I realize we were not going to interfere. True and I pledge to keep that promise. However, I have a question for you—just one. Agreed?"

Do you love her? True prepared to hear him say.

She was wrong. "Did Midgie tell you she was pregnant?"

"Pregnant!" Who asked the question—herself or Marty? Probably both.

Marty's eyes clouded with shock. His face blanched and the little blue vein along his left temple which always revealed extreme emotion ballooned. Shock turned to a radiance that rivaled the sun. His moment of Creation. His Day of Revelation. There was a sacred silence. Then Marty became human again. He grinned, appearing to True's startled eyes to rise up in the east and come down in the west, and threw his hat at the ceiling.

"Oh, Midgie, Midgie, Midgie!" Turning to his brother, now a respected doctor, he asked, "When?"

"You figure that one. When could it be?"

Marty's face turned scarlet. "It could happen like *that*? I mean— it would happened—uh—"

"In June—on your wedding night, to be exact," Wil said professionally.

"June, July—this is November—a little March hare!"

Marty was giddily happy in a way that set True and Wil laughing, neither of them having been privileged to see this side of him before. And then a new side—one of concern for another person. He would never be the same again.

"She ought to be taking care—not overdoing—"

"Midgie's sensible, she's not glass. I doubt that she's breaking a horse. Anybody can deliver a baby—"

"Not this one! She'll stay on her feet until her hands won't touch in front! Babies need fathers even before they're born—and mothers need specialists like you. Nobody discovered this but you. So don't count on me for Thanksgiving. I'm going to find my family. Whoopee!"

Thanksgiving Day dawned as bright as the good news. The Goldish family arrived in sheepskin jackets and fur caps of ancient vintage, bundled against the cold that Billy Joe predicted to arrive by noon. He was right. Wind poked at the chimney places by the time the roasted wild mallard ducks and dressing (with "thickened gravy" for Tex) were ready. Sage rivaled the sweet scent of nutmeg and cloves in the pies, and yeasty loaves of bread that Grandma Mollie would have envied—crusty-brown outside, feather-light inside—crowned the feast.

Crowded into the wee kitchen on benches of rough boards laid across sawhorses the diners waited, visibly salivating. How long had it been since the men had a home-cooked meal? And the expression on Mariah's face said this was her first Thanksgiving. Her sons, hair slicked with pomade or lard holding the middle parts intact, had controlled their manners as well. But their eyes were full moons.

As planned, Young Wil read a few brief praise passages from the Psalms, careful not to overexpose those for whom this might be their first encounter with the Bible. "Would each of you want to name something you're grateful for?" he asked upon closing the Bible. "Only if you wish."

"I dunno 'bout prayin'—" Slinger's voice trembled.

"Just saying what you appreciate can be a prayer," Wil said gently.

"Later it's important knowin' thangs—know how old Methuselah wuz?"

The look cast the foreman's direction told the questioning Billy Joe that he might not reach what's-his-name's age. But Slinger answered best: "Which birthday?"

Snickers from the group broke the ice. Tex said with innocent pride, "Me, I'm thankful I'm uh good shot! Brung down four wheat-stealin' ducks. Yep! I'm glad th' Lord gimme a good aim like Slinger's, even iffen he don' feel up t'braggin' 'bout it."

A home, they said . . . good neighbors . . . this dandy meal . . . and (from Augie and Mariah in fragmented English) *Gracias, gracias!* True longed to shout out the secret of her joy, saying instead, "Lord, thank You for love."

Billy Joe would be praying yet had the coffeepot not boiled over. The grateful men ate in silence, tossing down food with the same skill used to toss hay in the mow. Mariah brought out her guitar. They sang familiar songs of the range, then old hymns. The wind's brassy bass joined the singing to blow in the snow—winter's lock for the seeded wheat. *Praise the Lord!* "And please," True prayed in the secret closet of her heart, "let Your Word be locked inside these men's souls."

27
A Letter from Home

❧

THERE WAS NO word from Marty. There was, however, a long letter from Aunt Chrissy tucked into a bulky Christmas package marked OPEN EARLY. It was a struggle for True to wait until she, Young Wil, and Billy Joe could get back to the Double N before opening the box. It could hold a message concerning Marty or Midgie's whereabouts— better yet, both of them. But traveling home was long and tedious.

Snow had thawed, leaving the main road slippery and a bridge washed out—a gulch having turned into a short-lived river, trying the patience of men and mules. The animals were compelled to wade belly-deep and decided, with the poorly developed logic of mules, to stop in midstream. Billy Joe ranted and threatened, but to no avail.

"Git outta here, y'dum critters, lickety-split! Iffen we don' git there y'git no fodder fer uh week 'n no apple fer Christmas! Sech dum-dums," he said to True. "'Er maybe they're smart, knowin' they git my goat worryin' me into thankin' I won' be able t'buy th' yard goods fer my Mariah t'make them fiesta dresses fer yore mama 'n gran'mama fer gifts. Wil, I'm bettin' they don' budge!"

Young Wil laughed. "I'm no betting man, Billy Joe. But if I were, I'd put no more than a dime on such stakes. Mules, like people, like an occasional *please*."

"You joshin'?"

"Test my theory."

"*Please*, good brothers," Billy Joe said, falling for the gag.

To the surprise of all three riders, the beasts obliged. But valuable time was lost. Tillie suggested a new route home over higher ground to the south—took longer but had better drainage.

Shopping finished hurriedly, Young Wil bribed the mules with a sack of oats and loaded the wagon while Tillie asked permission to make twin Indians for the twins: a maid with braided hair and a brave wearing the paint of his tribe and carrying a fishing spear. "And, oh, True," she said happily, "Randy'll be back for Christmas week."

With some misgiving the three of them took the narrow trail overrun with brush and dill weed. Billy Joe was strangely silent as the mules strained up the gently rising hill, coming at length to the summit, crowned by a few wind-warped pines. A small creek led downward on the other side, emptying into what must be the McKenzie River, although True hadn't realized it was that nearby. The creek meandered at approximately the speed of the mules, narrowed, disappeared, then reappeared to pause where the ground rose again.

Billy Joe hawk-eyed the surroundings, obviously onto something. He was. "So thet's hit! I heered 'twas so—that th' Good Lord had emptied His pockets 'bout there, bringin' in more prospectors. Could'a landed anywheres, I guess—me, I ain't interested in chemicals, but I smell gold. 'N," he scratched his chin, "I'm wonderin' what it's agonna add t'our problems—farmin', railroadin', more feudin'!"

True now recalled the clump of men talking in low tones as they stood apart on the platform where the railroad terminated onto a spur. Then the orders for a pick, shovel, and five-cent pie tins.

Her thoughts were interrupted by a faint sound—familiar, almost music, or was it the wind playing in the struggling pines? There! Again the sad-sweet notes floating through the gathering darkness. Had the men heard? Both were silent, but wasn't Young Wil urging the mules forward an indication? True looked past him and was surprised to see a sheer cliff that seemed to plunge downward and end in midair. Below were darker splotches of darkness. Tents? Overhead the stars came out one by one to crown the heavens. And by their dim light she was able to make out the rocky gap. A green-rocket falling star sped across the sky, causing her to jump. It was only a falling star, but it illuminated the Mystery Man! And then she knew the source of the music: his harmonica.

She was glad to get home. Deciding to make no mention of the incident, True steadied her nerves by cutting the ropes of the enormous package while the men unloaded the wagon.

And there, as she had hoped, was the letter!

Dear Family:

Winters being harsher in the eastern part of the state, Miss Mollie and I decided to make extra quilts, hoping that their memories will keep you warm. You will find little patches of the past scattered at random—some of which I shed a few tears parting with: little scraps from your baby garments . . . Angel Mother's wedding gown for True . . . Marty's first rompers . . . Young Wil's first-day-of-school shirt (How he loved them both, the shirt and school!). I will leave the rest unexplained—although I suspect that all of you will recognize some of the colorful pieces Grandma Mollie stitched in so lovingly for your "something blue" to sleep beneath the first night. I think all of you were a little embarrassed taking along a quilt in June—and now it is I who sits here crying because all of you are gone, but together! Precious moments that bind us all into the loving family that we are . . .

True laid the letter aside, eyes misty with tears . . . partly from sweet sentiment, and partly because it was clear that Aunt Chrissy did not know that the four of them were no longer together.

Later she would read what Jerome and Kearby wrote—mostly school, how they were soloing in the cantata "Christmas Covers the World." O'Higgin was helping with the *grievshock* (*hot embers*) pantomime. *Come home!*

But first True felt an irrepressible urge to locate Angel Mother's diary, read it, and remember achingly what she could of the beautiful Vangie. It spoke as if written for True: "I will laugh when you laugh . . . cry when you cry . . . so long as you are together . . ."

28

Christmas Wish Granted

❧

TILLIE CASWELL DELIVERED the colorful Indian dolls for the twins' rooms the same day Mariah brought the fiesta dresses. As they helped True wrap the package for sending home, the two women each revealed staggering pieces of news.

"I found out who assisted Midgie—I suppose one could call it befriending—in her, uh, leaving. Michael St. John! I guess we should have known."

Yes, we should have known, True's heart echoed. *He would have no qualms.* But wait! Should she be so hard on him? After all, he knew nothing of the circumstances; he only saw a girl in need—a need with which he could help. In addition, he had the lovely living quarters on the train which was leaving the next day. And, she realized for the first time, he knew Midgie's conductor-father very well.

Mariah's news had to do with another matter. Excitedly she reverted to her native tongue. Tillie listened with eyebrows raised, then explained to True, shaking her head in disbelief as she spoke.

"The boys reported seeing a woman—pretty rare, you know. Seems she was down below the cliff by the gap." She tilted her head southward. "You know children—down there faster than jack rabbits and talking to her, no less! Can you believe she was selling barbed wire? A *woman*! Had rolls and rolls of the deadly stuff in her peddler's wagon. Mr. Caswell—Curly—is afraid to stock the stuff himself."

True looked at the women in dazed incredulity for a moment, then laughed. "If I understand correctly, you are saying that this woman is braver than—"

Billy Joe stormed in the front door, eyes flashing a warning at Mariah. "Not braver—more foolish! I tole you, wife uv my heart, that you warn't t'mention—"

"Now, now, Beetle," Tillie Caswell challenged. "Well! So Mariah spoke to me—as well she should have. You needn't stand there like a mountain lion ready to spring. What's the difference who sells the wire when it comes right down to it? Women have the same right—"

"Nobody has the right as the law stands, Tillie." Young Wil had entered soundlessly. "This is cattle country—open range. Livestock would cut themselves to pieces in case of a stampede."

"Then who would buy it?" True asked, not understanding. "I thought the commotion was over a woman's taking over a man's job."

"In a way it is. Only a cowardly man would allow that—and only a desperate, defiant, or ignorant woman would agree. It spells danger."

For reasons only he understood, Wil pulled True to him. Protectively. Almost savagely. "This spells more trouble."

Frightened, True pulled away as far as space in the tiny livingroom allowed. "Will somebody please tell me what this is all about?" Fear shaped into a frightening vision enlarging within her heart. *Supposing Midgie—in her desperation for money—or to get even—*

"About?" Billy Joe cut in bruskly, "It's about woollies! Sheep 'n cattle mix 'bout as good as water 'n oil. An' t'thank thet was sheep country we gazed 'p'on crost th' gap—"

"But why a woman?" True persisted.

"Women don' get hung—punished rightful er maybe not so rightful—but not hung by th' neck 'til dead!"

Marty rode in on Christmas Eve at the speed of the rising wind, its cutting edge predicting a blizzard. He had borrowed a one-eyed horse from a lean-to that Curly called a livery stable. The animal, sniffing its more royal cousins, whinnied, and, turning its one good eye to their protective shelter, stumbled forward. At the sight of the comical pair, True burst into uncontrollable laughter to keep from dissolving into a puddle of sentiment. *Oh, Marty . . . Marty . . . what a Christmas present!*

"The prodigal's home!" Marty called, obviously glad, although his eyes showed fatigue and disappointment. True knew even before he told them that he had failed in his mission. Midgie was among the missing.

"Not a sign," he said. "She seems to have vanished. And anybody knowing anything kept it under wraps." Marty shook his head in despair.

Questions with inclusive answers. Did Marty check with Midgie's father? Conductor Callison was on a run. Did he go home? Out of the question, Marty explained, letting True take his wraps as he rubbed blue-cold hands over the luxurious warmth of the little pot-bellied stove. O'Higgin had hung a rider onto their previous policies when he was here: no visits home until the year ended. There was to be total breakaway.

"Guess he thought it would be easier to swallow later."

Easier for us all, True thought sadly, glad she hadn't known.

"Wil," Marty said slowly—uncomfortable in his new role of asking favors—"can we keep the fact that I left here between us, you think?"

"I see no point in making mention," Wil said quietly. "Anyway, a man would be foolish allowing any agreement to stand between him and love."

Marty's face went white. "I've been a fool; God set me straight. But I can't stay on the straight and narrow without help—His and yours. Know what I want for Christmas?" he blurted with a gulp. "You both with me—I—I know where to find her—but I need you." His face was that of a pleading child.

Young Wil looked inquiringly at True. Stunned, she nodded.

"Wish granted," Wil replied. "Are you absolutely sure she's not *here*?"

Had he thought of the barbed-wire lady too?

29

Reunion

❧

THE LANDSCAPE WAS beginning to freeze over on Christmas Day, scalloping ruts of the isolated road with silvered ice, thereby dictating caution—a caution that Billy Joe ignored as he urged the team ahead of the approaching storm. He asked no questions, content to be a part of the drama. The boss men need pay no nevermind to anything. Wasn't he in charge? Too bad they were unable to partake of the sugar cured ham that Mr. Marty brought home. But his Mariah would fix it up fancy-like. And, yes indeedy, they'd have the hands at their table for the feast. Prayers? Oh, my, yes! The men would know what Christmas was all about before partaking of such victuals as the loving Lord, whose Birthday they were celebrating, had provided.

While True packed a few necessities for traveling, Young Wil called the men into the cabin and told them simply that the Norths must be away for the holiday. "Your Christmas gift," he said simply,"is an invitation to share this place while we're gone. It's too cold out there, fellows. Just be careful with fires—and keep an eye out for—well, any trouble. No, there's nothing special to do, except for yourselves. There is plenty of firewood—also plenty of split rails for living quarters of sorts. Why not nail together a kind of bunk for yourselves? I will try and find you a stove, giving you warmer quarters—"

He stopped when there were tears in the eyes of the men. Billy Joe snorted with disdain, then blew his nose and faked a cough.

The train was on time and they were able to board quickly. As True waved a handkerchief of farewell to a tearful Tillie, she was surprised to feel a lump in her own throat. Six months ago she would have seen this trip as an escape. Now she felt—well, how *did* she feel?

On the way, Marty disclosed his plan. Well, maybe it would work. Just maybe. It seemed to be a last resort, actually. The ghost of Midgie hung over them all like Marley's ghost over Scrooge in Dickens' *Christmas Carol*. It would continue to do so until the matter was resolved. True refused to think of the unspeakable possibility that something could have happened to her—some tragedy—although this *was* a very real possibility. She concentrated on the beauty around her instead. Nature had been so extravagant with her paintbrush here—and it was *home*. A growing sense of excitement welled up inside her as the familiar green cathedral of the forest closed in . . .

The old hotel was in the exact ramshackle condition it had been when the four of them had spent their honeymoon here. Even the help in the largest diningroom in Portland remained. Seated at the long "family-style" table—deserted except for the three of them—True watched a rotund waiter (part Indian, she guessed by the black hair spilling down over his shoulders, shining like polished niello), her mouth suddenly dry. There was something about him—not sinister, more secretive—which said the diningroom had been cleared because of their presence, although he went on polishing and repolishing the silverware with the corner of his apron. Face immobile, he applied a torch to the low-swinging chandeliers, turned them low, and marched toward the kitchen, straight-shouldered as if he were keeping step to a war drum. Did she imagine it, or was there a tilt of his shining head in their direction as a signal to some unseen figure?

She did not imagine it. The familiar face of the manager appeared at the swing-door. There was a flicker of recognition in his swarthy face. But before she could nod or smile, he disappeared.

For the first time she wondered how Marty came to decide on the hotel's being where he would find Midgie. It seemed most unlikely. The dryness in her throat worsened as she ruminated the impending confrontation if his plan for a meeting worked. For confrontation it would be—if Marty reverted to his usual pattern, letting relief give way to rage. Would he go at her tooth and claw? And Midgie—how would she behave? Let him bully her? Or would her emotional floodgates give way? She couldn't for a moment imagine that the insecure, frightened Midgie could take a meeting in stride. Probably she would catch sight of them and flee again.

Marty was obviously in a state of nerves. It was unlike him to talk so much. He veered from one subject to another with such speed that Young Wil was having trouble keeping up with him. About barley. About the scenery. About some person or persons who had been helpful, but failing to say who or about what. Then back to barley.

True forced her eyes to look out the window as the dove of twilight alighted on a tall fir which stretched to reach heaven, its needled peaks probing the blue as the light gave way. Shadows blended. Darkness settled comfortably over the land.

"Now?" a woman's voice broke into the sudden silence.

"Now," a male voice responded. And a large woman with a smiling face, bursting with obvious curiosity, set steaming bowls of soup before them.

Then she could bear it no longer. Casting a furtive look over her shoulder, making sure her employer did not see, she lowered her voice conspiratorially. "Th' missus is 'bout t'dine. Want I should tell 'er? Shock, y'know—her bein' in a family way 'n all. 'Course now it's no bizness uv mine—"

"You're right, it isn't!" Marty snapped. "The manager knew this was to be a surprise—unrehearsed—forgive me, but do go about your business. This is something I—we—must handle alone—"

The woman fled, almost colliding with Midgie. *Midgie!* Wearing a blossom-pink maternity dress, Midgie looked like a ripe peach. But it was the way she lifted her rounded chin, the simple dignity with which she carried herself, that tore at True's heart. Her smile may have been a bit fixed, but her eyes were lighted with a million stars. True held her breath as she watched Marty. No admonishing frown. No harsh words. After all, his face said, the score was even. Midgie had left of her own accord, but he had come searching in like manner.

Crushing his napkin into a ball, he flung it without aim. It landed in the soup, causing both of them to laugh. Make that four! All were bursting with mirth as Marty and Midgie ran to each other, arms outstretched.

Marty crushed her to him covetously. And nothing was going to come between them—not even their child! "Darling," he murmured.

There were a dozen "I love yous"—unself-conscious, all of them.

"I'm sorry—never again—" Marty's voice broke as Midgie put a *shushing* finger to his lips. "Never again is right—no more mention of our being apart. *Ever!*"

Midgie turned to True and Young Wil, eyes shining. "No, don't go! We're never going to be apart again. I'm starved—for the first time in months! For food . . . news . . . and love!"

30
Homecoming

❧

A SHRILL WHISTLE pierced the midnight air as if vibration of the rails were not enough to alert Slippery Elm of the coming train. The short trips between the community and Portland, although irregular in schedule, occurred more and more frequently now (hopefully building "good blood" between landholders and the railroad company). But the arrivals remained an oddity—an iron monster from other worlds bringing good news and bad. And there were always new faces, those belonging to a new segment of the railroad crew. Tonight there were more spectators than usual. The usual openmouthed gawkers appeared to be waiting for somebody who never came. The few heavily coated, bearded favorite sons leaned importantly against the sagging buildings, either to stall off trouble or start it. There were also a few stragglers, and tonight the Caswells. To welcome home the Norths?

The air was frigid, but Curly had no time for donning a hat. He had news that wouldn't keep—of that True was sure as she caught sight of his shining head, which tried to outshine the moon it reflected. As Marty helped Midgie to her feet and Young Wil pulled their travel cases from the overhead rack, True watched Mr. Caswell's keen eyes travel the length of the train as if one car were a treasure chest! He must have found it, for his face, so tense when he rushed onto the rickety platform, now suffused with color as he pushed forward.

Spotting the Norths, Curly addressed them all simultaneously:

"Th' newly appointed division superintendent uv th' railroad—yer jest in time, meetin' scheduled fer tonight or tomorrow, dependin' on

which side o'midnight yer railroad time declares. Trouble a'plenty—
'n—oh, I'm a-gettin' more 'n more narrow 'twixt th' horns, plum
forgettin' interductions." Curly was winded but rushed on. "Wil 'n
Martin, an' yore purdy wives, say 'Hello' t'Mr. Em'ry Keelin'. Th'
Norths, sir; they got special in'erest all over th' valley—not shareholders 'xactly, maybe more say-so 'cause y'gotta 'ave right o' way
—shake hands. Me, uh man's gotta come up fer air *sometime*, I
reckon."

"I was beginning to wonder," Mr. Keeling said congenially, favoring True and Midgie with a smile. "Ladies," he acknowledged, and
then turned to shake hands with the other men.

His warm, friendly manner compensated for his lack of physical
charm. His small eyes, above a skimpy mustache with a moth-eaten
effect, and a decidedly bulbous nose painted red with tiny veins,
looked out of place above the perfect tailoring of his suit. He kept
shrugging as if the blue serge coat and pants were a new mode of
dressing, a uniform of distinction.

A lot seemed to have happened in the short time they were away—
happenings True wanted desperately to hear about. But Tillie Caswell
had rushed to her and Midgie with outstretched arms in tearful
welcome, her words drowning out the men's conversation. "Oh my
darlings, my darlings—let me look at you—so *that's* the secret—a
baby," she marveled. "Oh Midgie, little Midgie," Tillie was weeping openly now. "You can't possibly know what this means to me—
but someday—"

Why had she paused? It was not the first time True had wondered
about Tillie's unfinished sentences and about her past. But now was
not the time to pursue the subject even in her own mind.

"Coffee, coffee!" The Caswells were ushering the party inside
excitedly. True tried desperately to marshal order from the chaos of
the two conversations. It would have been impossible even without
the train's endless backing and starting, punctuated by the metallic
grind of brakes.

"What's going on out there?" Young Wil asked (trying, True felt,
to mask his concern).

"Some new track laid—" the division superintendent began.

"More's comin', too, 'n fast—never saw men work s'fast—like they
wuz tryin' t'outwit some uv us—"

True's mind went back to Curly Caswell's breathless greeting. Just in time he had told Emory Keeling . . . right-of-way . . . "trouble a'plenty . . ." There was more, but her mind bolted back to the present.

"Cut *our* fences—let the prize Longhorns escape to the hills!" Marty dropped his cup with a clatter. "We have to go—*now!* Can you put the ladies up for the night, Tillie—what's left of it?"

"No! Absolutely not!" Midgie jumped from her chair, fatigue erased from her face. "I'm going with you—at least, to the Double N. That way I—we, True?—will be closer."

"You can't take the chance. There's apt to be violence—"

"There's always a chance of violence. We live in a violent world. You needn't stand guard. I won't run away again. An encore would lack the punch of a first-time performance."

Even though the situation at the ranch demanded immediate attention, True and Young Wil sought each other's eyes and locked. This was Marty and Midgie? Their first expression was one of amused incredulity. The sense of amusement turned to one of admiration and respect born of conviction. The couple had become Mr. and Mrs. Martin North, husband and wife determined to protect each other, come what may.

The drama was unfolding rapidly. Young Wil, like herself, appeared unwilling to interrupt. Not that the other couple needed help!

"I won't have you taking chances—the baby's too important—"

"To be born without a father!" Midgie finished. "Want to come with me to the—*ahem!*—powder room, True?"

Tillie followed them. The men, speechless, followed with their eyes. "We'll need horses, Curly," Young Wil said quietly, "for four."

Once alone, the women made no reference to the conversation. Neither did Tillie make mention of the crisis at hand. Other matters took priority where Mrs. Caswell was concerned. True was torn between the two. Ultimately, in those few short minutes together, she chose to concentrate on questions she knew Tillie would ask—questions which she herself had had no opportunity to pose. It was a ticklish situation—one of great sensitivity, requiring the choosing of words with utmost delicacy. And Tillie sensed as much along with True. She behaved as if about to unpack extraordinarily fragile crystal.

Neither needed have worried, for the new Midgie made it easy. "I am sure," she said, reaching skyward to relax her weary body, "you

both want a quick account of my activities—and, no, you aren't prying. I am only too happy to give account . I had to get away—you both
know that—find out where I stood with my husband—and look my
own self in the eye. I never knew who I was. Even in my prayers I
could never properly identify myself to God. There's still a lot we
have to learn. But we'll learn together—and we have God with us,
and all of you!"

"Did you—uh—learn anything about—yourself?" The question
seemed important to Tillie.

"I learned I'm not dumb. I took classes in grammar, manners, and
birthing. A baby needs a lady for a mother. Then I enrolled in a correspondence course to work on here—something new, called psychology. I learned how to listen to Marty, like we have to listen for
the answer when we pray. And, oh, I made no contacts except with
my father so he wouldn't worry. He paid my board without questions.
Let's go!"

31
Night of Horror

~

"IS ANYTHING HARDER to bear than waiting?" Midgie pondered.

"Bad news," True answered, wondering if she believed it.

Midgie had been pitifully happy to get home, running her fingers over every inch of the spick-and-span cabin. The place looked as if the ranch hands had cleaned every corner minutes ago, but the cold stove said they had been gone for hours. Now the minutes crawled even though a fire chuckled cheerfully in the wood range and there was a lot of talking to catch up on. Midgie put the kettle on and made a batch of cinnamon rolls. True set the coffee on to boil and mixed batter for sourdough buckwheat cakes. The men would be hungry, they told each other, once the cattle were rounded up. And it was natural for daylight to drag its heels in midwinter. Well, wasn't it? They guessed so, neither of them daring to check the creeping hands of the clock.

"We should look our best," Midgie suggested. She fluffed her hair on the sides becomingly and applied a bit of petroleum jelly to her eyelids and eyebrows. "I can't do much about this figure, thank goodness!" she giggled nervously. "Oh, let me cut you a fringe of side bangs like young women are wearing in Portland!" She snipped, held up a mirror.

True saw herself through Young Wil's eyes and decided she looked more than a little acceptable. Surely he would be here soon.

The coffeepot boiled over, causing both of them to jump.

They could read the Bible. Yes, they could. They tried but were unable to concentrate. They tried praying, too, with the same results.

297

The problem, of course, True admitted to herself, was that they were not listening for the Lord's voice, but for some sound that would reassure them that He was riding with their husbands. "The hands are studying the Bible," True began.

"My chickens?" Midgie interrupted, indicating inattention.

"They're fine."

Midgie's nerves were growing more taut. She must see them—now! True humored her. Bundling up and bracing against the wailing wind, they checked the cozily covered coops. The rooster's reassuring voice to his startled feathered hens fell on deaf ears. And the building (taking on the shape of a bunkhouse that busy hands were erecting) blind eyes looked at but did not see. Eyes and ears were fine-tuned to see and hear any clue that would tell them their men were safe.

There was sudden silence. Uncanny, coming as it did. Was the wind for or against them? Either way, it played a role. Without it, True heard the snap of a twig. It could have been anything. But some inner sense told her that it warned of a human presence. She stood passive for a moment, hoping that Midgie had not heard. If she could manage to get the other girl to safety—

The thought died before its birth was complete. A tug at her arm said Midgie had heard and was stifling a cry. Moments ago True had felt the place was terrifyingly empty of anything human—just broad open spaces leading up into the night-blue sweep of the hills beyond. That's where the danger lay. And now it was here. Enemies squatted behind every bush. Menace lurked behind each building. Courage was dissipating like a vapor touched by sunshine. Yet mingled with fear was a morbid curiosity—or was it a form of courage for Midgie's sake?—that hypnotized her.

True would have been unable to explain why she stood perfectly still, a reassuring hand placed over Midgie's. She only knew that later it seemed wise. Rooted where they were, the two were able to hear the hair-raising combination of banshee yells and gunfire high above them.

Gunfire! Her mind did a double-take. Think. She must think. But her mind was stampeding—*stampeding*, that was it! The word alerted her to the awful possibility of a stampede of horses and cattle ... animals reverting to their wild nature ... fleeing they knew not what, only to trample one another to death ... charging any barrier senselessly, impervious to injury of themselves or others. And the men—*oh, dear God, our men—help them! How does one cope with a stampede?*

Stop them—she must stop them. But how? She could only imagine the buildings giving way beneath the onslaught of hooves. Automatically she shielded her face from the mass of dirt and gravel which would come with such force that she and Midgie would be buried alive . . .

And then the incredible happened. Bounding up from nowhere, a shapeless form appeared in the shadows, and with the speed of a panther began closing and barricading gates leading into the corral. Would the fragile fence restrain the terrified herds? There were barrels of rock, she remembered, to be used in construction of more concrete irrigation troughs. With superhuman strength she bolted forward just as the bent-over form took the shape of a man, clearly visible in the light of the descending moon. Never mind his identity; he was an answer to prayer. "The barrels—I will help—" and suddenly they were pushing with more power than they knew they possessed. All three of them!

Three? "Midgie, get inside—no, *run!*" True's orders fell on deaf ears. Midgie was pushing alongside them. And the sound of hooves came closer . . . closer . . . closer. Until two strange things happened simultaneously.

Later True would discover that it was only a small stone which slipped from the barrel they were managing to shove inch by inch. But for now it might well have been a boulder rolling beneath her, causing her to lose her footing. She fell face down and lay dazed, forgetting the vital mission at hand, visualizing only the terrain along the ridge of the gap and the valley trough below it on the other side. The clump of dead trees standing spectral and black like evil spirits, almost unobserved at the time, flashed before her eyes. Fire, Billy Joe had said—fire set by arsonists, intended no doubt to warn somebody of something: Indians in order to protect their burial places—or were there any Indians here? Sheepherders warning cattlemen against barbed-wire fencing in open-range country? The other way around? Or something to do with the railroad building?

In that brief moment in the netherworld, True fancied seeing a horse half-concealed behind a dead carcass of a tree, and on it the

Mystery Man—not moving, but unharmed, as wild horses and long-horned cattle neighed and bellowed past, only to fall moaning and dying beneath the sharp hooves of other animals. For somewhere up there stretched a strip of wasteland, pockmarked with gopher holes, tumbleweeds rolling, and heaping themselves like skulls of skeletons in search of their bodies. It was into those gopher holes that the irrational animals would fall, as would the horses ridden by Young Wil, Marty, and the ranch hands—and the enemies in wild pursuit. The illusion had zig-zagged across her mind with the speed of lightning streaking the sky. And then it was as if a gentle but powerful voice spoke from the ramparts of heaven:

"Why seek ye the living among the dead?" That meant *life* . . .

In response, True raised herself on one elbow, only to grow rigid with terror again. Hot breath was fanning her cheeks, salivating tongues licking her cheeks. Wildcats? Wolves?

And then there was a warning whimper, followed by a bark of concern. *The dogs!* How had they escaped the world of madness, and what were they doing here?

Tonsil and Lung had gone opposite directions and now stood like statues at either end of the corral, noses pointed up the hill—waiting, knowing exactly what to do. True shook her head to clear it, some far corner of her mind realizing that they—like Marty—though late bloomers, had metamorphosed from anaphase to maturity according to God's plan . . .

Midgie, too, had fallen. "The baby, the baby!" she was crying out. The stranger was helping her to her feet with a deep-throated order.

"In the house, both of you—*now*! We're as prepared as we can be. Get beneath the bed—*now*—they're coming this way. These buildings will go down like cardboard—unless—you know how to pray, don't you?"

True, every muscle threatening to snap, dragged a protesting Midgie inside and rolled her beneath the bed, covering both their faces with great down pillows. In the process she felt a hot, sticky substance bathe her hands. *Blood!* Midgie was injured. *Oh, dear God, not the baby* . . .

And then came the thunder of hooves mingled with voices which attempted to command and soothe at the same time. The pillows drowned out direction, but two other sounds penetrated the feathers: The dogs were barking like commanders—first here, then there. And above it all the sound of harmonica music. Soft, sad, sweet, pleading, and—above all—comforting. Of course! She should have known —the Mystery Man! He would be killed!

But what was this? Silence. Silence which came to life with voices —some familiar, others not. "We—did it—" Midgie gasped through a mouthful of feathers, the ticking having split beneath her tight grip. Hysterical laughter rose to True's throat as wildly they stumbled out the back door. Oblivious to the heavy breathing of exhausted animals, the happy yelps of dogs in need of praise, and the disappearance of the Mystery Man, they were pleading with God for sight of their husbands.

32
Aftermath

❧

"**H**OW MANY HOURS has it been since you had any sleep, you amazing girl?" Young Wil's voice was filled with concern, but never once did his hands stop working as, together, he and True leaned over a wounded stallion. The stampede seemed like a page torn from an ancient history book.

"I'll bite. How many?" she asked flippantly. She ran a finger against the scratch on her face, her only casualty, and attempted a laugh. The laugh—after all the excitement (and goodness alone knew how many revolutions the hands of the clock had made)—was a winner of its kind. "Should I check on Marty and Midgie, or continue helping here?"

His capable fingers secured a bandage on the quivering animal's near-severed leg. "Stay with me, I think, True. I need disinfectant, and please hand me scissors from the black bag. The bull needs attention."

True obliged. "Think I should be studying for nursing instead of teaching—that is, if ever we get back to our books?"

"You've been wonderful. Without your talking with Midgie while I worked, do you realize that she could have lost the baby? And poor Marty—we'd have lost *him* as well if that happened! Poor guy—one broken arm and the other sprained—the iodine, honey. Wow! this is a spirited critter. Think you can hold this hobbler on his forefeet while I get a halter?"

Of course she could. She could do anything, even hold the world on her shoulders, until young Doctor North replaced it on its axis. Angel Mother was right: "So long as you are together."

"Speaking from the grave ," Grandma Mollie had said. True called it speaking from heaven. How far-reaching a mother's love was . . . and that's how it would be with her own offspring, hers and Young Wil's . . . their love so great that it needed to find expression in creating and nurturing . . .

It must be the same with other forms of life. For it was at that exact moment that Wil gasped, "Can you believe this—a young heifer deciding to give birth instead of waiting for spring? Steady, girl, steady—" he soothed the cow as he had soothed Midgie in their struggle to protect her unborn baby. "True—come, darling, can you handle this?" All the while he was grabbing for ropes and instruments, sterilized and folded neatly away in gauze. "How many animals have we worked on—more than were in the ark?"

"The clean and the unclean," True replied. "I still don't know who's who and what's what about this whole mess. Who went where?"

He tried to catch her up as they struggled with the frightened mother-to-be. His phrases were fragmented, and True had to guess the rest. But a picture formed in her mind as Young Wil gently lifted the beautiful bright-eyed calf and placed it on a saddle blanket beside the new mother's face. "Wake up, lady—wake up and see what you've got here. She'll finish the job and let him know—yes, it's a boy!—who's in charge. Then we'd better take him inside for the night and put Mama in the barn."

True nodded tiredly, admiring him and loving him more than ever before, while struggling to put together the story of this night of horror and triumph. Their losses were fewer than could have been expected. The wounded were attended—cattle, horses, and men. Billy Joe and two of the hands were on their way to Slippery Elm . . . sheriff would be here tomorrow . . . other men were repairing fences . . . bullets had come close . . . even knocked Slim's hat off!—but they were safe. Identity?

"The whole thing was like a combination of an Old World drama with all the characters wearing masks, and just about as pagan. Like three performances in progress at once—a tragedy, a carnival, and Shakespeare's *Comedy of Errors*," Young Wil explained as they moved from one wounded animal to another, stopping often to diagnose and treat.

But the scene came alive in her mind. Make it a musical comedy, she thought, wondering if he knew of the Mystery Man's role. Yes, it had all the makings of a classical play absurdly confused with a second-rate road show. The colorful background set the stage: the starry heavens as an arched ceiling for the theater; the beautiful-at-a-distance outline of the rocky gap as a backdrop; clumps of bushes and charred trees as the wings—all softly lighted by a sinking moon as the crowning touch.

The first attacking party, according to Billy Joe and the other men (each account varying somewhat), rode up the hill with a bravado designed to thrill any audience. And, oh, yes, there was an audience—the other actors! Unfortunately, either none of them had read the play or there was no prompter in the wings, because all the actors missed their cues. A leader (as yet to be identified) made use of extras instead of seasoned actors. "Sapheads," Billy Joe called them, "not knowin' nothin' 'bout how railroads git right-a-ways, jest out t'make uh slick buck," but having descended on Slippery Elm to drop a few hints here and there regarding plans to destroy property. The cattlemen, farmers, and sheepherders got the word and prepared accordingly. Then the "sapheads" made a fatal mistake: One of them attempted to recruit Slinger, the trigger-quick veteran. And so, instead of terrorizing the victims, the would-be "bad men" found themselves staring dumbly at real "bandits" ("Yep, yep, yep! That's us—bandannas 'n all," Billy Joe supplied). Meantime the plot thickened. Ill-planned by all, a strange crossover began. Men joined the wrong ranks, with the railroad gang making the gravest errors of all, beginning to shoot wildly—some of the shots hitting target—

At that point the story was no longer comical—or maybe it hadn't been all along. *It was just that I am so tired, so tired,* True thought fuzzily. But now concern replaced fatigue.

"How many were injured—and was anybody—?" True was unable to finish.

Young Wil met her gaze squarely."You know there had to be casualties, darling. But I did the best I could—"

Her breath came out in a strangled sob. "I know, darling—I know. I was so anxious—so afraid—" her lips whitened, the scratch on her cheek throbbing painfully, "I knew that with all that shooting, there would be—and oh, Wil, darling Wil" (she had sobbed at that point), "I know it isn't right, but I asked God to protect *you*—not thinking of how some other heart would break if—if—"

"Don't you know He would understand that?" Leaving his animal patient for a tender moment, he leaped to his feet and crushed her to him there in the barnyard, their combined tears streaking caked dirt and dried blood from their faces.

In a far corner of the lot, a cow gave a near-human moan. Duty pulled her wonderful husband away, but she followed. "Is there a way to know the number—and their names?"

"Slim found a list on one of the hired gunmen," he answered from a bent-over position. "He checked the roll, forcing them all to answer. Found several undesirables, wanted by the federal government. Tex also recognized several and will give testimony."

They were nearing completion, both of caring for the animals and finishing the story. But the critical questions remained.

True's voice trembled when she asked what she must know. "Were there—fatalities?" Then, remembering she had asked, "How many?"

"Four. It was inevitable. Two of the attackers shot each other, neither breathing by the time I could reach them. One rancher—and a man none of us knew." Did she imagine it, or did he pause? She could not be sure, heart fluttering like a caged bird in her throat and tears blinding her to the expression on his face. "The rancher begged for a priest. I could do nothing for him, riddled by bullets as he was, but—I—I explained that I was not a priest, not even a minister, but I could offer a prayer. Only God can repair hearts—or bodies either, for that matter. The rest of us just prescribe."

"Oh, darling—"

Young Wil tried to grin as he stood. "Don't cry, True—I can't bear any more pain. I found out the man's name and thought—"

"I could call on his wife? You know I will."

"We men can mend fences, and if we're lucky, patch up bodies—even mediate differences. But it takes a woman to give understanding and love. And by the way," Young Wil made a partially successful attempt at lightening the conversation, "you ladies were the real heroines—how on earth did you come to think up that barricade?"

She started to explain, wondering if she knew how, when the dogs came bounding out, rested, bright-eyed, and obviously demanding a medal in the form of a meaty bone. "There were a lot of main characters," True said, trying to match his mood of life must go on, "Tonsil and Lung among them. There is more to say, too, but it can wait."

"Well," he said with a deep sigh of relief, "my tummy can't. Oh, one good thing came of all this unspeakable tragedy: The cattlemen, farmers, and sheep owners joined ranks. As for the railroad—who knows?"

33
The Other Side of the Mountain

❧

WINTER CLOSED IN with tyrannical rule. The tongue of the little stream which used to trickle down the Double N's irrigation trough slowed and stopped in frozen silence. Hills surrounding the vast valley snuggled in their mantles of snow. In January they were patterned anew daily with tracks of furry animals seeking dark refuges for their long sleep. Then the pattern disappeared completely as all (including the widely scattered houses in the countryside) became a part of the white-sheeted landscape, locked in until April's key opened the door. But the plunge in temperature locked in the wheat as well. It was as snug as the Norths in their cabin and their faithful helpers, whose bunkhouse was certainly better than no shelter at all.

It was a time of togetherness, drawing them all even closer. The hired hands spent the days mending harness, whittling furniture (Tex having taught them the skill), and—with the aid of the dogs' keen noses—tracking down deer, venison being about the only fresh meat available. A cause for amusement was the young Texan's slipping (unnoticed, he thought) to the closest wheat field and trying in vain to penetrate the frozen ground with a trowel in hopes of finding a sprouting grain of his red wheat. One of the men had served as apprentice in a wagon-making shop. Together, in their spare time, the group worked on the wooden spokes and dreamed aloud of purchasing metal parts for wheels when conditions allowed for traveling to Slippery Elm. The ranch came first and foremost, of course, but just to supplement the income, mightn't it be wise someday to hang out a sign that said ON-THE-PREMISES WAGONMAKERS? Might be able to sell one for, say 25 dollars or so cash money—and look at the improvements that would make! Add profit from the wheat, maybe patenting the new strain . . . and the thoroughbred livestock and Midgie's chicken eggs . . . why, they'd all be rich someday! Life was simple and life was good. Actually, they were rich already!

And so they sang a lot, their rollicking cowboy songs a lullaby lost in the wind, except to the Norths. They too kept busy, Young Wil with his medical books, True with her educational journals, Midgie with her correspondence course, and Marty with his bookkeeping to try to figure how he could turn a profit here—and also reading everything he could get his hands on concerning the birth and care of the newborn. There were times, Young Wil whispered to True, when more of his reference books were in Marty's bedroom than his own. In fact, Marty was pushing himself. His gray eyes were too often red-laced and rimmed with lack of rest, and when exhaustion would grip him in her fist, he would drink more coffee and read on. It came as a surprise to them all when he began designing plans for a double-log house—very, very long, with wide windows looking out on a vegetable garden here and a rose garden there—a house befitting his countess and his heirs. So he planned to stay on? True prayed it could be so . . .

There was still time out for the young wives to make a few baby garments from the precious yardage they had on hand, and to bake with whatever their rapidly depleting supply of staples allowed. On baking day the men from the bunkhouse joined them by unspoken agreement. And there was also agreement that there would be Bible study and prayer service. Warm. Informal. "Jesuslike," Tex said of it.

True marveled at her husband's unfailing patience with the questions of the five men. Tex possessed a homespun understanding, a heartwarming legacy left by his grandmother. The boy would feel comfortable if Jesus rapped on the door, invite Him in, and bring a footstool for propping up His feet in front of the potbellied stove. Augie, in contrast, was possessed with the devil of superstition, having heard nothing except the dark predictions of God's unquenchable fire of wrath. Slinger, convinced that he had failed so miserably in life that no "Power up There" could forgive him, found himself more comfort in doubting One's existence than to face judgment which was already pronounced. That left Pig Iron and Slim, both wanting desperately to hear the "Jesus story" but hampered by wrong interpretations by people with closed minds, some of them ministers. True was amazed to hear their backgrounds, once their tongues were freed enough to share without shame—colossal ignorance thrust upon them by people who ought to know better.

Augie stumblingly blurted out his fears of being struck dead if he laid money on the altar . . . set on fire by the "burning bushes" . . . run over by chariot wheels while the dogs licked up his blood. Midgie's mouth made a capital O of horror. "So that's what he means by 'Los perros son muy mal' and runs from Tonsil and Lung," she whispered to True. "He's afraid of those gentle creatures—bless his heart."

"Augie," Young Wil said simply, "those ideas are enough to scare you to death—taken from scattered stories in the Old Bible and given the wrong meaning. One day we'll take them up one by one. Agreed?"

Augie was only too glad to nod affirmatively, his dark eyes aglow with new hope. Marty saw and said in the same simple manner, "Wil—if I may make a suggestion? Could we, you think, begin with the New Testament and then go back to the Old?"

"Indeed!" Young Wil agreed, causing Marty's eyes to light with pleasure.

Together, with steaming mugs of coffee and butter-and-egg cakes, they traveled through the Gospels, pausing frequently to iron out the wrinkles of misunderstanding. The men relaxed and began to enjoy themselves, actually begging for more. "It's like music in my mouth," Tex commented one evening, licking his lips as if tasting the words.

"There's so much I still can't get through my skull," Slim said, the lines in his face crisscrossed with complexity. "Sorry, Mr. Wil."

Young Wil nodded. "I know, Slim. There's a lot that none of us understand completely. Remember that God knows we lack the background of those who knew Him in the flesh—and then gave His story to the world. But the more we read and talk, the better we understand. The Holy Spirit helps us interpret—"

Augie cringed. "Eees like—uh, el—thee Holy Ghost?" He stumbled on ghost.

Thank goodness, True thought, my Wil understands Augie's fears. It was evident when he replied. "Let's not worry about that now, my good friend—just remember that God loves us and His Spirit helps *us* understand. You," he placed an arm around the Mexican man's shoulders, "needn't be afraid."

"Seems like it oughta be more simple," Slinger said slowly; "sez somethin' then rubs it out. I git wantin' t'believe, 'n along comes somebody sayin' it ain't so."

"If you went duck hunting, Slinger, what would you look for?"

"Ducks—hafta know what I'm lookin' fer."

"That's right—and if somebody tried to tell you it wasn't a duck?"

"Hit 'im in th' snozzle with th' butt uv my gat iffen he got twixt me 'n my aim, I 'spect."

The other hands snickered. Amusement lighted Young Wil's dark eyes, but he kept his face straight, his voice respectful.

"Without violence—maybe without convincing your fellow Nimrod—you'd know it was a duck no matter what others said."

"Meanin'," Pig Iron said slowly, "some uv other folks' opinions ain't a-gonna sway us none—just gotta keep a clear head."

"I think," Marty interjected, "that God's words are clear enough when it comes to teaching about His care for mankind such as us, about sin, repenting, asking forgiveness, and *knowing* it's ours."

"That's what faith is?" Slim asked in awe. "Believe 'n heaven's ours?"

"That's salvation fer y'all!" Tex said, boyish face lighted with pride in his formative theology. "Some folks go round 'n round over little ole nibbles uv th' Bible, git theirselves all hung up like a fence-breakin' steer in baling war—wire—but," suddenly he paused as if struggling with his own understanding, "how we gonna know 'bout which doctrines is false, Mr. Wil?"

"Remember what uh duck looks like!" Slinger said smugly. "I betcha these here ladies'd know, havin' plucked as many pin feathers as they have. Right, Miz True, ma'am?"

True hesitated, her eyes appealing to Young Wil. His smile reassured her and she spoke haltingly "I guess we have to turn to the Bible and see which messages are essential—I mean, if doctrines—beliefs—show up once, maybe twice, and no more, they're less important than what Mr. Wil has told you—those that are repeated over and over by prophets, Jesus Himself, and the Gospel writers, who told the story which saves us."

Where did the words come from? she asked herself. Why, the Holy

Spirit, of course! But the men had heard enough. She mustn't get preachy. Already their understanding was growing. They were learning enough so that through more reading and prayer they could live lives pleasing in the eyes of God. *And, I Lord, am learning right along with them.*

"How about another piece of cake?" True smiled brightly.

"Bravo, bravo!" The chorus came from several of the men. "Shore wisht we had a *git*-tar, Miz Midgie." True held her breath, but Tex covered beautifully. "Whatta trip in larnin'! Feel like I'd crost t'th other side uv th' mountain!" he said.

34
Blessed Are the Peacemakers

&

A GUEST "FROM the other side of the mountain" was soon to call on the neighbors of the Double N—the very day it warmed up, March first, to be exact. The magical month of March! Midgie's month of delivery. The expectant father was jubilant with expectation. True and Young Wil had never seen Marty like this, even in his childhood years. His behavior bordered on the absurd. *His* day was coming, Marty declared to anybody within hearing range. Not *Midgie's*, and not the *baby's* but *his*! The mood was contagious. Morale, which had remained surprisingly high during the imprisoning bitter cold, soared even higher with the burst of winter-pale sunshine.

It seemed fitting that Tex should come dancing in with a handful of rich, black soil—so shiny it resembled a lump of coal. "It's sproutin'—see, whadda y'all thank I been trying t'git acrost? Give 'er a week, two at most, 'n she'll shoot sky-high—see them roots? Th' sun's a-gonna shoot th' temp'ature up, drive out th' frost, 'n pull th' grain right outta th' grave by th' armpits! Give 'er a pair uv frog-stranglin' rains, 'n we can set by yonder winder 'n watch 'er grow. This strain'll explode like a cannon, I tell y'all. Best we git sharpenin' scythes 'n hook on th' cradles—" Tex paused to grin, "th' *other* cradle, 'sides th' one we been makin' fer Junior—"

The other hands looked at him darkly. It was the wrong thing to say. Here the cradle was to be a surprise, and he up and spilled his insides. Well, what was wrong with that? Everybody knew Miz Midgie was giving birth—*the Good Lord be praised!*—but so was

311

Mother Earth! So Tex waved his work-worn hands in an arc and raised a defensive chin. "I cain't 'spect y'all to 'preciate th' sight yore pore eyes ain't seen—a gold mine growin' topside. We'll be rich—tickle yore ears, men?"

"Mine are already tickled!" Marty declared with a look at Midgie as tender as the green shoot of wheat that Tex had found. She responded with a smile of total contentment, no more concerned with the preordained delivery awaiting her than Tex was with his own birth of nature, knowing as he did that a hailstorm could abort his dreams. A lot was at stake—turning points for both of them. Failure, for whatever reason, could change their lives. Was their faith strong enough to withstand it? True prayed that it was.

She cast a quick look at her husband, caught him off guard, and saw a flicker of concern cross his face. Well, why not? He had stood by Marty in fulfilling his pledge to O'Higgin, worn himself thin trying to point out to these men who trusted him the difference between Paul's terminology, for instance, of practices he considered "disgraceful" and "sin," the paving stones to death—and the doctrine of faith, which spelled out salvation and godly life. And now he shouldered the burden of bringing a new life into the world. Failures could weaken immature faith.

True had thought of his responsibilities and how he had met them head-on with such strength, born of his faith, so many times. And each time she had said, "Darling, you're wonderful!"

"I know," he would say smugly, knowing what to expect.

And he was right. "Wil North—" and then she would fold herself into a little fetal ball in his arms, safe and secure in his love.

Now, as her mind wandered, so had the conversation. What were they trying to do, outbrag one another? Rich? Of course, they would be. Sure, sure, the wheat would help—it *should*, this being wheat country. But don't underestimate the thoroughbred horses, the cows, and—

All within the kitchen stopped rambling conversation and vagrant thoughts at the sudden commotion in the corral. Horses were neighing wildly and the bull was pawing earth as if digging for oil. The source of their indignation was clearly visible through the sunlit window.

A crude, homemade, two-wheeled cart pulled by an enormous

beast was turning in at the gate. "Hallow! Hallow! Be there anybody home?"

"Mrs. Hancock, Anna-Lee Hancock," Young Wil said in surprise.

"A-drivin' Adam's off-ox," Slim marveled too innocently to be poking fun. "Th' lady's th' widder uv thet peace-lovin' juice harp player— 'n his name *was* Adam, what kept cows from millin' with that—"

"Harmonica," Slinger supplied. "You know, Miz True, th' feller what helped you 'n Miz Midgie—then started up t'lend us a hand. 'Cept some coward shot 'im in th' back!"

"Bad news, else she's been t' a fun'ral," Slim said darkly of the tiny-framed lady dressed in black from her high-laced boots beneath a cheap, somewhat skimpily gathered long skirt to the enormous bonnet which all but covered her pale face.

"I be bringin' thee a chair of which I no longer have need—'tis a high chair for the little one." Adam Hancock's widow had skillfully looped the reins around the cart's brake, stepped gingerly onto the thawing ground, and was lifting the piece of hand-hewn furniture from the back of the wooden-wheeled vehicle before any of the men could reach her and assist. Young Wil was first to take the chair. "We've met before, Mrs. Hancock. Perhaps you remember—"

"I remember," she said simply. "I be bringin' my appreciation likewise—and some good news to thee. Wilt thou be calculating the subject?"

True did so mentally. The railroads, of course. But where were her manners? She stepped forward, extending her hand. Introductions were quick and businesslike, and the young Mrs. Hancock, about the age of herself and Midgie, True guessed, declined an invitation to come inside.

Feeling at a disadvantage, True expressed sorrow at the death of their guest's husband. Anna-Lee's response was unemotional. "He is not dead. We Shakers believe our loved ones merely cast aside our earthly garments and change forms of existence, no more. Believe ye God be King?"

All nodded. "Then ye be peace lovers and lovers of the land that God meted out, knowin' it be ours to guard for Him, in peace with our neighbors. We do not fight. Neither do we be backin' away. It was my husband's assignment to watch over both sides of the hill. Music was his weapon."

And it got him killed, True read in the men's eyes. Some of them looked puzzled. Others, faces blanched, stood tongue-tied. This modest-appearing little mite was a brave one; she lived up to her beliefs all right! She had walked right in here and taken over "peacefully," while they—with muscle and brawn—stood speechless. There was sure a heap they'd need be asking Mr. Wil.

True's mind had tilted the same direction. Her husband had better prepare himself to explain how the Constitution guaranteed freedom of worship, and to use this as an example of how diverse religious groups could live in harmony—providing they practiced the first two Commandments and replaced prejudice with the charity that "neighborliness" demanded.

But for now True had lost out on the conversation, catching only enough to know that her hunch was correct: The news concerned the railroads. Eight men and one woman met in Slippery Elm, Anna-Lee was reporting—no, not herself. Shaker women took no part in business. 'Twas Mrs. Tillie "who be a shareholder too." The nine-member committee outlined a plan for presenting to the borrowed judge, a Judge Grover from Portland, and his assistant, Mr. St. John. Both men listened courteously. "Nobody be goin' around in circles, just questions and answers. 'Twas not they who caused bloodshed, 'twas outlaw masqueraders who had not the fear of God in their wicked hearts." Yes, Anna-Lee's black bonnet bobbed up and down, it was put to a vote, and the news was that there be an alternate route.

"You be meanin'—" Pig Iron began, then glowered when Slim and Slinger nudged each other at his copycat language. "*I* mean, we a-gonna join them bobtails? Jest surrender our property coward-like?"

"Them ragtag renegades cain't take our property—let 'em try!" Slim scoffed.

"Maybe not—" Marty said slowly (still unsure of his position on the Double N, *and*, True often suspected, often his manhood), "but they can make it so miserable that we would have to vacate."

Faces flushed with anger. The discussion showed signs of degenerating into wrangling. Young Wil, who had said nothing, opened his mouth, then closed it. Anna-Lee Hancock had seen the men's mood change. She had the facts, and with them an ingrained sense of fairness. Let her answer.

"Both be illegal, according to your laws. That be the decision rendered by Judge Grover. We have our rights and they have theirs. We joined hands against their injustice. And now it be fittin' that we join hands for compromise. Good day!"

The gallant little lady lifted her skirts and climbed into her cart with the same agility and speed used in climbing out. Then she was gone.

"I didn't even thank her," Midgie said. She was stroking the chair.

True inhaled deeply. "And I failed to invite her again—"

"She'll return," Young Wil said, "in time of trouble."

"Maybe there will be none," Marty said. "Things seem—different."

Slinger shook his head. "Blessed be the peacemakers," he muttered, tossing his gun on the table.

35
Time and Tide

❦

THE SOFT, WARM rains of April came, but Midgie's baby did not. The prospective parents fretted with impatience in spite of Young Wil's reassurances that babies, especially the first, often took their time. Being late was far better than being early. But True doubted if they heard.

The world around them underwent a wondrous transformation. The odds in favor of Marty's making the Double N a lasting success were good. And he, like the springtime world, had undergone a transformation. It was hard to remember his outrage at being compelled to come here, his little-boy tantrums, and his inability to see himself faintly resembling a man capable of achieving a distant goal. The change which began slowly gained momentum, becoming so big that he seemed incapable of putting a lid on his ambition. Getting the books to balance was the biggest challenge of his life—until now. Now his entire world was crammed inside these four walls. The cabin was no longer a prison. Within this castle was the sum and substance of life, his crown of achievement—the baby! His and Midgie's. God had blessed them without measure, giving them a partner in their battle here. They were the predestined victors of all odds.

Nature seemed to agree. Midgie's hens hatched out baby chicks so round and fat that they resembled buttery dumplings; and the sweet-pea seed she had planted last fall all but obscured the cabin with their twining, blossom-strewn vines. Gardens flourished. Slinger announced arrival of "th' finest colt this side uv th' Mississippi" with a whoop surely heard in Slippery Elm. But Billy Joe had to "up'n steal my thunder," he declared when the foreman elbowed his way through the admiring circle of male spectators to yell, "It's a girl—fact o'th' matter bein' it's *twins*, much alike as coupl'a peas in a pod—*yippee*!"

Tex removed his hat in awed respect. "Whadda y'all know?"

"*Niñas*—gurls—lady Norths?" Augie stumbled over the words, then threw his sombrero to the ground and propelled himself up and down on it. "*Dos*—not one God send—two!"

"Weight, 'bout 40 pounds, I'd calculate," Billy Joe said importantly. "Legs wobbly, but standin' a'ready—all 40 pounds dry weight!"

The men were stunned—all except Young Wil, who winked at True through the window. She was uncertain what the commotion was about but realized that there was a comical misunderstanding even before Slinger, already piqued, bristled. The North baby was nothing this simpleton should joke about.

"Now, man, you gotta be spoofin'—ain't humanly possible—"

Billy Joe cast a withering look of pity at his challenger. He aimed his quick tongue, always sharpened and ready, at his target and hit. "May th' Good Lord gimme patience with th' likes uv you! Now, who said 'twas *human*? It's yore bounden duty t'be knowin' which cows is about t'freshen. Purdiest thangs on this ranch, barrin' th' ladies!"

An audible sigh of relief circled the group. A few tittered then, all eyes darting between the sparring men as if attached to a single pull cord, then seemed to think better of it. "Calves," Slinger was muttering, "when you knowed you was all-time misleadin' us—betcha weighed 'em together jest t'impress us . . ."

"Keep it friendly, fellows," Young Wil smiled. And, knowing that this was only the men's way of friendly chitchat, he signaled True with a wave of his hand. They must make a trip for supplies.

Tillie Caswell's cheeks rivaled the color of the bouquet of wild pinks she had gathered from the east meadow and bunched into a copper kettle adorning the piano top. The reason was immediately apparent: The Reverend Randy Randall had come again. What was not apparent was his look of concern as he talked in confidential tones with—of all people—the "man with the beaver hat." True, who had all but forgotten the stranger, questioned Tillie with her eyes. And,

Tillie, instead of her usual palms-up response, averted her eyes ever so slightly as she rushed forward to embrace True warmly.

"Oh, I'm so glad you came—so glad of the early thaw glad to show you the mail!" she exclaimed breathlessly—a little *too* gladly, True thought. But Young Wil had entered, was shaking hands with Mr. Caswell, and was explaining that, yes, all was well with Midgie, but they must take care of business quickly. He doubted if Marty was up to the excitement of delivering his firstborn.

Tillie Caswell went for the mail, the skirts of her becoming gray dress swishing past her Reverend friend as if to whisper a warning. Randy Randall turned almost immediately to extend his hand while brushing away the heavy white hair which, when he was hatless, tended to fall into unwanted bangs over his glasses. He was talking away as Tillie had done, running sentences together, telling her that he had seen the Senior Norths and that they were fine and sent love. His owlish eyes held True's in a way that all but dared her to turn away. When at length his gaze released hers, the man in the beaver hat was gone. So was Mrs. Caswell—after accepting a note from the stranger.

"I don't understand; I simply don't understand," True said as they returned to the Double N. "It may be nothing—only I can't dismiss the idea of the man in the beaver hat. First talking to Marty, then the minister—and now Tillie. There's a missing link, but a link for sure."

Young Wil nodded in agreement. "Somehow I get the impression it has to do with Marty, but don't ask me what. I overhead mention of the railroads. They're all rooting for him and Midgie, you know, wondering what they'll do if the wheat fails—"

"It isn't going to fail!" No answer, so she thought aloud: "They could plant orchards—and there's always a market for vegetables now that the trains run more regularly."

"This isn't the Willamette Valley, darling," he reminded her gently. "It's better suited for grain and livestock. So's Marty. I do believe he's found his niche, and I would back away from suggesting a change. He has become more like this land and the people on it than he realizes. They'd switch their wives for total strangers before changing crops."

True squeezed his hand and laughed. "Good girl!" Young Wil visibly relaxed. "I was afraid we were on the threshold of interfering again." With that he shifted subjects.

"Did Tillie make mention of Anna-Lee Hancock?" When True shook her head, he continued: "They've met now that Mrs. Hancock must do the shopping. Curly filled me in on their background. A small band called True Believers came to the Oregon Country for the sole purpose of establishing peace. A few went seaward, and a few stayed here. That separated families. Persecuted, some changed names, which meant that they were never able to reunite. So I guess they added strangers to their list of abstinences—alcohol, tobacco, meat. They scarcely venture into society except to market their wonderful cheese and hand-carved furniture—just sustain themselves without friends."

"I was honored when Anna-Lee came," True said humbly, "and I am even more honored now." *But why are you telling me this?*

The answer came flatly: "Curly said Tillie pounded her with questions—about Marty. No more questions, True. He knows no more than that—the only subject, Curly says, which is closed between them. Tillie, by the way, seems almost cured—I'm the doctor, you know—so I prescribe . . . *this!*" He leaned over and kissed her soundly.

"*That*—without an examination?" True gasped when she could breathe.

"I know the needs of my patients," he grinned smugly.

"Wil North—" she began, then with a giggle, "continue treatment!"

The wagon creaked on, its riders silent with their thoughts—which True suspected, were very much the same, all of them questions. Now and then one of them spoke. *The Oregonian* carried a report of the agreement made by the railroads versus the homesteaders . . . another "Great Compromise," the story ran. "Not that morality and decency could be legislated . . . up to both parties," the article concluded. But the next edition would carry news that the government had found a peaceful solution, differing only in its verbiage, St. John had told Curly. True half-listened, her mind still on Marty. What did the letter to him from O'Higgin contain? She had only scanned the bulky one from Aunt Chrissy. No real news. And what did that enormous package from Portland addressed to *Mrs.* Martin North hold? Midgie had no Meier & Frank catalog.

Even before the din of voices, True felt a sudden urge to get home. The voices grew louder, more frantic . . . Billy Joe and sons . . . dogs . . . *Marty* . . .

Midgie gave birth with Dr. and Mrs. Wil North's aid before the foreman and the boys had unhitched the team. A perfect specimen—nine pounds ("dry weight") of manhood, a powerful-voiced welcome addition to the human race. A miracle with a red face. The apple of a weeping father's eye. The fulfillment of woman's destiny to a misty-eyed mother who felt worthy at last.

Doctor and "nurse" tiptoed out, leaving the parents alone for the sacred moment to marvel at birth, to reaffirm their love—and to pray. "The time came—babies know," Young Wil grinned with just the right shade of pride in his own wisdom. True slipped an appreciative arm about him. *"Time and tide . . ."* Yes, the time had come. Somewhere behind, the tide was rising . . .

36
Bearing of Gifts

❧

MARTY'S HEAD CONTINUED to float in the upper ozone layer. His heart lay beside Midgie (obediently in bed by his orders). His arms folded around the "March Hare" (no name yet good enough), whom he allowed nobody to touch except in "emergencies." But his feet were planted square on the ground. He was obsessed with one question: *Would he see even a small profit on the Double N?* He was beginning to doubt it.

"I question that we will break even in spite of all the hard work on the part of the hands—and the dedication of you and the rest of the family," True overheard him tell Young Wil.

"Are you forgetting living expenses?"

The two men were in the bedroom where Wil was examining the baby. In the kitchen, preparing gruel which the new mother asked for, True could feel Marty brighten. "You mean I can count that in?"

"Of course. It's a part of the profit—"

"I just take cash on hand and subtract expenses? If we break even, I'm not ready for the trash heap?"

"Oh, Marty, don't say things like that!" Midgie's voice held a note of pleading. Then it strengthened. "I simply won't have you speaking of my child's father in such terms—as if he were a loser! How could you be when—do you mind," she paused uncertainly, "if—if I go on?"

True was so touched she almost let the gruel boil over. And how good to hear her husband's deep laugh. "Set him straight, Midgie!"

"You're forgetting something, Father Martin North! You and I have fulfilled every fine line of that trifling agreement—every fine-printed line. You were to stay put—"

True sensed that Marty's head jerked up sharply in preparation for giving a reproving look if she made mention of *her* leaving. Perhaps that had been the plan. If so, Midgie shifted emphasis quickly.

"And I was to present you with a child! If Irish O'Higgin can't be happy with that, we can start somewhere else."

"You're wonderful!" Marty's voice broke. "But" (stoutly) "I don't think that will be necessary." Neither heard Wil's bag snap shut.

Dr. North found his wife wiping her eyes with her apron when he entered the kitchen. "Hey, none of that!" he said tenderly. Grabbing her around the waist, he danced her jubilantly around the kitchen while the gruel succeeded this time in boiling all over the stove.

Breathlessly, they wiped up the spoils and fanned the smoke out the window. Then they sat down while Young Wil gave True the diagnosis which the young parents had been sure of all along. "That is undoubtedly the finest baby I have ever seen—not a flaw. No man could do better!"

"*You* could!" True burst out, then blushed.

"Oho! Well, now—I'll take that under advisement. But not before the honeymoon! Do you realize, my darling, that we have never had one? I've been thinking—"

"Dangerous!" she teased.

"You'd better believe it! The year's up in—let's see, six weeks. By then we'll have cut the hay, sold off some livestock, and settled up with Marty. I know how much you want to get home—but I want to detour by way of Portland. I'll arrange to take my preliminary exam, and you can do the same. And then, Mrs. North, we will be alone!"

Marty's duty, as he saw it for the next week, was complete care of his son. He was deaf, dumb, and blind to other responsibilities, with his mind locked around his offspring. Why not indulge him, let him take command? True suggested. All of the ranch hands agreed, but Billy Joe did not. There was a man's work to be done. Wasn't Mr. Marty in charge out there, too? 'Course he was. Busiest time of the year approaching. The Double N demanded attention of the owner (wasn't that what he was to be?). Some things he didn't understand about this ranch, and there were times when he wondered who did.

But one thing he knew: Mr. Marty was strong as an ox—and sometimes about as dumb. Babies were woman's work . . . so . . .

It was Billy Joe who sent Mariah to Slippery Elm to spread the news. Just why Tillie Caswell "went nigh on crazy" was another mystery. None of his business, of course. At least (proudly) 'twas himself, "The Foreman, the Beetle, the Thinker," who found a way to get the new father back into the fields. Miz Tillie and his Mariah simply shooed Marty out of the house and took over. He'd learn in time that the baby was mortal.

Tillie Caswell arrived and dumped packages on the kitchen table, upsetting a bouquet of wild larkspur in her mad dash into the bedroom. "Let me see him!" she cried excitedly. Grabbing the baby from Midgie's arms, she pulled back a fold of the baby-blue receiving blanket and buried her face against the downy fluff of dark hair that already showed signs of a question-mark curl on top. "Oh, you darling—you adorable angel—that's right, hold onto Great-Aunt Tillie's finger!" Seating herself in the cricket chair, she began to croon softly as she rocked him back and forth. "Oh, you're just what Auntie prayed for."

Auntie? Great-Aunt Tillie? Her titles probably meant the same as Miss Mollie's calling herself Grandma. But even as she tried to convince herself, True felt a nagging sense of doubt—a doubt which she saw reflected in Midgie's questioning face . . . something in the woman's past perhaps, having nothing to do with the Norths.

There was growing evidence to the contrary in the days to come. That it had to do with the North family revealed itself with startling suddenness. Or was it sudden? Actually the signs had been there all along, True realized later—little tremors preceding a major quake, followed by a never-ending wave of aftershocks.

But for now the Double N was achieving an air of busy normalcy. The "March Hare" (Uncle Wil and Aunt True declared it disgraceful that the King of the Glass Mountain bore no name!) was a good baby from the beginning. He awoke with a lopsided smile and cooed himself to sleep counting his toes, allowing Midgie to regain her strength, while Mariah assisted True with the household tasks. The men, busy getting livestock to market and early crops harvested, ate ravenously. Midgie's other hens hatched out their broods, which ate as heartily as the men. Surely every cow in the herd brought in a new calf, which meant churning, making cottage cheese, and storing away hoop cheese to age. Gardens continued to flourish. So there were canning and drying. And the irrigation system encouraged the wild berries to grow rank and hang heavy with jelly-ready fruit. True had never worked so in her life.

Mariah took over the laundry and cleaning. It was while she cleaned Midgie and Marty's bedroom that—in the process of mopping the rough-board floor—her rag mop stuck. In trying to loosen it, she reached beneath the bed and jumped back white-faced to declare there was a body beneath the bed. "*Si, si,*—yes, yes—ees a body, *Señora!*"

True was thankful that Midgie had gone for a walk so there would be no panic. "I doubt that, Mariah, but let's see. There should be nothing there," she managed to say calmly. A little apprehensively she felt beneath the bed slats. What she found surprised her more than Mariah's wild imaginings. There it was—the package that she and Young Wil had brought home on their last trip to Slippery Elm and had given to Marty because it was addressed to Midgie. And there on top lay the bulky letter from O'Higgin—unopened. Why, when it might be of utmost importance?

Marty chose that precise moment to come to the cabin for a drink of water. "Quick! Put it back—before she gets in—*hurry!*" His voice revealed a sense of urgency. "Forgive me—I'll do it myself. It—It's a long-overdue gift. But the timing has to be right. After all," he grinned, "others came bearing gifts."

True watched as he pushed the long box back in its hiding place. Relieved and touched, she reviewed the offerings of Tillie Caswell—pound cakes, hazelnut cookies, doll-size nightshirts, and the daffodil-yellow rompers, embroidered DOUBLE N RANCH, for the baby to grow into. Mariah had made some practical, loose-fitting morning coats for Midgie until she could get her figure back into its hourglass shape. Perhaps what touched True most of all was the dainty nainsook set of matching full-skirted slip and dress (made boyish by a tiny Peter Pan collar) which all but swept the floor. Light as swansdown and white as a snowdrop, the infant's garments were handmade by none other than the thoughtful Anna-Lee Hancock, then sent over by Mariah. After all, it was not proper for her to come in person unless by invitation, once she had paid a "duty call." True sighed. She must call on Anna-Lee—

Then her mind went back to the unopened letter. The envelope was sealed, but her lips were not. She no longer walked on eggs in her brother's presence. "Marty, shouldn't you open O'Higgin's letter?" True asked outright.

He paled slightly but answered with equal candor, "Yes, I should."
"Then?"

"I'm afraid to, darling." Marty's voice was so low that True had trouble hearing. "Midgie and I have built something special here—"

"You certainly have, my darling! We are so proud of you!"

"Thank you," he said humbly, "without you—well, O'Higgin saw the need and saw to it that we *weren't* without you. And, you know, I think Providence had a hand in the arrangement. God knew, too."

True laughed. "Marty North, are you stalling? Of *course* both of them knew. What makes you think they would let you down now?"

Marty picked up the envelope, then hesitated. "We want to stay here so badly—"

"Open it!"

He slit the flap with shaking fingers, then scanned a page with a grin spreading across his face that made him handsome. Looking at the second page, he let out a whoop of joy. "They paid off . . . he paid off . . . we—we—we . . . oh, read it for yourself—there's more, but I have to find Midgie—YIPPEEE!"

"Marty, you'll wake the baby!"

"Of course I will! He has to know! Get up, King of our Hearts, let's find Mommie!"

He lifted his March Hare, rosy with slumber but smiling, from the cradle and hugged True all in one fluid motion. Then, taking seven-league strides, he was gone.

The letter was cause enough for elation, Young Wil and True agreed, as (by Marty's request) they studied the contents. *What* paid off? O'Higgin's railroad shares. *Who* paid off? O'Higgin—with the dividends met his loan. And, of course, *we* meant Marty and Midgie, who would be allowed to stay on, having proven up on the claim *and* in the eyes of O'Higgin, in accordance with "terms thereof." "Two things I find puzzling," Young Wil said just as Billy Joe barged in, "how did they know about the—baby?"

True was glad he caught himself before saying that it too was a "term."

"Tillie hightailed it t'meet th' train 'n sent a telegraph—*gram*, tellin' dry weight—sooo (smug in his hold on all the world's wisdom) he's a'comin'—no need readin' on—that ole talker'll tell whut 'stay on' is!"

What *did* it mean? Another gift?

37

Bewildering Revelations

❧

TRUE LOVED MORNINGS such as this. The world lay still in those magical moments of waiting for the mid-May sunrise. Although the air was motionless, yesterday's fragrances of sun-warmed hay mingling with the sweet breath of pink clover and early blooming petunias lingered on. There was no sound except for a few twitterings of wrens nesting in the tulip vine and the crowing of Midgie's rooster, whose wake-up call was timed so precisely that surely the young braggart had clockwork inside him. True let her eyes wander dreamily to the illimitable spaces above a mountain peak, purpled by the distance. "How beautiful, Lord, how beautiful," she whispered. "I understand Your meaning, 'Be still and know that I am God.'"

She stood very still, listening. It was almost as if God were whispering in return, reminding her somehow of His Master Plan, the intermingling of His children's lives—each a part of the other to light His world. Soon she would be going home. But this was home too in her ever-broadening way of thinking. It would be sad, leaving. But, oh, the joy of being back with family! Was that how Jesus felt when He ascended beyond that purple mountain and returned Home to prepare a place for those who chose to follow—torn between two worlds? What a strange thought. And yet it persisted as her mind gathered memories into a hasty bouquet as one plucks flowers before they can face. In spirit Aunt Chrissy and Daddy Wil stood beside her, offering love unlimited. Joining them was Grandma Mollie and her practicality ... Irish O'Higgin and his bubbling laughter coupled with such hallelujah-faith that it shook the rafters when he sang—devout and God-fearing, but always with a twinkle . . . Uncle Joe, dear Uncle Joe, taken so young from Aunt Chrissy (but not before he led the children—herself, Young Wil, and Marty—to the Lord), just as Angel Mother had been taken from Daddy Wil. Mother, tender and fragile as a white violet—so fair of face, so filled with beautiful thoughts. Oh, God was kind to let her memory remain so faintly yet so vividly, like a whisper of Himself. Mother . . . singing to her bees . . . ever saying that forgotten would be the long, dark winter when spring came over the hill . . . then they would look for a last venturesome snowdrop and a first daffodil that tied together the seasons . . . pruning the wayward lilac so other blossoms could see the light. Mother . . . lifting the wind-tossed rose to caress each petal into place . . . planting a marigold seed and teaching True the patience the seed must learn, patience to wait for the first warm rain. "Life," she wrote in her diary, "lies within each clod." And in that beautiful moment alone with God, True became a part of them all, one with her Maker—and overwhelmed with desire to leave a part of herself with all whose lives she had touched.

At that moment the sun topped the eastern hill to set the world aflame. And against that blinding color there appeared a familiar figure, easily recognizable at a distance by his usual black coat. A fish basket swung over his shoulder, but it was hard to tell if the good man was going fishing or returning. Either way, his long strides told her that he was in a great hurry. "True, True!" Randy Randall panted; "make ready for the onslaught—they're coming, all of them!"

This time *they* translated into such a horde that True found herself wondering if war had been declared. There were the infantry, the foot soldiers; the cavalry on steeds that galloped along as if delivering Paul Revere's message; and—well, what did one label those who rode in "chariots," namely, buggies and wagons? Had they all camped along the roadside to arrive so early? And what on earth were they doing *here*?

Billy Joe had linked up with the group somewhere, looking as if he should be blowing a bugle, waving a flag, or ordering "Charge!"

Dazed, True picked out the familiar faces: O'Higgin . . . Tillie Caswell . . . Anna-Lee Hancock (here by whose invitation?), wearing her dark cotton and looking a bit less pale. And was she seeing things?

Could it be? Yes, there was Midgie's father. Who had notified Conductor Callison of his new grandson? Eagerly her eyes scanned the faces, hoping in vain to see Aunt Chrissy, Daddy Wil, and Grandma Mollie. But they were conspicuously missing. Irish O'Higgin was living up to the letter of the law all right. Even though Marty and Midgie had met all the other requirements of the crotchety old man's will, O'Higgin would see to it that Uncle Artie's wish was carried out. After all, two weeks remained before the year was up. Only then could the young Norths be reunited with Marty's family.

It was the Reverend gentleman who collected his wits to greet them all. And it was Young Wil, Marty, and the hands of the Double N who returned the greeting—thanks to Billy Joe's wild dash into the fields to summon them. Midgie, who had been nursing the baby, came out and looked at the crowd uncertainly. Then, with a squeal of joy, she was in her father's arms, weeping and laughing. "Oh, Daddy, Daddy—come see him—oh, the beautiful baby—*hurry!*"

Subtract two from the group, True thought foolishly. But add two more. She had caught sight of two men laden with briefcases and books but moving with purposeful strides alongside O'Higgin. Their faces were familiar, but—

"Thomas J. Riefe," Young Wil, who had worked his way to her side, prompted in a low voice. Oh, yes, the hog-jowled president of Centerville's largest bank, holder of the mortgage on the ranch. "And the pink-skinned man wearing Ben Franklin glasses was Uncle Artemis' lawyer." True managed to nod. Oh, yes—Isaac Barney, who prepared the will.

The trio was moving toward where the two of them stood. O'Higgin was embracing her warmly, reintroducing the two men who stood as sober as undertakers, and telling Young Wil to go for Marty. They— the Norths, O'Higgin, and "associates"—must caucus while the others prepared the feast (feast?). Then Midgie's father, Mrs. Hancock, the minister, and "another" would be joining them to "shed light on the matter," after which there would be a mortgage burning and—

"Surprise! Surprise!" somebody was yelling tardily, followed by a chorus of congratulations. Then the group set to work in an orderly fashion—kindling a bonfire for barbecuing, unloading food, setting up tables. It was organized bedlam, while True felt herself being led into the cabin, wondering if she had spoken a word . . .

"So—tell me," Isaac Barney began as he peered over his half-glasses at Marty. "Has this been a banner year for wheat?" he said once they were seated.

"Yes, according to what I know of wheat's history here—" Marty began uncertainly. He shifted uneasily in his chair, looking at Midgie.

"Turn a profit?" The lawyers eyes were interrogation points of suspicion.

Marty flinched. "My husband is too modest," Midgie interrupted, adroitly walking between Marty and the owlish man. "You can examine the books for yourself. And," turning with a fond smile to O'Higgin, "I am sure you know," she said proudly, "that Tex's experiment with the red wheat was a whopping success. In fact, he developed a heartier strain—one which Marty feels he can patent. One seed company is interested—"

Billy Joe, not to be ignored, barged in. "Heered a part uv thet," he said, removing his shapeless straw hat, " 'n figgered you'd be needin' more input. Me 'n Slinger got ourse'ves th' finest herd uv Shorthorns in these here parts. Guess we all showed you city fellers a thang or two—eh, Mr. Wil? 'N Slinger's steeds claim second t'none—"

True saw the look of consternation that Mr. Barney aimed at the foreman. She also caught the tightening of Marty's lips, the look of doubt that crossed the threshold of his features. But his eyes filled with appreciation when he looked at Midgie. *We tried—even if we failed—*

"Pardon me, Mrs. North," Isaac Barney said, ignoring Billy Joe completely, "but I was examining your husband—"

"*Examinin'*, be ye?" O'Higgin's voice filled the kitchen and floated out the window. "We have a bank examiner here if there be a need—though his mission be more t'do with railroadin'. 'N there be a company detective seekin' out any hocus-pocus—so how come ye go scoldin' th' lass? Midgie here be 'is pardner—'n th' lad's one mighty lucky mon—man—'avin her likes. Many a lad's been known t'go cringin' through life, all fer th' need uv a good wife standin' by for cheerin'! Git on with th' terms 'n th' signin' over th' deed. I be satisfied!"

True's mind took a dizzy turn, then settled down to questions. So the banker's business must be the railroad shares. That figured, since they went with the original ranch, perhaps spilling over into the claim on which Marty and Midgie had proved up according to the agreement. The railroad detective puzzled her. Was there a stranger in the crowd? Perhaps, since she was too surprised to greet each guest individually—doing well to murmur welcoming platitudes. The talk was a rehash of the terms of the will, which she knew by heart. Interesting, yet she felt her eyes drawn to the window. And there she saw Tillie Caswell engaged in conversation with none other than the man who had been the object of so many questions in True's mind as to his identity—the "man wearing the beaver hat."

There was sudden quiet, broken only by the scratching of a pen. "We'll need your signature too, Mrs. North, as witness of the fact."

What fact? True had lost out. She looked at them all apologetically— a grave source of irritation to the lawyer, judging by his condescending be-kind-to-dumb-women look. His round face wrinkled, making him look somewhat like a withered apple. His eyes were tiny green flames. Oh, dear! But the others looked elated. Elated, yes—and, in Marty's case—overwhelmed. So something wonderful had happened. Young Wil cast her a look of pride, and he irritated the squat little lawyer still further by extending O'Higgin's defense of Midgie.

"Well, since we're passing out compliments—O'Higgin having said that Marty could never have accomplished all he has here without his wife—Marty and Midgie's saying that they could not have done so without me, may I add that I could never have fought the good fight without the most wonderful wife in the world—a little brattish, but wonderful!"

"Wil North," True began, forgetting that they had an audience. Then, quickly, "The pen, please—"

"'N th' lassie trusts us, begorry! Nice lassie she be. Observant one, too—noticin' th' mon—man—speakin' with Tillie. Might as well be callin' 'em in—her 'n th' detective. More compliments! Without Detective Dansworth there, th' one what be wearin' th' fancy hat, Tillie Caswell never coulda regained u hut be lost, includin' 'er sense uv whut was a-goin' on in God's great footstool. 'N," the great man lifted his chest high with triumph, "Martin North here woulda never known 'is background . . . *Come on in!*"

38
Things Always Turn Out Right

WITH HER BREATH coming hurriedly and her heart pounding, True listened to a resume of Uncle Artie's will. In the thin spots, something told her that O'Higgin and the lawyer acted in the capacity of the Supreme Court in its interpretation of the Constitution. Certainly she had never expected that she and Young Wil would be involved in something that Isaac Barney breezily waved away in rambling paragraphs as "spirit of the law." She concentrated with an effort.

"He—the deceased—wished him who proved up on the claim, that is to say, the *new* ground, to have this," he said, beginning to wheeze a bit as he fumbled in his black bag to draw a small prayer book from among the other papers. So—?

The lawyer held out the book with a questioning look in O'Higgin's direction. The response was immediate—and shocking. "Mr. and Mrs. Wilson North, Junior," he said with a ring of power in his voice.

But—but this was not right. There had to be some mistake. True's eyes moved to catch Young Wil's, but he was accepting the book and nodding as Mr. Barney's wheeze developed into a sneeze which sent the papers askew. "Ragweed," he said wiping his eyes and ordering that certain marked passages be read aloud.

"I'm not sure I understand—" True let her voice trail off uncertainly. "*You* were the heir," she said to O'Higgin. "And—"

O'Higgin let out a whoop of amusement. "Ye be wonderin' who owns 'said property,'" he mimicked. "Sometimes methinks these

331

lawyers be paid t'muddy th' water. Never mind, Barney, me good man. 'Tis best I tell 'em in plain English—jest be holdin' yore peace 'n *all* will read th' bloomin' paper if 'twould please ye."

The words tripped from his tongue lightly—rapidly but clearly—the flow unbroken by the arrival of Tillie, Anna-Lee, the Reverend Randy (carrying a Bible), and Daniel P. Dansworth (carrying his hat!).

Marty and Midgie were now owners of the original Double N, O'Higgin explained, while Young Wil and True owned the newly acquired property completing the vast acreage that Uncle Artie desired. The four were to "make no never mind" about him and his Miss Mollie. They would retain most of the railroad shares, as Superintendent Emory Keeling deemed proper, a few falling to the four joint owners, to whom he would turn over his proxy—all right, all right, Barney, make it "power of attorney"—as long as they could lift the burden from his shoulders. Why should a pair the age of him and his Mollie-gal have to traipse for meetings, voting, and signatures?

"None." The banker spoke for the first time revealing a mouthful of gold teeth which protruded enough to give his face a rodent-like expression. "I will take care of matters at the bank and keep you informed as to best investments, how to set up trust funds, and—"

The lawyer mopped his brow. "The reading," he reminded, obviously eager to complete the transaction and escape from Ragweed Ranch.

To everyone's surprise the Reverend Randall stepped forward. "A prayer book, I do declare—and my friend Artemis at that," he said in awe. "May I please see it once more? I read from its pages through the passing of the old man's spirit. It—it is a special book—the one I used for his own ceremony. Yes—Artie was married, but briefly. His beloved wife was taken early by a dread disease—but that is another story. He was hopelessly sentimental, but hid his true emotions—we were dear friends—dear, dear friends—"

"Well, *somebody* take it!" Isaac Barney said sharply, holding a finger beneath his reddening nose to forestall a sneeze.

The minister obliged by taking the book from Young Wil's hand. "Well, I'll be," he murmured, "the very words that Artemis and Miss Betsy said—and asked the congregation to repeat along with them—how about it, Irish?"

"You read 'em good feller, 'n we be repeatin'."

Wilt thou take this loved one . . . to have and to hold . . . to live as one, according to God's holy ordinance . . . forsaking all others . . . until one shall lay the other in the arms of Jesus?

True stood transfixed for a moment, aware only that the kitchen-window curtain moved in and out as if inhaling and exhaling. The wind had changed directions which meant that the sun was moving westward as if the day had held too much already. But there was more. Much more . . .

Her husband laid a gentle hand over the icy fingers which must be hers. "Well," he whispered, "how do you feel, my darling?"

"Married—oh, *very* married," True breathed.

His ardent dark eyes met her violet ones. "You'd better!"

Around their private world there was sudden stirring. "Only key parties are to remain!" Isaac Barney ordered. Tillie Caswell was saying, "Things always turn out right." And outside Mariah began the soft melody of a Mexican wedding song.

39

The Residue and Remainder

I T WAS A case of déjà vu. True felt the same premonitory thrill race up and down her spine that she had felt—had it been only a year ago?—when the bespectacled Isaac Barney pursed his lips and read the will of O'Higgin's uncle.

"And now," he said importantly licking his lips as if to taste his words in advance, "the residue and remainder—the most important item of all." Looking over his glasses, the lawyer spaced each word, pausing between to let his full meaning soak in: "Establishing—proper—identity—of—one—individual. *Martin North, do you know who you are?*"

There was a dramatic pause.

At last Midgie lifted her great eyes, so large that they looked unreal in her childish face. But there was nothing childish in her manner. "Tell them, Marty. Whatever this man has to say cannot touch what we have—together."

Marty's hand reached out to grasp hers as if for support, but his voice was strong. "I do not know my background, if that is what you ask. But it is unimportant—"

Isaac Barney cleared his throat. "It is *very* important to the persons who have worked so diligently to trace it for you."

Tillie could wait no longer. "Tell him, for goodness sake!"

From that moment on the Norths became spectators of a play which was stranger than fiction. And soon to join them in the grand-

334

stand was Isaac Barney himself. After all, he was outnumbered by those with speaking parts. But they could not rob him of his rightful position. So he sat back with an air of authority that one usually associates with a prime minister or other visiting dignitary ready to challenge irregularities.

Somehow Tillie Caswell took center stage first. "This is a great moment in my life—the moment I have hoped for, prayed for, since losing track of my precious Hildred, my niece, my baby, her parents being killed in an Indian raid. I looked and I looked—all the way from Mount Lebanon, New York, to Portland. There was no sign, no trail of the little angel I had raised in my own faith but encouraged to learn of her parents' beliefs in the Shaker movement. Then," Tillie sucked in a painful breath, "she broke my heart, marrying so young as she did to a young man whose name I didn't even know. Oh, how can I ever forgive myself for—for the dreadful words I said? But for me, she might be here—and to think I objected to a Shaker husband after having her learn—"

The Reverend Randall rose from his chair to place a comforting arm around the shoulders of his friend. "Tillie, don't! Please do not torture yourself. You tried—we all did! And God *did* hear our prayers. He sent us these helpful friends who, each in his own way, led us to—him—and now you have a remnant. A fine one, I might add!"

"If thou wilt allow me to speak?" Anna-Lee Hancock lifted a slender hand, the long sleeve of her black cotton showing wear at the armpits.

All nodded. "'Twas not thee who kept you apart. There was a time when those departing Mount Lebanon were not allowed to return. How be it then that the young woman did not bring the husband and come to thee?" Adam Hancock's widow shook her head. "'Pride goeth before a fall,' I believe the Good Book be saying it. And the Higher Authority saith, 'Blessed be the peacemakers.' Be there bitterness left in thy heart?"

"Bitterness?" Tillie Caswell's eyes widened in surprise. "Oh, no, *no*—just remorse—no, not even that, for God has forgiven me, given me peace, happiness—restored my soul and my family!"

The other woman's eyes searched the hills as if seeking words.

"'Twas worth the risk then of having coals of judgment heaped upon my head. If thou art at peace, thou willst be willing to restore me to the same state. So 'tis I who be seeking forgiveness for deceptions—shame I may have brought thee and thine house—"

"*You*? Not you, Anna-Lee! It would be impossible for you to offend," Tillie said reassuringly. "But," with a smile, "if it will make you feel better, what is this dreadful thing you have done?"

"I am the barbed-wire lady!"

An audible gasp circled the room. Then silence.

"'Twas my means of gathering information for thee—and bringing peace to the valley. My people make the wire as a means of livelihood without feelings of guilt. 'Tis better that barriers separate the cattle and sheep than that men slaughter one another, offending God. But our men dare not offer the wire lest they be hanged—leaving behind families—as I have lost my husband by bullets. Punish me if it be thy wish—"

"Nobody is going to punish you, Anna-Lee. You are courageous—a fine lady. And your husband died a hero, remember that! But I guess we are all wondering why you choose to to tell us this—and at this time?"

"It *be* the time! I sought for thee information nobody else could have found among those who knew that Mrs. Caswell's niece was one of us. I be the one who could get them to speak. Others, our enemies, knew of the railroad shares, wanted the wire, and—and—forgive me, exchanged information which made my dear husband able to sign verification papers—just be saying I am forgiven my transgressions—"

"Transgressions, me foot!" O'Higgin boomed. "You were a key witness. We be praisin' th' Lord for th' likes o'you! Now, 'tis a time to be happy, not a time to weep. Tell th' good woman, Tillie!"

"I love you for what you have done," Tillie Caswell said humbly, knowing that her wonderful friend would be embarrassed by a caress. "You are sure—all of you? It—it sounds too good to be true. Oh, bless you all—I could take no more heartbreak—you are *sure*?"

"Shure 'n they be shure, me bonnie one. Reassure 'er Dansworth!"

At O'Higgin's command Daniel P. Dansworth went into action. Opening a portfolio of papers, he shuffled through them with an expert hand. "The birth certificate," he said without inflection. "It puzzles me as to why the party involved never bothered to question the attending physician." Before there was time for a response, the railroad detective held up other supporting papers tracing the Missing Person across the nation from Mount Lebanon into Oregon Country—and finally the death certificate for both her and her husband. "Cause: drowning of the latter—that would have been the Great Flood which all but wiped out the valley. The lone survivor being an infant son—no name, of course, as the former, your niece, died in childbirth, without gaining consciousness. The child was born posthumously nothing but a miracle that he survived. It took expert skill!"

"Uncle Wil has that—together with faith which sustained us all."

Young Wil's voice was the first from the audience. The performance had seemed unreal. Not one mention of a name. The miracle baby, *Marty*! True hardly dared glance at him. Would his face be blank with shock? Would he revert back to his former state of rebellion, self-pity—resentments which even he had been unable to explain?

None of these! Marty, gripping Midgie's hand, leaned forward, face aglow as if he were an architect ready to build a house that lightning would bounce off. And, in a sense, that summed it up. His faith, much like the wheat, was ripening. God had opened the windows of heaven for him and Midgie, raining down blessings. Their house would stand.

True had a strong desire to stand on tiptoe and shout. It was with an effort that she brought herself back to the occasion's solemnity.

"Then my name was Martin all along—never mind whether first or last. Daddy Wil brought me into the world and the wonderful woman—Aunt Chrissy to Young Wil and True—was then the wife of Brother Joe, who saved my life in another way. And they took me in—as their own?" Marty's question needed no answer. "Oh, I owe them so much—as I owe the rest of you. Tell me the whole story— the part each of you played in locating me, giving me a heritage to add to the already rich one. We—Midgie and I—want to be able to hand it down to our son."

Everyone started talking at once, Tillie Caswell's voice rising above them all. After all, *she* had seniority, being the nearest relative—a great-aunt to one Martin North, which made her a great-grand-aunt to that precious "nameless child" (such a pity!). But *she* had a name for herself—"Grandy" she was to be called, and—The lawyer shifted positions. "Shall we say 'Case closed'?"

No, no, *no*! This man had a right to know the story—even asked for it. It seemed they were *all* doing some digging at the same time.

Fate brought them together. "*God!*" Reverend Randall corrected, repeating what Tillie had said before. How he stood by, helped search, *prayed*. "All roads lead to Rome," somebody quoted, bringing the slate-eyed detective in touch with Midgie's father and then to the banker because of railroad connections. Yes, Mr. Callison knew there were questions—even (*ahem*) problems when his Midgie came to Portland craving more schooling. O'Higgin's homework was done for him, actually. There remained only a verification by the late Adam Hancock—with one detail missing, the family tree. Being a man of mental muscle, a party wishing to remain anonymous had studied genetics extensively and had found O'Higgin to be a "long distance" cousin to the Martins! With that announcement, Isaac Barney gave up any idea of restoring order.

40

"If Music Be the Food of the Soul . . ."

IT HAD BEEN a long day. The weary sun sought refuge behind a white city of skyscraper clouds, pausing only long enough to light each window with red-gold light. Above the spectacle a crescent moon smiled in anticipation, while down the hill what had been a busy murmur of voices skipped several octaves, becoming an impatient ring: "Come, *come*, COME!"

In response, those in the small kitchen filed out one by one—all except Marty, who remained behind to check on his son. When Midgie would have remained with him, Marty shook his head. A look of hurt crossed her face briefly. Then she too went outside, where, the clamoring crowd reminded them all, it was time to view the sunset.

Again the overpowering sense of déjà vu. Had it *really* been a year since the four Norths came here scarcely aware of their mission? True wondered as she gripped Young Wil's hand, meditating with the others at the glory of the sunset. Truly, sunsets were beautiful here. One could see so far in the open country she had grown to love. In an odd sort of way, she would miss it. It occurred to her then for the first time that they were part-owners here. What would they do with the land?

The question went unanswered. Randy Randall was reading from Bible passages especially selected about friendship. And, bless their hearts, Tex, Slinger, Slim, and Pig Iron boomed out the heartiest *Amens* in the crowd. Augie, grinning widely, made his way to Mariah's side.

There, without aid of a musical instrument, the two of them joined in a soul-touching a cappella duet. In English! Their voices throbbed across the meadows, echoing and reechoing "What a Friend We Have in Jesus"—obviously planned in advance, as no words were spoken.

Marty politely waited until the hymn ended. Then he stepped to where they stood and said, "May I ask that my wife be allowed to join you in the next song?"

At Mariah and Augie's delighted smile, an amazed Midgie walked uncertainly to his side. Midgie's white face said plainly that she was remembering the shattering incident at the Roundup Barbecue. Marty was too—but in a far different manner, True realized, as he handed her the mysterious package she recognized immediately as the one he had kept hidden.

Fumbling at first, Midgie began tearing away the wrappings. Then, excitement growing, her fingers tore at the last scrap of paper and, with a squeal of joy, she flung open the box. As if handling a sacred instrument, she withdrew a deep-blue velvet carrying case, snapped open the hinges, and lifted a concert-size guitar made of the finest variegated rosewood. As tenderly as she handled the baby, her fingers stroked the ebony fingerboard's raised frets, three pearl position dots, and nickel-plated tailpiece. "Oh, Marty, Marty—" was all she could manage as the prolonged "Oh-h-hhhh" of onlookers rose to a chorus of "Play, Miz Midgie. Play. *Play*. PLAY!"

Misty-eyed but sure of herself, Midgie obliged, her gifted fingers strumming music from the steel strings that surely angel harps would find difficult to rival. Her touch was that of a master, delicate and commanding, as she entertained the speechless crowd with a repertoire of Schubert's serenades. Then, her eyes alight with a near-holy glow, she lifted her face to the stars. "Sing with me!" she called out gaily, and began with old familiar favorites. Hymns. Cowboy songs. And, finally, a simple Spanish song dedicated to Mariah and Augie. Spectators, unfamiliar with the language, hummed and whistled and laughed.

Midgie's already-flushed cheeks took on a deeper tinge. A breeze still warm from the sun and spiced with meadow grasses danced in to stir the curls at the nape of her neck. She was a daughter of the soil now—the vagabond impulses gone. And she was a mother! That accounted for the added shine, True thought wistfully. *Now, now, no coveting*, she scolded herself; *my time will come.*

Midgie (who, like True and Mariah, had changed hastily into the fiesta dresses) faced her cheering audience with a bright smile. Then, rising from the bench that Augie had pulled forward for her, she said resolutely, "I wish to dedicate the next number to my husband and then—"

But the soft strains of "Let Me Call You Sweetheart" drowned out the words which completed the sentence. The near-recklessness of her previous singing was gone, her voice almost pleading in its throbbing sweetness. True's heart turned over inside her, and without warning she felt her own voice join the other girl's. The others, too, joined them in a salutation of greeting and farewell, with love, affection, and kindness between. It was a love song of the heart. Midgie and Marty forgot the rest of the world.

Young Wil was making his way toward her when both of them heard the baby's wail for attention. "Uncle Willie will check on him." He managed to mouth the words to True with an apologetic grin. But the young lord and master of the household was already in the arms of his "Grandy" Caswell. And Young Wil was further detained by one of the men who wanted him to sample the barbecue. The crowd was starving.

In that brief moment Michael St. John stepped from the shadows to stand beside her. "Michael! You're here—I'm glad." And, oddly, she was.

He nodded, face altered by something resembling compassion in the gathering twilight. "If music be food for the soul, play on . . ." he said softly.

41

Anonymous Donor

AROUND THEM VOICES diminished to murmurous, near-inaudible conversation as people consumed unbelievable amounts of food. True felt no desire for eating; her mind was too filled with questions which could be answered only as the full story unrolled of its own momentum. A certain sad-sweet emotion swept her being, intensified somehow by Michael's unexpected appearance; or was it his Shakespearean quote, revealing a softer side to him than she had known, which undid her? He was a master of diplomacy, to be sure, but this was different.

True blinked in an effort to rid her eyes of unexplained tears. Michael mustn't see lest he misinterpret. The fragrant air was settling to the chill quiet of neardarkness. To regain composure, she looked up the incline to where the irrigation pipes began. The little ripple of water was willow-fringed now, the dark green of the leaves silver-dappled by the infant moon. A faraway coyote howled mournfully.

Michael cleared his throat, uncertain of himself for the first time. "You must wonder why I came—like," he said with an attempt at lightness, "the uninvited evil witch at Sleeping Beauty's christening. But remember," he rushed on, "that the seven good fairies were each to bear a good gift. So—will it change my image if I tell you that I have brought my token of affection?"

Caught by surprise, True could ask only, "Toward whom?"

"Everyone—but more especially you. Will you—drat it all, I hate it when I'm sentimental! So will you do the honors after I leave?"

"Of course—but what about your image? Aren't you holding something back? It would please Midgie and Marty so much and—"

"I prefer to remain an anonymous donor, True—so will you please?"

"Of course," she answered, her mind elsewhere. *Anonymous donor.* "Anonymous person." They had to be one and the same.

"You are the one," she said slowly, "who traced Marty's family, giving him and Midgie the identity they wanted. Oh, Michael, I'm so grateful—you did for them what you did for me in Atlanta—and I—I—am afraid I never thanked you properly."

"Please, no gratitude. Just a part of my job." Michael St. John ground the words out as if to recapture his stampeding composure and drag it back to safer ground. "I am a railroad executive. As such, I am compelled to trace backgrounds, locating the missing persons who hold shares. It's that simple."

"That isn't simple and you know it."

"It was in Marty's case," he replied quietly, having given up all attempts at levity. "A lot of the research was done already. I think you know that was necessary when he ended up in trouble by resorting to near-criminal means to stop the railroads from cutting through what he saw as land belonging to homesteaders. When records showed his link with the Caswell family, you can guess the rest. Martin North holds stock in addition to the Caswell shares—and that, my dear, is the gift I bear. The news, I mean—and a—a family tree for the baby—now be merciful and don't laugh—"

"I'm not laughing," True whispered unevenly. "Oh, Michael—"

Michael drew an uneven breath. At that point he could have embraced her and she would have considered it a friendly gesture. But he did not so much as touch her hand. He was, after all, a gentleman—a gentleman scroundrel perhaps at points, but a gentleman all the same.

Voices had risen again. True turned back to the platform in time to see the long, flapping garment, the Reverend Randy Randall's differentiating trademark, pushing through the crowd. Beside him were Marty and Midgie, both looking over the heads of all others in search, she somehow knew, of herself and Wil. It was the part she dreaded: the farewells.

"I must go." Turning on her heel, True would have joined them but was delayed by Michael's urgent plea for one minute more.

"True, I wanted you to know that Felice and I are no longer together. She has gone home—to stay—along with her pompous
brother—"

"I'm sorry, Michael, I truly am. A broken marriage—"

He sighed. "It was no marriage at all. Someday, if I am very, very
fortunate, perhaps I will meet someone—forgive me for bringing up
the past, but I met that someone once—and was fool enough to let
her slip through my money-grasping fingers—"

"It wouldn't have worked, Michael," she said gently. "And, as for
meeting another—surely you know that you are bound in the eyes
of God to Felice. Marriage vows are sacred and binding."

"Ours were neither—either in the eyes of our Maker—or ours—
not even legally binding. Felice plans an annulment—"

Shocked, True looked at him in disbelief.

"Our marriage meant nothing to either of us. Don't be embarrassed
by this, but it was never consummated—"

White-faced in the glow of outside lanterns, she faced him. "Why
are you telling me this?" she whispered.

"I feel a need to purge my soul," Michael said miserably. "You
promised to pray for me a long time ago, and I guess it is working.
I'm not a bad person at heart—just suffering from some wrong up-
bringing. And now guilt and disillusionment with the principles I was
taught to build my cathedrals on haunt me. Thank you for all you
have taught me."

"I have done nothing—nothing at all—except pray. God has done
the rest. Oh, Michael, I do want you to be happy—like I am."

He laughed. "I doubt if anybody else could be *that* happy. But—
who knows, as you say, what God can do? But just one last gasp before I surrender completely—let me say that if I didn't admire and
genuinely like that lucky chap of yours, I'd break his kneecaps!"

True, feeling a bit giddy from lack of food and the long, exhausting
day, laughed with him. "I think I've witnessed a miracle," she said—
not sure whether she spoke to Michael St. John or their Lord . . .

A radiant True joined her husband at the platform, now an altar.
He took her arm as she lifted the full skirt of her fiesta dress to clear
the rough boards. Taking their place beside Midgie and Marty, who
stood before the Bible-in-hand minister, True was surprised to have

a cocoon of soft flannel thrust into her arms by "Grandy." The March Hare! At first she held him gingerly, as a maid of honor holds the bride's bouquet—ready to relinquish him on signal. Then from the cocoon there came a gentle coo as a wee, pink foot emerged. Forgetting the onlookers, True pulled back the soft blue blanket and laid her face against the warm, satiny cheek, a flood of deep emotion coloring her face. But why was Young Wil so touched? Surely he had seen a woman's face caress a baby's a million times over. But not hers, she realized . . .

"Hear, hear!" True scarcely recognized Marty's voice. "As you know, Reverend Randy is here to perform weddings, comfort those who mourn—and christen our babies. Midgie and I want to dedicate this child to our Lord and Saviour—"

When his voice broke, the proud minister took over. "I christen Christian Joseph Martin North—"

Christian Joseph Martin North, sensing that unfamiliar arms cradled him, let out a lusty yell. Midgie reached for him. Making no attempt to hide her pleasure that this special child already recognized the loving hands of his mother, she leaned down to croon softly to the smartest child in the world—deaf to the rest of the ceremony.

Marty, standing straight and tall, listened intently as the minister read Hannah's promise to dedicate to the Lord's service the son she prayed for, followed by the words of Jesus: "Suffer little children to come unto me . . . for of such is the kingdom of God."

That was Marty's cue. With a nod from Randy Randall, the proud father stepped forward to delineate the March Hare's name. "I have found my own lineage through the birth of our child," he said simply. "By coincidence, both my natural grandfather and my wife's father bore the given name of Christian—and there are two further reasons for our choice. His mother and I wish to rededicate our lives to Christian service—and then there is my wonderful mother, the only one I have ever known, Midgie's Aunt Chrissy—" Marty's voice faltered. Midgie reached out one hand to offer encouragement, tears sparkling in her twilight-blue eyes, and he was able to go on. "Joseph, known as 'Brother Joe,' was her first husband's name. It was he who baptized Wil, True, and me, for he—God bless him—took me in as his son." Again the catch in his voice. And then: "They gave me the name of Martin—because Martin, I have learned through Tillie

Caswell, my great aunt—that's right—" he said above the gasp and applause, "Aunt Tillie, 'Grandy' to Christian, is family—as were the Norths, who befriended me when 'Brother Joe' was killed—"

There was a subdued sniffle, followed by a chorus of sniffles, with Tillie Caswell leading the Great Weep which swept through the audience. When at last Randy was able to break in, it was to announce the baptism of Tex, Augie, Slim, Pig Iron, and Slinger this coming Sunday. Unless there were others—? It was then that Michael St. John, the "anonymous donor," stepped out to offer his heart openly . . .

42
The Leaning Tower

❧

NIGHT RANG DOWN its curtain. The air tingled with the arid smell of smoke, a reminder that ashes were all that remained of the mortgage on Turn-Around Inn. The only sounds, besides the operatic croak of frogs along the riverbanks in Peaceful Valley far below, were the subdued dialogues between departing guests.

Had there ever before been such a night? So happy? So sad? So filled with mysterious events? A night of revelations for sure. Just went to show you (on this they agreed) that mankind neither knew all the answers, nor would he ever. The human brain could cram itself chock-full of knowledge, but wisdom belonged to God. Fact was, that creation time appeared to be a beginning, not an end. Why, creation was going on all around them. Pretty sobering, but the Almighty must have left the rest of the work up to His people, with so much remaining to do that He just kept on recruiting. Look at what He'd done with those "losers" hired on at the Double N. Would anybody have thought of *them* as being worth their salt? Anybody, excepting, that was, the Norths? Here those four young folks had come in acting like greenhorns and turned out to be mouthpieces for the Creator. They had downright surprised everybody—maybe even themselves.

Either way, the valley, including Slippery Elm, would never be the same. Just take a look at Miz Tillie's shining face. Look at the change.

Yes, take a *good* look—one that penetrated the heart. Tillie Caswell was darting from guest to guest making sure that every one

347

of them had a good look at the only remaining member of her blood-line—carrying on the family name and destined to change her world, maybe the *whole* world. He had restored her sanity and her soul. Christian Joseph Martin North in a place called "Slippery Elm" was unthinkable. The foul name must be changed. Better get started on that before that big-city lawyer left . . .

The "big-time lawyer," his face again crinkled with worry lines (which made him look all the more like a withered russet apple), was conferring with the gold-toothed banker, who was smiling like an acre of sunflowers. Life, the two of them communicated unwittingly, was all in how one looked at it. The hog-jowled banker Riefe, having surrendered the mortgage, was already dreaming up other schemes for the new generation. Let that worrying attorney sneeze and fret a spell over the change in ownership, heirs, and railroad dividends. No, that was the mysterious Daniel P. Dansworth's lookout. Fact of the matter, he was doing so now. And sure enough, the railroad detective had joined the two men. Must be smarter than he looked. Still, he'd had the help of them all, squeezing out information the way he did as subtly as the "Ole Deluder hisself." Never could have completed his search, of course, without help from Tillie Caswell and that Mrs. Hancock. Unbelievable that the little Miz Hancock (right sweet when a body got to know her) promised to bring the entire flock of Shakers to witness the baptism . . .

"Jest sum it all up this away," said Billy Joe, who seemed blessed with a thousand ears, "Ole Artemis was shrewder'n we give 'im credit fer!"

True's mind was spinning even more rapidly than her guests' as she bade them goodbye. Too much had happened for her to absorb. Sometime she must piece together all the impossibles, binding them into a patchwork comforter to warm the hearts of her children, even as she must copy lines pertaining to Marty's background from Angel Mother's diary. He and Midgie would want to share these words with little Christian, and the writings would be a fine accompaniment for the family tree which Michael had prepared—

Michael! True shook her head, hoping to make her mind absorb what her heart was unable to communicate—the greatest "impossible" of all. How did Samuel's writing express it? Man looks on the outward appearance, but the Lord looks on the heart? Billy Joe, the philosopher, had said it another way in speaking of his friend, Artie: "A chestnut, that one—prickly on th' outside, but onct th' burr's busted there's a right sweet kernel uv goodness inside."

Forgive me, Lord. Michael's been "bustin' out" all along—only I failed to notice, because I had judged and imprisoned him for life . . .

The last hands had been shaken furiously, the last shoulder patted, and the last tear shed. Now the guests were gone. The four Norths, still dazed, remained outdoors looking at each other, too weary for speech.

A sweet-breathed breeze drifted in from lingering lilacs. Midgie's rooster crowed lustily. Soon dawn would spread pink bolts of color lavishly over the foothills, followed by the prodigality of sunrise splendor of a new day.

O'Higgin, whose knees had given out, rose and shook himself like a hibernating bear. "Well, I guess ye be knowin' I'm gloatin', lad," he boomed, reaching out to pump Marty's hand. "Allus saw th' tide o' enthusiasm in ye but feared instability might be dashin' ye 'ginst a reef—"

"You had a right to your doubts. I was argumentative to hide my *self*-doubt. I was a leaner—couldn't tread water without Wil here and True—and now—" *Marty was bustin' out.*

"You have Chris and me, darling," Midgie said stoutly as she reached for his hand.

O'Higgin scratched his red curls. "Nothing wrong with bein' a leaner. We all be leanin' on God. If th' Leanin' Tower didn' tilt, who be hearin' o' Pisa?"

43

Beyond the Farthest Star

⌘

"I WILL MISS the dogs," True said, meaning it but choosing this time to express affection for Tonsil and Lung in order to hold sadness at leaving in check. "But I guess they need space—"

"As do Marty and Midgie need space, darling," Young Wil said reassuringly. "They're the ones you're concerned about, aren't they?"

"I realize I'm as pale as paper, but am I *that* transparent?"

"Young ladies are supposed to be pale—"

"Who says?" True giggled. Her husband had a gift for turning phrases. Endearing—and maddening. "Name your source of information."

"*Godey's Lady's Book* by Sara Josepha Hale," he answered with a teasing air of superiority. "Mind if I ask you a question?"

"Yes, but you'll ask it anyway," True answered, playing his game.

But the game was over. "Won't it be exciting, getting back to Portland's shops, buying yourself a dress or so—doing the things a woman enjoys?"

The game ended for her, too. "I *have* been doing the things I enjoy, darling. You know I've loved it all—being with you, working together. In fact," True said slowly, "I have considered abandoning teaching and doing an internship in nursing. I have crammed three years of schooling into two—and we could be together—one long honeymoon!"

Young Wil touched her cheek with a gentle finger. "You amaze me, my darling. You truly do—and what you say has validity. As a matter

350

of fact—" he paused to rummage through his coat pocket—"I have had no chance to tell you that I have confirmation of our test dates, and—" Young Wil paused to put a pencil hampering his search into his mouth while he located another envelope—"O'Higgin brought a note from the Portland doctor I was with—nothing to consider—but—"

True's heart missed a beat, then began to drum, drowning out the sound of vibrations along the rails which announced their approaching train. "An offer—?" she ventured.

"Something like that—sent my mind hurtling as fast as yon train. Ready, sweetheart?"

To board the train? Applaud the offer? Advise Wil to consider it? Or turn around and go back to the Double N? What she wanted to do was none of those. If only they could turn back the hands of the clock, finish their honeymoon, and return to the Big House afterward . . . back where Aunt Chrissy and Grandma Mollie were baking every known cake, pie, and cookie, grooming the already perfect grounds, and planning a "surprise party," while Daddy Wil rearranged the office furniture to accommodate his nephew's chairs and books and spread news to every patient that the prodigal young doctor was coming home. In bowers of flowers the twins would be planning every known prank. Even the river would sing a bit louder, practicing its welcome for their return to Paradise. All this O'Higgin had told them—and more—before boarding the train weeks ahead of them.

If only . . . if only . . . but time did not turn counterclockwise.

Young Wil, sensing her mood—even hearing the words her heart was speaking, it seemed—smiled a bit crookedly. "We have grown by the experience, my dearest," he said as he helped her aboard the waiting train. "We need make no decisions now; just" (and his eyes regained their twinkle) "enjoy this honeymoon!"

True's mood changed. She grew more and more excited as the train's wheels ground out the miles between Slippery Elm and Portland. One by one she shed her concerns, concentrating on the fun of seeing city lights again, reuniting with family, and discussing the challenges of decisions regarding their future. After all, God would guide them. Hadn't He always? And before decisions, a honeymoon!

Even the ramshackle train station failed to depress her, although it was smoke-filled and crowded by unsavory men, only a few of whom dragged off their hats in the presence of a lady. Young Wil's strong, sure arm guided her through. Outside the world was clean and fresh as only the Pacific Northwest knew how to make it—a secret formula of wind and rain and sunshine. True unknowingly blended in with it all perfectly—so perfectly that all who passed turned to look with admiration at the girl in a dainty pink-and-white frock, the style of which suggested an inverted morning glory as its ruffled hemline swept the newly constructed boardwalk.

Familiar salt air tickled the nostrils, and hawking calls of "Tax-*eee*, tax-*eee*!" by drivers licensed to transport passengers for hire by carriage rose above the scream of white-winged gulls wheeling in for a landing and the never-ending stutter of engines as ships put out to sea. "I had forgotten how noisy cities could be," True reflected to herself as Young Wil whistled for a cab. But he overheard.

It was good to hear him laugh boyishly. "Let us hope that we don't draw a buffoon driver who serenades us country folk in Italian! Things have changed so much."

Things had changed as well in the old hotel where twice Mr. and Mrs. Wilson North had begun a honeymoon, only to be interrupted. The basic architecture was of choice quality, bulging and looming in unexpected places, begging to be preserved. The additions to accommodate a more discriminating clientele had taken nothing away. Alterations scarcely showed beneath a new coat of shining white paint. Somehow True felt relieved. She liked change while needing permanence, branching out while retaining roots. *Concentrate on your surroundings, not your philosophy*, True cautioned herself.

Inside, the changes were more visible. Thick red carpets made it difficult to wade through the pile. Chandeliers sparkled with a million prisms, overdone but hypnotic in their faulty beauty. True glanced from the great entrance hall into the diningroom and noted that the family-style tables had been replaced with alcoves which whispered an audible invitation to intimate dining. But the corner alcove boasted a long window which picked up the shimmer of the river and the tree-lined street beyond. Following her gaze, Young Wil arranged a reservation for the table of her choice.

"Happy?" he leaned across that table half an hour later, after they had freshened up and True had donned the best dress she had with her, a periwinkle-blue silk she had taken to the ranch and never worn.

"Deliriously," she said with the blush of a new bride. The truth was that she felt like one—shy, dreaming dreams, with eyes only for her husband. Alone, just the two of them, for the first time. Certainly the cardboard walls of the ranch cabin offered no privacy. The memory spun her mind backward and forward in spite of her resolutions.

"I—I do wish I could lift the curtain on the next act—"

"None of that, Mrs. North," Wil admonished. "Only God knows the end from the beginning. We will do according to His will. We have the assurance that wherever our hearts lead, God's love will follow."

"Oh, Wil, darling Wil," she breathed, "you are blessed with the gift of reminding me to 'Consider the lilies.'"

He dropped his head humbly and reached across the table to close his hands over hers. "Our Father which art in heaven . . ."

True's voice joined his. But before they ask only for their daily bread, repetition of the Lord's prayer was interrupted. A waiter noiselessly padded to their table and laid a yellow envelope near the heliotrope centerpiece.

With an effort, they continued. Then, ripping the flap somewhat nervously, Wil read aloud: "ALL ARRIVING TOMORROW STOP BEST WISHES ON TESTS STOP LOVE STOP THE FAMILY."

For a moment they stared at each other in disbelief. And then, forgetting their audience, the would-be honeymooners burst into a fit of uncontrollable laughter. One night alone. One.

Young Wil was first to recover. Wiping his eyes, he managed one word: "Meantime—"

"Our honeymoon," she gasped, feeling almost giddy. "I don't feel like dessert."

Her husband leaped to his feet in a comical fashion. "Nor I!"

Inside their bedroom Wilson North did not turn on a light. "Come here, brat!"

"Wil North," his wife began, then stopped. It would always be like this. Their love begetting love—and more love—ringed by others.

In the protective circle of his arms, her heart soared high above the trill of the bluebird's song, a song telling of dreams which had never happened—but should have. And would! Released from earth's gravity, forever they would follow the invisible footprints of faith. Beyond the farthest star. And God's love would follow.

PART III

Love's
Enduring Hope

With love and appreciation
to
JANICE
the enduring glue
which held our Masters Clan together!

*Known unto God are all his works from the
beginning of the world.*
                    —Acts 15:18

*Decision of character will often give an inferior mind
command over a superior.*
                    —W. Wirt

Contents

1

Descending

ஒ

IN THAT MYSTICAL time of day when gray light precedes the coming dawn, the world held a wraithlike look. Smoke spiraling from chimneys of early rising farmers looked black against the billows of white clouds, which (like the vine-maple leaves) blushed with just the right amount of pink to whisper the change of seasons. Like a wheel at the top of its climb, there was a breathless pause before summer yielded to fall, and then the world would be white with winter. Inside the cozy cabins, fires would blaze as they hissed happily on the diet of pine-resin logs; and hominy grits, swimming in lakes of melted butter, would replace the garden greens of summer-gone. People drew close to nature, God, and neighbors.

Like the wheel, the rented buggy had reached its apex—as had True's heart. The beauty spread before her and Young Wil brought a lump to her throat. It was too much to digest. One could only look, remember, anticipate. And then would come the descending . . .

"Happy?" Young Wil drew the horse to a halt.

"Of course I'm happy—I'm with you, am I not?"

"And 'whither thou goest . . .'? There needs to be more than that."

True cast a quick look at her husband's face. His eyes were darkly luminous in the soft light which was beginning to flood the world with morning. Was *he* having doubts? His plans had always been to return to the Valley, finish his internship with his uncle, and then doctor back to health the people he loved so dearly. It was a dream which, though interrupted briefly, was about to resume.

359

"There *doesn't* have to be more than that!" True said with heart-felt conviction, resuming their conversation. "Your people are my people already. But even if they weren't—"

"I know, darling—I know. You would follow me to the ends of the earth, regardless, just as you did when we gave up a year to see Marty and Midgie through that crisis." His voice grew husky with emotion.

"I loved it!" she said lightly, reaching for his hand. "It's going to be wonderful to get back, though, Dr. North."

"Not quite yet," he smiled. All the same, he patted his vest pocket with pride. In it was his temporary license. "There's the year to put in with my uncle, the senior doctor, which I'll enjoy and appreciate. It's just that—"

"You feel a little queasy. Very natural, Doctor."

Young Wil grinned. "Thank you for diagnosing my case for me, an indication that you have the same symptoms. With test scores like yours, how could you doubt yourself?"

As usual, she had been transparent in his presence. He was wrong in what he read into her mood, however. It was something she her-self was unable to understand, so why try to explain? "Test scores are one thing, but standing before a roomful of proceed-with-caution young eyes is quite another. So I can understand how you tremble at the thought of deciding if the patient's tummyache is appendicitis or indigestion from eating green apples. So how *can* you tell?"

"Very elementary," Young Wil answered in mock seriousness. "Just look for peelings under the bed."

"Very good. And if you find a saddle instead?"

"He ate horseflesh, of course!"

"Wil North, you are destined to be a quack."

Together they laughed. *Please, Lord, I love this man You gave me; let me sustain him forever with a merry heart*, True's own heart whispered.

Aloud she said: "You will be a wonderful doctor—one who will crash through every obstacle and win out by sheer persistence and—" her voice lowered as she looked at the handsome man beside her, so clean-souled, so massive in spirit—"you will win confidence with your gentle manner. But you may be a shade too good-looking. Women have a way of falling in love with their doctors, so I may have to pull hair—"

He stopped her with a kiss.

The human mind moves swiftly. In the short time there on the rise overlooking the dewy Valley, True's mind did a quick review, beginning with the most recent chapter and thumbing backward. The landscape between a rapidly growing Centerville and Portland was unchanged—verdant, mysterious, inviting while the larger city remained impersonal, almost uncaring, so filled was it with newcomers . . . ambitious businessmen with flowing ties, sharp of eye and alert of ear in search of new clients. Yet the elderly man with neatly trimmed goatee and resonant voice had appeared sincere as he monitored their tests. Used to be a doctor, he said, and was Mr. North sure? Well, all right then . . . To True, the good man's wife had some words of caution, he said. But seeing their youthful enthusiasm and determination, he shrugged and handed them the forms.

It was hard to concentrate. The monitor kept waving blue smoke from a fat cigar their direction in the poorly ventilated room, while noise below the second-story window was deafening . . . street vendors' voices trying to screech out the quality of their wares above the cheers, jeers, and shrieks as men hand-cranked Portland's first backfiring automobiles. City life was not for them, True had said. That was good to know, Young Wil had replied after giving the matter some thought. At the moment she had supposed that he agreed wholeheartedly. But did he?

True drew a deep breath, trying to clear her lungs of the stifling memory and to dispel doubt. They loved the countryside—all of it.

Her mind went back to the Double N, its surprises and its victories. Marty and Midgie would manage. Of course, now that they had the baby, they must give thought to schools. And there should be a church. How strangely the lives of the four young Norths paralleled those of the generation ahead of them . . . Angel Mother and her love for Daddy Wil . . . Aunt Chrissy and hers for dear Brother Joe. How mysteriously God worked, holding them together, binding their hearts with ropes of love, when the Grim Reaper, life's last enemy, stole away Angel Mother and Uncle Joe. The brokenhearted spouses had found solace in their mutual grief, had married, and had held together the bewildered children . . . nourishing their faith and preparing them for service in their beloved Valley, but never making them quite understand their strange relationship.

"Would you believe," True asked suddenly, "that Jerome asked me just what 'kin' he is to you and me? I guess he wants to be called 'Jerry,' saying that the new minister thinks a new name's in order after baptism."

Unabashed by her out-of-context question, Young Wil answered with a grin of amusement. "I'd believe anything of that pair! Kearby told me how much she loved honeymoons—and when could we have another?"

"*Another*? If we ever have a *first* one I'll be surprised! Imagine an entire family's invasion—oh, well, it was fun! You know, Wil, they've grown up thinking of me as a sibling instead of as a cousin on their mother's side. Same for you: on their father's side, Marty an adopted brother . . . but we loved them, 'kin' making no difference."

"You're wonderful—let's go home!" Surely the mountain stream, darting in and out between laurel thickets and ferns, sang a welcome song as they descended.

2

Home Is Where the Heart Is

THE "BIG HOUSE," Daddy Wil's family home, came into view in spite of Aunt Chrissy's flowers' efforts to obscure it. There was the gnarled old apple tree which had served so faithfully as a shade for Angel Mother's beehives, still intact just as she had left them. True's throat tightened, so caught up was she with tender memories . . . her mother's singing lullabies beneath the tree . . . Daddy Wil's building swings for her and Marty . . . Young Wil's tree house . . . the fat apple pies from the tree's fruit.

One could tell the seasons by that tree—its pink pouting buds whispering spring, then bursting forth with fragrant Hallelujahs on Easter morn (*always* then, in her memory). The leaves served as umbrellas to shield the infant green apples, which blushed with promise of summer as the season marched on. And no matter how many of the forbidden fruits she, Young Wil (who was old enough to know better, said his uncle-turned-doctor), and Marty ate with salt (even though the green fruit put their teeth on edge), there were always ample left for pies, cobblers, dumplings, and the best jelly in the world. Come fall, the leaves warned of winter. There had been no more than three months of real school, since starting was postponed until harvest was over. Closing came when it was "plowing time"— with countless closures between due to inclement weather and flu epidemics . . .

It would be wonderful getting home. But if anybody had told her she would feel like this, True supposed she would have disbelieved it. Why, she was homesick (not quite the word, but she could think of no better) for the lonely, formless landscape, the vastness seemingly blotting out time and space as it stretched on and on into infinity. The land they had feared and near-hated and grown to love now laid claim on their hearts . . . the faultless summer skies . . . the beauty of sudden storms—awesome and humbling as blue-white lightning clawed at the sky's ceiling as if seeking a means of escape— and, yes, even somber winters that bandaged their small world, forbidding movement. She would, True thought with a small smile of surprise at the idea, even miss the strange winds which whimpered, sometimes sobbed, as if in pain. Here the wind gossiped among the pines during the languid days and hummed her to sleep with nighttime lullabies.

Unknowingly she sighed. Perhaps me foreign thoughts came from the incomparable beauty of this Valley: mountains and more mountains, some bonneted with snow which refused to recognize the seasons which the old apple tree foretold, others waving wispy clouds like white flags floating from the tallest peaks, so gently did the autumn zephyrs unfurl them.

"Come, come! Who but you could smile like Mona Lisa while wearing such a pensive expression? Wake up, my precious, we're home—and from where I sit, we are about to come under seige!"

How true—with the leggy twins, barking dogs, and mass of adults charging upon them! There was Aunt Chrissy in a starched apron smelling of sunshine and sourdough, Daddy Wil pointing with pride at the sign proclaiming NORTH & NORTH, M.D.'S., Grandma Mollie ordering breathing room for her "babies" in order to gain right-of-way, and O'Higgin's mellow voice singing the doxology: ". . . as it is now and ever shall be . . ." True could only think of Angel Mother's sampler HOME IS WHERE THE HEART IS.

3
Changes

❧

DURING THE FOLLOWING week, True saw little of her husband except at mealtime. And even then, although Aunt Chrissy had gone all-out to prepare his favorite dishes, he might as well have been eating day-old corn pone and drinking unsweetened juice of wild grapes plucked from the vine before ripened. She understood, as did her aunt and (she supposed) the wives of all other doctors, particularly rural ones. Daddy Wil must catch his nephew up on the condition of patients, what they could afford to pay (and when), which ones were housebound, and which could make office calls. They went through mountains of files, discussed medical terms and new findings, and arranged a filing system which "the women can help set up."

Chris Beth smiled patiently and turned her palms up. The gesture, so characteristic of her, said: "Oh, sure, sure! All we have to do is loaf around here anyway—cooking, mending, keeping an eye on two unbroken coltish adolescents, and, of course, teaching! Bring on the files!"

True giggled. Aunt Chrissy loved every minute of it—and so did she! Besides, the two of them needed time to do some planning. And, to her aunt's obvious delight, True wanted to renew her acquaintance with every square inch of her childhood home—the old mill, the yards, the gardens, but most of all the cabin that she and Young Wil would call home. So she only half-heard Daddy Wil say that Young Wil's book was still popular. (Needed same updating to increase royalties, of course.)

The mill was still, but the footlog which connected the two houses was still intact. Mossy but showing no signs of age, the log, anchored securely between head-high clumps of sword ferns, lay in contentment—seemingly unbothered by the silver-tongued prattle of the gossipy stream it spanned. One day they would rebuild the bridge which the flood washed away, but True resolved that she would never permit removal of the log. It would be like carving away a part of her heart, for the mossy log represented the magical rainbow-arch which had catapulted her from childhood to maidenhood—quickly, so quickly. One day she and Marty were outrunning Young Wil, their adored but sometimes strict keeper. The next day Wil had joined their play in a game of fox-and-hound chase. True had slowed (purposely, although this she would never admit). As planned, Young Wil caught her while the unsuspecting Marty dashed on in triumph. Triumph? It was she who won! Her adored Wil, pinning her arms to her sides in victory, stared at her with a new fire in his eyes. That same fire ringed her heart.

"You're my prisoner!" His eyes still burned into hers.

"Yes," she said. "And, yes, I will."

"Will what?"

"Marry you, of course."

"Now, listen, brat—"

True had laughed up into his face brazenly. Even now the thrill of awakening came back . . . the thrill of knowing that she had won by losing. They would marry and live happily ever after. And they had.

"Still daydreaming?" Chris Beth laughed like a young girl. "The place always brings back memories for me, too. Just wait until you see 'Honeymoon Cottage.' Uncle Joe and I spent our honeymoon days there, too—" her voice trailed off sadly. "The heart remembers—come on, my darling," she said, her eyes brightening with second bloom. "Love has many faces."

True could only gasp when they entered the cabin, inhaling so deeply that it hurt her chest, then exhaling in a ragged gasp. Was she dreaming? One could never relive the past. Yet Aunt Chrissy's bringing all of Angel Mother's beloved furniture back (even rearranging it as her sister would have done) brought back memories so sacred and so real that the years between melted away. She felt small again, as if she must stand on tiptoe to see the top of the fruitwood highboy where her mother kept the monogrammed silver hairbrush and hand mirror, great bouquets of flowers (always flowers), and her precious diary which kept the memories alive forever. The walls were a riot of color—needlepoint pastoral scenes, dainty pastel petit point baskets of fruit and kittens in quaint tent stitch, embroidery . . . punch-work . . . appliqué—all the work of Angel Mother's slender, childlike hands.

With a lump in her throat, True turned to the marble-topped wash-stand where her mother had placed the handpainted china basin and giant pitcher, the mirror above it lowered so that a child could comb her golden curls, admire them, then experiment with her still-new face, twisting it into sordid shapes. How her mother had laughed! Maybe, in a way, she had never grown up. Certainly she had never grown old. There had been no time.

Tears stinging her eyes, True reached to stroke the highly polished spool-and-spindle bedposts, then let her fingers trace the outlines of the double-wedding-ring design of the quilt that Angel Mother had stitched lovingly in remembrance of the ceremony at Turn-Around Inn, uniting her and Daddy Wil, Aunt Chrissy and Uncle Joe. And then . . .

"Isn't this the bed—" True began, then choked back a sob, remembering . . .

Chris Beth nodded. And then they cried together, sharing their loss.

"Thank you—oh, thank you," True said a few moments later. "I am at home here in every way. I love you all so much—"

When the sun waved scarves of golden mist against the sky, too blue to be real, Chris Beth suggested that they turn home. Days were shortening, she said, even though summer's warmth remained. True agreed reluctantly. Time, she needed more time—time to drink in the beauty of her beloved Valley. With her remained the conviction that every twig, every blade of grass, every bush and tree was a jewel in disguise. Actually each was a precious stone—a sapphire, diamond, turquoise, or amethyst that must be protected from The Forty Thieves! But evenings were shorter here than in the flatlands of the Double N. So she quickened her footsteps to keep pace with her aunt, wondering if she had answered the millions of questions hurled at her this afternoon. There was plenty of time, of course. Why then did she feel a sense of urgency—a hurrying to tie events of the past year together? To make herself understood?

"I hope I am doing a fair job of putting the 12 months into words, helping you see the changes in the hearts of Marty, Midgie, Young Wil, and me. All the time I was there, I kept thinking of how I would relate it all—make you see it, *feel* it. And now I find myself tongue-tied, wondering if all is truth—or if words trip me up, forcing me into the realm of imagination, confusing facts with Maud Muller's 'might have beens.'"

Aunt Chrissy understood. "Don't I know and love you all enough to read between every unspoken line? Words are always like that—often baffling the speaker. I guess only God understands our prayers when our mouths utter one thing and our hearts whisper another—and," she sighed, "our spirits try to approach His throne while our minds gather daisies or wonder what we are going to have for dinner. Speaking of which—"

Laughing, "mother" and daughter linked hands and ran through the goldenrods, reaching home just as the sun dipped behind the hills rimming the valley.

Twilight had darkened the living room, but neither of the men had bothered to light a lamp. Would they always be this engrossed? Probably. They always had been.

"Wilson North, you are ruining your eyes—and you a doctor!"

The senior doctor did not look up, but the corner of his mouth went up appreciatively, a characteristic his nephew had inherited. True tried to remember which the two doctors thought more important—heredity or environment. Did the apostle Paul know anything about this thing called "genes" when he spoke of nurturing one's gifts?

"I still think of taking more courses in nursing," True said as she set the table for four. But before Aunt Chrissy could answer, she spied Young Wil's favorite cake. "Snow on the Mountain," she called it—a towering devil's food cake topped with swirls of feather-light frosting, often tracked with small fingers that could not wait. But now the cake reminded her to look high up the peak of Mount Hood. Yes, snow still topped it, lines waving here and there by the fingers of nature. She had missed that mountain. And the cake. *Oh, thank You, Lord, again for family, love—and home.*

"You will get plenty of practical experience in nursing in school," Chris Beth assured her as she rescued a cast-iron pan of cornbread sticks from the oven, "as well as helping your husband here."

True nodded. "Will I find things changed, Aunt Chrissy—the people, the church, the school?"

"Very. But I will let you find that out soon enough. I had planned a little shopping trip tomorrow—then church Sunday . . ."

True was surprised to see the sign: ABE SOLOMON'S MODERN STORE. Somehow she had supposed the Solomons to be retired. They were here, she recalled, when Aunt Chrissy and Angel Mother came to the frontier from Atlanta so many years ago.

She was surprised again at the inside of the department store. It was more like two stores, the old and the new. One side of the enlarged building was indeed modern—some of the merchandise rivaling that shown in the finer stores in Portland. But the other side held a strange fascination, perhaps from recollections of the Caswells' store in Slippery Elm, a trip into the past and a store whose proprietors had become dear to her heart. But that too was a part of the past . . .

The Solomons had not greeted them. Instead, they were greeted by remembered smells: food (strong hoop cheese, bacon fat, and the pungent fermented odor of pickles in barrels); mixed leathers of harness (probably there since stagecoach days, as the bridles were gaudily tasseled and cowhide-bottomed); and straight chairs clustered around the same old bumper stove she remembered since childhood.

An even shorter, stooped Abe attempted to straighten from the sliding door leading to a rounded glass display case where he had been arranging spools of colored thread. As, with hands to his back, he continued the struggle, Abe said: "Hep yersef t'coffee brewin' on th' back burner. Bertie, come hep—*Bertie!*" the word came out in excitement when his watery eyes caught sight of True. "Miz Vangie!"

"Vangie's daughter," Chris Beth reminded him gently. "You remember True—and, yes, the resemblance is striking."

"Oh, yes—yes, or course. Th' ole noodle ain't quite what it once was. Can th' two doctors in yer family do much fer heads?"

Bertie Solomon bustled briskly from the back room. "As I live and die, she *does* look like her dear departed mother. I would've supposed 'twas a figment of Abe's mind—come, darlin', let me feast my eyes!"

After the inspection, True wandered into the "Better Dress" department and was surprised to find how expensive fiesta dresses were. Why, Mariah could make a fortune here! Not that she would move, though . . .

True forced her mind back to the present, fingering feathered bonnets and partially opening parasols. (Not opening them enough to admire the designs, of course. Mrs. Solomon would suffer a grand mal. *Everybody* knew it was bad luck to open an umbrella inside a building. Worse than breaking a mirror. That brought only seven years of misfortunes, but an open parasol—that could strike a body dead!)

Amid True's mental wandering, snatches of conversation between Chris Beth and Bertie reached her ears. How was Maggie? Mention of Bertie's daughter set the woman's tongue loose at both ends. Maggie was in the pink in every way. A real jewel, that girl. Took her time about growing up, but now she had the world's best husband . . . was the world's best wife . . . and kept the world's cleanest house. The Lord had forgiven her one transgression . . .

Actually there had been several, according to Angel Mother's diary—mostly those of casting verbal stones. True further remembered that Aunt Chrissy had felt a pang of jealousy of what Grandma Mollie called the "town harlot, even drest in red befittin' her profession—why, Wilson North wouldn' spit on her likes, jest pray fer her soul! Twarn't even reasonable entertainin' that green-eyed monster th' devil created an' named 'Jealousy' whilst Adam 'n Eve wuz namin' th' animals!" True smiled, recalling that she too had played hostess to the same sin of jealousy. How *could* she have suspected Young Wil of turning his affections to Midgie (of all people!) when she herself was in Atlanta? All women were geared for the unsaintly emotion, she supposed, when another woman came between them and the men they loved (real or imagined).

". . . and *so*—we're right glad to be welcomin' you and Young Wil back Sunday." Bertie Solomon was saying, leading True to believe her talk had never stopped. "I guess you had a good doctor over yonder, else you'd never have left. Young Wil bein' a young deacon almost from cradle days led most Valley folks to speculate he'd be a preacher like his Uncle Joe, rest his dear soul. Old one or young?"

Minister, True supposed Mrs. Solomon meant, and answered accordingly. "Neither. There is only a minister who visits periodically—the community being—well, different than our Valley." True paused, something warning her to choose her words, as the woman enjoyed tidbits of gossip. "The hub is hardly a town at all, and houses are far apart, since the ranches are widely separated. Or," she stopped suddenly when it occurred to her that Bertie probably meant a resident doctor, "if you meant physician, we have—*had* none at all."

Mrs. Solomon clucked her tongue, eyebrows arched in question marks. Thank goodness, Aunt Chrissy came to the rescue. "I have a list here, Bertie, and, yes, we will all be in church." She handed a scrap of lined paper to the news-hungry saleslady. "True and Young Wil came back just as we have planned all along. Now, about the list—"

Another customer came in, forcing an end to the conversation. True did not know him, but was to learn later that he was the minister of the church now called "Centerville Community Church." Her impression was that he was a man of great height. Or was that because Abe Solomon was attempting to rise again, unfolding himself like a jackknife, to match the stranger's six-feet-plus? The result would have been ludicrous had True's heart not gone out to the older man. *Why do we try to be what we are not, Lord?* her heart whispered. *Teach me to be more thankful for what I am and to use it for Your glory.*

Shopping completed, Chris Beth waited as Abe Solomon counted each penny twice, then prepared to pick up the flavorings, spices, and coal oil. True hurried to assist her independent aunt—only to have another stranger reach out a work-hardened masculine hand to cork the spout of the fuel container by expertly clamping a raw potato over it. "Keep it from spillin', Miss—yuh must be th' new teacher, a pilgrim hereabouts. Welcome—here, hand me th' bundle an' I'll be obliged to heist 'em all in th' buggy. Guess yuh got no man fer this."

There was no time to answer the well-meaning stranger in the linsey-woolsey shirt that was buttoned to his Adam's apple and topped by a suit coat badly in need of pressing. He must be smothering! He hurried out with the parcels, stumbling over an untied bootlace, and disappeared down the alley of the long street—much longer than True realized.

Before the young man reappeared, Mr. Solomon brought "Brother Prescott" for an introduction. "Brother" made him sound older to True than his facial features indicated. The face was arresting. She almost smiled at the silly description which crossed her mind when their eyes met. The Reverend William Prescott's patrician nose, delicately drawn (but firm) mouth, and deep-set eyes glinting like hardened quartz took him from the beginning of the twentieth century and changed him into one of Robin Hood's men. His eyebrows arched with interest.

"So this is the new teacher? How do you do, Miss North—how nice that you will be working alongside your mother here."

It was a perfectly natural mistake, his addressing her as Miss, one which Mrs. Solomon did not ignore (or wait for True to correct), adding every detail of the family relationship to her captive audience.

The minister apologized and then they spoke of church matters.

"I'm sure the congregation has grown as everything else has?"

"Not really," William Prescott admitted. "There are so many denominations. We've come a long way since the Lee and Whitman missions. Other Protestant churches keep springing up—Baptist, Congregational, Episcopal, Methodist . . . then the splinter churches . . . and Catholic—"

"Splinter churches?" True questioned with interest.

"Actually, we embrace all," the minister said with a certain degree of pride. "Some original members remained, and new people join us by letter."

True felt a tug of concern. "What about—persons not knowing the Lord? I know they are welcomed. But—well—I find myself wondering if," she smiled, "we address Christians only, as Paul spoke to churches?"

The question hung in midair. William Prescott appeared to be considering the role of the church while True was remembering needs which the circuit-riding Randy Randall had met in the wide valley around Double N.

Their conversation terminated when a customer needed a hundred-pound sack of sugar for preserving late-ripening pears. Too heavy for Abe, so would Brother William give him a hand? True tried to manage a departure, but not before Bertie had wedged in "a word of caution." Young women had to be careful—surely True had seen the interest the stranger showed. And, well, even ministers were *men!*

True felt strangely relieved to be starting home, the late-afternoon sun suddenly thrusting its fire through the horizon ahead. *Home,* her haven, an island floating in the world's immense sphere of sky. An escape? *Had* she found things different? Yes—and no. True felt, momentarily, like a stranger. A confused one, with a forced smile.

4
Introductions and Interruptions

THE CHURCH WAS smaller than True would have supposed. What happened to the plans for a building so large and expansive that it could accommodate "the saved" (converts who formed the congregation) and "the unsaved" (newcomers, as well as wayfaring strangers who had never met God personally)? The latter Nate Goldsmith described as folks "knowin' Somebody with a Mind put this Valley together but got no inklin' they're akin to 'im?" True wondered again if the growing population found what they were looking for in the other churches.

And then her eyes (and mind) wandered over the worshipers. The Norths had arrived late because one of the horses developed a sudden leg cramp which the two doctors (serving as veterinarians when the need arose) had to attend to. Jerking the cramped back leg into place by means of a rope took time, then more time as they soothed the frightened animal. How gentle the two men were, Aunt Chrissy pointed out in misty-eyed pride. And how patient their wives must learn to be. How did Aunt Chrissy manage? Chris Beth laughed at the question. "It takes time, faith, prayer—and understanding," she said as if sorting words carefully. "Remember, I've been a wife to both a minister and a doctor. Qualifications are about the same." Still, True was on the verge of saying that women (if anybody at all) should be called the "*Very* Reverends" when bedlam broke loose upstairs.

The twins!

Thank goodness style dictated that skirts were *two* inches shorter this fall, else Chris Beth and True would never have made it up the stairs before one twin slaughtered the other. Even so, both tripped near the top. Breathless, they were forced to be spectators of an ugly but comical scene. Kearby had cut herself some irregular bangs, the yellow fringe standing in peaks where the cowlick sprang. Their mother had tried in vain to explain to her brother that it was natural for a girl on the brink of young womanhood to pay attention to her appearance. Today, however, she had upset Jerry's cologne (tucked behind a photograph of Grandfather Somebody). Chris Beth's reasoning furnished the enraged Jerry verbal fuel. Grabbing her cork-bodied doll (joints allowing it to "walk"), the boy was dancing wildly around the hall, forcing the jointed legs to bend out crazily and singing:

> Down in the meadow where the green grass grows
> Sat little Kearby as fair as a rose!
> She sang and she sang—she sang so sweet,
> Along came her feller 'n kissed her on the cheek—

Furiously, Kearby wiped up the spilled cologne with her handkerchief. Waving it like a banner back and forth, she made a somewhat successful attempt to drown out his voice:

> Jerry's mad 'n I am glad
> for I know what'll please him:
> A bottle of ink to make him stink
> and I-know-who to squeeze him.

"Stop this silliness—*right now*, both of you!" Aunt Chrissy ordered in her best schoolteacher voice. "Open that window, Jerry, and give that cheap-smelling stuff some air! Kearby, True can even those bangs tomorrow. We will settle this later—and don't give me that I'm-not-going look, either of you."

Well, here they were in church, even though True wished they could have been in a more worshipful mood. The men undoubtedly were remembering the chestnut mare's leg (fortunately for the twins, who were still sulking). Aunt Chrissy, obviously still concerned, leaned over to whisper that she was glad True and Young Wil were here. They would be a leveling influence . . . and she jerked her head toward Kearby and Jerome.

True had nodded mindlessly, her eyes wandering. No new fall clothes—too warm. The ladies were still in their summer voiles or lawns, and so many folding fans waved back and forth that a small breeze stirred in the airless room. They wore, she noted, strands of ivory beads she had seen at Solomons'. And turban-style or roll-front "Cheyenne Effect" hats (so popular last year) had for the most part replaced sunbonnets, except for the few very elderly ladies and the wives of the Disciples with their carefully stitched white skullcaps.

Brother William prepared to go forward to occupy the pulpit. His face reddened and True could almost hear his grunt as he folded his giant frame to lace one shoe, methodically crossing and tying the strings. Rising to his full height, he carefully buttoned his suit coat and tightened his tie. He would choke when the fanning stopped.

Which it did when the congregation rose for the first hymn. Folding their fans, the ladies placed them in the racks ahead of them alongside the Christian publishing house advertisements, an assortment of combs and tortoise-shell hairpins—and, alas, wads of hurriedly stashed-away gum garnered from children's mouths.

The brief message was more of a testimonial. William Prescott had been a farmer, a progressive one, he said. But there came a call plain as day: "Come over and help us today—like the old hymn says." He had no choice but to stop plowing and say, "Here am I, Lord, send me." His "assignment" had been the Western frontier. On the way from Kansas he met the love of his life, a dedicated Shaker lady—

True's ears picked up the word, hoping the man would tell more about the dedicated woman he would have married had fever not struck her down. But he moved to family relationships: husband-to-wife, wife-to-husband, children-to-parents . . . and, finally, Christian fellowship. Amens filled the church, so True supposed that the members were satisfied. She was not. She wished that the minister had delved into the gospel story with as much enthusiasm and passion as his "feeling the call," as much live-forever love as his mention of his mate-to-be . . . Didn't giving one's heart to God come before walking in His tracks?

True's wandering thoughts came to a halt. A commotion similar to that which the twins had created earlier erupted with a squeaky opening of the church door, followed by a din of frenzied male voices. "Is there a doctor in the house? Quick! We gotta have hep—now!

Waylaid by hoodlums—er, Injuns—on th' way t'th' Bab-Baptis' church over yonder—wimmen, chil'drens are—gonna be kilt—doctor, doctor! Runaway horses—hep us find a doctor, Parson—'n the rest be prayin'—HEP!"

The two Dr. Norths were at the doorway, asking questions tersely of a man who was calmer than the others before the unnecessary details were finished. Number in party? Which direction? True could hear no more right now; Young Wil would tell her on their way. Her husband was all doctor, racing out the door without her as if whisked away by a whirlwind. No invitation, no goodbye—just a quick stop to pick up the inevitable black bag, trademark of his profession, and he was gone.

A growing heaviness encircled True's heart. It was hard to pin down—similar to (but strangely different from) an emotion she had felt back when . . . oh, that was it, *jealousy*! Pure, green-eyed jealousy. Another woman she could cope with, wrestle to the ground if need be! But how did one grapple with a man's work? *We have to talk, Lord . . .*

Brother William tried in vain to restore order. They must pray, he reminded them . . . and he wanted to introduce the new teacher. But people were filing out. All but the stranger who had answered questions. He was making his way to her. And then recognition came . . .

5
Comfort in Time of Affliction

❧

WITH HER USUAL briskness, Mollie Malone O'Higgin began herding the confused and frightened women into a corner of the church. "On your knees now, all of you. Know what it would feel like if 'twas your own out there? We're safe—our families are safe—we're in th' house of th' Lord. What better place for prayin' 'bout th' matter? With this many surroundin' th' throne, how can we fail? Git t' th' heart of th' problem, them out there in that runaway wagon—no mealy-mouthin'—"

Nate Goldsmith took issue with the words. "Now, be hearin' me, Miss Mollie! Prayin's fine fer women, but us men got a bigger job t'do—"

"Bigger than prayer?" True watched in awe, her own heart throbbing beneath the frilled lace jabot of her blouse as Grandma Mollie wilted her challenger with words. "I'm s'posin' yer all set fer formin' a posse, takin' th' law into your own hands. And on th' Sabbath—shame on you! Now, best you follow my man's example," she continued, pointing to where the big Irishman was already squatting beneath a giant Douglas fir. "You know th' Good Book tells us t'comfort one another in time of affliction. *O'Higgin!*" The three-octave rise in his wife's voice brought O'Higgin to his feet. "Nate 'n th' others'll be joinin' you. See that they make it!"

Without further ado, a low chorus of prayers began.

"What a vita' woman!"

The words were whispered, but True sensed their source. The man whose face she recognized was from the settlement just east of the Double N. Why he was here and why he sought her out she had no idea. And surely this was no time to inquire.

She could only nod to the Shaker and whisper in reply that they would talk later. Right now there was a greater need.

He understood. "A new breed," he whispered as if to himself, "a woman who braves hardship and danger to serve where she is needed."

"We all try to—here—"

"And elsewhere. Later—Mrs. North. God go with you."

The tall, sober-faced man covered the distance between himself and the kneeling men in two or three long strides. True dropped to her knees, overwhelmingly tempted to pray for her husband and Daddy Wil. But the others came first. The men she loved had put them there . . .

The sound of hoofbeats did not disturb the concentration of the women inside the church. The voices had reached a low, near-moaning chant while outside the men's ears were alerted. Generations of vigilance had entrenched in them the awfulness of truth. What happened elsewhere could happen here.

The stranger in their midst was equally conditioned. True sensed it. Dedicated to peace, he nevertheless faced reality. Evil existed; it was how one faced it that counted. She sensed as well that he had left the other men and knelt beside her. His inquiring glance spoke of his philosophy as his eyes locked with True's when she lifted her head slightly. Without words the two of them communicated as he reached a hand of assistance. As she rose soundlessly, True surveyed his face. It was younger than she had thought in their brief encounters at the few circuit-rider services near the Double N. The flourishing mustache that came to a point near his sunk-in middle, only to part divergently and curl upward in opposite directions, added maturity and proclaimed fundamentalism. But nothing in the gentle countenance resembled a holier-than-thou attitude—just acceptance of God's will.

He motioned her to the door, away from the other men, who—although prayers had stopped—watched the road and trails in silence. Unnoticed, the two of them stepped to the opposite side of the building.

"Begging your pardon, ma'am. 'Twas blatant of me to approach thee without permission." When True waved away his explanation, he continued: "I have not met thee formally, so may I be presenting myself as a God-fearing man on whom He has laid the burden of maintaining peace—one of the Brethren, Jeremiah of the Tribe of Benjamin. Jeremiah Dykeman be my earthly name. I salute thee in the name of Jehovah—knowing thou art my friend."

Although the introduction was lengthy, Jeremiah Dykeman did not seem to hurry. Neither did he do so in explaining his mission. He had led a group of "pilgrims"—no, he didn't know their name—over the hills and this far in their journey to Portland. Brutal, the trip had been brutal—ill-fated since the pack of mysterious riders had stalked them all the way from the community. Oh, how things had changed back there—but best keep on the story at hand.

"It makes no sense—it be so unnecessary—even before the volley of gunfire which sent the horses running out of control, I set the people doubting—disbelieving the Word I promised would guide us." The gentleman's mouth tightened. Breaking out of his amiable, sympathetic character for the first time, Jeremiah appeared to be wrestling for an answer within himself. "When God would have me demonstrate His faithfulness, I be leading them astray—milling, complaining, proclaiming life to be unfair, unpredictable, cruelly senseless—"

Sometimes it *can* be—or seem so, True wanted to say. Instead, she hastened to get back to the reason for the man's need to share with her in particular. "What happened on the way?" she asked.

"They demanded all our goods—and I be surrendering them instead of standing firm. 'Twas to save lives—only wouldst thou believe the peaceful gesture served only to arouse their ire? The sinful men fired on my people, killing a lad of 13—an innocent lamb—"

His voice broke. *A broken spirit. A contrite heart.* The phrases came unbidden. But what happened was not this man's fault. And the words were not intended to make such a dedicated man feel guilty.

"They would have fired anyway," True said helplessly. She stifled a sob and shook her head resignedly. "Some things are unexplainable. But," lifting her head, "whatever happened was not your fault—the important thing is that *you* have not lost faith." Lifting her head determinedly, and wondering where the words came from, she consoled, "You will bring them back together. Perhaps that is God's mission after all."

"Bless thee. We buried the lad along the trail—and I must be burying the past, preparing for the news ahead. Thou art thankful surely for law and order here, something we be lacking—although it be shameful that man be compelled to rely on any save God's law. We be obliged to the Norths, His servants—which be reminding me—"

The sound of hoofbeats came closer, then blended with wagon wheels. And then there were voices. Weeping. Wailing. Moaning. All told the story of tragedy. There were low words of consolation and encouragement, promises of justice, a reminder that already the culprits were in custody. Nate Goldsmith's voice rose threateningly, almost as if he hoped other would-be assassins were slinking in the brush. True was occupied with straining her ears for the sound of her husband's voice—so busy that she took little heed as Jeremiah handed her a sealed envelope . . .

6
"I Will Not
Leave You Comfortless . . ."

♋

"T RUE!"

Young Wil—oh, praise the Lord! And Daddy Wil assisting with
lifting the injured from a rickety wagon pulled by a pair of scrawny
mules.

"Darling—dearest—" True's words were lost in the deafening confusion of everybody's trying to talk at once. She lifted her skirts to
keep from tripping and ran into her husband's arms. He embraced
her briefly. Then, "I need you."

I need you. Three beautiful words amid all this horror. Mechanically, True ran to the buggy, opened the box on back, and pulled out
bandages and extra bottles of medication that he always carried in
addition to sterilized instruments in his black kit.

Around them swam a sea of faces, ghostly and congealed in silence,
eyes blank and expressionless with shock, or else angry and menac-
ing in their grief. The latter ones, hysteria their master, were beside
themselves, spitting out rash words, some punctuated with oaths,
verbally shaking their fists in the face of God. But True, like Aunt
Chrissy who had joined them, was scarcely aware. Fragmented conversation reached her subconscious—enough to communicate death.
But the job at hand was to minister to the living. True blotted out all
sights except the broken bodies in need of repair, all thoughts except
assisting the doctors—and all voices except that of Young Wil's low-
pitched voice ordering supplies or actual assistance as he set broken

bones and splinted them, or stopped the flow of blood and bandaged the open wounds. Surely these must be the most rugged souls on earth, gritting their teeth and bearing up when the painkilling drugs ran low.

"Keep talking to them. They need reassurance. The commotion out there's doing them no good," Young Wil whispered at one point.

In a white haze of single-mindedness, True said words she would never recall, soothed feverish foreheads, and held cold compresses to parched lips. Thank goodness, Nate had quieted down, and—hoping the Lord would forgive her if her befuddled thinking was wrong—True felt it was to Pastor Prescott's credit that he sensed this was no time to chastise the angry mob out there for irrational behavior or to force unwanted prayers. Instead, he followed Jeremiah's example and moved among them quietly, letting his calm presence be enough for now.

True was dimly aware of the passage of time. Fatigue was taking its toll. "How many casualties?" she asked wearily at one point, unrolling another bandage and cutting her finger as she snipped a length from the roll.

"Here—get some antiseptic on that," Young Wil said as he wound the gauze around a child's hand, held the cloth with his teeth, and secured the wrapping as True obeyed his order. "There you are, my brave little lad," he soothed, and to True: "almost finished—all ways—"

A movement close by caught True's eye, bringing her back to a fully conscious state. A second look brought eye contact with Aunt Chrissy, who was standing to stretch. True followed her lead, feeling as if a strong irritant had been rubbed into live, but wounded flesh all over her body. It was almost good to feel again—feel anything. "Are you all right, darling?" Young Wil's voice came from a long way.

True nodded, managing a smile. "My head feels like somebody had bored holes in it to let the devils out—"

"Now, where on earth did you hear about that?" Looking on the verge of collapse, he too managed a tired smile—tired but exhilarated, an emotion she too was experiencing.

"Something I read in one of your old medical books.'Bleed, blister, purge, and other appalling techniques,' it advised doctors."

"Grisly, dangerous, and painful, I'll wager. They stopped such quackery in the Dark Ages. 'Counter-irritation' I think they called it. The more excruciatingly painful, the more sure the cure—like some preachers of today!"

Together they laughed—and the world came back into focus again. There was still work to do. But they had worked together—a man-and-wife team—serving. Rising above fear, she had attended to the needs of others. And the result was surely what the Lord intended: True North had slain the green dragon of jealousy. She understood her husband's calling. The exhilaration rose within her even as she surveyed the bodies swathed in bandages around her. Now to cover them in case of delayed shock . . . Young Wil was rummaging in his bag for a disinfectant.

"Fatalities?" True asked as he poured the stinging liquid over her extended hands. "Ouch! That stuff's pure firewater—how many?"

Young Wil blotted her hands gently and kissed the bruised and blistered palms before handing the bottle to her and holding out his own hands. True gasped, "Oh, darling, you're a mess! Even your body's bleeding!"

"The blood's from others, sweetheart," he replied soberly. "There was one elderly lady, a mother and her new baby—and one of the attackers. Uncle Wil and I did what we could—and there was interference all the way. Grief-stricken men not trusting our methods—and—Ouch! that stuff *does* sting—there was real trouble when we medically treated the murderer. There were threats that we would swing from that gesture, so crazed were the men. There's no explaining to an angry mob that doctors are under oath to treat saint and sinner without discrimination."

"But the man died—" she said pensively.

"With an oath on his lips." The words tore at his throat, stinging far more, she knew, than the medication on his open wounds.

"I guess God deals with life in His own way. He looks after His own—bringing you and Daddy Wil back, and saving the others—"

"I've no sure answer for that, little nurse of mine. I only know that all of you prayed—and there is no greater earthly power."

It was a sacred moment between them, one that True regretted must be broken. Reluctantly she inquired about the bodies of the dead.

"We persuaded the survivors to remove them to Helwig's Funeral Parlor in preparation for tomorrow's burial—here in the cemetery."

True nodded, then mused aloud: "Why, *why*, Wil—why the slaughter?"

"It's insane—and these were not the only casualties. They looted and killed all the way from Slippery Elm—you were aware that they came from there, newcomers?" When she nodded, he went on: "They killed about a dozen fellow emigrants along the trail—shot one man in the back as he sat working on his harness. Paid looters, some say—"

Young Wil was busily picking up his dwindling supplies and handing blankets to True when the awful possibility occurred to her. "Wil!" she gasped, "what about Marty and Midgie—and the baby?"

His arm was around her when Jeremiah Dykeman joined them. "Oh, this is Jeremiah Dykeman, Wil. My husband—"

"I recall," they said in unison and shook hands.

"I be remembering thy kindnesses past," Jeremiah said warmly, "and see that the Good Lord be using thy skill and loving here as well. May I be posing a question? There is unrest, doubt, and fear in my flock, a need for reassurance that the transgressors are—are—punished."

"Apprehended," Young Wil assured him. "And we, in turn, need an answer to our concern. Our brother's family—are they—?"

"The letter will explain all. Mrs. North will tell you. As I be explaining to thy wife, 'tis a dangerous territory—uncivilized. But, yes, your family is under God's wing—in spite of all that has happened to them— begging your pardon. There be a need for my help in moving thy patients into the church with thy permission. Plans be that they will remain, some of the bereaved going to Turn-Around Inn, others elsewhere. Brother Prescott will lay the dead to rest come the morrow."

The funeral service was simple. The bereaved, in control now but with fury still roiling inside (judging by the tightened lips and clenched, white-knuckled fists), requested a common grave. No ceremony—just a hymn and a few words from the Good Book at the graveside.

William Prescott chose a passage from the Gospel of John. As he read, rain-darkened clouds appeared from nowhere, almost immediately releasing a deluge. Children scampered into the church. Adults covered their heads with whatever protection they could find—coats, blankets, hymnals. Grandma Mollie produced an enormous umbrella as black as the churning sky and held it over the head of the young minister as loudly he intoned the words in an attempt to make them audible above the whine of the wind.

Even so, only fragments reached the ears of those huddled together trying to hold a tarp over the little knot of mourners. The scene could not have been gloomier as the intended words of comfort faded in and out: "Verily, verily . . . I go unto the Father . . . I will not leave you comfortless, I will come to you . . . yet a little while, and the world seeth me no more . . ." Oh, dear friends, Jesus *will* send you a Comforter, and because He lived, these dear ones shall live . . . "

The clouds dispersed and the sun reappeared—comfortingly . . .

7

Evil's Bright Lining

❧

THE NEXT DAY was brilliant, the air rarefied by the rain. It was as if nature, having wrung the clouds dry before pinning them back against the blue, willed their bright lining to portend a message of hope. Little had remained of the night when Daddy Wil and Aunt Chrissy sent True and Young Wil home. Daddy Wil would take the first watch. The younger Norths were to get a bit of rest, have some food, and relieve the older couple in care of the wounded temporarily "hospitalized" in the church. They hadn't followed orders, of course. Dawn was ready to climb the silent hills; and there were preparations to make for patients which Daddy Wil and Aunt Chrissy undoubtedly would recommend moving to the Big House. The cabin, ready for their occupancy, could serve to house some of the overflow.

There had been no time for talk between True and Young Wil. Too, they were unnecessarily quiet in order to let the twins, shocked to silence, rest. As far as True knew, neither of the twins had spoken a word since the frightening episode began. It was their first encounter with disaster, cruelty, and sudden death. Western and Central Oregon were no longer "wildernesses." Only the vast area beyond the mountain chain to the East remained untamed. And that is where it all began . . .

Young Wil, his face still ashen with fatigue, helped True from the buggy—laden with fresh supplies and enough nourishing broth to hold body and soul together for the wounded until other arrangements could be made. They needed to hurry in, but True's eyes and then her footsteps were drawn to the single burial mound, washed flat by the rain. A retinue of shadows crisscrossed the single pine board which identified those who had perished. Head bowed, hands folded, True's heart murmured a silent prayer without checking the names of the interred, a single family.

She squeezed her eyes shut. This must never happen again, *never*. And then, behind stinging eyelids, came a nightmarish vision ... charred ruins of cabins which the crazed night riders had torched ... emigrant houses reduced to black rubble, perhaps with the remains of the owners still inside.

True shuddered, the faces of Marty, Midgie, and the baby floating before her horrified eyes. And then she felt the comforting arm of her husband around her. She faced him. He held her close. And just as quickly the horrible scene dissolved. Jeremiah had said they were all right ... the letter would verify that ... and that God needed her and her doctor-husband here for now. And once again she saw the world through the clear, crystal screen of yesterday's rain. The Comforter was with her ...

"In some mysterious way, known only to God, perhaps some good will come of this," True whispered as they started toward the church.

"Oh, my darling—" Young Wil's voice broke with emotion too deep for expression. "I wonder about the name—" but True did not hear.

There were some very positive outcomes of the tragedy, but they unfolded gradually, as well they should. Who felt like seeing—even looking for—the good in time of unrequited grief? For now, the problems at hand must be taken a step at a time, "each day sufficient unto itself."

Although True was unaware of it at the time, the disaster brought the Beltrans back into the full fellowship of the church. The Basque family from the high meadows (Rube and Rachel, son Burtie, and Watch, their giant shepherd dog) once tended the sheep in the higher elevations, undisturbed. Then had come the war between cattlemen and sheep-raisers.

"All bein' hardheaded, there wuz no reasonin'," Grandma Mollie had said. "The Beltrans drifted from one denomination t' th' other—finally despairin' with us all. Our deacons called, but th' timin' was all wrong," Miss Mollie sighed. "Keep hopin' th' Lord'll speak t'them—"

He did. How else could one explain their sudden appearance at a time when they were needed most? Young Wil was checking the condition of the patients inside the church while True followed, taking notes, answering questions, reassuring, soothing, offering a prayer when asked.

"We'll check for those needing hospitalization—" he began, only to be surprised by loud outcries of protest. Fear ran rampant and, deciding he had made a mistake, Dr. North began a retraction. He had his hands full until twin shadows, short of stature, blocked the light of the window.

"Welcome home, Miz North! Wife here 'n me bin thinkin' a talk with the Lord might do no harm. Seemed like a voice from up yonder tole us th' day."

"Mr. Beltran!" True sprang to her feet.

"Th' same." The Basque were people of few words, and so it surprised True that Rube Beltran looked around him and gasped, then turned her direction and gasped again. "Good people, folks like you we need—and purtier'n a cowslip—all growed up 'n filled out." Embarrassed, he stopped and lowered his voice. "Terrible thing. *Wife,* we got vittles?"

"We allus got vittles, Husband," she replied with simple dignity.

True turned to Rachel. "Thank you, Mrs. Beltran," she said, automatically reaching out to embrace the woman who was old enough to be her grandmother. The plain face of the other woman lighted with joy as if this were her first embrace for a long, long time.

Young Wil had risen to his feet. "God bless you both—we can do with some help. But first that prayer."

The four of them joined hands and, knowing the ways of the Basque people, the young Norths stood with them in a circle of silent prayer for a full minute. "Amen!" It was Rube Beltran who broke the silence. "Now, Wife, you be goin' home t'make ready, spreadin' th' news as you go. Steer clear o'them victorias—could cause a runaway."

That was the beginning of getting the wounded housed until the two doctors could declare their recovery complete. There would have to be decisions made, True was sure. But for now—she would take no heed of the morrow.

"What's a victoria?" she asked instead, swabbing a stab wound with iodine, then blowing on it to stop the sting.

"Used to be a four-wheeled pleasure carriage for the well-to-do—now another name for an automobile, the open passenger type."

"These automobiles," True mused aloud, as she recorded a temperature reading her husband gave her, "will they ever take the place of buggies and wagons—be practical for—"

"Doctors?" Young Wil grinned. "Not until there are roads—and that looks a long way off—here, clip this thread and we're finished."

The sound of wagon wheels said that the settlement had rallied in time of need as always. Some faces True recognized, others she did not. She only knew that for the first time she felt *completely* at home with these capable men in shirts that needed boiling or flowing beards in need of a barber (or were young and fuzzy-faced, like overripe peaches). On man, a stranger to her, was barking orders as if he had treed a squirrel, his bald head gleaming (her tired mind thought foolishly) like polished marble. Even on a dark night she could see to write a letter by its glow. *A letter* . . . yes, she must read the one delivered by Jeremiah. *But for now, O Lord, let the others take over . . .*

Busy days followed. Dog days, bridging late summer and early fall, brought sultry heat. A view from the dormer-windowed structure (considered a "must" on the upstairs roofs of the better houses in the East, in the preceding century) was about all Young Wil and True's temporary quarters in the attic afforded. Although True declared she would never be able to stand upright again for fear of bumping her head on a rafter, and Young Wil's shins were barked to the bone from stumbling over old trunks, the situation gave them a much-needed cause for laughter as well as a sense of satisfaction that the Big House was doing what life expected of it—housing the homeless downstairs.

It was from one of the windows of the houselike structure that True spotted the chokeberries along the stream separating the Big House from the cabin. Somehow, she supposed, she or Aunt Chrissy would make time for jelling them—if she could coax the twins to pick the fruit without a fight ending up with a basket emptied over the top of one or the other's head.

Then True saw Kearby and a girl about the same age, ragged and palefaced (Clarice Somebody, wasn't that the name?). The two had become inseparable; and Kearby, who was a good two inches the taller of the two, had asked permission to go through her wardrobe and share last year's school dresses with the young survivor of the tragedy. "The hems have been let out twice and some are faced—please, may I?" she asked True.

Aunt Chrissy must decide, but True agreed that it was a good idea. In anticipation of a "permission granted" from her mother, Kearby was helping Clarice into a gingham gimp when True confronted them about the berries.

"Oh, surely!" Kearby surprised her by saying. "Isn't this blue pretty on Clarry?"

"Lovely," True responded, glancing at the watch pinned on her starched white cotton dress, the closest thing she owned resembling a nurse's uniform. "I have some ribbons about that color—if you would like your hair braided—"

"Oh, yes!" The gangling girl's face changed, her marvelously large eyes lighting the world and inviting all to admire the new image she envisioned in herself. "I never had my hair fixed—Granny, she's the one I—I lost—had crooked fingers. But," Clarice lifted her head high, "she always wanted me to look pretty—stop hiding—said I was as withdrawn and sociable as a scarecrow." The childish voice caught in her throat.

"You're very brave," True replied with admiration. "I think it would please your grandmother to see you standing tall."

Clarice took the words literally. With a lift of the thin shoulders still higher, she walked gracefully across the dining room. "Where can we find a bucket?"

True handed her the granite one which the family had used for storing drinking water until a leak sprang in the bottom. Murmuring a polite "Thank you," Clarice marched ahead of Kearby, her mind obviously crowded with hopes and dreams never divulged. True hoped she would open up to Kearby; it would be good for them both. Then, to her surprise, Kearby turned and winked, the first sign of the old romping coltishness inside that True had seen since returning to the Valley. The girl was herself—yet different.

The next surprise came when Jerry whistled. "Hey, you two! Need some help? There are bears galore along that creek. And there's nothing they like better than berries—unless it's girls for munching!"

Kearby and Clarice stopped dead in their tracks. Then he also turned and winked. Jerry too was back, but with a change for the better, called maturity!

It was no surprise at all when Young Wil called (life was shaping up): "I need to go into Centerville, darling. Uncle Wil and Aunt Chrissy have things under control here, and we need medical supplies. Also (he inhaled deeply) I want to talk with one of the law officials—about Slippery Elm—"

True changed quickly into a skirt of bright floral material draped simply over a slip of plain color. She felt festive, ready to get away from the ordeal they had undergone. The pointed bodice was remimscent of Dickens' *Dolly Verden*, so with a smile she bent up one side of the burnt-straw sunhat and pinned it with an artificial rose.

Downstairs, Young Wil whistled a signal for departure. The whistle turned to one of admiration as True hurried out to meet him. "You look as if you stepped right out of *Barnaby Rudge*," he said, helping her into the buggy. Somehow she was glad he remembered the book they had read together—so glad that she abandoned the plan to read aloud the letter Jeremiah had delivered, enjoying instead the sun-warmed fields of goldenrod and the few bright leaves that floated down around them in the wooded silence . . .

"I've arranged for military escorts for those returning with Jeremiah," Young Wil told her on the way back. "The militia wants to check out conditions in Slippery Elm—the name stuck in spite of efforts to change it. People say it deserves no better—getting worse by the day."

"But the families who came here—why would they go back there?"

Young Wil inhaled deeply. "I looked around and there's simply nothing for them here. All the land's taken and nobody wants to sell—even if any of them had a dollar to call their own. As for jobs, there are none—seems the *good* times are over, a sort of depression in store. The poor souls would be lucky to find work for a quarter a day—and they couldn't surive. It's amazing what the money-grabbers will do when opportunity knocks—they'd charge 35 cents a night for a coyote hole. Don't look so remorseful, sweetheart. Jeremiah has a plan—"

They were home, his sentence unfinished. And the letter unread.

But something wonderful had happened! A sobbing Kearby ran to throw her arms about them both. "Clarice opened up—said the boy buried on the trail was her brother—" Kearby choked. "Oh, I'll never quarrel with Jerry again—no matter how impossible he is—I promised God—"

The sinking sun cast brilliant linings on the dark clouds of evil. God felt very near.

8
Decisions

T EN DAYS WINGED past, long days for the two doctors and their outwardly tireless wives. Grandma Mollie was equally busy, planning every detail for meals and carrying each out systematically. "Me Mollie-gal never did she waste a movement that I be knowin' 'bout," O'Higgin began. "Me—I be tryin' t'give 'er a hand 'n she sez, 'Git out from underfoot!' Ye lassies puzzle us men, but here be Irish stew she knows be me favorite. Fer th' sick, she sez, but me, I be findin' they's a-plenty still brewin'."

True smiled, accepted the enormous kettle, and brushed the red-bearded cheek with an affectionate kiss. "You two have a perfect understanding and you know it."

"Sure 'n we do," O'Higgin said with emotion. "Sometimes bein' apart 'as its advantages—clears up th' mind. A man's got nobody but 'is shavin' mirror 'n th' Almighty t' be answerin' to: Nobody but meself t'pat on th' back fer successes—iffen I could be reachin' me back anymore. Only problem bein' I had nobody t'blame fer me failure, either. What I truly need bein' alone fer—in short little spurts, mind ye—is meditatin' on the greatness of me Lord 'n Master. Praise be fer all them He be savin' from th' womb t'th' tomb. He brung through them what survived fer a purpose, jest as He be addin' to me years. They's purpose in guidin' us stumblers down life's twistin' path. He be testin' us—that's what! So I best be goin' hafta hep them what'll be makin' decisions bout leavin'. Got me some idees, somewhat like Jeremiah's, 'bout th' future. Wilson here 'n Young Wil's

a-gonna heal bodies, but th' Lord'll 'ave His 'ands full healin' th'
broken spirits. Them attackers was all beast.They be bound t'pay fer
ever' humiliation 'n revoltin' act—not t'mention th' lives they be
takin'. But we gotta pray fer 'em—'n pray just as hard fer healin' th'
others."

Winded, O'Higgin stopped, grinned, doffed his hat, and left singing an Irish folk song, his melodious tenor voice all but shaking the
needles of the surrounding firs. True wondered fleetingly why he had
made no effort to visit the "March Hare," young Christian Joseph
Martin North. Or, for that matter, why the proud parents had waited
so long to bring him to meet the rest of the family. But, with a frown,
she concluded that the answer lay undoubtedly in such harrowing
experiences as the senseless attack.

Thank goodness, the injured gave welcome indication of recovering rapidly. True attributed the recovery to her uncle and husband's
skill. Grandma Mollie said it was the good food, seasoned with heaping scoops of love. Could be their association with "decent folks,"
as Nate Goldsmith claimed. But on one thing they all agreed: God's
power was at work through whatever medium He chose.

Virgil Adamson concerned True. His broken arm was healed and
the splint was already off, since it was only a hairline fracture. However, his eyes looked vacant, and he wandered around, engaging in
disjointed monologue.

"Give him time," Young Wil said, carefully masking any concern
he might harbor. True often wished that doctors would stop writing
in their confidential black books and would instead discuss their
patients openly. But with pride she realized that this was her
husband's fatal attraction—his holding the Hippocratic oath with
near-sacredness, second only to the Bible.

"But what will happen to Clarice, his stepdaughter? He's all she has
by way of family, now that her grandmother's gone. And she lost her
brother along the trail. You know," she said, breaking the train of
thought, "we owe a lot to that girl—called Clarry by her grandmother."

They talked about the positive reaction which the twins—Kearby,
anyway—had had to Clarice's loss. But Wil had some news of his own.

"That accounts for Jerry's behavior," he said with a grin. "I approached the overdue subject of the constant bickering, only to be
stopped when I tried explaining about changes as we grow up. 'Now,

don't go telling me about the birds and the bees,' he said, his tone implying that he knew more about the subject than I do."

"Probably does, too, the way the younger generation talks now." The words were out—words that True found embarrassing. How did one go about *unsaying* something?

"Hey, thanks a heap, brat! I'm glad you have the grace to blush."

"I'm not blushing!"

"You are so!" Young Wil mimicked the twins. And without preliminaries, he reached out and drew her to him. She was sputtering mild protests and scattering records they'd been updating when Aunt Chrissy appeared at the office door.

"I should have knocked," she said with her still-beautiful ripe-olive dark eyes twinkling. "Another time might be better—"

"Yes!" Young Wil's dark eyes teased, too.

"No!" True gasped, trying to retain her dignity. Then, picking up the clutter to hide her pink face, she related the part of the conversation having to do with the children.

It surprised them both that Chris Beth said calmly that she believed Jerry was discovering girls, that he had eyes for Clarice.

"Oh, no—they're too young—"

"Now, now, True, don't go mothering Jerry as you did Marty," Young Wil said with authority. True made no effort to defend herself.

"The poor child will have her hands full taking care of Virgil," Chris Beth said, returning to Clarice. "He lost his wife and new baby. His first wife died when Clarice was born. She was in a family way and desperate. That was after the father was killed—and I suppose Virgil felt incapable of taking on two stepchildren when he married Clarice's aunt the very same day of the funeral. Anyway, the grandmother begged for her daughter's children."

True realized then that she had no idea what the girl's last name was. She had supposed it to be Adamson. Somehow it seemed important. Just how important time would tell.

The matter of Clarice and Virgil's relationship nagged at True's thinking. He seemed to see her as his anchor, who made him feel safe, no longer vulnerable. He was the child, she the mother. But Clarice was no more able to protect him than a fledgling could protect its parents. Although the grandmother had taught her well what

Clarice referred to as the "three Rs of reading, writing, and *religion*," she had held the child in the nest instead of teaching her to fly. Consequently, Clarice could make no decisions without consulting Kearby—even the simplest ones, regarding the clothing which Chris Beth had applauded her daughter for sharing. What should she wear? What went with which garment? Clarice accepted Kearby's opinion about trimming her hair and curling the bangs without question. Going against Grandma had been wrong, and going against the world amounted to the same thing. Virgil and Clarice's facing the "out there" was courting chaos. They needed roots . . . family . . .

Time was rocking on. There was talk of decisions to be reached. And all the while True became more troubled. Something half-remembered . . .

"What's your friend's last name?" she finally asked Kearby.

"Clarice? Hancock. Clarice Hancock. *Clarry*, she wants to be called."

Hancock . . . Hancock . . . where—? Of course! Anna-Lee Hancock, the Shaker lady back in Slippery Elm. And—the name on the pine shingle in the cemetery had been Hancock. Not Adamson!

9

The Letter

❧

NATE GOLDSMITH CALLED at the Big House shortly after True made the startling discovery about what surely must be a discrepancy in names on the pine-board marker serving as a headstone in the cemetery. He too had noticed the variance, a fact which disturbed the little man as much as the October heat that plastered his shirt to his chest, giving it the comical appearance of a bird cage.

Mopping the few remaining strands of hair across his balding skull, the deacon, president of the school board, and town crier panted out the news. "Sumpin' ain't right—I kin smell it," he declared. "First this Virgil man ain't havin' nothin' t'do with that purdy stepdaughter, 'n now he's clingin' like a leech. This stupor he's in is jes plain faked, if you ask me!"

"Nobody did," Grandma Mollie reminded him calmly. She had brought over some partially completed dresses for Kearby. "That was plum nice of you, chile, sharin' thataway with Clarry, pore little thang. So," she smiled in a conspiratory manner, "I up 'n felt justified in copying th' latest styles from Solomon's Ready-t'-Wear fer yourself."

"That's stealin'!" Nate said triumphantly, then leaped in to resume his discussion of them Adamsons, Hancocks, or goodness-knows-who from the post office's "Most Wanted" list. Course, some'd call him judgmental.

Mollie O'Higgin bit off a thread and spit it out as if it were dusty. "Stuff's rotten as dirt—probably been in stock 50-odd years."

396

"Like I wuz sayin', ole Virge is puttin' on—"

"It could be shock, Mr. Goldsmith." True spoke for the first time. Noting Chris Beth's nod of approval, she told the story of the Caswells back in Slippery Elm. How Tillie, having lost her niece in the flood— Marty's mother—Mrs. Caswell lost touch with reality. "Even yet she confessed to Young Wil that she feared sleep because in her dreams the baby had drowned along with his parents."

Nate was taken aback, but only temporarily. "We jest ain't got no more room in th' school—even considerin' them whut's leavin' fer them denom'national academies 'n that farmin' college in Corvallis. Course there's that orphants' school. But this here's public, 'n as president of th' board, I consider it's my bounden duty t'keep it free from opini'nated meddlers. Still 'n all, th' gova'ment's stingy—ain't givin' us no more less'n we want more taxes—and there's folks a'plenty feelin' tax money oughta build roads. Gotta give th' matter lotsa thought—my job's a big un, one I wouldn't 'spect yuh women t'understand—least of all *teachers*."

"Lay off, Nate!" Miss Mollie bit off the word as she had bitten off the thread.

Nate Goldsmith cringed. But in a wavering voice he was determined to make a last-ditch stand. "Jest thought y'ud welcome my 'pinion 'bout this man claimin' t'be in a stupor—how 'bout it, Doc?"

Nobody had seen Wilson North, the senior doctor, enter. "You know I can't discuss the case with you, Nate—even if I knew. Let's stick to school affairs. Have you set an opening date?"

Nate's face brightened with self-importance. "I'm a-takin' census now. Crops is most in, but I gotta come up with figgers. You women— uh, *ladies*—got 'bout time t'brush up on th' lates' in that Normal School—queer name, ain't it now?—in Mammoth—er, Monmouth, guess it goes by since 'twas lib'rated from zealots—"

"I'd hardly call them that, Mr. Goldsmith!" Chris Beth objected with a flash of her dark eyes. "Churches have been responsible for the establishment of our schools. And, as for zealots, we all have to be careful, don't we? Zeal is fine; but it's the people *within* the church—and there are some in our very own Centerville Community Church—who become fanatics and cause friction. It's the same with the schools."

"Amen!" Miss Mollie said loudly. "Seems t'me you'd oughta be concentratin' on gettin' set up fer school 'stead of stirrin' up talk."

At that point she threw back her head and gave a hearty laugh. "Sorry, but it's so ridiculous—your askin' Chris Beth 'n True here t'go back t'school. No matter what th' latest fashions are in learnin', cain't y'git it through that thick head what they've been through aidin' their men bring back t'life these unfortunates who's passed through hell on earth? You heerd what True tole 'bout that relation of Marty's 'n her with no doctor or preacher t'hep undo th' damage—"

True heard no more. Her own mention of Tillie Caswell had stirred the ashes of something near-forgotten. Overlooked, at least. And now Grandma Mollie's referring to it uncovered a live coal of memory.

The letter:

Mumbling an excuse, she hurried out of the room and up the stairs to the attic that she and Young Wil were still compelled to call home. She had given up attempts to keep their belongings in any kind of order, so it took several minutes to find the sealed envelope. How could she have postponed opening it? She knew the answer, or course. But what came first in life? Only the Lord knew what her priorities should be. And for now the letter was her top priority. With shaking fingers she clawed at the flap of the envelope, tearing off a corner of the single-page message that was signed by Midgie's childishly careful hand. She had known it would be . . .

10
"Where Is God?"

୶

TRUE SCANNED MIDGIE'S letter, her eyes glazed with horror,
then let it flutter from nerveless fingers. The dormer window above
a battered trunk framed the setting sun, the only ornament emboss-
ing a cloudless sky, its fading light draping barren fields that proclaimed harvest was indeed over. Somehow the dying light shroud-
ing the distant hills, defiling them with black shadows, portended
evil. Or was it the lurid, shocking pictures that Midgie painted?

"Relax," she commanded her rigid, shuddering body. When she
regained a measure of control, True wiped away beads of perspiration that glistened on her face. Then she recovered the letter and
reread its shocking contents. Again. And again. Even then she was
unable to absorb the words. For the first time in her life, True North
wanted to escape life . . . run away . . . no, cower in a corner like a
beaten child.

"Where is God?" she whispered helplessly, the courage inherited
from her aunt and demonstrated all her young life now dwindling.

"If you don't know the answer to that, guess who's changed addresses?" Her husband's voice—strong and reassuring, even as it
gently chided—brought True back to earth and into his arms.

"Cry it out, darling, then tell me about it."

Cry she did, as well as babble. "I want to leave . . . go away, just
you and me . . . you can establish a clientele anywhere . . . with me
helping . . . I'd rather be your nurse than a—a—teacher anyway . . .
oh, please . . ."

He could have chided her, patronized her, or even reasoned with her. Being Young Wil, wonderful man that he was, however, he came to her rescue slowly. Rather than pulling her back when she moved from the circle of his arms, he made no attempt to impose himself into her private world.

Instead, wisely and patiently the doctor worked his way slowly back into the conversation as if her thoughts made sense. "Where would we go?"

"Anywhere—even though I'm far removed from my mother's generation—and the ones that came long, long ahead—I know now that we never should have tried to adjust to this—this jungle of madness—called a frontier. It—it's not in my—what's the word, *genes*? A part of me's begging to go home—"

"Where's home, my darling?"

True, feeling as if she were coming out of a trance, hesitated. "Boston, maybe—back to a genteel society—or Atlanta—"

Atlanta. That was it. No, *Boston*. It was farther away . . .

"No!" Fully alert now, True found the thought repugnant. "I mean, oh Wil, I don't know. I—I just know I'm no coward. Running away settles nothing—we—have to take a stand, don't we? Against man's inhumanity to man—oh, pray that God will forgive me for my weakness. I've seen so much—and now this—but I should have been strong—"

Young Wil embraced her then. "I'm sure He understands, but—" with a feeble attempt at a smile, "I'm not sure I do—oh, is this the culprit? May I see it—or would you like a glass of water before we talk?"

"I'm all right—for now," True said, surrendering the letter when his hand reached out tentatively. "We'll find a way—as long as we're together—"

"And that's forever," he said tenderly. Then he began reading the letter.

For a fleeting second the letter was a knife thrust before Young Wil, daring him to make use of it. So fleeting was the expression that True might just have imagined it. Sensitive and caring, he always knew instinctively how to handle any situation. Right now, he recognized, was a critical moment in her own recovery. He would be careful. His nature and profession dictated that. But it would be foolish to deny his own emotion. All this showed in his face.

"Incredible," he said quietly, shaking his head in disbelief. "I understand how you feel—how *they* feel. Let's see if we can shed more light on Midgie's letter the second time around. Here, darling, come sit by me."

Young Wil shifted his long legs and moved from his sitting place on the bed toward the windows, careful not to bump his head where the rafters slanted above him. He patted the place beside him. True sat down, some faraway corner comforted by the warmth he had left behind. Unable to speak, she slipped a cold hand into his.

"My dear, dear True," he began uncertainly. The remainder he read without emotion:

> I don't know how to begin. I keep hoping I will wake up and find the past months have been a nightmare. We've tried so hard, and I am so proud of Marty. We should be so happy with the March Hare fat and healthy—and we would be if the Devil hisself—see, I can't remember how to say words proper? But the Deluder somehow found us all here, hid (hidden?) away—and he just up and set to work. If he was visible I'd shoot him—Daddy taught me to use a gun. But I guess I'd have to stand in line, wouldn't I? Oh, True, you'll know how to break all the awful news. Won't you say it with good words?

Things had changed, Midgie repeated Jeremiah's words as she plunged into the terrible story in her own way. Lots of people had come from Appalachia . . . good country folks but in need of everything from money to "learning." No ideas how to protect themselves—too used to old-time-religion preachers saying fear was evil. Then came the hoodlums—must've followed, demanding everything—*everything*—heirlooms, food, *women!* In their ignorance, Midgie went on, the misguided immigrants tried to live by some well-meaning preacher's interpretation of the Bible . . . see no evil . . . hear no evil . . . speak no evil . . . just surrender and "be led to slaughter without a bleat."

Would it have mattered anyway? Midgie wondered.

> The cut-throats took from the ones who tried to protect their families anyway—busted into the Goldish house, shattered a bottle over Billy Joe's head and—you know the rest. Poor, helpless Mariah. It's happened before—and this awful treatment brought it all back. Mariah's not normal, hardly speaks, and what she says makes no sense. And them innocent little boys saw it! No preacher . . . no doctor . . . and I don't know enough of her language to make her understand we love her . . . and that some way, somehow God will send help . . .
> Tillie Caswell (the baby's "Grandy") could be helped but—

Some of the words were hard to make out at this point, giving a clue to Midgie's own deep wounds. But Marty had not known, being too busy in the fall harvests (*so* bountiful). Then one of the hands went into town for supplies . . . heard the awful news and hurried home like Paul Revere, spreading the news . . . and picking up some news in return. There was going to be a turkey shoot that night . . . and the poor innocents saw no wrong in that kind of gambling . . . no danger either. So bad as they needed food, they were bound on going, all being good shots. Marty knew there'd be trouble, felt it in his bones, took the ranch hands and went . . . but the bandits beat them there, got tired of shooting in the match and shot the lights out . . . yelled, "It's a stickup!" and shot one Appalachian in the back . . . and laughed! Aimed at Mr. Caswell and shot before he could open the safe. Marty tried to protect Curly . . . but got his shoulder shattered by a bullet (not to worry, he would be all right now). "And they still killed Mr. Caswell—shot him clean through the heart. So now 'Grandy' ain't right either—sometimes 'sane-like sometimes not, keeps switching. Normal 'round Martin. Otherwise addled . . ."

"Hang on, all of you, we'll help." Young Wil said the words as if the helpless victims were in the room. Then he added, "when we can."

He turned to True then. "As if these were the only enemies—but there are others—rustling, dragging sacks of seed to do fall planting, only to have it eaten by worms before it germinates—if starving wolves don't beat them to it—"

"Hadn't we better go?"

"You know we can't, True. School's opening next week. Nate said so after you left the room—and our practice here—"

"—is more important than our brother?"

Young Wil sighed. "You know better than that! But think darling, what could we do at this point? And we are needed here—all of us. Thank goodness, Jeremiah met with the survivors here, and they all but accepted his invitation to share from their common storehouse. What will tilt the scale is your willingness to share that you are reasonably sure that some of them—Clarry, at least—belong to the Hancock family. Nobody listens to Nate, but you know the background—"

True wondered what her answer would have been had Aunt Chrissy not called to say that dinner was waiting. *Dinner*—sweet normalcy of the word . . .

Outside was cooler than inside the house. The men found it bearable in their stuffy office, but True felt as if her chest were caving in for lack of air. She felt hemmed in from all sides, making her realize that Aunt Chrissy was probably right in saying the situation was responsible—decisions from all sides. The two of them were sitting in the porch swing, its motion making True a little sick.

"We've talked these things over—and everywhere I run into a road that ends abruptly above a steep cliff with no way to turn back. I can understand how little Clarry feels," True said slowly, fanning the heat from her legs with the tiers of her gingham skirt.

"Mmmm?"

"Unable to reach a decision—and her past, like her future, hanging overhead, like twin ghosts over Scrooge in Dickens' *A Christmas Carol.*"

Chris Beth plucked a pungent leaf from a hanging pot of herbs. "Since so much depends on Clarry's attitude—at least, it *might* help these confused people—let's concentrate on her first. It might be easier for you to talk to Jerry. He and Kearby think you and Young Wil know a lot more about life than we parents." She sighed and bit into the mint leaf in concentration. "Then if he would talk with her— she opens up like a flower for him, is his friendly ear, hanging onto every word about his botany experiments. I guess this is what a boy his age needs, as Miss Mollie puts it, 'a somebody he can spark to.'"

True was unconvinced—at least, that so young a boy should be forming relationships. But Aunt Chrissy was much wiser than she . . . and his talking to Clarry sounded like a good idea.

It was. And a conversation True and Chris Beth overheard between their doctor-husbands explained why—as well as the *whys* of other matters.

Their own conversation had lulled, each buried in private thoughts, when the men's words floated out the window. Young Wil was talking in a troubled voice. A voice sounding tired, so tired.

"Yes—yes, I *do* hesitate to encourage another change for Clarry—

risk her trying to adjust to strangers again. I'd guess by nature the girl is timid and irresolute. Then the horrifying experience coupled with this stepfather—if he *is* that—caused her to further withdraw. But you know, Uncle Wil, there's something buried deeper. Even when she's with Jerry, she trembles at an innocently raised voice, flinches at a moving shadow, and near-jumps out of her young skin at distant thunder. It's more than her jumpiness, though. It's as if Clarry is so afraid of the world that she can't live with its ordinary sounds. True dropped something in the kitchen this morning and the child ran to hide behind the door—" his voice trailed off helplessly.

"Did our children notice anything irregular?"

True had a mental picture of Daddy Wil leaning back in his easy chair, arms lifted, hands laced together to pillow his head, while his nephew sat tensely on the edge of his own chair, brown eyes burning with such concern that they all but glowed in the dark.

"Notice? Yes, they noticed—but not the way an adult would. Or else they are excellent actors—or see something we miss altogether—" Young Wil stopped as if the words expressed a new thought.

"Meaning?"

"I'm not sure—Jerry and Kearby, during a truce, exhibit good manners and—well, sensitivity. They could have been trying to save Clarry from embarrassment—or, could it be that they see something's not right? Anyway, they turned Clarry's hiding into a game—"

"Which it is, more or less, a kind of hide-and-seek of the mind to blot out reality. Is that what you're saying? Cause for concern, yep—like this Mariah person—and Marty's Aunt Tillie, but—" his voice went with hands spread out in despair, "we've not come far—no powder I know will help the workings of the mind."

The air was charged. True and Chris Beth could feel it, as one feels electricity building just before a storm. But Young Wil's voice, while vibrant with excitement, was low and controlled when he spoke: "There's something out there—a connection between the body and the mind. I'd like to do some post-grad work—for my book—go to Portland—"

Where was God? With Young Wil, of course. As his mate would be!

11
Doubt Is Out!

THE BEST WAY to spread the news that Clarry (and perhaps some of the other members who were struggling with the decision of where to relocate and start anew) probably carried the Hancock blood in their veins was to tell the Solomons. Their store had a wider circulation than *The Oregonian*. In any case, the newspaper was slow at best in reaching the Valley.

True and Jeremiah made a trip to Centerville, and when they returned, Abe and Bertie both listened—Abe somewhat passively and Bertie with ears actually appearing pointed like a bird dog's. She "just knew" there was something strange about "that girl." She "just knew" there was something unnaturallike about her relationship with "that man" calling himself a stepfather. Best get them all out of here before they "poisoned the minds of our young folks." Take the North twins—

True quietly but firmly interrupted. "We know nothing about them, Mrs. Solomon. Let's not be judgmental. Clarry is welcome in our house. But," she paused, "if she has family—"

"Right! That would serve the purpose for hurrying their exodus—" Bertie Solomon stopped short, her face reddening. "What I'm meanin' is that those Shakers, Quakers, Breth'ern—whatever they are—could prove helpful. And," she raised her shoulders as if adjusting what she called "the full armor," "it's our Christian duty to give these folks a proper send-off. I'll volunteer spreading the news. Abe here can let Nate know. No time to do a lot. Still, we could send some wagons about the Valley collecting—you know, like we do when they's a fire."

405

Eyes aglow now, Bertie Solomon went into action. After all, wasn't
this a brilliant idea? And it was hers! Abe here could pass the word
to Nate Goldsmith. Depend on Nate to alert all the committees he
appointed himself to chair, well as the Board of Deacons and the Board
of Education. Folks didn't need cash money. Take those Basque
folks—still shearing woollies, dyeing, carding, spinning, and weav-
ing. Just look at the warm clothes other womenfolks could knit in a
hurry for that cold country "over there"! Her tone located the eastern portion of Oregon somewhere across the ocean.

"Now, Abraham, git th' mules hitched and git goin'!" Bertie
Solomon's command to her husband ended her soliloquy. "Apt as not
news'll carry to Salem and Portland. Glad them mule critters won't
have to be goin' into th' city. Even blinders don't help their skittish-
ness of trolley cars—it bein' all th' clangin' 'n zingin' that scares 'em
outta what few wits God allowed 'em, not that a body can blame 'em-
me, I'm not partial to trolleyin', all them sparks flyin' from wires.
Wonder if it won't be one of them contraptions that starts the fire
that consumes this wicked world!"

True smiled. "I doubt it," she reassured Mrs. Solomon. "Thank
you for all the wonderful ideas—"

"Which we will implement." Jeremiah, finished with his purchase
of a few essentials, paid Mrs. Solomon, her husband having begun
his mission. "I can add to the list of items most needed for thee—
dried fruit and beans, some staples—and a few learning books.
Knowest thou that there is no school and that the Tribe of Benjamin
teaches their own? Should we hope that Portland's State Board of
Education will share?"

"They will," Mrs. Solomon responded, and went on planning with
Jeremiah.

True's mind had gone back in time, remembering a similar situation as recorded in Angel Mother's diary. It was *this* valley which
was in its early stage of development then.

And the miracle of response, her mother had recorded, "enlarged
like the enlargement of their hearts." It would happen again . . .

Her train of thought shifted. Was this the time to share the contents of that sacred diary with Kearby? And what about Jerry? Saying
goodbye to Clarry would hurt him, followed by Kearby herself, providing she chose to attend the Wilbur Academy for Girls that True had

overheard her mention to Aunt Chrissy. Having "silly girls" under-foot was one thing, but being parted from them was another . . .

But, no, this was not the time. Opening the diary too soon would be like entering an empty tomb—no spirit. The timing must meet a specific need, answer a near-to-the-heart question. God would know when . . .

The die was cast. Once Jeremiah convinced the North family that Clarry was in all likelihood Clarice Hancock, and once Jerry com-municated the news to the girl, it was she who—taking strength from her idol—found courage to suggest returning with Jeremiah. And once the Solomons picked up the message, news spread like wildfire, gath-ering momentum as it traveled. There should be—there *must* be—a proper send-off.

"Sorta like 'The Little Red Hen' story," Grandma Mollie smiled indulgently to True later. "Who would bake the ham? *I will.* Who would roast the hens? *I will.* The same with salt-risin' bread, corn pone, an' sugar-spice cookies. After all, these folks hafta do more'n fill their bellies one night. There's gotta be leftovers fer sandwiches that stick t'th' ribs. No question, of course, *where* the feast is a-gonna be—"

"Turn-Around Inn?"

"Shore as shootin'! A kinda celebration—jest between us homefolks. Meanin' th' mortgage's paid—'n things is all right 'twixt me 'n my man agin, thanks t'you, Young Wil, Marty, 'n Midgie. By the way, you been hearin' from them? Guess no news is good new—" Miss Mollie paused to wipe her hands on the generous folds of her Mother Hubbard apron.

"But I *have* heard," True said, feeling a twinge of guilt that life had kept her too busy to share the frightening message in Midgie's letter. She blurted out the contents in one run-on sentence without stopping.

Grandma Mollie kept nodding her near-white mountain of hair as she rolled out pie crust with expertise that required no directions. Watching her twirl the pan on one finger, pricking the bottom with a fork as it completed a single orbit, True thought how representa-tive it was of this wonderful woman's life: no recipe, no waiting around for a Daniel Boone or a Davy Crockett to step from the pages of some book. Life was real. One learned by listening, learning, prac-ticing. God was her leaven.

"Write her," the older woman suggested. "Here, scratch my nose," she said, twisting her face and holding up flourdusted hands. "Thank you, sweetie—yes, send it by Jeremiah. I've a hunch he'll beat th' locomotive—serve t'git 'em all acquainted, too."

Of course! She would explain everything to her sister-in-law. And, yes, she must write to Tillie Caswell. Oh, if only she could go with this band, be the shoulder they so needed, hold them close and reassure them what they already knew but may have forgotten in the terrible crisis—that hope springs eternal . . . that love endures all things, hoping—*knowing*—that God will deliver them from the wilderness of despair. Like Grandma's pastry, hope needed no recipe—just practice . . . the only essential ingredient being love that endured.

The letters were difficult to write; words wouldn't come. Then True's busy mind piled them up extravagantly, only to find that they said nothing. After chewing her pencil, crossing out, and erasing, True finished bulky (though in her mind meaningless) letters and gave them to Jeremiah. His report would explain matters better.

"We should be there, but . . ." "We will be there when . . ." Young Wil's words echoed in True's mind: *when*? But this was the life of a doctor's wife, her tired mind said—more in acceptance than bitterness. This was where they belonged. Or was it with Marty and Midgie, their own kin, in time of trouble? Yes, they had "Grandy," but Marty's aunt needed more comfort than the young Norths. As backbones of the troubled community, none of them dared allow themselves to break down. They were the hope of Slippery Elm. They needed support—*now*. Not a year from now, when Young Wil's internship was completed . . .

It occurred to True then that, according to the conversation between the two doctors, it was her husband's wish to pursue the revolutionary relationship between the mind and the body. Biting her underlip, True felt her eyes fill with tears. *Forgive me, Lord.*

For it was as if He had spoken to her. What more appropriate timing could there be, what greater mission? So it took another year? And another? Maybe it was God's will that her husband discover ways to help people overcome those vague disorders loosely labeled "hysteria." Tillie Caswell, whose mind had taken in more than it could hold and overflowed with heartbreak, had retreated into a world of unreality. Would she, without professional help, recover a second time? And how about Midgie? Could little Midgie, with her insecurities and her hurts, remain strong in her newfound faith in God's love—and Marty's?

A sudden excitement tingled along her spine. What a challenge! True could hardly wait to see her husband, to tell him that she understood. Oh, praise the Lord, she understood! Why, right here were dozens of examples. Clarry—timid, shy, irresolute, afraid to fall asleep for fear of dreaming of the hell on earth she had undergone. If some medical key could help her unlock the torturous journeying into her past, perhaps she could overcome her fears of men. Men? True realized suddenly that the child *was* afraid of the man who called himself her stepfather. But he was in need too, else why would he cling to Clarry as he did? Shaking her head, True found herself wondering why the idea had never occurred to her. And now examples, as if in the flesh, paraded across the threshold of her own mind: Zeck McDaniel, who resorted to a wheelchair only when he felt neglected; Lizzie Talissman, who "mouthed off" (Grandma Mollie's word), then developed hiccups that went on for days . . .

"Who hath known the mind of God?" Without realizing she was speaking aloud, True—wide awake now with revelations she had never known before—continued to quote at random from Paul's messages to the Romans. "We have the mind of Christ . . . neither be of doubtful mind . . . fully persuaded in his own mind . . ." *Doubtful, persuaded, doubtful—*

Back and forth zigzagged the shining thoughts, upward like the nuptial flight of a queen bee, then coming back for a soft landing. *As a man thinketh, so is he.*

"Doubt is out!" The words came out joyously—just as the loving arms of her doctor-husband enfolded her. Understanding without words.

12
Goodbyes Without Tears

⤴

THE ENTIRE VALLEY must have shown up to see the ill-fated immigrants well-fed and well-stocked for the journey back to the part of Oregon in which they had stopped only briefly. Not a-tall surprising, Grandma Mollie said with a cluck of her tongue. Bertie done her work well. Never done anything by halves, that woman. Her tongue was her worst enemy, less'n its bridle was given a jerk in the right direction. Bertie Solomon could be nosy, git under a body's cuticles. "Still 'n all, she allus comes through in a crisis, as I explained to your Aunt Chrissy when, as a girl with a heart broke in half, she come to us. One o'God's miracles, that's what—and He's apt t' be turnin' out another from these poor souls. Jest you wait and see."

"He already has," True said, and then could have bitten her tongue.

Mollie O'Higgin chuckled as she motioned her husband to her for setting up picnic tables. "You've got that faraway look in them beautiful violet eyes—so like your Angel Mother's, except for th' look that closes a matter. O'Hig-*gin!*"

Fugitive bars of a song that her doll-like mother used to sing to the bees flickered across the screen of True's memory unfocused, then righted themselves:

> But to every man there stretcheth
> A high road and a low;
> And every man decideth
> The way his soul should go.
> The matter was settled. Her soul had taken wing.

It was the sunset hour when the group sat down to eat. Little heat waves, reluctant to let go of summer, pulsed along the foothills. Above the little flurries, the still-brilliant rays of the sun painted the evergreen of the firs brick-red.

"I will lift up mine eyes unto the hills, from whence cometh my help." O'Higgin's musical voice, still burred with Scotch-Irish, boomed above the singing of the little streams victoriously cutting through the ridges at near-right angles to form miniature emerald-green valleys of their own. The big, God-fearing Irishman repeated the passage.

The Appalachians clung to his every word, identifying with the brogue if not always understanding his words. He made "horse sense" to them. But where, True wondered, was the minister? In fact, where had William Prescott been all along? She had hardly caught a glimpse of him. How could a dedicated minister declare a "hands-off" policy?

Irish O'Higgin read the remainder of Psalm 121, then repeated: "I will lift up mine eyes unto the hills . . ."

True allowed her eyes to travel higher and higher up the hills until they loomed to mountains, where the green-garbed forests had never paid toll to the woodsman's axe. There the snowy peaks, still bright with sunshine, bared their jagged-rock fangs in defiance of the persistent remnants of the past season. Somewhere through those hills lay a gap through which tonight this group must pass. It threatened, while beckoning, in the mysterious silence.

In the distance a coyote howled. Then, closer, a gopher—rare for these parts—darted True's direction, quickly stealing a breadcrumb, then with Jack-in-the-box speed did a disappearing act. But not before True saw the yellowed teeth (bearing a startling resemblance to the jagged fangs of the gap) clamped down on the morsel in a death-grip. Thank goodness, the militia would be traveling with this group—although it puzzled her as to why they should make the trip at night . . .

After Jeremiah's prayer, with its *Thees* and *Thous*, passing of the food, mountains of it, began. The children, while obviously awed, shook their heads and waited with downcast eyes. Only once did a thin-faced lad speak. His single word was a question: "So'gum?"

"Sogum?" True asked gently.

"'Lasses—sirp." His head went down again.

Of course! Sorghum syrup, dipped in cornbread, as she recalled.

But before she could answer, a bonneted lady whose face was hidden by its dusty brim scolded in an embarrassed whisper, "Got none, Jasper! Shet yo' mouth 'n take yore pot-likker!"

Silently the mother ladeled a soupy substance drained from a black pot of overcooked cabbage onto a wooden plate and set it before the boy. "Want some?" she asked True.

How could anybody want *that*? The night air reeked sickeningly with its smell.

But Aunt Chrissy had taught her that it was an insult to refuse to partake of whatever was set before her. Well, she would just have to ask the Lord to forgive her for this whopper. "Certainly!" she said, knowing that she was about to be sick.

"Hit's fittin'," the faceless woman said defensively. "I been cookin' hit all day—only way hit's safe. Hast t'turn red." Then she saved the moment for True by replacing the tin plate serving as a lid.

"I let these folks browse in my garden," Nate Goldsmith's voice, with ill-concealed piety, announced from the far end of the table. "But, now, chil'ern, you'd best be eatin' our foodstuff as well."

The children nodded eagerly and the mountains of food shrank.

From that point on the woman and children remained silent. The men kept up a lively conversation. Planning perhaps for the journey? It was hard to tell, as their speech was so quaintly peppered with strange expressions that it might as well have been in a foreign tongue: "afeared . . . aidge o'dark . . . blatherskite wimmen . . . sunball." These phrases sounded innocent enough, but what followed did not: "Man hadda right fer settlin' whut matters shore 'nuf wid a gun—nat'rul as a-wearin' pants. Hadda right fer hidin' a still fer likker . . . hadda right fer takin' keer o' 'is fambly. Hadda right fer marryin' like he chosen, cousins 'n all—better'n furriners. Long ez he did'n vi'late th' Good Book—er fornicate outsiders . . ."

Truly ill now, True laid down her half-finished ham sandwich, excused herself quietly, and slipped away. She was sure nobody noticed.

One moment the world was tinted with rose-pink memories of sunset, and the next a gray-purple twilight had settled over the Valley like a bird readying for the night. A new-phase moon offered little light, making it impossible for True to make out the identity of shapes of a few strollers along the several narrow trails. She stopped, not wishing to disturb them. And then she was rendered unable to move.

Darkness could not blot out the identity of the voices, mingled though they were above the wail of fiddles in sad-sweet farewell . . . their only goodbye.

Jerry—Jerry and *Clarry!*

"I don't want to leave you!" Clarry's little-girl voice carried a tell-tale sound of tears.

"And I don't want you to go," Jerry choked, his voice breaking embarrassingly as he changed octaves from childhood to adolescence. "You don't belong with them, do you Clarry? I mean you've not always—"

"Lived among the mountaineers? No—he—uh, they—*we* have been from place—oh, Jerry, don't ask me any more—I *have* to forget what I—I—can't explain to you or myself. But I'll keep this forever—"

The musty scent of late-blooming roses reached True's nostrils, as shapeless as the horrifying suspicion that gnawed at her heart.

"I must take you back,"Jerry said with more maturity than True knew the boy possessed. The girl, openly sobbing now, and promising to write, clung to his hand as they passed within inches of where True stood gripping the body of a towering fir that graciously pulled her into its shadows.

The snap of a twig alerted her to the fact that she was not alone. The gopher? She shuddered. Another snap!

"Who's there?" Her voice trembled.

"'Tis I, the big, bad wolf."

"Wil—oh, Wil darling—" True clung to her husband with such force that her own muscles ached.

"Hey, I should do this more often! I saw the youngsters leave and was wondering if they should wander out here alone—then you—"

"How long have you been here?" Still clinging to him while accepting his handkerchief, she dabbed at her eyes. "What did you hear?"

"Everything. But my suspicions needed no confirmation, darling. Surely you put two and two together, knew that they are tasting first love—and remembering how sweet it is, especially when it endures—"

It was a beautifully romantic moment, one for which she had longed as time robbed them of togetherness. But the timing was wrong. As sweet as Young Wil's gestures were, his voice was light-years away.

True nodded against his shoulder—remembering. "I love you—I love you—but, oh, Wil, what about Clarry? Is she a prisoner? Has she—?"

"Been violated? Yes darling, I am sure of it—"

"You mean—?" True was unable to speak the words.

"I mean," he said softly, yet in a tone that betrayed unleashed fury, "*used*, molested, and left an emotional cripple. Incest is common—not against their code."

"By that beast—that terrible man claiming to be her stepfather—"

"We don't know that for sure."

The slight pause said he suspected it. "With a little encouragement I could hate Virgil Adamson—if that's his name," True said with uncharacteristic fierceness. "I could. I could. And," thoughtfully, "why was he so eager to remarry, right into the same family?"

Young Wil drew a ragged breath. "This only time will tell, darling. But dismiss bitterness until the facts are in. All our friends in and around Slippery Elm will be on the lookout. Then O'Higgin—"

"He's going?"

Young Wil nodded. "Sort of under the pretense of looking in on the Double N. Of course, he's dying to see the March Hare—"

"As am I! And as are Aunt Chrissy and Daddy Wil. Oh, Wil, why can't we—? But, of course, I know why a visit's out now."

Reaching up, Young Wil pulled a twig from the closest fir bough and plucked off the needles one by one as if he were studying it. "Back to O'Higgin—he plans to keep Clarry by his side all the way, then deliver her to Anna."

"And Virgil? What's to become of him? I guess he needs help. He's a human being—even if he *is* a subspecies. Oh, darling, we are sending them a pack of trouble. I thought we would be safe here, protected from trouble—but I guess," True said with a sigh, "the devil does his work well in all places."

"As does God! Maybe the Lord sent us these people to remind us just how needed we are everywhere. Their being here has served to convince me that the subject I want to pursue is essential. I will need your approval, your help—your understanding—"

A rare uncertainty stopped his flow of speech.

"Wil North," True bristled, "are you implying I wanted to return with this group without you? 'Until death do us part!' Not only will

I cling, I will cling tighter each year. I am your helpmate, your Adam's rib, so," True was talking rapidly now, her breath coming in little short puffs of excitement, "I will study with you—learn—and do *my* internship in the classroom. Maybe I have taken too much for granted. Maybe there are cases like this," she shuddered, "in our own Valley."

"There are such cases everywhere, put under wraps, of course. I was reading the Old Testament last night and found so many references that it overwhelmed me."

"But ours is the age of enlightenment. We are under the New Law, the love of Jesus—and He makes it all so plain about responsibility to the family. How could people claim ignorance?"

"Because," he said slowly, "they can't read, particularly in Appalachia. Law and order, civil or Biblical, comes by word of mouth. They have survived simply by their own laws, which hinge on two, I guess: 'Thou shalt bear arms.' They simply shoot down the stranger—meaning preachers, teachers, revenue officers . . . and every now and then when somehow a would-be peacemaker manages to break down the barrier . . . well, there's either a hanging of the victim or a lynching of the 'furriners.'"

Oh, dear God, I didn't know, True's heart whispered. Audibly she whispered, "No lawyers to defend them? You said *two* rules?"

"How could a penniless mountaineer afford a lawyer? There's occasionally a kangaroo court. But bear in mind that the population has intermarried—and worse!—that everybody's related. And Rule Two is: 'Thou shalt protect thy family!' They enforce it, welcoming no outside interference. That includes the law—and the Almighty Himself—God forgive them."

But they receive forgiveness by asking, True argued. *Ask?* Her husband shook his head sadly. One did not seek forgiveness unless one saw a wrongdoing. True must try and understand that for generations—was she up to hearing this? Of course she was! Else how could one help?

"Darling, they don't want to be helped—not now. Killing is a—well, a game up there in the tanglewood of laurel, ivy—and primitive thinking. It provides excitement in their dreary world. This handful of mountaineers sneaked away from 'the family' after hearing a hellfire-and-damnation sermon by a man who had never attended a school, his only qualification of his words being 'Leastwise, that's the way I heered hit.'" He sighed in a way that made True hurt. "And look what they found out here!"

There was a long silence broken only by the hoot of an owl in search of food. And then the fiddling changed to off-key hymns, as the pathetic fugitives had "heered" it.

"We must go back, sweetheart," Young Wil said, trying to coax her into a lighter mood. "Unless you want them sending out a searching party to eavesdrop like we did—"

"Oh, Wil . . ." True pulled back, clinging to the safety of the shadows. "Is there hope—I mean that these people will learn? After all, isn't it a good sign that they're stopping over in Slippery Elm—"

She stopped, realizing the folly of her own words. How could they learn with no schools, no seminaries—not even a preacher?

Young Wil must have read her thoughts. "Who can know the mind of God? I wish they could have heard some sermons of salvation here, but at least they have not killed each other, dancing in the victim's blood and then attending the funeral the next day! Come on, darling, we must—"

"That's the way I 'heered' it." Wil attempted a second lightness, which failed miserably. "I'm sorry I upset you—yes, there *is* hope. After all, their belief has roots in the Scriptures. Who knows but what they can shake off the ironclad conviction that folklore takes care of the rest . . . If they can take away a mustard seed of truth, it can sprout like mushrooms in the devil-darkened hollows. So, come, sweetie— no tears of goodbye. We'll pray instead . . ."

13
The Twain Shall Meet

IT WAS ONLY a fortnight from the time the newcomers left
Centerville until O'Higgin returned. Ordinarily it would have seemed
much longer to the families awaiting his return. But there was such
frenzied activity in the Valley that nobody chalked off the days after
the first night. Jerry moped. Kearby, seeming to sense that something
dreadful had happened to Clarry, steered away from all men—even
those within her family—and kept up an endless wheedling in favor
of having her parents send her to Wilbur's Academy for Girls. She won
her case and, with the aid of her father, was admitted, carrying with
her a near-perfect report card, a trunkful of attractive school clothes
(only to find that uniforms were required), and an outward bravado.

"Are you sure you want to do this, honey?" Aunt Chrissy asked
gently. Kearby's waspish reply canceled out her affirmation.

"Would my talking to her help reassure Aunt Chrissy?" True asked
Young Wil.

His answer was a shake of his head. "She's in no mood. We have
to allow youth to find its own level, like water. Now, darling, lighten
up as we probe the human mind together. Kearby, Jerry, and Clarry
are at an interesting stage in human development, weighing and re-
weighing their chances for success out there in the world which looks
exciting and frightening at the same time. Their insecurities come
out in mood swings—sometimes high, too high, like spirited starlings,
and at other times deliberately stoking the fires of pessimism. Follow me?"

417

Indeed she did. Wasn't she guilty of the same thing? Deliberately she dismissed her misgivings about those on their way to Slippery Elm, about the twins, about the somewhat empty feeling she had about the rather meaningless church here—about *everything*.

Young Will had told her once that when one took away something undesirable it must be replaced by something better—a more desirable substitute.

So she filled her mind with readying for occupancy the cabin that Aunt Chrissy had once occupied with Uncle Joe. The formula worked. It would be such fun for her and Young Wil to be alone for the first time! Picking and slicing every event that came their way was no way to live. Neither was her tendency toward overprotection. God would look out for them all . . .

"But," she smiled to herself, "I suspect He will leave ironing of those ruffled curtains, washing windows, and beating carpets to me!"

And almost in a "jiffy" (Grandma Mollie's word) the cabin was sparkling and the happy couple were moved in. "Just look!" she said with pride as her husband picked her up and carried her over the threshold.

"I looked," he grinned, easing her onto the bed, then sitting teasingly at a discreet distance. "Double Wedding Ring quilt . . . feather mattress, downy as a cloud . . . and . . ."

Impulsively he eased toward her, inching slowly, as if courting her anew. Then, leaning forward, he kissed her boldly with a force that caused her to blush. She was the bride again, but—

"The gingerbread! It's burning!" True jerked free with a giggle.

"Methinks the lady protests too much—"

True grinned wickedly, waved, and backed toward the woodstove.

Early the next morning school commenced. True had to forgo breakfast. She was too on edge to eat, so great was her concern for the day. Swallowing her coffee with a force that almost scalded her throat, she tried to rationalize her queasiness. *I have taught before*, she told her reflection in the hourglass-shaped mirror above the armoire in the larger of the two bedrooms which the small cabin afforded. *Yes*, the True in the mirror affirmed, *but that was only to fill out the year when your aunt was confined before the birth of the twins*. Teachers were hard to find then, Mr. Goldsmith had reminded her with a hint of warning in his voice. He would be on hand a lot, of course, in case she needed his help. One needed *his* kind of help in the same manner one needed laryngitis on the night she was to solo in a concert!

"Why so pensive, darling? You'll do well and you know it!"

Young Wil, bless him, with all he had to do (judging by the entries in the old ledger which served as an appointment book) took time to bring True another cup of steaming coffee.

"I'm not pensive!" True denied with too much feeling. Then, whirling, her mouth filled with tortoise-shell hairpins to hold her heavy hair in what she considered an appropriate "teacher hairstyle" halo, she mumbled a garbled apology. "I'm sorry—of *course* I'm scared. I—I've had no time to get things ready—room's a dis-disaster—and my hair absolutely won't behave!"

The last words came out as she sneezed. Pins flew in all directions like ill-aimed arrows, causing both of them to laugh. True needed the release but realized that her laughter sprang more from nervousness than amusement.

"Go ahead, laugh it out," Young Wil encouraged in the same manner he had urged her to cry so many years before when Angel Mother was taken and her little heart lay about her like shattered glass.

"It's just—it's just that I must look like Mr.—Nate Goldsmith when he—he spits that cud of tobacco—and it runs down on his chin—"

"Parting his beard like the Red Sea—yes, he's still on that filthy weed. Come here!"

True obeyed. Young Wil snapped the three top grippers on her high-necked pink blouse (which made her pink cheeks all the pinker). He then kissed the back of her neck where three gold curls, held prisoners by the pins, had escaped, and turned her toward him—drawing her close. And suddenly she *was* crying—crying her heart out as she had when his awkward adolescent arms had held her on the night of her mother's death, bringing comfort as nobody else could have. Even then she had known it was young Wilson North to whom her heart belonged.

"It's all been too much, sweetheart," he was saying now. "You held up commendably—perhaps too well—"

"Wil North!" True said with spirit, "are you going to read *my* mind, too?"

"I always have," he replied almost humbly.

The two doctor-husbands had hitched the buggy to the most trusted roan. Obediently he clopped along, like a four-legged clock, ticking away the time, telling Chris Beth and True that confrontation was near at hand.

The morning was bleak and sunless, with a hint of rain in the air, unseasonably cool after the heat. And now a brisk breeze was rising.

"I feel dressed all wrong," True said against the teeth of the wind, "and I feel a sense of foreboding in spite of my husband's sweet efforts to erase it from my day. If only I had my room ready—"

Chris Beth urged the roan forward. Then she laughed lightly. "Don't let Nate bully you, True dear. You provide a necessary service which cannot be imitated, and he knows it. Anyway," she inhaled, hesitated, and then burst out, "you have nothing to worry about. It was supposed to be a surprise—that old faker made me promise—Nate, I mean. But, well, so I won't be guilty of talking too much, the charge he brings against *all* women, let me give you only a hint. You have nothing to worry about, absolutely nothing. Just prepare yourself for a nice surprise—and a wonderful day!"

And then they were there.

The surroundings were dearly familiar, yet excitingly unfamiliar. True somehow felt she was drinking in the beauty of the land for the first time: seeing the mountain ranges fold one behind the other as if they were in motion . . . marveling at the green-upon-green of the hills looking so deceptively close. Patches of emerald-green, like the design on a five-point star, appeared stitched between the wispy clouds that climbed the hills and then stopped to rest. Then, like a backdrop, the purplish-blues began, peak after peak of towering heights— their heads capped by bonnets of snow—probing today's gray of the vaulted sky. Who could fully understand this glory? To True, it was as if God's voice thundered through the surrounding canyons, only to drop to a loving whisper in the fir trees and the mountain stream that flowed around her . . .

"Oh, the school has a new coat of paint," she whispered in awe, "and a new roof—oh, Aunt Chrissy, another room!"

"*And* another teacher," a man's voice said very close to her ear. The voice, like the surroundings, was familiar, yet so unexpected that it came from a stranger—a stranger who was tethering the roan to a shady oak and emptying a generous portion of what Young Wil had laughingly called the horse's "sack lunch"—fat, golden oats from a gunnysack.

"Good morning, Mr. Prescott," Aunt Chrissy said to the stranger's back. True stiffened and came out of her fog.

Prescott! What was the young minister doing here? Or were there two of them?

Not unless the Reverend William Prescott had an identical twin. No, she thought, the delicately carved features could hardly be duplicated, even in a twin! The finely drawn but firm lips curved into an engaging smile. But for some reason the deep-set eyes did not. They still reminded her of hardened quartz, and again she compared him with one of Robin Hood's men. Something about him—

"You are staring, Miss North," William Prescott said, eyebrows arched in amusement as he reached to help her from the buggy.

"*Mrs.*," True reminded him as she gingerly lifted the pegtop skirt an inch and accepted his hand simply because she was unable to alight without it. "And you are to please forgive my staring. It—it's just that I did not expect to see you here—and—"

She hated herself for fumbling for words. "Is this customary—I mean, for ministers to attend the opening of school? Is there to be chapel?"

"Whoa, one question at a time. Yes, it is customary for the new teacher to put in an appearance. And, yes, again, there is to be chapel. Unless you object?"

"Of course I do not object!"

"Mr. Prescott is to serve in several roles—teacher, preacher, and principal. We needed someone like him, as you will see," Aunt Chrissy told her.

True stood very still, listening to the drumming of the grouse and an occasional gobble-gobble of a wild turkey joining in protest of the invasion of their privacy. Nearby evergreen berries offered an abundance of fruit, and hazelnuts were in their prime. Probably that was what all the fuss was about.

Chris Beth, aptly described by President of the Board Goldsmith

as being "high-stocked with brains 'n allus busier'n a couple of hon-
eybees in a sweetbriar patch," tactfully moved on. She must have
suspected that William Prescott and her niece had something to settle
between them. It was true. But for the life of her, True had no idea
what. The man was arrogant, a characteristic unbecoming a minister. True was not even sure she liked him. He was learned as far as a
formal education went, but there was an aura of mystery that made
her suspect him. . . . It should be of no importance to her, but it was.

"You'll need to know the facts about the people with whom you'll
work—that is, if the mountaineers (only don't call them that) all show
up as promised." The man's tone made her sound like a newcomer.

True's chin jutted out defensively. "You forget that I grew up
here—" and there she stopped. "What do you mean *mountaineers*?
We have no mountaineers here, Mr. Prescott."

"Not by that name—they prefer being called 'Highlanders.' They
are really Scotch, but—well, it's a long story. I suggest that you take
a quick look up the mountains to your left. Or is that your blind side?
Maybe you would prefer not to look."

True ignored what she considered to be insulting words. The man
was impossible. But she did look upward and was surprised to see
that a narrow path sliced out the side of the almost-vertical wall of
the mountain. Up, up, up it went, sometimes losing itself as it jutted sharply to avoid an unexpected outcropping of jagged rocks. And
along the shocking trail were shacks, hastily erected of the crudest
logs, held intact by dried and cracked mud, and windowless. The
cluster of lean-tos, huddled together as if seeking protection by numbers and separated only by gawking, squawking chickens, extended
to the backbone of the mountain. A large, black pot swung from a
tepee of poles centered the pitiful scene, its immensity suggesting
that it was community property. There was no movement. Even the
trees stood windless in spite of the stiff breeze. And then hounds,
skin stretched tightly over their ribs as if there were no flesh between
skin and bone, appeared from all directions. They bayed without
enthusiasm and then sat down to scratch. There were no other signs
of life.

True was speechless. Were there children here—children she was
supposed to teach? Where had they come from, and when? "Who—?"
was all she could manage.

"Appalachia—Great Smoky Mountains. Starving, frightened, trusting nobody. Chestnut crop failed, and they had to leave—some, that is. Others are fugitives from the law. Either way, they're hostile, ready to shoot their way out of any situation that's threatening."

"But—but why didn't somebody try to get them together with the group we helped?"

William's laugh was without mirth. "Them they hate worst of all—totally different breed. O'Higgin can explain matters better than I can. I think he can crack the barrier. I can't offer any other hope—"

"*Can't* or *won't*?" True spoke the words before knowing she planned to—and then wondered why.

"Both!" he said tartly. "They're dangerous—stubborn—feuding—"

True sighed. "I must get to my room—but these people—well, 'East is East and West is West—'"

His voice was so low she could scarcely hear: "But the twain shall meet . . . someday . . ."

14
The Light of the First Day

⌀

STEPPING INTO HER classroom, True experienced a peculiar, otherworldly feeling. She had crossed into another time, another century—walking backward. All progress seemed to dissipate, and she was back at the beginning of the American frontier. She did not exist. In her place were Angel Mother . . . Aunt Chrissy . . . all who came before her.

She was unable to settle the butterflies in her stomach even though she had handled classrooms before. She wished momentarily that she were as cocky and overconfident as William Prescott. It was then that she realized he was neither of those. Of course not—he was scared silly! Sure, he had been in the pulpit, where he could and did hold his congregation at arm's length. But he had had no experience in teaching, where small human beings swarmed about one's feet seeking love, understanding, and "learning" as a swarm of bees clusters in search of nectar for honey. Nate Goldsmith had appointed him to be principal simply because he was a *man*, and because women, through no fault of their own, were not very bright. So unabashedly (lest Mr. Goldsmith, Aunt Chrissy, or True herself would think of him as a beginner) William Prescott spoke and behaved in an arrogant way which the more experienced would avoid at all costs. She smiled to herself. Here was Study Number One for Wil's book. And she had expected it to be a child . . .

Eyes adjusted to the dim classroom, True looked around her in amazement. Why, all was in readiness! There was a large brown crock filled with colored leaves on the work-table, where paper, pencils, and primers had been laid out with the same precision that one arranges the place settings for a formal meal. And right in the center of her desk lay a fat, rosy-cheeked apple for the teacher! Books, which had not been there before, lay in waiting on shelves which lined the walls. Where had they come from? And when?

Somehow she knew who had prepared the room even before William Prescott himself told her. He had entered the room quietly and his first words were, "Do you like it?"

"Like it? I love it—and what's more, I am deeply appreciative, Mr. Prescott."

"William, please, when the children aren't around."

True smiled. "I appreciate all you've done, William."

He colored, then managed a smile. "At least it earned me a smile, my first from you."

Was this what Wil's psychology book had described as a "compensatory act," one performed in order to gain favor or make amends for some imagined shortcoming? Perhaps she had made him feel it necessary. The thought made True feel a little ashamed.

"I have been unfair to you, Mr.—uh, William. Let's try again."

"My pleasure! Oh, the books—I've been boning up on Oregon history, and I find that people in this state are literary-minded. They pooled their books like their food and circulated them even before the first wagon trains—but I'm sure you're well-versed in history?"

"Quite well. Of course, Daddy Wil's a native and taught us that back in 1848 or so—anyway, when Oregon was a Territory—Congress set aside about 5,000 dollars for a Territorial library. Unfortunately it burned, and we're still struggling to increase our books—"

"Struggle no more." William looked complacent. "Your friend, working with the government and the railroads, has arranged all this, with more to come—"

"My friend?" Surely he didn't mean—

But he did! "Michael St. John, the railroad tycoon—and look at this. Mr. St. John himself collected writings by some of the fur traders, scientists, missionaries, and explorers such as Cook, Vancouver, Lewis and Clark, Slacum, and Wilkes—all careful journals, sort of travelogues. But the first works of fiction, too—you know, Moss with his *Prairie Flower*, Joaquin Miller, Edwin Markham—"

William Prescott was rubbing gentle fingers along the spines of the books. But True, excited as she was, felt her mind pulling in two directions, one part of it wanting to listen and the other part marveling at Michael's generosity.

And then the principal had her attention again. "Oh, here it is, True—I mean Mrs. North—"

"True's all right," she smiled, wondering if he heard.

"The best-known of all books written on Oregon is Frederic Homer Balch's *Bridge of the Gods*. What an interesting man! Born in Lebanon, Balch didn't attend school until he was 15 or so, and then very little. But he learned to read at home, and—here's what may appeal to our charges—his ambition was to make Oregon as famous as Scott made Scotland!"

"Scotland—yes, that may appeal to their background if—"

"But wait! There's more! The author converted to Christianity and burned the manuscript he was working on—said what he was working on was sinful!"

A little like Michael St. John. "Then—what—" True began eagerly, then stopped. Michael, in his new life since his own decision to walk with the Lord, was seeking ways to serve. He was a brilliant businessman but neither preacher nor teacher, so was using his money to furnish needed supplies. And, oh, how money was needed—both there and here. *Bless him,* she thought as her eyes misted over.

"You're wondering what contribution Balch made?"

True came back to the confines of the classroom with a jolt. "Er—yes. Yes, I was. If he burned the manuscript—"

"That was the one he was working on then. But he kept remembering stories of the Columbia River Indians which he'd picked up as a boy. Characters kept haunting his thoughts, begging to be born—writers being a peculiar lot, I guess. At last he took up his pen and wrote *The Bridge of the Gods,* but never lived to know it would make him famous. Just as well, perhaps, although it's sad, as it could have made him feel guilty."

"Oh, but it shouldn't! He made a great contribution—"

William was watching her closely. "You think we can remove guilt—shame—and fear?"

"God can!" True's reply was instantaneous. And then she realized that the man beside her was fighting an inner battle. She could hardly wait until tonight to share her news with her husband. But ahead lay the day. How long had they been talking, anyway? Only a few minutes, actually, but to True it seemed an eternity.

Aunt Chrissy's head popped through the door. "Time to ring the bell, Sir—that is, if we plan chapel the first day."

"Absolutely—but—" William turned to True, "take one quick look out the window and get a view of those who are waiting to meet Teacher."

The schoolyard swarmed with children. True hardly knew what she was expecting—but not this. The children were beautiful, though fragile to the point of looking undernourished. Flaxen-haired and pale, they looked like little celestial creatures.

Almost all were barefoot, some with feet bleeding from the jagged rocks in the winding mountain trail they had descended. But their clothing was clean and surprisingly well-fitted. Except for their tendency to clump together, removed from the other children jumping over lumber piles reserved (she learned later) for a new library building for community use, their high-pitched squeals of laughter rang like bells in the clean air, and one would not have thought them different.

Chris Beth peeked around the door frame again. "Ready?" she smiled.

True nodded absently, her mind on the contrast between these children and the others of Appalachia. Why the difference between the "Highlanders," who chose (she supposed) to climb higher, and the "Valley Folk," who occupied the rich river-bottom lands in their former home?

"The children—they're so tidy. I just never expected the difference—fact is, I never expected *them*."

"It never pays to generalize, does it now?" Aunt Chrissy chided gently, her eyes glancing at the tiny watch pinned to the bosom of her simple white blouse. "There was never time to prepare you for the onslaught, not that I know the whole story. O'Higgin will have more news. You and I had our hands full, and then some. There goes the bell!" Its clang announced "books time" to the eager newcomers.

But at the hall entrance where the children were lining up, Chris Beth paused, turning long enough to say, "About the clothes—Bertie,

Nate's wife, Olga, the Chu's, and all the Basque people, led by Rachel Beltran, collected outgrown clothing. Miss Mollie took a nip and a tuck and the proud parents 'biled 'em' in the black pot. The Solomons furnished notions. Oh, dear, here comes Nate! Shape up—make him feel important—"

Nate Goldsmith was wearing—to True's surprise—a white shirt with a stiffly starched bosom and collar, which being about two sizes too small, caused his Adam's apple to be thrust almost to meet his chin. Even his voice was strained when he strutted in to introduce the man at his side. Rolling his eyes without an attempt to turn his head, the Honorable President of the Board said importantly, "This here's Mr. Courtland," then turned his body to the immense shadow which loomed to shut all light from the door.

"Howdy," said the man wearing patched but clean overalls, his deep-set blue eyes probing True's. He removed the old felt hat which had been pinned up in front with a thorn and bowed in a surprisingly gallant manner.

"How do you do, Mr. Courtland?" True greeted him with a smile.

"'Bout as common. Glad t'have ye here—shore 'n we are. Now, Wife 'n me want that our little, Josie, Nellie Sue, Charming, Eliza, 'n th' boys be larnin' a heap—case we find we wanta go back thar as missionaries. Welcome a'gin, sweet Ma'am—'n iffen we kin he'p—?"

"I will let you know," True smiled, warming up to this proud, courtly gentleman. Mr. Courtland seemed to know.

"Here ye be now—bein' all Wife 'n me had t'offer. Want t'wear this t'adorn yore purdy hair?" His offering startled her to silence.

Nate Goldsmith winked at her—his signal that she must not refuse. Not that she would have. But why rob him of his joy in authority?

True accepted the long owl's feather and tucked it in her hair, realizing that with the feather standing at attention at the back of her braid she was sure to be a subject of ridicule among local children. She must look exactly like the ghost of a young Indian maiden.

Pleased with his simple, artless gesture, the man turned to go.

It was then that True froze. In his back pocket was the imprint of a gun, the handle barely visible above the frazzled top.

She did not hesitate. "Mr. Courtland, Sir, I'm afraid I must ask that you leave your gun at the door."

The man turned in surprise. "Leave me gun? Why I wouldn' be

drest without it—no he-man goes about half-drest." He patted his pocket. "Hit's my best friend—protects me 'n my family, provides food—why, I've promised me wife I be bringin' home th' meat. Planned on squirrel stew—"

"Which you probably will have," True smiled. "But I cannot have guns brought inside the classrooms. That is against our rules. Just lay the gun by the door, please. Then you can recover it as you leave. We are so happy you came," she said winningly.

The man grinned. Maybe he was getting soft—maybe a little hen-pecked—but, then he'd never met so brave a lady. Fine job she'd do. Yep, fine job!

The children's bright eyes all focused on teacher as pupils of all ages shuffled to find seats without a word. Above the tom-tom rhythm of her heart (either from excitement or a delayed reaction to her impetuous order to Mr. Courtland), True was dimly aware of two circumstances. These children, all with bisque-doll skins, were all ages even though she was to have beginners and chart-class. And here were the larger ones struggling to fit themselves into small desks (replacements for the battered secondhand benches). And there was the overwhelming, almost intoxicating, smell of varnish, new paint, and a strange food-smell similar to the odor of the strung-together pine cones, red peppers, garlic, and something else that True was unable to identify—a "good luck charm," said one of the children, that was as "important as a man's gun."

A man's gun. True tried to push the idea to the back of her mind as she assessed the group, wondering what to do about the assortment of ages and sizes.

The children's bright eyes remained glued on her. "Fine fix," True said to herself. She had never felt so helpless in her entire life. Preoccupied with the problems at hand, she took no notice of the amusement in the eyes of the local children whose parents she knew, so was unaware that they were about to explode into laughter. Actually, she might have welcomed it except that other matters were more pressing. In fact, they were closing around her—the children looking like giants.

One tiny girl, looking too young to be there, caught True's eye in an amazingly mature manner. What a lovely child! Fat-cheeked, with a high, rounded forehead and wide-open blue, blue eyes.

"Are yuh stuck, Teacher?" The voice rang out like a tiny silver bell. "Pray—thet's whut our maw does when her's got too much t'housekeep, 'n th' floor's all covered in slut's wool—"

"Shet yore mouth, Little Josie!" ordered the awkward boy of about 13 who was wedged into one of the desk seats so tightly that his breath came in difficult gasps. He was obviously the tiny girl's brother. Looking sheepishly at True, he volunteered, "We ain't 'posed t'be talkin— 'n anyways, our paw ain't so pious, jest shoots up the chim'ley lettin' sparks fly—skeers our pet pig 'way from th' table—"

The suppressed laughter exploded somewhat like one would expect from a shotgun. This she could handle. Raising a hand for silence, True said softly, "You must be members of the Courtland family. You are Little Josie—and you?" She turned to Little Josie's brother.

"Nathan—Nat—'n we's all Prim'tive Babtis'—don' talk uh heap—"

"Praying's better anyway," True smiled. "We'll be gathering for chapel and then—"

There was no time to discuss seating. William Prescott was pushing back the curtain which made the large auditorium into three rooms.

Nate was suddenly back. "He's a-gonna read 'bout Creation— th'light of th'first day—larnin', I guess he means—'n he's hopin' *you* larn somethin' too. Dangerous thang—disarmin' a man—sez you'll be payin' . . ."

15

And Then the Dark

❧

IT WAS INDEED an enlightening day—a day of discovery. It had thrown True only briefly when the children of the Appalachian families showed up. After all, "Come one, come all" was the motto of this Valley. Here was a new way of life with which she must become acquainted. Already she was planning home calls so that she could familiarize herself with their expectations. In fact, there was a certain challenge, a renewal of the spirit of adventure that she had come by naturally. It "ran in the family," according to Grandma Mollie. And to think, True had thought everything was under control here, that the Valley, beautiful and peaceful as it was, was finished. It had hurt when they left Slippery Elm, because of saying goodbye to Marty, Midgie, the baby, and all the new friends. But even more, she had known how much remained to be done. She still missed it, but now— well, thank goodness, God was in charge of the future. He had given her a new assignment, and He would help her fulfill it.

But she had to admit that it was a tough one. And just how much help she could expect from human sources remained to be seen.

True had hoped that Jerry would be around to help. After all, if all ages were to be scattered like the tribes of Israel, his presence would afford her a hand. But she should have known that Aunt Chrissy would want him with her. To their surprise he ended up with one Mr. William Prescott, who dangled a carrot before the boy's nose— one that was obvious to the point of being ludicrous. Except to Jerry!

It was not every young man who was appointed to the position of Junior Vice Principal!

Well, if ever a principal needed a helper, it was this one. True's own apprehension melted away in sympathy when she saw the violent trembling of William's legs as he read the planned passage. And he had an inattentive audience. The new children, although quiet, fumbled with their new supplies as if they were from the king's counting house. Even a sheet of lined paper was a treasure. They were lost in a world of magic, staring in fascination as if they expected the lines to disappear. But that accounted for only part of their preoccupation. They did not understand a word that this strange man was reading.

The Valley children behaved even worse. They were squirming and giggling. The squirming came from boredom, and the giggling, True finally realized, sprang from amusement at the feather perched in her hair. Well, Mr. Courtland was still there, taking it all in, so she would just have to put up with it. Afterward there would be a lesson on manners—she would see to that. Meantime, she shook her head at the gigglers, who went right on giggling while the Appalachian children saw and took her disapproving glance seriously. Their faces blanched and they laid the supplies down as if they were burning their hands.

When William Prescott stopped to catch his breath, the children's faces went even whiter, if such a thing were possible. Thinking they were in "big trouble," one small boy called out, "We declare, Teacher Sir, we don' know them words—never heered 'em—'n they skeer us— 'cause our Paw'll bust our britches—"

The principal's face went as white as theirs. He looked hopelessly at Chris Beth, then directed his question to True. "Uh, should I dispense with the reading—or have prayer—?"

A forest of small hands waved back and forth. True bit her lip. He had prepared the rooms but not his words or his heart. Obviously he was fearful of offering a prayer before this group of restless children, perhaps fearing their laughter, even though he was accustomed to praying from the pulpit.

"Pray," True said crisply, adding to herself, "you need all the prayers you can offer!"

"Don'chu know how?" The artless question came from the Courtland lad who was still squeezed into the tiny desk. "We do—but we don' wanna be throwin' off on you—less'n we git our hides tanned."

He glanced uneasily over his shoulder at his father, glad perhaps that the gun lay outside the door!

The fairylike creature called Little Susie stood up. "I kin—"

All the Appalachian children clapped as their hands went down. True cast an anxious glance at Mr. Courtland. To her surprise, he was smiling broadly.

"Go ahead, Little Susie," True said quietly, seeing that William seemed to have lost not only his poise but his voice. Was he in shock?

"Shet yore eyes 'n bow yore heads," the little girl said sweetly. And then she began an odd sing-song af words which obviously made sense to her peers.

Good Lawd, we thank ye-hey-tank-toodle all day—
Come 'bide with us, hey-tank-toddle, 'n take our sins away . . .

Feet tapped. Fingers drummed. And, with eyes still closed, the children swayed in a sort of trance, all singing the words unselfconsciously together with a certain charm that expressed deep emotion.

The day rocked on, frustration after frustration looming to destroy all hope that it would get better. First came the commotion of trying to place children where they belonged, which never materialized. For some reason William Prescott held fast to the idea that it was unwise. About the only thing he held onto, True sniffed inwardly, except a desk or chair to hold him on his feet!

"But why?" she asked quickly as he was drawing the curtains to separate the rooms again.

Glancing over his shoulder furtively as if he actually believed "Walls have ears," he whispered nervously. "You'll see."

What on earth bothered the man? But he was right. She did see.

There was no need to fill names in the register until the matter was decided. "Some of you are uncomfortable. Just bear with us and I'll try to get you older boys and girls into other rooms—or make some arrangement about desks—" True stopped, realizing that she had no authority to promise anything against the principal's wishes.

Wails of protest filled the classroom.

"I fit in here like a bird in a nest," one Huck Finn-looking boy objected . . . ragged overalls torn off just below the knees . . . barefoot . . . a cowlick . . . with a sprinkling of freckles crossing his stub nose . . .

gray eyes lighted with innocent objection. "Paw put me in charge of th' little 'uns—an' we gotta stick t'gether, us Prim'tive Baptists!"

It was the second mention of Primitive Baptists, so it must be an important matter. But there was no time to dwell on the thought; the overgrown Courtland boy needed attention. His father had left the room, so he was in charge. "Please, Ma'am, hit ain't good t'go separatin' us. Me, I kin fit in this here seat better'n I kin fit in with furriners—now, don' go thankin' I'm a scalawag—we love one 'nother—"

"Aw, Miz North, let 'em stay," the youngest Beltran boy put in on behalf of the newcomers. "Cain't you see . . ." His voice trailed off.

Oh, she saw all right! The Appalachian children were soft-spoken, well-mannered, and eager to learn. But they were not going to be pushed around. And they had no intention of making an effort to fit into a new group. That she saw—and something more. She saw, as Mark Twain must have seen, a moment in history, and she longed to preserve it because it represented a valuable record of a rapidly disappearing social order. She could learn much from these people . . .

The next lesson came with an "Eeeek!" as bedlam struck. The Valley children leaped to safety on top of their desks. The Appalachians remained seated, eyes puzzled.

"Dunno why they's sech skeeredy cats—hit bein' jest a skunk wantin' t'larn like us. Granny makes skunk oil fer us when we got the grippe—keeps 'em cooped like chickens, tho' I'd not be ahankerin' fer dumplin's," the Huck Finn character volunteered.

The fluffy little creature, blinking in the light, waddled down the aisle, nose twitching slightly as if others than himself contaminated the air, little front feet turned inward toward the white spot on his black chest, and tail up suspiciously straight—right toward True. It was all she could do to keep from leaping on her own desk. Then she saw the culprit—Huck himself. It was not what he did but something he did *not* do. His face was straight, too straight. It looked like a mask.

"Do you know anything about this—this creature?" True's stride, her route bypassing the trespasser, took her quickly to his desk.

"Me—yessum, some. I know they kin stink purdy bad."

He wouldn't lie. That would be "sinful." He would just withhold the truth, bypassing the facts no matter how long the dialogue continued. There could be no doubt that he had masterminded the skunk's appearance. But why give him the satisfaction of a scolding?

"You seem to know a lot about skunks—what's your name, anyway?"

"Ebenezer—named after my paw'n his paw—'n yessum, I know—"

"Then toll him out of here, Ebenezer!"

The boy stared at her blankly, his freckles standing out on stems. What had gone wrong? Why hadn't his plan worked? his eyes questioned. Aloud, he said, "What's *toll*?"

"Coax, beg, drive—do anything to get him out—"

"Oh, thet. Ain't no problem." Huckleberry Finn II stood with pride, took the striped creature by the tail, and marched out with all the dignity of a soldier goose-stepping off to war.

"Now," True pitched her voice low, exuding a calm she did not feel, "you boys and girls be seated, please, and let's get the register ready for tomorrow's roll call."

They complied, ready to right the wrong as well as regain the dignity they had lost temporarily in the eyes of the new children. One volunteered to write down names. Another would follow and write in addresses, while others would check with the preacher—no, the teacher—that is, uh, the principal, and ask for some other desks.

There was a general commotion as the desk-swapping took place, but at last it was finished. The helpers did a good job with the names, but when it came to addresses, they'd had no cooperation. The mailman wouldn't come "up thar," the children said. No need anyhow, since not many folks could read. They all knowed where t'other lived, which trees had notches carved, where there wuz a hole 'twixt th' rocks, or a rail loose in th' fence, so who needed this—what was it, address? Well, that part would have to wait until her house calls. For now she must show a few books that might hold appeal for the older children. Most were unable to read, but they would be embarrassed by *The Three Bears*. *Treasure Island* was entirely too difficult, although the plot would fascinate them. Thank goodness, most of the books had synopses. She could garner interest by reading these aloud. She must write to Michael, thank him, and congratulate him on his wise selections.

She wrote herself a reminder and added several others. Ask for a fan, since the room was stifling. And more firewood (the potbellied stove would gobble the rick outside the window). And surely the Board would understand a need for something other than the communal cup that

True suspected one of the mountain children had brought—a long-handled, hollowed-out gourd to dip into a tin bucket which was already rusting where water had run down the sides. Somehow her mind wandered to the other Appalachian folk who had gone to Slippery Elm. Those children had no school at all—no church—and—

Her thinking was split in half by a loud *clang-clang-clang* of a bell, the three clangs signaling lunch. Jerry must have told Mr. Prescott or rung the bell himself. She was about to explain to the new children when there was a nerve-curling clanging of the clapper which seemed to go on forever. Didn't Mr. Prescott know—

"Fire! Fire!" screamed the Valley children for the benefit of the new pupils, then stood at attention, awaiting Teacher's orders.

The Appalachian children panicked, some scampering like mice into the other rooms, others jumping from the windows. Someday perhaps True would laugh about this, but for now it was almost more than she could bear. And ahead lay the lecture she must make on how to conduct themselves in emergencies—maybe a few terse words for the principal himself. Imagine a fire drill on the first day!

Order restored, lunch ("dinner" to her new pupils) gave True reason to write herself another note. The contents of the "dinner pails" were so pitifully inadequate that she felt she was about to be sick. Thick, half-cooked "sow bosom" hung limply from between heavy, yellow biscuits. The rinds (bristles still intact) had not been removed from the pork. Surely something could be done to supplement the children's diet. Of course, there was pride to reckon with . . .

At last the day ended—almost. As True saw the children off, William Prescott shouldered his way through the group to stand by her side. The hand he pointed up the mountain trembled. Following the direction his finger pointed, she saw a shoulder-to-shoulder troop of mountaineer men, descending the mountain on sure feet, their hands on holsters strapped openly to the side-front of their bibbed overalls. She felt a bit queasy herself . . . but why had William fled?

True managed a smile and a wave of her hand. The men lifted their assorted hats and returned them to their heads. But they did not return her smile. Maybe it was fatigue which caused a sudden dread of the future. Momentarily, the hand of darkness clutched at her heart . . .

The darkness became real as she, Aunt Chrissy, and Jerry rode home in the gathering twilight. There was so much to talk about; but Jerry monopolized the conversation. Mr. Prescott said . . . Mr. Prescott made me responsible for this . . . Mr. Prescott made me responsible for that . . . and then, "This will be my best year, being in charge, then next year—well, I've got plans already. Mr. Prescott and me."

Chris Beth frowned a bit, then smiled. "I'm glad to see you so happy, darling. You never liked school so much before. And I know you'll do a fine job!"

Aunt Chrissy's words translated into: "This is the beginning of a change in our Jerry." And she would have been right. But for now True was unable to care. She was tired, tired . . . tired . . .

At home she fell across the bed, too exhausted to undress. Her husband was gone when she awoke the next morning.

16
The Return of O'Higgin

TWO WEEKS PASSED quickly as True worked her way through a wilderness of problems. "Do you think we'll ever get this year on its feet?" she asked Aunt Chrissy over and over. And always the answer was the same: "Of course we will—although I'm not just sure what the Lord has in mind. These children are so interesting—so unique—so *precious* in their own way. Sometimes," she said with a wistful look in her dark eyes, "I almost wish we didn't have to 'civilize' them—impose our standards on their simple ways."

"But we're doing it for their own good," True invariably protested. "And I doubt if we're going to *impose* much on them. Some of mine are as stubborn as mules—gentle and sweet, but not about to be persuaded to change their ideas."

They agreed that they must move slowly with the new curriculum. Chris Beth was in a quandary as to the children's insistence that they learn Latin. Each day one of the fathers came down the mountain to observe what took place where his child was supposed to be "larnin'." They themselves, almost without exception, were unable to read. Why then was it important that their offspring master Latin? "'Cause th' Good Book once was in thet speech till them whut s'posed they be a-knowin' more'n God hisself begun messin' up His words 'n tamperin' with our childrun's brains—got 'em all churned up—'n in danger of hell's furnaces. Latin, hit's gotta be like once 'twas—'n you teachers, bein' smart 'nuf t'read, know 'bout th' Lord God's wrath fer him whut changes one teeny word—er goes takin' hit out."

438

The most immovable of them all was a man by the name of *Goodman*. He was "hidebound on a-livin' up t'th' name like unto how th' Old Country ancestors tooken pride in hit." Like their blood-line, they had to keep away from "messin' 'round with silly games 'n fancy stuff which hafta be forged out in th' devil's workshop—hit's Latin er nuthin'."

True shook her head helplessly, feeling drained of her sanity. She knew the Latin words to "Twinkle, twinkle little star . . ." and that was the extent of her knowledge of the language. "What will we do?"

Aunt Chrissy laughed. "We will ask our husbands to help, that's what! For some reason I never understood, Jerry took an interest in your Daddy Wil's work and pestered him until he dragged out his old textbooks and helped him a bit. It's a dead language, but—"

"Better it be dead than all the teachers!" True said with a shudder, remembering that it was her frightful duty to disarm each mountaineer. It had become so routine that, amusingly they had begun to drop their weapons of their own accord. Which was not to say that William had not created a wall of fear, no matter how careful she was to conceal it, around her heart. One of the men would balk one day . . .

For the most part, the men were polite and appreciative, each making it abundantly clear that "facts" were what they had brought their families here for. Facts. Truth. "Light"—only to be found in Latin. But one man by the name of Hank-John Brown was different. He was surly, even angry—and seemingly very frightened. He made her uneasy with leading questions concerning the group from Appalachia which had come before his "flock." "Skeered, they wuz—'n well they oughta be. They's settlin' up t'do one day. Don' let 'em come near—don' want them nasty-minded filth tryin' t'mate up with our virgin daughters—no incestin' 'mongst us. An' we don' go co-minglin' 'mongst them what fornicates 'n desecrates—me, I be ready t'shoot any boy what goes courtin' me daughters afore he's got a chance t'draw! Don' go 'lowin any boy settin' near my girls—ye hear? I never shot me no woman—still—" he rolled bloodshot eyes to peer out the window where he had reluctantly dropped his weapon, and without so much as a "Good afternoon" he sprang from his chair, recovered his gun, and disappeared.

True felt almost out of touch with Young Wil. She was buried in a sea of work but had to postpone questions and relating incidents from

the classroom because of his demanding schedule. He kept long hours
(he was often still out on house calls at bedtime and did not awaken
her on returning), and then he spent hours working by lamplight on
his book. When there was a moment it was like doing battle with a
shadow to get her husband's attention.

"I wish you wouldn't work so hard, Wil," she said wistfully on one
of those rare moments. "There's a moon—a full one—just waiting
to be shared—"

True paused, wondering if he had heard. In the quiet, the music of
their private stream stole into the livingroom-dark. A bird twittered
and the mountains, wrapped in twilight's purple shawls, beckoned.

Hard work had burned away the daylight hours for them both,
stolen away a margin of togetherness she needed. Now, teasingly,
she paraded before him—flexing her muscles in luxurious pleasure.
"What a relief to move—we could walk—talk—oh, Wil—*can't* we?"

Wil's eyes had a faraway look in them. And the sheaf of papers
waiting on his desk told her the answer. Women could *make* time for
their husbands, she thought a little bitterly. But men—well, whoever
said, " 'Love to man is a thing apart; 'tis woman's sole existence' had
it right." She could tell him that Chicken Little was right, that the
sky was falling, and he wouldn't hear!

And, then without warning, True had a chance to test her theory.
There was a distinct crackle of brush right beneath the front window, a muffled voice, and then the warning cry of a bird of prey
closing in on its kill.

"What was *that*?" Young Wil was at her side immediately, a steadying hand on her arm. "Oh—I see." And his hand pointed at a great bird,
motionless in the darkening sky as if poised to reconnoiter before sailing in on silent wings to dive.

"Birds don't talk—you know that!" True said a little sharply because of her fear. Mindlessly, she pulled away and eased to the window, peering out in spite of her fear. There she saw a menace behind
every stump, a lurking danger behind each tree. Then her courage
floundered. But, hypnotized by the lazy blue sweep of the mountains
(where she was sure the object of her fear had originated), she felt
unable to move. Until some movement, some motion turned her
around.

Young Wil was not there!

True came to her senses then. She had sent the man she loved into a danger he knew nothing about. Perhaps even now, he was surrounded by mountaineer men with six-shooters dangling at their sides. Even now a shadow was crossing the yard—

"Wil!" she screamed in warning, and wondered later if her feet touched the braided rug even once as she rushed out the door.

A hand closed about her own. But it was not herself for whom she feared. It was her husband. "Let go of me—you—you—"

"Watch your language, Teacher!" an intimate voice whispered in her ear. "Some detective you'd make." But the mellow laugh gave away the identity of the shadow.

"Wil—Wil North—you scared me out of my wits—and if you dare tell me it's my mind working overtime—"

He was guiding her footsteps toward the door of the cabin. "My, my! What length some women will go to in order to get attention—"

"Only when they're neglected by their mates!"

It felt good to release all her pent-up emotion—no matter what the cost. And they'd have to talk now. Already she had postponed telling him about the odd manner of the mountain men dangerously long.

"Thank God I haven't made you hate me," Young Wil said fervently as he gripped her cold fingers in a warm, comforting grasp with such strength she wanted to cry out. But, oh, it felt good to hurt!

She was putty in his hands. But she had not imagined the sound!

As if reading her mind, as always, Wil closed the door behind them, the cozy room jealously guarding their privacy. "There was someone out there," he said flatly, "and I can't tell you not to be afraid because I have no idea who or why—but I *can* beg you to be careful, darling."

He slid down into his favorite easy chair, drawing her into his lap. True made no protest, winding her arms about his neck instead.

"Of course there was! And what do you mean—you haven't made me hate you? How do you know what evil lurks in my heart, you overconfident, impossible man? Talk about male ego—"

"Who wants to talk about it?" He buried his face in her hair. "But I'll answer your question before devouring you completely."

True snuggled closer with a giggle as in mock seriousness Young Wil said smugly: "Women *pretend* to hate us—hate being close to love, you know. But to despise me, find me loathsome, now that's different."

She nodded. "Something you're picking up for your research? Studying *me*, then generalizing about women? Oh, well," she faked a sigh, "I don't mind being your subject—and darling, although we've been apart far, far more than I'd like, I've been working right along with you—studying influences of—the newcomers—"

True poured out the whole story then, every detail. And when she finished, Young Wil said quietly, "I've known, sweetheart—and I've done my share of watching from a distance and praying. Now I'm even more afraid for you—and if anything happened to you—"

His voice broke in several places, and he held her closer as the darkness folded its arms around them.

Sunday brought three surprises. True glanced around, hoping to see some of the new settlers at church. Seeing none brought keen disappointment. But not to William Prescott, whose eyes surveyed the congregation anxiously. Relief spread over his delicately formed features, a reaction which still puzzled her. What was he afraid of?

Afraid? His sermon certainly reflected fear. It was as if he were two persons—except that she did wonder at his text. "Come now, and let us reason together . . . " he read from Isaiah. Somehow she felt that the passage had to do with his problem. Yet his poise surprised her.

The second surprise came at announcement time. Nate Goldsmith stood and with his usual pomp presented a report that one would expect to hear at a school board meeting. All was well, he said of school. Lots of new books . . . extension of the curriculum to include Latin . . . two new cedar watering buckets, a dipper, and individual paper drinking cups "fer hy-*hy*-giene, y'know, 'n a coupla privies fer th' same purpose." But, best of all, Nate said with a lift of voice, was the newcomers who visited school daily—and it was the "bounden duty" of others to do likewise. *O, no!* True's heart cried out. But the report was interrupted by a merry whistle. O'Higgin was home!

17

Understanding—and Lack of It

✃

A BURST OF applause greeted Irish O'Higgin. But it did not seem to bother William Prescott, who wanted to hear a report as much as the congregation. News of the "folks over there" was of even greater importance to him, True was sure. Somehow he fitted into a strange puzzle here involving both the group in Slippery Elm and those choosing the higher elevations here in the Valley.

"Greetings from th' goodly folks ye befriended, in th' name o' th' Lord Jesus Christ!" O'Higgin boomed, his merry blue eyes dancing with pleasure at the stomping of feet almost drowning out his words. "Now, be still, dear ones, lest me voice not be heard in God's hoose— *house!*"

Why, that rogue! He actually winked at his "Mollie-gal"! His boldness brought even more applause. True looked at Grandma Mollie, who sat there poker-faced. Not that she fooled anybody. Theirs was a good marriage, an inspiration to all who took marriage seriously, binding them with sacred vows—in contrast to the growing number who seemed to have misunderstood the terms. Did they really suppose the final promise was "until *divorce* do us part"?

O'Higgin doffed his plaid-and-tasseled tam-o'-shanter to expose a near-bald head (with the few strands of red hair that were combed forward to cover the loss failing in their mission). He compensated by allowing his always-abundant red facial hair to grow into an enormous beard.

443

"I be knowin' 'tis hard waitin' on a full report," the big Scotch-Irishman grinned winningly, waving a ruddy hand for silence. "'N ye kin depend on receivin' it—but first," and there was a rare near-pleading tone to his voice, "'tis patience I be askin'—patience whilst I be informin' me family. But this day jest 'low me t'tell ye them mountaineers Jeremiah 'n me be takin' t'be pasturin' in a new land be more ignorant than vicious—victims more I'd be thinkin' o'Blue-Ridge environs mix't with whut Young Wil here'd be referrin' to as heredity 'n ye old demon rum . . . their region was invaded-like by outsiders with dif'ernt idees. And-well, th' pore ignoramuses—they gotta be changin' er they're goners. Tempers flared when some Prim'tive Baptis' hiked up them hills t'tell 'em guns be a tool o'th' devil—'n a man caught aimin' one o'them tools at a brother, kinfolks er not, was predestined t' be takin' th' fire-stoker's hand 'n go Down There. No power on earth be able t'undo that—not even God."

There was an outcry of protest. But O'Higgin's powerful voice rose above it. "Now, ye gotta be rememberin' them mountaineers see their reflection 'n be believin' it—seein' theirselves as good folks who jest be misbehavin' onct in a blue moon . . ."

Not to worry, he declared. The believers separated themselves from "th' infidels" and, deciding they were "God's elect, chosen ones, baptized into heaven" before the Creator finished earth's foundation, up and got themselves out.

"But," and here O'Higgin's chest swelled with such pride that True feared the buttons would pop off his vest, "they're a-changin—shur'n they be! Ye gotta be rememberin' our Marty's where I be placin' him— right there in their midst—bein' no preachers thereabouts, 'n him 'n Midgie, praise be! jest up'n prayed 'n prayed 'til th' prayers be answered—they got it straight from above they gotta be fillin' in where them saddlebaggers leave off—you be knowin' 'bout them kind what used t'come through onct a summer—passin' th' hat—fervor dependin' on how much be put inside. Well, begory, t'God be th' glory! Onct our Marty be tongue-tied, 'n now th' words come a-flowin' like Moses struck th' rock!"

There was such a roar of shouts that True wondered which would go out the top of the building first—her sanity, or the roof itself, or, judging by his face, the Reverend William Prescott!

"Lots more t'be said—but ye, bein' devout like ye be, understan'—I kin tell by th' gleam in yore eyes thet a man bes' be sharin' with 'is family afore he goes spoutin' off too much. Some o'this is family talk—"

They understood, but with reluctance.

And now here they were, the family—the O'Higgins and the Norths. The setting, of course, was Turn-Around Inn. The weather had cooled mercifully, "'nuf t'thin th' blood," Grandma Mollie said. To which Aunt Chrissy had answered (with a secretive smile at True), "Yes, until we can get it thickened with fall's molasses."

A fire chuckled in the big fireplace. The kettle sang merrily of coffee to come. A gingerbread-scented woodstove made promises of its own. The newest litter of kittens tumbled in Miss Mollie's yarn, batting balls in unnoticed glee. O'Higgin opened his worn Bible, read selected passages concerning love, and called on Daddy Wil to pray. It all made a beautiful picture, one that would live forever in True's heart . . .

The rest of the evening was spent in one long soliloquy by O'Higgin.

"Brother, them Scotch-Irish be like unto yeself—'n thet be th' reason ye got so all-fired worked up, begosh 'n begory!"

The men were rugged six-footers—like unto the giants of Canaan who made the children of Israel look like grasshoppers, O'Higgin's monologue with himself began. Come to think of it, the story ran a heap like the Bible's account of spying out the Promised Land. Only it was King James who sent *these* giants out, well as the rawboned but "fertile as th' soil" women to America's shores. Supposed to intermarry and replenish the land with Protestants! Sad to say, they did more "fightin' than courtin'." They took up their muskets instead of their Bibles and did more washing down meals with stilled liquor than serving communion . . .

But the first immigrants were pure of heart—smart, too, sharper than a tack. They knew it was God's will that they build churches and schools. They knew rich land when they saw it, so settled in the valleys as pure and virgin as their women. All stuck together, helping offspring build cabins instead "o'pitchin' lots elsewheres." First crops were good but eventually the bottomlands could hold no more "'count o'them prolific girls a-marryin' at 12 or so turned out many as 30-some-odd wee lads 'n lassies."

So families pushed higher and higher up the mountains, where farmland grew more and more shallow, not near as productive as the womenfolk. By and by the folks up there got to be as uppity as the shallow soil and began a war of words, claiming 'twas God's will they eke out a living by the sweat of the brow. And that was easier to accomplish by using hoes "'mongst th' rocks 'n fern-feathered dells" than down in the bottoms where the oxen did all the sweatin'. The mellow soil produced enough corn for johnny ashcakes. Awful good with wild turkeys and acorn-fed coon meats. And already the trees were big enough to hide their whiskey stills—natural to have them, elsewise they'd be wastin' a lot of that corn as well as the wild fruits.

Each generation took them higher into the hills, where hunger prevailed. But they were too proud to admit it. They were deprived in other ways, too. No learning. No law. "No women fer th' lusty men with big appetites—so's they be gittin' theirselves all cantankerous t'live 'round." That spelled out the history of the intermarriages "'n worse."

By now the war of words had ended. Arguing was "ole woman's meat." Men wasted no time at it. "Shot other men dead 'stead." That was Giant Number One, a man's gun! The other was "th' Prim'tive Babtis' church—kinda germinated from th' Good Book, then went 'Calvin'—still makin' claim on Baptis', cuz o'th' duckin' required when they got religion." The shooting continued, as did the whiskey-making and the intermarrying "'n th' like, includin' concubines." Religion never changed a man's *ways*—just his heart. So the rest of their self-styled religion took its "proof" from superstition, dreams, and "visions" that they shared in white-faced fear. Now a body could shoot a blood-'n-gut mortal. But a ghost—well, now that was different.

The hate burning in their hearts shot its flames higher and higher among the mountaineers. Nobody dared invade their privacy. For sure, no trespasser would be coming back—except as a white-faced corpse. And that's where O'Higgin stopped, his face drained of all color. "'N that's what I be fearin's a-gonna happen t'my Martin-boy!"

The group tensed. Then, white-lipped, all tried to speak at once. After all, intriguing as this account was, it served only to give them insight into the tension between the two groups with whom they had dealt. It told them nothing concerning their own!

"Then you truly feel that Jeremiah's group is a threat to Marty?" Young Wil's question rose above the others.

"Could be—jest *could* be now." O'Higgin's near-bald head bobbed up and down, gleaming in the firelight like a polished marble. But True saw tears in his usually roguish eyes. He leaned forward, bracing his elbows on the still-open Bible, and cupped his bearded chin in the ham-sized hands. "Meself, I be takin' no pleasure in bearin' bad news—but best I tell ye I ain't feelin' tip-top 'bout me lad—er—"

"Midgie and the baby?" Aunt Chrissy cried out with seldom-heard alarm in her voice. "They're in danger too—was that what you were about to say?"

"O'Higgin! Don' you know better'n shatterin' all our nerves? You got no proof now—'n I'm not one bit sure the Lord takes a likin' t'such talk—less'n you *know*?"

O'Higgin looked remorseful but made no effort to amend matters, even though a scolding from his Mollie-Gal was more threatening than facing a grizzly bear.

True's thoughts deserted her body. She imagined herself in a tub of comfortably warm water, sinking into its depths, letting its warmth untie the muscles of her taut body. For a moment it worked. Then Daddy Wil's voice brought her back to the problem at hand.

"But if they're Christians, like they claim—"

"Nay, nay!" O'Higgin lifted a hand of protest. "I ne'er be sayin' thet—not onct did me ears hear mention o'Christian—jest Prim'tive."

"Well, they're that all right," Daddy Wil said crisply, "but they seem to know little about laying aside arms and repenting!"

"No exposure, shure 'nuf. Me lad be tryin', but he be no preacher— 'n then there be th' rascal namin' hisself Clarry's stepfather—reminds me—got a letter from th' bonnie lass fer Jerry—'n 'nother fer True—"

Jerry and True snatched for them hungrily.

18
Midgie's Letter

❧

ALTHOUGH THE HOUR was late, Mollie Malone O'Higgin busied herself in the kitchen of Turn-Around Inn. Hospitality kept late hours. A body just naturally felt better about matters when the tummy was satisfied.

"Skim the morning's milk, O'Higgin. This gingerbread behaved itself, all tender to th' touch 'n is deservin' th' richest cream."

The two of them argued, scolded, and laughed in their unique way which created the signs of a happy marriage. Jerry had taken himself upstairs, two at a time, in order to be alone with Clarry's letter. By now he would have read it three or four times. The two Wils were deep in conversation, eyebrows knitted in thought, voices pitched too low to be heard above the sleepy whisper of the dying fire. Outwardly it was a cozy scene, but the air was charged. A log shifted to break in half. The snap brought everybody to their feet nervously.

As the men sat down to resume their talk, True motioned toward a corner in invitation for Aunt Chrissy to join her. The up-ended logs sent a shower of sparks up the chimney, then burned like twin candles, making it unnecessary to light a lamp.

"Let's share Midgie's letter," True said quietly as she pulled two ladder-back chairs close together. Chris Beth waited in anticipation as True unfolded the three sheets of paper and smoothed them in her lap.

It was hard to read the squeezed-together words crowded so childishly together. True noted with a smile that Midgie had written on both sides, making the thin paper even more difficult to read. But she noted also that the language and the punctuation continued to improve.

The letter was so refreshingly "Midgie" that it was easy to forget the frightening news that was sure to follow. But at least the words started with the usual bundle of household news—another room added, a sunny corner papered with rocking horses and reserved for the March Hare ("we call him 'Christian' when we can remember"), next spring's bulbs planted ("you know how welcome they are in the confusing month of March, everything covered with dirty leftover snow, winds bitter and bound on taking out their fury on the world, all that mud . . . then up pop a million crocuses as numerous as stars, daffodils so gold and shining they almost sound their trumpets like Joshua's troops marching around Jericho seven times").

True paused to look at Chris Beth. Both were smiling, each knowing that tears of understanding were close to the surface.

Midgie, almost as if postponing the burdens of her letter, talked about the season at hand.

> I will never forget the beauty of autumn there. Marty and I will cherish the memories forever. But they are fading, no longer outdoing the special show of God's handiwork here. Remember, True, how fall days always look like a sunrise—the earth, the rocks, and the mountains declaring His glory? The whole world's a brilliant red such as described in Revelations . . .

Revelations. Midgie was working up to her own gradually. But first, didn't they want to hear about the family of friends there?

> Things were better for Tillie, the adorable March Hare's "Grandy." Midgie was uncertain which was a greater factor in the restoration of her sanity—love for her precious great-great grandson ("and, oh, lineage counts with Tillie Caswell!") or the come-to-stay arrival of Reverend Randy after Mr. Caswell's terrible fate. They were doing a lot to the store—

True wished that Midgie had gone on to tell more about their ministering to the newcomers. But instead she switched to other matters without indenting for paragraphs.

> Mariah and Billy Joe, the "Beetle" (True, noting Chris Beth's questioning eyes, took time to explain that he was once a bowlegged squatter who made claims of being Uncle Artie's foreman and did such a good job that Marty kept him on), had replaced their tent with a house. "A *real* house—well, a kind of lean-to, but cozy with a little-mouthed

fireplace and lots of wall hangings, all cobalt blue and turkey-red—colors that only Mariah could make like they belonged amongst the dresser with a cracked mirror, rag rugs, and strings of colored gourds mixed with red peppers and garlic! Mariah's so happy and keeps those knowing fingers busy sewing—her and Tillie—for the new folks—"

Once more, the letter stopped where it should have begun. There was news about each of the farmhands. And, oh, the best part:

Mariah was having them come for Thanksgiving—Augie, Tex (his new kind of wheat had done well and a government man was coming to take a look, might even buy some to recommend to a big seed company), Pig Iron, and Slim. All were modern-day disciples—how on earth could Marty do as much as he did trying to spread the Word without them? Not that Marty could do what needed to be done, but . . . well, back to Slim—his withered arm was on the mend and he was as good at breeding fine cattle as he claimed . . . oh, such longhorns, short-horns, Holsteins, Jerseys, and Ayrshires . . . right proud of them she was until the silly critters took to running like they were calves, trampling down her garden and the morning glories . . . good that roses had thorns. Of course, Slim was "getting on." That's why her heart was gladdened that he was seeing the Widow Grant even though the poor creature had her problems. Real plain woman, salt-and-pepper hair pulled back so tight that her scalp shows through. Tied up in knots, too, hands always moving, but it was plain to see that she was gone on Slim. Betrays herself by sucking her lower lip in every time she looks his way. Well, anyway, I'm going to ask her over for the holiday, too—a good start to get to know these strange new folks—hoping we can avoid trouble . . ." *more* trouble than they'd had. But who knew? Look how much trouble Abraham had finding ten good men. Did True suppose God might look with the same disfavor upon Slippery Elm in view of all this wickedness and destroy it like Sodom and Gomorrah? "Sin's great and grievous—like I'm about to tell you—"

True inhaled deeply and prepared herself for what lay ahead. Miss Mollie's interruption at that critical moment, although she was generally welcome in any circumstance, was a disappointment.

"I come in 'bout middle-way through, quiet as a mouse—was agonna tell our menfolks I'd added sourdough griddle cakes 'n maple syrup, it bein' so late 'n all . . . but," the older woman fanned herself with Midgie's envelope, "I got t' thinkin' thet's a good idee she's got, ain't it though? How's about we include them peculiar folks up th' mountainside? Yep," Grandma Mollie answered her own question, "we do it!"

"Begory! We do, me bonnie one!" O'Higgin, restored to his jolly self, boomed as he dumped a fresh armful of wood to rekindle the fire.

It was useless trying to read further. Midgie reluctantly laid the letter aside until they completed refreshments. Young Wil called Jerry, but there was no answer. When Daddy Wil suggested that boys this age needed a lot of privacy, his nephew nodded thoughtfully.

"Now," Daddy Wil surprised True by saying "I think I speak for us all when I ask that you share the rest of Midgie's letter with the entire family. I have a feeling we all need to know."

"I agree," True said woodenly. He was right. It was only that she, like Jerry, felt a sudden urge to be alone. Reluctantly she began:

> We don't know which way to turn. Things were bad before the new people came—and now it's so confusing we don't know who the enemy is. The militia is still here, our only protection. But they're more on the lookout for deserters and bootleggers—I do believe some of these men would make whiskey from other men's blood if they could afford the sugar! Mr. St. John—and saint he is, too, creating a library, only to have it torched—

A gasp went up from the listeners. "Burnt *books*! Thet be a downright sin in me mind. Think ye th' same? Best myself be there—"

"Best yuh be settin' yourself down, O'Higgin!" Miss Mollie declared, followed by a low-pitched, "But I'm beholdin' to yuh!"

The big Irish man poked the fire, then obeyed. "Go 'head, lass."

"Where was I?" True murmured, her mind more on Michael's new image than the loss. Books could be replaced—"Oh, here—" she said, a little embarrassed that she had allowed her mind to wander, "still talking about Michael St. John—"

> —thinks the railroad feud has died down. He's doing what he can to restore law and order, watches his men. But he can't be everywhere at once. Nobody can but the Almighty, and sometimes I think He's turned His back—what with all this cursing His Holy Name by some of these Appalachians. Why, True, they'll kill *anybody*—enemies, friends, kinfolks. The militia tried disarming them, but they crush skulls with sharp rocks. Oh, how they misquote the Bible (can't read it, of course) . . . and us with no teachers to educate them. No preachers to teach them about God's forgiveness and how to get it—and no doctors to patch up the wounds. So they bleed inside and out. Even the nonviolent Shakers have had to learn to shoot straight. That's where that sweet Clarry is—with Anna-Lee—or *was* till Virgil Adamson found her. The child ran here pale as a cauliflower . . . then disappeared. *Oh, how we need you . . .*

19
"Mica, Mica, Parva Stella . . ."

Exhausted THOUGH SHE was, True was unable to sleep when, as dawn was nearing, she lay down with senses spinning. Young Wil had insisted that she rest even though he and Daddy Wil had to respond to a call by a man who, faceless in the dark, waited at the gate of the Big House when they returned. "Hit's serious, Doc—Docs—needin' of you'ns—"

With a shock True realized later that she had heard nothing regarding the nature of the emergency. The words blurred together. Didn't these people realize that doctors' families had problems too?

"What should we do, Lord . . . *what*? Help us . . . we are stumbling . . . falling . . ."

A knock on the cabin door startled her. "Who is it?" she managed to mumble, feeling for her slippers.

"Jerry—" his voice came out uncertainly.

"*Jerry!*" True was wide awake as, barefoot, she hurried to lift the heavy board which barred the door.

"I—I heard part of Midgie's letter," the boy confessed.

"That's perfectly all right, darling—you're a part of the family," True assured him, managing to find a match to light the oil lamp.

"I know where she is," he said flatly.

"*Clarry?*" True whirled to face him.

He nodded without accepting her motion of invitation to sit down. "But I'm not supposed to tell—"

"You *must*—it could mean her life." True was having trouble breathing. Should she promise to keep her whereabouts secret? Bargain to get the truth? "*Tell* me, Jerry—*please*. I'll do my best to keep it between us—"

"With Kearby."

True caught her breath. "But how—I don't understand, Jerry."

He shook his head, face white with pain. "I don't either—that's why I have to go—Kearby can't keep her."

It was a delicate situation, one which should be faced with a clear head—certainly not by a person who was herself exhausted. *Think!* True commanded herself. *Move carefully . . . think before speaking. Let the Lord lead . . . if Jerry were convinced he knows best, would he have told me, when the girl's whereabouts were to be kept secret?*

At length True spoke. Did her words come out as thick as they sounded to her own ears? It was as if her tongue were too large for her mouth. "Sweetheart," she said slowly, "I know exactly how you feel, because I feel the same way—torn different directions—knowing that Young Wil and I need to be with Marty and Midgie, but needed here, too. I—I haven't had an opportunity to talk with anybody—so it's good that we can talk, just the two of us—think, plan, and *pray*—that's the first step, Jerry. We both know that."

He nodded while making a circle on the braided rug with the toe of his shoe. "You feel that way too—then you understand. But, True, I *have* to go to Clarry—don't I? I mean—oh, True—I *have* asked God— *why doesn't He answer?*"

True walked toward him. "Are you too big to be hugged, sweetie?" He made no objection, so with her arms about him in a comradely fashion, she was able to get the words out. "I'm guilty on that count, too, Jerry. We don't give Him time, really wait for an answer. We just make up His mind for Him. Remember the saying, 'Doubt is out'?"

Again he nodded.

Without warning the answer came—and in such a strange way that neither of them recognized it at the time.

The handful of pebbles tossed against the window could have been the gray-fingered dawn scratching to be let in by the two tense persons inside the cabin. The faces pressed flat-nosed against the panes were leering skeletons in the half-light.

Fright changed to indignation. Who were the intruders and why—

Jerry recovered first. "What are you doing here, Loren—Josiah—Billy Jack?"

The frightened faces withdrew, and their owners would have fled had Jerry not opened the door and commanded them to stop. "What's the trouble—why are you here at this hour?"

All talked at once. It was that new boy and his followers, Master Jerry (*Master Jerry?* True was intrigued by both the title and her young cousin's mature behavior). Bigger'n a growed-up man, they babbled, big knuckles he liked to use on littler kids. They said, "We—" more, but Jerry said, "Come on!" and, before True could collect herself enough to try to stop him, he was gone—the children at his heels. Taking a dark shortcut through the trees, the group was swallowed up in the now-pinking dawn. What was she going to tell Aunt Chrissy?

Why, the truth, of course.

Forewarned, True braced herself for the worst. And found it! The walls of the schoolroom were covered with brown spittle and the chalkboards were smeared with crude but explicit drawings. She would have to notify Mr. Prescott the moment he arrived.

Only he did not arrive. Instead there was a note on her desk stating that "business" had kept him away—and could they manage?

Anger boiled up inside her. Somehow he had known; nothing could convince her otherwise. This had gone far enough. Nate Goldsmith needed to know the truth—whatever it was—about William Prescott. Meanwhile, God would have to see them through this day. *Where was Buster?*

She found him quickly enough. The gawky giant-boy was sprawled at her desk, muddy bare feet crossed on top of her register. Sullen, insolent, vacant-eyed, the youth's swarthy skin covered with red pimples, he leered at her in a way that resembled pictures she'd seen of the devil himself.

"What are you doing at my desk?" True asked angrily. "Get your feet down *immediately*!"

Buster made no move to obey. "Nothin' else fits—wanna see iff'n ye're able t'make me move?"

"That won't be necessary," Jerry said from the door. "Move—*now*!"

Buster showed no signs of moving. True was dimly aware that this was a showdown of sorts, and that there was a large audience of spectators gathering—more than the sum of the three rooms added together. *More* students . . . from where . . . *Appalachia*? Buster was staring at her, daring her. But she ignored him, knowing that she must retain her composure. Knowing, too, that Jerry stood at the crossroads of his young life.

The overgrown bully looked mildly stunned. A woman not knuckling under was reason enough to raise the eyebrows, and an upstart kid ordering a he-man around was downright shocking. His bravado showed signs of weakening.

"Go chew yer cud, half-pint," Buster tried again, turning his attention back to Jerry. But "thet stupid kid glared at him!"

The onlookers laughed, causing indignation to flood his pudding face. Losing control, he began sputtering. Then, when the snickers continued, Buster's snake eyes narrowed as he stared at True. Why, he wasn't right, True realized. His eyes, slitted like those of a reptile, showed a sickness of the brain. He needed help . . . but Jerry needed protection . . . what was she doing here among the spectators?

But there was no time to move forward. Jerry had grabbed the muddy feet, flung them from True's desk, and—with a quick, fluid motion—grabbed the insolent intruder by the ragged collar of his dirty shirt. "Apologize for your bad manners. The lady's name is Mrs. North—or some of the pupils call her Miss True—"

"Thet ain't a-gonner be whut I call 'er—"

"Say 'I'm sorry,'" Jerry ordered, his grip tightening on the collar. "Say it *now*—if you want to draw another breath!"

And then came the surprise of True North's life. Buster cowered, his thin lips whitening as they shrank to a line. A snake. A *scared* snake.

"I—I—*let go*, yuh stumblebum—sorry I sed thet—*let go*—I uh— uh—cain't ketch a br-breath chokin'—"

"*Say it!*"

"I—I—did'n' mean nuthin'—Missus—jes' had—a—hanker'—t'swap out—'Howdys'—"

The mouth opened to reveal rotting teeth. The slitted eyes bulged. And his face turned a frightening blue.

"Let go, Master Jerry!" Chris Beth stood at the door, her composure reminding True from whom she herself had fallen heir to courage. Even in a crisis, Aunt Chrissy used a low voice in giving commands—also remembered to call her young son by a title of respect.

Jerry's grasp relaxed, but his eyes remained fixed on Buster, whose bluff had been called. What's more, he was in trouble—bad trouble. True felt her heart go out in pity for the bully whose image had tumbled. And now—

"I'm a gonner," he whined. "Thet man a-bustin' in's me paw, 'n he's pizen—he's a-gonna whup me—'n beat Maw 'cuz I ain't got me no brains—" Buster's entire body shook with fear.

"Whut's goin', shoolmarm? I brung yuh 13 a-needin' larnin'—'n don' see no hopes—better I line 'em up 'n thrash 'em one by one—"

The man's walrus mustache divided as he wiped tobacco from his chin. "Ain't got no sense—never learnt Latin 'n I heered ye cain't larn 'em—so's I best jest beat hit in—"

Jerry smiled, his composure regained. What he said was:

Mica, mica, parva stella,
Mirror quantum sis tam bella,
Splendens eminus in illo,
Alba velut gemma calelo.

"Well, I'll be a suck-egg mule—yuh young'uns behave!" The stranger removed his hat and flattened it against his belly, then stumbled out.

The rest of the day was unnaturally quiet. "I was proud of you," True whispered to Jerry at one point. "Twinkle, twinkle little star . . . My star's here—for now," was his reply.

20
Quiet—
and Then the Storm

❧

THE LINES WERE drawn. The children knew where they stood, and seemed comfortable with that. Discipline was something they understood. What's more, True felt an overwhelming relief that parents had learned to respect her, Aunt Chrissy, and Master Jerry. Mr. Prescott was another matter. He was still a question mark in their minds, as he was in True's. Why wouldn't a teacher—particularly a minister of the gospel—be seeking out these people, becoming acquainted? Why no home calls? Yes, she must talk with Nate . . .

But, True wisely decided, she would make no issue of the matter. An opportunity would present itself. And in the meantime she must fight the battles within herself. To be sure, the children were entitled to an education, a part of which was a better command of the English language. But how could she go about unsnarling their grammar while preserving their heritage, apart of which were their quaint, mystical idioms that was so much a part of themselves? "Paw, he's discomfortin' real bad 'n our meanness is a'tendin' t'worsen 'im" . . . "Come Sat'day last Maw went a'washin' body-cover clothes" . . . "Us'n cain't eat 'til th' noon-high sun sez 'tis th' dinner spell" . . . "Frawgs make music down by th' slough when they go courtin'." And, often as not, mixed in with what she had come to regard as their "hill talk" were such courtly words as "sires, dukes, and duchesses" occupying the "thrones" at their "gloaming supper."

Now that they had overcome much of their shyness, there was genuine desire shining in their bright (and often intelligent) eyes to mingle with the Valley children. But they shied away, sticking—in obedience to their parents' orders, True suspected—with their own clan, engaging in folksong games.

Gradually they attracted an audience. Well, could she help it if integration worked from the opposite direction? If only she could guide them into Sunday school through the local children. But for now a step at a time, True reminded herself.

Meantime, she made behavioral notes faithfully just as she made lesson plans which would include them all. She talked more with Jerry than with William Prescott, who had developed a peculiar twitching of the nose which would have been comical had she not suspected something serious as the cause, or Aunt Chrissy, who seemed preoccupied. None of them saw as much of the North men as they would have liked. But that was soon to change!

And meantime a letter came from Kearby. It bubbled with school news. Her grades were top-notch. She had made the girls' choir. There was to be a school party which boys would attend. And the head mistress was letting them wear bows in their braids . . .

True wished details were less sketchy about the co-ed party. She hoped it meant that Kearby was overcoming her fear, which had become a near-obsession since Clarry's ordeal (yet to be spelled out). But no word about Clarry herself. This, too, was destined to change. But for now there was relative calm. And the children were learning at a pace which surprised the two teachers, the teacher-principal, and his "vice-principal," Master Jerry. There was no change in those with learning disabilities, but they too had learned to socialize—consequently, were less disruptive. Even Buster. What a pitiful piece of humanity! The clumsy boy often came to school with purple rings around his eyes, obviously resulting from his self-described "long head" of a father.

"What should we do? I've met Buster's father, and he seems different—" True began, hoping for William Prescott's counsel.

"He *is* different," was the immediate reply. "A stubborn Scot. And, of course, we have a sprinkling of flinty Irish and close-mouthed Germans mixed in with the English gentry—"

"Yes?" True encouraged. But his mouth had clamped shut.

"I—we can ask O'Higgin to help. He'd love it. Then there's Nate's wife, who speaks German fluently—if you approve?"

He turned palms up. Why? Well, she would find out!

"You seem to know a lot about these people's background—"

"Yes," Prescott said bluntly and stalked out of the room.

All right. If he refused to cooperate, she would take the lead. Thanksgiving would be a good time. Which reminded her that Grandma Mollie wanted parents notified to come for dinner. She was already preparing, with help of the neighbors. Baking, mending . . .

It was a struggle getting invitations to parents. The children were overjoyed and labored over the notes with a dedication that was heartwarming. But to no avail. The parents, of course, were unable to read. But, even with the children proudly showing off their writing and then translating the words, the adults refused hands-down.

Bitterly disappointed, True made preparations for the holiday with her family and friends. Yes, of course, they would help, O'Higgin assured her, and agreed to show up Monday. "As fer their not bein' on hand fer th' Lord's celebration—well, now—iffen th' mountain ain't a-comin' t'Mohammed, Mohammed'll be a-goin' t'th' mountain, begory!"

"Yep, yep, thet we will!" Nate Goldsmith was jumping up and down like an undersized grasshopper. "Whar's thet principal?"

True motioned him aside. Nate trotted along behind her like a terrier about to receive a bone. Suddenly he spun on the heel of his boot, went back to pick up his loaded plate (although dinner was yet to be announced), and then joined her. They had the talk that True had planned. "Sumpin's mighty wrong—I sensed hit—" Nate said between nibbles. "Well," proudly, "I'll fix thangs—good!"

There were prayers and hymns. Disappointments dwindled. And outwardly the crackling fire and enormous bouquets of chrysanthemums, rivaling the color of the flames in reds and golds, spelled tranquility. But True sensed that it masked an undercurrent of premonition—one which she felt perhaps most of all.

"What did O'Higgin mean?" she asked Miss Mollie suddenly.

"We kin plan a feast fer school—maybe they'll come to thet—"

True was about to express doubt when the rumble of hoofbeats sounded and the air was split by a frenzied yell. A mountaineer man.

"Th' wound's opened up, Doc—one from th' gunshot—you gotta' be acomin'—you wuz right—bullet's gotta be tooken. Family's all riled—sayin' you gonna die afore Jim Haley. But I'm a-takin' you in—you 'n th' teachers here. They'll safen hit fer you. Comin' peaceable-like er do I hafta use force?"

A stillness fell over the great livingroom. Faces went rigid with fear. They were accustomed to hardship, but this was different. The people they loved most of all were in danger. And they were help-less. Even now, the stranger was fingering his coatpocket for a gun.

Already the doctors had their black bags in hand. Why the hesita-tion? True had recognized the man as the one who came for help at dawn the morning after Midgie's letter came. "Comin'?" The man's voice carried a threat.

"Of course—we're doctors," Young Wil spoke for them both. "But not the ladies!"

"It's all right," True said calmly. "They know us. Put away your gun, Sir!"

21
Death March

"CAIN'T NO ANI-MULE make hit up thet hill," the man's eyes, deep-set in their sockets, seemed to penetrate True's very soul. "An' ain't fair fer you city-gal women t'try."

Was he weakening in his decision? Her husband's life was on the line. She would beg if she had to. "We are pioneer women, Mr.—sorry, I didn't catch your name?" Bloodlines were important, making the question flattering—particularly when it was accompanied by a warm smile which turned on all the feminine charm of True North.

"Kimbell, Ma'am—Ryan Kimbell—'n" (hat in hand) "most call me Ry—'pendin' 'pon if they's friend er foe—'n you got yourse'ves a rep'tation of friend, but now I got hit 'pon my shoulders t'warn you, hit's damned iff'en you go'n damned iff'en you don't. Clear?"

"To us both." Aunt Chrissy's voice was steady, her eyes unafraid.

"Don't do this." Daddy Wil walked between them, taking each's arm.

"True is not going!" Young Wil's voice was a command rather than a statement. Their dark eyes locked.

"Wil North! Let go of me, there's no time to waste."

A grin of admiration creased Ry Kimbell's slim, weather-creased face. "Gotcha some gal-woman, man! 'N you better be grateful—whilst you try on savin' my brother's life, Miz North here's gonna be tryin' on savin' your'n. Fo'ks up thar trust 'er 'n I cain't say th' same fer you doctors . . . shudda done whut we tole you, bored a hole in th' skull 'n dug out thet lead—even iff'en hit meant 'is brains'd

461

leak out. No need fer a man's dyin' from a bullet, jest needed blood drained."

Chris Beth smoothed her husband's face and whispered something in his ear. Then, freeing herself from his protective grasp, she sidled back up to True. "We'd better waste no more time talking."

Already Young Wil was bringing the buggy that Jerry had hitched. "We'll follow your lead to the gap—then walk." True thanked him with her eyes.

"I'm a-bettin' my last sixpence all of you's not a-comin' back— but—" attempting a grin must have cost the man more than that, "I got me woodchoppin' shoulders iff'en they're needed fer survivors."

Sounds of their hasty departure drowned out the tearful farewells of those left at Turn-Around Inn and their promises for a prayerful vigil. There was not one among them who would not have changed places with their beloved North family, but reason told them that nobody hereabouts was qualified. God had given them special gifts.

"We shudda stopped 'em, blowed th' crazy man's head off," Nate Goldsmith was screaming, his words falling on deaf ears. His intended audience was already kneeling in fervent prayer. So fervent that nobody except Miss Mollie saw O'Higgin, Jerry, and Olga Goldsmith slip away to take a shortcut, unarmed but unafraid. They "spoke the language" of the Appalachians. Both meanings implied . . .

"I'd be cautious—hit's nippity-tuck your bein' able t'keep up—but I'm th' only hope you got," Ry Kimbell warned at the bottom of the climb. "A'ready we're on th' aidge o'dark-an' bear in mind hit's a death march we're on!"

Death march. The near-whispered words rose and fell in True's ears, filling the Valley with a dirge. But she squared her shoulders and, taking hold of her aunt's hand, motioned their guide ahead.

"Yea, though I walk through the valley and the shadow of death, I will fear no evil—for thou art with me . . ." *Lord, lead us!*

"Now," Ry said as he positioned himself in front of the procession, the ladies sandwiched between him and the two doctors who brought up the rear, "this trip don't pleasure me none."

It pleasures none of us, True thought, but saved her breath. The trail wound sharply upward, then became so steep that conversation was impossible. Several times Young Wil attempted to communicate in a low voice, breathing heavily. But True was unable to hear with her heart drumming like the muffled drum of the grouse. Her legs ached. She felt light-headed. And certainly her skirt was too long and too wide for the steep, narrow trail. It was all a bad dream.

If so, she, Aunt Chrissy, Daddy Wil, and Young Wil were to awaken suddenly and simultaneously. Back a way, True had been convinced that traveling conditions could be no worse. She was wrong.

There was the sound of churning water, tumultuous in its rush to the sea. So this must be where one of the rivers headed. There had to be a bridge—only there wasn't. Just an enormous log tossed across the depths without an anchor at either end. How on earth—?

Ry Kimbell's hobnailed boots saw him across and, surprisingly, the man offered a hand to Chris Beth, who reached to grasp True's, thus forming a human chain.

"Don' go lookin' down!" the mountaineer shouted above the roar of the water. "Th' logs is slippery-like, bein' barked in parts—keerful, iff'en you fall, there'll be a drownin' afore a shootin'!"

True gripped Aunt Chrissy's hand and felt her uncle's gentle hand supporting her back. He was trusting Young Wil to make it on his own. But, knowing her husband, True was sure that Wil's eyes were glued to his loved ones, readying himself to do whatever he must. She must try and make it. *Don't look down. Careful . . . catwalk . . .*

And then the log began to sway. A sudden dizziness overwhelmed her, the roar of the water below reminding her of the great height to which they had climbed. And then a piece of bark on which she had positioned her foot sideways gave way and the river rushed up to meet her.

"On your knees, darling, quick! Straddle the log—oh, would to God I'd had sense enough to leave you—"

Dimly, his voice penetrated. "Wil North—" True panted. And then she went down with a jolt that surely must have split her in half— one leg dangling helplessly on either side of the slippery log.

How her husband managed to bypass Daddy Wil, put his strong hands beneath her armpits, and all but drag her to safety would remain a mystery the rest of her life. As would the remainder of the death march . . . up . . . up . . . up toward the razor-sharp backbone of the mountain, with bottomless ledges dropping steeply from both sides.

And then the welcome sound of a rooster's crow! Something resembling civilization. *People*—never mind how dangerous!

A cabin loomed out of nothingness, unbarked logs, cracks chinked with mud . . . a pack of half-wolf dogs, and any minister would envy as large a congregation as was assembled, men wearing slouch felt hats, bibbed overalls, hands jammed in their pockets threateningly. Not a word of greeting. Something warned True to retain her silence.

The only light inside the crude cabin came from a sputtering candle which sent shapeless shadows in ghostly dance from the rough-hewn rafters to the bare floor. A man, white as a corpse except for a circle of blue on his left temple where the bullet must have entered, lay motionless across a straw-stuffed mattress.

"Is he—?" True swallowed the word, *dead*.

"In a coma—right, Doctor?" Young Wil addressed his uncle.

"Whet's that? Speak up so's we kin hear," one of the men ordered.

"Coma means unconscious, Mr. Kimbell—unaware of what's going on around him," True heard herself saying as the two doctor's examined the patient thoroughly. Aunt Chrissy, she noted in the unnatural silence, had opened the medical kits and spread the instruments on a sterilized cloth.

"The doctors will need a brighter light. Have you a lamp—uh—" Aunt Chrissy hesitated, then went on, "Which of you is Mrs. Kimbell?"

"I'll be answerin' fer th' widder," Ry interrupted.

True's chin shot up. "You'll do no such thing!" she said with spirit. "What's more, your brother's wife is *not* a widow. Chances are good she isn't going to be, if—" True swallowed and went on, "you call off your watchdogs and cooperate! Now—we need a lamp if you expect my husband and uncle to do the job you brought them here for."

Several of the men stepped forward threateningly, one reaching for a double-barreled shotgun lying across a moosehead rack. "Rest up, fellers, th' gal-woman's a real lady—a *teacher* lady, braver'n a wildcat. *Clara Belle!*" Ry Kimbell spoke with proud authority.

As the men looked on in awe, Clara Belle Kimbell answered, her body pressed against the wall. "Yessum, I have a lamp." The sweet-faced woman in a faded calico dress and no shoes on her feet stepped from the shadows. She slipped from the room with surprising grace that whispered of a better environment than this once upon a time.

There were no further interruptions from the bystanders. Teachers were smart, a whole "covey" smarter than doctors. They, not "medical quacks," were the ones what were to "larn th' young'uns."

And wasn't that the whole purpose of being here? So they could learn and take back their learning to Appalachia? Most teachers could "tote a tune."

Clara Belle was back, the rubbed-brass lamp she handed Chris Beth chasing the monstrous shadows away. "What more?" she asked through tightset lips which spelled fear and grief-in-restraint.

"Some boiling water, Clara Belle—I'm True, by the way—and some extra sheets just in case—"

"What else were you going to ask for?"

Without hesitation, True answered: "Prayer."

The next few minutes were critical. They determined whether her husband would live or die. Clara Belle knew it. And True knew that not only a man's life but their entire future lay in the hands of the two doctors. But they must be inspired by the greater Hand . . .

Clara Belle turned her back to stand in the corner in silent prayer. Young Wil took note, spoke a few low words of consultation with his uncle, and—motioning all others from the room—called the wife of the dying man to his side.

Outside a strange jumble of conversation was in progress, something akin to the Tower of Babel's confusion of tongues. Latin . . . German . . . English filled with idioms . . . and English in classic form.

True and Chris Beth glanced at each other in wonderment, while their ears were attuned to their husbands' simple explanation of the task that lay before them—praising the Lord for Jerry, O'Higgin, and Olga Goldsmith, who could communicate with the enemies-turned-friends.

Did Clara Belle understand that the bullet was pressing against *this* part of the brain? Dr. Wilson North, the senior doctor, showed the quiet woman a hastily drawn sketch. That removal could cause massive hemorrhaging? *But wasn't the young doctor here a specialist, writing a book on the matter?* Not exactly . . . he was doing a different type of research . . . but, yes, it would help, Young Wil tried to explain. *But they thought it was safe?* The eyes of the stanch lady were filled with confidence. They were gentle men. And she had prayed. So, "What are we waiting for? I trust you both."

"Your approval," Uncle Wil said quietly, a somber note in his usually jovial voice. "We are uncertain as to whether your husband can withstand the operation—and yet, if we don't remove the bullet—"

"He won't pull through? And if you *don't* operate?"

"He—what's his name, Clara Belle—did I hear you say Grady?" At her nod, Young Wil went on: "I have to tell you the truth, my dear, and I know the decision is hard. But you are a strong woman—you will bear up—" he paused to nod at True, his signal to embrace the brave woman facing the starkest alternative of her life, "so let me tell you that even if Grady lives, there may be brain damage— blindness—"

So sure was Uncle Wil of the wife's decision that he and Aunt Chrissy were pulling the lamp closer, adjusting the tasseled shade, and placing the instruments in order of their use. True's arms were folded about the woman, one of her hands wiping away the beads of perspiration from the cold forehead. Clara Belle turned pleading eyes to meet hers.

"You're a woman—what would *you* do, Mrs. North?"

"I would go ahead—*now*. Your husband is dying, my darling."

Clara Belle clung to her momentarily. Then, letting go, "Proceed!" she said loud and clear. "Mrs. North—True—help them. I'll pray—"

The rest was a horror story. People tried to crowd in, morbidly curious. "Stay out—all of you! You're using all his oxygen," True ordered. Outside, she heard Jerry, O'Higgin, and Olga's voices promising to explain every step providing they would stay put. They obliged.

"Razor—have to shave off the sideburns . . . antiseptic . . . ether . . . " True and Chris Beth handed the supplies from the table, each trying to breathe naturally as the sickly-sweet odor of the anesthesia closed around them. A first incision . . . an order for a sponge . . . forceps . . . and then the blessed words: "Close up! We're finished— and he's breathing!"

True came out of her reverie as she heard the men's voices outside burst into a hill-splitting shout. The crowd closed in—and her husband's arms closed about her. "You did it, my darling—you saw me through!"

22
Turning Point

❧

IN THE DAYS that followed, the seriousness of the circumstances under which Young Wil and his uncle had performed the life-threatening operation struck True with full force. How impetuous she had been, leading, as it were, the men to do the job at what amounted to gunpoint! Why, they could have been killed—all to save the life of a man they didn't even know. And for what reason? At times, an inner fire grabbed at her insides, squeezing, burning, rendering her almost helpless in a delayed reaction.

And then, just before her mind and body melted, it all made sense. Like a sudden parting of the clouds after a storm, the world righted itself. Her hope for peace gained sturdiness. Could it be true—the way God sometimes performed His miracles? Did He sometimes send out stern reminders that peace is a fragile thing, hanging from threads and pinned in a fear-conquering manner by small acts of love-in-action? The premise, then, was that peace was never rock-solid. But the underlying concept, God's love, had proven sound. It could be demonstrated only by human hands—hands that did His will. And hearts that endured?

Surely, yes!

The week after the ordeal brought a swarm of incidents to reveal that circumstances were dramatically altered among the mountaineers, and consequently between them and those in the Valley below.

"How is Mr. Kimbell?" True inquired of the children.

467

"Mendin'." It was Buster who loved to report. "Safe fer th' docs up thar now. Fo'ks aint' never 'lowed sech a'fore."

So Young Wil and Daddy Wil—probably taking turns—were making house calls. Why hadn't either made mention of this? But she knew why, of course: They did not wish to worry her and Aunt Chrissy. And, with a wry smile, neither did they wish to become "hen husbands" tied to their wives' apron strings. It was important that they nourish the new image of themselves.

"One day I will visit your homes," she promised instead, and was surprised at the look of amazement in the eyes of her charges, which now numbered 65! Well, thank goodness, most of them came from large families. "Maw'll be right proud," came from all directions.

"The children tell me that you plan home calls." William Prescott said one day as the children sat in circles (now mingling groups), having lunch. His tone registered disapproval.

"It is time—actually overdue," True said a bit defiantly.

"I wouldn't encourage it—you are often foolish."

Foolish? True felt a dart of anger shoot through her heart. "Why are you avoiding these people like the plague, Mr. Prescott?"

"William."

Her anger enlarged. "All right, *William*—what are you afraid of?"

His eyes took another arrow from his quiver. Then, spinning on his heel, the principal, now drained of anger, replied simply: "I am one of them."

Shock kept True from responding. And after that there was no time.

Christmas was nearing, and Grandma Mollie, unbeknownst to True, had assembled the Valley women together for quilting covers for the mountain folk. The ladies seemed better informed than True herself of their troubled history . . . starving for food back in the Blue Ridge country, both for body and soul . . . feuding between clans (some saying that one or the other groups had been responsible for the attack on the wagon train, its refugees now in and around Slippery Elm). Little solace they'd found here . . . just new entries in the catalog of catastrophes. Just more blood and sweat. Working on shanties with bare hands seven days a week . . . too proud to accept help . . . breaking around boulders that an earthquake couldn't budge . . . soil so "pore up thar" that it wouldn't produce enough for one square meal, planted as it was by hand around those immovable objects. Took a year readying the land and, discounting the bugs and varmints, there was the weather. A body could just about count on a frog-strangling rain to wash away what little soil they had.

"Well," Mollie O'Higgin said proudly, biting off the string dangling from the final knot of another finished quilt, "things are improvin', thanks t'them wonderful Norths, well as my Irish—not to mention Olga here! But we can't be settin' down on th' job now—come on—hep me hoist this quilting frame so's we can git another underway."

"They'll be comin'?" asked Bertie Solomon. "I'd have supposed their kind would be stone-deaf to invitations—"

"They're coming!" It was Chris Beth who made the announcement quietly from the doorway, where True stood beside her. The two of them had made the trip to share the good news as well as check on progress.

The applause was deafening—as was the jabber of what O'Higgin would have called a "roomful o'women all a'talkin' at onct, bless em!"

By gathering bits and pieces of the talk, True and Chris Beth were able to piece them together like one of the complicated quilts.

Plans were made. There would be food such as those pretty-eyed children had never before seen—and enough to take home. Since the school was neutral ground, there could be a brief program (maybe some Bible, although Brother Prescott had been behaving mighty strange lately, and rumor had it that those folks didn't take kindly to "educated preachers" anyway). But mostly there would be games with prizes! Clothes all wrapped up in disguise. Shoes which the Solomons said were just a wee bit dated. And more—bundles and bundles underneath the biggest tree in the forest. Couldn't be called "charity" this way. "Now, here's whut we're a-gonna do . . ."

"Can wars end like that—I mean—maybe we're expecting too much," True, ears still ringing, said on the way home.

"There could be a temporary truce—a start—" Aunt Chrissy's voice trailed off.

"Is something bothering you, Aunt Chrissy?" True had been concerned for some time now over the distracted look that her aunt wore.

There was silence as the buggy creaked on. "Aunt Chrissy—"

"What?" Chris Beth said with a start. "Oh, yes—it sounds fine."

True reined the horse to a stop in a shaded strip of woods. "We'd better talk. What's bothering you—other than our common concerns?"

Her aunt fidgeted, then answered slowly. "I—we almost never have time to talk. I—I was glad you asked no questions—but wondered why not."

"About William Prescott—I was wondering the same about you."

Chris Beth disregarded the question. "About Kearby—Thanksgiving."

"Her not coming home? I *did* wonder—but thought with only a day—"

"It was more." Aunt Chrissy's voice sounded almost sad. "Her excuse sounded flimsy—just a note saying she had a friend who came first."

True had never felt more guilty. Kearby meant Clarry—and she was bound by her promise to Jerry. She would talk to Young Wil . . . but, no, the promise included him!

"I'm sure Kearby meant just what she said," True murmured. Then, gathering strength: "She'll be here for Christmas. You'll see!"

Just how she was going to arrange that was beyond her at the moment, but arrange it she would. She would begin by talking with Jerry, then writing a letter to Midgie. Midgie! Guiltily, True realized that she had been in such a turmoil that she had not answered Midgie's letter—although the problems in Slippery Elm occupied equal time with the problems here. How did life get so complicated?

Now she broke the silence. "Aunt Chrissy—surely you aren't entertaining any idea that Kearby is—well, involved with some boy?"

Her aunt's head jerked erect. "Is there a possibility?"

"No!" True said flatly. "Don't ask me how I know. I just *do*. It's only that we are all so overwrought. It is easy for doubts and fears to creep in. Tell you what," she said brightly; "let's pray."

And, there in the shy-cathedral of the eternal evergreens, with the sun shining through the stained-glass windows of the autumn-painted maples, the two women clung to each other and prayed for the hope that endures . . . although, surely the Lord in heaven knew that it was theirs already . . .

True followed through with all her promises, writing a hasty note to Midgie, asking an update and promising a lengthy letter later, then concluding with a Midgie-like postscript: "Can't you arrange to visit us?" The opportunity to talk with Jerry came about naturally. He would show her the shortcut to the mountain settlement, he volunteered when she made mention of home calls. On the way, she asked him to release her from the irresponsible promise regarding Clarry's whereabouts. He was remorseful that his mother was worried. He would see what he could do. But, meantime, he was adamant about keeping the promise. A promise was a sacred thing. "Remember your wedding vows?" The question startled True to silence.

23

Revelations, Uncertainties—
and a Promise!

CLIMBING THE MOUNTAIN was easier the second time. The shortcut route was shorter, of course. But there was something more, something True would have been unable to define: a new source of strength, a stabilizing energy that quieted her heart and gave her the peace and strength to see her through the crises to come.

They stopped by the Kimbell cabin first. Clara Belle met them at the door, her features softened by the miracle which had taken place here. "Can you come in?" she asked a bit uneasily. "Grady ate his breakfast—and heartily—but I—I am doubting if you would care for cornmeal mush."

"Oh, we ate hours ago—and it's best we not disturb your husband," True said quickly, saving this gracious woman further embarrassment. "Actually, Master Jerry and I stopped in order to check on Mr. Kimbell's condition—"

"And," Jerry interrupted, "to invite you both to be our guests at the big school program—dinner, games, a program planned by your children. It would please us all so much!"

The woman cringed. Her lovely eyes turned toward a fleecy, lamb-shaped cloud that appeared to be grazing on a distant high meadow of sky. But she was not seeing the view. She was seeing some specter beyond True's cone of vision. "I went to such a celebration once—and the ladies wore lovely gowns—" Clara Belle looked down at her bare feet, trying to cover one with the other.

"You will wear such a gown yourself," True declared rashly. "The Solomons are too busy to make calls but want to do something special for you—"

Sheer joy flooded Clara Belle's face. "You mean—*clothes*?"

And then she seemed to fade back into an earlier century, a world of omens and witchcraft—a world that doctors and teachers could not comprehend. Bringing together the two worlds could only feed the jaws of evil. True had never before witnessed such a mixture of faith and joy, wiped out as one erases a blackboard.

And then an amazing thing happened. From inside, Grady Kimbell called out in an unbelievably strong voice, "We'll go—we owe 'em thet. An' count on th' young'uns—"

Some women would have wept, but Clara Belle said simply, "I'm obliged to you, Mrs. North. We will bring wild holly and mistletoe."

"Well," Jerry grinned as they turned away, "there goes my Christmas money."

True's heart swelled with pride, but she dared not risk a reply. Tears would embarrass Master Jerry, who was emerging into manhood at the speed of a bullet sure of its target.

"This is the Craytons' place," Jerry whispered when another cabin— shanty, really—loomed out of the trees. His announcement was verified by Sammy Joe's sudden appearance at the crazily slanted door.

"Teacher," he gulped, trying to swallow the chunk of cold cornbread he had stuffed in his mouth. "So'ghum!" He all but choked as he pointed to his mouth in an announcement he need not have made. Rivers of the thick, brown substance flowed down from each corner to drip on the bosom of his shirt. "Maw!" he managed to yell before going into a spasm of coughing.

True decided against entering when she surveyed the yard. Pigs wallowed in ankle-high waste—both animal and human. The stench was unbelievable as the morning sun sucked steam from the soggy filth.

Maizie Crayton, wearing an ill-fitting apron-dress, answered her son's call. "Ye be our brood's teachers, I'm a-s'posin'—stop tryin' t'show off, boy!" The woman pushed at her hair, which may have been combed a month ago, although True wondered about that. "Yep, we be a-comin' t'th' blowout et th' school. Glad we be thet they's larnin' stump'n more'n me 'n me ole man got knowin'. Las' church doin' we go'ed to didn'n make no mention of th' Almighty—jest ranted 'bout some feller named Calvin. I reckon ye be knowin' 'im?"

True mumbled some kind of feeble response, an overwhelming nausea threatening to take over. How could they contend with such living conditions? And she was expected to teach their children?

She would have picked up her skirts and fled down the mountain except that Jerry was steering her limber legs toward a tall, slender woman who stood in the yard of another shack, waving a hand in welcome, her beautifully cut features carving into an uncertain smile.

"I am Mrs. Courtland," said the lady, who in her ragged garments maintained dignity with a touch of regality. "You and my husband have met. Please come inside."

Courtland. Oh, yes, of course. The man who had come to school the first day armed. How in the world did he win this fair lady?

The children, so like their mother, ventured out—as tidy as they were at school, one part of True's mind thought as the other part wondered in surprise at the warmth and color around her. Everything was clean, spotlessly clean. A million questions flooded her mind. What had held them together—this strange group? There was squalor here, and filth—and yet there was also a certain grandeur that harked back to their pure-strain past.

One of the children brought True a chair. The child was, she realized, less at ease than her hostess. And Mrs. Courtland had noticed.

"You are wondering," she said gently, "what has bound us together?"

"I—I'm sorry that I stared. It—it's just such a contrast—"

A ray of sun came through the spotless glass of the east window, picking up gold lights in Amy's (she learned Mrs. Courtland's name later) crown of hair and bouncing back from a pewter pot filled with colored leaves. "Our proud heritage, I guess—born and bred in us—a sort of snobbishness, really." She laughed softly. "Imagine my choice of words—snobbish—when," her soft voice took on a distaste as if she had bitten into bitter fruit, "we would be begging were it not for our stiff-necked pride. Oh, Mrs. North, help our children see what our ancestors saw." Amy leaned forward in her intensity. "You are our last hope—you, your family—and I should like to include the teacher or preacher—which is Mr. Prescott?"

"Both—and I regret that he has been unable to call—"

"So do I, not that he would have been welcome by some."

True drew a deep breath. "He seemed to sense that. May I ask if you know why, Mrs. Courtland?"

"Amy—and I should like to address you as True. It gets so lonely for me. Seeing you is like—well, going home—being with my own kind. I know that makes no sense—"

"It makes all the sense in the world—Appalachia being home to you, then coming into another—well, culture. You see, my mother and my aunt came from Boston after attending school in Atlanta." True told her then about her mother's diary, how two young girls had come to the American Frontier with romantic notions, only to feel lonely and homesick. She stopped short of mentioning more, and ended instead by telling of her own search for her roots in their homeland.

Amy's eyes were shining. "Yes," she said dreamily, "I confess that I miss the Blue Ridge, but it goes back farther back to the courtyards where lords and ladies strolled through formal gardens . . . drifting away in the misty past of the moors. I hear ballads that I have never heard but somehow passed down to me in these few heirlooms, ancient letters, and stories told and retold through the generations when there was no question who God was. You see, True, we are not all repulsive. We have blue blood flowing in our veins."

"Oh, my dear," True protested, "I never thought of you as such! The God you knew then is the same now. It is ourselves who in one form or another draw a curtain between. Maybe we can rediscover that lost past together. Originally, the purpose of education was to teach children to read His Word—and, in your way, you have tried to preserve that. Even your men want that back. I am so glad that we had this illuminating visit—it's like—well, walking backward into the past—"

Amy Courtland rose slowly from her chair and glanced through the back door. For her husband? Perhaps it was time to go, True suggested. But Amy detained her with a timid hand placed on the cuff of a simple blue dress that True wore. "Lovely—" she said, and then: "Not backward, but forward, like seeing more clearly through the glass that Paul wrote about—catching a glimpse of what was, yes, but what is to be—if we can bring them together. I want to move forward—"

True nodded. "Yes, take a stand as you have taken in accepting our invitation to the Christmas festival."

Amy smiled radiantly in anticipation. "We can hardly wait—even my husband, who, as you know, is a master at 'taking a stand.' But wasn't it Oliver Wendell Holmes who said, 'It's not enough to take a stand; we have to know what direction we're going'?"

True nodded. How wonderful to meet someone here who spoke her own language! And, strangely enough—as is always true when people open their hearts to one another—she was learning much from this woman. "I believe," she said slowly, "that it's possible to go forward without letting go of the past. It is the Bible which has shaped our lives—and, even though most of its foundation is built on the past, its truths endure. After all," she tasted the words and found them sweet, "it is our common heritage. Isn't our culture somewhat the same—coming back in little glimpses that bless our lives?"

"Precisely. And I hope, dear True, that you will remember and preserve the good in us—bits of our language in poetry and song—forgetting the crudeness—when we are gone . . ."

"*Gone?*" True's mouth felt dry with disappointment that she would have felt impossible just an hour ago.

"You surely must have known that was our plan—to learn from you and have you teach our children so we can take it back to our people?"

Had she known? True found it hard to remember. But suddenly she wore a new yoke, that of preparing the children as *missionaries.* It was a tremendous responsibility—almost terrifying. But hadn't Jesus promised that His yoke was light? Joy replaced the terror.

How little did she know that the next stop was surely arranged by Satan himself in an effort to wipe clean the slate of her buoyant spirit, to rob her heart of its joy . . .

"One more stop," Jerry said. And, in her state of euphoria, True did not protest.

An older woman—tall, gaunt, and angular, with once-lovely golden hair now snarled and twisted like a rope around her head—met True and Jerry at the door in answer to their knock.

"Yeah? Whatcha be wantin'?" she asked suspiciously.

Jerry explained their mission, to which the half-hidden face lighted up. "So ye be comin' to' call? An' git th' lowdown on folks up'n th' mountains, I betcha. Well, now, I be th' one ye best see," she said, her gossip-loving tongue licking the thin, pale lips. "Bes' ye set a spell. Ned, he be gone, so git askin'!"

The children slipped inside, sticking their heads in curiously, only to be ordered out by their mother. "Yer paw's a-gonna be late. So set y'se'ves down without a peep 'n git eatin'."

The children sat down at the rough-board table without ceremony—taking no time to wash up, although there was a basin by the back door. Memories of the pigs came back, and True longed to leave but felt herself being pushed into a rickety chair without invitation.

"Jest as well yuh know th' truth. Me—I be knowin' a heap 'bout both bunches, meanin' them whut lef'. Bad—really bad, thet mess—a whorin' bunch, even 'mongst theirse'ves! I be scarred by th' mem'ries they lef —men usin' li'l-girl folks lack they wuz women—'n all th' while a-claimin' to'be full'a religion. Course some of 'em wuz trespassin'—comin' in whur they had no bizness t'git loose of th' lawmen. Take thet 'un whut raped a chile—crippled 'un—'n married th' mother cuz she wuz a-gonna be birthin' a bastard-chile. Musta knowed it'd be a girl he cud be usin'. Got 'erse'fshot—th' woman—'nkilt in th' gun battle a-comin' hereabouts, I heered—hate 'em all, we do, but," she rolled her colorless eyes, refusing to meet True's penetrating gaze, "we live by our own code so didn' have nothin' t'do with th' attack—"

True found herself wondering about the truth of her statement. No longer in a hurry, she leaned forward, every muscle tensed. "The man—the trespasser—what was his name—Mrs.—?"

"Trevor—my name, thet bein'. As fer 'is name—let's see, I be forgettin'—but I'm recallin' a name. Coulda been 'is wife-woman's er her bastard-chile—'twas C-C—I be' forgettin'," she sighed, "too much biz'ness needin' me here."

The Trevor woman was hedging, but she had given True what she wanted to know. Her concern now was for Jerry, but his mind seemed to be elsewhere. The girl's identity would hurt—in case it was Clarice—

"Is there something we need to know here, Ma'am?" he asked politely, causing True to exhale audibly. All clues pointed to the awful truth.

"Oh, lots. One of yore chi'drun down there—ain't saying' who, mind yuh—saw with 'er own eyes th' hangin' of 'er maw. Th' Paw bein' a real devil cuz of strong drink—even a-threatenin' t'do th' same thang t'li'l ole Lucy iff'en she so much as breathed a word, sayin' he'd toss 'er body on top of th' grave fer raven food—"

It was Jerry's turn to become sick. True saw it in his eyes. And his nostrils were actually turning green. But Jerry shook his head. "Why," he asked, spreading his fingers apart and looking at True desperately, "would God let that happen?"

"It's hard to understand, darling. I get confused myself—but we have to remember that God doesn't *want* it to happen. But there's so much wickedness in the world and we are here to help Him combat it—"

Mrs. Trevor snorted. "He's forgot us—ain't no way t' com'cate with 'im, cuz we forgot 'is language—thet's why we gotta be larnin' Latin. Yep, thet's our deadliest sin—we up'n forgot 'is way of talkin' so th' Almighty paid us back good 'n planty. Jest plain forgot us fer punishment—we're all doomed fer th' fiery furnace."

Deep emotion swept True's mind and body, shaking her very soul. But how could she respond? *Put the words in my mouth, Lord.*

"God understands all languages, Mrs. Trevor," she said slowly. "All He wants to hear is that we are sorry for our sins—and that we love Him and will serve Him—then some of these things will not happen—"

The woman's mouth gaped open. "Now, how kin thet be?"

Jerry's color was back. "Because," he said with a bold lift of his young chin, "we will all love one another as He loves us. *But*—" Jerry hesitated, seeming to sense that it would take more to convince these people, "as for the Latin, we are teaching it, and maybe one day we can send a minister back to the Blue Ridge country—"

A look of horror crossed the angular face. "'N git 'im kilt? A ed-ja-cated preacher—back thar? I cain't begin t'tell yuh how many's buried in th' chestnut groves—with no tombstones. Which reminds me," her eyes brightened like a vulture having found a bountiful supply of carrion, "rumors got hit thet a few slipped outta them hills 'n is plannin' on goin' back totin' them big words. Know anybody fittin' thet mold? Could be a—teacher—er—well, speak up."

True's heart missed a beat. And surely her body was sheeted over with ice. One wrong word and William Prescott would become a missing person right here in their own Valley . . .

It was past midnight when Young Wil found True propped in bed trying to concentrate on lesson plans. "Darling!" he exclaimed in surprise, "those violet eyes should be shut, proving you're in slumberland." He came to lie on his stomach beside her. "What's the problem? Don't deny it—I see it on your face—" and then his arms were around her, "Oh, little sweetheart, I've made you cry!"

In that tender moment he let her sob out her account of the day. "Oh, maybe the man who monitored our tests was right in questioning us about being sure we belong here," she said at last. "*Wil North, you knew!*"

"About it all," he said smugly, then with a kiss, "We'll have the best Christmas ever!"

24

A Most Amazing Christmas

THE BEST CHRISTMAS ever? True and Young Wil were to remember his words forever. In a way his prophecy was right—one brimming with wondrous amazement, as if the Star of Bethlehem's beams had led the mountain people into the Valley and stopped immediately over the school. Steeped as they were in superstition, half-truths, and folklore, it was an omen once the events of the evening came to a close. And to them the "larnin' place" would become forever "Th' Church of th' Nativ'ty."

That was the miracle—the miracle which made the world shine briefly with "best ever" glory.

But it was an evening filled with perplexity as well. "Fear not . . ." the angels had sung. But it was raw fear which clutched at True's heart—no, she mustn't feel like this, else the Baby Jesus would have been born in vain. Somehow she must achieve a certain peace. "Lord—oh, Lord, my God," she whispered over and over as the evening unfolded, "stay with me—see me through . . ."

The crowd began congregating early. Before dusk the auditorium was overflowing, the guests spilling outside and not seeming to mind as the black-velvet of the Christmas sky was lighted by a million brilliant stars, twinkling as if to upstage the Star which had led them here.

True had a blurred-together impression of candles glowing among sweet-scented evergreens . . . children's eager faces scrubbed until they were as rosy as apples . . . and a general milling of friends and

480

strangers offering to help the Valley people set out the makings of a feast. There was a feeling of breathless waiting—anticipation—which seemed to hark back to the hills of Judea.

But where was William Prescott?

"It's imperative that he be here," True whispered to Aunt Chrissy. How glad she was that she had shared the mixed emotions of the home calls. Somehow her aunt had a way of coaxing her gloom to fade, even wiping away her fears of inadequacy by repeating her own misgivings as a beginning teacher. And, as for her fears—well, yes they were well-founded. But one did not run from them. God had an oversupply of ivory-tower dwellers already. And now, Aunt Chrissy was speaking as calmly as then.

"Yes—if our program is to go the way we planned," she smiled, "but" (and she consulted the small, enameled locketshape watch pinned to her shirtwaist blouse) "there's plenty of time. He could have been delayed—"

"*Way*laid, you mean!" Jerry said in a small voice. "Mr. Prescott promised to be here early—and he always keeps his promises."

Jerry had behaved so calmly when they visited among the mountain people. Why was he so nervous now?

"Teacher, I cain't git these angel wings on straight—do angels hafta have wings?" True's fingers trembled as she helped adjust the wings. And then she, Chris Beth, and Jerry were surrounded by excited children who eyed with longing the giant fir decorated with Miss Mollie's gingerbread men. "When'll we eat 'em?" "When do we have supper—before or after the program?" "Why are we so late?" "Teacher—I—I—forgitted—*forgotten*—my lines 'n my paw he'll be hoppin' mad—oh, I 'member. Let's git startin'!"

Outside, the flaming fire had dwindled to brilliant red coals. Just right for setting the coffee to boiling. But the program was to precede the meal, and there was still no sign of the principal.

"Get your father, Jerry," Chris Beth said quietly. But there was a note of urgency in her voice.

Both doctors responded to the summons. Yes, it was odd. And people were getting restless. The O'Higgins were keeping up a lively conversation. But for how long? Yes, it was best to switch plans, have the meal first.

Jerry made the announcement and the shout of glee was reassuring. Maybe things weren't that bad after all, the teachers told each other in an effort to shake off the feelings of apprehension.

"Did ever y'see people so hungry? Fine thang, th' board's decidin' t'feed th' multitudes." Nate Goldsmith had managed to shoulder his way through the people who stormed the table, most of them refusing to stay in an orderly line. "Yep—good thang—"

He waited just long enough for a compliment. When none came, he blurted out the matter which had brought him to True's side. "Now, whar's thet principal of our'n ? He's done a heap a peculiar-like thangs," Nate paused to wipe gravy from his chin with the back of his hand, "but this 'un takes th' prize!"

True was able to move away when one of the small boys, too young for school, tugged at her skirt. He just had to "go"—and would it be all right to "git 'hind a bush cuz hit's dawk 'n people's cain't see. Nate grabbed a small, uplifted hand and hurried him away.

That gave True a chance to rush to her room. Why hadn't she thought of it before? Maybe—just maybe—William Prescott had left a note again. That was most often his way of dealing with situations.

She was right. Propped against her desk copy of *Elementary Latin for Teachers* was a bulky envelope bearing her name.

Quickly she turned up the wick of the kerosene wall lamp, tore open the flap, and read the first line, stared at it with disgust, and thrust the pages under a stack of spelling papers to be graded. Her face was flushed with anger when she hurried back to the group, where the women were hastily picking up the remains of the meal and packing them into containers for the guests to take back with them. The games were already in progress.

There was a general state of confusion as children played the musical-chairs game, the winner of each stop of Mr. Beltran's harmonica being allowed to open a package of clothing. True welcomed the opportunity of organizing the squealing children and their excited parents into something resembling order. It helped her work off the fury churning inside her. And by the time the game (in which everybody won a parcel) ended, the fury had turned to fear, triggered by a fragment of conversation reaching her ears above the pandemonium. Two men, whose faces she was unable to see, were whispering.

"Yep, thet's th' way I heered hit—sad-like, 'ceptin' he 'ad hit comin'. He's been astin' fer hit fer a long time—"

"Agreed—but, whut a hor'ble way t'be leavin' this ole vale of tears—swingin' by th' neck like he wuz. Pore man, rest 'is sinful soul, wuz 'lowed t'hang thar still breathin' fer hours, 'cordin' t'reports—yuh know, dyin' by inches. 'Course he 'ad it comin'—"

The voices drifted away, leaving True frightened, remorseful, and sick . . . *sick* . . . had she ever been so nauseated? That's when she prayed as she had never prayed before. "Oh, give me strength to get through this, Lord. Surely something good can come of this . . . let us somehow get Your blessed message of love across to these lost souls. . . ."

Dead, William Prescott is dead.

The words pounded at True's temples as Jerry maneuvered the children through the Nativity Scene while parents, caught up in a spell, leaned forward in pride and wonder. If the young actors stumbled over their lines, nobody noticed. It was the first time their parents had seen their own children perform—and, for most, the first time they had heard the message of Christmas.

God is at work here, True's heart whispered one moment. The next, it harked back to the dark world into which He had sent His Son. *Dead, William Prescott is dead . . .*

Olga Goldsmith rose to play the secondhand piano which the church had found at the Saturday afternoon auction in Centerville. The Jericho Singers, the all-male chorus formed by the church, followed. Moments later their voices filled the church with carols with what Grandma Mollie often described as "awful majesty," bringing tears to the eyes of the listeners. And then—one by one—the listeners joined in the singing, bodies moving slowly back and forth in a strange rhythm, known only unto themselves, their eyes closed as if seeing another Christmas, one so different that it could have happened in Appalachia—or beneath the silent stars of Bethlehem.

So caught up was True that again she forgot the terrible present. An inner voice seemed to be proclaiming that things would never be the same. The people, including the scoffers, had begun the long journey home—ready to savor the splendid misery of the climb.

And so their hearts were prepared for O'Higgin's reading—not the account of the Holy Birth, for they had *witnessed* that, but Isaiah's prophecy of God's Gift which offered freedom from captivity and salvation to a world "as filled up with sin as this very night—'nuf t'make a body shake, lest he be of a mind t'hear!":

For unto us a child is born, unto us a son is given; and the government shall be upon his shoulder; and his name shall be called Wonderful, Counselor, The Mighty God, The everlasting Father, The Prince
of Peace . . .

"And t'think He be born lovin' th' likes o'me—'n all of ye, good
brothers—th' whole wicked world." O'Higgin closed his worn Bible,
tears of joy streaming unashamedly from his merry blue eyes. *Oh,
praise the Lord for O'Higgin—and for the person who had presence
of mind to invite him to fill in tonight*, True whispered in her heart.

Young Wil. It had to have been Young Wil. He always knew how
to right the world when it spun off its axis. And hadn't he said this
would be the best Christmas ever? The stream of people pushing their
way forward to pump the Irishman's hand proved him right. What
could they do to help? How could they find out more? Was it true
that the Bible he read from "tole hit same as in Latin"? That being
so, maybe they had ought to learn reading, too, not waiting for the
offspring to be spreading the gospel. And was it true—"Swear on yer
maw's grave"—this gift was for everybody, even women and children
who could be mighty ornery?

Overcome, True slipped out the side door and into her room. The
wick had burned out, extinguishing the light. True shivered as she
fumbled for a candle and then a match. How could it be so dark when
there burned in her heart such remorse that it threatened to ignite?
How the words seared, scorched, and pained. *Dear True: I deeply
regret that I will be unable to attend the program. It is better this
way . . .*

Better! When hours later he was swinging from a tree?

Laughter, unrelated to mirth, clutched True's throat. "I laugh because I must not cry," Abraham Lincoln had said.

And then a hand reached out to touch hers in the darkness . . .

25
Aftershocks

❧

THE TOUCH ON True's hand must have been startling, but she had no clear memory. No memory either of her husband's concern when he caught sigh of her face after he had lighted the lamp. But the words in William Prescott's letter would linger forever . . . at first to shock her, then to haunt her, and later to take a place in the orchestra pit of her mind as an overture to introduce an unfolding drama—a drama with climax after climax, seemingly without the usual falling action which led to an ending.

"What is it, True? What has happened, my darling?"

Without awaiting an answer, he gently removed the letter from her trembling fingers. "Sit down," he pleaded, "and try to relax. Everything's under control—people are filing back up the mountain. There, hear the singing, the caroling—darling, *please* sit—"

Young Wil pushed her gently into the chair at her desk. "I'll read it aloud if you wish. I've a hunch it's from Prescott. Right?"

Yes, and he's gone—forever. You'll be reading the words of a dead man. That was what she wanted to say but could find no voice.

Maybe it would be better if she never knew the contents. No—what was it Aunt Chrissy said about God's having enough ivory-tower people already? If she had a part in his demise, she would never forgive herself. Yet if she never knew, she would feel equally guilty.

"Read it," she said at last through stiff lips. "I have to know—"

"'Dear True: I deeply regret that I will be unable to attend the program. It is better this way,'" Young Wil began, pausing where

485

True had left off, his brow puckering. "We could wait if you aren't up to this."

"I'm up to it," she said, feeling stronger. He read on then, his voice never faltering but his head shaking in disbelief at points.

You are more capable of facing the audience than I. In fact, I would fear for my very life, as I have no way of determining who among them are friends, if any, and who are the enemies. For, yes, I have enemies among the mountain dwellers, people sent here from the Blue Ridge country to spy me out and bring me home for punishment. Don't ask me why an education is a sin—it just is, like trying to escape and "mate-up with a furriner—jest lack th' Good Book warns 'gainst." Can you imagine my suffering, True? I am asking no sympathy, mind you, just begging you to understand.

My father was what is commonly called a "liquorhead"—hard-working when he was sober, but that was seldom. And a real devil when he was drunk, cursing and beating my mother. She forgave him, saying it was Bible-like to forgive. And we little ones believed her, saint that she was. The child of a minister who harked back to more enlightened times, she was less superstitious, more steeped in the true meaning of the Bible and better educated than those around her. "William," she used to whisper as she heard my prayers at night, "you have a fine mind. If something happens to me, take the cash I have put away from the egg money and use it for an education. You are different. You can change this place, put it back together for the Lord. I have dedicated you to Him, promised. So your destiny is pre-ordained. I will watch from heaven—"

I used to cry myself to sleep about that. Lose my mother? It was unthinkable. What would I do? She was the only one I could talk to, the only one who loved me, the only one who cared. Imagine growing up with eight brothers (most brandy-drinkers like my father) and five sisters who were afraid to speak aloud. But I could dream. Wasn't I pre-ordained to melt down the golden calf of their drunkenness and absolute love of bloodshed? Oh, the blindness of it all. You see, the mountain folk gloried in their "religion," calling the senseless killing "pleasin' t'th' Lord—regular human sacrifice." That was just the way the world was, one tired-looking lady told me when she caught me crying after an emotional funeral—God's plan, and nobody could change it.

Oddly, my father made no objection when Mother started me to Sunday school. Hetty Amerson didn't know any more than I did, he said after two drams of brandy and just before he'd reached the beating stage. So he guessed the teacher'd not be "contaminatin' my mind with notions of changing things. Only the ignorant could praise the Almighty." Learning was sinful. It was trying to steal God's wisdom, so man could take control.

I guess I didn't learn a lot from Miss Hetty, except about David. He was my hero. I made myself a sling, gathered up a secret pile of stones, and waited for a giant (the devil himself, I guess) to hack his way through the bushes past the whiskey stills so I could destroy all evil. As the years passed, with no giant appearing, I grew weary of waiting and gave more thought to my well-meaning mother's plans for me. But the call I was supposed to hear never came—or maybe I wasn't hearing it above the gunfire, cursing, and screams of heartbroken widows on weekdays and the drunken shouting of the Primitive Baptists in response to a "Revival Preacher" (unordained) who confided to me that he had to "get gloriously drunk" to keep up his courage. But he did know how to read, and he taught me secretly. I wondered why he never read the Bible, but he explained that he had it memorized—only would be "shot down" if he quoted from it "proper." True or untrue, I will be forever grateful for his "You can do it, Sonny, you being a lot quicker than the others. And, as you know, there's only two kinds of folks—the quick and the dead."

And then my mother died. It still hurts remembering but I've managed to put it all behind me except her last words, "Remember, William—remember." I promised. That night my father went crazy, drank brandy like it was lemonade, while I shrank in a dark corner and wondered if he would beat her after the spirit had left her body. But he worked off his frustration by hammering together a pine coffin for the burial, then joined his cronies in the tobacco dryer in a game of strip poker. When he'd gambled away our last cent but refused to strip off his long johns, one of the men shot off his mouth and then his gun. That meant a double funeral—biggest one ever. Thousands came to the celebration, some on foot. Some of the bereaved (kin counting down to thirtieth cousins) had to camp outside, and I could hear their moanings and groanings all the night before. The women kept it up as they dished up food following the "divine experience" of the two of them going together. The men, of course, had finished their wailing, having uncorked a jug for getting brandy-eyed. That was the day that set me wondering what life was all about. How could God love us and yet will these things to happen, while some said it was pre-ordained before Adam was formed and others just laughed at their bloody hands, saying they'd helped the plan along? I slipped out and sat under the sweetgum tree and prayed the best I knew how. And the answer was that this was wrong. But I heard no voice thundering from heaven. It was left up to me what to do about the money in the sugar bowl. I realized finally that I had no choice. Everything was pre-ordained . . .

"Poor William—if only I had known," True whispered at that point. Visions of a hanging body, gasping, and then going limp tore at her heart. As if the rope were about her own neck, she could say no more, need as she did to share her suffering.

"There would have been nothing you could do, True."

Her voice came then in rasping gasps. "You—can't—can't mean it was—*pre-ordained?*"

"Of course I don't mean that! I mean that the man had to find his

way, make his own choices. Forgive me if I sound abrupt, darling.
It's just—well, I believe that we should stop here—"

True shook her head vigorously. Young Wil bit his lip and read on:

And so I ate of the forbidden fruit from the sugarberry bush growing
in the graveyard just to prove to myself that I wouldn't die of dysen-
tery. But I felt sick and ran, stepping on graves in my haste—then
running faster when I remembered that this would bring their ghosts
back to get me. You see, I didn't believe these things because God was
in charge; but I could not escape the superstitions of my childhood. I
am still afflicted at points. I guess your husband will understand that,
being as informed as he is in the workings of the human mind. But I
am not paranoid. I know my life is in danger and that it has been since
I slipped away wearing a hand-me-down suit with red suspenders
which caused the other students to laugh when I entered school.

You know the rest, the important parts, at any rate. You've heard
it from the pulpit. And, as you know, I was never an inspired minister—never able to bring the gospel message. Maybe, I decided, the
Quaker girl I loved was right, the Voice I thought I heard being that of
my conscience at having failed my mother. Why not try teaching for
awhile? But it wasn't right either. And then when I saw my people
again, it came! I knew what I had to do—do now before I was killed.
I must go back and try to get the message of God's love across. Yes, I
know the danger, but I am willing to lay down my life . . . I can no
longer be a Jonah . . . God has found me . . .

"Why, thet dumbell—crazier'n horseflesh! I allus knowed he wuz
queer in th' head. Expectin' us'll be organizin' a searchin' party—
thet's whut—'bout as apt t'happen as bein' bit by a snake with four
legs!"

It was Nate Goldsmith. True, eyes closed and face covered by her
hands, had been in another world, totally oblivious to the one which
briefly she and Young Wil had escaped. Neither of them had been
conscious of the silence outside nor the quiet footsteps which brought
an audience now lost in the shadows beyond the pale halo cast by
the flickering lamp.

Without looking around, she answered now, tonelessly and without emotion: "William Prescott is dead."

The blue haze, as William had described the mountains of his
childhood, closed in around her. The room was alive with the sound
of voices, voices filled with questions. But to True the world lay
hushed, the spirit world more real than the cosmic one over which
man had dominion. *Or did he?*

"True, True darling—look who's here!" Young Wil was gently shaking her shoulders. "*Look!*"

But she was unable to turn. "They hanged him—others found him—swinging from a tree—"

"Who be ye talkin' of, lassie? Be ye meanin'—"

O'Higgin was unable to continue. "Leave th' lassie be," he said at last. "She'll be a-sharin'—oh, could ye be meanin' *he*—he be Brother William?"

There were more questions which True was never sure she answered correctly. But she communicated with the one person who knew the truth.

"The man they found was—it has to be—my stepfather!"

The voice was low and musical, almost childlike. Only one person sounded like that. And it was that voice which brought True to her senses.

"Clarry!" she gasped. "Oh Clarry, *are you sure?*"

"She's sure. 'Twas I who brought the message." Jeremiah stepped from the shadows. The fog was lifting to reveal faces. Only True North could not trust her eyes. It couldn't be. *It just couldn't!*

26
What Christmas Is All About

TRUE SLEPT LATE the next morning—if one could call it sleep. The small remnant remaining of the night (when at last all were in bed) she had spent dreaming of roaming the Great Smokies, not bodily but as the "voice in the wilderness" trying to prepare the way for William Prescott's arrival, pleading his cause—only to realize that she was neither seen nor heard. She was transparent and voiceless—struck dumb, rendered helpless. The dream was so real that right now she touched her body, tested her muscles, just to make sure she was of the flesh.

The events of last night had an illusory quality as she tried to piece them together. Bit by bit it came back . . . the program . . . the principal's letter . . . his demise . . . no, he was alive. It was Clarry's father who was hanged. *Clarry!* Thought of the girl brought True from her reverie. Clarry was here—Clarry, Kearby, Jeremiah—*Midgie!* Fully awake now, joy flooded her being, sending blood flooding the body that was very much flesh indeed! Midgie, Marty, and the *March Hare*. It was the warmth and sweetness of the drooling baby, pink-cheeked and heavy-lidded from need of sleep, snuggled against her bosom which restored her sanity. A baby . . . a squirming real-life baby who sucked his thumb and dimpled at her even as he fell asleep. The baby Chris . . . the Baby Jesus . . . that was what Christmas was all about . . .

A faint sound came from the livingroom. Young Wil would probably have had breakfast and be working on his book. He was incorporating the notes that True had made in the classroom and on home visits. Jerry,

490

she smiled to herself, would have gone back to the Big House before the birds knew it was morning. He had volunteered to sleep on a cot here at the cabin so Kearby and Clarry could have his bedroom. Now she must join them all before O'Higgin and Grandma Mollie (who had taken the overflow of guests) returned. Time was short, and—

The noise again, a sort of scraping, as if a reluctant door were being forced open. Something cautioned her not to call out her cheerful "Good morning, darling!" as she usually did on the seldom days that Wil was home. Instead, she slipped into the daffodil robe he loved and gently turned the knob, hoping to find him at his desk. She would put her hands over his eyes, give him three guesses, knowing very well she would be drawn into his lap instead.

Clarry! But what was she doing here? Dusting to surprise her? The girl was propping a note against a cologne bottle. A *goodbye?* True was about to call out when she noticed how cautiously Clarry was moving, something clutched in her hand—something bright and sparkling as only a circle of pearls centered by a beautifully cut sapphire jewel could be. *Her mother's brooch!*

True stood transfixed, unable to believe her eyes, as she watched Clarry hesitate and then white-faced, thrust it into the pocket of her sweater. "Clarry!" True found her voice as the girl reached for the latch to let herself out quietly. The jewel box was gaping open, so there could be no mistake.

"Put it back, Clarry," True said calmly. Her voice was sorrowful but grave.

Clarry turned with a little half-sob, her young face twisted with fear. "I—never—oh, Mrs. North—I beg you to believe me—I *never* took anything before—"

"The word is *stole*, Clarry. And, yes, I believe you—so replace the brooch. It belonged to my mother and is far more precious to me than it could be to you."

Clarry's face looked blank, as if she were unable to comprehend the words. "Precious? I—I—didn't think of the pin's importance—I mean—*that* way. I—oh, Mrs. North—"

"True."

The girl looked even more stricken. "You—you would be kind— after what I've done—I thought—thought maybe I could sell it—" Clarry gulped, "and run away—"

"Put it back, Clarry. Nobody can solve a problem by trying to outrun it. And no amount of money would be worth the price you would pay—"

"You—you mean—you'll report me to the militia? Oh, Mrs. North —*don't*, I beg. Some of the soldiers came with us—to make it safe when they brought us out of Slippery Elm—while it's under martial law." Fear turned to defeat. "Yes, that's what you'll have to do—but (remorsefully) I deserve it—"

Head down and shoulders slumped forward, Clarry walked—*crept*, really—to the highboy, placed the piece of jewelry back onto its blue-velvet bed, and closed the lid. The sound reminded True of the finality of the carefully controlled metallic click of a coffin lid. The child was burying all hope—her very life—in this heartbreaking interment. But she must guard against being too soft if she wanted to help Clarry. She was *not* a bad girl, but what she had done was wrong. Understanding must wait.

"You have returned my property, Clarry. But I am unable to help until I know the truth. So, forget punishment, and explain what it is that you are running away from. Your father—stepfather, whatever he was—no longer has a hold on you—don't be afraid."

Silence stretched between the two of them as long as True could endure it. "Sit down, Clarry. Take the slipper chair. I'll sit here in Dr. North's desk-chair. He doesn't seem to be around."

"No," Clarry said in a small voice as she eased her thin frame into the slipper chair with a puzzled look "I—uh—heard his uncle say there was a call—somebody's appendix—then I—oh, Mrs. North—uh, True— I'm so ashamed—I slipped in—and the devil told me to—steal it—"

True inhaled deeply. Already some of the Appalachian thinking, or rationalizing, had rubbed off on the orphan girl, although she was not "one of them."

"What," True said, choosing her words carefully, "do you suppose the *Lord* would have told you?"

"To leave it alone—but I couldn't take time to ask Him a favor—"

"God always has time, Clarry. But He deserves an explanation— and so do I. Why did you do it, darling?"

When the word of endearment slipped out, Clarry opened her eyes to look at True in admiration. And her whole lurid story came out.

True knew that "that terrible man" was not her father, not even her stepfather, didn't she? Virgil never married her mother, just bullied her into living a lie. Because (the girl hung her head) "I am a bastard—dirty, unlovable—disgraced."

"You are none of those things," True said softly. "We will talk about that later. But, for now, please stay with your story."

"I loved my mother—but she neglected me—I guess," the lovely girl said bewilderedly, as if she were making a new discovery, "she did the best she could, giving me to Grandma, only I was stolen time and time again. I loved her," Clarry's voice was defensive now, "oh, I loved my mother so much—but she was afraid of *him*, afraid of disgrace—afraid of everything—even afraid of loving me. I guess that's just the way life is—people can't change what they are—"

Clarry looked up at True. There was no change in her facial expression. And, although the tragic eyes did not blink, a tear trickled down one cheek. "I guess you hate me."

"I do not hate you and you are wrong about people being unable to change, Clarry, but go on with your story."

"I need to know what's going to happen to me—now that you've found out what I'm like. And," her voice strengthened a bit, "what does my family, such as it was, have to do with the pin I—I stole?"

"I want to be fair. I respect the law, but I want to hear your side of the story. We've never really talked. Try to trust me."

Incoherently the story came out then—the ugly truth told in words that tumbled over each other as if they had been bottled up far, far too long. Virgil Adamson was downright brutal. He beat her when she tried to protect herself, and, being a coward like her mother, she guessed, she—well (a shudder shook her body) allowed herself to be abused "the other way." Then he got involved in robberies, killed some people, too. He forced her at the age of nine to sell stolen jewelry because, he said, her mother was in need of a doctor and would die without the money. He was sent to prison, telling Clarry that she was his accomplice and would be put in the cell with him if she told. A group of grim-faced women from some church placed her in an orphanage. All she could remember was a high iron fence with a locked gate and that there were no other girls her age—mostly boys who snickered when they saw her and spoke in loud whispers behind the angry-looking matron's back about taking her out in the woods. That's why she ran away to find an aunt. The woman meant well, Clarry guessed, but she scarcely had enough for herself, and she called her niece a burden. And then *he* escaped . . . and the whole sordid affair commenced again. Grew worse, in fact.

"And now he's dead—and I find myself *glad*—do you understand? Glad, *glad, glad*! Only they're going to find me—"

"Who, Clarry?"

"The outlaws with him—they'll think I helped before so I'm helping now. So I should know where the stolen money's buried—"

"Do you?"

"No! I've been living with Miss Anna-Lee, and she's good and kind, but she can't protect me. And besides, I don't want to embarrass her— and—if those church people find me, they'll send me back to that horrible place. Oh, can't you see why I *had* to run away? Kearby has been so kind—but I'm a burden to her, too—and hiding me out of the way like she's been doing is bound to get her in trouble—that's all I've ever caused is trouble—can't you see why I did it?"

Poor child. Poor innocent victim who had seen nothing but the power of evil. How could one expect her to recognize the power of good? Compassion overwhelmed True, and she was about to reach out to the child who saw her as judge and jury when Clarry crumpled to the floor and crawled like a legless reptile to coil at her feet. True was so taken by surprise that she was unable to move momentarily— just looked with horror at the stricken face, so pale in dismay and distress at her confession that surely the blood had been driven from her young heart.

True regained her composure, slid down beside Clarry, and cradled her in her arms. "Nobody will harm you, darling—we love you."

"You—you *forgive* me? If only I could have known you—*forgive me*?"

"Yes, darling," True said gently, "that's what Christmas is all about."

27
Life Must Go On

❧

A WEEK WAS not enough, but it was all they had. And True was grateful for the seven days. It seemed symbolic somehow: The Lord had created the entire world in that length of time. The North family must somehow rebuild two worlds from chaos and somehow bring them together, even hang a sun in the sky, for there must be a shedding and spreading of light. Just why the burden rested on their shoulders nobody seemed to know. Except Aunt Chrissy, that is.

"Because," she reassured Marty, Midgie, and the O'Higgins as they shelled walnuts for the holiday puddings that she was late in making, "we are His 'Chosen People'."

She cast a misty-eyed smile at Daddy Wil, who smiled back tenderly, the message saying they would never forget the details in Angel Mother's diary. "We can be proud of God's choosing us as His elect. The holy election puts us in the governmental position of the Supreme Court justice—it is for a lifetime."

The three younger ones did not understand. Jerry laid down the two walnuts he had been pressing together to break the shells, and rubbed his reddened palms. "I've a feeling this goes far back. Tell us about it, Mother. There seems to be some mystery."

"The works of th' Lord are always mysterious," Grandma Mollie volunteered. "O'Higgin, cain't yuh keep th' fire goin'? Add a log!"

Chris Beth continued, "You're right, Jerry; but it is True's story, recorded by her mother in a diary. We are all mentioned, except you and Kearby, the end being before you were born—before your father

495

and I were married, in fact. He was Vangie's—Vangie was True's mother, my sister—before Vangie—left us." Her voice broke.

All seemed caught up in emotion. The room lay in solemn stillness except for the occasional crack of a shell and the muted hiss of the backlog that O'Higgin had heaved into the widemouthed fireplace as it cast alternate fading and flaring lights—shadows dancing against the homey wall hangings. Homey. And it was Christmas. Yet the atmosphere seemed subtly portentous. So much was at stake.

It was True who broke the silence. "I think," she said with just a hint of unsteadiness in her voice, "that the time has come for sharing the diary with you, Jerry—you, Kearby—and Clarry. I want her to read it too."

Clarry's lips whitened. "What! *Me?*" Her voice was strained, humiliated. And her eyes, just before she lowered them, reflected a look of betrayal, their message clear: "I trusted you—and you let me down, just when I thought you understood. You promised we would never speak of the unpardonable thing I did—and now I am at your mercy, without defense. You will see that I'm punished—and you are wrong about God's love. I am *not* an innocent victim—I'm bad, *bad*, BAD. Nothing can change it—I was born that way—"

The look broke True's heart. She had a difficult role to play. "Of course you are included, Clarry dear. The diary will bring all the family skeletons out of the closet—let you see that none of us is perfect, although sometimes we adults try pretending we are. We are all sinners until we confess our sins and ask forgiveness—and then we become perfect through His love. All of you are old enough to see us as we are—"

O'Higgin slipped a stubborn walnut beneath the rocker of his chair and came down on it hard. The crash might well have heralded the end of the world.

"O'Higgin!" Miss Mollie's voice filled the room. "Talkin' of sinners—what's under thet thatch of red hair—anything? Causin' us t'jump outta our hides 'n need a doctor!"

"Now, now, me Mollie! There be two in this room—'n be 'avin' ye a peek et th' fruits of me labor. A perfect nut!"

"You got thet one right!" she muttered.

Laughter filled the room and the tension was broken. True cast a quick look at Clarry, whose eyes were shining, lighting her lovely face with relief that came close to spelling happiness. *Oh, praise the Lord!*

"We were going to make fudge, remember?" Kearby reminded her brother. "Come along, Clarry."

The girl cast True a heartbreakingly touching look of gratitude as she followed the twins into the great kitchen, where she would take part for the first time ever in Christmas preparations. And something told True that Clarry Hancock's mind was making preparations for Jesus' coming into her heart. One need not travel, for within each heart lay a Bethlehem . . . an inn where ultimately each mortal must decide whether there is room . . . and, one by one, those True North loved were deciding.

True wanted—*needed*—to talk with everybody individually, but time forbade. The only real group togetherness was at mealtime. And then there was such a joyous babble that she wondered if anybody heard a word anybody else said—except when it was quiet and Jeremiah prayed his beautiful prayers. Otherwise it was a natural pairing-off dictated more by priority than choice.

Chris Beth, obviously wanting to spend more time getting to know the "New Marty," recognized that her son must talk business with Irish O'Higgin. She longed to hold her first grandchild, too, become acquainted with his adorable baby-ways. True could see the desire in her eyes. But Aunt Chrissy rendered him to Grandma Mollie, who—for the first time ever—allowed others to do the work while she rocked, sang, and (according to Midgie's hurried whisper) "spoiled him rotten." However, Chris Beth was able to spend some needed time with her daughter; and for some unaccountable reason she seemed worried about Kearby.

Clarry monopolized Jerry's time, who looked "moon-eyed," Nate Goldsmith observed. He had come, of all the improbable times, to deliver a wagonload of books and brightly illustrated maps with real roller-cases which could be fastened to the wall! True sucked in her breath with admiration and surprise. Oh, what a boon—but who on earth was the benefactor?

Nate, chest out with pride, took time to spit (and keep her guessing) before his announcement. "Thet railroad feller—what's th' name? Oh, Saint Something—right fittin', ain't it now?"

"St. John—Michael St. John." For some reason True wanted to cry. Biting her lip instead, she turned a few pages joyfully and managed to thank the President of the Board. "They—Marty 'n th' others—knowed 'twas comin'—jest no time fer grabbin' hit in their hasty exodus. Bad, thangs is bad thar, I'm a-tellin' yuh—did'ja know 'bout th' hangin'— I'm a-meanin' t'other one, th' straw-stuffed dummy, strung up lack thet Virgil outlaw, hung on a rope in—uh—uh *ef*—some big word—"

"Effigy," True supplied, then in horror, "did Clarry see?"

Nate spat again. "Nope! Thet's why th' militia scampered 'em all out—'n I'd be guessin' with a pinch of relief, too, whut with th' meanin' of th' hoax. 'Twas a warnin' to 'em, yuh know, but now with th' new marshal—"

"There's a marshal?" True interrupted, hope rising inside her.

"Hasta be—with marshal law—ain't thet how they said 'twas?"

Disappointed, True tactfully explained the difference between the needed marshal and the "martial law" temporary takeover by troops. But she doubted that Nate listened. He was too busy stroking the treasure he'd delivered and asking Jerry's whereabouts. The boy could help unload, he said, since 'twas his bounden duty (importantly) long as he'd have to fill in for that sneak of a Prescott. After all was said and done, 'twouldn't change things much. The young man had been packing the load anyway.

"Jest whut he—Jerry, that is—seen in thet cowardly calf beats me. But would'ja be believin' he claims Prescott he'ped him make up 'is mind t'be a teacher—decided faster'n greased lightnin'—when he shudda tooken a run-ago at 'im—"

"A *what*?" Thrilled though she was to hear of Jerry's ambition and eager as she was to get the precious cargo unloaded, there was a point to make here. "I've never heard you use that word."

Nate removed his slouch hat and scratched where his hair used to be. "Ain't jes' fer certain—reckon I borried th' word—"

"From the mountain people," she smiled. "We all rub off on each other, don't we? Oh, here's Jerry—"

Young Wil, finished with house calls, joined them. Boldly he kissed a curl at the nape of her neck, then just before she could hiss "Wil North—mind your manners!" her husband took a look at the wagon-load of supplies and whistled. "What a blessing! If you can manage, Jerry—you and Nate—I'd like some time alone with Clarry, please."

Daddy Wil and Jeremiah were strolling toward the ever-gurgling stream, buried deep in conversation. About the need for a church in Slippery Elm? Probably. It occurred to True then that the school was in need of a pastor too. In True's mind it had been for some time. Surely there was a minister who could win the respect of the Appalachian folk through gentle persuasion—kindness, patience, peacefulness, and understanding—then emphasize salvation, spelling it out, making it clear, pounding the pulpit if he must!

And then her thoughts changed. Oh, here came Midgie! They needed to talk and talk. But first, just to hold one another. *Close!* Men would never understand, they admitted laughingly, that crying together sometimes spoke louder to women than words. Chris Beth, looking out of the upstairs window, where she and Kearby were having their mother-daughter talk, looked down on the scene below. And history repeated itself. True and Midgie were herself and Vangie. The diary would tell—also reveal the fears in her own heart. And that was, at this point, how it should be . . .

The warm embrace had covered a lot of ground. It spoke of undying affection. It spoke of happiness found with men they loved. It brought back tender memories, shared dreams, and the need of togetherness for the four of them, just as Mary Evangeline North, heart breaking with the ache of temporary parting, and wasted body wrenched in pain, had written her final entry in her diary: . . . *so long as you're all together.* That would have been Uncle Joe, Aunt Chrissy, and Daddy Wil, the bereaved husband. Angel Mother, in human form, would be gone, but her spirit would linger forever. It was here now—with her and Midgie.

But there were other things to talk about, a world that the two of them shared—had helped to build, in fact. And now it was crumbling. Unless, of course, True and Young Wil would come back . . .

"Oh, darling, we can't consider a move—can hardly plot our future —until life levels here. It makes me ache to talk about it—"

"Then I will tell you the news." Midgie's dimpled smile brightened her round, girlish face with a lightness that True was sure her sister-in-law did not feel.

And talk they did, words tumbling out nonstop as if they must be spoken on deadline—which in a sense they must. The ranch hands had taken over, refused to leave, saying they'd help restore law and order . . . still trying to "teach Bible" . . . but Midgie wondered if 'twas smart, seeing that they needed schooling . . . needed a preacher too—but, oh, True, there was a teeny-weeny chance . . . the Reverend Randy having just taken over handling of the Caswells' business . . . and, yes, Tillie *had*, by the grace of God, become her old self since losing her husband . . . not that it would last without some doctor like Young Wil who knew the workings of the mind. Same for Mariah. Back to help Spanish tongues speak English while Tillie did it the other way 'round. But as for morality, what little the handful of decent folk had been able to instill had shriveled up and died, forcing decent God-fearing people to bear arms— allowed by the Constitution, but was it Christian? Midgie wished True could see how beautiful their house was now, spring bulbs sprouting already, bumper crops harvested, and ground "turned under" and allowed to fallow just before casting Tex's new strain of wheat. The cattle were multiplying and trying to replenish the earth as if they'd just stepped from the ark . . . same for the horses, real thoroughbreds . . .

True savored every word, but waited for Midgie to run down before bringing to the forefront questions which she knew were of critical importance to them both: the newcomers, the Appalachians.

At last Midgie inhaled deeply, almost painfully. "Your turn—you knew, of course, that Virgil Adamson was hanged?" She shuddered.

"Yes, I heard indirectly." True gave as complete an account as possible, except for Clarry's attempt to take the brooch. And the two of them pieced the story together, including the girl's flight from Slippery Elm. The stories coincided, including her reasons.

"Fear?" True said. "Didn't Anna-Lee befriend Clarry when she found she was a relative of her husband's? Couldn't Clarry look to her for protection?"

"Maybe I can understand better than you, True. I can identify with her, remember. Our backgrounds are different from yours—and, yet, we don't want to bring humiliation to those we love. But there's more—lots more. Clarry has real reason for being fearful. That awful gang Virgil Adamson was involved with will get to her if they can. So we might as well turn her over to them and get it over with if she returns. In fact, she would endanger us all—I'm so confused—but, darling, I don't dare take her back until the gang's rounded up, which will be the case when we get home to the Double N."

True could see the logic—could even see the wisdom of keeping her here—but, she evaded, it would be risky, too. Clarry and Jerry shouldn't see so much of each other day and night. And that's what it would amount to with Jerry's taking over—well, it would rest with the family. And with Clarry. That was another consideration. Young Wil would know how to talk with her. And the diary would help—at least, in letting Clarry know that she was not alone in being illegitimate. "But you were not abused," Midgie pointed out. "Oh, True, that leaves scars that even love can never wipe out. If you were there, we could form a little group—open up, talk things out—Clarry, Tillie, Mariah—me. You could lead—"

"But I am not there," True pointed out tiredly. "Let's see what develops, involve the Lord in this. And, meantime, I guess it will fall on our shoulders to deliver food to some of the needy. Feel brave enough to help? When you see more of how the Appalachians try to exist here, it will help you understand those in your area who, in their blindness, are at war with each other."

Midgie fidgeted. "I saw enough at the program to scare me—but," with a lift of her chin, "I will come. I—I can't help wishing one of the men—no, this is my Christmas gift. I had no time to prepare gifts, and I'm sorry."

True put her arms about Midgie and felt her trembling. "Don't be afraid, Midgie dear—" she paused, a bit shaken herself at the parallel between Aunt Chrissy's reassuring Angel Mother, remembered from the diary—"just keep the peace of Christmas in your heart. And, as for gifts, we had no time either—our Christmas is giving to the poor. Remember that the Baby Jesus grew up . . . walked among the poor . . . and, like the Star, said 'Follow me.' I—I'd rather sit safely by the fire and make popcorn balls—don't I owe that to my family? But—Midgie—think about what I owe *Him*. A pilgrimage— to a land of hunger . . . misery . . . and hate-filled faces. Yes, following is risky . . ."

They delivered the food but said little of the journey. On Christmas Day six bewhiskered men of the mountains brought down a roasted pig, its eyes still intact and the skin rubbed in alcohol "t'tighten th' hide fer cracklin's, savin' need t'scrounge round fer soothin' sir'p fer th' stummick afterwards of a square meal."

The family dinner was festive. But True and Midgie, recalling the pig sty, refused pork. Nobody noticed, as all were talking at once, Clarry and Kearby most excited of all. *Clarry was going to the academy with Kearby.* Just like that? How—? True, her eyes locking with Midgie's said Christmas was a sacrifice. Life must go on . . . and everybody would help. . . . They had handed the needy a Star.

28
End of a Silver Silence

~❧

EVERYONE WAS GONE and the world lay in a silver silence.
Nature had tiptoed in and dusted the Valley with the first snow, a
grim reminder that winter was a reality of life. But it locked in the
peace of Christmas in a mystical sort of way, just as the harsher
freeze to the east would lock in the winter wheat at the Double N.
Too, the quiet allowed time for reflecting as well as getting the
school in order.

There had been a frenzied rush readying Clarry for the unexpected
departure with Kearby. Fingers, the few sewing machines, and Mrs.
Solomon's "Alteration Department" worked far into the night adjusting "dresses that didn't sell" to fit Clarry's slender figure. It was
Jerry's admiring glances which brought to light a deeper relationship
than his mother or older sister had allowed themselves to accept.

"It keeps happening over and over—history repeating itself," Chris
Beth marveled. "How did your mother have so much foresight?"
There was both admiration for her beloved sister and a concern for
Jerry (which she tried to conceal) in her weary face. "I'm glad you let
them share the diary—the girls, that is, since Jerry was bogged down
with the school supplies—do—do you think things are serious between him and—?" Somehow she seemed unable to say the name.

True smiled. "As serious as they can be at this tender age." She
was about to suggest that they waste no time fretting over it when
she caught sight of the paleness brought on by her aunt's own words.

It all came to her then, the high-tide of revelation nearly sweeping her off her feet. "You are remembering Young Wil, aren't you?" she whispered, "Young Wil—and me—conceived out of wedlock like Clarry?"

"Oh, darling, *no!*" Chris Beth dropped the flatiron back on the bed of coals she had raked onto the hearth and rushed to take True in her arms. "If I ever, *ever* gave you reason to believe—oh, my darling, you come close to being my favorite child, if I would allow that."

True hardly heard. Her own mind was seeing too many parallels. Somehow she managed to mumble out her feelings.

Aunt Chrissy pulled True's head to her breast, stroking the golden curls back from her damp forehead the way she used to do when a bad dream had awakened True from troubled sleep. "There *are* similarities—I mean in our relationships—even with the changes. You have grown up knowing that we believe God brought us here for special work, and that it is to continue down through the generations."

Yes, that was true, True admitted to herself. And now she wondered if it had been her aunt or herself whom she doubted. Young Wil had told her as they studied together that the mind was tricky, not always reliable. That it tended to shift certain characteristics from self to another. But—

"I'm sorry, Aunt Chrissy—I shouldn't have said that. But," sitting upright, "what has any of this to do with Jerry's attraction to—perhaps love for—Clarry?"

Aunt Chrissy considered the question with puckered brow. "Her background," she said at length, "is so different. She has been through so much. I guess, to be truthful, I am afraid that her values—no matter how much she hates her past and what that man has done—make her more aware of her power as a woman. I don't want that for Jerry! But I'm wrong in assuming the worst, darling—I know that I am. You see, I am remembering what loose tongues did to your mother—and I don't want that happening to Jerry and Clarry, poor child—"

"I know," True said in a small voice; "it's all in the diary. I know, too, that scars will remain, as with Midgie. But Clarry is working her way through this. Young Wil is keeping me informed and says she will forgive herself of wrongdoing, real or imagined, once she realizes that God has forgiven *her.*"

"Oh, darling, yes, yes. Sometimes I wonder if we mothers aren't bad for our children." Her attempted laugh faltered. "Is there something more you want to ask me? You still look troubled."

As True watched her aunt dampen her forefinger and test the heat of the iron, she remembered that she too must iron some white shirts for her husband. But she could not bring the conversation to a close until she had an answer to a question which had nibbled at her mind for far too long already. Sprinkling the starched shirts could wait.

Aunt Chrissy had begun the tedious job of ironing the pleated bosom, waiting—but not pushing—for an answer. When it came, she looked startled. "Jerry and Clarry I can understand, I guess. But why are you so concerned about Kearby?"

There was a quick intake of breath before Chris Beth said in a low voice, "I didn't know it showed. But her unnatural fear of men after Clarry's experience, followed by an about-face worries me. You see, Kearby told me, when we talked, that there's a boy she wants to bring home—brother of one of her friends there. Oh, just tell me I'm a goose!"

Relieved, True threw back her head and laughed, feeling the tension inside her melt into nothingness. "Is *that* all! All right, my precious aunt, you are a goose—a wonderful, normal, much-loved 'Mother Goose'!"

As True ironed and Young Wil worked on his book that night, the wind outside took on force, pushing against the invisible in a way that made her uneasy. Such a strange wind, advancing and retreating, like a mighty army. It played up and down the scale, discordant at one point, harmonizing at another. The room filled with smoke, making it necessary to open the door against a wall of wind.

"Did—you—get the—information you wanted—from Clarry?" True panted as they pushed against the door together.

"Here—stick this underneath while I hold it open." Young Wil managed to reach the fire shovel with his foot and kick it to her. Done!

In the freezing cold, True ventured to interrupt him again. "Did you?"

Young Wil looked up vaguely. "Clarry? Oh—ah—yes. I'm transcribing my notes—nothing confidential, I guess—" he paused to gather up papers the wind had scattered, "as she said she'd revealed the temptation to take the brooch."

He resumed his writing. *Confidential.* Young Wil respected that. But of course he would. Why should she have felt guilty for respecting it too? Relief swept over her. *Forgive my humanness, Lord.*

As they locked up for the night, Young Wil looked up at the somber January sky. "Snow tomorrow. Better get your boots out—my hands are frozen. Let's turn in and snuggle."

Warm in her long flannel nightie and secure in her husband's arms, True no longer felt uneasy. She listened until the wind grew hoarse and hushed its voice and Young Wil's even breathing told her he was asleep, then gave a contented sigh with no premonition of the greater storm which was building around them.

The next morning the world was white, with time, space, and substance tucked beneath the blanket of snow. School was to resume today. And the silver silence would be broken—ending in a number of ways . . .

29
Calm Before the Storm

そ

JANUARY, TRUE THOUGHT later, was the silver lining of an invisible black cloud. The North family (which included O'Higgin and his Mollie-gal), the Valley folk, and the mountain dwellers settled into a routine which Young Wil referred to in his doctoral dissertation (to be published in book form) as "a successful period of adjustment." Grandma Mollie sniffed and said 'twas more like the wolf and the lamb dwelling together. But Isaiah never made mention of what happened when the wolf sniffed fresh blood, did he?

To True it was much like the prophet's account of the restoration of Israel. *Peaceful.* So she encouraged her class to memorize the verse, "Sing unto the Lord, for he hath done excellent things . . ." After all, her prayers were being answered, her every wish granted. Didn't Michael's contribution to the library, followed so soon with textbooks and school supplies, stand out as a shining example?

The children stood in awe at the new materials, their eyes saying that Christmas was here to stay. They violated her rule by leaving their desks without permission and clustering around her. "Le's see, le's see . . . move, yuh upscuddle, lemme see . . . Teacher, Charmin' cain't see, her brother's a mean'un greedy 'n tetchious, allus packin' a gredge . . . *move!*"

True, as excited as the children, regretted that she must restore order. "Here, let's find Oregon on the map." Wordlessly their clumsy fingers located the Appalachian country, having no idea whether to

507

trace their fingers east or west. It was as if they knew of no world outside their place of birth, even though they were now relocated.

Making note of their lack of knowledge, True asked that they wash their hands before opening the new books which two of the older boys would distribute. Again, the look of enchantment as they touched, smelled, and clutched the beautiful books to their hearts. True turned away to hide the tears. This was their first exposure to books with all the pages intact and unspotted by sorghum or lard.

Learning took on a new meaning for them. All embarrassment, bewilderment, and reluctance to learn faded. These books were *theirs,* not at all like the missionary barrels "of stuff," they said. True encouraged them to talk about the contents of the barrels. "Funny hats, right-smart purdy onct, but et up by moths . . . store-boughten lard buckets, right nice fer dinner packin'—'cept bottom's rusted outta th' critters, 'n thar warn't no bails . . . funny corset-thangs (*giggle,* *giggle*) fer fat womans . . . shoes thet hurt cuz of long nar' toes, not no buttons neither . . . some books whut was too colored-up fer readin' 'n pages tored outta 'em."

Then Buster's voice rose above all others. "Paw wuz hoppin' mad, built a far hottern hades 'n us'n all burnt 'em 'n roasted sow belly. Sed us foks don' be needin' no char'ty."

Sickened, True turned away to hide the horror she felt. *Think of something else,* she willed. She remembered then that Buster's teeth looked much better. Oh, yes, of course. Her wonderful husband had taken a retired dentist with him on some of the house calls. Which reminded her to tell the children that the doctors were coming in February to weigh and measure them. "Then," she smiled, "each of you will have a health record all your own. We'll learn how to take care of ourselves and (rashly) be fit enough to do battle with a lion like Daniel!" That she regretted, because one tiny tot said she'd be searching "fer th' jawbone of th' ass."

True seemed the only one flustered by the Bible quote. It was then that a strange notion crossed her mind. They were ignorant because they had no learning opportunities. But they were open and open-minded. What came out of their mouths was innocence itself. They appreciated what the Lord provided, no matter through whom He doled it out, and they instinctively recognized His "good gifts" above the pitiful crumbs from do-gooders' tables. *Are they more civilized than we are?* A new sense of responsibility swept over her.

For the remainder of the week, True allowed the children to draw maps, label them, and try to pinpoint the ocean, mountains, and valleys. By Friday parents were coming en masse to see what all the commotion was about. That was when they decided to tackle reading for themselves . . .

All this True wrote in a letter of appreciation to Michael. He answered promptly, telling her that he had arranged through Meier and Frank's to have shoes of all sizes delivered, suggesting that Solomon's Store put on a "sale."

Meantime, Midgie responded to True's more detailed letter to tell of a similar experience with the missionary projects. "It was all disgraceful and degrading," she commented, then went on to relate how the contents were put to use in Slippery Elm, "only it would have been far better if they'd been sent up in flames like your people there. Poor darlings—they break my heart in half! Marty found bloody footprints—human ones—in the snow and hoped there would be some decent shoes. What did he find? Junk, *awful* junk! But the Appalachian people were so cold, feet all frostbitten, you know, that they grabbed at anything. It would be a riot if it weren't so downright pitiful—like having your heart carved right out of you. Why, True, it's not one bit uncommon seeing one of the men at Tillie's store wearing a frock-tailed coat over his ragged coveralls. One woman bought green satin shoes with heels sky-high to go with her shapeless calico that's worn so thin it's like gauze. She stumbled off the gallery of the store—nearly drowned in the rain barrel, and what did she say? First question was, "Oh, what 'bout my bee-u-y-fullest shoes in th' world?"

Midgie went on then with family news and views. True loved her sister-in-law's every word—the information and the amusing way in which she expressed herself. Midgie had managed to "study up" on her grammar and learned to communicate well without sacrificing her own unique personality. *If only I can accomplish that here,* True thought.

Quickly she scanned the remainder of the letter. There were papers stacked eye-deep on her desk and notes to prepare for Young Wil, some checking on Jerry (oh, dear, she had neglected him!), and so she read the next paragraph without really absorbing it.

"Things are still bad, even with help of the militia. They plan to get more help . . . but a bigger problem . . . well, let's not worry, but they've discovered she's gone . . . may go gunning for her . . . "

In fact, serious as the situation was in Slippery Elm, True had to smile at Midgie's constant reference to their need of Young Wil and herself. Not that she doubted it. But Midgie was so obvious . . .

Aunt Chrissy was as happy as True with all the supplies. They planned together for hours, listening always to Jerry, whose ideas were sometimes better than their own. Nate had managed to have the state issue a "Temporary Substitute Certificate" for Jerry ("nobody possessed 'nuf brains t' be askin' his age—'n me, I don't volunteer"). Aunt Chrissy was happy, too, about how faithful the girls were in writing home from the Academy. Her mind seemed to be at rest *now*.

"Sometimes," she smiled happily, "I think it's all too good to be true." That was before the wolf smelled blood, True supposed later . . .

30
The Smell of Blood

❧

IN SPITE OF the Appalachians' progress in other ways, one thing was the immovable object: They refused to lay down arms—unless their weapons were within reach. Old habits die hard. "Back home" men slept with their rifles cocked. Sure, things were changing here. Folks voted other folks in and voted them out. But in the long haul, did it matter much? Violence hid behind every bush no matter where a man was. The bulging hump of a mountain in these parts was as good a hangout as the brooding monsters of the Great Smokies. And what did the government care? Best a man be prepared. Even the Good Book said so.

The Norths prayed together often about the feuding mountaineer spirit that seemed to hold the people together. Actually, it was their source of pride. What help was a newfangled gas buggy if a man had no money? they reasoned. And who cared about that smart man called Edison—somebody who almost got himself killed trying to put lightning in a lamp? Both changes were more dangerous than bullets—and did nothing to protect a man's family. Better have a neck like a hoot owl that twisted round and round so he could keep watch behind him, that's what. And keep his powder dry.

"If only we could set a good minister in here—somebody like Joe," Wilson North said one evening. To which Aunt Chrissy replied that there would never be another like her former husband. "But," she reminded them all softly, "he left the torch in our hands. We must carry on."

That was when the two doctors began to approach the men with proposals that they put away their guns. To no avail. Everywhere the answer was the same: "We'd be kilt 'fore a week took leave!"

"I suppose," Young Wil said, his voice carrying a hint of defeat, "they're right, carrying grudges as they do. And somehow they're unable to bring together their new thinking—even after turning their lives over to the Lord—and the lifestyles which have been instilled in them. It's like—well, they continue living on an island unaffected by change."

"Don't give up, darling. I refuse to allow those weapons in my classroom," True began, and then stopped. After all, the guns were left within reach. "You're right, darling—we'll just have to keep working on it. Eventually something will show them the need for law and order—or will it? Change has to come from within. It's something that only God can do."

Young Wil's head jerked erect. "Are you aware that they claim to be studying so they can take the gospel back?"

"And how do they propose to present it—with a gun?"

"Actually, I think they're homesick for the most part—the men, anyway. Most of the wives seem more content, safer. But," he shook his head, "I keep hearing how good it would be to get back where the land is free of bullies calling themselves 'the law.' Better, they say, to be free like the Constitution promises—free to make their 'home brew,' kill if need be, and just watch the buzzard sail without flapping wings over cows that might be a little lean, but that was true only because they were allowed to be free—it's confusing."

"But," True said determinedly, "it's not futile. Somehow we have to shake them awake. And we will!"

"We? It well may be circumstances."

"Wil North, stop trying to scare me!"

For the first time her husband did not laugh or tease. His concern was too deep in the very core of his heart, she realized.

In February the weather grew milder, snow turning to rain. Snow thinned in the Valley, leaving the ground to look like threadbare carpet under which lay a bog of mud. It was a nuisance, but better than a shift of the winds to bring the warm Chinooks, triggering sudden thaws, mountain slides, and the threat of floods. The mountain children, still surrounded by snow in the higher elevations, were too excited to notice. They were getting health charts!

True watched with admiration as the two doctors examined them (often having to soothe the girls' fears and dry their tears), especially noting the reassuring way both her husband and her uncle weighed, measured, and made records while gently talking of proper foods to eat and the value of cleanliness. He knew that the eager children would take the message home. How true! Before the end of the month, parents were coming. First out of curiosity, then to ask shyly if maybe this would be a "purdy good idee" for them all. Young Wil cautiously caught True's eyes and winked.

"If you wish, yes," he said with just the right amount of hesitation. "Ladies first—and then, you men. Without your guns, of course."

True was relieved to hear one man actually joke, "I dunno, Doc. M'gun she packs a lotta weight!"

Maybe they *were* getting the message across in small doses.

And then a miracle happened! True received a surprise letter from William Prescott. He had arrived safely at his home country and was amazed at the reception he had received. A retired minister and his musically inclined wife had broken the ground for him—worked their way into these people's hearts somehow, and introduced William as if he were a stranger. Old-timers had clustered around him, some with suspicion, others just curious that an outsider would dare invade their territory—and, True could almost feel his shudder, some drawing knives and brandishing guns. And then—would she believe that a big square-ox of a man (noted for his "killing ways," William learned later) stepped bravely forward to say, "Don' I know yuh, boy? Ain't yer mammy th' one whut usta bake th' ashcake fer eatin' with th' wine in mem'ry of th' dead et fun'rals?" He'd thought there would be another funeral, he said, when he nodded. But instead, the people were afraid of "Ox," and when the giant of a man asked him to his cabin for hammeat that night, there was an opportunity to explain his mission here. "Lordymercy, man," his host had observed privately, "don' yuh know whatta chance yer a-takin'? Still 'n all, iffen yer wantin' t'preach, tain't none of nobody's bizness, 'n I'll take keer of yuh bes' as I kin— bein' a shot lack I yam." Mr. Leady was a powerful man (both ways) . . . so there was hope . . . now, would it be possible that the Norths would be willing to allow Jerry to come and help . . . ?

True threw the letter aside, horror rising to the surface. Send Jerry? *There?* Why, the man was mad. Stark, raving mad . . .

It was days before she could bring herself to finish the letter.

"Dr. Miller, the minister who helped me here, is tired and his wife is not too well. He would like to move to a milder climate for her benefit, but has no desire to retire. I have described Oregon and they would like your permission to come there. They are sweet, gentle people, but he is a fundamentalist—meaning that he sticks with the message of salvation, gently. Mrs. Miller is a teacher and will help in the classroom . . ."

True's heart soared then. And before it seemed possible, the family had relayed the message to Nate, who called a meeting of the deacons. And the Millers were invited to visit. Jerry's going was out of the question, of course. And, to True's surprise, Jerry agreed. "Besides," he grinned, "you couldn't get along without me—and neither could Clarry, maybe Kearby either."

The Millers were all he proclaimed them to be, and more. The day that Dr. Miller preached his first sermon in the Valley, the church was packed. Not an empty pew, with heads poked in at the windows. Those heads belonged to mountaineer men who claimed they'd not be caught dead in a church. "Well, now, ain't thet jest th' bes' news ever? That'd mean 'nother fun'ral," one of the insiders growled.

The man outside whipped out a knife. "Two of 'em—" he growled.

That was when the preacher, ears attuned to signs of trouble, said in a gentle but authoritative voice, "If all will lay down your weapons—guns, knives, rocks, anything which would harm your brother—we will get started."

Mumbling that the preacher wouldn't last a week hereabouts, the newcomers obeyed his request. After all, preachers had bewitching powers—last time they saw one shot right betwixt the eyes, the cows gave bloody milk the night of the ice-cream social. Real scary. Preachers were a threat—particularly this one—not like a saddlebag one who filled his stomach and flew like a bat out of torment. But this one, well, he was a puzzlement. Didn't shout. Didn't do much to make a man mad. Hard to hate a man whose words came as sweet as spring rain. There were questions needing to be asked, of course. Was he

"Prim'tive?" Did he baptize or just "dry clean"? Why, even their kids knew better than dabbing down like Tuesday's ironing. Every gosling they owned had been baptized in the waterbucket. Better listen to this one, yep, lest he be casting a spell—

Well, by gum, the man made sense and he had a sense of humor. Never saw preachers laugh before—and make them laugh at themselves. Like saying "Hardshells are hard to crack—so I don't look for one immediately—"

But he got one anyway. He made the glory of God's love sound so appealing that one woman shouted right in the middle of the sermon. That caused the man at the window to interrupt, "Shout hit out, Preach. Cain't hear a word 'bove that thar hyst'ery." From another window came an "Amen!" And, when Dr. Miller invited all wishing to hear more about the road to heaven to gather up front where he would talk with them personally, there was a stampede. Better get the lowdown here. Education used to be the enemy. But—well, maybe they were getting soft in the head, thinking that maybe the enemy *was* ignorance . . .

The man was hard to figure out. Maybe that's what kept them coming. One thing was certain, he wouldn't take "No" for an answer. First man they'd met who was so all-fired determined—and had a remedy for every excuse they had for not bringing their families to church. No shoes, they told him, and he up and took the whole mountainside to Solomon's Sale. Bertie said later that she and Abe never done such a booming business. Of course, they had to depend on volume, she grumbled. The Valley women were downright huffy, called it false advertising to offer only shoes, so they just had to mark down all the stock.

Well-shod now, the men ran short on excuses. And this preacher was a bold one, coming at all hours of the day without warning. Made it right hard to keep a man's business to himself. Most had given up the stilling and bootlegging, but liquor—like guns—was a necessity, wasn't it?

Gradually the mountain men began to wonder about their lifestyles. If they were wrong in their thinking, they were in a terrible fix with the Lord. The presence of strangers would hex the flowers, they'd been told. Why, then, did the daffodils bloom more golden than

31
Warning Unheeded

THERE WAS NO time to warn Aunt Chrissy and Jerry. Time was of essence. The mountaineers must know the awful news. And, more importantly, they must know that "their kind" was not responsible. Else there would be civil war—and the fragile thread holding them together would snap. This True was thinking as she took the short-cut where the underbrush was thickest and blackberry vines tore at her long skirt and the laces of her boots as if to hold her back. Maybe the children would alert Mrs. Miller. She could take over in an emergency and—

But there was no more time for thinking. The tumultuous sound of rushing water told her she was nearing the stream. Fed by the river, it would be near flood-stage. And she must cross it by footlog. A quick survey told her that the high water had set the log swaying and that it was slippery from waves which washed against it with such force that they broke to course over the poorly anchored makeshift bridge. True looked away, hoping to overcome the seasickness she felt in the pit of her stomach.

But she couldn't afford the luxury of being sick. A moment's hesitation could mean loss of life! Not once did True think of her own life as she hoisted her skirt and set a tentative foot on the swaying log. It shifted warningly, but only dimly was she aware that she was in trouble. Closing her eyes momentarily, she let go of her skirt and balanced her weight by stretching both arms out the way she did when she, Young Wil, and Marty tried mastering the art of tightrope

518

"Prim'tive?" Did he baptize or just "dry clean"? Why, even their kids knew better than dabbing down like Tuesday's ironing. Every gosling they owned had been baptized in the waterbucket. Better listen to this one, yep, lest he be casting a spell—

Well, by gum, the man made sense and he had a sense of humor. Never saw preachers laugh before—and make them laugh at themselves. Like saying "Hardshells are hard to crack—so I don't look for one immediately—"

But he got one anyway. He made the glory of God's love sound so appealing that one woman shouted right in the middle of the sermon. That caused the man at the window to interrupt, "Shout hit out, Preach. Cain't hear a word 'bove that thar hyst'ery." From another window came an "Amen!" And, when Dr. Miller invited all wishing to hear more about the road to heaven to gather up front where he would talk with them personally, there was a stampede. Better get the lowdown here. Education used to be the enemy. But—well, maybe they were getting soft in the head, thinking that maybe the enemy *was* ignorance . . .

The man was hard to figure out. Maybe that's what kept them coming. One thing was certain, he wouldn't take "No" for an answer. First man they'd met who was so all-fired determined—and had a remedy for every excuse they had for not bringing their families to church. No shoes, they told him, and he up and took the whole mountainside to Solomon's Sale. Bertie said later that she and Abe never done such a booming business. Of course, they had to depend on volume, she grumbled. The Valley women were downright huffy, called it false advertising to offer only shoes, so they just had to mark down all the stock.

Well-shod now, the men ran short on excuses. And this preacher was a bold one, coming at all hours of the day without warning. Made it right hard to keep a man's business to himself. Most had given up the stilling and bootlegging, but liquor—like guns—was a necessity, wasn't it?

Gradually the mountain men began to wonder about their lifestyles. If they were wrong in their thinking, they were in a terrible fix with the Lord. The presence of strangers would hex the flowers, they'd been told. Why, then, did the daffodils bloom more golden than

Gabriel's horn this year? A body could almost hear them blast. And who wanted to be caught doing something that might infuriate the Almighty if the end was close?

The only thing wrong with all this, the Norths realized later, was that the Valley became dangerously satisfied. And the satisfied rose is one whose petals are about to fall . . .

The petals of their blind optimism dropped on a day when one would least expect it. The rains had dwindled to misty curtains which parted to show the sun's face. Hope for peace was gaining sturdiness— just melting away gradually, in True's mind, much like the snow. Enough to let the valleys make their annual promise of spring—apple buds pink (in what farmers called "popcorn stage") and ground almost ready for plowing, while up on the mountains wild lilacs trailed like purple waterfalls. The sun was so sensible, too, holding back its warmest rays, which would melt the snow too fast and overfeed the river, creeks, and streams. Yes, peace was a fragile thing.

Oh, it was good to be alive! Mrs. Miller, the sweet-faced, iron-gray-haired wife of the minister, was coming today. School would be out soon. But she wanted to get the feel of it for next year so Jerry could get back to his studies. And other good things were happening in True's life. Young Wil had told her he was going to finish the dissertation on time, timeliness being of utmost importance to the august body before whom he must read his work in what they called his "orals." Midgie had written that the Reverend Randy was staying on and had plans for organizing a church. She *thought* there was another reason, but time would tell. And then there was the flow of letters from Kearby to Aunt Chrissy and Clarry to Jerry. Both girls were ecstatically happy, as was Jerry. And Clarry was *safe* . . .

So when and how did it all begin? One moment True was arranging the bucketful of spring beauties with pussywillows. The next moment there was chaos. She hadn't so much as noticed the shift of the wind—its breath now too warm and dry, sucking away the sound of approaching hooves or voices of the riders.

"Trouble, Teacher—*bad* trouble." Little Josie's small voice held fear but no hint of danger. The child probably referred to the wind, which True now heard for the first time. The dread Chinook! Apprehension rose inside her. Her thoughts were busy with plans for getting the children home early when the door burst open, scattering papers about the room in wild disarray.

Suddenly above the roar of the wind there were shouts and angry voices. *Oh, not now, children.* "Pick up the papers and close the door," she ordered in an attempt to restore order. But the shouts grew louder.

"Let go of m'sister, dirty bully! Teac-*cher*!"

"Git th' gals, that 'un—'n t'other side 'er—yuh little weasel, git them teeth outta m'leg yuh half-pint b_____"

The word he used was unacceptable, and the voice was that of a man! True whirled, her vision blurring as she saw some of the children curled into little balls for protection beneath their desks . . . others forming a human screen around the horrifying scene of three masked men trying to pin down two of the larger girls . . . and the remainder clinging to her skirt for protection. What on earth? "*Get out!*" she shouted wildly.

"Wanta be kilt—all of yuh—'n smell yore teacher's blood?" One of the men dragged the screaming girls away. The other aimed a gun at True. "Git goin'—got 'em both, Adamson's gal 'n yer sister as hostage!"

They rode east into the wind—*with the wrong girls . . .*

31
Warning Unheeded

֍

THERE WAS NO time to warn Aunt Chrissy and Jerry. Time was of essence. The mountaineers must know the awful news. And, more importantly, they must know that "their kind" was not responsible. Else there would be civil war—and the fragile thread holding them together would snap. This True was thinking as she took the short-cut where the underbrush was thickest and blackberry vines tore at her long skirt and the laces of her boots as if to hold her back. Maybe the children would alert Mrs. Miller. She could take over in an emergency and—

But there was no more time for thinking. The tumultuous sound of rushing water told her she was nearing the stream. Fed by the river, it would be near flood-stage. And she must cross it by footlog. A quick survey told her that the high water had set the log swaying and that it was slippery from waves which washed against it with such force that they broke to course over the poorly anchored makeshift bridge. True looked away, hoping to overcome the seasickness she felt in the pit of her stomach.

But she couldn't afford the luxury of being sick. A moment's hesitation could mean loss of life! Not once did True think of her own life as she hoisted her skirt and set a tentative foot on the swaying log. It shifted warningly, but only dimly was she aware that she was in trouble. Closing her eyes momentarily, she let go of her skirt and balanced her weight by stretching both arms out the way she did when she, Young Wil, and Marty tried mastering the art of tightrope

518

walking so many years before. Added to childhood memories was that of her more recent crossing. Déjà vu . . .

"Never look down!" True could almost hear Young Wil's warning. So, eyes wide open now, she fixed her gaze on the safe side of the log where she would set foot in only seconds if she kept her wits about her. The roar of the water said she was past midpoint. She was going to make it! And then a piece of bark let go of the parent trunk. There was no time to right herself. She was falling . . . falling . . . falling. The moment seemed to stretch into eternity.

God looks after fools, her husband was to tell her later. Surely He must have reached out and grabbed her, breaking the fall. Else how could she have landed with a violent jolt astride the log—almost senseless but safe? Her teeth ached. Her head swam dizzily. But somehow she must manage to pull her legs from the swirling water, which was getting higher. Soon the log would float away. She must *crawl*.

With superhuman strength, True jerked her petticoats free of the snags which had entangled them but perhaps saved her life. Cautiously, she pulled one leg at a time onto the slippery log and, in a dazed state, began to crawl and claw her way onto the opposite bank.

Surely the Lord told her to look back. And that glance over her shoulder gave her access to the most terrifying view of her life.

The children were crawling, one by one, behind her . . .

"Get back!" she tried to scream. But the teeth of the wind bit into each word, leaving no sound. She would have to direct them by hand.

Waving a hand frantically, True caught the eye of the first little girl. Who? She had no idea. The curtain of rain was blurring the picture, warping small faces grotesquely so that they were beyond recognition. How many were in this army? All the mountaineer children, undoubtedly.

She signaled them to crawl and pointed to her face. Bless their hearts! They understood and, like a trail of ants, they kept creeping toward her, eyes fixed on her face with complete confidence. She understood, understanding humbling her heart. How thankful she was that she had felt only yesterday to read them the story of "The Great Fisherman"—Peter—who must keep his eyes on Jesus to avoid sinking into the churning depths of the sea.

The log tilted crazily and, although True suppressed a scream, the faces focused on hers were calm and trusting. "Come on—that's it—stand up and jump, darling—*jump*—I'll catch you!"

The leader was close enough for True's words to penetrate. The tiny figure rose on unsteady legs and leaped. *Little Susie!* True held the frail body to her while directing the second child to jump.

"Run, both of you—run as fast as your legs will carry you! *Jump!*" she ordered the third and fourth children. "Go home quickly and tell your parents it was strangers—nobody from here—who kidnapped the girls!"

The procession seemed endless and the log was no longer visible. True had never prayed so hard. "*All* of them are coming—Lord, help me!"

At last it was over. The children scattered, dodging outcropping rocks, sliding down and getting up determinedly, never looking down to the valley floor. True lost all sense of direction in the gathering darkness. Somewhere she heard the welcome clang of a cowbell. They must be getting near to one of the cabins. She concentrated on her footing. "Uptilted," the folk who lived here described this part of the mountain. "Straight up" would have been more apt, True was thinking as her foot slipped and the wind did the rest. She fell, head striking something hard and solid . . .

She must have lost consciousness. Someone was wiping her face and speaking soothingly, but the words were garbled. "Children . . . told . . . said the doctors came . . . ready to care for . . . wounded." Jerry? Yes, the voice was stronger now. The words made sense.

It was too late, he said. Too late. The men went crazy. Ignored the message and, arming themselves, rode away. *They were going to kill every Appalachian in Slippery Elm. There would be a slaughter . . .*

32
The Legend of True North

⁊

SOMEDAY TRUE WOULD be called a vital, courageous woman in the annals of Oregon history. Even the pines would whisper her name as future generations told her story. She weighed and measured everything with those heaven-blue eyes, then tackled the job, big or little. Not a mean bone in her body, but spirited as a young pony— and often just as playful. Her young heart was molded from love, hope, and faith—and talk about endurance! Nobody ever figured, for instance, how she managed to get all those children across that flimsy footlog in time—Just before the whole contraption hurled itself down the raging torrent, angered at the delay. If ever a man had saved so many lives he'd have been awarded a medal.

But for now she felt like a failure through and through. How could she have imagined even in her wildest dreams that she could cut through the lineage of generations, take this one back to their fine heritage, build on it, renew their pride in a single year? They were so hungry in mind and spirit. And she could feed them! Hadn't she seen them bloom out, only to shrivel beneath the slightest pressure, renew their feuds, become actually violent over trivia? They had an iron will and, worse, seemed to take actual pleasure in finding a reason to keep their feuds alive. She had failed.

And she was so tired, so tired. It was hard to raise her head from the pillow to take the broth that Aunt Chrissy almost forced her to drink. Hard to move beneath the covers, but easy to remain in bed.

521

Ordinarily, she thought foggily, she would have flatly refused to stay
put when she was ordered to bed by Young Wil—

Young Wil! Reality was replacing the blind alleys through which
she had passed. Where was he? What had happened? And for the first
time, True pulled herself upright, fumbling for her robe.

Gently her aunt pushed her back. "Oh, my darling, you had us all
so scared! But not too fast—easy—give yourself time."

Time? There was no time! That was the last she remembered
clearly. What followed came back in fragments with voids between.
Never mind the blow on her head . . . not when people were killing
other people . . .

It *all* came back then. Jerry's bringing her to one of the cabins on
the mountains. Men making a litter . . . bringing her home . . . so they
weren't all gone? True must have spoken aloud, for Aunt Chrissy
filled her in. "Remember Young Wil's departure, sweetheart?"

True nodded with a half-smile. "What a foolhardy thing to do, brat!
Can't I trust you to stay out of trouble. This is a nasty blow, Uncle
Wil. Give me a hand—I have to go, but, yes, you stay. We never know
what'll happen. I'm glad you sent for the girls—*hold still!*"

"Wil North," True managed to mumble numbly, "you—are—
bos-sy—"

She may have argued or pleaded—or had she dreamed that part?
Either way, he was as convinced as she that one person could save
the world. And now he was gone . . . but would she have it otherwise?

"School's dismissed," Aunt Chrissy went on to say. "The roof was
blown off—and the children are in no condition to study. Kearby and
Clarry are home—and you know why. It was a case of mistaken identity. The kidnappers could return—now, stay put—"

"I'm hungry! And then there are a million things I must do."

But first she must learn the facts. And they came from all sources.
Faster than True would have believed possible.

The first night True sat up, a woolly blanket wrapped about her
and her toes toasting before the widemouthed fireplace where a blazing fire cast friendly shadows leaping over the waxed furniture in the
Big House parlor, a surprise guest came calling. At the loud, persistent knock, Kearby and Clarry scampered to the kitchen. Jerry rose,
hesitated, and picked up Uncle Wil's hunting rifle.

"Not on your life!" Jerry's mother sprang forward and grabbed the gun. "We do *not* settle problems that way. *No violence.* You know that."

Jerry stood straight and tall. Then he decisively opened the latch.

Without prelude, a bulky, rain-soaked man burst into the room. True's shock was so great that her eyes could focus only on the puddles of muddy water forming around the enormous boots, worn so thin that two toes were visible. *Mr. Courtland, the man she had disarmed!*

"Ain't no social call, this," he said, nervously twisting his hat and glancing with combined awe and uneasiness around the cozy room. "I jest had t'tell of circumstances 'mongst our people. It's beholdin' I am t'yuh, Miz North. Yer one fine lady—and brave'rn them three whut walked through far—*fire*—in th' Good Book—not gittin' their feet burnt! Savin' m'baby, Little Susie, 'n all th' rest—depend on us t'be rewardin' y' all with 'nuther of them roasted pigs. God bless ye—" he wiped his eyes, almost overcome with emotion. "Guess I better be sittin'. Th' rest'll take a spell . . ."

His story began.

There was a great commotion as the men from Centerville cantered into Slippery Elm, which was all but deserted. Just beyond, a great group had congregated to see the outcome of a "dilly of a fight" which was a downright peculiar one. Two men had married twin sisters (cousins, of course, all being inbred). The women got caught in the rainstorm, one making it across the rain-swollen stream and the other stuck on the other side. Well, the husbands were waiting and the one closest to the river grabbed what he thought was his wife, but 'twas the twin. When the stream settled back to normal, the other man crossed to get his wife. Only problem was they got themselves the wrong women. That was history.

But this was now—in this storm. Seems like when they found out the difference the men decided they'd better get trading, might even have to offer "boot." Trouble was, the "confounded women" didn't want to change back, and the men were madder than hornets. The principle of the thing, you know. So they were all yelling like bats outta you-know-where. Now should they get shooting or act like their wives said? Could mean 'twas meant to be . . .

A preacher—kind of funny-like one—came. Randy Somebody.

Must have been "Prim'tive," for he said they'd have to switch back. Had those men crying and saying they hadn't meant any harm— wanted to be baptized while the creek was high. Preacher had a hard time telling them they'd all be drowned. But they said 'twas fine. They'd die clean—

True found herself wanting to burst into laughter. No wonder the girls, who had summoned enough courage to peek around the door facing, were stifling snickers. But what had this to do with the critical situation between the two groups of Appalachian people? Chris Beth asked. "And you girls," she called over her shoulder without turning, "get the coffee boiling. Our guest must be chilled."

Oh, but it did have something to do with it! Mr. Courtland's weathered face crinkled into a smile. "God's way of lettin' tempers cool— 'n do His mir'cle! Sudden-like there wuz a tug on this arm here—'n then on 'tother. 'N, bless Pete, thar they wuz—my gals—my *beau-tee-fulest* li'l gals in this ole worl'! Safer'n a pig in a poke!"

The big mountaineer took leave as unceremoniously as he had entered—refusing coffee and refusing to answer any more questions. Two of his boys had taken their sisters home. Now he must be with their mother.

There was no sleep at the Big House that night. Where was Young Wil? What had happened to cause the release of the two Courtland girls held captive? Who was responsible? True would feel better if Grandma Mollie were here, only to have Jerry blurt out, "She's with the men— insisted that the bereaved womenfolk would need comforting."

"With them?" True said dully. "You mean—why, I didn't even know O'Higgin went, and now you tell me this. Grandma Mollie in Slippery Elm," she repeated, unable to believe her ears. "Has everybody gone crazy?"

"Up there, yes, I'd be-a-sayin' thet's accurate-like." There had been a prolonged silence as True's question hung between them. And now it was answered by Miss Mollie herself. "I let myself in th' back way. O'Higgin's tetherin' th' horse thataway. Like ourse'ves, th' nag gits winded—"

"Oh, Grandma Mollie!" When True sprang to where the big woman had sunk wearily into a rocker, she was followed immediately by the rest of the family, all chorusing, "Tell us—*tell* us!"

"Leave me Mollie-gal ketchin' a wee bit o'air!" O'Higgin boomed as he slammed the kitchen door against the wave of cold morning air. "Yuh wanta tell hit—go ahead—after yuh stomp them muddy boots!" his wife ordered in her scrubbed-clean household voice. Of course, in the end, it was the two of them who gave the account as they saw it.

The Reverend Randy had himself a real problem, a bear by the tail, they said—even before the Centerville army came looking for trouble.

Early in the year as it was, 'twas time to store barrels of liquid spirits to mix with the other kind of Spirit that preachers always hoped to generate in their summer tent meetings. No real problem, mind you, amongst the Slippery Elm folks—Reverend Randy and Marty (oh, what a pair!) had just about dried that place out. Until the arrival of "that clan." Humph! Claiming that 'twas a necessary part of the revival—had to have communion, didn't they? Now Randy and Tillie refused to deal with the stuff, so they brought their own to peddle. Sold it, too, at a whopping profit, until Randy ordered them out—called them a tribe of Gypsies and worse, a "den of thieves." Mad to the core, they were all out to get Randy. But would you believe the mountain folks who came riding in to make trouble ended it? Leastwise, stalled it for awhile.

The rumor made the rounds somehow. And one big mortal just up and preached himself! "'Tain't God's will we go shootin' preachers—guess that'd take us all to th' fiery pit yer so 'feared of yuh fled th' homeland! Whatta bunch of cowards 'n hypocrits—hellbound! Thet preacher's right! No wonder our child'urn's a disgrace, built of th' same dust as their parents—'n jest as dirty! Know why? *We made 'em thet way!*"

There was a mumbling amongst the crowd, then silence so thick you could serve it on a platter. Even the katydids hushed making music. Hearts began hammering like a cabin was being roofed. And then!

"Hit ain't right," another man yelled from the angry mob of uninvited guests. "Us wantin' t'lay down arms lack we do, 'cuz we're seekin' out a edju-ca-shun 'n wuz seein' th' light—'til yuh done this hor'ble thang—stealin' our innocent virgins—ye servants of th' devil!"

There was a terrible commotion then. *Terrible.* Everybody on the opposite side of the river drew their guns, then, appearing to think a minute, replaced them. But their protests were so loud that "that body of peacemakers—you know, th' wonderful kinfolks of Clarry's—heard and just boldly marched into all, singin' praises like th' katydids—" Miss Mollie began, only to be interrupted by her husband.

"Begory! They jest up 'n poured all thet rot-gut into the risen river, they did, they did! Howled like wildcats, eh, Mollie-gal? Th' owners, they be. Whilst some of them thet be pretenders of faith took on th' notion 'twould be a good time fer bein' 'baptized in th' spirit— down stream, that be!"

"Irish is a-tellin' hit straight—'ceptin' fer th' vital part! Turns out them Appalachians wuzn't responsible a-tall—"

"Right ye be, me lassie! Right ye be! But t'git back to me version, th' hypocrits wantin' t'be' baptized in th' spirit' got theirselves one whoppin' surprise. Our folks up 'n whipped out guns—and me, I be wishin' fer me bagpipes t'celebrate—feelin' 'twas justified usin' weapons in sech case as this be—"

"Killin's never justified, O'Higgin!"

O'Higgin laughed and did a jig. " 'Twarn't necessary. Them cowards jest dropped t'their knees 'n begged fer mercy—hard tellin' if they be a-pleadin' t'th' Almighty on 'is throne er them thet be on th' riverside!"

True shook her head. Unbelievable, all of it. But where was her husband? Yet what she must ask was: "If they didn't, who did? I mean, who took my students?"

"Oh, thet—" Grandma Mollie shrugged as if that were a minor part of the whole scenario. "Why, 'twas th' crooks seekin' Adamson's loot. Th' militia arrived, found 'em, 'n hauled 'em off t'court without takin' time t'tear down their ugly faces from th' post-office wall, 'n guess whut!"

She was about to say that the awful war had ended, that folks would go on to tell about the legend of True North . . .

33
"Starbright"

⤴

THE NEXT DAY dawned bright and clear—just right for turning the calendar to "April." True woke up early, feeling refreshed and completely restored. The morning star still lingered in the west when she stole out of the Big House and hurried to the cabin. She must clean house and have sourdough pancakes ready for mixing when Young Wil arrived. This was the day her husband would be home— her heart told her so. She unbraided her hair, brushed it vigorously, and then—allowing it to cascade down her back—knelt at the window still in her robe. "Good morning, Lord; there is so much to thank You for—and one of them is for hanging the stars in the sky—stars to light the night—and stars of hope—"

Again she looked at the star, its brilliance lighting the horizon. Who said one must pray with eyes closed? Hers were wide open, lighted with awe at God's handiwork. "Starlight, star bright—" she incorporated into her prayer, so lost in wonder that she failed to hear the little squeak of joy which the cabin door always gave when someone entered.

"'First star I see tonight'—and it's tangled into your hair."

The words were soft, tender, almost reverent. "Wil—*Wil*! Oh, my darling—my darling!"

True was in her husband's arms, held with such tenderness that it seemed almost a sacrilege when he kissed her ear and whispered, "What's for breakfast, my little heroine?"

527

Over pancakes, Young Wil rounded out the story, made it come alive for True. No need pretending, he grinned as he poured honey generously over a third helping—he was scared, just plain scared. He, Marty, the Valley folk who went along with O'Higgin, and the two ministers decided it was prudent not to interfere unless the situation got out of hand. Did they have a hand in the truce? Well—he guessed so—who could say? The outcome, of course, had to be an answer to prayers which flooded heaven. But who could have guessed *how* God would choose to go about it?

True laid down her fork. "I just never dreamed—are you aware of how much the two clans *hated* each other? It was a prime example of the irresistible force meeting head-on with the immovable object— if such a condition were possible."

"You don't believe that can happen, huh?" he grinned over his coffee cup.

"I doubt it. Some day that force would come up against something that proved it to be irresistible—or the immovable object would budge —I think. I'm not smart like you—so you tell *me*."

"Not smart? Ha! Women have always been our superiors. They just have the good sense to keep it to themselves. I quite agree with your logic, Mrs. North, but—let's suppose it *were* possible?"

True shook her heavy hair, pushing at a curl that kept falling over her right eye. She squinted in concentration, then turned palms up.

"Both would be consumed by friction."

"So," she said slowly, "that's how it happened—and they both realized they would be destroyed—here and in the hereafter—"

Young Wil looked longingly at the stack of brown sourdough pancakes. "Get thee behind me, Satan!" Then, wiping his mouth determinedly and refolding his napkin, he returned to the Appalachians. "Of course, they disliked giving in—kept chipping away at trivia—which church was *The Church*—amusing claims about Luther, Wesley, even John the Baptist (claiming he was a Primitive, of course!). But what clinched the deal was, of all people, that bold little foreman of the Double N! Billy Joe marched up and stood between the armies separated by a river and stubborn thinking.

"Now looky here, folks. D'yuh honest-to-Pete think th' first question our Maker's a-gonna ask is, 'Which denomination wuz yuh?'"

The Reverend Randy, taking advantage over the sudden silence, moved in to outline the plan, the *real* plan to salvation, raising his voice until it rang against the mountain. (The Slippery Elm folk needed a message of "th' ole-time religion" through the mouth of a "God-fearin' man whut wuzn't a-feared t'speak up.") Dr. Miller followed, wading right out into the threatening current of the water, and talked about living out that Plan. "Are you aware," the big man with the gentle voice asked, "that first and foremost we are to love God with all our hearts—the first commandment—and that *all* the others relate to man's love for his brother? Think about it," he pleaded.

Billy Joe, overcome with the limelight he had captured, wasn't about to lose it. "Ever hear of shootin' yer neighbor 'cuz yuh love 'im so much—did'ja, huh? Yuh gotta minister to 'em—thet's whut—'n thet means bustin' up them stills, so as not t'take advantage of another man's weakness like a bunch of buzzards—understan'? Otherwise, ye cain't go 'round askin' t'be baptized—thet'd be empty as some of yer thick skulls! Wanna git into heaven—huh?"

They understood.

Young Wil consulted his pocketwatch and whistled. "I'm late—"

"Late! Wil North, you've had no sleep for a week!"

He laughed. "Now who's being bossy? You, the *perfect* model—want to spoil your reputation?"

"*Perfect?* Who said *that?*"

"All of them—both sides! Poor Billy Joe's moment of glory was short-lived. All began babbling about how it was you who taught their children right from wrong and the children brought the ideas home. Come with me while I shave."

True lifted the heavy kettle, wondering if there was enough hot water. Fortunately there was. She hurried to the bedroom and poured the white china washbasin full. There was a burst of steam and immediately the mirror above the washstand was fogged over. Before blotting it clean, she looked at her blurred image, unable to recognize her reflection. *Who am I, Lord?* her heart whispered. *Just what do You expect of me?*

The moment passed. Seating herself on the slipper chair nearby, she asked a long series of questions, listening raptly while her husband filled her in between practiced strokes of the straight razor, making neat ravines through the mountains of white lather. Yes, of course, he saw Marty's family. Helped celebrate the March Hare's birthday, in fact. Midgie loved the tiny gold ring that True ordered through Meier and Frank's with "Chris" engraved inside along with his birthday. "She probably told you the details," Young Wil said, reaching sheepishly into his back pocket to pull out a crumpled envelope. And, yes, he had a chance to talk briefly with Tillie, though not long enough to find out the secret of that glow on her face. Anna-Lee had been in touch with Clarry.

"She wants the girl back and is perfectly capable of teaching her at home—they all prefer that, you know. There's a real change in Clarry—and I," he paused to wrap a hot towel around his face and mumble through it, "give you credit for that, too. She identified with the diary—says our generation is repeating the history recorded, and," removing the towel, he looked straight into her eyes, "that theirs will carry on in the same tradition. Now, don't ask where she fits in—I think you know. Just be prepared to use that fatal charm of yours on Chrissy—uh, Aunt Chrissy—one hill at a time. Now, no more questions—do I have a clean white shirt? Oh, all the hands send love, and of course an invitation to visit. And no begging's necessary," he grinned, buttoning the starched shirt that True had laid out wordlessly. "We'll go just as soon as this book and exam are finished, I promise. Button the top, sweetie."

True wanted to rush into his arms with a squeal of delight, but something bothered her about the way he kept talking as if to head off further questions. What was he withholding?

"All right, out with it!" she said suddenly. "Something's wrong."

She had expected him to remind her of the time. Instead, he sat down on the edge of the bed and motioned her to join him. "Yes—something *is* wrong, having nothing to do with the reconciliation—at least, not directly." He dropped his head into his hands. Alarmed, True placed a supporting arm about his slumped-over shoulders and waited.

"What I saw there made me sick. And I don't know how to handle it. If I explain the medical facts, they're sure to equate it with 'God's will,' predestination, or God's way of showing His wrath for their sins. Some of the problems we can solve with a health program such as you have going here. Education's slow, but it will get them there eventually. But meantime—well, help me figure out what to do."

They were going blind, almost all of them. Young Wil's voice choked with emotion. They called it "sore eyes" and washed them with salt water, which was like pouring oil on a spreading fire. The eyes burned worse. They clawed and tore at them because of the irritation—yes, there was a name for it, *trachoma,* according to Uncle Wil's medical book. And the prognosis was worse than what they endured now. Blurred vision first, then the eyeballs would dry up in their sockets—blindness. And (True was sure he almost gagged) then there was another kind of problem, with eyes rolling around in their skulls. This afflicted the newest generation. Unable to focus. Couldn't read. Could hardly see to feed themselves. Research showed that some, maybe all, of the problem was due to intermarriages practiced over a long history. Of course, there were other problems. Typhoid had begun cropping up. Fortunately, he had vaccine to begin an immunization program—but they needed three injections—and then there was lung fever, hookworm, and trichinosis from a heavy diet of pork—

One of Young Wil's fists struck the opposite palm with a *whang!*

Sickened, True tried to make her voice sound steady. "One hill at a time, darling—remember? Go back. I'll finish the school year and join you. Then we can get answers and help from the State Department of Health when you're called to Portland—"

"I've been summoned. The date is April fifteenth." His voice was flat with acceptance of failure. "And you can't leave—not now—"

"Things will work out, darling. We *won't* surrender. Let's pray!"

There was no progress in getting the roof on the school repaired. Men promised to help, but they had problems with damage at home. All this aroused Nate Goldsmith's ire so that his screams of rage would have done credit to a bull moose. The school remained without a roof.

Feeling depressed, True suggested to Chris Beth that they get an early start and pay Miss Mollie a call. It would be good for them all. Taken by surprise, the older woman gathered up her colorful scraps and rolled them into a bundle while trying with one hand to hoist the quilting frame to the ceiling. The result was a scattering of diamond-shaped scraps all over the floor of Turn-Around Inn's parlor.

"How lovely!" The guests hurried to give their hostess a hand. "Who will receive this—oh, *these,* two of them! A full-size and a wee one?"

"They're promised—leastwise, in my mind. A surprise, sort of."

True laughed. "Is the pattern a secret, too?"

Grandma Mollie relaxed. "Not on yer life—'tis 'Star Bright'!"

34
Volunteers for Jesus

❧

EASTER!

Never before had Centerville Church held such a crowd as was in attendance the following Sunday. Word had circulated that the mountaineers were coming en masse. And then there were the faithful of the Valley. In addition, there were newcomers—actually well-known, but strangers to the church. Probably out of curiosity, True whispered to Aunt Chrissy.

Well, they couldn't have chosen a better day, Aunt Chrissy was to whisper back, tears coursing down her cheeks . . .

Dr. Miller shook hands with them all as they entered, calling the regulars by name. "Punkie" Perkins, who claimed to be an atheist, was noted for being on the defensive. "What kind of doctor are yuh—treat animals er human bodies?"

"I treat men's souls," Dr. Miller answered with a smile.

A little flustered, Punkie muttered, "Well, yuh got'cher work cut out fer yuh here 'bouts. Want me t'plead fer mercy?"

"God does." The gentle answer sent Punkie slinking into a corner.

That set the mood. The mountain folk, scrubbed, starched, and well-behaved, overheard and, with a look of pity at the man, marched with unexpected dignity to the very front pews.

Dr. Miller related the incident in Slippery Elm without emotion. "What they need more than cash contributions is love and understanding, and eventually some teaching *by people who understand.* What they need are recruits."

532

The closing song rang out:

A volunteer for Jesus, a soldier true,
Others have enlisted, why not you?

One could see the exhilaration in faces of the "Uplanders" as they stormed the pulpit. "Yuh ast fer recruits, yuh got 'em—learnin' t'read th' Good Book 'n cleanin' up th' mother tongue, well as our sinful ways, Doc—'n who can be understandin' better'n us?"

Dr. Miller could not argue with that. Neither did he seem to doubt the good people's sincerity. A few low questions. A pumping of hands. Tears. And there were those who said Punkie Perkins crawled out the back window to escape being mobbed.

It was then that Jerry, followed by Kearby and Clarry (holding hands as if for strength) walked down the inclined aisle. "You asked for volunteers," Jerry's voice wavered only slightly. "Here are three. We've dreamed of faraway places—China, Africa—and talked about the needs in Slippery Elm. But that's a long way off. We just want to answer the call right now—then go back to school to prepare ourselves. 'Study to show thyself approved,' I think the Bible puts it—"

The minister was too overcome to do more than put his arms around them. That's when Chris Beth commenced to cry. Not that she cried alone.

The touching moment was shattered by Nate Goldsmith's bull-moose voice. "Now, how 'bout some volunteer *laborers*? None of this puts a roof on th' school." A few hands went up, but not enough to shake a roof. "Well," Nate looked at them pityingly, "'As ye sow, so shall ye reap.' Guess yuh'd ruther jest shut th' door in young faces—end th' year—"

The protests the little man expected failed to come. There was a shout of glee from the children instead, then another round of applause when O'Higgin suggested that the Valley ladies pack barrels of dried fruit, smoked meat, and usable clothing for the Centerville Appalachians to take to their Slippery Elm brethren. "Hard it be, ye should be knowin', t'pray on a empty stummick—want I should pronounce the benediction?"

Dr. Miller nodded. The congregation joined hands. The benediction was powerful.

35
Some Went, Others Stayed

⤜

CLARRY RETURNED THE diary to True the day she departed to finish the school year with Kearby. There were tears in her lovely eyes. "I am torn between three worlds?" she said. "Kearby's world, this beautiful Valley—and, yes, uh—Jerry—and Anna-Lee Hancock, who is my family. But the diary helped. I am not the first to wonder which direction I must take—eventually—oh, what a beautiful Easter—"

There was a sudden blast of April-sweet air as the door was flung open to admit O'Higgin into the cabin. Had he knocked? Or eavesdropped?

"Th' top o'th' mornin' to ye, lassies!" he smiled with a doff of his hat, then picked right up on the conversation. "Decisions never be easy, me bonnie one. Think back on Christopher Columbus—think 'twas easy fer 'im t'set sail on a square ocean? Then th' Pilgrims, so we be worshipin' as we be choosin'—tho' sometimes I be needin' t'borrow me a school dictionary t'tell what brand o'faith most lay claim to. Be thet no matter—long as we love Jesus—oh, 'twas right proud o'ye I be yesterday, lass! Then there be me own ancestors—rest their souls—who be makin' th' greater contribution t'history, them what lef' when th' potato crops failed er them whut be stayin' t'build back? Who be th' quitter? None o'them," he answered himself. "All be hearin' th' voice o'God—jest like you, lass—jest like th' clan bustin' up on th' mountainside—some gonna be stayin' jest like True and her Young Wil—"

534

There was no chance for Clarry Hancock to reply, for Kearby had come to bid her goodbye. Chris Beth was with her to hurry them along, but even so they were delayed by an unexpected turn of events.

Clarry's serious mood disappeared with a dimpled grin, a reminder of how young she was. "Did you show True his picture?"

Kearby's face reddened. The glance she gave her mother from lowered eyelids was uneasy. Chris Beth met her daughter's eyes levelly. "We have always been open, Kearby—all of us—as a family. I have no idea who *he is* and have no intention of prying—"

True walked over to embrace her cousin, whom she thought of as Baby Sister. "Who is the Mystery Man, sweetie? Want to share him?"

Kearby's lower lip trembled as if she were on the verge of tears. Clarry's regret at her question showed in her face. But, to the surprise of them all, Kearby lifted her chin, shoved a hand into an overstuffed bag, and, after fumbling for some time, pulled out the photograph of the young man. Young, yes, but older than these girls, one glance told True. The thin, bespectacled face held a certain charm. What was the look? Determination? Dedication? Whatever, it was appealing. And True said as much, praying that Aunt Chrissy would soft-pedal her concerns.

And she did. "Is this the young man you wrote about? Why haven't you brought him for a visit? The brother of a friend, you wrote?"

Little lights of joy flared in Kearby's face and the words tumbled out. Kevin was wonderful. Handsome in a mature way, enough older to make boys her age look silly. How much older? Nine years, maybe, and *so* brilliant and devoted to his college work—going to be a minister like Uncle Joe. Kearby was *so* glad Mother understood; she could tell by Aunt Vangie's diary that the sisters had seen so many kinds of love . . . Young Wil's for his teacher (Chris Beth) . . .

Mother's for Uncle Joe, then Daddy . . . and don't forget (triumphantly) that Young Wil was as much older than True as Kevin is my senior. "Of course, we have to make decisions . . . a long time from now . . ."

Wagons loaded ("lock, stock, 'n barrel," Nate described it), the mountaineers left just short of April fifteenth. Even in the excitement of the self-proclaimed "evangelists'" departure, the date set wheels turning in True's head. The date was significant . . . well, of *course* it was . . . the day Young Wil was scheduled to make his presentation before the august Board. And she could go! Why, the roofless school had proven a blessing—letting the mountaineers take their children and leave for Slippery Elm and allowing her to go with her husband!

A sea of faces swam around her . . . beautiful blond angels . . . and, in contrast, those with midnight hair and eyes (proof of a comingling of genes) . . . and those with carrot-red hair and a sprinkling of freckles marching across small noses. And then there was Buster—big, brutal Buster, who had learned to deal with life in his own way. Books were a waste of paper for the onetime bully, but he had powerful muscles and a will of iron. God could make use of more like him. If Buster could learn the value of obedience, anybody could. After all, no matter what one's "doctrine," wasn't obedience a key word? "I ain't never gonna be full of frivol a'gin, Teacher, all cuz of you loved me 'n learnt me Jesus kin put th' likes of me t'work. I dun made my paw see th' light." "Boy's right," his hardheaded, giant father (who once met life with balled-up fists) agreed. "Ain't a-gonna lay a hand on nobody 'ceptin' t'try healin' their souls. But yuh kin betcha life I'm a-gonna meet thet incestin' headon—gonna bury hit, 'n be a pallbearer fer th' fun'ral!"

"Now, be rememberin'," O'Higgin blew his nose and began, "ther' be no disgrace in failure—"

Mr. Courtland saluted smartly. "Lessen ye blame it on somebody else!"

The children made a great production of saying goodbye, weeping, holding to True's skirts, and worshiping her with their eyes. True withheld her tears until they were out of sight. And then she wept bitterly, for a part of her heart was gone.

36

The Outside World

⌒

ONCE, AT THE top of the rise leading out of the Valley, True looked over her shoulder for one last look at the painted scene spread as far as the eye could see. Orchards in full bloom. Gardens lushly verdant with promise. And newly scarred land which—after removal of the conifer trees—became "black gold" to tillers of the rich, raw land. Every person she knew and loved took on substance in a new form, as if momentarily God gave her a peek into their very souls. "You would be proud of us, Angel Mother," she mused as if she sat alone in the buggy seat—"those who left to fulfill God's purpose, and those who remained behind for the same reason."

Young Wil pretended not to see her wipe away a tear. "And now, it's on to Portland!" True smiled. Then she laughed aloud. "Do you realize that we're going to get that honeymoon at last?"

The room felt stuffy. Her eyelids felt heavy, so heavy. Maybe she was coming down with—what was that horrible eye disease? True wondered vaguely if Young Wil had incorporated—*trachoma*, that was it—in his case studies. But listen, she must *listen*. Someone, a portly gentleman with a stern face, was introducing Young Wil. Their future lay at stake.

"Gentlemen," her husband was saying, "before presenting my paper, may I present my wife, True North, without whose help I would have been unable to conduct the live research. *True!*"

Taken by surprise, she stood. Aware only of a spattering of polite
applause by the men, she concentrated on his opening statement: "We
are caught in a decade of change. And, lest we move too fast—no
matter what cries out from the human body for help—there must be
research and case studies. Science alone is not enough, unless we test
it. Medicine is like a limpet at midtide struggling to be at home on
the land of the past and the sea of the future. Tenaciously and nos-
talgically, too often sentimentally, one foot desperately clinging to
the anchor of certainty of home remedies while the other reaches for
the unknown. Our glory lies in seeing ourselves as guardians—riding
out the tide of untested trends. What have we in common in this hall
today? We are doctors, under oath to treat the flesh and—according
to my thesis—*the relationship between the mind and the body*. Call
it Mental Health!"

The men listened respectfully. Then, they—like her—became so
absorbed that her "studies," combined with her husband's observa-
tions, took on flesh, walking and talking up and down the aisles,
crying out for help—and getting it. How? By conviction that someone listened . . . understood . . . and cared . . .

"Oh, darling, you were eloquent," True whispered shakily as hand-
in-hand they left the men to caucus for what might be hours or days.

"I had *you*. I watched your eyes, pretending the committee cared
as much—and, in a way, I guess they do. Time will tell. What we
need is oxygen to clear our brains!"

"You mean noise to numb them—let's take a walk—and not
think."

Eagerly they descended the stairs and were about to go out the front
door when Young Wil stopped. "Oh, I need to see these people," he
said, reading aloud: "STATE DEPARTMENT OF HEALTH AND
WELFARE."

True understood and sat down on a bench against the wall. Then
feeling suddenly weary, she closed her eyes—only to have them fly
open at the sound of Michael St. John's "True North!" and then teasingly, "We have to stop meeting like this!"

True felt genuinely pleased to see him, and invited him to sit down.
"Only for a moment," Michael said. "I guess we are both wondering
what brought the other here."

True explained, and he was sympathetic. "I would spend no time worrying over the doctor's 'pass' or 'fail' chances. He's a bright man, True, and among the most dedicated. As for the needs of our mountain people, nobody is more aware than I. I wish," he said slowly, "that God had shaken my shoulders before He did—think of what I could have done back there in Atlanta for the deprived—"

"It is never too late, Michael. I am proud of you—but, tell me what you are doing here."

His face lighted up. "I'm working on getting a school in Slippery Elm—so much red tape—but I might as well make use of the pull I have with some of the powers that be. I know them all through my holdings in the railroads, which, as rumor has it, may come under government control. Then," he inhaled deeply, "I am giving thought to entering the political arena. Washington could use some tough but caring men. 'Congressman St. John'—how about that, huh?"

True smiled in encouragement but had no time to reply. The head of an austere woman who looked for all the world as if she had been sucking on a lemon popped out of the "DEPARTMENT OF EDUCATION" door. "Mr. Alexander will see you now—*only* you," she added with a forbidding look.

The old debonair Michael returned. He winked at True boldly, making sure that the man-tailored woman saw. "Where are you staying?" he called over his shoulder.

"We call it 'Honeymoon Hotel'—ours—"

A look of near-envy crossed his face. The woman remained at the door, her eyes narrowing in suspicion. For Michael, laughter, even in the face of uncertainty, came easy. True found herself joining him now. For that she was always grateful, as it was the last time she was to see him in person, although his face would smile triumphantly in *The Oregonian* the next election year. And his name would be engraved one day on the ST. JOHN SCHOOL in a town once called Slippery Elm.

Young Wil was smiling when he came back. The health department was going to send a committee to Slippery Elm to "investigate matters." That must surely translate into help, since nobody could fail to see the need.

But she said nothing, for no misgivings must spoil his mood. Why, her husband was whistling under his breath in a way she had not

heard him do for what the mountain people would call a "coon's age."
Unbidden, more of their colloquialisms swarmed back—"noisome"
. . . "brutishism" . . . and such Biblical words as "verily, verily" . . .
"hireling" . . . "at cock's crow" . . . "I say unto you" . . . "art" (for *are*).
Stop this, True ordered her mind. But she realized then that the people
she had grown to love and understand had perhaps come closer to
the original language of the Bible than some of the other interpreters.
What's more, they had left more than a speech pattern which would
crop up unexpectedly now and then among descendants of the original Oregon settlers as the years went by. As for herself—well, they
had done more than take away a part of her heart; they had left a part
of theirs in return.

Young Wil was still whistling. Should he—in the city? It seemed
almost inappropriate to express one's joy here. Well, proper or not,
money couldn't purchase from her the thrill of seeing the exuberance
in her husband's face. He looked downright little-boyish as he stopped
at the building's exit and said, "'*Eloquent*'? Did I really do that well—
or," hesitating uncertainly, "just how do you define the word?"

His speech, he must be talking about. Young Wil, who was always
so sure of himself, should take to heart her adjective? True felt like
whistling herself! "Eloquent?" (How *would* she define it? He just
was!) "I guess," she said slowly, "eloquent is saying the just-right
words—and no more."

"Oh, darling!" Young Wil grabbed her up and swung her around.
"I'm going to buy you the prettiest dress in Portland!"

"Wil North," True gasped in embarrassment, "put me down! What
will people think?"

"That we're in love!" he laughed triumphantly before setting True
on her feet. "Everything's coming up roses—you've made me feel it!"

True was giddy with happiness. She might as well have been sip-
ping liquid ambrosia from the peak of Mount Olympus. Oh, God was
good!

Outside, True could only gasp at the scene spread before her. Where
were all these people going in such a hurry—ladies sweeping grandly
down the boardwalks with heads held so high True marveled that
they didn't trip over their pointed-toe shoes? And look at those hats!
Bedecked with flowers and ribbons, the brims were so large it was
bewildering that the elegant ladies could avoid colliding with one

another. Most had male escorts dressed in proper black (resembling undertakers to True). The men held their heads just as proudly. They were shod with glistening shoes and spats and carried canes without needing them!

Sighing, True cast one glance at the simple blue broadcloth suit she had bought on the "Better Dress" rack at Solomon's. Imagine her thinking that the brooch would look too ornate for Young Wil's presentation! "I'll take you up on that offer for a new dress," she said.

Not that he could hear her above the earsplitting noise. The metallic grind of trolley wheels against their tracks. The clopping of horses' feet against a hard-surface street. The screams of vendors. The backfiring of automobiles. And, above it all, the shrill whistles of seagoing vessels mingled with whistles of smoking manufacturing plants. Why, the very sun was blotted out of the sky periodically as something resembling standpipes belched out smoke. A veil of (True shivered at the word) Stygian darkness overhead.

It would be good to see light, even artificial, inside a store.

In an exclusive boutique True passed over the frilly finery, settling instead for a dark, up-to-date suit, but agreed with the saleslady that the rose-pink blouse was right. A hairdo? True looked at the elaborate coiffures of the boardwalk strollers and knew it was foolish to have a professional do her hair, only to cover it with a hat . So which? At Young Wil's urging, she decided on the hairstyling. Her reward was his gasp of admiration at the nest of golden curls on top, the back caught up smartly in a figure eight.

"One of those wagon-wheel things the other ladies wear would spoil it. But come with me—" So, he had been window shopping?

Smiling, he led her into a millinery shoppe next door. "Oh, so this is your lovely wife," the milliner said kindly, "and here is what your husband has in mind—three pink ruffles which fit snugly between the becoming curls and the stylish figure eight."

This time it was True who gasped. She was no longer the country mouse. Why not be frivolous—maybe even a bit dramatic? But, no, not the ostrich boa. Nothing else, thank you. True walked out of the shoppe holding herself in a stately manner, wondering (with an inner giggle) if she "swept" along instead of walking . . .

The beautiful honeymoon-week was magic-filled. Unaware that admiring glances followed wherever they went, Mr. and Mrs.—no,

Dr. and Mrs.—Wilson North II strolled the boardwalk unfalteringly. They held hands seated in the privacy of an intimate alcove where a young man with a celluloid collar served them . . . attended theaters and operas in the afternoons . . . and strolled the beach barefoot at night . . . then attended a formal church service on Sunday—the only place, oddly, where they felt ignored and ill-at-ease. The congregation faced forward during the service and each other afterward, ignoring the strangers in their midst. Fellowship? A foreign word . . .

April twenty-second? True would remember the date forever. They were enjoying a leisurely breakfast in bed when the telegram arrived.

"Oh, no!" True's laughter filled the room, almost upsetting her coffee on the tray she balanced on her propped-up knees. "If that's the *family*—"

"It isn't." Young Wil had scanned the yellow sheet and begun to dress. "The committee has reached a decision. I must report now—"

He was pale and his hands shook, causing True's own heart to pick up tempo. She helped him adjust his tie and held out his coat. Too soon he was gone. For a year they had worked on a twin aim. Now he must stand before these men with rapier-sharp minds and hear their reaction to: 1. the problem; and 2. the solution.

The door swung open. Young Wil was back with his report. He grabbed True, still in her robe, and danced her around the room. "Did anybody ever tell you that you have the most beautiful eyes God ever used to complete a perfect face?"

"Wil North!" But the swing of his hands erased all solemnity. They went for the idea . . . bought the book and wanted another. *And* how soon could he assume duties as Chief-of-Staff at the big hospital under construction?

37

Crossroads

❧

"IT'S ALMOST MAY." Young Wil's statement pointed out the obvious. True knew, as he knew, that both of them had made small and meaningless conversation since boarding the train at Portland bound for Slippery Elm. Anything to avoid the decisions lying ahead.

Her husband tried again. "I hope," he said, running restless fingers through his thick hair, "we remembered gifts for everybody back home." They were at the crossroads and—

Question: *Where was home?*

True smoothed the folds of her old blue broadcloth. It seemed more appropriate to save her new purchases for some special occasion. "I think so. Diaries seemed appropriate for the girls—and Jerry, for some reason, has always wanted a feathered quill . . ."

A new pipe for Daddy Wil. Aunt Chrissy was right—he would never get away from chewing on the polished reed stem of his ancient corncob pipe, which often went unlighted. The newer ones, meerschaums, had celluloid stems. Aunt Chrissy would love the white India embroidered silk parasol with scalloped edges . . . and wait until Grandma Mollie saw the hardwood cabinet for her spices. *Spice!* The very word sent True's senses reeling . . . Miss Mollie's big kitchen with the monstrous cookstove, its warming closet always filling the air with the memorable fragrance of spice (which never quarreled somehow with the yeasty smell of rising sourdough). And then there were the seasonal smells—honeysuckle mingled with orchards in bloom in springtime, jam-ready grapes ripening in the summer sun,

543

and the fingers of fragrance that reached out from every cranny when she baked the great, clove-stuck hams. True inhaled deeply, realizing that she was seeing the rails ahead through a blur. They never should have left—

Quickly, Young Wil picked up the conversation. "O'Higgin will love the *Song-Leaders' Manual* I found, all the new hymns included. He can read notes, you know—me, I'm a follower, but able to keep up by following his hair-raising baritone which shakes the rafters."

They summed up together then. A leather ledger (name embossed in gold) for Marty . . . an assortment of silk lilacs, daisy wreaths, and roses so real that one could almost smell them for Midgie, a dream-come-true . . . a hand-painted rocking horse for two-year-old Chris . . . a white ostrich feather fan for Mariah (on sale) . . . and, for Tillie and Reverend Randy, the most extravagant gifts of all. The delicate translucent-pink china cup with 22–karat gold on the fluted edge for Tillie's collection would be the most beautiful thing she had owned since leaving her Eastern "socia-whirl" world in search of her niece, who would prove to be Marty's mother. She was starved for beauty. And, as for her dear friend, the minister, he needed a new Bible to replace the aging one from which he tried to teach. The leather-bound one, complete with colored maps and a comprehensive concordance, would thrill his soul and make it well worth the unbelievable price.

By now the Norths' cloud of concern had lifted and their excitement grew by the minute. They laughed over the other purchases— all practical. The ranch hands would be overjoyed with the burlap bags of new grain, the platform scale, the riveted cream cans, the improved dilution contraption for separating cream from the milk, and the new-style automatic rotary churn with a hand crank. *Oh, there went the whistle!*

True grabbed her paisley bag while Young Wil busied himself with the overhead luggage. "Where's the candy?" His words were garbled because he was holding the brim of his hat between his teeth.

"In the baggage car—horehound, peppermint sticks—oh, darling, *look* at the hills of home!"

Her husband looked at her sharply, then realized that True was not fully aware of her words; she was too engrossed in the view. How could she ever have thought of the landscape here as benign? The straight-up cliffs following the curve of the rushing river, less heavily forested than the Valley beyond the "hum,"were beautiful in their own way. Roots of the giant oaks clung to the eroded cliffs—gnarled and inspiring in their fight for life—amid boulders that even now were shifting colors like a kaleidoscope, the patterns of light and shadow always changing. In the back country, clumps of leafless field lilies sprang up in unexpected beauty, and occasionally a person could find the near-extinct trillium among the wood violets in glades of sword fern. Strange that now even the savage-billed vultures sailing in search of the carcass of a baby lamb or calf had a certain charm—graceful in their near-still wings which flashed iridescent-purple against the sun. They were doing the work that nature intended. Scavengers though they were, the giant birds cleared the landscape, preventing disease. How life had changed True's outlook! She saw the balance of nature in a new way. A new balance, too, in people—all fulfilling God's purpose one way or another . . .

And it was quiet. So quiet. The city seemed far away. Just a restful silence that restored her soul—

And burst her eardrums! "Surprise! *Surprise!*" Surely a million voices changed wildly, the echoes bounding back from the canyon walls.

What on earth! Who—? *Who!* Just everybody she and Young Wil had ever known—both here and in the Valley! Aunt Chrissy . . . Daddy Wil . . . O'Higgin waving his shillelagh . . . Grandma Mollie waving her best silk handkerchief. True's eyes were unable to focus on them all, except that some inner instinct told her that all those for whom she and Young Wil had purchased gifts were *here*—and that Midgie and Marty (holding the March Hare) were elbowing their way through the crowd.

"Midgie—oh, Midgie darling—you're *pregnant!*" True gasped in surprise as her sister-in-law reached out in an effort to embrace her. "Talk about being 'great with child,'" she panted. "That's me—due for 'travail' any minute—when are you and Young Wil planning—" (a family? Yes, when?) . . .

Backslapping, hugging, everybody talking at once. Portland's noise could never rival *this!* And Tillie screaming above several heads, "I knew you'd come—I knew you'd make it for our wedding. I *knew* it!"

How on earth did little bowlegged Billy Joe, the B make it to Young Wil's side? "Midgie oughta be delverin 'bout th' same time as th' prize heifer! Guess she—th' boss's Missus—ain't a-gonna let a thang like thet keep'er from holdin' the big blow-out—sez yuh done hit afore 'n kin do it a'gin—brang the girl-chile into th' world—"

Grandma Mollie shoved him aside. "Me? I'm a-gonna stan' up with th' bride 'n groom—Cousin Tillie 'n thet wonderful preacher-husband. Brangs back mem'ries—how I stood alongside yore precious mother a-holdin' Marty whilst Chris Beth took 'er vows—with our precious Vangie lookin' 'bout lack Midgie here—double weddin' lack yours—"

When she paused to blow her nose, O'Higgin interrupted, "Wonderful mon Cousin Tillie be takin'—wonderful mon—"

"*Man*," Miss Mollie corrected between blows of her nose.

Jerry exclaimed excitedly, "I'm hiking up through the Gap. They'll be here tomorrow—both factions of the Appalachians—but somebody ought to tell them we've arrived safely."

"And, besides, I can't wait," he might as well have added.

Tomorrow the children would be swinging to her skirts, all talking at once as the adults were doing now. True was glad that she and Young Wil had run what must have been all the candy stores in Portland in short supply. She was glad, too, that their choice of gifts for Tillie and Randy were their most elegant purchase. Just right for a bride and groom. And, how could she have chosen a more suitable outfit for a wedding? Not that she and Young Wil would be in the wedding party. The day belonged to an older generation, which was as it should be. The world needed to know that love was not reserved for youth, but that true love, blessed by the Spirit, endured timelessly, each year more precious than the one before. She wondered who would perform the ceremony—and then she saw Dr. Miller. Shovel in hand, he was helping dig the barbecue pit.

Oh, they had thought of everything! True felt she would burst with happiness. She was sure she could *hear* the vast acres of wheat growing . . . that the daisies which usually folded their white-petaled lashes at sunset wouldn't sleep a wink tonight . . . and that the May moon rising over the Gap truly *was* made of green cheese.

A small tug at her skirt told True she was not alone. In a nursery-rhyme mood, she swung little Chris up and around dizzily. His golden curls bounced, his laughter rang out merrily, and her own skirt billowed like an inverted mushroom. "As I was going to St. Ives . . ."

St. Ives! Why, that was it, of course. Michael, his life dedicated to service, undoubtedly would be led to build a church. It was no curse to be wealthy, but God expected good stewardship—money was not to be flaunted but shared to help others. Meantime, she and Young Wil would enjoy their moment of glory as "godparents" . . .

38

"Whither Thou Goest . . ."

꧂

IT WOULD BE a night of pandemonium. Hammers would ring out as the ranch hands nailed together a platform for the ceremony and the Grand March musicale to follow. Cookstoves would gobble up wood faster than the men could split the stovewood. And the "good wives" would be doing everything a good woman was supposed to: baking . . . making last-minute nips and tucks in the handsome blue-over-white gown which only Mariah's clever fingers could adjust from a "stout women's size" pattern to a "young-matron" appearance (the nervous bride's only concern being that her wealth of long hair would be dry enough to crimp into a becoming style, the back being somewhat like True's—True *would* help?). And flowers . . . flowers everywhere . . . who took that cake frosting recipe? It was lying right here . . . "Men, stop that poundin'. Want this weddin' cake t'fall? . . . Children, stop runnin' thro' th' archway else no cake fer yuh tomorrow!"

A week . . . wasn't that how long Young Wil had to decide? The Portland offer would be the greatest opportunity of his life—one of the three directions which they must decide between, True reviewed in her mind. And yet her heart knew a strange peace even when the options changed from three to four! Because she had made her decision already . . .

True's eyes scanned the crowd for her husband. There was a compelling urge to talk with him, say the things she'd been unable to find words for on the train. Her eyes met Chris Beth's instead. Her aunt laid down her apron and shouldered her way to where True stood.

"You look lost, darling—missing your mate? I understand—you and I are only half-people without our Wils! They're talking together," she frowned, "a little too seriously for all this—"

Aunt Chrissy made an arc toward the enlarging group. In her hand was a stack of envelopes. "In the commotion, I forgot your mail."

True thanked her and began thumbing through the packet, not sure she knew what she was looking for. Was it the letter from William Prescott? If so, her subconscious was working overtime. The man was out of their lives. Totally and completely. Well, wasn't he?

In the subdued light of a low-burning lamp moments later she was ripping open his envelope and scanning the contents. He had survived the "murderous wilderness" (as others called the Great Smokies—those who predicted he would never come out alive). He loved the mountains and wondered how he could have ever left home, no matter what the reason. The enmity, for the most part, was gone, but remnants of doubt remained. There were those who advised him to be "a mite mo' keerful." Old rancors died hard, so he was compelled to work on forgiveness along with the three Rs—there being no enlightened preacher. True, there hadn't been a "killing or a stilling" for a long while, but disease was taking the populace faster than the shotguns used to. Oh, the wasted potential . . . fine minds falling to ruin . . . healthy bodies of former generations wasting away, neglected. Were they really any better off? Fires that once raged were now a bed of ashes. "I guess," he wrote in near-conclusion, "I've done little more than sink an axe in a giant oak. But where helpers would once have been executed, the people now pray for them—only their belief in God is waning. If He doesn't answer prayer, what's the need of it all?"

True closed her eyes in an effort to withhold the tears. William Prescott had no right to do this to her! Casting his own burdens on her—or *were* they his own? Behind her eyelids flashed visions. Sights and sounds that were somehow familiar, reminders that God created it all and—in some strange way which she did not fully understand—put every man in charge of his brother.

She hovered too much, Young Wil had told her. But how did one escape? Again she saw them, heard them, *dreamed* them. As they were and as they ought to be. Hordes of worshipers in a large church . . . singing, shouting, even allowing for an even distribution of those with colored skins, heretofore "horsewhipped" if they came near . . .

the mellow voices of a black choir whose only musical accompaniment lay outside the church, the soft melody of running water, swift and glistening, as pure as their souls . . . and then the evening-gloam . . . the sad-sweet calls of the whippoorwills chaining themselves to the hearts of all who heard. For sure, "hit was a-gonna rain . . ." Beautiful Appalachia restored . . .

True did not hear Young Wil tiptoe into the room. "Oh, here you are, my love," he said, tactfully ignoring the letter in her hand. "I'm guessing you had to rest a bit. Small wonder—and to think! *Mañana* will be worse. Oh, the tumult . . . Lung and Tonsil will bark their fool heads off . . . the March Hare will bark the shins of every guest with that 'Kiddie Kar' we have yet to present. Soooo, Young Doctor North prescribes a walk for his beloved patient—but not alone, *never alone*—"

It was the last two words that undid her, let the dammed up wall of tears come in a cleansing flood. Too long, too long, she had held them back . . . the sea was so wide, her boat so small . . .

They walked in the silence of the moonlight, holding hands but not talking. At length Young Wil said quietly, "The letter was from Prescott, wasn't it? Wanting us to join him—help out?"

True nodded, so sure was she that this was what the unread ending amounted to. Waiting for no words, her husband said, "Has Jerry seen the letter?"

"Jerry?" she repeated dully.

"Your brother—remember?" Young Wil was teasing, actually teasing her. And already love was working its magic. The situation was no longer a problem, and peace came stealing back. Her feet, like her heart, were light—wanting to leap ahead without dread or fear.

"He will enjoy it. And have you thought of Kearby and her young man? I am looking at the future through a peephole and seeing it clearly," Young Wil continued as if inspired. "I know the signs—they're all there for the four of them—and four brilliant young minds could shake those mountains."

"A teacher, a preacher—*and* perhaps a doctor. Did Kearby tell you that she was interested in medicine? Well, so is Clarry somewhat—darling, if anything should happen—uh, to me—I want Clarry to have Angel Mother's brooch—if she's family—" True said out of context.

"I understand, but nothing's going to happen to you, my sweet. You have work to do, remember? Sooo, shall we talk about our future?"

"All night if you wish, Dr. North," True said gaily. "You have some decisions to make—me, I've made mine!"

His next words made her wonder if he heard. "You know, standing back there on the platform, as you cast your eyes to the hills, it seemed to me that we stood at the crossroads of our future which melded into all the problems of the world—"

"—and that windswept platform became an *everywhere*, all the people becoming one," she finished for him. "I know. And there we stood, wondering which road to take, never knowing where the others might have led. Crossroads are lonely. To endure—or to let go—"

Surely Angel Mother, who had devoted her short adult years to righting a wrong in her mind, must be agonizing for True—understanding because choices were so hard for the child-mother. Or was she rejoicing that her beloved Valley had become a seeding ground for missionaries produced in her own family? Oh, why should memories come alive now? The softness of her singing to the bees . . . telling Bible stories . . . sharing adventures of successes and failures of pioneer life . . . popping corn. Daring to dream. And, most of all, filling the firelit room with the silver tinkle of her laughter. Aunt Chrissy had been the one with the quiet resolve, the courage which Angel Mother wanted for True, her wish granted. But the love for all that was beautiful, the silvery laughter, and the dreaming had been the legacy of the flowerlike creature who gave True birth.

Flowerlike? Yes. But fragile she was not. Else why, when Mary Evangeline North wrote the final entry in her diary—a message of goodbye—had the very foundation of the family been shaken? Why had it taken so long for them to see that she was plucky, too, seeing them through every crisis in another way? Only it was sad—but God had known. And only He knew His plan for the daughter she adored and her young husband . . .

Oh, dear, now I am weeping again! Have I no control?

"Darling—what have I said? *Oh, forgive me!*" The words wrung from Young Wil were filled with remorse.

True raised her eyes, twin violets in the moonlight, and allowed him to dry her foolish tears with a big white handkerchief that smelled faintly of antiseptics. "Forgive you? I am the one who begs forgiveness. Time just turned backward, so indulge me—and remember, Wil North, that it is vain and foolish not to forgive!"

"Brat! Oh, you little *brat*! Sunshine and shadows, that's you, you.

But I love it—all," he grinned his endearing grin, "except for the woman's way of winning. You know we men are pushovers—that to us the most powerful flow of water on earth is your tears."

"I wasn't expecting them, darling. It's just that I was thinking back over the years—*analyzing*, if you need a medical term—our wonderful family, thinking of how each is a part of the other, a powerful influence. It seemed so sweet, and yet so sad. There are several kinds of *sad*, you know."

He inhaled deeply. "Smell the clover? I think I understand. Fragrance is not its main purpose, but is a sweet added benefit. Forgot I was poetic, didn't you—or assumed that if I made a rhyme it would be about parts of the body?"

"Ummm—like the heart? So back to our thesis, Doctor. Ours is a choosing, I guess, like the clover. All the choices you face have important purposes, but you must decide what *your* purpose is—test it, see if you chose what is right for you, or if its added benefits are too appealing to resist. There! We're even! You didn't know that I hid a brain beneath my bonnet!"

"You know you're bright, so stop fishing for compliments, but—" Young Wil paused, and when he spoke again the teasing was gone, "I'm glad you mentioned the Blue Ridge. Don't let Prescott's letter upset you too much. The outlook is brighter than he knows, I think. The old 'popskull' stuff is just about a thing of the past—too many Revenue officers keeping watch for even the backsliders to risk bootlegging, and the townsfolk have either grown leery or no longer have a taste for the fiery drink. And there's hope for the economy, too, according to word I pick up at the medical conferences. Coal mines are opening—bringing new hope—"

"Which you and I never lost."

"Right, sweetheart." He took her hand but did not turn around. That meant their talk was unfinished. "As I see it, we will not be choosing between a land we love, an area where we are needed, and a job with a great future. I would say that they're somewhat the same. There's always need for love, understanding, service—so it boils down to what my most precious piece of property desires!"

"Wil North! I'm not *your property*—oh, yes, I am, darling—"

He squeezed her hand, the muscles tightening in intensity. "You have reached a decision, so help *me*."

He did hear.

"Yes—yes, I have." She dreaded the words. But they must be said. "It depends on when—or *if*—you plan a family. Children's needs would be the first consideration."

She had thought it would be easier. Why was her heart pounding?

Leaning down, Young Wil pressed his warm cheek against hers and the grip on her hand tightened even more. "I leave that to you," he said, but his voice was husky. "Frankly, it's a novel idea, I confess— I guess there has been too little time to give it proper thought."

"I—I thought all men wanted a son?"

"To carry on the family name?" He chuckled. "Marty seems to be doing well enough in that area. And there's Jerry. Or did you suppose me to be so egotistical that I must make it my lifework to make sure that my genes are handed from this generation to the next—or, perish the thought, that I must create in my own image?"

True giggled. "In a mixed-up family like ours, none of that seems important. And, as for your last question, well, God has done that for you—created in *His* image."

There was silence. They walked on, and True noted that the grass was growing damp with dew. They should be getting back. Even the slant of the moon said so. There was Tillie's hair to do. And yet, as warm, intimate, and revealing as their talk had been, something was left unsaid. It hung between them, unfinished.

"I guess I need to confess something," True said slowly, "since it was I who brought up the matter of a family. So I confess that I have given it little thought—oh, not that I am opposed—you know how I adore Chris. He is a part of us. It's like joint custody—we never *own* our children, do we? It was so with my seeing Midgie through her pregnancy, your ushering him into the world, and," True laughed, "my trying to take care of him, only to have him snatched away by Marty!"

"Marty and Midgie needed a child to hold the marriage together. We have no such need—and, in most cases, I would declare that to be a wrong reason for bringing a child into the world. Their case seems different—as I guess all cases are. Generalizing is dangerous."

True agreed with him, then, with a rush of words, said that she felt less need to create than to love and serve those already created. *All* of them. All over the world! Most parents *wanted* to love but simply didn't know how. They, too, needed her—

"Mother Eve."

Young Wil spoke the words tenderly, softly, not spoiling their implication that she was greatly blest. It was True who spoke at length.

"I have always felt that if it is God's plan, He will send us children by the dozens—and that will be fine. We need not concern ourselves. And even then I would want to help others—learn to love—"

"Mother Eve," he said again. "And your preference on my job?"

"I didn't say preference. I said I had reached a *decision.*"

"Well?" True fancied he was not breathing.

"I have decided that we must listen—listen with our hearts—else we may miss the still, small voice of God."

"Sooo," his voice shook ever so slightly as if he wrestled to regain control, "we herewith put it all in His hands—and go forth to enjoy the wedding feast?"

"Exactly."

"But—who can say where God will lead? What about *you?*"

As if by signal, they stopped and faced each other. This was the moment which counted. But True was prepared. " . . . whither thou goest . . ."

She could say no more, and neither could he. But the way he embraced her spoke of a reverence unknown by the human tongue, a *knowing* which said: "God will walk with us wherever the road. If we stay, He will stay. God needs help in good conditions and in bad. And who are the winners? Those who listen and follow."

True was halfway to heaven already—here in her husband's arms, and there among the throbbing stars. A wellspring of laughter, born of joy, bubbled up inside her. She drew back slightly.

"Darling," she said solemnly, "I just couldn't have been a Mother Eve."

"And why not, prithee?"

"I could never have thought up a name like *Hippopotamus!*"

Together they laughed. Joyously. Triumphantly. And the hopeful hills sent back their laughter, its echo reaching "far beyond the heavens" . . .

Leaving in the human heart a love everlasting . . .
And the strength to endure . . .
For: "Happy is he whose hope is in the Lord."